THE PEACOCK AND THE PEARL

THE PEACOCK AND THE PEARL

Jennifer Lang

St. Martin's Press
New York

Library of Congress Cataloging-in-Publication Data

Lang, Jennifer
    The peacock and the pearl / Jennifer Lang.
        p.   cm.
    "A Thomas Dunne book."
    ISBN 0-312-08871-X
    1. Great Britain—History—14th century—Fiction.
    2. London (England)—History—To 1500—Fiction.
    I. Title.
    PR6062.A5325P4   1993
    823'.914—dc20   92-34394
                                                     CIP

First published in Great Britain by
HEADLINE BOOK PUBLISHING PLC.

First U.S. Edition: January 1993
10 9 8 7 6 5 4 3 2 1

To my father, Russell Lang
a piratical capitalist and great survivor

Oh pearl, a delight for a prince
To set flawlessly in pure gold:
Among orient pearls, I can with confidence say
I never found her peer.
So round, so radiant in whatever setting,
So small, her sides so smooth
Whenever it came to judging bright gems
She, to me, was above all others.
Alas! I lost her in a garden,
She fell from me through the grass.
I pine, mortally wounded by the force of my love
For my own pearl, without a blemish . . .

Translated from *Pearl*, late-fourteenth-century
poem by unknown poet

CHARACTERS

The House of Plantagenet

Edward III, King of England
Alice Perrers, his mistress
The Princess Joan, widow of the Black Prince, eldest son of Edward III
Thomas Holland, Earl of Kent and Sir John Holland, her sons by a previous marriage
Richard of Bordeaux (later King Richard II of England) her son by the Black Prince
John of Gaunt, Duke of Lancaster, son of Edward III
Constance of Castile, his wife
Katherine Swynford, his mistress
Henry Bolingbroke, his son
Thomas of Woodstock, earl of Buckingham, son of Edward III

Nobility

Robert de Vere, Earl of Oxford
Henry Percy, Earl of Northumberland
Earl of March, heir to Richard II
Earl of Salisbury
Earl of Warwick
Earl of Arundel
Michael de la Pole, Earl of Suffolk
Thomas, Lord Berkeley

Knights

Sir Edmund de Cher
Sir Nicholas de Cher
Lady Elizabeth de Cher, their mother
Agnes Proudfoot, Sir Nicholas' betrothed

Sir Tristram de Maudesbury, retainer to Lancaster
Robin Swynbrook and Godfrey, his squires
Lady Isabel de Maudesbury, his mother
Martha, her maid
Sir Robert Knollys
Sir Hugh d'Aycliffe, retainer to Northumberland
The Sieur de Chevigny, sometime Champion to the Black Prince
Sir John d'Ypres
Sir Philip Mansell
Sir William Whittington
Lady Joan, his wife
Sir Thomas Percy
Sir Perducat d'Albret

Church

Simon Sudbury, Archbishop of Canterbury
William Courtenay, Bishop of London
John Wycliffe
Robert Hales, Prior of the Knights of St John, and Treasurer of England
Abbot Blake of Cirencester Abbey
William of Tresham, sub-Prior of Cirencester Abbey
Father Luke, a parish priest
Father James, a charity priest
Brother William, a Franciscan
Gervase de Haen, a monk
The Prioress of the Convent of the Sacred Heart
Sister Agnes, her Chaplain
Sister Teresa, sub-Prioress of St Helen's by Bishopsgate

City of London Merchants

Mercers

Adam Staple, Mayor of London, 1376–77
Richard Burgeys
Matilda, his wife
Mariota, her daughter
Alice, his daughter
Joanna, his daughter
Thomas, their son
Dickon and Owen, his apprentices
Joan and Anna, his maids

John Fressh, Alderman
John More, Alderman

Grocers

Nicholas Brembre, Mayor of London, 1377 and 1383–86
Idonia (sister to Margaret Philpot), his wife
John Philpot, Mayor of London, 1378–79
Margaret Philpot (sister to Idonia)
Adam Karlyll, Alderman
John Hadle, Mayor of London, 1379–80

Drapers

John of Northampton, Mayor of London, 1381–83
Petronilla, his wife
Robert, William and Roger Comberton, his brothers
Idonia, Petronilla's daughter, married to Roger
Katherine, John and Petronilla's daughter
Matty, his cousin
Adam and Will, his apprentices
William Essex, Alderman

Fishmongers

William Walworth, Mayor of London, 1380–81
John Horn, Alderman
Walter Sibil, Alderman
Kurt, an apprentice

Goldsmiths

Adam Bamme, Alderman
Robert Launde, Alderman
Nicholas Twyford, Alderman

Vintners

William Tonge
Richard Lyons, Alderman

Cordwainers

John Constantyn
Alice, his wife, daughter of Richard Burgeys
Roger and Harry, their sons

Rebels

Wat Tyler
John Ball
Ben Smale

Other

Black Nick, a sea captain
Sam, his henchman
William Gryffard, Merchant of the Staple at Calais
Bridget, a maid
Roger Tambard, a minstrel
Joe Mercer, a Scottish pirate

Those marked in bold type are recorded in history.

PROLOGUE

Aquitaine, 1371

The young squire gazed out over the ramparts at the spectacular view laid out before him. Rolling plains, shimmering in a haze of heat, stretched uninterrupted to the majestic mountains on the horizon; in the middle distance a gleam of water revealed where the River Lot wound placidly on its way to join the Garonne. It was good land, blessed with an abundance of sunshine and rain and rich fertile soil. The slopes on either side of the river should have been covered with fat grapes slowly ripening on the vines in the hot summer sun. Instead, the earth was bare, laid waste by constant pillage. War had cut a great swathe through some of the fairest land in all France and there was nothing left to harvest.

Immediately below the castle, the houses of the town huddled up against its walls. The squire could hear the sounds of people stirring. A late cock chased the dawn with his cheerful clarion call and was answered by the musical cackling of his hens searching for food. It made the squire feel hungry and for a moment he considered making a foray into the town, then discarded the idea. It was too soon since the last raid. The hens would barely have laid enough eggs to make it worth his while.

A sudden movement in the court below caught his sharp eye and he stiffened, instantly alert. A short, squat figure, clad in clerical black, was hurrying across the grass, with something so furtive and urgent in his gait it boded ill for his purpose. The squire, delighted with this diversion, leant over the edge of the crenellated battlement and addressed the fugitive in ringing tones.

'Good morning, Father. You're up early. Where are you off to in such haste?' The priest looked up startled, then scuttled away round the corner of the court like a well-fed rat. Quick as a hawk, the squire dropped from his perch on the ramparts, darted into the keep and down the narrow twisting stairs into the open space below. Running with light, swift steps across the inner bailey he pounced on his quarry by the outer door.

1

'I asked you a question, Father,' he said with a grin. 'What's amiss? The devil got your tongue this morning?' But the priest did not respond with his usual unction, nor try scolding him for lack of respect. There was something about the fat man's expression, the sweat of fear which clung to his pallid face, the desperation with which he was trying to twist out of the squire's grasp which made the boy suddenly uneasy. 'What's the matter?' he asked, the hair on the back of his neck beginning to prickle with alarm.

'Plague!' muttered the priest looking round him in terror. 'We're dead men unless we leave at once, this minute. It's in the town, they say, and here in the castle. Your commander, he's already down with it.'

Plague! The word wiped out all the bright promise of the morning. The young squire's limbs turned to liquid and his stomach heaved. He could scarcely breathe for the pounding of his heart. Fear, irrational, uncontrollable fear, took possession of his mind.

'Quick', the priest was plucking ineffectually at the squire's fingers which were still clutching his arm. 'We must flee while there is still time' The squire did not stop to think of his duty to his master the knight who lay dying in his chamber, of what his flight might do to his companions in arms, of the effect on the townspeople if the occupying garrison were suddenly to leave the castle empty and unguarded. Fear had him in its grip. Although he was too young to have known the terrible devastation of the Black Death, he had heard tales enough from the survivors, and subsequent outbreaks of the disease had kept the tales alive. Too well he know what lay in store for anyone who caught the plague – the vomiting and the spitting blood, the sudden shivering, the dreaded scarlet blotches, the black boils, the delirium and the unbearable agony which came without warning, carrying off its victims in a few hours. The fear which had at first paralysed the boy, now suddenly galvanised him into action. Scarcely knowing what he did, he dropped the priest's arm and ran, as if pursued by all the devils in hell, into the outer bailey. The Gascons working in the stables stared in astonishment as the squire seized a saddle at random and flung it onto his horse. The little rouncy, quick to catch its master's mood, backed away nervously, sidling and fidgeting while the boy struggled with the harness. When he tried to bridle the animal, the horse threw up its head and bared its teeth, thoroughly unsettled, while the boy, sobbing and cursing, tried to coax it within reach. At last it was done and he led the plunging horse out of the stables at the run. Without a backward glance he leapt into the saddle and galloped out of the castle, leaving the priest to make what way he could on his own two feet.

In a large cool room at the top of the keep, the commander of the garrison lay in a canopied bed. He was a young knight of barely seventeen summers, strong in bone and muscle with a body tuned to perfection by a youth spent fighting in the service of the Black Prince. The plague, however, was no respecter of physique. It could lay waste the most perfect physical specimen in less time than it took to hold a tournament. The knight was delirious, fighting a whole host of diabolic creatures who would not be vanquished. First it was a helmless knight with live coals for eyes burning into his brain, lips bared like a savage wolf, riding at him full tilt, his levelled lance dripping not blood but a thousand writhing serpents. Next he was in the forest, wrestling with a great wild beast which was tearing at his groin with fangs sharp as dagger points. Then he was on the plains of Najera and the hot sun was baking down on his bare head, an army of dead knights was advancing towards him and from a hundred hoarse throats came the cry: 'Come with us!' But he fought them one by one with all the strength of an indomitable will and an unconscious instinct for survival. He knew who his adversary was: it was death and he would not be conquered. Though his body was on the rack and his mind in hell, he would not give in.

Then there came a time when he was free from pain and struggle, floating somewhere in the corner of the chamber looking down at the poor body writhing in such agony on the bed. He saw a figure bending over the bed, dabbing at the angry scarlet patches with a cloth and he marvelled that any man had the courage to come near a plague victim in the hour of his death. Was it the priest he wondered, with a strange sort of detachment, come to save his soul from damnation? If so, where was the sacred pyx, the wine and the bread? It could not be the priest. If it were not the priest then damnation awaited him on the other side of the void. Eternal damnation or a return to the torture on the bed – in his pleasant state of peace it did not seem to matter to him which he chose. He watched with a detached interest the figure labouring so fervently over his body. He was lancing the great black boil on his groin, squeezing with infinite care the poisonous liquid from the swelling. It seemed a shame that so much effort should go unrewarded. With a tinge of regret for the unknown adventure waiting in eternity, he left the peace which lapped him round like a soft cloud and returned to the battle on the bed.

A searing pain was twisting and turning through his limbs, like an angry eel seeking new places to strike. The wild beast was still gnawing at his groin and he tore at it with frantic hands. A face was bending over him. He grasped the creature by the beard and to his surprise felt hair between his fingers.

'God's blood, are you a devil come to torment me?' he gasped.

'No devil, nor angel neither,' the creature replied, 'just one of your archers atrying to help 'ee, and I'll do it better if ye leave me head on me shoulders.'

3

'You can't love life much to court death in here with me,' said the knight, letting him go.

Lord love 'ee, sir, the plague don't strike twice. I beat him back in the forty-second year of King Edward afore we came out here and it looks like you're going to do the same. These four days past you've been fighting the bugger, and them as lasts as long as that usually makes it.'

The knight lay back and contemplated survival with surprise. He didn't feel as if life was a very real possibility. He wanted to go on talking to the man but his weakness was too great. He could feel himself sinking back into the haunted world he had barely left and braced himself to meet the horrifying creatures that inhabited his mind. But the archer had done his work well and instead of delirium the knight fell into a dreamless sleep.

When he woke up the archer was still there, standing by the window with his hand up to his eyes. There was something about his intent watchfulness that made the knight instantly wary.

'What is it?' he asked.

'It's the French, your honour. A small party. Three knights and their squires, well mounted, with no more than a score archers and men-at-arms on foot.'

'Well, don't just stand there, you fool, get down to the gate and see it's secured. Put some men to guard it, I don't trust these Gascons. Get the archers up on the battlements and when they're within range, shoot the knights' horses from under them. Send my squire here to help me and if he's afraid of the pestilence, say if he doesn't come the French'll get him first.'

'Your squire's gone,' replied the archer, still watching out of the window. 'The first hint of sickness, he and the priest hopped it, devil take them, which gave the men-at-arms and archers the excuse to do the same. There's not any left that's not sick nor dead.'

'Well, get up on the ramparts. You ought to be able to keep a small party like that at bay, if you shoot straight.'

'The townspeople are running out to welcome the French now, sir. We couldn't hold the castle against the town and the French, not without our full complement of archers. We're done for, your honour.'

'Get my sword,' said the knight, struggling to get out of bed.

'You'll not stand, let alone wield a sword,' said the man, turning from the window at last.

'I'll be damned if I let a Frenchman take me lying on my back,' said the knight between his teeth. He swung his legs over the bed, pulled himself up by the bed curtains and tried to stand. To his surprise he found he could not control his limbs and he fell in a crumpled heap on the floor like a rag doll.

'There, I told 'ee so,' said the archer, helping him up. 'You'd best lie down again. Even the French'll never kill a sick man in his bed.'

'Go to the devil,' swore the knight. 'Get me my sword and something to cover my nakedness.'

The three French knights who approached the great hall an hour later with their squires were rejoicing at the ease with which they had taken the castle. The native population in the town had given them a rapturous reception, their men-at-arms and crossbowmen were stationed on the battlements, and already the Lilies of France were floating above the keep. They walked into the great hall totally unprepared for the sight that met their eyes.

A knight sat at the head of the long table which ran down the centre of the room. He was in full armour save for his helmet; his sword lay on the table in front of him. Behind him stood the archer leaning carelessly on his longbow, playing with a sharp-tipped arrow between his fingers. The three Frenchmen paused on the threshold and crossed themselves in terror. The still figure of the knight, with his ghastly pallor and staring eyes sunk far back into his head, looked for all the world like a corpse.

'I know you and your countrymen have good reason to fear an English bowman, but don't be alarmed, my archer will not shoot you.' For all its weakness the mocking voice sounded human enough and it spoke in French. They drew their swords and advanced cautiously into the room. 'Do not be afraid, God has delivered this castle into your hands and we are, as you can see, at your mercy.'

One of the French knights pulled himself together. 'You surrender yourselves and the castle?' he asked, marching purposefully towards the table. The young Englishman tried to pick up his sword, but his hand shook so much he needed both hands just to turn it round and push it hilt first towards his captors. He sat back, gripping the edge of the table, fighting against the exhaustion that threatened to overwhelm him.

'If you will tell me your name, sir knight,' said the Frenchman picking up the sword, 'and give me your pledge not to try to escape, we can arrange details of the ransom later.'

'Escape?' said his captive with a flicker of a smile. 'I can barely stand.'

'Of course once the ransom is agreed and I have your pledge, you will be free to return home to collect it in person if you wish,' pursued the Frenchman.

'Ransom,' echoed the Englishman shaking his head slowly as if trying to clear it.

'Yes, ransom,' prompted the Frenchman, 'but we can discuss the price later when you have recovered more.'

'I am your prisoner to do with what you will,' replied the young Englishman, 'but no, I'll not give my word and there'll be no ransom.'

5

'But it is customary,' stammered the Frenchman. 'If you will not agree to the ransom, then we have all the inconvenience of keeping you prisoner with little or no recompense for our pains.'

'Kill me then,' the knight replied, dragging himself to his feet. 'It will not be difficult for I am half dead already.' So saying he took a step forward, clutched at the edge of the table and pitched forward face down into the rushes at their feet.

PART I

'If no love is, Ah God what feel I so?
And if love is, what thing and which is he?
If love be good from whence cometh my woe?
If he be wicked, a wonder thinketh me...'

Chaucer – *Troilus and Criseyde*

CHAPTER 1

London, 1377

Early in the morning on the Feast of St Valentine in the fifty-first year of King Edward III, Joanna Burgeys was walking down West Chepe from the Mercery. The sky was only just beginning to lighten and a fresh wind whipped her skirts round her ankles as clouds threatening rain scudded across the heavens. Passing the open door of St Mary le Bow, she heard the murmur of a chantry Mass and said a swift prayer for the souls of the dead.

Today being a holy day, the streets were quiet, the shops closed, empty of vociferous apprentices crying their wares. All, that is, but the shops selling food. Reaching Bread Street, she sniffed appreciatively the delicious smell of new-baked bread. It made her feel hungry. The street was long and narrow, the upper storeys of its tall timber houses leaning towards each other so far that they formed an arch across the street which almost shut out the sky.

Halfway down the street a little knot of people had gathered outside the Church of All Hallows and Joanna paused to see what the attraction was. A friar was standing on a wooden block haranguing the crowd. 'Are the abbeys poor?' he was saying. 'Does the Bishop of London dine on bread and water? You, my friends, know what poverty is, but do the priests? How does the Church keep it's vow of poverty and chastity? We are formed in God's likeness and they treat us like beasts.' A Lollard, thought Joanna, with a tiny shiver of excitement. I wonder he dares preach such heresies right outside the open door of All Hallows Church. She would have liked to stay to listen to more but she had an errand to do and dared not linger.

At the cookshop the lark pie was ready for her. She put it carefully into her basket, fascinated by the sound of scratching and twittering from beneath the pastry.

'Will they really sing when it's opened?' she asked in wonder.

'Wouldn't you if you was a lark and put in a pie, wouldn't you sing when the lid was off?' the pieman demanded with a grin. She pon-

9

dered for a moment, trying to imagine what it would be like, and was about to ask him if he didn't think it cruel when she heard the sound of shouts coming from outside the shop. She darted out of the shop and stopped in dismay. The whole street seemed full of running figures. Bakers were sweeping the loaves off the counters outside their shops and hastily putting up their shutters. She could hear the cries growing nearer. 'Foreign bastards! Flemish devils!' They were after the Flemings again. She hesitated and a stone hurtled past her cheek. Then she felt a hand tugging at her skirt and looked down to see a poor creature crouching at her feet. He had a white, pinched face half hidden by a mop of black hair, and his teeth were chattering with terror. She turned back to seek shelter with him in the cookshop, but it was too late. The shopkeeper already had his shutters up and his door barred. Street riots were bad for business. Two or three Flemings ran rapidly past her looking over their shoulders with frightened, hunted faces.

'Run!' she said. 'I can't help you now. Save yourself while you can.' He gave her a despairing look and broke into a queer sort of broken hop, for one leg was so withered and twisted the simple act of running was beyond him. It made her angry and she put down her basket and turned to see what she could do to help delay his pursuers a little.

There were more Flemings now, about a dozen of them, pushing and shoving each other in the narrow street, slipping in the refuse lying in the middle of the road, fighting each other in their anxiety to escape. One of them collided with Joanna and propelled her into the street. She was swept along with them like a leaf in a storm, pushed and pummelled, unable to resist the urgent press of bodies, forced to run with them or be mowed down. Another stone flew past her head and she ducked. The shouts from behind were coming nearer.

'Clubs! Fishmongers!'

'Send them back to Flanders where they belong.'

'Clubs! Grocers!' How well she knew that cry of 'clubs'. She had heard it often enough from her father's apprentices. It was their rallying cry.

She glanced behind her and saw a mob of them, clubs raised, howling like a pack of hounds closing on its prey. She could smell fear, see it on the faces around her, feel it in her own quickened heartbeats. She was pushing and fighting now, each minute expecting to feel a numbing blow from one of those clubs behind her, tripping over her skirts, trying to get out of the relentless current of human bodies bearing her along. The shouting was all about her, louder than her laboured breathing, the drumming in her ears and the screams of the unfortunate Flemings behind her. She caught her foot on the hem of her skirt, tripped, tried to save herself, failed, and fell headlong. The breath seemed to explode in her body as the feet hit her. She curled herself up into a ball and covered her head with her arms, fending off the blows as best she might. With her cheek pressed against the cobbles and her nose buried in the rotting contents of the gutter, winded and frightened, she did not even notice the stench or feel the water oozing beneath her.

After what seemed an eternity the shouts became fainter and she dared to breathe. Cautiously she raised her head. Most of the Flemish workers had melted into the numerous side alleys leading down to the river, pursued by the more energetic and fleet of foot. Battered, bruised, breathless, Joanna sat up and it was then that the returning apprentices, deprived of their prey, caught sight of her.

'A wench,' they cried running back with whoops of glee. A new fear gripped Joanna as she realised that now her plight was much worse. Before she had been a helpless spectator dragged into the crowd by its momentum. Now she herself was the quarry and it was too late to try and escape. Individual apprentices were easy enough to handle, but in a gang like this, with their blood roused, what might they not do?

She waited, muscles tensed for the moment when rough hands would seize hold of her and a dozen teasing, reckless, smelly, fishmongers force her to do – what? A sudden picture of the day when little Anna the kitchen maid had come home, her smock torn, her lips swollen, blood smeared on her bare thighs, flashed through Joanna's mind.

'Merciful Mother protect me,' she whispered, scrambling to her knees.

They were crowding round her, jeering. A clod of mud whistled through the air and as she ducked to avoid it, another hit her on the temple. The blow made her catch her breath, but it also drove away her fear. She scrambled angrily to her feet. Hands shot out and caught at her, spinning her round.

'A wench, a wench, a poor little Flemish wench,' they chanted. 'Dance for us, weaver. Dance!'

'Fools!' she shouted, striking out wildly at the probing hands. 'I'm not a Fleming. I'm a master mercer's daughter and the mercers will see you all tried in the Mayor's court if any one of you dare lay a finger on me.' A derisive cheer went up and too late she realised her folly.

'A mercer!' they cried. 'Hey look, lads, come see what we've caught. A mercer wench – pretty sight, ain't she? A mercer's brat in the gutter.' Her linen cap had been knocked off and her hair hung down in two untidy braids on either side of her face. Her cheeks and nose were smeared with dirt from the gutter. Rude laughter ran round the circle of teasing faces and a rough hand shot out to tweak one of her braids. She flung back her head defiantly. Tears stung her eyes as he wound the long thick hair round his wrist and pulled her towards him. Furious, she brought up her hand and dealt him a stinging blow across the face with all her strength. He reeled back cursing and his companions crowed with delight.

'Hey, Kurt,' they called, 'are you going to let the little spitting cat of a mercer get away with that?' Kurt lunged for her and she leapt backwards. Her heel caught in the hem of her skirt and she fell down at his feet in the mud.

'Lay her, Kurt,' they screamed, eager tongues wetting parted lips. 'See, she's waiting for you.'

A heavy body pressed her to the ground, hands seized her scrabbling fists, an overpowering smell of sweat, fish and ale made her retch, and a hoarse excited voice in her ear shouted, 'Love me sweet, love me.' Rough hands were pulling at her ankles, trying to force her kicking legs apart, while all the time his great weight was crushing the breath out of her body. It was harder and harder to struggle. His face was barely an inch away. She could see his little piggy eyes, dark with excitement, peering down at her, feel his hot breath on her cheek, see his mouth, wet and loose-lipped, coming closer. His teeth were bared. Frantically she wrenched her head aside. His hand caught her chin in a vice-like grip and forced her head backwards down on to the cobbles. She dredged her dry mouth for the last vestige of saliva and spat full in his face.

'By God's blood, I'll make you sorry for that, you little hellcat,' he swore.

Her head was swimming. She longed to close her eyes, to shut out the red ugly face bearing down on her, to seek refuge in oblivion. But she must not. She must fight. She must defy him. She had only her will. 'Blessed St Mary, save me,' she prayed fervently.

Suddenly the weight on top of her lightened. She heard shouting. The cruel hands relaxed their grip. Through the hard cobbles beneath her she felt the reverberations of iron-shod hooves. Her tormentors were running away. Slowly she sat up.

A knight was sitting on his horse, gazing at her. A weak ray of February sun shone through the narrow gap between the houses above onto his golden hair. She blinked. Had she died and gone straight to heaven?

'Are you hurt?' he asked.

She stared at him blankly, unable to believe her eyes. He swung a long leg over the back of his horse and dismounted.

'Did they hurt you?' he repeated, handing the reins of his horse to his squire. She shook her head, too bemused to speak. He held out a hand to help her to her feet and frowned as she grimaced with pain. 'You don't look very good to me,' he said.

'I'm all right, I think.' She smiled at him shyly as she tried to brush some of the dirt from her kirtle. 'No broken bones, just bruises.'

'What happened?'

'It was a 'prentices riot, the fishmongers were hounding some poor Flemish weavers again. I got caught in the riot and knocked down in the rush.' She blushed hotly. She could not possibly tell so magnificent a person the sordid details of the real peril he had saved her from.

'The city's altogether too prone to riots,' he said, frowning again. 'Things have come to a fair pass when a child like you is not safe to walk the street in broad daylight.'

'I'm not a child, I'm turned sixteen'. He was clearly taken aback and she realised that she did not present a very dignified picture. She turned away from him and began hunting in the unsavoury contents of the gutter.

'What are you looking for?' he asked.

'I seem to have lost one of my shoes,' she said, holding out a blue-stockinged foot.

'Never mind the shoe,' he said, apparently unmoved by the sight of her well-turned ankle.'You can ride on Orion. Is your home nearby?' She looked doubtfully at the big stallion. The horse was fidgeting nervously, head flung back, ears pricked, listening intently. The squire was having a hard time controlling him.

'I'm not sure I wouldn't be safer walking.'

'Orion's all right, he's just a little excited, that's all. With all the noise and shouting he probably thought it was a battle. He's a trained war horse and he loves a battle.'

Joanna watched the knight walk up to the impatient stallion and begin stroking his neck soothingly. He wore chain mail and over it a blue surcoat with red lozenges running diagonally across; a long sword hung at his hip. He was quite the most beautiful person she had ever laid eyes on. The horse was settling under the soothing hand of his master and Joanna suddenly thought of how it might be to feel that hand on her own body. A stab of longing shot through her so sharp it left her trembling.

'There, he's quieter now,' said the knight. 'But we'd better be going. He gets impatient if he's kept standing still for too long. Where do you live?'

'In the Mercery,' she said, still in a daze. 'It's not far from St Mary le Bow, on the other side of Chepe.'

'Come, let me help you up,' he said walking towards her. 'They must be worried about you at home.'

'Oh!' She gave a shriek and the horse flung up his head and stamped nervously. 'The pie. I quite forgot the pie.' She darted off towards the cookshop, while he stared after her in amazement.

'Would you believe St Valentine could be so cruel, Robin?' he said to his squire. 'To send me a damsel in distress who is not only the plainest wench I've ever clapped eyes on, but mad to boot. If I kiss her, do you think she'll turn into a fairy princess?'

13

'She has lovely eyes,' said the squire with a sigh, 'and her smile, did you not see her smile?'

'The trouble with you, Robin, is you're too susceptible,' replied the knight with a grin. 'But you can do better than a kitchen wench.'

'Look,' called Joanna running back with her basket held aloft like a trophy, 'a miracle. The pie is unharmed, and I found my shoe – right outside the cookshop. Isn't that lucky?'

Very fortunate, for Orion is getting impatient again,' said the knight drily. 'May I help you into the saddle?'

'Since I've found my shoe, I think I'd better walk,' she said eyeing the horse with suspicion. 'Besides, it will be better for the pie.'

'As you wish.' He looped the reins of his charger over his arm and fell in beside her.

All along Bread Street the shutters were opening, the loaves were being put out on display once more and the shopkeepers were crying their wares.

'What do you lack!'

'Fresh bread, good sirs.'

'Goodwives, what will ye buy?'

'They get back to business quick enough,' said the knight. 'What was the riot about?'

'Oh, it was the usual business of the 'prentices harassing the aliens. They don't like foreign workers taking their jobs,' she explained.

'I don't blame them for that.'

'But there are not enough freemen to do all the work there is. Father says that if only the aliens were allowed to be free, like the others, there would be more work for everybody and the price of cloth would come down. Father's a mercer,' she added proudly. He did not look particularly impressed and she realised that to a knight, a mercer was not perhaps a very important man.

'Why don't they make 'em all free?' he asked.

'Because the victualling guilds won't let them. They want to keep the price of food up. But what with having to pay high wages and buy expensive food to feed the workers, everybody but the victuallers will be driven out of business, so Father says.' He frowned and she decided that she had not explained very well. In truth it was not an easy matter to explain, especially when she was out of breath from the effort of keeping up with Orion's energetic walk.

'Are there many riots like the one today?'

'Oh no, and the Flemings usually get away. As you see, the shopkeepers are used to looking after themselves. It was just stupid of me to get caught.'

'It seems things have come to a pretty pass when innocent women and children cannot walk about the streets without being knocked over by rioting 'prentices. Why doesn't the Mayor do something about it, or is he a fishmonger too?'

'No, he's a mercer, but I doubt if anybody can control the fish-mongers when they have a monopoly of the sale of fish in the city. If it weren't for them, we'd all starve. Besides, many of the aldermen are fishmongers or grocers or vintners, and the Mayor is not strong enough to act on his own.'

'That's what this city needs then,' he said, 'someone strong enough to knock all these warring guilds' heads together. Someone like my liege lord. He'll soon put a stop to all this rioting when he takes control of the city.' She looked at his badge, a red rose, circled with gold thread, embroidered on his surcoat and wished she could remember which great lord it represented. Her brother Thomas would have known.

They had come to the end of Bread Street and turned into the wider thoroughfare of Chepe. The city's principal marketplace was without its usual stalls, but people were coming out of St Mary le Bow after Mass and standing about talking in little groups, while the wind whipped their cloaks and the long flying tails of the women's head-dresses into billowing sails. Orion snorted and danced sideways along the cobbled way, which made a group of stout matrons leap onto the steps of Chepe Cross like a flock of geese startled by a fox. Joanna laughed and looked up at the knight, but he was too busy controlling his horse and did not notice.

At the top of Wood Street, Joanna paused, reluctant to let him nearer her home lest any of her family meet him. He was so miracu-lous, so utterly the embodiment of all her most secret dreams that she wanted to keep him all to herself.

'I shall be safe enough now,' she said. 'Our house is just down there on the left.' He nodded and she tried not to notice that he seemed relieved.

'Joanna's my name,' she said, shyly offering him her hand.

'Goodbye, Mistress Joanna.' He bent gallantly over the grubby fin-gers and brushed them lightly with his lips. Then with one easy move-ment he leapt onto Orion. The horse wheeled the instant he felt the weight on the saddle and plunged forward, but the knight checked him so fiercely he reared up, hooves pawing the air. Even as she backed away from those flashing hooves, Joanna marvelled at the way the knight sat his plunging mount so calmly. Then they were gone, trotting down West Chepe towards St Paul's, scattering peo-ple from side to side. With her hand, which his lips had touched, pressed against her cheek, Joanna watched until he disappeared from view.

The sound of Bow bell brought her out of her daydream. Normally she would have stopped to listen as the church bells from every quar-ter of the city chimed in unison. Five times a day the bells rang, and each individual bell had its own particular note. By their insistent clan-gor every citizen fixed the pattern of his daily life and it was a sound

15

that Joanna never grew tired of. But not today. Today the great cascade of harmonic sound pealed trouble, for it told her she was late. She would get a beating, for certain. Worse, she might be made to miss the feast.

She began to run. If only she had not loitered on her way this morning, had not stopped to listen to the friar outside St Hallows Bread Street, she might not have been caught in the riot. If she were to be punished for being late, it would be her penance for listening to such seditious talk. But then if she had not been caught in the riot she would never have met the knight. Any punishment was worth the bearing for that.

CHAPTER 2

William Gryffard, a merchant of the staple newly arrived from Calais, heard the bells of the city ringing for the terce as he rode down the Royall, so named for the well-fortified tower built at the top of the street which housed the Queen's Wardrobe. His destination was Nicholas Brembre's house in the Royall, a substantial stone building set back from the street in its own large garden, which, with its courtyard, storehouses, orchards and carp pond, was as fine as any knight's dwelling. Brembre, a grocer married to the vintner's daughter, Idonia Stodeye, was one of the most powerful men in the city. Stodeye's other daughter, Margaret, was also married to a grocer – John Philpot. In the city of London it was necessary to belong to a guild in order to trade in the city at all, but that did not mean that men like Brembre and Philpot had to limit their interests to pepper and spices. They dealt in wool, wine, wheat, metal, fish – and money. They were merchant capitalists, traders buying and selling raw materials rather than making goods. Some of them advanced money to the government or held office under it, lucrative posts such as the Customs or the Mint. They owned property in the city and land outside it. They married each other's children, widows and wards to preserve and extend that property. They were a close-knit, intermarried clique in whose hands the real power of the city lay.

William Gryffard would have liked to have been one of them. But he did not belong to a guild. As a stapler he was responsible for collecting the tax on all the wool exported through Calais. He had power of a sort but nothing like the influence of these London merchants. They had political power. The king relied on the guilds for money and a degree of stability; in return the guilds were granted special privileges: the right to wear liveries, to control wages and prices, to search and condemn any goods which were below standard, and to elect the Mayor whose power within the city reigned supreme.

As Gryffard rode into the courtyard of Brembre's Inn, he met the grocer coming out with his wife, elaborately attired as for a feast.

'You here, Master Gryffard?' said Brembre. 'Do you bring me news from Calais?'

'Not much of import,' replied Gryffard. 'I've come to seek news from you this time. London's in trouble, it would seem.'

'Then you'd better come with me,' replied the other. 'Richard Burgeys the mercer gives a feast for the Mayor. The Mayor's no crusader, he'll avoid trouble if he can. We've got to try and put some steel into him, make him stand up to Gaunt.' So saying he set off briskly, the light of battle in his eye. Gryffard dismounted and fell in beside Idonia, the grocer's wife, reflecting not for the first time what a dangerous man Nicholas Brembre was to serve.

Gryffard believed that the only way to survive all the risks and uncertainties of a merchant's most hazardous calling was to know more than his rivals. News was something which Gryffard prized beyond gold and precious stone. It was his life blood, the vital fuel which fired his success, something for which he would pay most highly or risk much. He had a far-flung network of informers who kept him supplied with a thousand secrets, mostly unimportant trivia, but nothing was too slight to be of interest, for it was with such unimportant details that he built up the very formidable sum of knowledge which enabled him to keep ahead of his rivals. Because he always seemed to know everything before anyone else, he had acquired an almost sinister reputation and there were those who even believed he was in league with the devil. Gryffard was not displeased. Anything which caused fear in other men was worth holding on to, so he encouraged them to believe in his demonic infallibility and kept his secrets to himself.

Gryffard was aware that in the city of London a struggle for power was taking place between the victualling guilds who provided food and the mercantile guilds who produced goods. The year before, Sheriff Northampton, a draper and leader of the mercantile guilds, had led an attack in Parliament on the victuallers and their friends. Richard Lyons, a vintner and alderman of Bread Street, was one of those who had been impeached for, among other things, using his position as collector of the wool subsidy to export wool elsewhere than to the staple at Calais, and imposing duties on wool and appropriating some of the monies raised to his own use. Gryffard had some sympathy for Lyons who was, he felt, a victim of the Sheriff's zeal. The next time Parliament met it had been packed with powerful friends of those who had been impeached and all of Northampton's work was undone. Gryffard wanted to know which side in the struggle was likely to win. Brembre was the man most likely to be able to tell him.

On the short walk from the Royall to the Mercery, Gryffard tried to discover something of Richard Burgeys, the mercer who was giving the feast. It was a name he did not know.

'Burgeys is a man to watch,' said Nicholas Brembre. 'It's my belief he'll lead the Mercers Guild before long.'

'Do you think he'll be Mayor?' asked Gryffard.

'I think he'd like to be,' was Brembre's laconic reply.

Burgeys' house was a narrow-fronted, two-storey, stone building. The shop was on the ground floor and an outside staircase at the side led to the living quarters. Up this staircase a soberly dressed, thin man with a long, solemn face was helping his pregnant wife.

'John of Northampton!' exclaimed Brembre. 'What is Burgeys playing at, I wonder?'

'Perhaps he wants to unite the city against John of Gaunt,' said Idonia.

'That's what we all want,' retorted her husband impatiently. 'If only some of these mercers and goldsmiths could see where their best interests lie, but they're trying to hunt with the hawk and run with the hounds. Richard Burgeys now, he's a mercer and as such a friend of the Mayor, who supports Northampton. But he's not committed, I'll swear by that. I should like to win Burgeys to our cause. We need strong guilds like the Mercers with us and Burgeys, when he's Master, could bring them in. He has the will to do it,' he added, leaping up the stairs in Northampton's wake. 'If it was worth his while.'

A stout oak door at the top of the stairs led directly into a long, rectangular room, laid end to end with long trestle tables and already crowded to overflowing with merchants and their families. Gryffard recognised several men of importance. There was John Philpot, Brembre's bother-in-law, talking to William Walworth, a fishmonger, as he washed his fingers in the scented water provided, while further away John of Northampton was consorting with Adam Staple the Mayor and two others whom Brembre informed him were John More, also a mercer and friend of Northampton's and Adam Bamme, a goldsmith.

'Any friend of Nicholas Brembre's is welcome in my house,' said Burgeys cordially as Brembre presented the unexpected guest. 'Tell us, Master Gryffard, how was your journey from Calais? I trust you had no trouble from the French?'

'It wasn't easy,' Gryffard replied with a grimace, 'the closest I've been to a Frenchman yet. We only escaped through God's good grace and the diabolical cunning of our sea captain.'

'Did they get any of the others?' asked William Walworth.

'There weren't any others.'

'Crossing the Channel in a lone ship, that's risky, surely, these days?' put in Adam Bamme.

'It is, but I can't always wait for a fleet. I like to come and go as I please,' replied Gryffard with a shrug. 'The sea captain seemed to think it would be safe enough and thanks to him it was, although I wouldn't like to repeat the experience.'

'Could be useful,' said Burgeys. 'I've a warehouse full of wool just now; I'd like to get it across to Calais without having to wait for the next fleet.'

'Master Philpot introduced me to this fellow last Michaelmas,' Gryffard said. 'He's an arrogant knave, but he knows his business, I'll say that for him. Mind you, I wonder if he doesn't have a pact with the devil. While we were all on our knees during the worst of it, praying to St Nicholas to bring us through, our captain was standing up on the poop of the ship with arrows falling like rain all about him, laughing. It was as if he knew they couldn't hurt him.' Gryffard crossed himself hastily. 'He sailed his ship right under the Frenchman's nose and shook his fist at him, before letting loose a shower of arrows into their galley. There's something inhuman about that fellow when he's dicing with death.'

'Black Nick's not in league with the devil,' said Philpot with a laugh. 'He's just a good seaman who's not afraid of the French. I'll tell him to come and see you, Master Burgeys, he's always looking for business.'

They took their places at the high table. The Mayor Adam Staple and his Sheriff John of Northampton sat on either side of their host. Then Philpot, Brembre, Walworth, Bamme, More and, at the end of the table, Gryffard. A good-looking boy with a marked resemblance to Burgeys approached the Mayor bearing a brimming silver-gilt cup and cover. On bended knee he lifted the cover with one hand and with the other proffered the wine to the guest of honour. It was gracefully done.

'The cup-bearer has the air of any squire trained in a knight's household,' said Gryffard to Brembre.

'Burgeys' son is to be a lawyer, he's apprenticed at the Temple,' replied the grocer.

A thickset young man was starting with fierce concentration to carve the roast peacocks. With his tongue protruding slightly from his mouth he carefully laid the first slice in the alms dish in the middle of the table, gave thanks to God, then seized hold of the peacock's leg and began wresting it from its socket with belligerent determination.

'The carver,' Gryffard probed, 'who is he?'

'That's John Constantyn, a master cordwainer, married to Alice, one of Burgeys' daughters by his first marriage,' Brembre informed him. 'I suppose he was the best Burgeys could do for her at the time, but he's grown more ambitious for his children since then, so my wife tells me.'

Gryffard looked around him curiously. The hall was not large,

20

hardly large enough for the number of people Burgeys had asked to his feast, but there were silver cups on the cup board behind the high table, and best beeswax candles by the hundred upon the walls. Spread out on the table were roast ducks, a lark pie, an eel stew, a spiced chopped meat dish garnished with crayfish tails, a dish of bream and a pink jelly and custard. Just for a moment it almost spoilt Gryffard's appetite to think how much it had all cost, and he studied his host with renewed interest. A man who from small beginnings was aiming high, he thought, with a son training to be a lawyer and the Mayor at his feast. A risk-taker too, perhaps, if he was prepared to send his wool to Calais without waiting for the wool fleet and had the temerity to ask both Northampton and Brembre at the same time. Risk-takers were vulnerable, thought Gryffard, picking up a duck's leg and tearing the meat off carefully with his teeth. How much would Burgeys risk to become Mayor? He might never get the chance if John of Gaunt, Duke of Lancaster, had his way.

John of Gaunt, the King's third son and uncle to Richard of Bordeaux, the heir to the throne, was showing every sign of wanting to take London into his own hand in direct defiance of the Mayor's power granted by charter from King John more than a century earlier.

'The King'll not outlast another winter, God save him,' said Philpot, 'and then heaven help us all when Lancaster makes his bid for the throne.'

'He'll not overrule his nephew, not when Richard of Bordeux's been formally acknowledged heir apparent in Westminster,' said Adam Staple.

'A ten-year-old boy!' exclaimed John Philpot. 'A man like Gaunt isn't going to let a boy stand in his way to the throne.'

'What I can't understand,' said Adam Bamme, 'is if Gaunt's so set on the throne, why is he stirring the whole of London against him now? He's either a bigger fool than we take him for or else he's very sure of his position, to act in such an arrogant manner.'

'Gaunt's always been an arrogant fool,' retorted Philpot. 'He thinks that might, and the King's favour, is right. But he'll find he can't do with London as he does with his estates in the north.'

'It's no good talking about what's going to happen when the King's dead,' put in Nicholas Brembre leaning across Philpot and directing his words at the Mayor. 'The question is, what are we going to do about him now?' All the men seated at the high table turned to look at the Mayor. Adam Staple took a quick gulp from his wine cup.

'This Bill of his, to extend the Earl Marshal's power of arrest in the city,' he said uncomfortably, 'it may not pass through Parliament.'

'Of course it'll pass through Parliament. Gaunt has it packed with his retainers,' retorted Nicholas Brembre. 'Gaunt intends to take the

21

city into the King's hand and if we don't do something to stop him we'll lose all our liberties.'

'How do you propose to stop him?' asked Bamme.

'I think Bishop Courtenay has given us an opportunity,' said Brembre, 'in summoning Wycliffe to appear before convocation at St Paul's to answer the charge of heresy.'

'And I think the Bishop's been most unwise,' retorted John of Northampton. 'This is not a trial of heresy, it's a trial of strength between the Bishop of London and John of Gaunt. Since the people of London will side with their Bishop, it will only inflame the city.'

'Exactly,' replied Brembre.

'What do you mean?' demanded Northampton angrily.

'Why, only that it's time the Duke of Lancaster was made to realise that the people of London will not dance to his tune. A good riot might give him pause for thought.' Brembre stared across the table at Northampton, a piece of peacock impaled on the end of his dagger, his eyes bright and challenging. Northampton's fingers tightened instinctively on his own knife.

'The trouble with you, Nicholas Brembre,' the conciliatory voice of Staple broke the silence, 'is you take too many risks.'

'And the trouble with you,' replied Brembre, not in the least reconciled, 'is you don't like trouble.'

'Who does?' said the Mayor with a shrug.

'I wouldn't have thought of the Duke of Lancaster as a reformer.' Richard Burgeys was anxiously trying to change the subject.

'Gaunt's befriending Wycliffe does not stem from any religious fervour,' said Adam Bamme. 'He's using Wycliffe as a tool to try to break the power of the bishops and Bishop Courtenay knows it.'

'I don't like riots,' said John of Northampton. 'Riots can very easily get out of control. There is too much riot and disorder in the city as it is. We lay ourselves open to a charge that we are not fit to run our affairs.'

'My daughter Joanna was involved in some sort of fracas in Bread Street this morning,' put in Burgeys and turned to summon his son. 'Thomas, ask your sister to come here, will you?'

Idly Gryffard watched the girl approach the high table, appraising her with a knowing eye. She was not pretty, he decided. Her mouth was too soft and full, her chin too square; her face, framed by her fine linen cap, had none of the oval symmetry he liked in women. She wore a pale gown which for all its costly miniver trimming only emphasised her essential ordinariness. She squeezed awkwardly between the close-packed tables and came to stand beside her father with an expression of mingled apprehension and defiance, and Gryffard guessed that she was no stranger to being summoned to account for herself.

22

'Joanna, will you tell us exactly what happened this morning?' Burgeys said.

'It was nothing, just the 'prentices hounding the aliens as usual. The Flemings mostly got away, I think. It didn't last very long.' She did not look at him. With eyes downcast she twisted her fingers together in the folds of her skirt. The child's hiding something, thought Gryffard, instantly alert.

'Do you know which apprentices they were?' asked John of Northampton. The girl glanced swiftly round the table and bit her lip.

'You must answer the Sheriff,' said her father.

'It was the fishmongers and grocers,' she said, raising rich, amber-coloured eyes to her father's face. Her eyes were far from ordinary, Gryffard noted in surprise, full of a soulful mystery he did not expect.

'But the Flemings escaped and no one was hurt,' Philpot prompted gently.

She nodded.

'Then I should think you can go back to your dinner,' he continued with a smile, 'since no harm seems to have been done.'

She turned, relief flooding her face.

'Just a minute,' said Adam Bamme, pointing a duck's wing at her. 'You were hurt, Mistress Joanna, were you not? Are those not bruises I see on your temple and cheek?'

'It was a flying stone hit me, it was nothing,' she said quickly. She was lying, Gryffard knew. But why?

'A pretty girl gets knocked down by a bunch of apprentices running amok,' he said with just the merest hint of irony, 'and nothing happens to her save a bruise to the temple. This city must be a great deal safer and more orderly than many I know in France or Flanders.'

She looked at him and a slow blush spread over her face and up to the edge of her linen cap.

'You told me you had come to no harm,' said Burgeys angrily.

She looked down miserably at her feet.

'Come, Mistress Joanna,' said John Philpot kindly, 'we are all of us concerned about you. If anyone attempted to molest you today they must be punished.'

'They did try to... try to...' She stopped, embarrassed, and threw a look full of eloquent appeal to her father.

'They tried to rape you,' put in Nicholas Brembre brusquely.

Her head came up like a horse suddenly reined back by too brutal a hand. 'That's right,' she flashed. 'But they didn't succeed.'

'Who rescued you?' demanded Gryffard, drawing a bow at a venture.

'It was a knight,' she whispered, but there was fire now in those eyes.

'A knight rescued you?' exclaimed Burgeys. 'Why did you not tell me this at first?'

'I didn't think it important, and I was late and in a hurry to get ready for the feast.' She was looking at the ground again.

'Who was he?'

'I don't know, Father, he did not tell me his name.'

'This knight, you say you do not know who he was but he must have had a coat of arms,' said the goldsmith.

'There were five red lozenges conjoined in bend on a blue shield.' She knew how to read coat armour, Gryffard observed and wondered who had taught her.

'Did he have a badge?' asked Philpot.

'It was a red rose,' she said.

'Lancaster!' exclaimed Brembre. 'He must have been one of John of Gaunt's retainers. I wonder what he was doing in the city.'

'He said something about trying to make the city a safer place for women and children to walk in,' the girl offered.

'By Christ's sweet mercy!' Northampton glared at Brembre. 'It is as I say, unless we can manage our own affairs better, the King will have good cause to intervene and we will lose all our liberties. Can't you see the harm you are doing to us all by this stupid campaign against the aliens!'

'And I say unless we stand together and fight for our liberties, we shall lose them anyway,' retorted Brembre staring back fiercely.

'You can go back to your table now, Joanna,' Burgeys intervened hastily, 'and tell the minstrel he can begin his tale with the second course.'

Gryffard watched her making her way back to the women, pondering what it was she had been trying to hide and why, but forgot all about Joanna as he noticed for the first time a beautiful girl sitting at table with the women and helping herself to a piece of lark pie. How gracefully she did it, he thought, watching her entranced. She was the embodiment of womanly perfection, with a delicate oval face, small rosebud mouth, hair pale as flax, and her eyes, although he could not see from this distance, he was sure would be cool and grey. Joanna was sitting down next to this pearl and Gryffard wondered with a quickening of his senses whether she could by God's good grace perhaps be another daughter of his host. That would make the mercer a very interesting man indeed.

As the minstrel began his tale, William Gryffard applied himself to the dishes of the second course now spread in profusion upon the table and thought that here might be the entry into London's powerful monopolies he had so long sought.

The minstrel sang of Arthur's court and of Queen Guinevere's lover. The room grew dark as evening approached; some slept, others

talked in whispers among themselves and the rest listened spellbound. Wandering round the hall, the minstrel embellished his familiar tale with never-ending quests, coloured it with mysterious wild beasts, added many damsels in distress and wove it into intricate patterns with Lancelot the bravest, most brilliant of knights conquering all – except his fatal love for Guinevere.

Matilda Burgeys awoke with a start when her eating knife fell from her lifeless hand onto her trencher with a clatter. She looked round anxiously to see if anyone had noticed and saw that the minstrel as he sang of love was looking straight at Mariota, and that she, wooed by the magic of his music, gazed back enraptured. Angrily Matilda stared down at the white damask tablecloth. Mariota should be married, could have been any time these two years past. She was sixteen already and far too pretty not to have a husband. Only Richard would not see it. He favoured his own daughters more than hers. Today was proof positive. Why, even after Joanna's wicked behaviour earlier this morning, Richard instead of banishing her from the feast had singled her out, summoning her to the high table in the middle of the feast. No wonder the child was rebellious and disobedient. A small neat darn on the cloth caught her eye and she moved her manchet bread to cover it. It irked her that a master mercer should have a darn in his best damask cloth and that his wife should not be allowed a new one for such an important occasion as this.

Glancing up, she caught Margaret Philpot's eye upon her and looked quickly away again. What was it about the woman that made one feel so inferior? Surreptitiously Matilda studied Margaret Philpot. She was dressed in a scarlet gown, its wide sleeves lined with marten fur right up to the elbow. Her hair was plaited and coiled into two meshed gold cauls on either side of her face, surmounted by a wide, ornamental, padded roll of bright red silk. Round her neck hung a single jewel on a ribbon, which flashed ruby red when it caught the light. Matilda had been beautiful once but she had borne and buried too many children and her beauty had faded. Sorrow and disappointment had left its mark on a face that had once been as perfect as Mariota's.

The minstrel was finishing his tale. The servants brought more candles for the iron prickets fixed round the walls and began sweeping the scraps from the tables into the alms dish to be carried outside and given to the poor. The tables were being folded away. At the far end of the room, two of the apprentices were on their knees acting as chargers for the Constantyn children who, with imaginary lances levelled, were letting off their pent-up energy in a splendid re-enactment of the minstrel's tale.

'That was a good tale the minstrel told,' said Margaret Philpot. 'Where did you find him?'

'The Mayor had him for his Twelfth Night feast,' replied Matilda proudly. 'Roger Tambard's the best minstrel in the city.'

'And expensive, I daresay,' said Idonia Brembre.

'Eleven shillings and eight pence,' Matilda told her, 'but I don't think that's too bad, not when you consider he provided the trumpeters as well.'

'Not bad for such a handsome man, don't you think, Mariota?' said Margaret Philpot. Mariota watched Roger Tambard making his way back to the minstrel's gallery above the carved screen at the end of the hall.

'I liked it well enough,' she said with a tiny shrug, 'but I prefer dancing. Joanna's the singer of the family.'

'I like to dance,' said Margaret Philpot looking round the room with careful deliberation, 'but I can't see anybody here worth dancing with, except the minstrel. Don't you agree, my child? But of course one cannot dance with the musicians.'

'How wonderful to be young and longing to dance,' put in Petronilla Northampton, easing her aching back.

'It's too near Lent for dancing,' objected Matilda, feeling unsure, now, whether the decision had been a wise one.

'Oh, Mother, couldn't we?' begged Mariota, and Matilda, looking around her flustered, caught Petronilla's sympathetic eye.

'You are fortunate, Mistress Burgeys, to have both your daughters still at home,' Petronilla said soothingly. 'Our last was married at Michaelmas and I miss her sorely, especially with this new baby coming.' She may have meant it kindly but Matilda felt unjustly accused. She could not bear the shame of having two marriageable daughters still at home thrust in her face before all these well-dowered supercilious women.

'I'm afraid we shan't have Joanna with us much longer,' she said with a quick spiteful glance at her stepdaughter. 'She's to go to St Helen's Priory at the beginning of Lent.' Joanna gasped and the colour drained from her face. Matilda began to feel better.

'A nun!' exclaimed Margaret Philpot, turning bright, inquisitive eyes on the stricken Joanna. 'How will you like that, Joanna?'

'I'd hate it! She knows I'd hate it!' declared Joanna in horror.

'But what about the singing? You should love that.' Margaret Philpot was clearly enjoying herself. 'Of course the chastity would be tedious, but you can have some fun even in a nunnery. We stayed in one, didn't we, Idonia,' she turned to her sister, laughing. 'Do you remember there was a nun expecting a baby at cherry time! It must have been one of the monks from the abbey nearby. They were constant visitors.'

'We stayed there for more than a week,' her sister agreed. 'It was so very comfortable. Better food than you get in most houses in the city.'

'Perhaps you should reconsider, Joanna,' said Margaret Philpot, her eyes twinkling.

'Joanna will do exactly as her father bids her,' put in Matilda sharply. 'It costs enough to send a girl into a convent. You should be grateful that your father is prepared to do so much for you.'

'There's a great deal to be said for the life of a nun if you have the vocation,' said Petronilla Northampton quietly.

'But I have no vocation,' said Joanna stubbornly.

Turning away from her set, angry face, Matilda saw that the Mayor was preparing to leave. 'Come, Joanna, Mariota,' she said, sweeping them before her. 'We must prepare to bid the Mayor farewell.' With the departure of the Mayor, Matilda relaxed a little. The stranger Nicholas Brembre had brought came to compliment her very prettily on her feast, the food, the music, the damask tablecloths and finally her daughters. By the time he had finished she was convinced that he was quite the most chivalrous man she had met. It did not escape her attention that while he addressed her, his eyes occasionally slid to where Mariota stood demurely at her side and she conceived the idea that here at last might be someone Richard would consider a worthy suitor for Mariota. It was certainly time. She made up her mind. She would brook no more delay. Joanna should be packed off to the nunnery forthwith and Mariota married before the year was out.

CHAPTER 3

Joanna lay in bed in the communal chamber off the hall where the family slept and listened to the familiar sounds around her. From the big bed in the corner where Father and Mother Matilda slept, she could hear muffled grunts and snufflings, like the noise dogs sometimes made wrestling together in play. Often she and Mariota had lain together smothering their laughter and wondering what their parents did in the curtained seclusion of their bed to make such a noise, but tonight Joanna was too miserable to think of anything other than her own plight. A nun! She was to become a nun.

Beside her, Mariota lay sleeping peacefully and Joanna snuggled up closer, seeking reassurance from her sister's warm, naked body. Mariota had been sympathetic, had wept even at the thought of Joanna being sent away. 'Who will brush my hair for me when you are gone? Who will I confide in?' she had asked piteously. Mariota had beautiful hair, long, silky and pale, pale gold. When braided it always lay in neat coils not like Joanna's bright chestnut tresses which fought her, whatever she did. Joanna was not envious of Mariota. Her stepsister could not help being so beautiful and good, but she did at times envy her the silken glory of her hair. Mariota had been sympathetic, but she had been no help. It did not occur to her that anything could be done to save Joanna from the nunnery.

Thomas had been much more positive. 'A nun!' He had gone into peals of laughter. 'Can you see our Joanna a nun? By the blessed saints, Mother's not serious?' And when Joanna had assured him that she was, he had shaken his head and vowed she would have to run away from home. She couldn't possibly be a nun.

Joanna lay and listened to the steady rhythmic snoring of Joan the maid curled up asleep with little Anna the kitchen maid on a pallet on the floor. Where could she run to? There was her own sister Alice – dear, kind, practical Alice. But the Constantyns had enough mouths to feed as it was and Alice, Joanna knew, would never encourage her

28

to disobey Father. With longing she thought about the knight, her rescuer, and imagined seeking him out at John of Gaunt's Palace of
Savoy. He had rescued her once, might he not do so again? But what
could he do? She had no idea what a duke's palace was like, whether
knights had ladies there with them. Besides, terrible thought, he
might not want her. She tossed and turned the whole night long, trying to think of some way of escape. One thing she knew. She would
not, could not be a nun.

At daybreak, unable to bear the torment any longer, she slipped out
of bed and dressed in the cold grey light of dawn. She would take her
trouble to St Mary's and ask the Virgin for help. Joan, yawning sleep-
ily, was pushing her pallet back underneath the bed and looked up in
surprise.

'It's all right, Joan,' whispered Joanna. 'I'm going to early Mass.'

The servant shrugged and shook some pieces of straw out of her
rough woollen kirtle. 'Say a prayer for them as has too much to do to
be always at Mass,' she muttered.

The Church of St Mary was dark and cold. Pools of light from the
guttering candles threw wavering shadows on to the vivid pictures on
the walls. The side chapels with their sleeping stone effigies were
shrouded in gloom. Groups of people, huddled in their fur-lined
cloaks against the cold, were talking together in the nave. They were
mainly fellow mercers and their families. Joanna knew them all, but
this morning she did not stop to speak to anyone. She lit a candle and
placed it reverently in front of the picture of the Virgin.

'Blessed Mary, Mother of God, don't let them do it,' she prayed.
'Don't let them send me to St Helen's Priory. I'll do anything, if you'll
only grant me this one thing. I'll,' she paused and tried to think of
some sacrifice worthy of the occasion. Then for the first time the
uncomfortable thought occurred to her that it was not perhaps very
tactful to ask the Virgin to be spared life in a convent. Maybe God
wanted her to be a nun. She knelt on the cold, stone floor in front of
the shrine and shivered apprehensively. Would God call? Behind her
she heard the tinkle of the bell at the altar, calling the congregation
to attention. The priest began to chant the introduction to the Mass.

Joanna stared up into the calm face of the Virgin, barely discernible
in the gloom. There was something in the face which reminded
Joanna of Petronilla Northampton. Then she remembered how yesterday at the feast Petronilla had bemoaned the loss of her daughters.
An idea popped into her head. Could she not go into the
Northampton's household, to help Petronilla with the new baby? It
would give her time – time to meet the knight again. Get her away
from her stepmother. Petronilla had seemed kind. She might prove
to be an ally.

The melodious plainsong was reaching its climax. The tinkle of the bell sounded behind her again. It announced the solemn moment of the Mass. Slowly Joanna rose from her knees and turned towards the altar reverently; the priest was performing the familiar ritual of the magical transubstantiation of the bread and wine into the body and blood of Christ. Uplifted, Joanna knew that she was not alone. God and the Virgin had plans for her quite different from her father's.

She hurried back home as soon as Mass was over, hoping to catch her father on his own. She had never before dared to seek him out unbidden, but today she must do it, she must be brave. One of the apprentices was taking down the shutters of the shop.

'Hello, Joanna, where have you been? You're up early.'

'I've been to Mass,' she said. He pulled down the narrow wooden counter which folded up against the wall of the house.

'Got a guilty conscience then?' he asked with a grin.

'Unlike you, I don't go to Mass only when I've got a guilty conscience,' she retorted. 'Is Father in the warehouse, Dickon?'

'He's in the counting house. You in disgrace again?'

'No, I am not, but you will be if you don't keep your long nose out of other people's business.' She pushed past him into the shop. Bales of silks, satins and velvets lay stacked from floor to ceiling on three sides in a rich rainbow of colour. The fourth side lay open to the street, protected from it by the narrow counter Dickon was busy polishing. A fine carpet covered the floor and opposite the street a small doorway led into the warehouse behind. Two apprentices were busy moving more lengths of material from the warehouse into the shop. At the far end were two small cubicles. One was where the apprentices slept, the other was the counting house.

Richard Burgeys was sitting on a high stool in front of a sloping desk, writing in a large ledger. He was handsome, hard-working and lord of his household: on him rested the burden of their wellbeing; round him revolved the entire household's daily care. Joanna hesitated in the doorway, overwhelmed by the enormity of her presumption.

He looked up. 'Why Joanna, what are you doing here at this hour?'

She let out her breath in a small sigh of relief. He was not, after all, cross with her for invading his sanctuary. He must still be in a good mood after yesterday's feast. 'I've been to church,' she said.

'Already? You're back very quickly. Was there no one there wanted to hear about our St Valentine's feast? I would have thought the description of Mistress Philpot's headdress alone would have taken more than a paternoster time.'

Encouraged, she ventured across the threshold. 'Father, I wanted to speak to you, alone.'

'It must be a matter of great moment,' he said with a smile. She clasped her hands tightly in the folds of her gown, took a deep breath

30

and could not think how to begin. In his hand he still held the quill pen, poised over his ledger. She watched a drop of ink fall from the pen onto the clean parchment of the ledger.

'Well, child, I haven't got all day,' he said gently. 'What is this matter which is of such importance that it cannot wait until we meet at the dinner hour?'

'Father, is it true that you are going to put me in a nunnery?' she blurted out. He started, frowned, tried to look her in the eye and failed.

'And if it is,' he said getting up, 'it is not for you to question my decision.'

'Father, what have I done that you should want to shut me up in a terrible prison for the rest of my life?'

'St Helen's Priory is not a prison,' he said frowning. 'Convents are for the gently born, they normally only take daughters of knights or better. I'm doing the very best I can for you. I know how much you love music. You will be able to sing all day to your heart's content.'

'If I promise never to lose my temper again –'

'Joanna, why must you insist on believing that I am sending you to St Helen's as some sort of punishment?' he interrupted. 'I am doing it because I love you. I must make provision for your future. The world is a cruel and uncertain place and if anything happens to me you will be thrown upon its mercy. The best that could happen to you is that the brothers of the Guild would find a home for you, and I do not want you dependent upon uncertain charity. In the nunnery you will find an outlet for your undoubted intelligence, if you will just be patient and learn all that they can teach you. Why, you could even become a prioress one day. Think how proud that would make me. You would be the equal of a noblewoman.'

'Could I not get married?' she asked in a low voice.

'Joanna, you're almost seventeen. I've tried to find someone suitable but it's not easy.'

'I know,' she whispered, 'I know I'm not very beautiful, but I'd make someone a good wife. I can read and I can write almost as well as Father James. I'd be loyal and faithful and look after my husband's interests when he's away.'

'Joanna, you don't understand. Marriage is a question of money – of his money and of your money. I had hoped to marry you to Walter Pritchard when he finished his apprenticeship last year, but after the bad harvest, his father had nothing with which to set him up in business and he had to take a job as a journeyman mercer with Master John More.'

'Well, I'm glad of that, I'd hate to be married to Walter Pritchard.'

'Then I tried to get John Budge. He would have been a very good match for you. His second wife died of the sweating sickness at

Lammas time and I thought it would be a very useful connection. But it appeared that he had it all settled with the widow of one of his old apprentices.'

'John Budge!' she exclaimed.' But he's an old man!'

'He's a very good skinner, Master of his Guild twice and a member of Common Council.'

'His face is all pitted from the pox and he walks with a terrible limp. I'm glad he wouldn't have me.'

'There,' he exclaimed, angry at last. 'Nothing satisfies you. Matilda is right, you have been too much indulged. A convent is the only place for you. When you have grown accustomed to the idea I am sure you will see that.'

'Please, please no, Father,' she cried. 'It will kill me to go into a convent.'

'You will do as you are told,' he said severely. 'Now go and make yourself useful to your stepmother, you've wasted enough of my time already.'

She stared down at the floor in dismay. She was making such a mess of it and he was losing patience before she had even explained her plan. He had turned away and was busy writing in the ledger once more. She threw herself on her knees beside his desk. 'It's Matilda, isn't it?' she said. 'She wants to get rid of me. She can't stand having me in the house. She hates me.'

'What nonsense. Matilda treats you like her own daughter. It is your fault, Joanna, if there is trouble between you for you have never been able to treat her with the respect due to a mother.'

'Mistress Northampton said yesterday that she misses her daughters now they've all married. Could I not go there, to help her when her baby comes?' She waited with baited breath while he went on writing in the ledger. He did not seem to have heard her. She laid her hand on his arm. 'Father, John of Northampton might be Mayor one day. Wouldn't it be useful to you if I were there?'

'It would indeed,' said a mocking voice behind her. She looked over her shoulder and saw a huge man standing in the entrance to the counting house, almost blocking out the light. He had a mane of thick dark hair flowing onto his shoulders, and a bushy black beard covering most of his face. His padded gambesons were worn and stained but there was an indefinable menace about his appearance which made Richard Burgeys instinctively reach for his dagger. Joanna jumped up.

'What are you doing here?' she demanded, too angry to feel frightened.

'My business is with your father, young lady,' he said. 'John Philpot sent me.'

'The sea captain?' Burgeys asked and relaxed a little as the man nodded. 'Joanna, you may leave us. Go and make yourself useful to your mother.'

She glared at the figure standing in the doorway. How much had he heard? His eyes resting on her face were amused. She hated him for his intrusion, for his casual scrutiny, for the way he stood in the doorway showing such interest in her affairs. But she was not going to let a ruffian like that deflect her from her purpose. Turning her back on him, she leant over the desk.

'Will you speak to the Northamptons, Father, please?' she whispered.

'Yes, yes, child, now run along and leave us. I've important business to discuss.' She was not convinced, but what could she do? Her father was getting impatient. Reluctantly she turned to go and found her way blocked by the objectionable intruder.

'Aren't you going to get out of my way,' she said with a toss of her head.

'Only if you ask me nicely,' he retorted with a grin. It was too much. All morning she had been fighting to control her temper. Now she finally lost it. She picked up the ink bottle from the desk to hurl at his head, but he was too quick for her. Her wrist was caught and held. Eyes that were piercingly blue stared down into hers.

'Let me go!' she hissed, glaring at him angrily. 'How dare you molest me in front of my father in his own counting house?'

'I apologise for my daughter's rudeness. I'm afraid I've been too easy with her. I don't beat her nearly enough.'

'Don't beat her on my account,' replied the intruder, releasing her with a grin. 'I like a show of spirit in a woman. It's a sign of a passionate nature.' He moved away from the door and Joanna, shaking with fury, scarlet with mortification and close to tears, ran past him out into the warehouse.

Richard Burgeys watched his daughter go, then studied the large man standing in front of him somewhat warily. He looked more like a pirate than a respectable sea captain. 'Are you the man who brought William Gryffard from Calais?' he asked.

'The very same,' the huge man replied with a surprisingly graceful bow. 'Black Nick at your service.'

'You've also shipped goods for John Philpot and his friends, I'm told. Were they satisfied with your work?'

The sailor inclined his head. 'John Philpot is my friend,' he said. Richard Burgeys felt unjustly rebuked. There was something about this man that made him hard to question. He almost dismissed him then and there but he thought of his warehouse full of wool and restrained himself. He had only recently gone into the wool exporting business and had discovered that there was more to sending wool to Calais than just buying well in England. It was easy enough getting the wool to London, the difficulty was shipping it across the Channel with England still at war with France and Spain taking France's part. He could wait for the wool fleet but he did not want to wait. He had to pay only a third of the cost of the wool at the outset but the settlement day for the rest was approaching. If he could empty his warehouse now instead of waiting for the wool fleet, he could exchange it in Calais for a cargo of silks and fine velvets, import them into England, sell them at the end of Lent and be in a very good position to settle with the wool growers and buy more before the Italians got the best of it.

'I've a load of wool I want taken to Calais. Can you do it?' he said, making up his mind.

'How much?'

'Come and have a look at it,' said Burgeys.

They went out into the warehouse and walked round inspecting the wool and discussing the terms which the sea captain laid down.

This man they called Black Nick might look like a brigand but he knew how to drive a hard bargain, Burgeys thought ruefully as they made their way between the bales.

'Do you insure your cargo?' The captain asked after they'd finished viewing the stock.

'I can't afford to,' replied Burgeys. 'I'd lose all my profit. You're my insurance. I'm told you lead a charmed life.'

'I've been lucky so far,' replied Nick. 'My ship's faster than the French and I've some good bowmen among the crew, but nothing's certain about this business. The sea's a bugger when roused and the wind's as fickle as a woman. I tell you this, I fear the sea more than the Spanish or the French.'

'They told me you feared nothing,' said Burgeys.

'A man's a fool or a liar who says he's not afraid. If you want to play safe you should spread your cargo over a number of different ships.'

'If I wanted to play safe I'd wait until the wool fleet was ready.'

Black Nick gave a great shout of laughter and stretched out his hand. 'A man after my own heart. It's a deal then.'

'Where is your ship?' asked Burgeys flexing his crushed fingers gingerly.

'She's lying just off Billingsgate.'

'When do you sail?'

'Not before the trial of John Wycliffe at St Paul's. I don't want to miss all the fun.'

'Do you think there'll be trouble?'

'Bound to be,' said Nick cheerfully. 'Especially since the Earl Marshal's taken one of the Bishop of London's clerks prisoner and locked him up in his inn by Aldgate. I doubt if the Bishop'll stand for that. The city's like a field of straw in a dry summer. All it needs is a little spark to set it alight, and you can count on our good Duke of Lancaster to provide the tinder.'

When he had gone, Burgeys sat staring before him deep in thought. Black Nick was right. There would be trouble when John of Gaunt brought Wycliffe to St Paul's, Brembre would see to that if Gaunt did not. Burgeys did not trust Brembre, his ruthlessness and arrogance unnerved him, and yet he knew that if ever he was to attain his great ambition to be Mayor, it was with men like Brembre that he would have one day to deal. Unless John of Northampton dealt with him first. John of Northampton could succeed Adam Staple at Michaelmas. He was a sheriff of the city and an alderman. He had a large following among the mercantile guilds. If John of Northampton became Mayor, he would use his power to destroy the victuallers and their supporters. Burgeys frowned as he suddenly remembered his daughter's impassioned plea to be sent into the Northampton household. It would be very useful to him to have a daughter there, if Northampton won; and if he lost, there was still Mariota.

Mariota was the jewel in his household. Many suitors had come to him asking for her hand in marriage but none of them were worthy of such a prize. He had been proud of her yesterday. She had outshone all the women who had come to his feast. Mariota would be his entry into the charmed circle that held the city in its power. If he could just find a husband for her who was a friend of Brembre and the victuallers then he would be one step nearer to the seat of power and control of London – as Mayor.

Meanwhile, there was Joanna to be disposed of. Matilda would not wait much longer. At the thought of Matilda his flesh began to tingle, aroused by memories of a most satisfactory conclusion to his Valentine's Day feast. Matilda knew how to make him comfortable when he kept her happy. She had been very loving last night, warm and soft and pleasurable. He would speak to John of Northampton today. If he agreed to have Joanna, it would save him the dowry he would have to pay St Helen's.

Richard Burgeys hitched himself onto his stool, arranged his velvet gown more comfortably round his knees, and applied himself to the abacus. He wrote some figures down on the edge of his ledger and considered them carefully. Then he smiled, well pleased with the result of his calculations.

CHAPTER 4

On the nineteenth day of February, John of Gaunt, Duke of Lancaster, brought Wycliffe to St Paul's Cathedral to answer to the Bishop of London. The Duke came in force, with the Earl Marshal of England, Henry Percy of Northumberland. Each great lord was accompanied by some twenty retainers, knights clad in polished steel, over which they wore a surcoat emblazoned with their own coat of arms. It was a formidable display of strength and also a brilliant spectacle, a moving tapestry of vivid colour, in the midst of which walked John Wycliffe with his four advocate friars in their sober cassocks of grey, white, black or brown. A small colony of doves in a garden full of peacocks.

Sir Tristram de Maudesbury was humming to himself as he rode along. Thoroughly bored with the daily sessions of Parliament at Westminster, he looked upon this expedition to St Paul's as a most welcome diversion. Orion was prancing and jiggling with excitement, tossing his head and snatching at his bit in a way which his rider found highly stimulating. He ran a steel-gauntleted hand down the stallion's arched neck and felt the great strength of the taut muscles bunched up in eager readiness beneath his fingers. He loved the sense of power that controlling an unmanageable stallion like Orion gave him.

The Strand wound through open fields beside the Church of St Clements Danes and the cloistered walls of the Temple, founded by the Knights Templar and now an inn for lawyers, and on past the Convent of the White Friars and the turreted manor of the Bishop of Salisbury with its gardens stretching down to the River Thames. The knights rode three abreast and the peasants working in the fields on either side watched them pass by, mouths agape. One of them raised his hoe in salute and Orion swung sideways in instant outrage.

'You want to watch that horse of yours,' said Hugh d'Aycliffe, one of Percy's retainers, riding alongside. 'He almost had my leg that time.'

'He'll be all right presently,' said Tristram straightening the horse with a quick jerk of rein. 'He's an intelligent animal, you see, he knows from the extra weight of my armour that something's up. He's expecting a battle, always gets over-excited at the thought of a bit of fighting.'

'I can't think why you have to ride a war horse about the town,' replied Hugh. 'I wouldn't dream of bringing mine out on a job like this.'

'Orion's all right,' Tristram repeated shortly, not liking to admit that he had only one horse. 'It's this cursed priestly stroll. I can't think why that Wycliffe fellow must choose to walk all the way to St Paul's. You'd have thought he would need his breath to answer the bishops when he gets there.'

By the River Fleet they fell into single file to cross the narrow bridge. In front of them lay London, the largest city in all England. Tristram stared up at those formidable walls, with the tangle of church spires, turrets and thatched roofs breaking the skyline behind. A glittering prize, he thought, magical, indomitable, and teeming with rebellious citizens ready to defy the most powerful baron in the kingdom. It would not be easily taken.

'Do you think there'll be trouble?' he said hopefully.

'I shouldn't wonder,' replied Hugh d'Aycliffe. 'The Duke must be expecting some, else he wouldn't have brought us all out in full armour. Percy and Gaunt mean to teach the city of London a lesson this day, I'd swear by the Holy Rood.'

The horses' iron-shod hooves rang on the cobblestones as they entered the city beneath the carved stone of the Lud Gate and the big bell of St Paul's began to toll. Slowly they rode up the hill past the Convent of the Blackfriars towards the stone silhouette of St Paul's Cathedral dominating the city. The churchyard was a seething mass of merchants, master craftsmen, apprentices and journeymen, all trying to crowd into the cathedral.

'Jesu, the whole of London must be here,' swore d'Aycliffe.

'By St Michael, I hope not, for I've never seen a more unattractive bunch of people all gathered together in one place,' replied Tristram, dismounting and leaving Orion to his squire. 'See if you can quieten him down, Robin, and don't let any of these grubby townspeople touch him, you know how he hates being handled by strangers.'

'Not much chance of that,' said Robin with a grin as Orion reared up and lashed out purposefully with his two front feet. The flying hooves missed a plump baker's leather basinet by a hair's breadth and the man ducked his head and ran squealing with fear towards the entrance into the cathedral. Laughing heartily, Tristram began to elbow his way through the crowd to where John of Gaunt and Percy sat still mounted, talking to Wycliffe.

'Well, Tristram,' said the Duke smiling at him, 'what do you think of the Bishop's congregation?'

'Pretty disorderly rabble, Sire,' said Tristram drawing his sword. 'We'll have to force a passage for Your Grace.' But Wycliffe laid a restraining hand on his arm.

'Put up your sword, young man,' he said. 'These people have come to hear what I have to say as well as the Bishop. Rough handling will only make them angry and harden their hearts against God's truth.' Tristram gazed round the churchyard at the people who were pushing and struggling around the door of the cathedral, noted the leather headpieces they wore, the occasional steel breastplate, the stout clubs carried by the apprentices.

'These people haven't come to listen to anybody,' he said scornfully. 'They've come to make trouble, and trouble is what they're going to get!'

'Bravo, sir knight,' said Percy with a grin. 'We'll show them who's the master in this city, by St Michael and St George we will.'

'I beseech you, Your Grace,' implored Wycliffe, 'let us enter the house of God peaceably.'

'By all means,' replied John of Gaunt. 'Tristram will ensure that no man lays a finger on you, or your fellow friars, and that this rabble here listens to what you have to say in respectful silence.'

'God's truth is not helped by forcing men to listen,' protested Wycliffe. 'No good will come of arousing their anger, I beseech you, do not handle them too roughly.'

But Tristram did not stop to listen. Shouldering his way towards the great west door, he was followed by the rest of the retainers who with judicious use of shield and sword hilt soon cleared a path down which Gaunt and Percy strode into the cathedral.

It was dark in the church after the bright morning light outside, and at first it seemed to Tristram that he was confronted by an impenetrable mass of humanity. He drew a deep breath and immediately regretted it. The stench was stupefying. Wrinkling his nose in distaste, he considered lowering his visor, but decided that he would then be able to see almost nothing at all. As his eyes grew accustomed to the gloom, he was able to discern above the heads of the people the distant figure of the Bishop of London, waiting in the chancel, surrounded by priests and supporting clergy. Resolutely he began to attack the wall of people in front of him, kicking out with his spurred feet and digging his steel-clad elbows into unprotected flesh as he forced a way up the longest nave in England.

'Watch what you be doing,' shouted a man angrily, rubbing his bruised shoulder, and Tristram grinned as he dealt the man a quick blow with the flat of his sword, before forging onwards, impregnable in his armour, leaving a trail of muttered curses, raised fists and ineffectual retaliatory kicks in his wake. At the other end of the cathedral the Bishop of London was making his way to the head of the choir steps, carrying the great gold cross of his office in front of him like a banner.

'What sort of entrance is this you make into the house of God? Throw down your weapons, or by St Peter I'll have you thrown out of this church.' The Bishop's powerful voice rang out angrily. It carried right into the furthermost corners of the cathedral and was greeted by a howl of approval.

'By God's light, that's fighting talk,' muttered Tristram as Henry Percy pushed forward angrily.

'Proud prelate!' shouted Percy. 'Do you dare tell the Earl Marshal what he shall or shall not do in his own city?'

'The Earl Marshal cannot abuse the sanctity of God's house in any city,' retorted the Bishop with a threatening wave of his great gold cross. Behind Percy came Gaunt striding arrogantly down the narrow aisle his retainers had forged for him. Wycliffe, head bent, hands folded as if in prayer, crept apologetically behind him. The Duke paused when he reached the chancel steps and stood, one foot on the step, head thrown back, his hand on his sword hilt. The blue and red velvet of his sleeves, the three ermine tabs on his chest, the lilies and leopards of his surcoat, the gold of his coronet glowed in a shaft of sunlight streaming through the painted glass of the eastern window, but no more radiantly than the Bishop's richly embroidered ecclesiastical vestments and jewel-encrusted mitre. Church and chivalry glared at each other in mutual defiance, while Wycliffe waited, a sad, patient figure in his grey gown, until the Duke seized hold of him and pushed him up the chancel steps towards the Bishop.

'We have brought you your heretic,' announced the Duke. 'Bring him a seat, he's tired after his long walk.'

'He can stand,' replied the Bishop from his vantage point above. With long, swift strides, Lancaster leapt up the steps towards him and the Bishop was forced to draw back to avoid being knocked down. A rustle of expectancy ran though the packed nave. Tristram heard it with the familiar thrill of excitement tinged with fear he always felt before a battle. It wouldn't be long now!

'A seat!' shouted Lancaster.

'And I say he shall stand,' the Bishop shouted back. With an angry gesture, Lancaster pushed the Bishop in the chest. A long growl of protest, like distant thunder, rumbled round the cathedral.

'The Duke threatens our Bishop. Down with the Duke!'

Encouraged, the Bishop waved his golden cross at Lancaster who raised his arm as if to strike the sacred emblem from the Bishop's grasp.

'Kill him!' The voice from somewhere in the midst of the nave was immediately followed by uproar. The nave became a sea of writhing, shouting figures, climbing onto the tombs, clinging to the window ledges and the carved-stone traceries of the pillars, all baying for blood. Tristram swung round to face them and knew that the trouble he had so eagerly sought was here.

'Get the Duke and Percy out through the Lady Chapel and take the priests with you,' he shouted to the knight beside him, pulling down his visor. 'We'll hold the nave.'

'Kill him!' The cry rose up from a thousand throats as the people pressed forward. The knights linked arms in line abreast in front of the entrance to the chancel, forming a steel chain. With feet wide apart and well-tuned muscles tensed, they stood firm as the first wave of human bodies broke against them. There were cries of pain as flesh met steel, and Tristram grinned inside his visor. They'd teach these unwashed rabble a lesson all right. The people at the front fell back, afraid of the knights, but from behind they were still pushing forward, trying to reach their Bishop in the chancel. Gradually the knights were forced backwards, inch by inch, towards the rood screen behind them.

Tristram braced himself and held on grimly. In front of him all was chaos. The whole nave was a mass of seething, struggling bodies. Without purpose, or direction, they jostled each other and screamed abuse at the Duke of Lancaster. Candles swayed on their prickets, the rood screen creaked ominously. Sweat drenched his body and ran into his eyes, his muscles cracked as he braced himself against the wall of bodies while all the time his mind was racing. This was no good. They were trapped, pinned against the carved wood of the rood screen behind his back. If he should lose his balance now and fall he would be done for, weighed down by his heavy armour he would be as helpless as a beetle on its back. Painfully he turned his head and through the narrow slits of his visor caught a glimpse of a grey gown disappearing through the Lady Chapel. Pray God the Duke and Percy had got safely out of the Dean's door which led out into the churchyard.

With a great crack the rood screen collapsed and in the confusion Tristram seized his chance. He drew his sword and kicking aside the bodies which lay at his feet he charged through the struggling masses, calling on the other knights to follow. The first few yards were easy. The crowd, frightened by the collapse of the rood screen, were now trying to get out of the cathedral. Instead of the tight-packed mob pressing forward, there was now only a row of retreating backs scrambling to get out of the way. Laying about him with the flat of his sword and kicking at any soft bundle of human flesh which might lie on the floor to impede his progress, Tristram fought his way towards the distant door at the end of the nave, carving a narrow passage through the sea of swaying bodies, like a reaper cutting a swathe through a field of corn. All around him the people muttered curses and angry protests, but they were not brave enough to turn on him; everybody was too anxious to get out.

Halfway down the nave the going became tougher. Tristram could no longer use his sword to much effect as his arms were pinned to his side by the great press of humanity. A club caught him a glancing blow on the side of his helm, but there was nothing he could do to avenge the attack. In front of him a knight was struggling through the press and he recognised the arms of Hugh d'Aycliffe. A man stumbled and fell hard against Hugh's knees, who took a staggering step forward, clutched at the nearest body, only to be beaten off, and began to topple. Tristram grasped d'Aycliffe beneath the steel plate of his shoulder, braced his powerful legs, and steadied the knight. Hugh kicked the fallen body from his path and with arms linked the two knights struggled shoulder to shoulder until at last they reached the great west door.

Outside, Tristram looked round eagerly for his horse, ready to mount a full-scale charge against the mob, but the fleeing crowd had lost all taste for the confrontation and were disappearing swiftly into the neighbouring streets and alleyways.

'By St Michael, I'm glad to be out of there,' said d'Aycliffe leaning against the stone wall of the cathedral to catch his breath. 'What a stinking, unruly mob these Londoners are. I'm in your debt. If you hadn't saved me back there I'd very like have been trampled to death.'

'You'd have done the same for me,' said Tristram, removing his helmet and mopping the sweat from his face. 'I think the Duke got safe away.'

'So much for the Bishop's trial,' said Hugh with a laugh. 'I doubt if he'll summon Wycliffe to St Paul's again in a hurry.'

'I wish they were not in such a hurry to run off,' said Tristram, looking round the emptying churchyard wistfully. 'I'd like to teach these craftsmen a lesson, something they might really remember us by.'

'We'd be better employed finding out what has happened to our liege lords,' replied Hugh. 'They may want an escort back to the Savoy Palace.'

'The Duke's to dine in the city today, with Sir John d'Ypres in Cornhill.

'Then we might as well dine in the city also. The excitement had given Hugh an appetite. 'Do you think we can find a tavern that's open?'

We can try,' said Tristram.

In Philpot's Inn just off East Chepe, Margaret Philpot was flirting with Black Nick. She was dressed in a tight-fitting, long tunic of bright red,

41

with a sleeveless loose surcoat decorated with the Philpot arms impaling those of Stodeye. Her headdress, the fashionable new Crespine, consisted of two cauls of stiff gold wire confining her hair either side of her face, with a jewelled filet round her brow. She wore no veil or wimple and her bared throat was long and slender and white. In her lap she held the lute which he had just given her.

'There seems to be much coming and going since the Bishop's visit this morning,' she said bending over the lute and plucking a chord. 'What do you think it can all be about?'

'I should think they are discussing what is to be done about the prisoner Lord Percy has shut up in his inn,' he said. She looked at him in surprise.

'Has Percy got a prisoner?' she asked. 'How do you know?'

'The whole city knows it by now,' he said with a shrug. She studied him curiously. He was large and unkempt, and his padded leather jerkin was stained with salt from the sea, and yet she knew that he was more than he seemed. Her husband treated him like a friend rather than a servant and there was about the man himself a certain nobility of manner, a confidence which belied his impoverished appearance. That, combined with his air of suppressed power and the careless virility of the man, she found very exciting. In vain she had tried to prise his secret out of him. John Philpot when appealed to only laughed and told her not to meddle in what did not concern her. Meanwhile Black Nick flitted in and out of her life, brought her presents and paid her elaborate compliments, but never showed any signs of falling a victim to her charm. It made him irresistible. He was standing staring down into the street though the open window. It irked her that she did not have his full attention.

'This prisoner at Percy's Inn,' she said, 'what is so important about him that it brings all these people to our house at the dinner hour? Has not everyone at some time had a prisoner in the cellar?'

'It is part of an alderman's duties to keep the peace in his ward,' he replied, 'not the Earl Marshal of England's. It is an infringement of the city's liberties, if I read the matter aright.'

'Will there be a riot, do you think?'

'Very probably. The scene in St Paul's this morning was somewhat riotous, but Gaunt and Percy's retainers prevented it from getting out of hand. Don't you wish you had been there?'

'No, no, of course not. I should have hated it. All those people pushing and shoving. I should probably have torn my gown.'

'Riots can be exciting,' he said. 'Danger and power are like strong drink to a mob, like love. Men lose all sense of reason and act like animals.'

'Love! Surely you are not comparing love to a riot?' she said, laying down the lute. At last she seemed to have his attention.

42

'Why not? Don't you think there should be danger in love – a little spice to make the meat more palatable?'

'Are you a dangerous lover?'

'It depends on the lady,' he said, his eyes on the bare triangle of flesh between her throat and her breast. 'Some ladies are soft and sweet as April showers and have to be wooed with gentle words and a light hand. Others are hot and fierce like the summer sun; they like to be taken by storm or beaten into submission.'

'And which kind do you like the best, Nick?' Her eyes held his expectantly, returning the bold challenge of his stare.

'I like them all – in their season,' he replied with a grin. She was disappointed. She did not know what she expected from him but always he left her feeling tantalised and cheated. She wanted him at her feet but he had not so far shown any signs of proclaiming himself her slave.

'You're not a constant lover then, she said with a frown.

'Constant!' He threw back his head and laughed. 'Tell me, Dame Margaret, what is this constancy the troubadours sing about? I have yet to find it, in woman or man. Constancy is for the poets and the minstrels, but it is not for you or me.' He bent over her and caressed the long column of her white throat delicately. Her flesh gloried in the feel of his strong fingers tracing the line of her low-cut tunic. She held her breath, waiting. His face was so close his beard brushed the side of her cheek and the feel of it sent a shiver of expectant desire through her body. His hand inside her tunic reached her breast. Suddenly he stiffened. Into his eyes there came a watchful look. He stood up. The door opened and William Gryffard walked in.

'Black Nick's wanted in the great hall,' he said.

There were several men standing around the fire in the great hall: Nicholas Brembre, John Philpot, and another grocer, Adam Karlyll; three fishmongers, William Walworth, John Horn and Walter Sibil.

Gryffard followed Black Nick into the hall and Nick was conscious of him lurking behind him in the shadows, his watchful eyes roaming from face to face, taking no part in the conversation.

'We want you to do a little job for us, Nick,' said Philpot, handing him a goblet filled with wine. 'We want you to lead an attack on the Earl of Northumberland's inn at Aldersgate and rescue the prisoner he has chained in his dungeon.'

Nick drank deeply from the wine cup and smacked his lips appreciatively. 'I've hardly enough men for that,' he said.

'We don't want you to use your men,' put in William Walworth, 'we want you to lead the citizens of London.'

'Shopkeepers, apprentices, craftsmen!' Nick was incredulous. 'You want me to take Percy's Inn with them?'

43

'There will be thousands of them,' pointed out Brembre.

'Against trained knights in armour, they'd be massacred.'

Walter Sibil, a large man, well dressed in a flowing furred gown which failed to disguise that his bulk came not from hardened muscles but from well-indulged flesh, contradicted Nick confidently. 'Knights can't fight properly in narrow streets. There's no room for them to charge. Separate them and pick them off one by one. Go for the horses. Fighting on foot in full armour, a knight wouldn't stand a chance alone against enough determined men, even unarmed shopkeepers.'

Nick studied Sibil thoughtfully. 'Since you know so well how to pit a rabble against knights, why don't you lead them yourself?'

'Master Sibil can't lead an attack on Aldgate,' put in Walworth quickly, 'as Alderman of Bridge, it's his duty to preserve law and order.'

'There will be no knights at Percy's Inn,' Nicholas Brembre assured Nick. 'Percy is with the Duke of Lancaster at the Savoy. The city is aflame. This morning there was a near-riot in St Paul's. Now is the time to keep the trouble stirring. All we want you to do is lead them in the right direction, the mob will do the rest.'

'I don't like using men I can't control,' said Nick. 'It's a dangerous game when you start playing with the power of the mob. A mob is like the sea, it's lethal when whipped up into a storm.'

'Of course it's a dangerous game,' said Brembre, his eyes glittering, 'but you do not win in this life by playing by the rules. Rules are all very well for the joust or the tournament. There you can ride with coronals on your lance and swords rebated. But in war, would you fight with blunted weapons?'

'In war,' retorted Nicholas, 'you fight with trained men, not a rabble of malcontents whipped up into a fury of hate and vengeance by their own grievances.'

'You have to fight with the weapons you can find,' put in Philpot. 'The Duke of Lancaster can find a hundred knights to fight for him, but he cannot use them in the city and in the city it is numbers that will win. The city is aroused, gangs of apprentices are roaming the streets looking for trouble. It is our only chance. If we can just gather them together into one determined mob, no amount of trained men can combat that.'

'And afterwards, my friend,' asked Nick quietly, 'who takes the blame for having led this daring raid?'

'They will not know who led it,' said Philpot. 'It will appear to be a continuation of the trouble in Paul's this morning. You and the prisoner will be halfway to Calais before the city has calmed down sufficiently for Gaunt to dare to take reprisals. Then when he does, it will be the Mayor and sheriffs who are blamed for not having maintained

44

law and order.'

Black Nick drained his wine. They all watched him anxiously. 'Very clever,' he said at last. 'The city riots and thereby demonstrates to Gaunt and Percy it will not stand for interference from him. Gaunt learns that he cannot force his way in the city. But the Mayor is discredited.'

'Exactly,' said Brembre. 'We have to stop Northampton and his friends now, while we have the chance, otherwise the control of the city will be in the hands of a bunch of ignorant craftsmen. It would be worse than John of Gaunt. When all is over, we will be the peacemakers. We will go to the King, ask pardon for the city's offence. A scapegoat will be sought. We will get rid of that mercer Adam Staple and his friend John of Northampton the Sheriff. We will be able to choose a Mayor more to our liking. The city will be once more in our grasp. There will be benefits for all, once this is over.'

Black Nick grinned. 'Well then,' he said, putting down his wine cup. 'I'd better start while this mess of porridge you've stirred up is still on the boil.'

CHAPTER 5

In the Mercery, Matilda, Mariota and Joanna were sorting linen in the bedchamber. It was something Matilda liked to get done before the season of Lent began. But today she was finding it hard to concentrate on the condition of her sheets and tablecloths.

'I do wish I knew what had become of your father,' she said fretfully. 'He should have been back from St Paul's by now.'

'Don't worry, Mother,' said Mariota, 'he's got the apprentices with him. They'll not let him come to any harm.' Joanna laid a damask cloth carefully in the coffer and tossed a handful of thyme over it. The knight would be at St Paul's with the Duke of Lancaster. Oh, if only she could be there too instead of shut up here sorting linen, when the whole city seemed to be on the move. All the men had gone, the apprentices as well as her father, even Hanklyn the cook. Men had all the excitement and women nothing but waiting and anxiety. Suppose there were fighting? She pictured the knight on his powerful stallion charging down Chepe with his lance levelled, and then realised with a guilty start that he would be charging against people like her father.

'Joanna, mind what you're doing!' Matilda's voice cut sharply across her thoughts. 'Can you never do anything right? You'll have to be more alert when you go to the Northamptons. I can't see Petronilla Northampton being as patient with you as I have been.' Joanna held up the damask cloth she had been about to put away in the coffer. It had a tear.

'Give it to me, it wants mending,' said Mariota.

'Yes, give it to Mariota,' Matilda said. 'I wonder what Mistress Northampton will think when she sees the sort of stitches you make. Though I daresay Petronilla does not have to sort through a pile of worn-out table linen trying to make it last another season, when it's fit to be given away to the poor. Why a master mercer cannot have new linen at all times on his table, I cannot think. The warehouse is full of the finest cloths, of every kind. Jesu, what's that?'

Joanna ran to the window and leant out to see into the street below. She could hear shouts and running feet and caught a glimpse of a stave and a head covered in a leather basinet.

'More men running towards Chepe,' she said. 'There must be trouble.'

'The saints protect us,' wailed Matilda, clutching her breast as she sank down upon a rail running round the foot of the bed. 'He should never have gone. I begged him not to go to Paul's this morning. They should none of them have gone. What will become of us if anything should happen to them? Oh, how my head aches just to think of it.'

'Perhaps you should lie down, Mother,' suggested Mariota, laying a sympathetic hand on her arm.

'Lie down? How can I? My head is throbbing so, it feels as if it is going to burst.'

'We could make you a tisane to help you sleep,' went on Mariota persuasively. 'It's no good worrying yourself into a frenzy. If you sleep a little now, then they'll be back before you're awake, you'll see. Wouldn't that be better than listening to every sound and imagining the worst?'

'I'll go and get some rue,' said Joanna quickly, glad of an excuse to escape. She whisked out of the room before her stepmother could protest.

The hall was bleak and empty, smoke-filled from the two large logs smouldering in the fireplace. On the table the dinner dishes lay cold and unappetising, waiting for the men of the household who had not returned. Joanna hurried through the gloom and down a narrow wooden staircase which led into the warehouse below. She picked her way between the sacks of wool piled high on every side, slipped the bolt on the small door beside the counting house and let herself into the garden. There she paused and listened. All was quiet. She wandered slowly into the herb garden and began looking for the rue needed for the infusion. She found it and knelt down to pick the young blue-grey shoots, when suddenly she heard a sound like a low moan coming from the direction of St Paul's. She stood up, clutching the herb, and listened intently. The moan seemed to be rising to a chant.

Something exciting was happening out there, and the temptation to know more was overwhelming. It seemed to Joanna that she could not face the uncertainty and the suspense any longer. The idea of going quietly back to the bedchamber, of trying to calm Matilda's fears and looking for tears in linen cloths while the whole city was up in arms was insupportable. She told herself that the tisane could wait. What Matilda really needed was information. She would not go far, just to the end of Wood Street. In Chepe somebody might have news, you could see St Paul's from there. If anybody had any news, she would get it there. Scattering rue in her wake, Joanna ran across the garden to the little wicket gate leading into a lane which ran down the side of the house.

Wood Street was deserted. All the shops in the Mercery had their shutters up. She ran quickly down the street. The houses on either side had a strange blank look to them with their shuttered shop fronts and counters folded up against the wall. Above her head the overhanging windows gave nothing away. She reached the wide thoroughfare of Chepeside and found it deserted also, shutters closed, stalls hastily removed. She climbed onto the steps of Chepe Cross and stared up the hill. Dark clouds massed above her head but gave way to an eerie band of light outlining the great stone mass of St Paul's Cathedral, its high spire reaching calmly into the stormy heavens.

'Kill, kill, kill!' The roar of the mob was clearly audible now; it was coming closer, and not from St Paul's but from further over to the right towards Aldersgate. Joanna froze as she heard it. It was a terrible sound. She began to regret the impulse that had made her leave the safety of the walled garden at home and turned to go back. Better Matilda's constant carping than to be caught out here by a mob like that!

It was then that she saw a riderless horse careering down the hill from St Paul's, his caparison flapping wildly as he ran. She stared at the five red lozenges emblazoned in diagonal stripes across the blue of the caparison and recognised them instantly. Without thinking she leapt out into the middle of Chepe waving her arms at the runaway. The frightened animal slithered to a bucking halt, snorted through flaring nostrils, wheeled, and set off at a gallop the way he had come. She stared after him in dismay. Where was his rider? The knight – her knight — was lying helpless somewhere, at the mercy of the mob. 'They've killed him,' she thought setting off up the hill in pursuit. 'Blessed Mary, Mother of God, don't let him be killed.'

Mindless now of everything save the man who had haunted her dreams these past five days, she ran towards the swelling roar of angry voices with only one thought in her head, to find Orion's rider. Fear, not for herself but for him, lent her feet wings, closed her mind to all caution, and her ears to the howling of the mob. She had reached the College of St Martin le Grand, almost opposite St Paul's, when a wave of human bodies came sweeping out from Foster Lane and carried her with them into St Paul's churchyard. With an agility born out of desperate need she clung to the gate and watched horrified as the frenzied crowd hurtled by.

'Kill, kill, kill!' they chanted – apprentices, journeymen, master craftsmen, respectable citizens who had lost all idea of their own identity in the frenzy of mob violence. All around, people were shouting as they ran, punching the air with their daggers, baying for blood. 'Kill, kill, kill!' The intoxicating chant fired their blood and drove them on regardless of aching muscles, bursting lungs and wildly beating hearts. 'To the Savoy! Down with Lancaster! Kill, kill, kill!'

Suddenly Joanna caught sight of her brother Tommy running in the crowd. She barely stopped to think what he was doing with such a rabble but launched herself at him, clutching at his arm with both hands. 'Stop, Tommy! Help me!' she shrieked.

'Mother of God,' he swore. 'Joanna! This is no place for you.'

'Tommy, you must help me. There's a knight lying somewhere, maybe he's injured, maybe he's dead. We've got to find him.' She was dragging him out of the path of the mob into the sanctity of the cathedral garden. He tried to fight her off, but she was two years older than he, and desperate. 'Please, Tommy.'

'God's blood, Joanna, can't you leave me alone,' he shouted at her. 'Why should I drop out of this perfectly splendid riot to help a knight? We've come to fight them, not to help them.'

'Tommy, you've got to help me,' she said clinging to his arm. 'It's the knight who rescued me on St Valentine's Day. Something must have happened to him.'

'Sweet Jesus, Joanna, he's one of Gaunt's retainers, we can't help him now. The mob would tear us to pieces.'

'He saved me,' she said obstinately, 'from *rape*, Tommy. Look, they've nearly all gone now. In a minute we can go and look for him.'

He gave an exasperated sigh. 'All right, he said. 'What do you want me to do?'

She looked round the deserted churchyard. The horse was there, in a corner of the churchyard, panting and shivering with fright, ears back, head turned to where the last of the mob was disappearing round the side of the churchyard towards Lud Gate. Joanna watched him helplessly. She did not know what to do. Now that the mob had gone, the excitement was dying out of her. She was out of breath, she had a stitch in her side from running and it was raining. She felt hopeless, but Tommy was standing looking at her with the expectant look he used to wear as a little boy, when, before he had been sent away to the Temple to learn to be a lawyer, she used to lead him into childhood scrapes. He had followed her blindly then and would do so now. If only she knew where to start looking.

'Was there a battle?' she asked, trying to pull her scattered wits together.

'No battle. We attacked Percy's Inn, but there were no knights guarding it. We got the prisoner out that the Earl Marshal had no right to be keeping. Jesu, but that was fun. You should have seen the startled face of the clerk in the stocks when we dragged him out of the cellar. The poor devil thought we'd come to kill him, I swear, not to set him free.'

'If there weren't any knights at Percy's Inn,' she said, 'he must have come across the mob before that.' With a sinking heart she listened to the fading screams of the mob disappearing down Lud Gate hill. She was beginning to feel sick.

Suddenly the horse made a wild dash out of his corner, skidded to a halt in front of a gravestone, threw up his head, lips stretched back in terror, then darted into the corner again. She looked round anxiously to see what had frightened him and saw a flock of stray sheep nibbling the grass round the gravestones. Her relief made her want to laugh.

Tommy was staring at the placid animals. 'They shouldn't be there!' he exclaimed. 'They probably escaped from St Nicholas Flesh Shambles. Of course, the sheep might have been released by the mob, but maybe the riderless horse is connected in some way. It's not much to go on, but it might be worth a try.'

'Bless you , Tommy,' she said, taking his hand. 'That lawyer's training's done you good! We'll start there.'

The Shambles, or flesh-market, contained several slaughterhouses for the butchers and was full of penned animals which had been brought to the city to be slaughtered and sold. Pigs, sheep and cattle raised curious heads above their pens as Joanna and Tommy walked into their midst. One startled bullock threw up his head and gave a great bellow of alarm, and Joanna nearly jumped out of her skin with fright. Then at last she saw him, a steel-clad figure lying on his back in the middle of the Shambles. Impossible to tell whether he was alive or dead, impossible even to tell who he was, save for the shield lying face down in the mire. Thomas rubbed at the smeared blood of offal and animal entrails with his sleeve and held it up for her to see. There were five red lozenges running diagonally from the top corner of the shield to the bottom.

Joanna looked down at the still figure and was overwhelmed by a feeling of utter helplessness. The bullock in the nearby pen let out another tortured bellow and, turning quickly, she saw the knight's squire come riding up leading the frightened stallion.

'Is he hurt?' he asked.

'I think he's dead,' said Tommy, frightened.

'Oh, I shouldn't think so,' said the squire, dismounting. 'Stunned most likely. Here, hold the horses, can you, while I get his helmet off.' He knelt in the slime of animal entrails and removed the helmet. 'He's not dead,' he said, 'but he's certainly stunned.'

'Will he be all right, do you think? asked Joanna weakly.

'He will be, if we can get him out of here,' said the squire.

'Well, what do you suggest?' asked Tommy struggling to hold Orion, who was still thoroughly unsettled and taking great exception to the animals in the pen nearest to him.

'Isn't there a convent near here we could take him to?'

'There's the Convent of the Grey Friars opposite. I'm sure they'd help,' said Joanna,. Now that her worst fears had been allayed, her natural optimism and practical sense were beginning to re-assert themselves.

'Stay here then, while I find out,' said the squire and marched off.

'He's a cool one,' grumbled Tommy, 'ordering us about like a couple of serfs. He's hardly as old as I am and not half as big. I could best him in a wrestling match any time. What call's he got to go leaving me with the horses as if I were some sort of stable lad? This big beast here's already tried to sink his teeth into my arm.'

'He'll be back soon, Tommy.' She knelt on the ground and took the knight's head in her lap. Underneath his helmet he wore a padded leather cap which completely covered his hair. She gazed at his long curling eyelashes and chiselled nose with wonder. He reminded her of one of the stone effigies lying on top of the tombstones in St Paul's Cathedral. She shivered and crossed herself, praying to St Michael, patron saint of soldiers, that the squire would hurry and come back.

When the squire did come back he looked crestfallen. There was no trace left of the confident young boy who had taken charge so quickly.

'The Grey Friars won't have him, they said they couldn't take one of Lancaster's retainers into their convent, the Bishop of London would never forgive them. I told him the Duke of Lancaster would never forgive him if he didn't but he slammed the door shut in my face.'

'What are you going to with him then?' said Tommy. 'You can't leave him here and you can't take him to the Savoy, not with that mob on its way there.'

'I don't know,' said the squire. He looked very young and helpless all of a sudden, a small, fresh-faced youth in a red and blue surcoat and jaunty red cap who for the first time in his life had discovered that the great name of Lancaster did not open every door. He looked at Joanna enquiringly. They both did, Tommy and the squire, the rain beating down on them and their wet hair clinging to their faces. They were just boys of fourteen, halfway between child and man, who knew how to fight but had not yet learnt how to think for themselves.

She looked down at the unconscious man with his head in her lap. He would know what to do if he wasn't lying unconscious in the mire of St Nicholas Shambles. A fierce, possessive determination gripped her.

51

'We'll take him home,' she said decisively.

The squire looked dubious. 'You Londoners are not very friendly towards the Duke's supporters.'

'You haven't got much alternative,' Tommy told him sharply. 'You'll have to trust us. He did my sister a good turn not long back. We're in his debt.' The squire turned and stared at Joanna in surprise.

'I'm sorry,' he said. 'I didn't recognise you. What a piece of luck.'

'Why else do you think we bothered with him,' retorted Tommy. 'If my sister had not been in his debt we'd have left him to rot here, I can tell you.' The squire doubled up his fists and turned angrily towards Tommy, but Joanna intervened quickly.

'Be quiet, Tommy!' she said. 'We must get him on one of the horses.'

It was not easy lifting him in his armour. Joanna was surprised how strong Robin proved; for when at last they finally managed to get the unconscious man up onto the saddle, Thomas was panting hard from the exertion, but the squire, who had borne the greater share of his master's weight, seemed hardly out of breath. Thomas, she could see, looked at him with new respect.

'We'd better get rid of your badge before we go any further,' she said. 'Here, Tommy, let me have your dagger.' She cut the red rose of Lancaster off the squire's surcoat and stuffed it up his sleeve.

Later, when they arrived in Wood Street with their burden, Joanna was relieved to see that the houses were all still closed and shuttered.

'Open up quickly, Mariota,' she called, standing in the middle of the street outside her father's house. Almost immediately her stepsister's frightened face appeared at the window of the bedchamber above.

'Blessed St Mary, Joanna, where have you been? We've been worried sick,' she said.

'Someone's hurt,' replied Joanna. 'Open the door for me, will you?'

'Is it Father? Has something happened to him?' Mariota leant further out of the window, trying to see beneath the overhang.

'No, no, it's not Father, but hurry, Mariota,' urged Joanna. Mariota's head disappeared and, not long after, the big oak door at the top of the steps leading up to the hall swung open. Matilda and Mariota peered anxiously down.

'Joanna!' exclaimed Matilda angrily. 'I might have known I could not trust you on a simple errand even to the herb garden without your getting into some sort of trouble. Where have you been, you evil child?'

'Mariota, run down and open the shop,' put in Tommy. 'Quickly, we must get him inside before anybody sees him.'

Mariota stared in startled bewilderment at the dishevelled squire and the steel-clad body lying across the saddle. 'Who is it?' she asked. 'Is he dead?'

'Not yet, but he will be soon if we don't get him off his horse and into the house,' said Thomas. Matilda exclaimed and Mariota continued to stare and it seemed to Joanna that they would never open the shop, but at last came the welcome sound of the shutters being opened. With difficulty they eased the unconscious man off the horse and carried him carefully inside.

'Who is this you've brought home with you, and where is your father?' demanded Matilda.

'I don't know where Father is,' said Joanna as they laid the knight down among the bolts of silk, velvet and fine wools.

'You've no business to bring a stranger here, Joanna,' insisted Matilda. 'No business at all. Running about the city when the whole place is in an uproar. What about the tisane you were going to make for my headache? What about that? Where's my tisane? How dare you run off when you know how badly I was feeling. I've been waiting all day for news of your father and now you come back bringing me nothing but more trouble.'

Joanna never heard a word. The knight's face was the colour of parchment and she did not know what to do. Joan might know. Joan always knew what to do in a crisis. Ignoring Matilda, Joanna darted past her, into the warehouse and so into the garden. Pray God she would find Joan in the kitchen.

The kitchen was a small, oval, wooden building standing on its own in the middle of the garden. It had a large open fire in the centre of the room with a hole in the roof above it to let out the smoke. A large pot hung on a hook above the fire and a heavy oak table ran down one side. Joan as sitting at the table deftly plucking a chicken and Anna, the kitchen maid, was busily pounding spices.

'Well, here's a to-do, Mistress Joanna,' said Joan staring at her in surprise. 'The whole house's been turned upside down alookin' for 'ee. Where've you been then?' She listened while Joanna told her story, plucking at the feathers on the chicken with quick rhythmic jerks of her fingers while a cloud of feathers settled on the floor around her feet.

'I don't reckon as you ought to have brought him here,' she said when Joanna had finished. 'Suppose he dies on you?'

'He'll not die,' said Joanna. 'I'm not going to let him and you must help me. Matilda's useless, and Mariota and I don't know what to do.'

Joan laid the bare chicken on the table and wiped her hands on her ample thighs. 'Stunned you think he is,' she said, scooping up a pile of feathers into her apron. 'We'll try burning some of these under his nose then. Now you run down to the cellar and fetch up a bottle of the mistress's peach brandy wine, what she put down last Lammas time. That might revive him. And Anna, bring a brand from the fire.'

When Joanna got back with the brandy she found the knight still laid out on the floor of the shop. Mariota had bundled up a length of best Flemish wool as a pillow for his head and the acrid smell of burning feathers filled the air. He showed no sign of returning consciousness. Joan laid aside the burning feathers and tried to pour brandy down the unconscious man's throat, but it only trickled out of the corner of his mouth and onto the floor.

'Perhaps we ought to find a doctor,' said Joanna, kneeling down beside him on the floor. He looked alarmingly still. 'Where's Tommy?'

'He's holding the horses,' said the squire, busy removing the camail which protected the knight's neck and shoulders. 'Here, help me with his armour.'

Joanna began struggling with the stubborn leather buckles binding the plates of steel on his shoulders. As she did so, she looked once more at his face. His eyes were open, blue as the sky on a fine May morning. He gazed at her blankly for a moment while she held her breath. 'Sweetest maiden, let me kiss you,' he said, suddenly clasping hold of her hands. Matilda gasped.

'He's not himself,' said the squire quickly, 'he doesn't know what he's saying. See, he's swooned again.'

Joanna let out her breath in a long, slow sigh. His hands, lying loosely on top of hers, seemed to burn her flesh and she waited desperately for him to open his eyes again.

'Who is he? asked Mariota, gazing down at him.

'And what's he doing lying in our shop?' demanded Matilda. 'That's what nobody seems to want to tell me.'

'He's the knight who rescued me from the fishmongers. When we found him lying senseless in St Nicholas Shambles, we had to rescue him. We had to bring him here. The Grey Friars wouldn't have him,' Joanna explained impatiently.

'I daresay they wouldn't,' retorted Matilda bitterly, 'and if the Grey Friars wouldn't have him, I don't see why we should either. Oh, why is your father not here? He should never have gone out to St Paul's this morning. Or if he did, he should have come straight home as soon as the trouble started. He had no business to leave us alone and unprotected with the city in an uproar like it is. Have I not enough to bear without this as well?'

Joanna was not listening. She was watching the knight. They had finished removing his armour. He lay on the floor dressed only in his tight-fitting jupon and particoloured hose. His body was the body of a fighting man, broad-shouldered, narrow-waisted, strong, powerful and well-muscled. His hair was the colour of ripe corn. Joanna gazed at him longingly, trying to imagine what it would have been like if he had kissed her before he swooned again.

'Mariota,' Matilda's sharp voice brought Joanna out of her trance, 'find something to cover him with. We cannot leave him lying near naked on the shop floor.'

'So that's the knight who rescued you, Joanna,' said Mariota as she fetched a length of Flemish cloth from of the shelves.

'Why didn't you tell me he was so handsome?'

It was then that Richard Burgeys returned. He walked into the shop and the first thing he saw was Mariota tucking some of his best Flemish cloth round a recumbent form.

'Dear God,' he exclaimed stopping dead in his tracks, 'who's been hurt?'

'Oh Father,' said Mariota leaping to her feet and grasping him by the hand, 'you are safe and well? We have been so worried about you.'

'So!' said Matilda. 'You are home at last. God be praised! What had Wycliffe to say that it took so long?'

'The trial broke up in confusion,' said Burgeys laying down his sword with his eyes still on the covered form, 'but who is it that you are tending?'

'Sir Tristram de Maudesbury,' said the squire, coming forward.

'And who may you be?' asked Burgeys, more and more bewildered.

'My name is Robin Swynbrook, squire to Sir Tristram.'

'And how, pray, did you get here?'

'Tommy and I brought them,' said Joanna getting up from her knees.

'Thomas, where's Thomas?' asked Burgeys sharply.

'He's with the horses outside, Father.'

'Well, that's something, I suppose. For a moment I thought it might be Tommy lying there.' He took off his leather headpiece and addressed himself to the squire. 'Now tell me how you and your master come to be here.' Robin glanced at Joanna anxiously and she smiled at him reassuringly.

'Sir Tristram and Sir Hugh d'Aycliffe were dining in the city,' the squire explained. 'After dinner we were riding past the Queen's Wardrobe when we heard the sound of a disturbance. So we rode to investigate. In West Chepe we came across a great mob chanting and shouting and at their head a huge black-haired fellow with wild eyes and a bushy beard leading them towards Percy's Inn. Sir Tristram charged them and they gave way before him but that was the last I saw of him until I found Orion grazing in Paul's yard. I guessed he must have come down somewhere. Charging on cobbled streets isn't exactly what he's trained for. So I rode around looking for a likely spot. He must have come down among the pens in the Shambles. We found him lying there senseless.'

'Who found him?' asked Burgeys, plainly bewildered.

'I found him, Father,' said Joanna, 'I had to help him. He's the knight who rescued me from the fishmongers.' Anxiously she watched her father. He frowned as he tried to make some sense of the tale. Suddenly he glared at her.

'This knight who rescued you from the fishmongers, Joanna, didn't you say he was a retainer of the Duke of Lancaster?'

Joanna nodded guiltily and dared not meet the squire's embarrassed, imploring eyes.

'Fools!' shouted Burgeys. 'We can't have a liegeman of the cursed Duke in my house. Get him out of here.'

'But Father, what would you have me do, when the Grey Friars wouldn't take him?'

'You should have left him where he was.'

'Leave him to die at the hands of the mob?' she said horrified.

'If Gaunt wants to wage war on London, he and his retainers must take the consequences,' replied Burgeys fiercely.

Joanna looked at the knight lying at her feet. Nobody was going to take him from her. 'Father,' she said, 'I think we ought to get a doctor to look at him. We've tried everything we can to bring him round but he doesn't seem to be stirring.'

'A doctor! I can't have a doctor here, it would be all round the Mercery before prime tomorrow. You don't realise what trouble you've brought me, Joanna!'

'Joanna always brings trouble,' said Matilda with a sniff.

'Father, it would be worse if he were to die,' said Joanna slowly.

'Are you going to let her foist us with this stranger?' demanded Matilda bitterly. 'Are you master in your own house, Richard Burgeys, of is it for Joanna to say who comes here and who does not?'

'If he dies,' said Joanna, ignoring her stepmother, 'then we shall have the Duke of Lancaster to account to.' Burgeys glared at her but her gaze held his steadily.

'Put up the shutters,' he snapped. 'Do you want the whole world to know he's here? It's a mercy some busybody hasn't been in here already, wanting to know who's been hurt. Lucky for us there's nobody in the streets. And somebody tell Thomas to get rid of those horses, they're bound to draw attention. There's a woolman further up the Mercery behind Wool Street. He's got a good stable at his house. He'll doubtless take them for a while.'

'I'll go,' said the squire jumping up eagerly and Joanna could see he was thankful to escape.

'That's right, you go with my son,' said Burgeys, 'he'll show you the way. And mind you don't tell the woolman anything. Tell him we've got some Italian wool merchants staying with us until the city's calmed down. They're about the only men I know could afford a horse like that one outside. And on your way back, call at the apothecary and see if you can get something to bring this knight of yours out of his swoon.'

Joanna flung her arms round her father's neck, 'Oh thank you, Father, the saints will bless you for such a good deed.'

'Of course he can't stay here,' said Burgeys disentangling himself with a frown. 'A lot of customers I'd have left if they knew I'd befriended a liegeman of the Duke of Lancaster.'

'We can hide him in the warehouse,' said Mariota. 'Joanna and I can take care of him. He won't be any trouble. Nobody need know that he's here.'

'And what about me?' exclaimed Matilda. 'How am I supposed to run this house with a wounded fugitive in the warehouse and my whole household attending to his needs every minute of the day?'

'We have no alternative,' said Burgeys. 'The damage is done now that he's here. Joanna is right, if he dies, the Duke of Lancaster may hold us all accountable. We must keep the man, at least until he recovers his senses. But he must be hidden. No one must know he's been here. If it gets out that I've one of Gaunt's retainers hidden in the house, they might ransack it as Percy's Inn was ransacked today. The servants and the apprentices must be told that their very lives are at stake if a word of this is breathed abroad.'

'Blessed Mother have mercy on us,' said Matilda crossing herself, 'it's all your fault, Joanna. I thank God that soon you'll be out of this house, though if Master Northampton knew what trouble you are he would never have agreed to take you. And don't think you can come back here if you do not please them, for you can't. I've had enough. It's a nunnery you should be going to, and that is where you will end up, I'm sure of it.'

But Joanna simply smiled. She was not to go to the Northamptons for another week and meanwhile the knight would be here in the warehouse, and she intended to spend all her waking hours tending to his every need. A week was long enough; anything could happen in a week.

CHAPTER 6

Northampton's Inn was situated down one of the lanes leading off Thames Street, the long, narrow thoroughfare which ran parallel to the River Thames. Known as the Hood, it consisted of a number of stone buildings – a dye house, stables, warehouses, bakery and kitchen – arranged round a paved courtyard in the shape of a square. At its heart lurked a bare central hall, open to the roof beams, with a two-storey bay at either end.

On the day after the riot, Petronilla Northampton sat weaving in the solar, a spacious room on the top floor of one of the bays, over-looking the river. It served as the master bedchamber and Petronilla's sitting room. A large bed took up the whole of one corner, its hangings of blue silk decorated with Northampton's merchant's mark. In another corner was the loom. Weaving was something Petronilla did when she felt troubled. The rhythmic throwing of the shuttle backwards and forwards, the careful control of the coloured wools on the wooden frame in front of her, the satisfaction of watching the pattern grow before her eyes, she found very soothing. It took enough skill to occupy her mind without making too many demands on her concentration. The chattering loom shut out the noise of everything else, and for a while she was able to exist in a small , calm world of her own.

A shadow fell across the loom and she looked up. Her husband was standing staring down at the intricate pattern she had created and from the expression on his long, pale face, she knew that he was very worried.

'Is it bad?' she asked.

'About as bad as it could be.'

'Did they reach his palace?'

'No, the Bishop of London stopped them on the road, thanks be to God. But not before they had killed a poor priest who tried to remonstrate with them on the way. There was nothing we could do, nothing. The mob was utterly out of control. The Bishop flung him-

58

self in front of them in the Strand and threatened them all with excommunication if they did not give way and depart peaceably to their homes. By God's mercy they listened to him in the end, else there'd have been murder done on a huge scale.'

'And Gaunt,' she asked, 'what will he do now, do you think?'

'It's rumoured that he's sent for reinforcements from the north, that he means to attack the city.' He was pacing up and down the room restlessly, his hands tucked into the folds of his long fur-lined sleeves.

'The King would never let him make war on London, it would be madness,' she said.

'The King is old and sick and cares only for that strumpet Perrers,' said Northampton bitterly. He was standing with his back to her, staring out of the window, clenching and unclenching his fists behind his back. Awkwardly she got up from her stool and went to the window to stand beside him, gazing down at the calm waters of the river in the distance.

The King had been young once, she thought. Edward III had been only fifteen when he succeeded his murdered father fifty years ago. For three years the kingdom had suffered terribly as the young King had struggled for power against his mother and her favourite Roger Mortimer. But Edward grew up fast. By the time he was eighteen he had the country fairly under his control. Mortimer was hanged at Tyburn and the King's mother confined in a cloister. Wise, capable and brave, like his grandfather Edward I, the King had brought prosperity at home and prestige abroad. Many men had made fortunes out of the war with France, and the great victories at Crécy and Poitiers had made English armies feared throughout Europe.

'It's sad to think of the King now, with all his glory gone,' said Petronilla, watching the boats on the river with their bright, painted sails tacking to and fro like dancers weaving in and out in the pattern of the dance. 'Do you remember the pageants and the tournaments when the Black Prince brought the French King back after Poitiers? How the city welcomed him as he paraded his royal captive through the streets. I don't think we'll ever see the like of them again. If only the Black Prince was alive now, he would never have let John of Gaunt go so far.'

'The King doesn't care, he lets Gaunt do what he likes,' said Northampton, staring morosely at the busy wharves beneath him.

'I'm sure the King won't let Gaunt make war on the city,' she persisted. 'He knows too well what civil war can do. He grew up with it. Can't you go to the King and ask him to mediate?'

'Adam Staple tried. The King won't see him. God protect us from old men who have outlived their usefulness. It's Gaunt we should be talking to now.' He began pacing up and down the room again and she leant wearily against the windowframe watching him with a sense

59

of helplessness. If only this pregnancy did not make her feel so exhausted, she thought, then she might feel better able to help him with his difficulties.

'I don't trust Philpot and Brembre,' he said, suddenly swinging round to face her. 'They're likely to try to make capital out of this. Brembre knows the King well, he lends money to him. Suppose they go to the King at Shene and make their own deal with him?'

'Would it matter, as long as it brings peace to the city?'

'Matter!' he exclaimed. 'Of course it would matter. It would set back our cause by years. Adam Staple would be bound to go and a mayor of their choosing take his place. It may even be Brembre.'

'Would that be any worse than John of Gaunt and Percy taking the city into the King's hands?'

'It wouldn't be much better,' he said. He stood in front of her, took both her hands in his. 'Don't you see, Petronilla, if they succeed unchallenged they will have the city for their own ends. Already the price of fish is twice as much in London as it is in the rest of the country. The poor are being starved so that the fishmongers can grow fat on the proceeds – what else are they to eat except fish? They can't afford meat. Brembre and his friends have grown rich on favours from the King. They will soon be as powerful as Gaunt. What good is it having our own independence if our rulers become great overlords who do not care for the wellbeing of the craftsmen in this city? What's freedom worth then? What's the difference between Gaunt and Percy or Brembre and Philpot? They are all barons who have become too powerful.'

She gazed up at his pale, taut face. His eyes, burning with the intensity of his purpose, transfixed her. He was right, he was nearly always right. 'How can I help, John? she said, invigorated by his crusading spirit. But, he stood looking through her, as if at some vision of his own. Then he dropped her hands.

'Richard Burgeys is bringing his daughter here after dinner,' he said abruptly.

'Today! But I thought she wasn't coming until Ash Wednesday.'

'She's coming today. I saw him this morning at the Mayor's house and he's very insistent that we have her now or not at all.'

'Dear God, what's the girl done!' exclaimed Petronilla and her heart sank. She did not feel nearly strong enough to take someone's difficult daughter into her household. 'I suppose it's some love trouble. It might be the minstrel – I noticed she was very taken with him the night of the feast. Oh dear, I wish she could have waited until after this baby was born.'

'She's coming to help you with the baby,' put in Northampton impatiently.

'What am I going to do with a beauty in the house?' she said, staring out of the window across the river, where above the houses with their gardens running down to the distant bank a line of treetops marked the open country to the south.

'Find her a husband, of course,' said Northampton, resuming his restless pacing. 'It shouldn't be too difficult. Burgeys is on the way to becoming quite a rich man, I shouldn't wonder.'

'If he's so rich why has he not found her a husband himself?'

'He's been too busy building up his business to have the time or the money for marrying off his daughters,' said Northampton. 'From what I've heard, he uses every penny and much more besides to stock his shop with the finest goods a mercer can. He's always overstretched, buying far more on credit than is prudent, but the gamble seems to have paid off. Now he's buying wool like any merchant capitalist. He sends his son to the Temple to be a lawyer instead of apprenticing him to a fellow mercer and seems able to afford a nunnery for his daughter. He's an ambitious man and I don't want him falling into Brembre's hands.'

'There will be trouble with Matty,' she said, frowning. 'I had hoped to have her betrothed to Adam before the Burgeys girl came here.' Matty was a cousin of John of Northampton, an orphan whose family had died in the plague of 1348. Too poor to be sent into a nunnery and too plain to attract a husband without a dowry, she had become a permanent fixture in the Northampton household. As such, she made herself very useful, but Petronilla never gave up hope of marrying her off to one of the apprentices.

'Adam knows where his best interests lie,' said Northampton, 'and if he wants to prosper as a master draper he would do well to marry Matty and benefit from all the trade I can pass his way. He knows that as well as the next man.'

'I daresay he does,' said Petronilla with a sigh, 'until he catches sight of the beauty. Common sense tends to fly out of the window once a young man's fancy turns to love.'

'Well, there's no question of his marrying Burgeys' daughter. She can do much better than one of our apprentices.' Northampton was stern. 'So be careful. We need Burgeys, Petronilla; we need all the support we can get.'

'But your support in the city is huge,' she said. 'I'm always being told that the people will do anything for you.'

'The poor, the journeymen craftsmen, the minor guilds, but it is the great companies I need to help me defeat the victuallers. The Mercers and the Goldsmiths Guild, for instance.'

'You have the Mayor on your side and he's a mercer.'

'He may not be Mayor for much longer and the mercers are a law unto themselves. I cannot count on all of them. John More is on our side, but Burgeys sits on the fence. That's why I want you to do this

61

for me, my dear.' He took her hands in his again and peered down solemnly into her face. 'It's not asking much, you yourself said you missed your daughters now they've gone from us. You will do it, will you not? To please me, to please Richard Burgeys? I need his support.'

'Blessed Mother, I wish I'd never said it!' exclaimed Petronilla, leaning her back against the cold stone of the window embrasure and gazing at her husband's worried face. He was a good man, for all his revolutionary fervour. He never beat her, never forced her to do his will and if she always ended up doing it, it was because she wanted to help him, because he had persuaded her that his will was best. She gave his hands a quick, encouraging squeeze. 'Let's hope she has a nature as sweet as her face, then maybe I shall be grateful for her presence after all. If things are as bad as you say, then a beautiful young girl may be just what we need to cheer us,' she said with a smile.

Petronilla was resting on her bed in the solar, with Katherine her youngest daughter keeping her company, when Matty came to tell her that she was wanted in the hall. 'I said that you were resting, but he said to tell you Master Burgeys is here with Joanna.'

'Yes, well, of course, I must go and welcome the girl, Matty,' said Petronilla, levering herself up off the bed and trying not to notice Matty's grimly disapproving expression. She had tried to explain at dinner about this addition to the household, tried to make out that it was for Matty's convenience as well as her own that the girl was coming to help with Katherine and the new baby. But Matty had insisted that she needed no help, that Katherine did not take kindly to strangers, that it would upset her to have someone new looking after her at a time when her mother would be taken up with another baby. Well, thought Petronilla, straightening her cap in front of the polished steel mirror hanging on the wall, let's hope the girl can win her round. I really don't feel I have the energy to go on trying. Aloud she said, 'See if you can help Katherine with her spinning, she's beginning to learn, but every now and then she gets the yarn into a terrific tangle.'

Entering the hall a few minutes later, she paused in dismay, completely taken aback to find that instead of the beauty she had been expecting, Richard Burgeys had brought the elder Burgeys child who seemed about as cheerful as a mourner at a funeral.

'Why, this is Joanna, is it?' she blurted out in surprise. 'But aren't you the one who was going to be a nun?'

'I'm not going to be a nun, and no one can make me,' declared Joanna, glaring at her fiercely.

'No, of course not,' said Petronilla faintly. How could she have been so tactless!

John of Northampton whisked Richard Burgeys quickly away to look at the latest consignment of cloth in his warehouse, and

Petronilla was left alone with Joanna who remained standing where her father had left her, scowling down at her feet. Joanna did not look as if she was going to be an easy presence in the household, thought Petronilla as she watched the men depart, inwardly cursing her husband and his political aspirations. She was no beauty, that was certain, not in that brown kirtle and plain blue surcoat anyway. So at least there would be no trouble with the apprentices falling in love with her. Matty could rest easy on that score. She's trouble though, thought Petronilla, studying her carefully. I shouldn't wonder if her spirit is as hard to tame as that bright chestnut hair struggling to spring from the two lumpy braids coiled untidily on either side of her face. There was determination in that chin, passion in the soft, full mouth, fire in the amber eyes. God, no doubt, had some purpose in sending the girl to her but she would need all His help to fulfil it. Resolutely Petronilla braced herself. The best way to meet trouble, she had found, was usually head on.

'Now look here, Joanna,' she said firmly, 'I think we had better get a few things straightened out right away. I daresay you came here only to escape going into that nunnery you hate so much. You didn't want to leave home and you feel they were glad to be rid of you. Is that it?'

The girl gave no sign of having heard, but just went on staring at her shoes as if in a trance.

'Well, I didn't want to have you either.' Petronilla was beginning to get annoyed. 'I'm doing it to oblige your father. But I don't put up with bad tempers, disobedience or unwilling work, otherwise you go straight back home and that probably means into St Helen's Priory. I can be a hard taskmaster, as hard to please as any Prioress, so you had better decide whether you want to stay and to try to please me or whether to go home again with your father now.'

Still the girl said nothing. Petronilla was surprised and a little disappointed. She had thought the child had more spirit. Expecting to provoke her into some sort of life, she had been prepared for rebellion perhaps, even loss of temper, but not this helpless indifference.

'Are you listening to me, Joanna?' she said more sharply than she intended.

The girl looked at her then, but with such bleak misery in her face that Petronilla was shaken. She was reminded of an injured dog they had once had to kill. The dog had bitten everyone who had tried to help it, she reminded herself ruefully.

'I'm sure that Matilda Burgeys has taught you to sew and spin and weave,' she said more gently. 'I don't think life in our household will be very much different from being at home, and my little daughter Katherine is looking forward to your coming.'

'Mother Matilda tried to teach me, but I'm afraid I'm not very good at it,' said Joanna in a low voice. Petronilla's heart sank. What was she to do with her? If the girl was so determined to be miserable, perhaps she would be better off in a nunnery after all. 'Let's go and find Matty,' she said, abandoning any further attempt to get through to the child. 'She'll show you where you are to sleep.' Matty's implacable hostility was no more than her new attendant deserved, she thought with a sigh as she led the way out of the hall and up the winding staircase to the solar in the bay above.

Afterwards, Joanna could remember little of that first day in the Northamptons' household. It had come as a shock to find that Petronilla was not the gentle Madonna-like lady she had imagined her to be, and she had been vaguely conscious of some hostility from Matty as she showed her where to put her things. But her mind and her heart were so firmly left behind in her father's warehouse, with Sir Tristram de Maudesbury, that almost anything anybody said to her left her completely unmoved.

She drifted through the rest of the day in a daze, remembering how he had looked, lying on the pallet in the apprentices' cubbyhole at the back of the warehouse. The joy when he had come at last to his senses again. How he had teased her when she tried to make him drink the posset that Joan had prepared. How they had laughed when he had upset it all over her skirt and how Matilda had scolded when she had come and found them laughing, insisting that Sir Tristram needed rest, not clumsy girls who could not even give him a posset to drink without spilling it all.

That was this morning. Then she had been bundled unceremoniously out of her father's house and into Northampton's at least a week earlier than had been planned, and she did not know why. Unless it was her punishment for bringing the knight home yesterday. It still seemed extraordinary. If her father was so angry that she had brought him to the house, surely he would have banished the knight as well? But he had not. She had been removed from the house, despite all her beseechings and pleadings, while her knight lay still hidden in the warehouse, tended by Matilda and Mariota, and tolerated, she was almost sure, by her father. It seemed the grossest sort of joke played by fate, to have provided her with the opportunity of such unimaginable bliss and then to have snatched it away from her so cruelly.

She took her place for supper that evening in the hall, still miserable and bewildered. The Northamptons themselves had already supped in the small chamber below the solar, as they only ate in the hall with the rest of the household at dinner in the middle of the day. The household was a large one. Apprentices, journeymen drapers, the dye master and his two assistants, the cooks, as well as several women servants were all seated on benches on either side of two long trestle tables which ran down the centre of the hall. Joanna picked at her food, unaware of the curious stares of the apprentices, and of Matty's attempts to ensure she receive the last of the mutton broth, the smallest piece of baked white bread, the lump of beef with the the the most gristle in it and the piece of cod which had nothing but bone. Joanna was not interested in the food, nor in the conversation around her. Her mind was back in the Mercery, where she longed to be. Then one of the apprentices leant across the table and winked at her.

'Your father's been trying to palm off second-class goods then?' he said with a grin.

'I don't know what you mean,' she said indignantly. 'Father sells only the very finest quality.'

'Cutting it a bit short of the yard perhaps,' suggested another. 'The mercers always were sharp.'

'We'll know all about it when the Master and Wardens of the Mercers Guild have searched your father's shop tomorrow,' hissed Matty, gazing at Joanna's bewildered face in delight. 'There's no smoke without fire, they say, and they wouldn't be going to make a search if they didn't know he'd got something to hide.'

'It's not true.' Joanna gazed at them in horror. 'Father's never had faulty stock in his life. He only ever sells the very best.'

'Oh, but it is true,' said Matty with great satisfaction. 'Isn't it Adam?'

'True enough,' said Adam. 'John More's apprentice, Will, told me himself. Met him in Chepe this afternoon on his way to tell one of the Wardens, says his master's a bit embarrassed having to go there so soon after that grand feast on St Valentine's Day.'

'Bit of a change for him, feast one day, condemned stock the next,' said Matty nastily. But Joanna did not hear her. She was thinking quickly. A search of her father's goods would not matter, not normally. He had no faulty stock, of that she was sure. But if the Master and Wardens were to find Sir Tristram hiding in the warehouse, it would be a disaster. He must be warned. Tristram must be spirited away before the search.

She looked round the table at the alien faces surrounding her. There was no one here who would help her. No one she could trust. She must go herself.

The rest of supper she sat wrapped in thought, desperately thinking what she could do. She could not go now, not after curfew; it was too dangerous to cross the city after dark and besides, she might not be able to find the way. It would have to be tomorrow, very early. If she were to slip out of the house at prime, pretend she was going to early Mass, she might be able to get to the Mercery and back before anybody missed her.

But next morning, hurrying across the paved courtyard with eyes downcast and a pious expression on her face, she was surprised by Petronilla.

'Why Joanna, where are you going so early in the day?'

'To Mass,' stammered Joanna. 'I always like to go to the first Mass of the day, it's more peaceful then and I can listen to the music better.'

'And yet you have no vocation,' said Petronilla with a smile. Joanna looked at her uneasily and wondered whether she suspected anything. 'I too feel the need of God's help and advice this morning,' Petronilla went on, 'so shall we go there together?'

There was no help for it, Joanna had to accompany Petronilla to All Hallows the Great in the Ropery and afterwards wait in the cold, dark nave while Petronilla greeted friends and exchanged news.

'Nothing good, I'm afraid, this morning,' said Petronilla shaking her head as they began to walk back along the Ropery. 'Everyone is waiting for the Duke of Lancaster's revenge against the city. It's very bad for business.'

The Ropery, so called because mainly ropemakers lived there, was a short stretch of Thames Street between the Church of All Hallows the Great at the top of Church Lane and the Church of All Hallows the Less. The smell of tar and hemp hung in the air and already one or two seamen from the ships anchored out in the river were examining ropes which hung in great festoons outside the houses. Petronilla owned all the land from the Ropery to the Thames and between All Saints Church and the steelyard. It had been part of her dowry when she married her first husband. On the walk back to the Hood, Petronilla told Joanna that the rents were overdue for collection.

'The troubles of the past few days put it right out of my mind.' she said. 'We'll make a start this morning. You can help me, Joanna. It always takes a long time. If trade is good then they're too busy selling rope to stop and pay. If trade's bad then you have to listen to why they haven't got the money.'

'What do you do if they have no money to pay?' asked Joanna, while her heart sank. Petronilla seemed determined not to let her out of her sight this morning; she would never be able to get away to warn her father.

'They usually have, even when they say they haven't,' replied Petronilla. 'You have to be very patient, bully and plead, bully and plead, until they weaken. I never force them when I know they really haven't got it. There's no point. You can't take what isn't there. I try to help them over the bad times with a little food and occasionally some good advice and just wait until prosperity returns. It usually pays off. Gratitude makes them better payers in the end. It will be good for you to learn how to do it, then you can take over for me when the baby comes. You might find it more interesting than working in the house.'

In vain Joanna wracked her brains for a way of escape. She resigned herself to having to wait until dinner time. Perhaps then she could slip away. Pray God it would not be too late.

Later, while they were in the solar getting ready to set forth, Petronilla sat down suddenly on the shelf round the bed, her hands on her side.

'What's the matter, Mistress Petronilla?' asked Matty anxiously. 'You look ill.'

'It's nothing, I shall be all right directly,' said Petronilla a little breathlessly. 'It's my own fault, I should never have eaten that bread after Mass this morning. I'm always better if I wait until noon before I break my fast, but I was so hungry and it smelt so good straight from the bakehouse. I'll just sit here and rest a little, then Katherine can help me sort through the linen, won't you, my pet? But I'm afraid I don't feel up to collecting rents this morning.'

'Let me go for you,' said Joanna, seizing her chance.

Petronilla studied her thoughtfully. 'I wonder if you could manage it,' she said. 'It's only the Ropery. If you take one of the apprentices with you, you should be safe enough. Will's a good lad. He's been with me several times and knows how much each shopkeeper owes. Yes, take Will with you, he'll show you what to do – and don't listen to any excuses from the ropemakers.'

'Could I not go for you?' said Matty.

'No, Matty,' said Petronilla, holding out her hand with a warm smile. 'I need you here.' Matty shot a look of triumph at her rival, but Joanna, all too pleased at this heaven-sent opportunity, had already fled from the solar, unaware that the freedom she had been granted was in the nature of a test.

She found Will in the long, rectangular warehouse across the courtyard from the hall, busy stowing bales of Brabant linen and Flanders cloth that had recently been unloaded from a ship tied up at Hay's Wharf.

'You couldn't have come at a better time, Joanna,' he said straightening up slowly with a grimace. 'My back is about ready to break.'

'Mistress Petronilla wants you to go to the Ropery to collect the rents for her,' said Joanna.

'What, all on my own?' he asked, surprised.

'The mistress is sick, she ate too much new bread this morning,' explained Joanna. 'She says can you manage without her?'

'I suppose I can. I'll certainly be glad to have a try, anything's better than unloading this stuff,' he said with a grin. 'Aren't you going to come and keep me company? Some of these rogues react better to a woman's persuading.'

'No, I can't. I've got an errand to do for her elsewhere,' she replied vaguely. He accepted her excuse and went off to the counting house to fetch the tally sticks.

Holding her breath, Joanna walked towards the stone arch which led into the street, trying not to hurry, keeping her eyes straight ahead and steeling herself not to glance guiltily over her shoulder. It was not until she had passed the Church of All Hallows the Great and had left the Ropery behind her that she dared to breathe again and quicken her pace.

She flew along Thames Street without a second thought for the consequences of what she was doing. Her mind raced ahead of her to the Mercery and to Sir Tristram de Maudesbury, and the joy of being able to see him again, until she was suddenly jolted out of her daydream by the sound of someone calling her name. She looked round guiltily and to her horror saw the merchant of the staple coming round the side of the high stone wall of the steelyard.

'Goodday to you, Mistress Joanna,' called Gryffard. 'Are you going my way, by God's good grace?'

'I'm on my way to see my family,' she said faintly.

'Your family?' he queried, puzzled.

'I'm in John of Northampton's household now,' she explained, hoping devoutly he would not pry any further.

'I'm on my way to Chepe,' he said. 'I'll walk with you. The city's not very safe yet after the riot. I'm surprised that the Northamptons let you go on your own. Things have by no means settled down.' He had watchful eyes, she thought, disconcerted, and hoped he was not going to ask her a great many difficult questions. Picking up her skirts carefully she walked on, pretending to give her full attention to avoiding the many puddles in the road.

'Is this your first visit home then?' he asked. She nodded, cursing the bad chance that had brought him across her path on this of all mornings. 'Yet it's still less than a week since your father's feast,'he persisted.

'A week's a long time when you're homesick,' she replied quickly.

'Ah, to be young and impatient and think a week a long time. At my age a year seems to pass all too soon,' he said. She looked up at him to see if he mocked her and nearly walked straight into a heap of refuse lying in the gutter. He seized her elbow and guided her carefully round the obstacle.

'I'm surprised your father sent you into Northampton's household,' he said still holding her arm. 'I'd have thought he had more sense.'

Almost she confided in him then. He was looking at her with such interest and she was much in need of sympathy. But there was something about those penetrating eyes of his which made her feel that once started she might not be able to stop and that to tell him too much would be a mistake. So she smiled at him warmly instead and went on walking in silence, quickening her pace a little as they turned into the Walbrook, in the hope that he might become too out of breath to question her any further. But though he may have claimed age, he kept pace with her easily. A small stream ran down the side of the street and women were busy washing their linen in its muddy waters.

'Where does your father get his wool from?' asked Gryffard presently. She looked up at him startled.

'Father's a mercer,' she said. 'He sells silks and velvets and the best damasks.'

'But he deals in wool, because he's got a cargo going to Calais with Black Nick, the sea captain. I wonder if he means to sell it at the big Pash Mart in Antwerp at Easter or perhaps St Denys Fair at Paris.'

'I don't know,' she said, surprised that he knew so much about her father's trade but happy to be at last on what seemed a reasonably safe topic. 'I thought he bought here in London at St Bartholomew's Fair. Sometimes he likes to go to Winchcombe in the summer, although he says even at Winchcombe it's almost impossible to get fine linens.'

'I'm going to the Cotswolds myself in a few days,' he volunteered. 'Perhaps your father and I could go together.'

'Aren't the roads very bad at this time of the year?'

'They can be, but that's all the more reason for going. The worse the travelling, the fewer the people willing to attempt it. I find it pays to get ahead of the Italians; their purses are very deep and there is little wool left worth the buying when the Italians have passed by.'

They walked on for a time after that in silence and Joanna began to wonder when he would take his leave. When they reached Wood Street and he was still at her side, she stopped and held out her hand.

'Thank you, Master Gryffard, for accompanying me so far, but I need not take you any further out of your way,' she said as firmly as she could.

'But it isn't out of my way,' he replied, taking hold of her arm again and guiding her into the Mercery.

Anxiously Joanna searched the street ahead for any sign of a deputation from the Mercers Guild. The shops down either side were open, dark caverns of secret delight, concealing all kinds of richly coloured finery. The apprentices were busy crying their wares, but there were fewer people about than usual. Outside her father's house, she paused and looked about her apprehensively. A broad-shouldered merchant was considering a length of velvet lying on the counter and his girth shielded her from Dickon's inquisitive gaze. Further up the street, Owen was crying their wares, trying to attract one of the few passers-by into the shop.

'Shall we go in?' said William Gryffard.

Joanna stared at him aghast. Now what was she to do? She tried to think of some polite excuse, but he was already shepherding her down the lane which ran along the side of the house towards the steps leading up to the main door. She went with him, her heart thumping in her breast, aware that there was nothing she could do to prevent his coming in without arousing his suspicions. He seemed to have an uncanny knack of getting his own way without even asking.

CHAPTER 7

Anna, the little kitchen maid, opened the door. 'Mercy if it ain't Joanna!' she exclaimed, standing in the doorway mouth agape.

'Yes, it's me,' said Joanna seizing hold of Anna's arm and propelling her firmly into the hall. Somehow she had to prevent William Gryffard going down to the counting house, 'Is my father at home?'

'The master 'e b'aint be 'ere,' Anna informed her, peering over her shoulder at William Gryffard. ''E went out soon after prime.'

Joanna was stunned. It had never occurred to her that her father might be out. What was she to do now? Somehow she had to get rid of the merchant of the staple and get down to the warehouse, fast, before the Master and Wardens of the Mercers Guild arrived to make their search.

'Find Mariota,' she whispered into Anna's ear. 'Tell her to come to me here in the hall – quickly!' she added, pinching the girl's arm hard. The girl was simple. Would she understand? Would she hurry? 'And bring some wine,' she shouted after the fleeing maid. Pray God she doesn't bring Matilda, thought Joanna, looking anxiously round the hall, half expecting her stepmother to jump out at her from among the shadows.

Gryffard was standing quietly in the middle of the room, watching her. There was something about him that made her feel uncomfortable, something in the way he waited there so calmly, sympathetic eyes resting on her face, as if waiting for her to blurt out the truth to him. He was a man, she felt, who was used to getting at the truth. What did he want?

She turned her back on him and began trying to poke life into the one wet log lying in the hearth. Instantly he was at her side, flinging on more wood, fanning the smouldering logs, helping her get some sort of a flame going.

The rustle of skirts brushing through the rushes on the floor made Joanna turn round quickly. Mariota! God be praised!

'Why Joanna, whatever is the –'

'William Gryffard brought me,' interrupted Joanna, flying across the hall and flinging her arms round her sister's neck. 'Keep him here,' she whispered, 'the Guild's coming to make a search'. Mariota's slender frame stiffened in her arms and all the colour drained from her face, her calm grey eyes gazing at Joanna blankly.

'It's good to see you again, Mistress Mariota.' From over her shoulder Joanna saw Gryffard coming closer and she gave her sister a last frantic shake of warning before releasing her. 'I remember you well from the St Valentine's feast but my memory, I find, did not do justice to your beauty.' His gracious words brought some of the colour back into Mariota's face but she still looked bemused and frightened.

'I'm sorry Father isn't here to welcome you, Master Gryffard,' Joanna said quickly, terrified that Mariota might start asking awkward questions in front of this stranger. 'Do you know where he went, Mariota?'

'No, but he shouldn't be long, we're expecting him back for dinner.' Mariota was looking far too shaken to be safely left alone with Gryffard. It wouldn't take him long to worm all their secrets out of her if he chose to do so. But what else could she do? thought Joanna in desperation. Time was running out. Unless she got down to the warehouse immediately, the Mercers Court would be upon them and it would be too late.

'Where has that girl got to with the wine?' she said, deciding to risk it. 'Master Gryffard, I'm sure, must be thirsty after his walk. I'll go and see if I can hurry her up.'

He did not answer, too busy settling Mariota on a stool by the fire. He seemed disposed to pay elaborate compliments and she was rewarding him with a bashful, sidelong glance from beneath her long lashes. Relieved, Joanna recognised it as one of her sister's most effective weapons in a considerable armoury of flirtatious equipment, and Mariota was never happier than when receiving and encouraging tributes to her beauty. As Joanna ran down the winding stairs into the warehouse it suddenly occurred to her that perhaps Mariota had been the reason for William Gryffard's visit to the house today.

In the warehouse all was quiet. She hurried to the small room the apprentices slept in. There was no one there. Where was he? Had he already gone? But no, his surcoat and shield were lying propped up in the corner.

'Sir Tristram,' she called forlornly, staring down at the empty pallet with a terrible feeling of loss. Had he had a relapse and died? She heard a step behind her and whirled round. He was standing in the entrance to the little cubicle and at the mere sight of him her legs turned to jelly and her mind to a confused muddle incapable of rational thought.

'I thought you were Mariota,' he said.

'And I thought you were dead,' she replied. He laughed and she laughed with him, for a moment forgetting all her troubles in the magic of his presence. He was dressed in a fur-trimmed gown of her father's, his long sword hanging from a silver girdle round his waist. Even in this uncharacteristic attire he looked impossibly handsome, especially when he smiled at her.

'You're better,' she said inanely, transfixed by his smile.

'You disappeared, and there was no one to throw soup at me,' he said, teasing her, 'so I got up.'

'You can't stay here,' she said, suddenly remembering, 'you must go at once.'

'But I don't want to go, not yet. Not now you're back to look after me. Not now I'm feeling better. I've been a great trial to everybody and now I want to make amends. Besides, I promised Tommy a lesson in swordsmanship when he gets back.'

'Tommy?'

'Yes, he's helping Robin take the horses back to the Savoy today. I didn't think Orion was very safe in that woolman's stable.'

'But you can't stay here,' she said, 'the Mercers Court are coming to make a search of father's stock, they'll be here at any moment.'

'A search?' he repeated, plainly baffled.

'Yes, for faulty stock. A guild has the right to search any member and if the stock proves sub-standard, it is condemned. They'll turn the warehouse inside out.

'Don't worry,' he said, his hand clenching on his sword hilt, 'I'll see that they don't get a close look at your father's goods. How many of them will there be?'

'But you don't understand, she said hastily. 'It's not his goods – father's stock is beyond reproach. It's you they musn't find here, else Father will be ruined. No one will trade with him again, not once they know he's sheltered one of the Duke's retainers. And it's all my fault for having brought you here in the first place.'

He leant against the entrance to the little cubicle and regarded her ruefully. 'You want me to go now, this minute?'

'I'm afraid you'll have to,' she said, peering past him anxiously into the empty warehouse beyond. 'There's a merchant of the staple upstairs in the hall and I don't know how long Mariota can keep him occupied. Do you think you're well enough to walk back to the Savoy?'

'Oh, as to that, apart from a sore head, I'm not much the worse.'

'Come with me quickly then,' she said bundling up his surcoat and handing it to him. 'You can get out through the garden into the lane down the side of the house. You'll be safe enough in the city dressed like that.'

'I'd feel safer in my armour,' he said picking up his shield.

'That'll be all right here.'

'Where are you going to hide it?'

72

'There's no need to hide it,' she said, leading him out into the warehouse. 'Father often deals in armour. There's nothing wrong with him having some armour in the warehouse.'

'How do I know he won't sell it?'

'Father's not a thief,' she flashed quickly, then blushed with shame when she realised he was teasing her again. He laid his shield beside the rest of his armour in the corner of the warehouse and followed her out into the garden. She unbarred the door and peered cautiously out into the lane. 'It's all right now,' she said, 'there's nobody about.' He was standing looking up at the house and she gazed at his broad back, longing to say something that would let him know how much he meant to her, but the very intensity of her emotion left her tongue-tied.

'I never thanked you properly for what you did that day in saving me from the fishmongers,' she stammered. It was a poor substitute for all the tumult of love that was in her heart.

'It was nothing,' he said with a shrug. 'You and your family have risked much more on my account. Maybe one day I shall be able to repay the debt.' He was still staring up at the house and she watched him, holding her breath, desperately willing him to kiss her before he left. 'Meanwhile,' he said suddenly turning and grinning down at her, 'the sooner I'm gone, the more relieved you'll be, isn't that so?'

She shook her head wordlessly, gazing at him with her whole heart in her eyes.

'Adieu, Joanna.' He touched her cheek lightly with his finger. 'I'll be back – for my armour.'

Mute with the agony of her longing, she watched him stride quickly through the door and out into the lane. Now that he was gone, all the wonderful things she had wanted to say to him came tumbling into her mind and she cursed herself for a simpleton for having let such a golden opportunity escape. Fool that she was, she had not even told him where to find her!

'Joanna!' The harsh, unwelcome voice calling across the garden brought her back to reality. 'Whatever are you doing here? Sweet Jesus, am I never to be rid of you?' Matilda was hurrying round the corner of the kitchen like an agitated hen, her linen veil flying out behind her. 'Where is he? Where's Sir Tristram?'

'He's gone, Mother Matilda.'

'Gone! Where's he gone to? He never said anything this morning about going.'

'He's gone back to the Savoy!'

'Back to the Savoy! But what about the sugar loaf I've had made for his dinner? I don't understand. He's not well enough to leave. He's only just left his sick bed. It's madness!'

Patiently Joanna explained about the search and the reason for Sir Tristram's rapid departure.

'I don't believe it!' protested Matilda indignantly. 'Your father in all the years he's been a mercer has never had a search for sub-standard goods. You're making it up. I don't know what your reasons for meddling are, Joanna, but I warn you, if you try anything like this again I shall insist that you are removed from the Northamptons' household forthwith and sent straight to the Priory.'

'Don't worry, Mother Matilda,' replied Joanna bitterly, 'if Petronilla Northampton finds out I disobeyed her this morning she will throw me out into the street anyway.'

'You mean you came here without the Northamptons' permission? Little fool! They'll never take you back now.'

Desperately Joanna tried to make Matilda see beyond her own pre-occupations. 'I couldn't ask for permission to warn Father about the search, they would think he had something to hide. And I couldn't tell them about Sir Tristram, could I?'

'Somebody must have told someone about him,' wailed Matilda, 'else why are the guild coming to make a search? And your father not here – oh, why is he never here when he's wanted? What are we going to do?'

'It's all right,' soothed Joanna, 'now that Sir Tristram has left there's nothing to worry about. Let the Wardens search the shop and the warehouse, they'll find nothing to Father's discredit.'

'And what of the merchant of the staple in the hall with Mariota now? What will he think when the Wardens arrive? Do we want the word going back to Calais that Richard Burgeys is suspected of selling sub-standard silk?

Joanna had forgotten all about Gryffard. She bit her lip and looked at Matilda with scarcely concealed irritation. 'You must get rid of him, Joanna,' her stepmother went on. 'You brought him here, you must take him with you when you go.'

'I can't, I've got to get back to the Hood, before the Northamptons discover I've gone,' said Joanna.

Swiftly Matilda moved to the garden door and shot home the bolts. 'You're not leaving here without him,' she said, grasping Joanna firmly by the arm and dragging her across the garden towards the house. 'You had no right foisting him on us without any notice like this and me in my everyday gown too.'

'I couldn't help it. I didn't ask him to come, he just followed me in.'

'Well, maybe he'll follow you out again,' said Matilda pushing Joanna in front of her through the warehouse door. Then seizing her once more by the wrist, she marched her up the stairs to the hall.

Mariota and Gryffard were drinking wine by the fire. Mariota sat gracefully erect upon her stool listening to him with apparent fascination.

'You found her,' said Gryffard, turning to greet them with a friendly smile. He looks pleased with himself, thought Joanna, and hoped it was Mariota's company rather than any unexpected revelations which had so humoured him.

'Yes, I found her,' said Matilda, 'but I'm afraid she has to return immediately, for she has promised the Northamptons to be back in time for dinner. I wonder whether we could trespass on your kindness and ask if you would be good enough to accompany her back to the Hood. I don't like the child walking about the city on her own at this time.'

'And quite rightly,' he replied, draining his wine. 'I shall be only too happy to be of service. My errand in Chepe can wait for another day, when perhaps I can take the opportunity of calling upon Master Burgeys and renewing my acquaintance with Mistress Mariota?'

'Farewell then, Master Gryffard.' Mariota graciously held out a small, white hand for him to kiss. 'Take good care of my sister, won't you?' She got up and embraced Joanna warmly. 'Come and see us again soon,' she said kissing her.

Joanna returned her embrace with a heavy heart. How easy for Mariota to say that, she thought, when she doesn't know the trouble I'm in. It would be a miracle if she succeeded in returning to the Northamptons undetected.

Walking back to the Hood, Joanna tried hard not to think about the problems which lay in store for her there, but her mind could fix itself on nothing else. She would not even have minded if Gryffard had plied her with questions. At least it would have provided her with some distraction for her tortured mind. But he now seemed too preoccupied with his own thoughts to pry into hers.

Chepeside was abustle with people going about their ordinary business among the jumble of market stalls with their bright coloured awnings, like bees flitting from flower to flower collecting pollen on a hot summer's day. Some of them were gathered in little groups talking earnestly, no doubt discussing the danger the city was in from the Duke of Lancaster's revenge. Joanna watched them enviously, too concerned about her own immediate disgrace to have any anxiety left for the peril of the city. She longed to loiter, to delay the moment of reckoning when she would have to account for her inexplicable behaviour, but Gryffard marched her firmly onwards, and it occurred to her as they passed the church of St Mary le Bow that she must get rid of him before they got to the Hood.

Bow bell began to chime and then one after the other in a joyous fanfare of sound the bells from every church in the city pealed.

'You'll be late for dinner, I'm afraid,' Gryffard said.

'I know,' she replied, finding inspiration. 'But so will you, and it will be because of me. Where do you dine today?'

'With Nicholas Brembre in the Royall,' he said.

'But that is on our way, and it's not much further to Thames Street.

There's no need for you to miss your dinner in order to walk all the way with me. I shall be perfectly safe. The city's quiet enough.' To her surprise he acquiesced quite readily and for a moment it amused her to think that his stomach took precedence over his gallantry. She bade him farewell outside Brembre's Inn in the Royall.

She walked more slowly through the Vintry, towards Dow Gate and the Ropery, trying to think of what she would say to Petronilla Northampton, but no plausible explanation presented itself to her. Even in her own eyes her behaviour had been inexcusable and she could not possibly tell them the truth. So she walked on, fearing the worst but hoping for a miracle.

Dinner was already well advanced when she entered the hall and she realised with a fearful sinking feeling that she could not have chosen a worse moment at which to make her return. The Northamptons, the chaplain and the secretary were seated at the table on the dais and below them the rest of the household ranged in descending order of rank along the benches down both sides of the laden trestle tables. A deadly quiet fell upon the assembled company as Joanna made her appearance. A sea of faces turned in her direction, while what seemed like a hundred eyes examined her curiously. Burning with shame and scarlet with embarrassment she remained just inside the carved screen, unable to move, consumed by a passionate desire for the floor to open and swallow her up. It was far, far worse than she had imagined.

'Come here, Joanna.' It was John of Northampton who summoned her. Her legs were shaking so much she could hardly move. Slowly, she forced herself forward, eyes fixed upon the rushes at her feet, hands clasped together tightly at her breast. Like a condemned prisoner on his way to the block, she approached the high table at the other end of the hall. She knew the eyes followed her, she could feel them boring into her back – and the whispers, running round the room like mice in the wainscot.

'Where have you been?' His voice, quiet and cold, asked the inevitable question.

'Home,' she whispered.

'Why?' They would beat her, that was certain. But would they send her away? Biting her lip, she stared down at her feet and waited for the storm to break.

'Answer me.' His voice was quiet, controlled and patient as any confessor's. She did not dare look at him.

'I don't know,' she mumbled. At her feet a piece of chicken bone lay buried in the rushes and a small colony of ants was busily swarming over it.

'We were worried about you. You father gave you into our care and when it was discovered you were missing, the whole inn had to be tuned upside down in search. My apprentices have wasted valuable time combing the neighbourhood. I think you owe me an explanation,

76

don't you?'

'I'm sorry,' she mumbled again. It had never occurred to her that the Northamptons might be concerned about her disappearance. It made her feel worse.

'Why did you go home, Joanna? Why did you leave this house without a word to anyone?'

'I don't know,' she repeated helplessly, staring down at her feet. The ants were dragging the bone through the rushes; slowly, step by step, they were moving it by sheer force of numbers. Joanna watched them, wondering with a detached fascination where they were taking it.

'Joanna, look at me.' The voice, suddenly sharp as honed steel, rang out in the hushed, expectant silence of the hall. She looked up, startled, into his long, pale face and saw no mercy there.

'You ran away and they sent you back, is that it?' Petronilla intervened, leaning forward a little from her seat beside her husband. 'We cannot keep you here against your will, Joanna.'

'It's not against my will,' she mumbled. 'I had to go home, I cannot explain why, but I had to go. I didn't run away, I always meant to come back. I wanted to come here, I did. Ask Father if you don't believe me.'

'It doesn't matter,' said Petronilla with a sigh. 'I thought I made it plain to you yesterday that I would not brook disobedience in my household. I gave you a responsible task this morning, to see if you could be trusted. You betrayed that trust and I have learnt my lesson. I'm afraid that you are no use to me here. You will have to go back home.'

'Please, Mistress Northampton, don't do that. Give me one more chance,' pleaded Joanna. In her desperation she had quite forgotten about the interested audience behind her. She ran to Petronilla's side and threw herself down on her knees beside her chair. 'They'll send me to the nunnery, I know they will.'

'You should have thought of that before you went,' said Petronilla, hastily turning her head away. 'A convent is the only place for a girl like you. I can see that now. I can see why they had to get rid of you. There is nothing more to be said. Now go to my solar and wait there for me. A little fasting and reflection may bring you into the right frame of mind for St Helen's Priory.'

Numb with despair, ignoring the fascinated household who had been witness to her disgrace, Joanna slowly left the hall and climbed the stairs up to the solar. Her fate, it seemed, was sealed. No amount of pleading would move the Northamptons to change their minds, and she knew that if she were sent home, Matilda would see to it that her father could not be won round again. She could almost hear the doors of the convent closing behind her. Aimlessly she looked round the solar, and her eyes alighted on Petronilla's prie-dieu in the corner. Throwing herself down on her knees before it, she prayed for a miracle.

CHAPTER 8

In the hall Petronilla was finishing her dinner with difficulty, unable to get Joanna out of her mind.

'Of course we cannot keep her now,' she said, as if trying to convince herself, 'not in the face of such rank disobedience. The child is utterly untrustworthy.'

'No, of course not,' replied Northampton firmly. 'I can't think what Richard Burgeys thought he was doing foisting such an unruly girl onto you at a time like this. Clearly a nunnery is the best place for here. I'm very sorry, my dear, to have put you to all this trouble.'

Petronilla ought to have been glad that he took her part so readily, but she was not. There was something about the child, something about those huge, pleading eyes in the resolute young face which pulled at Petronilla's heartstrings, that and the curious dignity with which she had walked past the packed tables in the hall, ignoring the curious stares of the whole household. There was an indefinable quality in her which, if properly nurtured, might bear some surprising fruit, thought Petronilla. She could not help feeling that in sending Joanna away she was failing in God's purpose. But how could she keep the girl after such wanton defiance, how condone such behaviour? Nobody in her well-run household defied her authority and got away with it. Joanna was trouble, she reminded herself sternly; she had sensed it from the start and the sooner her disturbing presence was out of the Hood, the better it would be for all of them.

She pushed back her chair and got quickly to her feet – too quickly. Her swollen belly made her clumsy and as she stood up she lost her balance, clutched at the table, failed to reach it and fell over backwards into the rushes. Pain shot through her side so sharp it took her breath away.

'My dear, are you all right?' Northampton was bending over her, helping her to rise.

'Of course I am, so stupid of me,' she said a little breathlessly as she brushed the pieces of straw off her skirt. 'I'm so large now it makes me awkward. I forget sometimes. Sweet Jesu!' Another pain stabbing through her made her double up in agony. Her husband's anxious face swam before her eyes, and she groped for the chair behind her, feeling her legs go weak. He caught her as she swayed and helped her back into the chair.

'It's the baby,' she gasped, gripping the table in front of her so hard her knuckles turned white. 'I think he wants to come into the world before his time.' Pain was stabbing through her now like a knife thrusting in and out of her abdomen. She looked at the circle of anxious faces gathering round her and tried to smile reassuringly. Dimly she felt their supporting hands as they helped her to her feet. The ground before her rose and fell through a haze of pain as she stumbled across the hall. They half carried, half dragged her up the steep stairs to the solar. In agony she collapsed upon the board running round the bed, aware of a frightened Joanna being driven out of the room by Matty, opened her mouth to remonstrate but another stab of pain, more intense than the rest, turned the words into a scream.

The pain engulfed her like a burning sea breaking on her body in great vehement waves. Like the sea, the waves varied, some broke gently and were almost bearable, then would come two or three great crushing breakers, hurling themselves upon her and driving the breath out of her body in a cry of agony. Occasionally, as the pain ebbed a little, she was conscious of her surroundings, of her hair hanging in two loose braids over her breasts, of someone wiping away the sweat which ran down her face and into her eyes, of hands gripping hers, of the midwife's arms supporting her on the birthing stool.

Some time later the doctor came. Petronilla glanced at him in the midst of her agony and caught a look of helpless concern on his face. 'I'm going to die,' she thought. 'Poor John, how will he manage without me at a time like this? I must not die, not yet. Not with the city in this turmoil. John needs me, there is so much to do.'

The pain searing through her belly was relentless now, growing out of her womb and attacking her whole body. She leant against the midwife, writhing on the birthing stool while her women stood and watched her helplessly. The doctor and the midwife whispered together and shook their heads. They gave her acrid herbs to chew on and bathed her head with rose water, they held her frantic hands and told her to be brave. But Petronilla was unaware of anything save the unbearable agony of the child struggling to be born. It seemed to her pain-crazed mind as though she were poised over a pit of hell with a hundred devils stoking the fire which reached up from below and threatened to devour her.

'Hold me,' she screamed to the midwife, 'don't let me go.' Amid the flames she seemed to see Joanna's stricken face, the huge, pleading eyes staring up at her in bewilderment, and she made a vow to God that if He permitted her to live through this ordeal, she would let Joanna stay.

Banished from the solar with Petronilla's scream ringing in her ears, Joanna had fled to the women's dorter, a long, narrow attic above the stables. It was dark and cold there, but in all the large complex of buildings which made up the Hood, it was her only refuge. There Joanna waited, not knowing what to do. She had enough experience of Matilda's many birthings to know what ailed the mistress of the household, but Petronilla was a stranger and apart from a brief feeling of pity she did not dwell much on her suffering, she had too many problems of her own to worry about.

Crouched in the gloom on the straw pallet which served as bed for her and Matty, Joanna contemplated the consequences of her folly. She realised that she had thrown away her only chance of a future outside the convent, yet looking back over all the excitement of the past few days, she did not see how she could have acted differently. In her misery she went back for comfort to the few moments she had spent with Tristram alone in the warehouse, treasuring every word and gesture, and it was then she suddenly remembered how empty the warehouse had been. The piled up bales of wool had gone! Had Nick collected the wool – and stumbled on Tristram? She did not know but it helped to have someone to blame other than herself for her misery.

Hadn't William Gryffard said that Black Nick was to take a load of wool for her father to Calais? She sat bolt upright on the straw.

'It was that demon Black Nick who betrayed us, I'm sure of it,' she muttered. Angrily she jumped to her feet and began pacing up and down the small attic thinking about the ugly man who had humiliated her in front of her father. He would betray anybody, of that she had no doubt! But why? Then she remembered something else. Robin, the squire, had said that the attack on Northumberland's Inn had been led by a man with a bushy black beard and wild black hair. Black Nick! She was surprised he had not attacked her father's house openly, but then perhaps he did not want to lose a good customer. This way was much more subtle.

As the long afternoon dragged slowly into evening, Joanna worked off some of her anger and pain on devising torments for the man who indirectly, it seemed, was the cause of most of her suffering. Although there was nothing she could do to punish him, it made her feel a little better to be able at least to blame someone else for her troubles.

By the time the Angelus sounded, Joanna was very hungry, and when soon afterwards two laundry maids came into the dorter, she wondered whether perhaps she might be allowed into the hall for supper.

'How fares Mistress Northampton?' She asked tentatively.

They stared at her, whispered together, crossed themselves and hurried out of the dorter. Joanna watched them go, dismayed. A little later, a distracted Matty appeared. 'Can I do anything to help?' asked Joanna, jumping up. 'I feel so useless sitting here.'

Matty stared at her blankly, then without a word started rummaging in the coffer at the end of the room where they kept their clothes. 'Could I not take care of Katherine for you?'

'Stay away from her. Don't you dare touch the child! shrieked Matty. 'Have you not done enough harm already, with the mistress on her death bed?' She too crossed herself and hurried from the room.

'Merciful Saviour, they think it's all my fault,' thought Joanna, now truly frightened. She could not possibly go down to supper. Too exhausted to think any more, she undressed and, kneeling on the bare wooden floor in her smock, committed herself into God's keeping, resigning herself to a long hungry night of wakefulness. But God was kind. No sooner had she crept beneath the blankets on the pallet bed than sleep, deep and untroubled, claimed her instantly.

She woke to the sound of the bells ringing for prime and stretched luxuriously. the previous day's fast and the long night's sleep made her young body tingle with health and energy. The straw pallet was empty and, with her mind still hovering on the brink of sleep, Joanna lay and listened lazily to the bells. Dimly she remembered Matty getting in beside her some time just before dawn and with remembrance she came fully awake.

Springing out of bed, scattering the blankets in a heap on the floor, she hurriedly began to dress. There was no one in the room. She was still struggling with the buttons down the front of her gown when Matty appeared.

'The mistress wants you in the solar right away,' she announced, her lips folded tightly over her turned-down mouth.

'Mistress Northampton?' stammered Joanna, staring foolishly at Matty. 'Then she's not...'

'No, she's not dead, you'll no doubt be sorry to hear,' retorted Matty. 'And she wants to see you now, this minute!'

'But I haven't done my hair,' gasped Joanna, seizing the mass of tumbled chestnut curls and trying to tame them. 'Matty, won't you help me braid it, please.'

'I've work enough to do without acting lady's maid to those as lie in bed all morning,' said Matty with a sniff, seizing hold of one of the blankets and giving it a vigorous shake. 'But I shan't mind helping you pack your things when you've seen the mistress.'

At least, thought Joanna as she left the dorter with her hair bundled untidily into yesterday's cap, if I am to leave the Hood today it will give me great pleasure to slap that Matty's face before I go.

Standing outside the solar a few minutes later, Joanna did not feel nearly so belligerent. Dismissal awaited her on the other side of that door and there was nothing to be done but face it with what dignity she could muster. Fervently she wished that she had not overslept this morning, that she had had time to braid her hair neatly. Then, taking a deep breath, she pushed open the door and walked into the room.

Petronilla was tucked up in the big bed, lying with closed eyes and a peaceful smile on her face. A small bundle tightly wrapped in linen lay beside her. Joanna crept to the foot of the bed and stood there shifting from foot to foot, wondering what to do. Petronilla's eyes opened.

'Isn't he beautiful?' she said, twisting her head and gazing at the tiny scrap at her side with maternal pride.

Joanna stared down at the screwed up little red face atop the linen bundle and could not agree. 'He looks very like you,' she said and hoped the fond mother would take it as a compliment.

'Do you think so? I'm not sure he doesn't look more like my daughter Idonia when she was born.' Joanna didn't really think the infant looked like a human being at all, so she said nothing.

Petronilla was plainly exhausted. Her eyes began to close again and Joanna wondered whether she should leave the room. But where was she to go, and what was she to do? She could not spend the rest of her life hiding in the women's dorter. It was better to know her fate and to face up to it now. She drew a deep breath.

'You sent for me, Mistress Northampton,' she murmured.

'Yes, of course, so I did,' said Petronilla. Her voice was weak and tired and there were dark blue shadows under her eyes. 'God has been good to me, Joanna, He has spared me and He has given me this beautiful babe. In gratitude for God's mercy and in honour of a vow I made, I will give you another chance. You may stay with us if you wish.'

Completely taken aback by this unexpected reprieve, Joanna fell on her knees beside the bed and seized hold of Petronilla's hand. 'Oh, Mistress Northampton, you won't be sorry, I promise,' she whispered, a sob in her throat. 'I will serve you to the last breath in my body, by the Blessed Virgin I swear it.'

'I'm glad to hear it, Joanna,' said Petronilla with a smile, 'for I feel as weak as a kitten and there is a great deal to be done. Now go and do something about that wonderful hair of yours, then you can bring me some bread and ale, for I must get my strength back as soon as I can.'

Matty was furious when she heard the news. 'You've bewitched her, that's what you've done!' she exclaimed. 'Evil, you are, I knew it the very first moment I set eyes on you. You've brought nothing but trouble to this house from the moment you came, and Mistress Petronilla is too good to see it.'

'What nonsense, Matty. What evil have I done? The mistress has just been brought to bed of a fine healthy son. What harm is there in that, may I ask?'

'Time will tell,' Matty muttered, glaring at Joanna full of jealous suspicion. 'The midwife said that the child came out of the womb silent as the grave and she had to smack him several times before he took his first breath, then instead of a great lusty cry, he made just a whimper. You stay away from him and from the child Katherine, I'll not have you meddling with either, putting the evil eye on them.' But Joanna took no notice of Matty, she was too relieved at being allowed to stay.

Matty's forebodings proved well founded, however, for the new baby died the next night, just two hours after he had been hurriedly baptised by the Northamptons' chaplain. Petronilla took it very hard. She lay in the large bed in the solar, staring up at the embroidered tester above her head, her hands continually straying to the empty place beside her. She took no interest in the running of her household, content to leave everything in Matty's charge.

Matty used her power to see that Joanna was kept in the background as much as possible and given the most menial tasks to perform. When Matty discovered, to her delight, Joanna's ineptitude with needle and spindle, she heaped all the sewing and spinning she could find upon her rival, then complained daily to Petronilla about Joanna's bad work. 'I daresay the child will improve with practice,' was all Petronilla would say but Matty was content to wait, confident that the steady litany of Joanna's faults and shortcomings would eventually wear out even Petronilla's patience.

Joanna bore it all with as much stoicism as she could muster, determined to give no one cause for casting her out. She went about the many menial tasks Matty found for her meekly, biting back the angry retorts that burned in her brain, aware that she had an enemy, but unable to understand the reason for Matty's implacable animosity. She had no friends, Matty saw to that; the women treated her with scarcely veiled contempt and the apprentices, when she had any dealings with them, seemed bent on either provoking her into losing her temper or in enticing her into trouble. It was not in her nature to turn the other cheek, but whenever she was tempted to let fly, Joanna thought of the convent and the black-robed nuns shut in behind its high stone wall, and forbore. John of Northampton she barely saw; he was hardly ever at home and far too preoccupied with the city's troubles. And so she kept herself to herself, enduring her loneliness as best she could and trying, when she lay beside Matty's stiff resistant back on their straw pallet at nights, not to miss the warm comfort of her bed at home and Mariota's confidences in the darkness.

When Matty saw that Joanna was not to be driven into rebellion by these methods she began muttering about spells and witchcraft. This, too, Joanna tried to ignore, but when the women drew away from her in the dorter and Matty refused to share her straw pallet any longer, she realised that resignation was not enough. If she was to survive in the Northampton household, she would have to get the better of Matty.

Petronilla, Joanna decided, was her only hope. Somehow she had to appeal to the mistress over Matty's head, show her that there were ways in which she could shine. But how, when Matty kept her busy with tasks she was so bad at? Joanna frowned as she jabbed savagely at the linen tablecloth she was mending. Try as she might, the stitches were neither neat nor even. Matty knew her weaknesses, and there were all too many of them. The whole household was beginning to accept Matty's opinion of her; pray God that she had not already poisoned Petronilla against her.

The next morning Joanna dressed very carefully, braiding her hair neatly and tucking it out of sight beneath a clean linen cap. Then when Matty was out of the way, she slipped unobtrusively into the solar. Petronilla was dressed and seated in front of the loom, but her hands were idle in her lap.

'Why, Joanna, whatever brings you here?' she asked, looking up.

'I wondered if there was any service I could do for you, Mistress Northampton.'

'I don't think so.' Petronilla gazed listlessly out of the window. 'Matty sees to all my needs. She has been invaluable.'

'I thought you might like me to read to you.'

'Can you read, Joanna?' asked Petronilla in surprise.

'Yes, Mistress Northampton, and Father James says I write a fairish hand. Father James is the chantry priest who gives us lessons.'

'Unusual accomplishment for a girl.'

'Well, I'm not very good at spinning and weaving, so I learnt to read and write instead. Sometimes I even help Father in the counting house, when the apprentices are away buying stock, and he's teaching me how to use the abacus.'

'Well, I don't feel like doing sums today, I'm afraid it might make my head spin.'

'And I'm sure the weaving makes it ache, so wouldn't you rather I read to you?' persisted Joanna.

Petronilla seemed unable to make up her mind. She sat gazing at Joanna with a vacant look in her eyes, which frightened the girl. Turning away, Joanna espied a pile of books on the shelf running round the bed.

'How wonderful,' she said. 'I've never seen so many books. All we have at home is a book of hours and the lives of the saints.'

'And doubtless you know them both by heart.'

'I like the lives of the saints best.'

'Yet you have no wish to emulate them.' Joanna looked at Petronilla uncertainly. Her face was grave but lurking somewhere in the depths of her grey eyes there was the gleam of something approaching a twinkle. God be praised! Beneath the sadness and forbidding manner there lurked a sense of humour.

'I don't think God wants me to be a nun,' she replied with a quick conspiratorial smile.

'Why, Joanna, you look really pretty when you smile,' said Petronilla, startled.

Greatly daring, Joanna swiftly bent down and scooped up the pile of books. 'What would you like me to read?' she asked.

'Do you know the poet Langland?' Petronilla was becoming interested in spite of herself. 'If Langland is to be believed, even in a cloister pretty girls can get into plenty of trouble.' She got up from her stool in front of the loom and came to sit on the side of the bed. 'Langland was a chantry clerk,' she went on, selecting a book from the pile Joanna still held. 'When I was a girl he brought out the first edition of *Piers Plowman*; since then he has added many new cantos and fresh passages. This is his latest edition.' She leafed quickly through the book on her lap and finding the place she wanted, handed it to Joanna. 'Let us see what you can make of him, shall we?'

Joanna had never heard of *Piers Plowman*. She read hesitantly at first, very conscious of Petronilla sitting at her side. Then, as the extraordinary ideas and fascinating imagery gripped her, she read on entirely absorbed. There was Sloth the parson, who could neither sing nor read, but who could find a hare in a field better than a *beatus*. There were monks who had no pity on the poor, though money rained on their altars. There were friars preaching for their private profit, pardoners selling false pardons to cheat poor people of their gold, nuns squabbling in convents. Joanna looked up.

'Is it all true?' she asked, her expressive eyes round with amazement.

'True?' Petronilla shrugged. 'It's a story, an allegory, like the minstrels' tales, but Langland is only saying what Wycliffe says in a different way.'

'I suppose it's not surprising when people are forced into convents against their will. You can't expect them to keep their vows in the same way that a really convinced nun might,' commented Joanna.

'That's a very cynical thought for a child of your age. I can see we shall have to keep you out St Helen's Priory if we possibly can. We don't want you becoming another Dame Peronelle, or leading some poor misfortunate monk to eternal damnation.'

'I'm no Dame Peronelle,' said Joanna vehemently. 'If I took my vows, which I shan't, I should stick to them.'

'Even if a handsome young monk came and swept you off your feet?' teased Petronilla.

'A monk!' exclaimed Joanna and, at the sight of her horrified face, Petronilla burst into laughter.

She was still laughing when the door opened and Matty, leading Katherine by the hand, walked into the room. Matty stopped on the threshold and, at her look of dismay, Joanna felt almost compensated for the many, many times she had forced herself not to smack that long, miserable face.

'Ah, Matty,' said Petronilla. 'Joanna has done me so much good, she has been reading to me from *Piers Plowman* and I had almost forgotten what a wonderful book it is. I have read Langland many, many times, but listening to Joanna is like coming upon him afresh, seeing new depths and new visions. I have been brooding too much on my own sorrow and it has made me idle. I think I will come down to the hall today for dinner. You would like that, my pet, would you not,' she said scooping Katherine up into her arms. 'And tomorrow Joanna shall read to you too.'

After that Joanna's position in the household improved. At some time nearly every day, Petronilla would send for her to come to the solar. There Joanna would spend many a happy hour reading, or sometimes writing letters for her mistress. Matty complained that Joanna was behind with the mending. 'Get one of the other women to do it,' replied Petronilla. 'Joanna is far too useful to me here.' It was then that Matty realised her brief period of power was at an end. She confined herself to dark mutterings and a jealous protectiveness towards Katherine, but the rest of the household were quick to change their tune. Joanna the outcast was now the mistress's favourite, and they discovered when they treated her well that she was far kinder than Matty and much more fun. The apprentices stopped their teasing and vied with each other in trying to win one of Joanna's rare and wonderful smiles.

Petronilla, watching the awkward, unappreciated girl blossoming in her new environment, was amused and astonished. Never had a vow been easier or more rewarding to keep. In encouraging Joanna, she was able to overcome her own sorrow and even, for a time, forget her anxieties for her husband and the future.

CHAPTER 9

As John of Northampton had feared, Nicholas Brembre and John
Philpot were received by the King at Shene who succeeded in making peace between his son, John of Gaunt and the city. The price of
peace was disgrace for the Mayor, Adam Staple, who was deprived
of his office. To the people of London, Nicholas Brembre was the
hero of the hour. It was no secret that he had been behind the successful attack on the Earl of Northumberland's inn and now he led
the successful deputation to the King. He had met force with force
and won, and he was duly elected Mayor in Staple's place. The Duke
of Lancaster had no alternative but to accept the election of the one
man in the whole of London most strongly opposed to him. The Bill
to extend the Earl Marshal's rule over London was not heard of
again, the murdered priest who had met his death at the hands of the
mob on the way to the Savoy was conveniently forgotten, but the
Duke of Lancaster did insist on some form of public penance.
Brembre agreed to organise, in honour of the Duke, a procession to
St Paul's Cathedral and the day chosen for the procession was the
Annunciation of the Blessed Virgin Mary.

On 24 March, Joanna came into the solar at the Hood to find
Petronilla with her head buried inside the painted Italian chest at the
foot of the bed. She turned when she heard Joanna come in, her arms
full of soft green wool.

'I don't think this gown fits me so well since poor little James's
birth,' she said. 'Why don't you try it on?'

Surprised, Joanna self-consciously shed her ash-coloured stuff
gown and struggled into the new one. It was a straight sheath of
green wool, with a round neck and tight, buttoned sleeves to the
wrist. Petronilla had her head buried once more inside the chest.

'I think this cream surcoat will go very well over the green of the
gown,' she said straightening up. 'Why Joanna, how thin it makes you
look, as willowy as that sister of yours, I vow.'

'Maybe the Lenten fast has improved my figure a little,' said Joanna with a grin. The surcoat with its wide neck and large cut-away armholes hung straight to the ground, setting off the tight-fitting undergown to perfection.

'Now we need a headdress,' said Petronilla, studying Joanna thoughtfully. 'I've seen a way of wearing a veil which is very pretty. Shall we try it?' Without more ado she wound Joanna's two thick braids into circles on either side of her head. Then she fixed a metal circlet round the girl's brow and draped a veil partly over and partly under it, swathing her throat and tucking the ends into the bodice of her gown. 'Better than I would have dreamed possible,' she said standing back to admire her work. 'I always knew you were a beauty, it just took a little bringing out, that's all.'

'I'll never be a beauty like Mariota,' said Joanna with a sigh.

'Just look there then,' said Petronilla, turning her round to face the piece of polished steel hanging on the wall, 'and tell me that you're no beauty.'

Joanna looked. She hardly recognised herself in the streamlined stranger peering back from the mirror. Her face, framed by the soft folds of the veil, seemed all eyes and mouth; her neck seemed to stretch up to her ears, and the loops of her hair supported the veil on either side of her head so that the shape of her face was altered to a fashionable oval.

'I do look better, don't I?' she said, staring at her reflection in astonished delight.

'You look wonderful, ready for the penitential procession to St Paul's tomorrow.'

'The penitential procession!' exclaimed Joanna, turning to look at Petronilla. 'You mean I am to go?'

'Indeed you are to go,' Petronilla assured her. 'John wants as many of the household as can be spared to accompany him. He's afraid the citizens of London may be chary of showing their penitence to the Duke of Lancaster.'

'But a procession,' Joanna's eyes glowed with excitement, 'surely everyone loves a procession?'

'Let us hope so,' said Petronilla with a wry smile, 'otherwise the Duke might have cause to complain that the city does not accord him proper respect.'

When they reached the Guildhall the next day and found only a small crowd shivering outside in the chill March wind, it seemed as if John of Northampton's doubts had been well founded. Joanna was disappointed. She had been expecting all the city's guilds, grouped together in their different liveries beneath their colourful banners, with musicians, torch bearers and singing priests; the sort of exciting, moving pageant which took place when the Mayor rode to Westminster to make his oath of office.

'Do you think we're too early?' she asked Adam.

'No, we're not early,' said Adam. 'Master Northampton's not aiming to wait long for the Mayor, not for Master Brembre. The master's hoping to have arrived last with his own show of strength, I'd say.' John of Northampton had brought with him his brothers Robert, William and Roger Comberton, their wives, and William's two eldest boys, as well as his five apprentices, his chaplain and his secretary.

Joanna looked about her curiously. It was a peculiar crowd, huddling together in little groups, whispering and staring at each other warily. She saw her father, talking to Adam Staple and two or three other mercers. He smiled at her and nodded, but did not approach. She was hurt, and wondered whether he held her to blame for the search of his shop. It would not be surprising, she thought, knowing Matilda's skill in twisting the truth to suit her own view of things. She longed to speak to him, to hear how everyone was at home, to find out how the search went, to tell him the truth, but she did not dare launch out alone into that hostile crowd. Adam saw her wistful gaze.

'Your father'll not dare speak to you here, not now in front of all the others,' he said sympathetically. 'We're out of favour now Brembre's Mayor.'

Joanna was startled. She was so used to being blamed for everything that she found it hard to believe that her father's behaviour towards her was due not to anything she had done but to political expediency. She glanced quickly at the Sheriff to see if he noticed. John of Northampton was talking earnestly to his brothers and seemed sublimely indifferent. He was a striking figure in his scarlet alderman's gown with his gold chain of office round his neck. Beside him Petronilla and his brothers' wives were grouped together, their fur-trimmed mantles sweeping the ground and their veils floating from their elaborate headdresses in the stiff breeze like the billowing sails of the Thames river barges. Joanna thought they looked magnificent in their solidarity. She felt proud to be with them. She raised her head and glared haughtily at her father. If he did not want to speak to her he was a fool.

Suddenly, a rustle of expectancy ran through the crowd and they all turned towards the Guildhall. Nicholas Brembre, the new Mayor, was striding purposefully through the stone arch while behind him walked several other aldermen in their scarlet gowns. Joanna recognised William Walworth and John Philpot escorting Margaret Philpot on one arm and her sister Idonia, the lady Mayoress, on the other. Strolling in their wake, dressed like a courtier in tight-fitting tunic, long particoloured hose and short cloak thrown casually over one shoulder came Black Nick, his hood pushed back from his head and lying in festoons of bright-coloured cloth halfway down his back. Joanna hardly recognised the impoverished-looking sea captain with his faded gambesons in this splendid apparition, yet there was no mistaking those broad shoulders, that fierce beard and strong black hair standing up round his head and doing battle with the wind. Petronilla's daughter Idonia, the wife of one of John of Northampton's brothers, Roger Comberton, was staring at Black Nick curiously.

'Is that the Mayor?' she asked.

'No, that's not the Mayor,' said Petronilla. 'That's the Mayor over there, talking to Adam Bamme the goldsmith.'

'He looks as if he ought to be Mayor, even though he is so ugly,' said Idonia.

'Dame Philpot doesn't seem to find him ugly,' said Cicelia, William Comberton's wife. 'Perhaps it's his air. He carries himself like a king. The Mayor had better look out.'

'Perhaps it's Master Philpot who should look out,' said Petronilla's daughter, watching Black Nick as he leant forward and whispered in Margaret Philpot's ear. She turned and laughed at him over her shoulder. 'Although what she sees in such an ugly man I cannot make out.'

'Perhaps being so ugly he has learnt to put himself out for women,' said Petronilla with an amused smile. 'Don't we all love a man who pays us attention? An ugly man whom no woman can resist, wouldn't that be a fascinating combination?'

'Dame Philpot certainly seems to find it so,' replied her daughter. Joanna, listening to them, thought it quite impossible that any woman could possibly find such an incarnation of evil attractive.

She watched Margaret Philpot begin to greet the various aldermen, laughing, kissing, welcoming them all. There was something about her, the spontaneous gaiety in her lovely face, her musical laughter, the warmth and sparkling vivacity with which she enfolded everybody she talked to that appealed to Joanna enormously. Margaret Philpot seemed fun and the magic of her touch transformed the little groups of people holding back from one another in suspicion and fear.

When she reached John of Northampton, Margaret greeted him warmly, although she did not attempt to kiss him on the cheek. 'How good of you to come, Sheriff Northampton,' she cried gaily 'and with so many of your household. Our procession will be so much the better for the numbers you bring with you.'

'Unfortunately I cannot bring enough to make up for all the others. I fear John of Gaunt will not be impressed with the sincerity of our penance,' replied Northampton solemnly, but Margaret had already moved on and was pressing condolences on Petronilla for the death of her baby.

'I know too well the sorrow and the heartache, for I lost two of mine in swift succession last Lammastide,' she said holding Petronilla's hands in hers and gazing with genuine sympathy into her face. 'But who is this you've brought with you today? Not another daughter-in-law, surely?'

'This is Joanna Burgeys,' said Petronilla calmly. 'She is helping me to forget my sorrow and to get on with living.'

'The nun!' exclaimed Margaret clapping her hands to her breast. 'I would never have recognised her. So you escaped the convent after all, my child, and to good purpose, I can see. I would never have recognised you, you're so improved. Are you not the musical one? I too adore music. I have this very day taken delivery of a new harp from Vienna brought to me by Black Nick. You must come to Philpot's Inn and sing with me. Will you come?'

Joanna glanced awkwardly at Petronilla, longing to accept but uncertain whether she should.

Margaret's eyes danced mischievously. 'You cannot refuse me, you know, not now my brother-in-law is Mayor,' she said.

'But I don't want to refuse you,' said Joanna, touched by Margaret's warmth. 'I love singing.'

'Very prettily said,' murmured a deep voice in her ear, 'you should go far.'

Joanna turned quickly and found herself staring up into the very blue eyes of Black Nick. How dared he, she thought, biting her lip to check the angry words which sprang to her mind. After all that he had done to try to injure her and her family, how dared he stand there looking so utterly unrepentant? There was something in the way his eyes raked her, from her veiled head to her patterned feet, which made her feel glad she was wearing the new clothes Petronilla had given her. She dropped her eyes quickly, fixing her gaze upon his well-muscled calves. Not for anything would she allow herself to be challenged by that bold stare.

'Dame Philpot is right,' he said. 'The improvement is truly remarkable.' Much to her chagrin Joanna felt a slow blush spreading up her neck below her veil. She looked up.

'And you!' she retorted before she could stop herself. 'You've prospered, I see.'

'And been well rewarded,' he said with a grin.

Margaret Philpot took hold of Nick's arm. 'The Mayor is ready to depart. If we don't start soon we shall never reach St Paul's in time for vespers.' Relieved to be rid of him, Joanna smiled gratefully at Margaret. Black Nick was a villain and a blackguard; she would have loved to say something to wipe the provocative smile from his wicked face, but she guessed that there was nothing she could think of sufficiently wounding to pierce the thickness of his skin.

Nicholas Brembre was marshalling the crowd into some sort of order, issuing wax candles to the apprentices, striding about the courtyard with the vigour of a conqueror while people jumped to do his bidding. Joanna looked at John of Northampton waiting with his kin and his household to take his place in the procession and was surprised by an expression of bitter defeat on his long, pale face. He no longer looked magnificent in his isolation, she thought with a shock of dismay, he looked an outsider.

Leaving the Guildhall, the procession wound its way slowly through the Old Jewry, along Honey Lane and so into Chepeside. No cheering crowds lined the streets to watch it pass; no laughing women leant from the overhanging windows to speed it on its way; a few people, filling pitchers at the water standard in Chepe, stood silently watching as the quiet, apologetic snake of richly dressed citizens walked solemnly by. To Joanna it seemed a terrible anti-climax. All her joy in having been included in such a special occasion seemed to have vanished and now, instead of jubilation, singing and pageantry, all she was left with was a long walk uphill in a cold wind.

The bells began to ring for vespers as they reached St Paul's Gate. Listening to them, Joanna remembered the last time she had stood in Paul's yard, the violence and terror, the fearful unrestrained power of the mob. Now they were here to do penance for that day. How beautiful the bell sounded, a glorious harmony of different chimes borne on the wind as all the churches of the city heralded the last service of the day. So different from the shrieking of the mob baying for blood.

The memory of that day brought back the memory of Sir Tristram. All her hopes and dreams and longings, which had to some extent been quietened by the new interests and satisfying day-to-day activity at the Hood, suddenly came flooding back. It was of Tristram she was thinking as she entered the cathedral, of Tristram as he had looked when she said goodbye to him in her father's garden, of Tristram as he might look if he were to see her now in her lovely new clothes. Blessed Mary, Mother of God, she prayed as she entered the cathedral, please let me see him again.

With the beautiful sound of plainsong drifting down from the monks gathered in the chancel and the wax torches making little pinpricks of light, the procession wound its way like a long glow-worm through the mysterious dark of the cathedral towards the high altar. Joanna forgot her disappointment in the procession and even for a time her hopeless longing for Tristram, as she abandoned herself to the pageantry of the Mass, to the magic and the mystery of the solemn act of penitence which seemed beyond earthly pomp and show. It was not until later that she became aware that the cathedral was not as empty as at first she had supposed. A glint of steel in the light of the candles, a clink of metal on stone during a pause in singing made her pulses quicken. There were knights sharing the Mass! John of Gaunt's retainers must have been sent to witness the city's penance.

She peered around her as the priests flitted to and fro in front of the high altar, like moths in the summer darkness, searching for a glimpse of red on blue. But it was useless to look for coats of arms in the dark shadows of the cathedral. All she could see was the occasional gleam of chain mail. Her heart was beating so fast she could scarcely breathe. He must be here. It would be too cruel if he were not. Surely the Blessed Virgin would not let her down now.

The Mass, which had seemed so full of magic and meaning, now became interminable. To Joanna it seemed an eternity before the last Amen had been sung and the procession began slowly wending its way back towards the great west door. Looking about her eagerly, Joanna emerged into the twilight of the churchyard and saw a group of horses waiting in the care of their squires. Robin was walking Orion up and down. She recognised him instantly. Without a thought for the Northamptons or anybody else in the procession, she darted across the grass of the churchyard.

'Hello, Robin,' she said. He stopped and gazed at her, startled. 'Don't you know me, Robin Swynbrook? I would have thought after all we'd been through together you would not cut me dead in Paul's yard!'

'By all the saints! It's Mistress Joanna.' He seized her hand and kissed it fervently. 'You must excuse me, but you look different somehow.'

'Different!' she laughed. 'I hope you're not going to say my new gown doesn't suit me.'

'No, no,' he stammered, blushing up to his ears. 'It suits you very well.'

Looking over her shoulder she caught sight of a group of knights walking out of the cathedral with that stiff-legged walk peculiar to men whose legs are encased in meshed steel. Tristram was deep in conversation with another knight. His head was completely covered by his camail, but she would have recognised his straight, chiselled nose and prominent cheekbones anywhere. She felt light-headed, reckless, all her senses tingling with expectancy. She moved closer to the horse and tentatively stroked his arched neck.

'He seems quieter today,' she said with a smile so bright Robin caught his breath. 'I hope he's well.'

'Well enough,' replied the squire. He was gazing at her with the light of adoration in his eyes, a completely new experience for Joanna, and it gave her confidence. She glanced once more over her shoulder. Tristram was standing on the steps of St Paul's Cross, silhouetted against the setting sun, shouting for his horse. He looked as bright and pure as a crusader, she thought, fresh from the conquest of Jerusalem.

'Robin, by God's blood, do you expect me to walk all the way back to the Savoy tonight?' Tristram cried. 'Bring Orion over here, if you can take your eyes off that pretty girl for a moment.' Her knees went weak. Carefully she approached the Cross and stood in front of him.

'I'm Joanna Burgeys,' she said in a low voice, 'don't you remember me?'

'Joanna,' he exclaimed. 'Of course I remember. Are you here with your family?'

'Father's here,' she said breathlessly, 'but I came with the Northamptons. I live with them now. Northampton's Inn is down by the river, behind the steelyard.' She could hardly get the words out, she was trembling so violently, but somehow she must make him know where he could find her again.

He didn't seem to be listening. He was gazing out over her head, searching the churchyard and frowning. She wondered if it was because the procession had been such a mean, paltry affair.

'Do you think the Duke will be disappointed that there were so few of us come to offer penance for the city's fault?' she asked timidly. 'We may be few but our feelings are none the less sincere.'

'I think the Duke is thoroughly tired of London and all its citizens,' he said with a shrug.

'I hope you don't agree with him.'

'Oh no, I think some of London's citizens are quite exceptional,' he replied looking down at her at last, 'especially the women.' She gasped and stared up at him. He had paid her a compliment! She, whom nobody ever noticed, was thought exceptional by the most wonderful man on God's earth. She watched him, her heart hammering in her breast, eyes alight with love, waiting for him to say more, but he was once again staring out across the churchyard, scowling. What was amiss? She could see her father talking to the Mayor and Black Nick hovering behind. Sir Tristram seemed to be watching them too.

'Don't think my father unfriendly because he does not come and speak to you, he won't speak to me either today. I think he's very anxious not to offend the new Mayor.'

'No matter,' he said still staring out over her head at the procession as it was falling into line. 'I've been very adequately recompensed by his daughter.' She clasped her hands together against her pounding heart and stared up at him transfixed with joy.

'Joanna, the procession is almost ready to leave, what are you doing loitering here?' John of Northampton was standing behind her and the sight of his grave face brought her back to earth.

'I'm sorry,' she said quickly, 'but this is the knight who rescued me

94

from the fishmongers. I have been trying to thank him.'

'So this is your rescuer.' Northampton looked at Tristram. 'It was a good deed you performed that day, sir knight, and a great sadness to me that it should have been necessary. I have tried to find the culprits but without the help of the Fishmongers Guild I can do nothing.' Tristram merely looked puzzled.

'Master Northampton is sheriff of the city,' explained Joanna hastily.

'If the city would only let the Duke of Lancaster help,' said Tristram severely, 'London would be a much more law-abiding place, but it appears that my liege lord is rejected by all the people he most desires to help. Why can't you trust him?'

'Perhaps we misjudge him,' replied Northampton mildly. 'But you must admit his actions are not calculated to reassure us that he means to respect our rights and liberties.'

Tristram shrugged. 'Well, I don't know much about rights and liberties. I think loyalty is more important.'

'The trouble is there are sometimes too many kinds of loyalty,' said Northampton.

'The only loyalty I know is loyalty to the King and loyalty to one's liege lord,' Tristram told him loftily.

'The city cannot be coerced,' Northampton replied. 'Look at this procession, for example. The city's leaders are here, the Mayor, the aldermen, the sheriffs, a few of the guilds' masters, but the people stay away. We cannot make them publicly penitent, and nor can your liege lord.'

'To the devil with the people,' said Tristram, taking Orion's reins from Robin. He set foot in Robin's cupped hands and vaulted easily into the saddle. 'They will follow whither they are led. Where are their leaders leading them now?'

Joanna could have stood and feasted her eyes on him forever, marvelling at the graceful way he sat his horse, at the sheer beauty of his features and the wonder of his mailed strength.

'Joanna, what are you waiting for?' said Northampton sharply. 'Go and tend your mistress and tell my wife I will be with her directly.'

Joanna glanced up at Tristram. She longed for one word of farewell, for one hint that perhaps she might see him again, but Tristram was concentrating on controlling the plunging stallion.

She walked slowly back towards the others, glancing over her shoulder for one last glimpse of Tristram, sitting as if moulded to the impatient stallion, head bent to catch what Northampton was saying. So engrossed was she that she caught her foot on the edge of a gravestone, stumbled and would have fallen had a strong arm not caught her firmly round the waist.

'Watch where you're going,' said a deep voice in her ear, 'a churchyard's no place to be playing Hoodman Blind.' She knew that mocking voice only too well. Why did the wretch always get in her way?

'Let me go,' she said angrily, struggling to free herself, but he held her firm. As well might a rabbit escape the clutch of a predatory hawk.

'Ungrateful girl, do I get no thanks for the service I've rendered? You wouldn't want to get grass stains on that fine cream surcoat.'

'Thanks!' she exclaimed, her indignation almost robbing her of speech. 'I'm surprised you dare show your face here after the part you played in the city's riot.'

Black Nick glanced carelessly round the churchyard. 'John of Gaunt's knights don't frighten me,' he said. 'I'm much more afraid of you and that wicked temper of yours.' He was looking down at her with the devil's own mischief dancing in his eyes. A short time ago she would have struck out, biting and scratching like an angry kitten, but she had served a hard apprenticeship in Northampton's household, learning to endure the teasing and the taunts when she was out of favour. Now she drew a deep breath and forced herself to stillness within his encircling arm. Not for anything would she give him the satisfaction of making her lose her temper.

'The procession is about to leave,' she said quietly, though her eyes flashed, 'will you release me, please?' He let her go, and stood staring down at her thoughtfully.

'Are you sure you want to walk all the way back?' he asked. 'There's a litter taking some of the ladies back to the Guildhall. I could find a place for you if you like.'

'No thank you,' she replied, 'I can easily walk.' The knights were riding out of the courtyard, the plumes from their helmets streaming in the wind, a rich panoply of moving colour which left the churchyard the gloomier for their going. She watched them disappear from view, straining for one last glimpse of Tristram, ready to wave if he should turn round. He did not.

'It will be cold now the sun has gone down,' Nick persisted, and she wondered crossly if he had to be obeyed in everything.

'I never catch cold,' she said with a toss of the head. Then she saw her father coming towards her over the grass.

'Joanna, you look well, my child. I can see that life in Northampton's household suits you. I hope you are making yourself useful there.'

'Why don't you ask him yourself, Father?' she said as she knelt to kiss his hand.

'I hope that there is no need for me to ask,' he replied. 'I hope that my daughter can be trusted to be of service and not to let me down.'

There was not much she could say to that. So she asked after her family and was reassured that all were well.

He turned to the sea captain. 'When do you leave for Calais again?'

'I don't know, Nick replied vaguely. 'Probably not until after Easter.'

'Good, I should have another cargo for you by that time,' Burgeys told him. Joanna clenched her hands angrily at her sides, How could her father trust the man, did he not realise what Black Nick had tried to do to him? She glanced quickly at the sea captain and found him watching her with a decidedly calculating look in his eyes. There was so much she wanted to say to her father, so much she wanted to ask, and that blackguard knew it, which was why he was standing there preventing her from speaking to him. The villain!

Northampton joined them. The procession was beginning to move off. Petronilla had refused to ride back in the litter with the Lady Mayoress and her friends, and Northampton was worried whether she was strong enough yet for the long walk back.

'Can you not persuade her to accept the Mayoress's litter?' said Nick.

'My wife is not one to put comfort before principles,' Northampton responded grimly, 'and nothing would induce her to share a litter with the present leaders of the city.'

'Then let us hope her principles do not prove to be the death of her,' said Black Nick with a shrug. Unfeeling wretch, thought Joanna. She took her leave of her father and hurried to where Petronilla was taking her place in the procession and fell in behind her, schemes for the discomfiture of Black Nick seething in her brain. One thing was certain, she must get Mistress Northampton's permission to go home at the earliest opportunity and warn her father about the man to whom he was so confidently entrusting his cargoes.

But soon she forgot all about Black Nick. Walking through the darkening city, with the lights of the wax torches bobbing and twinkling in front of her, she relived the all too brief encounter with Sir Tristram, recalling in minute detail every look, every word a hundred times over, savouring each precious syllable he uttered. He had remembered her. For a delicious moment she allowed herself to imagine that he had thought of her as much as she had thought of him. Now he knew where she lived perhaps he would visit her. Anything seemed possible. Hope had been re-kindled and was dancing through her veins like the flickering torches lighting the procession on its weary journey home. Joanna did not feel tired, nor did she feel the cold, for she walked on air.

CHAPTER 10

There is nothing in life so uplifting to the spirits than the expectation of love requited. For the next few days Joanna lived in an enchanted world of eager anticipation. Petronilla, listening to her singing around the Hood, remarked to her husband that the child seemed to be happy with them at last.

'Settled down, has she?' said Northampton. 'But I wonder whether, now that you are over the birth of poor little James, you wouldn't want to send her back home. There can't be a great deal for her to do here.'

'I'd rather not,' said Petronilla. 'That is, if you can afford to keep her. She's an odd girl, I'll grant you, a little too quick to anger sometimes, although I think she's learning to control that temper of hers, but she has a wonderfully warm and loving spirit. Her mind is keen – I like that, and she learns quickly if she's interested.'

'Well, as long as she's of some use to you, my dear,' he gave her one of his rare smiles, 'keep her for as long as you want. One more mouth to feed doesn't make much difference to us, God be thanked.'

'It's interesting, isn't it,' mused Petronilla, 'how God's purpose works out. I only took her in the first place to please you, and then kept her because God spared me when I thought I was sure to die. I never thought I should come to be so fond of her. In fact I don't think I would ever have got over James's death had it not been for that child and her extraordinary ways.'

'I think maybe you're right and that God sent her to us for a purpose,' Northampton agreed, taking her hand in his and staring down at it thoughtfully. 'That knight who rescued her from the fishmongers, I've asked him to dinner.'

'You've asked a knight to dinner?' exclaimed Petronilla in surprise. 'When?'

'Tomorrow. I met him talking to Joanna in Paul's yard after the penitential procession.'

'But we can't give a feast, not in Lent.'

98

'There's no need to give a feast. He can dine quietly with us in my chamber. I want to talk to him. He could be very useful, Petronilla. He's one of Lancaster's retainers and maybe he can arrange a meeting for me with the Duke.'

'Why?' she asked, staring up at him, perplexed.

'I'm beginning to think that in John of Gaunt lies our best hope.' He released her hand and wandered over to the window.

'I don't see how John of Gaunt can help you. The city hates him.'

'I know,' he said, 'that is why the people have united behind Brembre. But there will come a time when they hate Brembre more. Brembre has used his influence with the King to get a settlement to his own advantage. But the King cannot last much longer and when he dies, what then?'

'Then Richard of Bordeaux will inherit the throne.'

'A ten-year-old boy surrounded by ambitious men! If the kingdom breaks up into factions when the King dies, it will be John of Gaunt who will hold the balance. He is by far the strongest and most powerful baron of any at court.' He began pacing up and down the chamber, his long face tense with suppressed excitement.

'Particularly if he has the support of London,' she said. 'Is that what you are so anxious to tell him?'

His restless pacing brought him once again to the window and he stood, staring out across the rain-streaked wharves to the grey river beyond.

'We need his support as much as he needs ours,' he answered her at last, 'that is what I shall tell him.'

She joined him at the window.

'What for, John?' she asked. 'To betray his brother's trust? To disinherit his ten-year-old nephew as soon as the old King dies? Are you so determined to get your way in the city that you would offer to help Lancaster defy God's chosen successor? If you do that, then you will surely reap the whirlwind.'

He looked into the steady eyes gazing up at him with such anxiety and love. He could have told her not to interfere in matters that she did not understand. He could have thrust her violently from him. But he had never, in all the time he had been married to her, laid a hand in violence upon her. For Petronilla had brought him not only her money. She had brought him her wisdom, her loyalty and her uncanny ability to smooth all sorts of troubles from his path. It was important to him to justify himself in her eyes, for in many ways she was the voice of his conscience.

'You know that there are things I want to do in this city,' he said, 'people I want to help – small, weak people who cannot help themselves. You know that it is their freedom as well as ours that is at stake: freedom to use the labour and the materials we want to produce the goods we need; freedom to buy the food we need to feed our workers at a fair price. I cannot do this without power, political power in the city. I believe that Brembre deliberately encouraged the riot to discredit Adam Staple and then used his influence with the King to have himself elected Mayor in Adam's place. If I am to defeat such men, I too must have influence with whoever is effectively governing the country.'

'Even if it means plunging the country into anarchy?' she insisted.

'If I am to defeat men such as Brembre and his friends then I cannot scruple as to the means I use, since they do not.'

'Can you not remember what it was like when the old King was a boy? Is all that he has done to unite the country to be thrown away?'

'It will not come to that,' he said, turning away from her. 'John of Gaunt will not overthrow his nephew, of that I am sure. But when the boy is on the throne, the government of the country will be in the hands of those who hold the most power, and I believe that it will be John of Gaunt. I have no influence with the others, but if I can make a friend of Gaunt now, perhaps when the time comes he will be able to help me. It is all I can do.'

She was silent, gazing out of the window at the rain, thinking of the recent turmoil in the city and her husband's failure to prevent it.

'Oh, my dear,' she said, 'I wish you would take care. Have we not trouble enough in the city as it is, without becoming involved in a struggle for power between the great lords as well?'

'You must trust me, Petronilla. When have I ever been wrong?' He took hold of both her hands and smiled down into her anxious eyes. 'Will you devise something delectable for the young knight who comes to dine with us tomorrow?' She knew it was no use arguing any longer. It was time to be practical.

'I must try and find a new way to dress carp, I suppose,' she said with a sigh, 'and we could have swan. But I don't think we can have musicians, do you?'

'Definitely not musicians, but I don't see why Joanna should not sing for him,' suggested Northampton.

'Why, John,' she said, smiling at last, 'what a good idea. I would never have thought of that.'

'I know I may seem a dull goat at times, my dear, always thinking of politics, but at least I can still surprise you.' He raised her hands to his lips and kissed them tenderly.

'Pray God you may go on surprising me for many more moons,' she said, casting off her misgivings, 'as I shall try to surprise you – with tomorrow's feast.'

What first struck Petronilla when Sir Tristram walked into the Hood the following day was what a very handsome young man he was. The second thing that struck her, much later when he was seated at the table in the chamber off the hall, was that he was a disappointed one. She looked at the dishes of the first course which littered the table – the stuffed pike, the roast swan, the pickled sturgeon – and could find no fault with them. The cooks had laboured since dawn preparing this dinner and she herself had spent most of the morning in the kitchen supervising their labours or in the chamber making sure that it was properly swept and strewn with fresh herbs for the occasion. All that lay within her power to make this dinner a success had been done, but now, watching Sir Tristram's handsome countenance, she could not persuade herself that she had succeeded.

Northampton was earnestly explaining the complicated state of city politics while the knight ate his way morosely through all that was put in front of him, and Petronilla feared that he was not listening to a word her husband said. As the meal progressed and Sir Tristram also wolfed his way through the 'eggs' fabricated from fish roe, the 'ham' slices, made with salmon for the pink meat and pike for the fat, Petronilla felt that all her clever contrivances had been wasted. It would not have mattered if she had fed him on bread and split-pea soup, for all the attention he paid to what was put before him. What did he expect, she wondered, and why did he come if all he was going to do was sit there and eat? Did Gaunt not feed his retainers at the palace?

'So you see why it is so important for me to have private audience with the Duke?' Northampton concluded, and from the blank look on the knight's face, Petronilla knew she had been right. He had not listened to a word.

'My husband is very anxious to speak to the Duke of Lancaster alone,' she said leaning across the table and pouring wine into his empty goblet. 'He thinks you may be able to help him to do this.'

Tristram regarded her quizzically over the top of his goblet.

'We need the Duke's help,' she persisted.

'A fine way you have of showing it,' he replied, drinking deep from his wine. 'I doubt if my liege lord is interested in London or its citizens any more.'

'Then why did you come to dine with us today?' she asked gently. She saw her husband frown and knew he thought she had gone too far. But somehow she had to get this young man's interest, or the whole scheme would fail.

'The Duke does not know that I am here,' he said, absently spearing a lamprey with his knife and popping it into his mouth. Petronilla sighed. She didn't seem to be doing any better with him.

'Will you not speak to the Duke for me?' Northampton pleaded.

'I'll speak to him if you like, but I cannot promise that he will see you,' replied Tristram with a shrug. 'And now I must be going.

101

There's a practice joust at Smithfield this afternoon, a mêlée, and I lead the Duke's men against Percy's retainers. I don't want to be late.

'But Joanna is to sing for you and there is a confection of figs, raisins and almond slices yet to come,' said Petronilla, 'It is a dish invented by a cook to the French King. My cook is renowned throughout the city for his tailles.'

'If Joanna is to sing, then I must wait to hear her,' Tristram said politely and Petronilla jumped up and whisked out of the chamber to fetch Joanna.

Music was not something which meant a great deal to Petronilla, but listening to Joanna singing, even she could not help but be struck by the purity of the girl's voice. She closed her eyes and was reminded of a lark pouring out its song of welcome to spring. It made her feel restless and opening her eyes she saw that Joanna was singing with her eyes fixed on the knight's face and they were shining with joy. Merciful Mother, the poor child was in love with him! How absurd love is, she thought with a sigh. What hope has she, loving a young god like that? Yet how natural. How could an impressionable girl like Joanna not love him, especially after he so gallantly rescued her from the fishmongers?

She looked at the knight curiously, he could not help but be aware that Joanna was singing solely for him. But Tristram was now talking quite animatedly to Northampton and did not seem to be aware of the musical treat being poured out for his benefit. Petronilla felt a sharp stab of irritation for her husband. Why could he not forget his purpose at least for long enough to let Sir Tristram appreciate Joanna's song? Idly she wondered whether the knight was married. He was found to be, of course. But what if he were not?

A dream began to form in Petronilla's practical mind which surprised even her with its audacity. Suppose they could get Sir Tristram for Joanna? There was no reason why she should not look as high as a knight for her husband. Her father would no doubt be able to provide her with a substantial dowry. Any man who sent his son to train to be a lawyer and had the means to send his daughter to a convent was quite likely to pay highly to get a knight into his family. It was a perfect plan. Burgeys would be in their debt for ever, Joanna would forge a link with the Duke of Lancaster's household and love, for once, would triumph.

But later that night, when Petronilla revealed her plan to her husband as they lay together in the big bed in the solar, Northampton was not impressed.

'Really, my love, I cannot think what has got into you. If I didn't know better I'd say you were suffering from spring fever. Joanna has no hope of a man like that. Whatever makes you think she might?'

'Why not? She has spirit and determination enough, and she has money. If Richard Burgeys is doing as well as you say he is, he can dower her well enough for any knight, and would be for ever in our debt for arranging it.'

'There must be dozens of merchants' daughters in the city of London who have as much,' said Northampton. 'She needs more than wit and will. She needs exceptional beauty, for one thing, to captivate a man like Sir Tristram.'

'There may be dozens of richer, more beautiful girls in the city, but it was Joanna whom he rescued from the fishmongers. Fate has thrown them together and if we could but help her a little, who knows what we might not achieve?'

'I'm not sure that we would be doing what was best for her if we did,' objected Northampton. 'I must confess to you that I was disappointed with Sir Tristram de Maudesbury. He's neither a good talker nor a good listener. The only time he took an interest in anything other than his food and drink was when he was talking about Gaunt's campaign in France and then he was completely unaware of what a disaster that had been.'

'But he's so handsome and Joanna loves him so,' protested Petronilla.

'Love,' scoffed her husband. 'What has love to do with marriage?'

'I thought,' said Petronilla running an exploratory hand gently over her husband's naked body, 'that love was what we had.'

'Indeed it is,' he said taking hold of her hand and kissing it, 'but we've been lucky.'

'Couldn't Joanna be lucky too?' asked Petronilla, trailing her fingers down his chest and over his flat stomach towards his groin.

'Petronilla, I don't know how you can be so obtuse,' he said, pushing her hand away. 'You know the sort of love the poets sing about, what Joanna fancies she feels for that handsome young man, is not what holds marriages together. What she feels is passion – destructive, dangerous passion which distorts the mind and ruins the senses. What we have is what comes when two people work together and respect each other, as we do. Love is the yeast in the dough of our marriage, it helps it to rise above all the trials and tribulations we are sent to bear. Passion destroys marriage. Surely you know that?'

'But wouldn't it be wonderful if just for once a girl could marry the man of her dreams,' said Petronilla wistfully.

'It would be disastrous,' retorted Northampton. 'What can Joanna offer a retainer of the Duke of Lancaster? He has been trained only to fight, to hunt and waste his every groat in riotous living. Money is something he never has to think of, for in addition to being well paid for his service in the field, he is also clothed, fed and housed by his liege lord. Whereas Joanna has been brought up with a proper understanding of the power of money, that it is not for spending but for using to make more. She has been taught to count the cost of every-thing. He just takes what he wants, when he wants it, and never thinks of who has to pay.'

'All the more reason why he should marry someone like Joanna,' said Petronilla, nibbling his ear playfully.

'I can't think what's got into you tonight,' exclaimed Northampton, twisting away from her in the darkness. 'I think that young man's bewitched you as well as Joanna. You didn't look for a knight for your daughter. You were happy to marry her off to my brother Roger. Weren't you?'

'No, I didn't look for a knight for Idonia,' said Petronilla with a sigh, 'but it was you, John, who wanted to get to know the Duke bet-ter. Remember? Think how useful it would be to have Joanna in the Duke of Lancaster's household!'

'I know, but now that I've talked to him I don't think he'll be much use to us. Forget this madness, my love, and go to sleep. I very much doubt if we shall ever see that young man again.' He turned over on his side with his back to her and within minutes his wife could tell by the steady rhythm of his breathing that he was asleep.

Petronilla lay staring up into the cavern of darkness above her head, thinking about what it was to be sensible. Joanna was very far from being sensible, and she would suffer all the consequences that her unruly and passionate nature would bring upon itself. But those who plumbed the depths also scaled the heights. That joy which had shone from Joanna's eyes as she sang for Tristram today had been glo-rious. Just for once, Petronilla wished she could be like Joanna. Then she sighed. John was right, of course, she was mad to think of such romantic nonsense. She could not think what had got into her. It must indeed be spring approaching, or a surfeit of fish. 'How glad I shall be when Easter comes at last,' she thought as she curled up round her husband's sleeping form, 'then we can get back to eating sensible food again.'

Joanna, happily unaware of the hopelessness of her case, was still dreaming of her knight. As the long, dull season of Lent at last came to an end, she threw herself into the great Easter rejoicings with gay abandon, performing all her tasks with such enthusiasm that the whole household could not help being affected.

'What's got into you, Joanna,?' teased Adam. 'I've never seen such a change in anyone, singing about the place all day long. The way you've been behaving recently, anyone might think it was you I was going to marry, not Matty!'

'What makes you think marriage to you would make me want to sing,' retorted Joanna with a toss of her head. 'I'd not marry you if you were the last man left on this earth, so there.'

'Wouldn't you?' he said, trying to slide an arm round her waist. 'I'll tell you what, Joanna, I'd much rather it was you. You're a pretty girl when you smile and I should hazard a guess you'd be much more fun in bed than poor Matty.'

'Why marry her then if you don't fancy her?' asked Joanna, warily dodging out of the way of his encircling arm.

'I've got to marry someone. My apprenticeship is up at Pentecost and if I'm to set up as a master draper on my own I need all the help I can get from Master Northampton. He's always made it plain that the only way I'm going to get that is to marry Matty. Time's run out for me, you see, Joanna.'

'And what better wife could you get than Matty? She's a hard worker and expects little enough from life. She won't always be complaining when money's short while you are making your way. She's very good with children, too.'

'I'd much rather have you,' he said making another grab for her.

'Me? I'd be a terrible draper's wife,' she said, dancing out of his reach. 'You know what a temper I've got. I'd frighten away all your customers!'

'I'm serious, Joanna! Won't you marry me and help me to set up shop behind the steelyard? You won't regret it, I promise you.'

'And bring down Master Northampton's wrath upon me, not to speak of Matty's? No thank you kindly sir.'

'The mistress would soon bring him round, you know what a favourite you are of hers, and once we're married and away from here you'll not need to worry about Matty ever again.'

'Well, I'm not going to marry you, Adam, and so you'd better make the best of Matty. I think you'll be surprised at what a good wife she'll make. She's been a different person since the betrothal. If you just show her a little kindness, she'll be your devoted slave in no time. Isn't that what you want?'

'You know it's not,' he said catching hold of her arm and pulling her roughly towards him. This time he was too quick for her and she could tell by the look in his eyes that he had stopped teasing and it was no longer a game. The fingers digging painfully into her arm were very strong. She stood still, knowing that to struggle would only provoke him more.

'Let me go, Adam,' she said staring at him coldly. 'Do you want me to tell the master, or Matty, that you have no respect for your betrothal vows?'

'Jesu, but you're a tough bitch!' he said, frowning as he let her go. 'But it's time you were married, Joanna, all the same.'

'Now don't you start,' she said laughing nervously. 'All anybody can think about just now is marriage, it seems. I've had enough of it.'

'The trouble with you is you're too choosy,' he said bitterly, 'and if you're not careful you'll end up in that nunnery after all. Probably it would be a good thing – it's about all you're fit for.'

The scene with Adam unsettled Joanna and try as she would she could not get his parting jibe out of her head. He was not the first person to have accused her of being choosy. What if everyone were right? Time seemed to be rushing relentlessly by and what had she achieved? She kept hoping that her knight would seek her out, but the weeks passed and there was no sign of him. There seemed no future for her save marriage to someone like Adam, or St Helen's Priory, and she was not sure which was the worse fate. Gradually her mood of euphoria was replaced by one of despair. Her days seemed pointless and her nights torture as Matty poured out into her unwilling ears eager plans for the future. Night after night, when Matty had at last drifted off into a dreamless slumber, Joanna lay beside her, wide-eyed in the darkness, wondering forlornly what was to become of her.

One day at the beginning of May, when she was helping Petronilla in the counting house, she was jolted out of her preoccupation.

'Would you like to go home, Joanna?' Petronilla asked.

'Home?' replied Joanna, fear making her mouth dry. 'You want to be rid of me?'

'No, no, I don't want to be rid of you, not even when you are feeling downhearted, as you are just now. But I've just realised you've not been home since you came here. At least not with my blessing,' she added with a smile and Joanna felt herself blushing with shame. 'I'm afraid I've been very selfish not suggesting it before. So I thought that perhaps after Mass you might like to spend the rest of Sunday with your family.'

Home! Joanna had hardly thought of it for weeks, but now a whole host of memories swept into her mind – of her father, of Mariota, even of Matilda – and suddenly she was overwhelmed by a great wave of longing to see them all again. She leapt to her feet and hugged Petronilla impulsively. Things would not seem so bad once she had been home, she was sure, and she might get news of Sir Tristram.

Joanna could tell by the few beggars huddled at her father's door that it was nearing the dinner hour when she arrived in the Mercery. As she entered the hall, Mariota was just coming out of the bedchamber. She was wearing a green gown of fine wool whose loose folds clung to her slender form and swirled about her as she moved. Her hair was unbraided and lay in a smooth, silken mass beneath a netted caul. Joanna gazed at her, all her new-found pride in her own improved appearance seeping away like water from a cracked pitcher.

'Oh Mariota, I'd forgotten how truly beautiful you look,' she said, envy and love for her sister struggling together in her breast.

'Joanna! You've come at last!' cried Mariota, running forward with a little skip and throwing herself into her sister's arms. 'How good it is to see you. I thought you were never coming home again.'

Love won, as Joanna hugged her back, warmed by the genuine delight in Mariota's welcome.

'Oh, Joanna I've missed you so.' Joanna thought she detected a tiny catch in the soft voice. 'Could you not have come to see us before this?' She held Mariota at arm's length and studied her carefully. The beautiful face was a shade paler than usual and there were smudges beneath the grey eyes which, she thought ruefully, in anyone else would have been ugly but which in Mariota only made her look enchantingly vulnerable.

'What's wrong, Mariota?' she asked gently.

'I thought you might have come before, I thought you might have been here for Easter. So much has happened and I've had no one to confide in.'

'I couldn't come before. Mistress Petronilla didn't suggest it and I didn't dare to ask. That time I came before, it was without her knowledge. You've no idea how nearly I was sent home. I've had to work so hard to win her round after such a bad start. I've become almost as good as you, Mariota. You wouldn't know me now, but it wasn't easy.'

'But you're happy. I can see that you're happy,' Mariota said with a deep sigh.

'Yes, I suppose I am happy,' said Joanna. 'Mistress Petronilla is sometimes hard to satisfy but she's always fair and has taught me so many new things. The books she has, you've no idea, Mariota, of all the wonderful tales there are in some of her books.'

'You're lucky then,' said Mariota, with another, deeper sigh.

'Dearest, whatever is the matter?' Joanna asked, taking her sister's hands in hers. Two large tears formed in the corner of the lovely grey eyes, trembled on the edge of the long lashes, then slid slowly over the soft bloom of Mariota's cheeks.

'Oh Joanna, I'm so unhappy,' she said.

'What is it? What's the matter? Is somebody ill?' asked Joanna in alarm.

'No, no! Mother's got one of her headaches, but that's not unusual. Father's gone to the Cotswolds to buy wool and you know how upset she gets when he's not here.'

'What is it then? You can tell me.' But Mariota only shook her head in mute despair.

'Joanna!' A familiar voice shouted and Joanna turned to greet Thomas as he bounded into the room. 'By all the saints it's good to see you,' he cried, seizing her by the waist and twirling her round. 'We thought we'd never see you again, didn't we, Mariota? That you'd got too grand for the likes of us now that you're in Northampton's Inn. Does Mother know you're here?'

107

'She's lying down in her chamber,' Mariota told him. 'She's got one of her headaches.'

'Where's Father?' Thomas asked.

'He's gone wool-buying in the Cotswolds?'

'Wonderful, isn't it?' said Thomas. 'They bicker away all day like master and journeyman, yet Father never leaves the house but she goes immediately to pieces!'

'Do you think I should go and see her?' asked Joanna.

'I wouldn't if I were you,' said Thomas. 'You know how you always manage to add to her distemper. Mariota's the only one can manage her.'

'She's sleeping now,' said Mariota. 'Why don't you go and sit with her after dinner?'

'There's a wrestling match in Moorfields this afternoon,' said Tommy. 'Some of the fellows at the Inns are going – Dickon and Owen too. I thought I'd go. Wouldn't you like to come and watch me after dinner?'

'Of course,' said Joanna. 'Do you think you'll win?'

'I think I've got as good a chance of winning as anybody.'

'But what about Mother?' objected Mariota. 'Someone must stay with her.'

'Joan can stay with Mother,' said Tommy. 'It'd do you good to get out a while, Mariota, you look a bit peaky. Can't have our beautiful sister losing all her looks, now can we?'

'Pay no attention to him,' said Joanna, seeing the bright tears trembling once again on Mariota's long lashes. 'You know how he always likes to tease. Tommy, you can be thankful you're not all alone helping to run the house. It can't be easy looking after Mother while Father's away.'

'Mother's all right,' said Mariota gently, 'it's just she's not very strong and the least little bit of trouble makes her head ache so.'

'Mariota, do come,' urged Joanna. 'If Dickon and Owen are going, think what it'll mean to them if you're there to watch?'

'I'd love to come,' said Mariota doubtfully, 'but I'm not sure whether I should.'

'But I've so much to tell you,' pleaded Joanna, 'and I want to hear everything that has happened since I've been away.'

'Oh, very well, but we musn't be too long.'

'We won't be. I must be back at the Hood before curfew.

Dinner was a lively meal. Thomas sat in his father's chair with Joanna and Mariota beside him and the rest of the household crowded along the benches on either side. Joanna felt happy to be back at home, surrounded by people she had known since childhood, with Joan's round red face beaming at her across the table. She was sorry to have missed her father but there was no doubt that without his or

108

Matilda's presence the atmosphere at dinner that day could be one of raucous and unrestrained merriment. Hands shot out to break off pieces of fine white bread and dip it in the bowls of bean porridge; the flagon of ale was passed swiftly backwards and forwards across the table; Tommy and the apprentices kept up a continual flow of banter, shouting at each other across the table as they attacked the meat stew, the ox-marrow fritters, the pasties and the frumenty. It was all so different from the ordered formality of Northampton's Inn, and Joanna, laughing heartily at one of Tommy's cruder quips, realised how much she loved and missed them all. If only Mariota, delicately crumbling a piece of white bread between her fingers and hardly eating at all, had not seemed so sad. Joanna longed to be able to offer comfort but knew that Mariota would not confide in her until they were alone and so instead she asked Tommy about the Inns of Court. He pulled a long face and groaned. He hated the law, he told her, his mouth full of capon pasty. What he really wanted was to be a knight like Sir Tristram. Sweet Jesu! she thought, gazing at him in surprise, not Tommy too!

'You can't be a knight without a manor, and lands and lots of serfs,' she said, eager to talk about him but afraid, too, of where the conversation might lead.

'Then I shall become a mercenary and raise a great company like Sir Robert Knollys and be the terror of France,' he said, attacking a large piece of pork with savage thrusts of his dagger.

'It's not as easy as it was when Sir Robert Knollys was starting out,' said Mariota. 'Then the Black Prince was winning battles all over France and there was loot and ransom money for everyone, but now the French have learnt caution. They won't fight us on land. They do far better making war on our ships in the Channel.'

'Sir Tristram says if only Parliament wouldn't be so mean and would vote the money for a big enough army for Gaunt to take to France, they'd win just as many victories as the Black Prince. If I went as his squire I'd win my spurs on the battlefield and come back rich and famous, like Knollys.'

'But Sir Tristram already has a squire,' Mariota pointed out.

'I thought you hated John of Gaunt and all those who serve him,' put in Joanna, puzzled.

'I did, but that's because I didn't understand. I listened to Father and he doesn't know everything. All he and his merchant friends can think of is that war costs money, but when you listen to Tristram you can see all the opportunities war has to offer. The glory and the excitement of battle as well as the chance to become rich overnight. Those lawyers at the Inns have one foot in the grave. By the time I've made money at the law I shall be too old to enjoy it.'

'People get killed in battle,' she said.

'And I could die in my bed of the plague tomorrow,' he replied jauntily. 'Come on, Joanna, can't you see that a knight has a much jollier time than a lawyer?'

'All I can see is that Sir Tristram has made a complete conquest of you,' she said uneasily.

'Well, he hasn't made one of me,' Mariota exclaimed suddenly with a toss of her head. 'I don't know what you all see in him. Father's right, Joanna should never have brought him to the house.'

Joanna let out her breath in a long, slow sigh of relief. All the time they had been talking about her knight she had been far too conscious of Mariota. A tiny doubt, a shadow of fear, which had been growing stronger and stronger throughout the meal had been laid to rest. Mariota did not like Sir Tristram! Whoever she was breaking her heart over at the moment it was not the knight. Sweet Mary, Mother of God, I thank you, she breathed, prepared now to listen to Mariota's troubles, real or imaginary, with true sympathy.

When they set off after dinner for Moorfields, the two apprentices ranged themselves possessively on either side of Mariota, determined to protect her from the attentions of any marauding stranger they might encounter on the way and at the same time vying with each other for her favour. Joanna, watching their antics in amusement and pleased to see that Mariota was beginning to revive under such an onslaught of gallantry, found herself walking alone with Tommy.

'Tommy, what's wrong with Mariota?' she asked.

'Love, I suppose' he said scornfully. 'What else is ever wrong with Mariota?'

'But she never has any trouble with her lovers,' said Joanna. 'She always has them at her feet.'

'Well, there's always a first time. We haven't heard so much about the secret lover recently and I wonder whether he might have grown cold.'

'Secret lover!' exclaimed Joanna. 'Do you think she really has a secret lover? It's so unlike her.'

'I don't know,' he said with a shrug. 'I thought you might tell me. You and Mariota always share each other's secrets.'

'You forget, I've been away from home for so long. Before I went away she was over her ears in love with Tambard the minstrel. You don't think it could be him? Father would never let her marry a minstrel.'

'I think Father wants this merchant from Calais he's gone off to the Cotswolds with. He's rich as Croesus, so we're to believe, and he's hand in glove with the new mayor.'

'William Gryffard!' Joanna was horrified.

'Why, what's the matter with him? He seemed a decent enough sort of a fellow.' By this time they had reached the city wall.

110

'He's pleasant enough,' she said as they passed through the narrow archway of Cripplegate, one of the six gates of the city, and out into the country beyond. 'Too pleasant, too anxious to please. I don't know what it is about him, but he makes me uneasy. Perhaps it's because he's so watchful.'

'He'd have to be watchful, wouldn't he? He's a merchant of the staple, always looking out for people trying to cheat the wool tax. Mariota'd be lucky to get him, I'd say. It would be a very good match for her. If she marries him she could queen it over everyone.'

'But what of Tambard the minstrel?'

'She can't marry a minstrel, Joanna. You said yourself, Father would never allow it. And even Mariota's not stupid. Anyway, whatever she thinks of him, this merchant wants her, of that I'm sure. He was here last Sunday just before they left for the Cotswolds. Gryffard could hardly take his eyes off our Mariota. Had Dickon and Owen in quite a stir, poor bastards.'

'Poor Mariota.'

'Poor Mariota indeed! She'll be pleased enough with the idea once she gets used to it. He's a rich man, isn't he? Told me he plans to build himself a new house when he settles in London. If he courts her a little, brings home some fine wool from the Cotswolds, shows her a little devotion, he'll have her eating out of his hand in no time.'

'Tommy, I'd no idea you knew so much about how to woo women,' Joanna laughed. 'You've become quite a cynic! Who's been teaching you such worldly wisdom?' He blushed and she looked at him with new eyes. He had grown since she'd last seen him and she realised with a shock that her baby brother was no longer a boy.

Moorfields was a green expanse of marshy land. On the drier parts there were playing fields, with archers' targets and football grounds, while cows and sheep grazed on the lush grass of the swamp. Further away stretched unbroken country, dotted with farms and villages, to the wooded hills of Hampstead and Highgate. Joanna gazed about her in fascinated delight at the colourful scene. The place was swarming with Sunday crowds, some playing games, some practising at the butts or with the quarterstaff, others wrestling, young men showing off their prowess for the benefit of the giggling maidens who had come to watch them. Children were darting in and out of the crowds playing tag or getting into mischief. Merchants strolled in the spring sunshine with their wives, parading their fine clothes and enjoying the air.

Dickon and Owen were soon put out of the wrestling, but Tommy fared much better, until he was finally vanquished by a huge blacksmith. Undeterred, he went off with some of his fellow students to the archery butts. Mariota seemed happy enough consoling her discomfited admirers, enquiring solicitiously if they had taken hurt and praising them for the skill and bravery of their performance. Joanna watched her sister's flower-like countenance and saw that she seemed quite recovered from the melancholy which had possessed her before dinner. She reminded herself that Mariota's passions, while always heartfelt, usually only lasted until another more exciting suitor presented himself, so maybe Tommy was right and Gryffard would win her round. She did not doubt that he would prove a persuasive suitor. And if he didn't, then Mariota would not hesitate to obey their father's wishes. Obedience! thought Joanna wryly, with a pang of pity for the secret lover. Obedience would always win over love, at least where her sister was concerned.

Left alone, she stared about her. Everybody seemed to be there. A pedlar was working the crowds with a trayful of ribbons and trinkets, a friar with his begging bowl, a pardoner doing brisk trade in selling pardons for next week's sins, even a man with a dancing bear on a chain. Then she noticed a gaily-coloured litter. It was carried by two black slaves and Joanna gazed at their ebony skin in startled curiosity. A small crowd had gathered to stare in wonder at these exotic bearers and the lady in the litter, who, thoroughly enjoying all the excited interest she was causing, was leaning out of the litter buying trinkets from the pedlar. She looked up and caught sight of Joanna.

'Why, it's the little nun,' she said and with startled surprise Joanna recognised Margaret Philpot. 'Are you still in the Northampton's household?'

'Yes, Dame Margaret,' replied Joanna, approaching the equipage warily. Margaret looked her up and down, her eyes full of curiosity.

'And has Petronilla found a husband for you yet?'

'No' Joanna looked down at her feet in embarrassment.

'But you are in love?' Joanna flashed a startled glance at Margaret Philpot and a slow blush spread over her cheeks and up to the edge of her wimple. Margaret's eyes sparkled. 'Who is he? Is he here?' she asked, looking round eagerly.

'No, no he's not here, that is.' Joanna broke off in confusion.

'You must come and tell me all about him,' said Margaret, patting her hand. 'Why have you not been to see me? You promised to come and sing with me, you know, and I hate people who do not keep their promises.'

Joanna bit her lip, not knowing what to say.

Mistress Philpot's eyes danced mischievously. 'You must come next Sunday, after noon. The Northamptons cannot possibly need you on a Sunday. I am in darkest despair since my little dog died and I do so need cheering up. You are good at that, so Petronilla says.'

'I'll try, but I'm not sure that I can,' stammered Joanna. She longed to accept such an exciting invitation. There was something about Margaret's sympathetic interest which made her feel that here was someone she could confide in. Here was someone who would not feel that her dreams of the knight were nothing but mad fantasies which must be exorcised as quickly as possible. But would she be allowed to go? If Petronilla preferred to walk all the way back from St Paul's Cathedral when she was desperately tired, rather than share a litter with this woman's sister, how would she react if Joanna were to say she'd been invited into the enemy camp?

'What's the matter, don't you want to come?'

'Oh yes.' Joanna raised her expressive eyes. 'But it's so difficult for me. I mean, that is, I don't know what Mistress Petronilla may have planned for that day.'

'Well, you tell Mistress Petronilla from me that the Lady Mayoress is coming to my house on Sunday,' said Margaret laughing gaily, 'and that I request your presence to help me amuse her and if the Sheriff knows what's good for him he'll see that you get there.' With that she tapped Joanna playfully on the arm and had herself carried away, still laughing.

CHAPTER 11

'I wonder what she wants,' said Petronilla when Joanna told her about Margaret's invitation.

'She only wants cheering up,' replied Joanna. 'Her pet dog has just died and she's in darkest despair.'

'Lucky Mistress Philpot if the only cause for despair is the death of a pet dog.'

'Would you rather I didn't go?' asked Joanna, trying to hide her disappointment.

'Of course I'd rather you didn't go, but it would not be wise to defy the Mayor just now. You'll have to go, but don't let Mistress Philpot's nonsense turn your head. You can't believe a word she says. And if she's entertaining the Mayoress, you had better have something new to wear.' Joanna looked down at the cream surcoat she was wearing, the same one Petronilla had given her, and felt embarrassed.

'I was going to ask Father for something out of the shop to make up into a new gown,' she said, unsure whether she ought to accept more charity from Petronilla. 'But he's gone to the Cotswolds buying wool.'

'When your father is home again he can repay me himself with some fine silk from Brabant,' said Petronilla soothingly, and Joanna accepted her offer gratefully, hoping her father would not mind.

The following Sunday she set out for Philpot's Inn dressed in a pale cream gown with loose sleeves trimmed with fur up to the elbows and a surcoat embroidered in green and red. Her head was partly uncovered and her hair dressed over the ears in the 'ram's-horn' style, braided with a large boss at each side of her head, over which her wimple was fastened by pins. She hoped she looked elegant and fashionable enough for the Philpots, but she was not at all sure.

Petronilla had said that she could not possibly fail to find Philpot's Inn, for it was a large house, even bigger than the Hood, in a lane just

114

off East Chepe. But when Joanna reached the wide thoroughfare of East Chepe there were several lanes leading she knew not where. As it was a Sunday, the shops were all closed and shuttered, and there was no one about to put her on her way. A friar was walking towards her and she considered asking him for Philpot's Lane, but she was afraid he might ask for alms and she had nothing to give him. He saw her and immediately confirmed her fears by stretching out his begging bowl.

Covered in confusion she plunged down the nearest lane, hoping it was the right one. It was narrow and dark with the overhanging upper storeys of the houses on either side almost touching each other above her head. Immediately she realised there could be no houses of the rich here and looking up nervously saw a woman leaning out of a window. Her hair was hanging loose around her shoulders and she was dressed only in her smock. Joanna was about to ask her for Philpot's Inn when the door below opened suddenly and she had to leap out of the way to avoid being knocked down by the large man who came out of the house. The woman leaned farther out of the window and blew him a kiss. He looked up to salute her carelessly, and Joanna recognised Black Nick. She gave a gasp of startled surprise and he spun round, dagger in hand.

'What the devil are you doing here?' he asked roughly.

'I'm looking for Philpot's Inn,' she said in a small voice, eyeing his dagger warily.

'Well, you won't find it in Slum Lane.' He seized hold of her arm and marched her roughly away in the direction of East Chepe.

She stumbled along, half running, half walking, propelled by the relentless grip on her arm. Embarrassment at having caught him visiting what she guessed was a woman of ill repute and the attempt to keep up with his long strides rendered her for a time speechless. He effortlessly avoided the piles of debris littering the lane but it was not so easy for her.

'For pity's sake,' she said breathlessly when she finally stepped in a puddle, 'let me go. Just because you've been enjoying yourself with some filthy whore, there's no need to drag me through the dirt.' He stopped dead in his tracks and dropped her arm so abruptly she nearly fell.

'And what would Mistress Joanna know about whores?' he demanded.

'If you could please just tell me the way to Master Philpot's Inn, I'll bid you farewell.' He was staring down at her, his dark brows drawn together angrily. He looked even uglier when he was cross, she thought. Ugly and menacing.

'And what business does Richard Burgeys' daughter have with John Philpot?'

'I've been invited, by Dame Margaret,' she said, rasing her chin defiantly.

'I'm on my way there myself, as it happens,' he told her. 'I'll take you.' He set off up the narrow street, only this time not quite so fast and Joanna, to her extreme vexation, had no alternative but to trail lamely in his wake.

Accustomed as she was to the sombre spaciousness of the Hood, Joanna was quite unprepared for the warmth and colour of the hall in Philpot's Inn. A huge fire burned in the hearth and hundreds of candles blazed from the wall prickets, lighting the hunting scenes depicted on the walls and adding a mysterious quality of life to the painted gods and goddesses gambolling though the thickets and forests. Beside the dais stood a long board bearing an array of gold and silver drinking cups, a dazzling testimony to Philpot's wealth. Two or three men were gathered round the fire drinking wine and one of them, she saw with apprehension, was Nicholas Brembre, the Mayor.

'Nick!' exclaimed John Philpot detaching himself from the group and walking towards the sea captain with outstretched hand. 'We had completely given you up. Margaret expected you for dinner and insisted we wait for it, until the food grew cold and my stomach noisy; protest drove me to defy her.'

'I'm sorry, but I had pressing business to attend to,' he said, casting a glance at Joanna hard with challenge, but she was far too overwhelmed to think of betraying him.

'Who's this you've brought with you?' went on Philpot, noticing Joanna for the first time.

'She's Richard Burgeys' daughter, I found her wandering about the city looking for Philpot's Inn. Dame Margaret's invited her, it seems.'

'Of course, I remember you,' Philpot said kindly. 'I'm glad you've come to see Margaret, she's been very down since the poor little dog died.'

'Tell her I'll bring her a monkey when I come back,' said Nick, accepting a large goblet of wine from his host. 'Alice Perrers has one and they're all the rage at court. I'm taking a cargo for an Italian merchant direct to Italy via the Straits of Gibraltar.

'When are you going to stop playing hazard with Spain and France and join my fleet?' asked Philpot. 'You're just the man we need to lead it against the pirates.'

'Nick grinned. 'I'd sooner you did something about the French and the Spanish.'

'That would take more ships than I could finance,' said Philpot, shaking his head. 'You want to talk to some of the churchmen who advise the King.'

'Churchmen? By God's pity, what do churchmen know about fighting wars?'

'With two or three good ships under a leader like you we should be able to catch that pirate Joe Mercer,' persisted Philpot. 'How about it?'

'I'd as lief be on my own. There's more profit for a man by himself.'

'And more danger too,' put in Brembre suddenly. 'If you persist in going on your own you'll get taken by the French or the Spanish, or the pirates, and spend the rest of your life at the oars of that galley of yours instead of on the poop!'

'It won't be the first time,' said Nick with a shrug.

'I suppose I shall have to wait until that damned galley of yours gets sunk underneath you, and pray to St Nicholas that you live to tell the tale,' said Philpot. 'I could make you captain of the best fighting cog on the water now. It would be a sight safer.'

'I'm far more likely to end up as meat for fish if you put me in a fighting cog and send me out looking for trouble,' Nick laughed, 'and I'm too fond of life to die yet awhile. There's too many lovely women on dry land to throw myself into the arms of some mermaid. No, I don't mean to spend many more years at sea. Don't think I don't know a man's luck runs out in the end. One or two profitable voyages and I shall have enough to fit up a second ship. Then I can find myself a rich wife and settle down to an easy life ashore like yours.'

'Marriage!' Philpot roared with laughter. 'I don't see an old rogue like you settling down to marriage. She'd have to be mad to take you, eh Joanna?' Joanna jumped and blushed. She thought they'd forgotten her and had been standing uncomfortably in the shadows wondering what she should do.

'If you could direct me to Dame Margaret,' she stammered.

'Why of course, my dear child, she's in the solar. Nick, show her the way. I know Margaret will never forgive me if I keep you from her, but don't be long. I've got some wine at Bordeaux you can bring back for me, if you're going to Naples. I'd like to talk to you about it.'

'Ah, you jealous old scoundrel,' said Nick with a laugh, 'you don't trust me with her, do you? But Joanna here will be her guardian angel, won't you, Joanna?'

His effrontery was incredible, thought Joanna, following him in perplexed silence out of the hall. His familiarity with this grand house and his obvious friendship with the Philpots seemed so out of keeping with his appearance in the stained gambesons the first time she'd met him.

She followed him up a spiral stone stair to a gallery which overlooked the hall. He was whistling a tune she did not know, a gay, melodious tune, and in a detached corner of her mind she noted with surprise that his execution was perfect. What was he doing here in this house where they treated him as an equal and he behaved with all the careless arrogance of the nobly born? It all contrasted so mysteriously with his trade as a sea captain.

At the top of the stairs he stopped whistling and Joanna heard the sound of a harp coming from the solar.

'The harp is Dame Margaret's latest passion. I trust that you can hold your own against such a fascinating instrument.' He threw open the door and stood back for Joanna to enter.

The solar was a small, comfortable room with a large bed, a blazing fire and one wall completely covered with a fine Flemish tapestry. The floor was strewn with fresh herbs and their fragrance was the first thing Joanna noticed as she stood hesitating on the threshold. Margaret Philpot, head bent over the harp, did not look up. She was dressed in a pale-blue, fur-trimmed gown. Her brow was plucked bare in the manner of the court ladies and her headdress the most elaborate Joanna had ever seen. The sleeves of her gown were tight to the wrists with long streamers of silk hanging from the elbows, which floated backwards and forwards as she played. On her finger a bright jewel the size of a thrush's egg flashed as it caught the light from the candles. On a stool by the fire, in a close-fitting gown of green velvet, with a surcoat of fine cloth-of-gold patterned with beasts, birds and intricately mingled foliage, sat her sister, the Lady Mayoress, bending over her embroidery. She wore her hair unplaited, brought forward in two parts from the back and coiled into a jewelled case on each side of her head, attached to a metal filet.

Joanna, gazing at such elegance in dismay, felt immediately inadequate in her borrowed plummage. She shifted her weight uncertainly from foot to foot, waiting for them to notice her, overwhelmed by the feeling that she was an outsider who had no place in such a tranquil scene, until a firm hand in the small of her back propelled her forward, and she half ran, half fell into the room. Margaret looked up with a startled cry and the harp twanged discordantly. She frowned, then catching sight of Nick leapt to her feet.

'Where have you been, you wicked man?' she said giving him both her hands and a warm smile. 'I've been expecting you since noon.'

'I've been busy,' he said, raising a sardonic eyebrow at Joanna. She gazed back at him stonily.

'How was your voyage? Did you have trouble from the French?'

'Enough,' he replied carelessly, crossing over to the fire to greet the Lady Mayoress. Idonia Brembre laid aside her embroidery to give him her hand to kiss, but there was an air of condescension in her manner. Clearly she did not share her sister's enthusiasm for this ugly man.

'How long do you stay in the city this time?' Margaret asked.

118

'Not long, I fear,' he replied. 'Your husband and his friends have wheat and wool, and much else besides, which they are anxious to see safely across the Channel. I cannot keep them waiting, even though it takes me away from lovely women like you.' He picked up one of the long streamers which hung from her elbow and ran it carelessly through his fingers. 'If I do not go, there will be no money for elaborate headdresses, or fine lace, or scarlet silk to line the inside of your sleeves.'

'Stay and sing with us,' she said, pouting at him.

'Alas, beautiful lady, I cannot, not today. Your husband awaits me in the hall, and I dare not dawdle. But I have brought you Joanna. She will sing for you.' He turned on his heel and strode out of the solar without so much as a 'by your leave' to the Mayoress.

'So, Joanna, you came,' said Margaret walking over to the harp and plucking idly at the strings.

'I came,' said Joanna awkwardly. 'Did you not think I would?'

'I wasn't sure.' Joanna began to wish she hadn't come. Somehow Mistress Philpot didn't seem to be as pleased to see her as she might have been.

'I can't think what you encourage that black-haired rascal for,' said Idonia, plying her needle vigorously. 'He's only a sea captain after all.' Joanna glanced at the Mayoress and wondered if she was the reason for Margaret's lack of spirit today.

'He may be a rascal,' said Margaret, 'but he's a daring and an audacious one. Don't you think he's attractive, Joanna?'

'I think he's the ugliest man I've ever seen,' Joanna exclaimed vehemently and Margaret gave a thrill of laughter.

'Well then, let us forget him. What shall we sing?' She ran her fingers over the strings of the harp. 'What sort of music do you like, Joanna, plainsong, ballards, roundelays?'

'Whatever pleases you,' said Joanna, confused.

'I think perhaps a love song.' Margaret struck a chord. 'Amour et ma dame aussi/Votre beaute m'ravie,' she began to sing. 'Come, Joanna, sing it with me.'

'I'm afraid I don't speak French,' said Joanna feeling foolish.

'But you must speak French!' exclaimed Margaret. 'No well-born lady should be without it.'

'There seems so much to learn,' Joanna sighed, 'I've only just learnt how to master the abacus.'

'The abacus! You don't want to waste your time counting. Is that all they teach you in the Northampton household? You must learn French. I will teach you, but not today. Today I shall teach you a love song.'

Margaret played and Joanna began to hum, cautiously at first, then as she mastered the melody with growing confidence.

Margaret nodded approvingly. 'You have a good ear, child. I wonder if you can learn words as quickly.' She began to sing.

'She is coral of goodness, ruby of rightness
She is crystal of cleanness and banner of beauty
She is lily of largesse periwinkle of prowess
She is marigold of sweetness and lady of loyalty
For her love I cark and care
For her love I droop and dare
For her love my bless is bare
And I was all wan

For her love in sleep I slake
For her love all night I wake
For her love I'd mourning make
More than any man.'

She had a full-throated, melodious voice, and Joanna tried to follow her, groping for the words, concentrating on learning them as quickly as she could to please Margaret, loving the music, her soul awash with the soft waves of sound coming from the harp. As soon as she had mastered the words she began harmonising on her own, thinking, as she sang, of Sir Tristram. Without realising it, she unconsciously changed the pronoun from 'her' to 'his'.

'For his love I cark and care, for his love I droop and dare,' she sang, her pure sweet voice soaring above Margaret's in perfect harmony. 'For his love in sleep I slake, for his love all night I wake' – so caught up in her dreams that she didn't hear the door open nor see Black Nick enter the room, and it wasn't until he joined in with a melodious deep baritone that she came out of her trance. The song died on her lips. He walked over to the harp, still singing. He was looking at her with a sort of startled awareness. Was something wrong? thought Joanna, and her hand crept up to her hair to see if her wimple had come adrift. Everything seemed to be firmly in place.

'You sing very well, Joanna,' said the Mayoress leaning forward and smiling at her quite warmly. 'You and Margaret made a most pleasant duet together.' Joanna glanced at the sea captain who was still looking at her, and then at Margaret, watching him thoughtfully. It made Joanna feel uncomfortable.

'I don't think Black Nick likes my singing,' she said.

'Indeed I do, Mistress Joanna,' he replied. 'You sing like a lark. For whom, I wonder, would you droop and dare?'

Blushing, confused and angry, she turned away from those penetrating blue eyes and stared into the fire.

'Joanna's in love,' said Margaret with a little laugh.

'I can see that,' he said. 'I wonder, does he know?'

120

Joanna clenched her teeth, watching the leaping flames resolutely. Hateful, hateful, man! But she would not lose her temper.

'You unchivalrous wretch,' chided Margaret. 'Do you expect to be made a party to our secrets? We do not pry into yours, all those important affairs you men discuss when you ban us from the hall.'

'Fair mistress, I go,' he said with a mocking bow. 'I would not stay blundering in your bedchamber when I am not wanted. Come, Joanna, I'll see you safely back to the Hood.'

'No, you need not go.' Margaret stretched out a slim white hand. 'You'll surely stay to supper?'

'My lady,' he said, taking the proffered hand in both of his and looking deep into her eyes, 'you are the light of my life and the guardian of my heart, but alas I must take my leave, for it is almost time for vespers and I must get this child home before dark. She is not fit to be left wandering about the city on her own.'

'Of course she shall not go alone,' put in Margaret quickly. 'She shall have one of the servants to walk her back to Northampton's Inn. Stay and sup with us.'

Joanna listened to them arguing over her as if she was not there and felt excluded and alone. Now that Black Nick had come, Margaret no longer wanted her. For a time she had felt part of an enchanted elite, now she felt an outsider again, and it was all his fault. She would not walk all the way back to the Hood in his company.

'Alas, I cannot stay,' he told Margaret. 'My life is run by the wind and the tides and I must get back to my ship to make ready.'

'You're not setting sail tonight?' Margaret asked in dismay.

'At dawn tomorrow. Are you ready, Joanna?'

'If you are in a hurry to get back to your ship,' Joanna said as calmly as she could, 'there is no need for you to accompany me. I can easily find my own way back.'

'It's on my way,' he said abruptly.

'Come and visit me again as soon as you can, Joanna.' Margaret held out both hands to her. 'There is so much we haven't talked about yet.' Her face was so full of interest and sympathy that Joanna could not help but be mollified.

'Thank you, I will,' she said, 'just as often as Mistress Northampton can spare me.'

'And then you can tell me all about your true love,' whispered Margaret in her ear as she kissed her. Joanna blushed and hastily went to take her leave of the Mayoress. Behind her she heard a low, throaty chuckle but looking over her shoulder all she saw was Black Nick's broad back as he leant over the harp.

'Try and visit my sister again soon,' said the Mayoress drily, 'I'm afraid she may be in need of much diversion once that rascal catches the tide.'

'Come, Joanna,' Black Nick, now standing by the door, was growing impatient. There was nothing for it but to give in gracefully.

Joanna maintained a dignified silence on the way back to the Hood, her eyes resolutely fixed on the road. Nick whistled the tune that Margaret had taught her. But he stopped as they turned into Bridge Street.

'So you succeeded in pursuading your father to send you into the Northampton's household,' he said. 'I wonder why. I would have thought it would have been much more to his advantage to have placed his daughter with the Philpots. Wouldn't you have enjoyed that more?'

'Mistress Northampton has been very good to me,' she said.

'That wouldn't be too difficult,' he replied. She was startled into looking at him and immediately regretted it. His eyes were dancing wickedly and there was something in the way he was looking at her that, try as she would, she could not prevent the hot colour sweeping up her throat and into her cheeks.

'I doubt if you can do your father much good through the Northamptons,' he said. 'Northampton's finished. Take my advice and stick to John Philpot and his friends.'

'What is it you want?' she demanded, anger making her reckless. 'How can you talk of my father's good when you have done your very best to ruin him.'

'I? Ruin Richard Burgeys?' he exclaimed, stopping in his tracks in amazement. 'Why should I want to ruin one of my best customers?'

'That's what I asked myself,' she said. 'Yet why did you send the guild to search his shop?'

'You really are the most extraordinary girl. Why should I do such a thing? I never meddle in a guild's business. When was this?'

'Soon after the riots.'

A cart laden with stone was creaking up the road from London Bridge and he drew her against the wall out of its way.

'Tell me about it,' he said, looking down at her with furrowed brows. 'What happened?' Too late she realised that she was in danger of revealing the closely kept secret. If Nick was truly innocent then he would know nothing of Tristram's having taken sanctuary in her father's warehouse and she certainly did not want him to find out now.

'Nothing happened,' she said, shrugging off his protective hand and walking on down the road. 'The guild searched his shop and found everything in order. Father never has anything but the very best quality.'

'Then no harm's done.'

'Except to his reputation. Father has never before been searched for sub-standard stock.'

'Reputations are not made by guild inspections, they are made by fair trading and if, as you say, your father always keeps only the best, his reputation will speak for itself.' She did not reply and they left Bridge Street and turned into Thames Street as the bells began to ring for vespers.

'Is that why you hate me so much,' Black Nick asked suddenly, 'because you thought I had set the guild on your father? I swear by the Rood I had nothing to do with the search of your father's house.'

What could she say? That she hated him for his arrogance, for his overbearing mastery of everyone who crossed his path, for his laughing, predatory eyes, for his ugliness? She bit her lip and walked on in silence.

He caught her arm and swung her to face him. 'Joanna, will you not admit you have been mistaken? Come now, let us be friends. There's my hand on it.'

As he reached towards her something inside her seemed to snap. 'Why is it you must have every female at your feet?' she shouted angrily. 'You cannot bear anyone who does not play your foolish love games. You are not content with whores and other men's wives, you want me as well.'

'Not for foolish love games, they are for whores and other men's wives,' he said grinning at her. 'I want you for my friend.'

'No,' she almost stamped her foot in her rage, 'I will not be your friend.'

'Enemies then,' he said with a bitter smile. 'I warn you, Joanna, you will find me a hard man to cross.' She tossed her head and began to walk swiftly away from him towards the Ropery, but he seized her roughly by the arm again and forced her to walk beside him.

His fingers bit deep into her flesh, but she clenched her teeth and scurried along with Petronilla's cream gown bunched up in her other hand, leaping as nimbly as she could over the debris in her path. By the time they reached the Hood, she was quite out of breath. He let her go then and strode off towards the river. She watched his retreating back with relief. If there was any justice in life he would meet his end at the hands of the French or the Spanish and she would never see him again.

CHAPTER 12

Mariota stared critically at the image of herself in the polished steel hanging on the wall of the bedchamber. Her beauty never failed to give her immense pleasure; from it she derived her strength, her serenity and her self-satisfaction. She took it very seriously; it was to be cherished and worked at, particularly the crowning glory of her waist-length hair which every evening had to be brushed by Joan until it hung like a curtain of pale-gold silk, before being plaited again for the night.

Slowly she turned in front of the mirror, looking over her shoulder as she did so, never taking her eyes off the image reflected in the polished steel. The gown she wore was of finest Italian silk, coaxed from her father just before he left on his wool-buying trip, and many, many hours of careful stitching had gone into its making. It showed off her neat, slender body to perfection. Her compliant hair was coiled in two immaculate braids round her ears, framing the perfect oval of her face; her skin was as clear and unblemished as when God had made it. She was not surprised when she saw the startled admiration leap into people's eyes whenever she entered a room; it was her reward for all her work and care, and she was glad that her beauty gave so much pleasure.

'Mariota! Are you not ready yet?' Matilda burst into the chamber in a flurry of agitation. 'You cannot keep him waiting much longer. He grows very impatient.' Mariota smiled at the image of herself over her shoulder, a provocative, tantalising smile.

'I'm coming, Mother,' she said. These last few weeks she had thought that the magic of her beauty had failed, that for once a man who had been everything to her, and she to him, had actually grown cold and forgotten her. It had shaken her to the very core of her being. But now at last he had come back; he was waiting in the hall. Indeed he had been waiting this last half hour while she prepared herself. As she took one last lingering look into the mirror, she knew that she had it in her power to bring him to his knees. Did he deserve any better after all the anguish he had caused her?

'Mariota, do you want to lose him?' protested Matilda bobbing up and down behind her, trying in vain to catch sight of her own reflection. 'For sweet Jesu's sake, stop preening in front of that steel and come with me, do. He'll leave without seeing you and what use your best silk gown then?'

'He won't leave, Mother,' said Mariota with supreme confidence. She picked up her skirts, just enough to show a glimpse of her small feet in their red, pointed slippers, and followed Matilda out of the chamber and into the hall.

Sir Tristram de Maudesbury was pacing up and down with swift impatient strides, but he stopped as soon as Mariota appeared and she could tell from the expression on his face that all her careful preparation had been well worthwhile. She gave him just time to catch a glimpse of her slender ankles, then let the pink silk fall onto the rushes and began to walk slowly towards the hearth with eyes downcast and the fine silk of her gown brushing seductively against her limbs.

'Here she is, Sir Tristram,' said Matilda, bustling across the hall, her veil and hanging sleeves flying behind her like a ship in full flight from the pirates. 'I'm sorry you've had to wait here all alone for so long. Master Burgeys is away from home, buying wool in the Cotswolds, you see, and there is so much for us to do in his absence. I'm afraid the household is all in a terrible muddle.'

'The Cotswolds? I've just come from there,' he said.

'Just think, you might have passed him on the road.'

'And if I had done, I would gladly have given him escort back to London,' the knight replied.

Mariota said nothing. Peeping at him coyly from beneath her lashes she could see that all the time he was talking to her mother, he watched her avidly. She stood still and let Matilda ramble on, knowing from his disjointed responses that he was not really paying her mother any attention and was waiting in delicious anticipation for the moment when Matilda would leave them alone together.

At last, after she had described all the discomforts of her most recent indisposition, had bemoaned the inadequacies of the apprentices and the trials and tribulations of running the household and the shop in her husband's absence, had apologised for the lack of any good Rhenish wine, Matilda finally made some excuse about finding something he might not be ashamed to eat and drink and bustled away in the direction of the kitchen. Mariota waited with eyes downcast, knowing, with all the certainty of much practice in the art of dalliance, that her very stillness was driving him mad.

'Mariota, have you nothing to say to me?' he burst out as soon as her mother had left the hall. 'No word of welcome? After what passed in the garden the last time I was here, nothing?'

She looked at him then, a swift upward glance of her long-lashed grey eyes and then back down at the rushes on the floor. 'I have tried to put what happened in the garden the last time we met out of my mind,' she almost whispered, 'since it clearly meant so little to you.'

'Do not say that, Mariota! I have thought of nothing else.'

'I have watched the moon, which was full that night, wane without a word from you,' she said, her eyes full of gentle accusation. 'It has waxed to full and is once more on the wane and only now do I hear from you. I thought you must have forgotten us.'

'Forgotten you? How could I ever forget you?' he said.

It was music to her ears but not for anything would she let him know it. She slipped past him and sank down gracefully on a stool in front of the great stone hearth.

'Mariota, speak to me,' he implored.

'What do you want me to say?'

'That you've missed me as much as I've missed you.'

'Pretty words, but how am I to know that I can believe them? You spoke many pretty words to me before and then disappeared and I had to learn to forget them all.'

'What could I do? My mother was on her death bed. I got word at the Savoy when I returned that night. I left at daybreak, and well nigh killed poor Orion on the way.'

'And was she dead?'

'No, by God's good grace she rallied and by the time I reached her had begun to recover.'

'My father can reach Northleach in under a week and he hasn't got a war horse like Orion to ride,' she mused, 'yet you have been away for almost two months.'

'What do you want me to do, neglect my duty to my mother?' he exclaimed angrily. 'By God's death, I nearly did. If I'd thought you'd have come with me I'd have taken you with me and married you on the way.'

Marriage! Never in all the things he had said to her since he had first recovered consciousness on the floor of the warehouse had he mentioned that magic word. It was the end to which all her scheming had been bent, but until this moment she had doubted whether the power of even her beauty was sufficient to make him overcome the undoubted disadvantage of her birth.

'You could have written,' she said without betraying a trace of the triumph which was coursing through her soul. 'You disappeared without a word and I thought you had forgotten all about me.'

'Mariota, I swear by Christ's blood, you have never been out of my thoughts,' he exclaimed vehemently. She looked up quickly. He was standing in front of her, legs apart, his hand on his sword hilt, staring down at her almost beligerently. 'Whereas, I don't believe you thought of me at all.'

She held his gaze for a brief poignant moment, smiled a small, sad smile. 'I did miss you, a little,' she whispered and dropped her eyes again. She heard his intake of breath, glanced up and surprised such a look of naked desire on his face that she was frightened. 'I can't think what is taking Mother such a long time,' she said nervously, getting up from the stool and edging away from him. 'I know she will be back any minute.'

'I want to marry you, Mariota,' he said, devouring her with his eyes.

'Father's away, we can't do anything until he gets back.'

'And when will that be? I can't wait much longer for you, Mariota.'

He was standing so close to her, she could feel his hot breath upon her cheek and see the pulse beating in his throat. Oh, where was Matilda? 'I don't know, but he's usually back by Pentecost,' she said a little breathlessly. 'Can you wait till then?'

'Wait for what?' said Matilda marching into the hall with Anna in her wake, bearing on a trencher a pile of pancakes and a flagon of ale. Mariota let out a small sigh of relief.

Most of her lovers had been either callow young apprentices or old men, and she had easily been able to control the passion which her beauty aroused in them. But this knight was different. There was a suppressed violence about him which was disconcerting. Definitely he was not like any of her other suitors. He was, of course, infinitely superior to them all and more madly in love with her than any of them. Through her surpassing beauty she had achieved all that she had wanted and more than she had dared hope for. Nevertheless, just for now she felt it would be safer if she were not alone with him too long. He had courted her before he went away, but never this ardently. She put it down to the love philtre of coriander seed which she had introduced into his wine cup the day he went away. It had done its work well.

As Matilda vociferously administered food and drink to their distinguished visitor, Mariota stood quietly by her mother's side, her mind full of bright visions of the life she would lead as Sir Tristram's wife. Lady de Maudesbury, what a wonderful name! She would go to court, she thought dreamily, and unimaginable new realms would be opened up for her beauty to conquer. Why, if the King were to last until she could be married, then she would even go to the new King's coronation! Blessed St Christopher, bring Father back soon, she prayed, refilling the knight's cup with ale and smiling serenely into his face. He was so handsome, a perfect match! Together they would outshine the whole of the Duke of Lancaster's retinue.

Richard Burgeys returned on the Sunday after Ascension Day. It was not long after sundown, but Joan and Anna were already clearing away the supper dishes from the hall. Mariota greeted her father calmly and waited, full of joyful anticipation, savouring the moment when she would tell him her wonderful news. Matilda threw herself upon her husband, alternately welcoming him home and fussing about his late arrival, wringing her hands over the pile of unappetising fragments in the alms dish about to be carried out to the poor at the gate.

'I don't want anything to eat,' said Burgeys, sinking down onto one of the benches which had not yet been put away for the night. 'I've supped at Philpot's Inn.'

'Philpot's Inn?' exclaimed Matilda. 'You went to Philpot's Inn before coming home first to your wife and family? That's a fine way to treat us!'

'Peace, Matilda,' he replied wearily. 'I'm tired and hot and dusty after riding through the heat all day. Don't plague me now.'

'Did you have a good trip, Father?' asked Mariota, kneeling down to help him off with his boots.

'The best ever. Your father is about to become a very rich man,' he said pinching her cheek, 'and you and your mother will be able to hold your heads up high with the best ladies in the city. Now bring me a flagon of ale, there's a good girl, for my throat is parched.'

'I see, so you supped at Philpot's Inn but they gave you no wine,' put in Matilda. 'Has his wine, too, turned to vinegar like ours and no new wine bought this two years past?

'No, he had some very good sweet wine just arrived from the Levant but the streets are so dusty I've worked up another thirst just riding down Candlewick. The city's like a furnace in this hot weather and dry as a tinder box. I hope you've kept the water butt by the front door filled.'

'Of course we have, Father,' said Mariota. 'Tell us about the Philpots. Are they well?'

'They're well and they gave me news of Joanna. She's been there several times, it seems. Dame Philpot seems to have taken to her. She's very pleased with our Joanna. I'm beginning to think it may be time to get her out of Northampton's household. His day is over, there seems no doubt about that. If Dame Margaret would have Joanna at Philpot's Inn there's no knowing how far she might go.'

But Matilda was not interested in Joanna. 'Had John Philpot any news of the King?' she asked. 'Nobody seems to know how he is. They say Alice Perrers never leaves the bedchamber, that he never goes out and that now everything is in John of Gaunt's hands.'

'John Philpot doesn't think the King will last the summer.'

'Father, if the King dies, will John of Gaunt become Regent?' asked Mariota.

'May God forfend,' he said crossing himself. 'If that devil should ever rule, we shall all perish!'

'But if he does,' she persisted, still kneeling at his feet, 'would it not be useful to know one of his retainers?'

He glared down at her, frowning. 'Has that young knight of the Duke's been to the house while I've been away?'

'Certainly he has,' put in Matilda, 'and he's only waiting for your return to speak to you about Mariota.'

'Speak to me about Mariota?' said Burgeys blankly. 'Why, what has Mariota done to upset him?'

'Don't be a goose, Richard. Mariota never upsets anybody. He wants to marry her. Just imagine! My Mariota married to a knight, living at the Savoy Palace and going to court! She will be Lady Maudesbury and go before Dame Petronilla and Dame Margaret and all the ladies in the city. I can't wait to see Dame Philpot's face when I tell her.'

'Then you'll wait until doomsday,' said Burgeys angrily. 'Mariota is not going to marry any retainer of John of Gaunt. I have other plans for her, and I'll thank you not to meddle with them.'

Mariota leant back on her heels and stared up at her father aghast. It had never occurred to her that he might not permit her to marry the knight. Why, Sir Tristram was the best, most wonderful husband any girl could hope for. He was handsome, nobly born, young and madly in love with her and yet her father was actually saying that he had other plans.

'Father,' she said, looking up at him imploringly with the tears trembling on her long lashes, 'if you do not let me marry Sir Tristram, you will break my heart, truly.'

'That's enough, Mariota. I don't need to discuss what I want to do with you. I've work to do.' He got up, brushing away the hand she had laid imploringly on his knee, and began to beat a hasty retreat towards the warehouse.

'Mother!' she implored. 'Can you not make him see that I must marry Sir Tristram?'

'Must!' Burgeys shouted. 'God in heaven, girl, you're not with child by him, are you?'

'Father! No!' sobbed Mariota utterly shamed by the accusation and completely bewildered by the injustice of it all.

'Don't worry, my angel,' soothed Matilda, 'your father will not ruin your happiness. I'll not permit him to throw away a chance like this for the sake of such a stupid thing as politics.'

Through her tears Mariota watched her father storm angrily out of

129

the hall. He was a tyrant, a hurtful, uncaring despot. How could he believe her capable of sinking so low as to lie with a man before she was married? It was an insult to the power of her beauty! It seemed inconceivable that her wonderful future should so suddenly have been reduced to such sordid dimensions. Sobbing uncontrollably in her mother's arms, it seemed as if her whole world had collapsed about her ears.

'There now, my little love,' crooned Matilda, 'Calm yourself. Between us we will bring your father round. He is tired just now and very full of all that he has been doing. But when he has been at home a few days, he'll put all this nonsense out of his head. He knows where his comfort lies, of that I'm sure.'

Richard Burgeys reached the sanctuary of his warehouse feeling more annoyed with Matilda than at any time in their fifteen years of married life. Burgeys' first wife had died giving birth to Joanna when he was struggling to establish himself as a master of his trade. His marriage to Matilda, then the lovely young widow of a well-established and prosperous mercer, had brought him the house in the Mercery, another baby girl – Mariota – to provide for, a few reliable clients and some remarkably valuable stock. It had been the beginning of his prosperity. In marrying Matilda all those years ago, he had been able to look beyond the limits of a mere shop in the Mercery to a future which would, with God's grace, take him perhaps even as far as the Guildhall. But it had not been easy. He had worked hard and he had prospered. He had used the money he had made to create more, but there never seemed to be enough for all his ambitious schemes. If he were ever to be Mayor, Burgeys knew he had to rise above the average merchant's parsimonious tendency to trade with only a limited number of familiar clients, taking small risks and expecting small profits. Now, as a result of this journey into the Cotswolds with William Gryffard, all kinds of lucrative opportunities lay within his grasp and he was not about to let Matilda jeopardise any of them.

Burgeys sat down in his counting house and opened his ledgers. At the thought of what he had done on this trip his heart began to pound with excitement. The risks he was taking were quite considerable, but the rewards would make him a rich man at last. Never before had he bought so much wool at one time, far more than he could afford. Gryffard had leant him the money for the first payment and even hinted that he would make it easy, when the wool arrived in Calais, to get many of the sacks passed by the staplers without paying tax.

Burgeys had no illusions about Gryffard. Just now Burgeys had something that Gryffard wanted – Mariota. It was in Gryffard's interests to promote the prosperity of his future bride's father, and he,

Burgeys, would be a fool not to grasp this opportunity with both hands. Gryffard was the kind of man who was going far. Already he was a good friend of the Mayor and the ruling families in London. Why, his own reception at Philpot's Inn this afternoon had been proof of that. As soon as it was known that he was an emissary of Gryffard, they could not do enough for him.

Once Gryffard and Mariota were married and settled in London, there would be no end to the ways in which the merchant of the staple would be able to help him. Gryffard had already made that quite plain. What had Sir Tristram to offer to compare with that? Only his title and his good looks, neither of which would be of use to anyone but Mariota. As soon as they were married, the knight would carry Mariota off to his manor and that was the last either her father or mother would see of her. When Matilda realised that, she would come round to his way of thinking, he was sure. Just for a moment his spirit quailed. The last time he had beaten his wife, he had spent a very uncomfortable few weeks indeed. But he must be firm. He could not let Matilda ruin everything for some romantic whim.

When Sir Tristram rode into the Mercery the following evening, Richard Burgeys was in his shop helping Dickon to set it to rights after a busy day. He was in a cheerful mood, for he had dined well. Neither Matilda nor Mariota had referred to the knight again and he was beginning to think that domestic harmony was assured. It was with displeasure therefore that he watched Tristram dismount in front of his shop, but he hid his feelings beneath a professional manner and immediately tried to interest his noble visitor in a bale of white marbled silk embossed with vine leaves and red grapes. But Tristram did not even glance at this fine example of the mercer's wares; he looked over his shoulder instead at the small group of curious onlookers who were gathering around the door of the shop and staring mouths agape at the knight, at his squire, and at the two splendid horses fidgeting impatiently under the squire's care.

'A word with you, Master Burgeys,' he said peremptorily.

'I'm at your service,' replied Burgeys, placing his hands palm downwards on the counter and waiting with an expression of bland enquiry on his face. Tristram frowned and glanced once more over his shoulder at the interested spectators.

'Not here,' he barked. 'In private.' Burgeys raised his eyebrows and began to roll up a bale of marbled silk. He would enjoy telling this condescending young god that he could not have his daughter for a wife.

Tristram was losing patience. To the delighted surprise of the onlookers, he vaulted neatly over the counter and seized Burgeys by the arm. 'The warehouse'll do,' he said. 'It's private enough by my recollection.'

Burgeys found himself being forcibly propelled through the back of the shop and into the cavernous warehouse beyond as if he'd been nothing but a sack of wool. Once out of sight of the spectators, Tristram relaxed a little.

'By the saints, Master Burgeys,' he said in what was obviously meant as a more conciliatory tone, 'if you knew what I'd come for you'd not have been so anxious to avoid me.'

Richard Burgeys was furious but he did not dare show it in front of this powerful young man. He led the way into his counting house with what dignity he could muster and perched himself on his high stool behind a barricade of ledgers.

'We shall be private enough in here,' he said. 'In what way can I be of service to you?' Tristram looked round at the ledgers, the abacus, the bottle of ink, the quill pens and his lips curled in disdain.

'Surprising though it may seem,' he said, 'I wish to marry your daughter.'

Arrogant young dog, thought Burgeys, and then he suddenly remembered something Margaret Philpot had said to him yesterday. 'Which one?' he asked craftily. 'I have two daughters not yet married.'

'Why, Mariota of course,' said Tristram, clearly startled.

'A pity,' sighed Burgeys. 'Mariota is already spoken for.'

'I don't believe it!' exclaimed Tristram in dismay. 'She said nothing to me about any other man. What do you mean?'

'You have been courting her behind my back and without my permission!' exclaimed Burgeys, letting his anger get the better of him. 'If this is the way knights behave it's not my idea of chivalry.' Tristram scowled and his hand went to his sword. Burgeys recalled the feeling of those steel fingers on his arm as he had been marched unceremoniously through his own counting house and trembled behind his ledgers.

'If it's the dowry that worries you,' said Tristram still scowling, 'I'll take her in her smock if need be. I have a good manor with a house, flocks of sheep and serfs aplenty. My mother has kept everything in order since my father was killed at Poitiers. Your daughter will live there like a queen, wanting for nothing. You can stay with her whenever you come buying wool. Why, I might even sell you some of mine.'

Burgeys stared down at his ledgers and just for a moment he was tempted. If this foolish young man was prepared to take Mariota dowerless, just think of the money he would save! A merchant's daughter married to a knight and without dowry. What a triumph! Life with Matilda would be easier too if he did not have to cross her in this. But then he thought of William Gryffard and he knew that it was useless. Mariota was in pawn to the merchant of the staple and this arrogant young knight would have to look elsewhere.

132

'As I said, she's already spoken for,' he mumbled into his ledgers.

'Is she betrothed?' demanded Tristram. 'Has she made her betrothal vows?'

'That is none of your concern,' said Burgeys grasping firm hold of a ledger and looking defiantly at Tristram. 'I have told you that you cannot marry Mariota and now I must ask you to leave.' Would he go without committing violence? Anxiously Burgeys watched the knight. It was clearly a battle between his natural instinct to fight and his duty as a knight not to use his strength against a helpless adversary. Chivalry won.

'May I bid her farewell?' He made the request through clenched teeth. 'I should like to pay my respects to Dame Burgeys your wife, who has been kind and welcoming to me always.'

'I'm sorry, my wife and daughter are resting in our bedchamber. I cannot allow you to disturb them,' said Burgeys, angry that the young man had the arrogance to throw Matilda's approval in his face. His anger helped him to shepherd the knight through the warehouse, into the shop and so out into the street. Tristram made no attempt to force his way into the house, and Burgeys breathed a sigh of relief as he watched him mount his powerful stallion. The horse wheeled and the knight let him have his head, scattering spectators. A worried frown creased Burgey's brow. Would the knight accept his defeat sensibly or would he try and seize Mariota without permission? Burgeys had heard tales of such things happening. It was a pity that Gryffard had gone straight to Calais from Bristol and not come back to London. It would have been much safer to have had the betrothal vows made and the knot securely tied. He would have to watch his daughter carefully. Not that he did not trust her to obey him. Mariota would never commit an act of voluntary defiance, but what of Sir Tristram? He did not know how much he could rely on that young man's chivalry.

CHAPTER 13

William Gryffard arrived in London on 20 June, and the next day rode into the Mercery shortly before noon. Deep in thought, he walked his horse along the middle of Wood Street, oblivious of the cries of the apprentices declaiming their masters' wares. Across the counters, bright bolts of silk lay in wait to tempt the susceptible passer-by, and lengths of velvet hung in voluptuous folds from poles jutting out into the street. But Gryffard was impervious to temptation, for his mind was totally absorbed. He guided his horse carefully through the throng towards the Burgeys house, pondering the use he had already made of the information he possessed and what further advantage could be rung from it before the news finally spread.

Richard Burgeys was in the shop, helping Owen roll up the lengths of fine silks and damasks as the noon bell began to toll. 'Well, here's a good morning when it brings you to my door, William,' he said coming out into the street as Gryffard dismounted. 'I didn't look to see you until the Eve of St John.'

'Nor me neither, but we had as fair a wind from France as any I've ever known, with no sign of the French or the Spaniards, God and St Christopher be praised.'

'Owen will look after your horse,' said Burgeys, leading the merchant into the shop. 'Did Black Nick bring you ?'

'He did, and a fair-sized cargo of yours, so he tells me. He's anchored below the Bridge. I tell you, my friend, you're going to be a rich man before Michaelmas; by the time you've sold what that black-haired ruffian's got in his holds you'll have paid for all your wool before it reaches Calais. That wool will fetch a deal of money, enough to buy some very fine wares. You ought to go over to France yourself as soon as you can. It's too much money to leave to agents to spend for you. Go to Antwerp or Bruges, there's treasure enough and to spare at the great Michaelmas fairs. You could be the envy of all in the Mercery with your Brabant lace, Italian silk, Flemish tapestries.'

'I'd like to go, of course I would,' Burgeys seemed hesitant, 'but there's so much to do here. Why, since I've been back I've scarce been out of the counting house except to go to Mass or a meeting at the Mercer's Hall. I've become a Warden of the Mercers Guild since I saw you last,' he added proudly.

'It's time you got another apprentice or two,' said Gryffard. 'The tide is running in your favour, my friend, and you must learn how to make the most of it. What do you have apprentices for if they cannot look after your shop for you? You should concentrate on buying the best and finding the money. I tell you, you're a merchant capitalist now, not a shopkeeper. Do you think the Bardi or Paruzzi got where they did by staying at home poring over their ledgers?'

'You're right,' said Burgeys and Gryffard could see that he was enormously pleased at being compared to the great Italian merchant princes.

'You'll dine with us, I trust. I don't know what Matilda's got for dinner, but I know she and Mariota will be pleased to see you.'

Gracefully, Gryffard accepted. Of course he would dine with them, it was the reason why he had come!

He followed Burgeys upstairs into the hall, full of excitement at the thought of seeing Mariota again. It was a sensation completely new to him. Even to himself he would not admit how much she stirred him. He had had women aplenty, mistresses and whores in many different cities all over Europe, but never once had he considered marriage. Mariota was different. There was about her something so aloof and yet so tantalisingly desirable it created in him a longing which nothing could satisfy save possession.

While Matilda apologised at length for the dinner, describing in the minutest detail all the dishes she would have liked to have prepared for him and listing all the malevolent happenings of fate which had contributed to their absence from the board, Gryffard feasted his eyes on Mariota. She was wearing a simple undergown of bleached linen with a surcoat of wine-coloured silk. Her hair was covered by a tight-fitting wimple which framed her face and accentuated its oval perfection. This simplicity appealed to him. She was like an uncut jewel awaiting the skill of the goldsmith. It would be his pleasure as her husband to deck her with all the riches his ingenuity could devise. He would be the goldsmith who would refine and polish the jewel and reveal it in all its beauty. All men would envy him his priceless possession and he would guard it carefully.

He watched her, at her father's bidding, take her seat at the table beside him, waiting for some sign that she recognised he had a claim on her, but she gave him no encouragement. She was so near, he could smell her flowery fragrance, yet he did not feel she was close to him. She was mysterious and unapproachable and he found her more

135

intoxicating than the finest wine from France. He reached out for the flagon of ale and filled her cup with a hand that shook a little. She said nothing; indeed, so far she had addressed not one word to him, but he was not dismayed. He liked quiet women – quiet and obedient, that was what he liked.

He was feeling so pleased with her that he decided to make Burgeys a present of his momentous news. After all, the Death Crier would soon be out proclaiming it in the streets; it would do no harm to make Burgeys a party to the secret now.

'The King dead!' exclaimed Burgeys pausing with his cup halfway to his mouth. 'May God have mercy on us all. What will happen now? Do you think the Duke of Lancaster will accept his nephew as King? If he doesn't, there'll be civil war, for the city'll not stand for it.'

'I don't think it's in the Duke's interests to start a civil war,' said Gryffard. 'He has too much to lose. There's hardly a country in England where John of Gaunt does not own a manor, besides most of Lancaster, Derby, Lincoln.'

'Does that not mean that he could raise the country if all his feudatories were to support him?'

'But would they? And there's London – the Duke has seen what the citizens of London can do when roused.'

'That's just it, what will happen to London now the King is dead?'

'The Mayor is on his way now to Richmond, with John Philpot and one or two others, to plead with the young King to settle the city's quarrel with John of Gaunt.'

'What can a ten-year-old boy do?'

'It is what the Duke can, or cannot, do that matters,' replied Gryffard. 'It's my belief that he does not intend to snatch the crown.'

'You believe that a man as proud and as powerful as John of Gaunt will submit to a boy?'

'It's not the boy he's submitting too, it's the forces behind the boy. If we can show the Duke there is a majority against him, if we can gather all those who are opposed to the Duke in unity against him before he has time to realise what is happening, then he will have no choice but to submit. That is the purpose of the Mayor's visit to Richmond.' He did not add that it had been his own intelligence of the King's death that had enabled the Mayor to act so quickly.

Alice Perrers had been alone with the King when he had suddenly been stricken with an apoplexy. It had not taken the King's mistress long to realise that he was in his death throes and that she was about to lose her unique position of power. While the King lay fighting for his last breath, Alice had made the most of those last precious moments to look after herself. She had seized what jewels she could and fled from the chamber and from the palace. A serving man who had been in Gryffard's pay for some time had come straight to him

136

with the news and Gryffard had made good use of it. Yes, the Mayor had been grateful to him, thought Gryffard, and his gratitude would prove useful one day.

'Does it mean that there will be no Marching Watch on the Eve of St John?' said Mariota, breaking her silence at last. 'I was so looking forward to it. The procession passes right past Mercer's Hall and we were to go there to watch from the balcony. There was to be a supper in the hall and Mother and I have been making garlands to hang from the balcony. I cannot bear it if it has all to be put off because the King has died.'

'I can understand how disappointed you must feel, Mistress Mariota,' said Gryffard with an indulgent smile, 'but the period of mourning will only last three weeks and then there will be the coronation to look forward to. Compared to that, what is even a Midsummer procession? I hope you've got some cloth-of-gold and crimson silks and taffetas in that cargo of yours from Calais, Richard, for it will be at a premium now with a coronation coming. You'll be able to charge twice the price for it.'

'And I hope that you will let your family have some of it to make up into something new before you sell it all,' put in Matilda quickly. 'The family of a Warden of the Mercers Guild should be a credit to his trade and not having to make do and mend all the time.'

'When have you and Mariota not been a credit to me, my love?' replied Burgeys soothingly, but she was not to be so easily put off. She launched into a vigorous tale of mended linen and gowns cut down into surcoats and for a while it was beyond her husband's power to contain her.

'Mistress Mariota, I hope I shall have a chance to see something of you while I am here,' said Gryffard while her parents argued, 'for I shall not be going back to Calais until after the coronation. I have bought a plot of land just south of the Priory of St Helen's and I very much hope that you will come one day and look at it with me.'

'I doubt very much that I shall be able to do that,' she replied, her eyes on her trencher.

'It would grieve me greatly if you do not,' he insisted.

'You've said yourself that we shall be very busy in the next few weeks. I do not see how I shall be able to get away. I must help my father as much as I can.'

'I'm sure your father will not mind your spending time with me. I am sure he would not like his daughter to tire herself out with work when it is not necessary.' She looked at him then.

'My mother needs me too,' she said, her grey eyes full of a cool disdain. 'She is not strong. She's plagued by headaches and suffers a great deal. I cannot leave her alone much.' Then she got up and started helping the maidservant to clear away the dishes from the

137

table. He watched her thoughtfully, noticing with his senses how gracefully she moved and with his mind considering her words. So she did not welcome his suit! But it was of no matter, she would do as her father bade her. But what of her mother? Was Matilda, too, opposed to the idea?

'I am having plans drawn for my new house in Cornhill,' he said turning to Matilda. 'I hope you and your daughter will come and look at them with me on the site. It may be that Mariota can suggest some improvements.'

'I can't think why we should be interested in your house,' Matilda said sharply. Gryffard drew in his breath and looked at Richard Burgeys in surprise. Surely he would rebuke his wife for her rudeness, but Richard looked away uncomfortably. Was he not master in his own household? Gryffard smiled grimly to himself. Here was a point he had left out of his calculations. Mariota's coolness did not worry him. She was young and impressionable and he had been away for many weeks. The colder she was to him the greater the pleasure when he finally brought her to succumb. But the mother ought to have been overwhelmed at the prospect of such a match for her daughter. Who else could possibly be better? Unless it were the knight. The knight! He had always regarded the knight as a danger, which is why he had tried to dispose of him while he was still hiding in the Burgeys warehouse, but somehow the man had been spirited away before the Guild's search. Perhaps Sir Tristram had come back to dazzle Mariota and her mother with his youth and chivalry. But he fancied he had the edge on the knight now. Burgeys was tied up so tight he could not possibly give his daughter to anyone else, no matter what.

Mariota was bringing a dish filled with water for him to wash his face and hands.

'I've brought you a present,' he said drying his hands on the linen cloth she carried over her arm and getting up from the table. 'It has been crafted by one of the finest silversmiths in France and I hope it pleases you.' She put down the basin of water and he could see that in spite of herself she was interested. From the purse hanging at his belt he produced a chain of fine Florentine silver chased with lover's knots and the letters W and M entwined.

'Why, it's beautiful,' she murmured, running her fingers over the delicate work with obvious pleasure.

'Allow me to put it on for you,' he said. She stood still and compliant while he laid the chain round her slender waist and fastened the clasp. He looked at the snake of silver gleaming in the candlelight against her wine-coloured surcoat, and felt well pleased.

'Thank you,' she breathed, her eyes on his gift, her fingers stroking the delicate filigree.

'It is nothing,' he shrugged, 'and quite unworthy of your beauty.

But there will be more, much more once you are mine.' She looked up startled and then quickly away. But he had seen enough in those cool grey eyes to know that he had not been mistaken. She was already a little more than interested. It would not take too much to bring her round.

By the time Gryffard left, the Death Crier, clad in a tunic ornamented with death's-heads, was parading the streets of the city. With him marched the Guild of All Hallows carrying crosses and robed in black. 'Good people, of your charity pray for the soul of our dear brother King Edward' he cried, 'who departed this life at the hour before vespers yesterday.' Women leant out of the windows, masters and apprentices poured out into the streets, craftsmen paused in their work to hear the news. In the Death Crier's wake the people bowed their heads and crossed themselves, then huddled together in worried groups pondering the news and its implications. That evening the churches would be full, as the people went to pray for the soul of their King, and afterwards to talk about what it would mean.

Joanna and Petronilla were in the Ropery collecting rents when they heard the news.

'We'd better get back,' said Petronilla. 'This is what John has been dreading. I don't know what it will mean, but there's sure to be trouble.'

'The poor little boy,' said Joanna, thinking of the ten-year-old Richard in the palace at Shene. 'He's so young to be King. His childhood is over now, I suppose.'

'If he does become King,' said Petronilla. 'King or prisoner – only he won't live long as a prisoner, I shouldn't think.'

'Poor little boy,' repeated Joanna sadly.

When they got back to the Hood they found that Northampton had already heard the news and gone out.

'Well, there's plenty of work to be done,' said Petronilla rather brusquely. 'We must get all that undyed broadcloth down to the dyehouse. Black cloth for mourning will be in high demand, we must make the most of it while we can.'

The next few days were ones of anxiety, hard work and gloom. John of Northampton was hardly at home and Petronilla was clearly preoccupied and worried. She relieved her feelings with work and the whole household was kept very busy. Joanna and the apprentices worked from dawn to dusk in either the dyehouse or the warehouse, or selling yards and yards of black cloth in John of Northampton's shops, or in the counting house writing up the ledgers.

When Northampton was at home Joanna tried to keep out of his way as much as possible. His long face wore a perpetual scowl, and she was terrified of incurring his wrath. From him they heard that the young King had asked the city to submit without reserve to his will

139

and that the Mayor had agreed. John of Gaunt was persuaded to meet the city's leaders at Westminster and there the Duke's quarrel with the city was at last successfully resolved. The danger of civil war had been averted by the intervention of the Mayor, and the city's leaders and the people of London could go about the business of mourning their King in peace.

Joanna thought that now perhaps the black cloud of anxiety and gloom might be lifted from the Hood, but if anything it seemed worse than ever. Nothing seemed to please Northampton, and Petronilla too was being difficult, exacting impossibly high standards for every task and driving them all very hard. As Joanna fell upon her pallet bed in the women's dorter at night, she thought with longing of Philpot's Inn and wished she could be allowed to visit Margaret again. To Joanna the death of the King himself did not mean much. She was too young to remember his past glories. Edward III was just an old man who had outlived his luck, a silly old fool ensnared by the wiles of his unscrupulous mistress and unable to control his overbearing sons. Joanna had never seen him ride in triumph through the city's streets with countless captured French knights in serried ranks behind him. Crécy and Poitiers were just names which old men went on about for too long when in their cups and the French a nation of cowards who would never fight.

It was the boy King who fascinated her. He had brought peace to the city and she could not help the feeling that a bright new age was dawning. She longed for the period of mourning to be at an end, to escape from the depressing feeling of hopelessness in the Hood, to be able to visit Philpot's Inn again and listen to Margaret's gay, outrageous chatter; to talk of Sir Tristram and let Margaret feed her hope with wild plans of ways to ensnare him for a husband.

After three weeks of solemn mourning, Edward III was laid to rest among the tombs of the Plantagenet Kings on the Confessor's mound at Westminster Abbey, and the city was able to look forward to the coronation festivities. There was to be a tournament at Smithfield the week before the coronation and Joanna was immediately flung into darkest despair lest the Northamptons in their present isolation would decide not to go. This fear was put to flight the day after the funeral, by Matty, of all people.

'Look what the mistress has given me,' she said, proudly producing an embroidered belt. 'It was to be for my bridal, but the mistress gave it to me today so that I could wear it to the tournament.'

'The tournament! Are the master and mistress going then?' asked Joanna, trying to sound as if she did not care.

'Of course, he's still Sheriff of the city, isn't he? They'll be going and so shall I, to take care of Katherine.'

Joanna did not question her further. Not for anything would she give Matty the satisfaction of knowing how much she longed to go to the tournament, but for the next few days she went in fear that the rest of the household were to be left behind. The demand now was not for black but for scarlet and cloth-of-gold, and work in the dye-house and shops increased as they laboured to satisfy it. Petronilla was preoccupied and unapproachable and Joanna did not dare ask her outright. But as the day of the tournament approached and preparations in the Hood reached fever point, it became clear that the whole household was to be allowed to go.

Joanna surveyed her meagre wardrobe sadly. Apart from the two gowns she had brought with her from home and which she now hated since they showed her at her very worst, there was only the green gown and cream surcoat that Petronilla had given her. It would have to do. Tristram had liked her in it well enough when she had worn it for the penitential procession. She wondered if there would be a chance to speak to him at the tournament, or whether he would be too busy fighting. The thought of seeing him made her heart beat so fast she felt she would suffocate in the stuffy dorter. She went to sleep beside the snoring Matty on the pallet bed, dreaming bright visions of Sir Tristram riding out on Orion to topple every other knight on the field.

CHAPTER 14

On the day of the tournament the Northamptons arrived at the jousting ground early in the morning, just as the sun was rising above the Priory of St Bartholomew. In the centre of the meadow stood the lists, a rectangle 150 yards long by 100 yards wide surrounded by a stout fence made of stakes driven into the ground. Displayed around a second, higher fence were the banners, shields and crested helmets of the knights who were to take part in the tournament. Joanna gazed in bewildered excitement at the brilliant colours in countless combinations on shield and banner, at the strange devices and heraldic animals, at the rows of helmets crested with stags or boars or dragons and their gaily coloured plumes hanging over the edge of the stockade. She longed to stay and look for Tristram's arms, but Northampton would not wait. The ground outside the stockades was already seething with people who were not privileged enough to sit in the stands. The young and agile were perched on top of the barriers, others were jostling for position near the cracks between the boards where they might be able to see something of the jousting when it began.

Shouldering his way through the crowd, Northampton led his party towards the loge reserved for important members of the city and their families. Already the lower tiers were filling with bright splashes of aldermanic scarlet as merchants and their families greeted each other and set about finding somewhere to sit. None of the aldermen greeted the Northamptons, however, and nobody made way for them. Not one hand was raised in welcome and Joanna glanced at Petronilla in dismay. What were they to do in face of such hostility? They could not return to the milling crowds outside the stockade, yet where were they to sit?

Petronilla was gazing at her husband with so much pride and trust that Joanna felt, for an instant, reassured. John of Northampton, grim-faced but determined, seized his wife by the hand and strode up into the stand without a glance behind him, brushing aside the protes-

142

tations of the men and women in his path, bumping against their knees and treading on their feet without a word of apology until he reached John More, who managed to make a space for the two of them. It was courageous and effective and Joanna could not help admiring him for the way in which he had set them all at naught, but it left no room for his followers.

'What shall we do?' moaned Matty, fingering her new embroidered girdle as if it were a talisman. 'We're not wanted here, that's very clear. I suppose we'll have to stand outside with the common folk. Poor little Katherine, she'll be able to see nothing.'

'That we shall not,' retorted Joanna, studying the tiered rows of wooden benches in front of her resolutely. What John of Northampton could do, surely they could try to follow? 'Come on, Matty, there's still some room left at the top of the stand.'

They clambered up almost to the top of the stand, ignoring the grumbling protests from those already in possession, until they reached a bench which was occupied by only two stout matrons.

'This bench is reserved for friends of the Mayor,' one of them objected as Joanna was about to sit down. 'He's the one who's saved our city. He's the one who's made peace with the new King and brought John of Gaunt to his senses. You're with the Sheriff Northampton, I saw you come in. What's Northampton done for any of us, that's what I'd like to know? It's time he went. Sheriff Northampton's no friend of the Mayor and he and his have no place here.'

'Well, I'm sure the Mayor doesn't want a fight now that everything has been settled so peaceably,' said Joanna with her sweetest smile, 'so try and throw us out if you dare!' She plonked herself down, dragging Katherine and the trembling Matty with her. The woman glared at her angrily, and Joanna stared back, her amber eyes flashing defiance, hoping that the woman would not dare to make a scene here. For a moment she was not sure, then the woman turned away and Joanna knew she had won.

Delighted with her victory, she promptly forgot about her tiresome neighbours now muttering angrily to each other and peered down eagerly at the lists below, at the plumed helmets and the banners, wondering which was Sir Tristram de Maudesbury's. Where was he? She gazed out across West Smithfield. The remains of an early morning mist hung in swirling patches above the flat meadowland, garlanding with ghostly tendrils the knights' pavilions which had sprung up like giant flowers at the far side of the Fields. Was he there, in one of those tents, being armed by Robin? In the centre of the stand opposite was the King's loge covered by a gold and red striped silk canopy, surrounded by the empty benches reserved for the court.

The Mayor arrived and took his seat in the centre of the city's loge way below them. Watching him and his entourage settle themselves on the benches, Joanna caught sight of Mariota, sitting not very far away from the Mayor. How did Mariota manage to be in so prominent a position? she thought with a tiny twinge of envy. Then envy gave way to pity as she saw that sitting by her sister's side was William Gryffard. Poor Mariota, did it mean she was going to have to marry the man after all? Just then Mariota turned round to speak to someone behind her and Joanna, waving furiously, tried to catch her attention. But Mariota did not wave back. Then a great fanfare of trumpets sounded, and Joanna forgot all about her sister as she craned forward eagerly to see what was happening.

A procession was slowly entering the field from behind the hospital of St Bartholomew. First came the squires riding the knights' huge war horses. Joanna gazed at them entranced, searching among all the riot of colour for the red lozenges on the blue field and thought she saw Orion, snatching at his bit with his customary impatience, and Robin struggling to hold him to the sedate walking pace of the procession. Next came the ladies of the court, mounted upon palfreys, and each lady led a knight by a chain of gold. It was a dazzlingly pretty sight and Joanna, gazing at them in awe, realised for the first time the enormity of her dreams. This was his life, she thought; these beautiful ladies in their brightly coloured silks and taffetas, with their jewels and elaborate headdresses, were her rivals. What hope had she against such birds of paradise? How could she ever hope to win his love?

The ladies and their knights were followed by a party of nobles, and Joanna watched as a child arrived, dressed all in white and riding beside a woman whose cloth-of-gold cloak reached from her shoulders to the tail of her palfrey.

'Look, Katherine,' said Matty, as all around them a great cheer arose from the spectators, 'there's the King. How small he is, to be sure.' The young King dismounted unaided from his horse, while a tall, spare man went to lift the Queen Mother down.

'There he is,' said Matty suddenly, and Joanna, startled, followed her gaze and saw a tall, golden-headed knight escorting a beautiful lady into the Lancastrian loge opposite, and for a moment she held her breath. The lady sat down in the principal seat in the centre of the loge and Joanna realised that the knight was not Sir Tristram at all, but his liege lord, the feared Duke of Lancaster.

'That's not him!' she exclaimed and then bit her lip in vexation. In her disappointment she had been about to betray her secret, and to Matty of all people. But Matty, equally preoccupied, was staring excitedly at where the more agile spectators were clinging precariously to the top of the fence round the lists.

'It's Adam,' she said waving frantically at her betrothed. 'There, he sees me. Blessed St Mary, he'll fall!'

144

'He will if you go on waving to him like that,' said Joanna. 'Don't encourage him.'

The knights were mounted now and on their heads they wore their great crested jousting helmets. Joanna gazed at them, completely indistinguishable in their armour, at the plumes bobbing so jauntily from on top of those evil-looking helmets, at the horses with the heraldic symbols emblazoned on the cloths which covered them from flowing mane to tail. It was a heroic, spine-chilling, magnificent sight. The trumpets sounded again and her soul leapt to the call as the splendid mass of steel began slowly to resolve itself into a cavalcade which wound away behind the lists and disappeared from view.

Next came the business of proclaiming the combatants and Joanna craned forward, trying in vain to hear what the heralds were saying. Realising that it was useless, she resigned herself to having to wait until Tristram appeared upon the field. Katherine was growing restless and she took the child on her knee, trying to distract her with stories and little snatches of song until the action began. At last, with what seemed like half the morning gone, the trumpets sounded again, a great long fanfare of triumphant sound which brought forth a knight at either end of the lists. The heralds made one more unintelligible pronouncement.

'Who is it, who is to fight?' asked Joanna as an expectant hush fell upon the spectators.

'Can you not be quiet,' snapped her neighbour. 'We've come to watch the jousting not answer your questions all morning.'

Joanna bit back an angry retort and gazed down at the two knights waiting at each end of the lists. One bore a simple broad stripe of black on white running horizontally down his shield and the same on the horse cloth. On his helm a lynx lay couchant. The other knight had small squares of green on gold and his helm was crested with a stag's head erased. The squires were clinging to the excited stallions, waiting for the signal to release the bridles.

The trumpets sounded, the squires ran for the barrier, the impatient coursers plunged forward, and Joanna held her breath as the two knights hurtled towards each other with lances levelled. They met with a great crash of steel and Joanna closed her eyes in terror. Surely they would both be killed by the impact! A sigh like a wave breaking on the shore arose from the spectators, and Joanna, expecting the worst, opened her eyes fearfully. To her amazement both knights were still in the saddle. One of the knights had a broken lance and he was riding back to the barrier to get another one from his squire. Then both knights returned to the far end of the lists, wheeled and once again headed straight for each other. This time Joanna watched wide-eyed as they met with another resounding crash of steel on steel. She saw one of them reel in his saddle but remain mounted. At the third encounter, another lance was broken and the winner declared. Joanna was disappointed. She did not know what she had expected, but she wished she knew more about the rules of the joust.

The day wore on and as joust followed joust, she became more accustomed to the clash of armour, the crack of breaking wood and the terrifying spectacle of knight thundering down on knight without anybody being hurt. So far no one had been unhorsed and yet, judging by the cries of approval from the spectators, there was much to admire in the blows the knights managed to inflict on each other. She longed to have someone beside her who might explain in detail what was happening. Matty was no use, fidgeting and complaining about the heat and the dust. Katherine had fallen asleep in her arms. The other women around her were busy discussing their latest lying-in. Nobody seemed to be very interested in the dramatic struggles being fought out for their entertainment below.

'It's so hot,' complained Matty, wriggling on the hard bench beside her. 'Are you not thirsty, Joanna?' Joanna did not reply. A horse had come crashing down with his rider as two knights met and for a time both horse and man were trapped against the wooden barrier that ran down the length of the list.

'See, the ladies in the Lancastrian loge opposite are drinking wine brought them by a page,' continued Matty. 'If only Adam might be allowed up here to sit with us. I'm sure he'd get us something to drink.'

'Aren't you interested at all in the jousting, Matty?' snapped Joanna.

'Yes, of course, but I wish we knew more of what was going on.'

Joanna shut Matty out of her thoughts and gazed again at the two knights now tilting at each other below. They met together with a resounding crash, wheeled, trotted to the end of the lists and then spurred at each other once again, lances levelled, shields held across their bodies.

A great wave of longing for Tristram swept over her and she wished passionately, with every vibrant fibre of her being, that she could be there among the ladies of the Duke of Lancaster's retinue, waiting for her knight to fight for her, instead of stuck up here with all these ignorant city merchants and their wives.

When the heralds announced an intermission before the mêlée, the loge began emptying as the spectators went in search of refreshment. Katherine woke up and wanted a drink. Matty complained that she was hungry.

'How long do you think it will be before they start again?' she asked. Aroused from her daydreams, Joanna looked about her.

'I don't know, but we'll not find out by sitting here. We might as well go and see what we can find.'

'Do you think we dare? We might lose our place.'

'Then we shall not be the only ones,' said Joanna. 'You stay here if you like, but I'm going in search of a drink for Katherine. She'll never last the day else.'

'I'll come with you, then,' said Matty, jumping up hastily. 'I'm not staying here on my own.'

Outside the lists, West Smithfield was like a fair, with booths of every kind doing a very brisk trade. Crowds were milling about jostling each other and gulping pasties and winkles. There were pedlars, and pardoners, and friars with begging bowls. The booths selling food or drink were surrounded by a pushing, struggling crowd of boisterous men, all trying to quench their thirst and fend off hunger before the start of the mêlée, which was to be the highlight of the day.

'Where is your Adam, Matty, when we need him?' said Joanna, scanning the crowds in dismay. 'We'll not get anything to eat or drink without a strong arm to aid us.'

'I don't know where he is.' Matty plucked anxiously at Joanna's sleeve. 'Perhaps we ought to go back to the loge. He may even now be trying to find me, for he knows that's where I'll be.'

'If he comes looking,' said Joanna, 'but I'm not prepared to count on Adam's chivalry at a time like this.'

'Well, what are we going to do?'

'We're going to walk about until we see somebody we know who'll help us,' Joanna told her with far more conviction than she felt. 'Tommy or any of the apprentices – they must all be here somewhere. It's just a question of finding them.'

'They're probably all sitting on top of the barriers,' whined Matty. 'They won't want to lose a place like that and I shouldn't be a bit surprised if we lose ours, and all for nothing.'

'You go back if you want to, I'm not giving up yet,' said Joanna resolutely, and then she saw him, the one person in all the city she most wanted to avoid – Black Nick, bearing purposefully down upon her.

'Well, if it isn't Joanna Burgeys,' he said when he reached her side. 'Not lost again, are we?'

'No, I thank you. I'm not lost.' Joanna tilted her chin and stared out over his shoulder at the seething multitudes. 'Matty and I have just come out to stretch our legs.' He looked her up and down thoughtfully.

'You may not be lost, but you do look very hot,' he said grinning at her.

'Oh, we are hot, and hungry and thirsty too,' said Matty. 'But we dare not go near the ale booths for the crowds around them, and there's nobody here to help us.'

'What, no knight to do your bidding? You surprise me.' He raised a sardonic eyebrow. 'Still, if you don't mind accepting the services of a rascal like myself, I shall see what I can do for you.'

147

'Oh, would you,' breathed Matty before Joanna could refuse. 'We shall be for ever in your debt.'

'It will be my pleasure to be of service,' he declared, raising Matty's hand gallantly to his lips and quite spoiling the effect by the look of triumph he flashed at Joanna as he did so. 'Wait here.' Joanna, full of vexation, watched him stride off. Why was it that he always managed somehow to play the part of rescuer when he was the very last man on earth that she wished to be beholden to?

'The Blessed Virgin be praised, are we not in luck?' cried Matty, delighted. 'What an enormous man. See how they make way for him. I shouldn't think anyone would want to tangle with him.'

'No indeed!' said Joanna bitterly, watching him shouldering his way through the crowd gathered round the ale booth.

'Strong but gentle, a true knight errant,' Matty enthused. 'Who is he?'

'He's a wicked sea captain with a heart as black as his hair and beard, and if you knew some of the things he's done, you'd no more ask his help than the devil incarnate,' retorted Joanna and was delighted to see the stupid smile wiped from Matty's perspiring face.

'Joanna, don't talk like that.' Matty crossed herself fearfully. 'You always think the worst of everyone. How can you say such things when he's been so kind to us?'

'Kind!' exclaimed Joanna. 'Black Nick's not kind, he's only doing it because he knows it will annoy me so.'

'Why will it annoy you? Are we not both faint for want of food and drink. Why do you always have to act so contrary, Joanna?'

'You don't understand,' Joanna went on, determined to punish Matty for inviting Black Nick's attentions. 'I tell you, he preys on helpless maidens, seduces them and leaves them ruined without a thought as to what will become of them. Knight errant indeed! The very word is defiled when you think of it in connection with that man.'

'Has he not tried to seduce you, then?' said Matty quickly. 'Is that why you hate him so much? I'm not surprised, no man would want you, Joanna! Not with your hot temper! Adam says you'll die an old maid.'

A lifetime ago Joanna would have been hurt and angry, but she had become used to Matty's waspish tongue by now. Why bother to explain that she did not care what any man thought of her save one, and that one so far beyond her reach that it was useless even to dream about him. The thought made her feel wretched.

Black Nick came back bringing a brimming flagon of ale and a somewhat subdued Adam. Matty, whose sensitive soul must have been more affected by Joanna's dire description of Black Nick than at first appeared, grabbed hold of her betrothed and bore him off with her, refusing to drink the ale Black Nick offered her and clasping little Katherine to her breast with such a look of terror that Joanna could not help but smile.

'What have you been saying to frighten her so?' laughed Black Nick. 'I declare you must have painted me blacker than the devil himself to drive that hungry maiden away so prematurely. I could swear she would have done anything for a cup of ale and a piece of pasty.'

'Matty is very fond of her betrothed,' said Joanna primly as she sipped the ale he proffered. 'All day she's really only been interested in looking for him. I doubt if she cares about the jousting at all.'

'Fortunate fellow to have inspired such devotion,' he said, using his dagger to cut up the pasty he had brought and handing her a piece. 'I hope he manages to live up to her expectations.'

'He doesn't have to,' said Joanna through a mouthful of pasty. 'For Matty it is enough that she is to be married, to have a husband and one day a house of her own.'

'Whereas Joanna Burgeys wants a knight in shining armour. Is that not so?' Taken completely unawares, she swallowed too much pie and choked unbecomingly. Blushing, she glanced at him quickly. Was he teasing her, or had he somehow guessed her secret? All the laughter had gone from his eyes and he was looking down at her intently with what seemed to her to be a great deal of scorn. 'Sir Tristram is not for you, Joanna,' he said. She looked down at her feet, shocked, humiliated and hurt. Dame Philpot must have told him! The confidences which she had poured into Margaret's sympathetic ear, and for that ear alone, had become a joke no doubt between them.

Anger saved her pride, anger and a fierce determination not to let him see how bitterly she felt betrayed.

'How dare you!' she hissed, throwing back her head and glaring at him, her magnificent eyes flashing fire. 'You're not content with what you've got. Why should I be? You want to own your own ships! You, who are nothing but a poor sea captain, you want to be a merchant prince! To that end you will risk your life and doubtless sell your soul! Why should I be any different? Why should I not aim high too? You want me to be like Matty and take an apprentice, or do as my stepmother wants and take the veil. But I shan't do it! I swear by the Blessed Virgin, I'll surprise you yet.'

'You never cease to surprise me, Mistress Burgeys,' he said and the laughter was once more back in his eyes, 'and I certainly don't want you to take the veil. That passionate nature of yours would definitely be wasted in a cloister.'

'That's all you can think of, isn't it?' she retorted, not in the least mollified. 'You wouldn't understand the sort of love which lasts a lifetime, a pure, unselfish love which doesn't look for gain or expect to be requited. The heroic love of a Lancelot or a Criseyde.'

'Heroic!' He almost shouted with laughter. 'You think that knights are heroic because they charge at each other with a wooden pole and still remain in the saddle! It's not difficult to hold a lance and hit your target when you practice doing it every day of your life. But don't forget that the creatures inside all that shining armour can be small and mean, soft and slimy as a snail without its shell. Forget about all that knight errantry, that's minstrels' tales. It's not like that any more. They're men, like any other, with all the faults and sins of men.'

'Pay no attention to him,' said a cheerful voice in her ear. 'Nick doesn't like tournaments. He thinks jousting is a waste of time. Is that not so, Nick?'

Joanna whirled round and found the Philpots standing beside them.

'Well, and how are you enjoying your first tournament?' Margaret asked her. Joanna could not look her in the face. This woman whom she had thought such a warm and trustworthy friend, had betrayed her most treasured secret to Black Nick, of all people. Confused and embarrassed, her anger draining out of her and leaving her helplessly vulnerable, Joanna could think of nothing except the need to escape.

'Joanna thinks it is all quite noble and uplifting,' Nick's mocking voice cut across her muddled thoughts, increasing her agony. 'Like Camelot reincarnate.'

'Do you, Joanna? Why, I think it's been very tame so far. I hope the mêlée will be more fun.'

'Except for that poor Gascon knight, the Sieur de Pavignac. It cannot have been much fun for him,' put in John Philpot.

Margaret shrugged. 'His destrier is not worthy. The beast was frightened, I'd say. If he recovers he should get himself a better war horse.'

'Nonsense, it wasn't the horse, it was bad riding,' said John Philpot. 'He'd not have come down if he'd held to a straight course. Don't you think so, Nick?

'I don't know, I wasn't there. Let Mistress Joanna be the judge. Was it the horse or the rider, do you think?'

'I don't know,' mumbled Joanna, wishing he would leave her alone. 'I couldn't see what caused him to fall, not from where I was sitting.'

'Couldn't you? Where are you sitting then?' he asked.

'It's far up in the stand, and I think I ought to be getting back there else I may lose my seat.'

'Lose your seat? What nonsense,' declared John Philpot. 'Are you not with the Northamptons?' Awkwardly Joanna explained that there had not been room enough for everybody in their party.

'Poor Joanna, it can't be much fun being with the Northamptons today, no wonder you look so unhappy,' said Margaret sympathetically. 'I tell you what, why don't you come and sit with us for the rest of the tournament? You can't have your first tournament spoilt for you just because of what that obstinate troublemaker Northampton brings upon himself.' It was a heaven-sent chance to get away from the hostility and discomfort of her perch at the back of the stand into more congenial company. Adam could look after Matty and Katherine. They were not her responsibility anyway.

Joanna's despondency began to lift, like the early morning mist, warmed by Margaret's friendly interest. It really wasn't possible to be cross with her for long. She was too sweet and too much fun. Perhaps she could not help chattering about other people's affairs, reasoned Joanna. Black Nick had no business throwing the knowledge in her face like that, trying to break up their friendship, like as not! But he'd not succeed, nor spoil this wonderful day.

Joanna accepted the invitation with her most radiant smile.

'Come along then, we don't want to miss the mêlée.' Margaret took Joanna's arm. 'Sir Tristram's bound to be taking part in that.' Joanna could not help shooting a quick, self-conscious glance at Black Nick. But already he was striding away from them and she hoped it was the last she would see of him that day.

Sitting beside Margaret Philpot, Joanna listened as the herald announced a general tournament mêlée between Thomas, the Earl of Buckingham for the King and his elder brother the Duke of Lancaster, with twenty of the bravest knights among their retainers, to be fought for the honour of St George and the King. The prize was to be a gold noble to each knight on the winning side and an additional prize of one of the King's best falcons to the knight adjudged most worthy. The combat was to start on horseback with the breaking of spears, but might then be pursued on foot with the flat of the sword as the only weapon. The lances must have coronal heads to cull them and the swords were to be blunted by heavy lead foils. A knight would be adjudged *hors de combat* if he were unhelmeted, lost hold of his weapons, or if any part of his body touched the stockades round the lists.

The marshals finished shouting the rules, the heralds yelled '*Laissez aller*' and scampered for safety over the barricades, the gates were raised at either end and forty opposing horses thundered down the field towards each other. They met with a crash that shook the whole field. Bloodcurdling cries almost drowned the clash of arms, while the wild high whinnying of the stallions rent the air. It was the most terrifying, yet exciting spectacle that Joanna had ever seen and she clutched the edge of the wooden bench tightly as she strained forward, searching the confusion of horses and men for a glimpse of Sir Tristram's red on blue. But it was impossible to pick out colours and symbols amid such apparent chaos. All she could see was the flash of drawn swords, the flaring nostrils of excited horses, the slow agonising fall of a steel-clad figure as a knight was unhorsed, while all around her echoed the crack of splitting lances. Soon there were not

151

many left mounted. Men struggled together hand to hand, or lay helpless on the ground in danger of being trampled by the plunging riderless horses.

Then she saw him, still in the saddle, a red plume flying from the crest of his helm and the red lozenges running diagonally across the blue caparison on Orion's heaving flanks. She let out her breath on a long sigh of wonder and realised that until that moment she had been too frightened for him even to breath.

A knight, all in black armour with green plumes fluttering from his helm and on his shield a row of green seahorses, was bearing down on Tristram who wheeled in time and the two knights met with a resounding crash, rocked backwards in their saddles, righted themselves, wheeled and rode at each other again. This time they did not break away after the impact but stayed locked together shield to shield. Then, as Orion reared, Tristram was dragged from the saddle, but as he fell he brought with him his opponent.

'Oh St Michael aid him,' prayed Joanna in terror, as both knights crashed to the ground.

'It's all right,' said Margaret, much amused. 'See, they are up already.' Opening her eyes again, Joanna saw Tristram draw his sword and set about the other knight with vigour. The two men were well matched and fought on for some time. Then suddenly, as Tristram raised his right arm, his opponent brought his sword down on his gauntleted hand with a crashing blow. Tristram's sword spun from his hand.

'Wasn't he wonderful,' breathed Joanna, sinking down beside Margaret. 'Who was that he was fighting?'

'The Sieur de Chevigny, no less, sometime champion to the Black Prince when he was alive. He's one of the best jousters in the land. Your knight acquitted himself very well.'

The only knights still mounted were Lancaster and Buckingham who were now about to ride a course against each other, for although the rules of the tournament allowed any knight to engage any other of the opposing side, it was still normal practice for the two princely leaders to be reserved for each other. The two brothers faced each other at either end of the lists. Lancaster waved his lance as a signal and they spurred down the field, as they had done on countless occasions as boys practising in the tilt-yard. It was gracefully and elegantly done, the lances held precisely horizontal, the snorting destriers kept on a dead straight course, the shivering impact of the lances square on the opposing shields, and the final neat thrust sideways of Lancaster's lance which knocked the helmet up and off Thomas's head, where it dangled by the lacings from his gorget.

Joanna was filled with a sense of wonder at such perfect artistry. Black Nick was wrong, she thought. How could such men as these be cable of a mean or cowardly act? They were the champions of all that was good and noble. Their glorious chivalry set them apart from more ordinary mortals. He was jealous, she thought suddenly. He too felt the yawning chasm which separated him from this enchanted world. He hated them because he was not like them.

The royal knights were now riding up to the King's loge. They bowed low before their ten-year-old nephew. Then the heralds announced that the tournament in honour of St George had been a draw and that the knight adjudged to have been most worthy was the Sieur de Chevigny.

'I think Tristram should have had the falcon,' said Joanna, eyes shining with pride.

'Tristram will have another chance tomorrow,' said Margaret.

'The best of the single combat is always reserved for the second day. Lancaster is to give a feast at the Savoy Palace tonight, so let's hope your knight is able to keep his lance steady in the morning.'

CHAPTER 15

Sir Tristram de Maudesbury scowled down at the trampled grass on the floor of his tent. He was dressed in a chain-mail shirt with a square neck and elbow-length sleeves, the skirt reaching to his thighs. His armour, burnished and polished by Robin since the previous day's fighting, hung upon the walls. Tristram picked up his sword in both hands and held it straight out in front of him, eyeing the shining blade critically. Not a tremor, not the merest hint of a quiver shook its tempered steel. Despite a night of feasting and carousel, his hand was as steady as a rock. A purplish swelling on his sword hand bore testimony to the blow he had received the previous day and he flexed his wrist, bringing the sword up suddenly at right angles, then moving it from side to side, testing the injured hand. Satisfied, he twirled the sword once or twice round his head and with a lightning downward blow severed a shaft of sunlight.

Absently he put the sword down, once more lost in thought. But it was not of the day's fighting that he was thinking, it was of a pair of cool grey eyes set in a perfect oval face, of a small rosebud mouth he should have kissed when he had the chance, of a slender graceful form which had once, for the briefest interval, lain soft and yielding within his arms and which now seemed, for some quite inexplicable reason, to be beyond his reach. Impossible, he thought, picking up his sword again and running his fingers along its blunted edge. It could not be that she was beyond his reach for ever. He would not accept it. It was unthinkable.

The silken flap was twitched aside and Robin slipped quietly into the pavilion.

'Is she there, Robin?' asked Tristram, fingers tensing on the sword hilt.

'She's there, not far from the Mayor on the right of the royal box.'

'Same as yesterday?'

'Same as yesterday.' Robin picked up the breastplate and began to buckle it on over the chain-mail hauberk.

154

'Is that pestilential stapler with her still?'

'Yes,' said Robin, passing the leather straps over the knight's shoulders and round his waist.

Tristram assimilated the information in silence while his squire placed the padded arming cap on his head and tied the chin strap. He could not understand the girl. She, who before he went to Gloucestershire seemed ready to fall into his arms the minute he mentioned the word marriage, now resisted all his attempts to either see or speak to her alone. She was only obeying her father, of course, and Tristram cursed himself for not having asked Burgeys for his daughter's hand before he went away. He'd have given her to him then, he was sure of it, but meanwhile this stapler had appeared from Calais – plague take him – and was even now sitting at her side. Well, he would show that scurvy merchant a thing or two today. Robin was bringing the vambraces and Tristram held out his arms in front of him, tensing his muscles.

'She looks more beautiful than ever,' said Robin, buckling the steel plates onto the knight's arms. 'She's wearing pink today. It suits her. In fact she's more enchanting in her simple pink gown than all the court ladies with their elaborate headdresses and embroidered surcoats put together.'

'Careful, Robin, don't you go falling in love with her as well, for then I'd have to fight you too and I don't want to have to start looking for another squire.'

'Never fear, she's beautiful, I'll grant you, but I lost my heart to her sister before ever I set eyes on the fair Mariota,' replied Robin with a grin.

'What! You're not still enamoured of that odd child – what's her name?'

'Joanna.'

'Joanna. By all the saints, Robin, why can't the mercer give her to this wool merchant?'

'Perhaps because the stapler, like you, prefers the other one.' Robin fixed the tail flap of the chain-mail skirt up through Tristram's legs to protect his groin.

'It's a sinful waste, throwing away a beautiful creature like Mariota on a fellow like that. I cannot understand why. It can't be money. I even offered to take her in her smock but he would not listen.'

'Perhaps it's the Duke,' said Robin. 'The Londoners have little love for our liege lord. It may be the mercer's afraid of upsetting the Mayor or some of his friends. He was fairly pissing himself with fear the night we brought you to his house, terrified someone would find out he was harbouring a retainer of Lancaster's.'

'But that's madness! He must know that the Duke's protection is better than anything he can find in the city. Besides, that's all over now. The Duke has made his peace with London.'

Robin, on his knees fixing the long rowelled spurs to Tristram's feet, said nothing. The knight scowled down at his squire, his mind still grappling with the enigma of his rejected suit. She was being forced against her will to marry a man who was utterly unworthy, of that there was no doubt. Apart from anything else, it was his duty to rescue her.

Robin was nearly finished now. He got to his feet. 'The blacksmith has managed to beat out that dent where the Sieur de Chevigny caught you on the hand,' he said as he fetched the great steel gauntlets lined with leather. 'I think it's as good as ever it was.'

'I was a fool to be taken in with that old trick,' said Tristram pulling the gauntlet carefully over his injured hand. 'I just hope I get another chance at de Chevigny today.' He flexed his powerful fingers experimentally. 'The blacksmith's done a good job.'

'Hugh d'Aycliffe's squire's been betting on his knight unhorsing you,' Robin told him.

'I'm not worried about d'Aycliffe,' said Tristram with a grin. 'I was only unhorsed yesterday because that brute Orion thought he was in a real battle and was trying for a kill with his forefeet. I hope you took d'Aycliffe's squire's bet.'

'By St George, I did. It seems an easy way to make some money. I just wish a few more would be as stupid. Orion ought to be better today. Yesterday's mêlée will have taken the edge off him.'

'Maybe the animal'll listen to me now. Give me my helm and then go and see to Orion. Walk him about a bit, don't let him get too excited.'

Left to himself, Tristram eased the great jousting helmet onto his head. It fitted tightly over his padded leather cap. Now he was ready. He stood in the middle of his tent, waiting for the call of the trumpet, and thought about what he was going to do. It was a good plan, one which ought to please her and appeal to the crowds too. But would it work? Would the King agree? Would a ten-year-old boy understand the nature of the request he was going to make? He ought to. The Black Prince's son must have been taught all the finest points of chivalry. He should be delighted. But what of Burgeys? What would his mean trader's mind make of it all?

Tristram frowned beneath his helmet. Here in front of this huge crowd he'd show them all. She couldn't resist him then and her father would know what it was like to have a knight pay court to his daughter. What chance the merchant stapler then?

Joanna sat on her cushion beside Margaret Philpot and watched Mariota, sitting next to William Gryffard just in front and a little bit to the left of them. Her sister puzzled Joanna. There was no denying that she looked very lovely in the pink silk gown which set off the chased silver belt round her slender hips to such advantage. She was bareheaded save for a bright pink ribbon round her brow; her beautiful hair, coiled in braids round her ears, looked as pale as flax in the sunshine. William Gryffard possessively monopolising her certainly seemed to think so, which was not surprising, but what fascinated Joanna was that Mariota did not seem to mind. She seemed to be flirting with him perfectly happily and Joanna, remembering Mariota's dark despair on her last visit, found it hard to believe. Yet watching her now with the merchant of the staple dancing attendance, she did not look like a girl who was suffering from a broken heart. Joanna was amused and at the same time a little envious. It must be so much easier to be good and obedient, she thought ruefully, if you could fall in love to order. Then suddenly a knight appeared at the far end of the empty lists and she forgot all about Mariota. A murmur of surprise ran through the packed stands as Tristram rode slowly towards the King's loge.

'Doesn't he look wonderful,' breathed Joanna watching in adoration as Tristram reined up in front of the gold and red striped canopy.

'They all look the same to me,' said Margaret. 'But what's he up to?' The little King was standing up on his great carved chair talking to the knight. 'He must be asking the King for some special favour. How intriguing, I wonder what it is.'

A page was sent scurrying to fetch Nicholas Brembre and Margaret gave it as her opinion that the Queen Mother was consulting with the Mayor. Then the trumpets sounded and the herald announced that Sir Tristram de Maudesbury had asked for permission to fight for the hand of the lady he loved. Joanna listened with bated breath as the herald pronounced that Sir Tristram's choice was a daughter of a merchant of London. Any knight wishing to challenge him was to come forward.

'A master stroke, by the Rood!' exclaimed John Philpot, delighted. 'That'll be the Mayor's doing. Very clever. A retainer of Lancaster's fighting for one of our people. Good, very good. That'll show them that the Duke's quarrel with the city is really over. I wonder who she is?'

Tristram was bowing to the King, turning away, but he was not riding out of the lists, he was coming towards them. Joanna sat as if moulded out of stone, the words of the proclamation ringing in her ears like a peal of bells. Nearer he came and yet nearer; a wild, crazy hope was tearing her apart. According to the minstrels' tales, knights who fought for a lady's hand usually craved a favour to wear. Could it be that he was coming to ask for such a favour? Never in her wildest dreams had she dared to hope for anything so wonderful as this. He was nearly opposite now. Blessed Mother, was he reining Orion back? Dear God, if you love me let him stop now, Blessed Saint Mary Mother of God let him see me. She was shaking so much she did not know if she could stand. Merciful St Cecilia, she had nothing to give him!

But Tristram did not stop. He rode past, a few yards only, then he reined Orion back so fiercely the great horse reared back on his haunches. He was looking straight at Mariota.

'Demoiselle Burgeys, I crave a favour to bring me luck,' he cried in ringing tones that all might hear. Mariota stood up while all the ladies of the court craned forward to have a look at her. With unhurried grace she untied the ribbon round her brow and tossed it, blushing becomingly, to her knight. He caught it on the point of his lance and the crowd cheered madly. Then he rode slowly and triumphantly to the end of the lists, while the spectators cheered and Orion danced, beating the ground with his great forefeet and swinging his quarters from side to side, but never getting the better of the knight who sat immobile on his back.

Joanna did not see him go. Utterly destroyed, she shrank upon her cushion while everything swam and danced before her eyes. She was going to be sick. She was going to faint. Desperately, desperately, she wished herself back at home, or with Matty at the back of the stand, anywhere but with Margaret, who knew all of her secret and would try to comfort her.

'Don't worry, Joanna,' said Margaret, 'it's only a game, just a piece of play-acting to add a little spice to the jousting.'

But Joanna knew that it was not a game. Everything had suddenly fallen into place. Sir Tristram was Mariota's secret lover and she had been a blind, susceptible fool not to see it. Tristram had been in the house with Mariota for days while he was recovering from his injuries during the riot and what more natural than that he should fall in love with her? Every man did, so why not the knight? She had not guessed because she had not wanted to.

'Oh look, Joanna,' Margaret was saying, 'how very diverting, that nice William Gryffard is leaving. It's difficult for him, I suppose, but I can't feel it's right for him to leave. He would be better to laugh it off. He must know the knight chose the wrong daughter. It was you he meant to choose, Joanna, of course it was, but it's probably difficult to see with those great helmets on. Is your sister actually betrothed yet? Oh dear, I hope William Gryffard does not take it all too much to heart, it would be a pity to lose him now. What do you think, John?'

'Difficult for the fellow,' said John Philpot. 'Of course Gryffard cannot possibly fight him. Only knights can take part in a tourney.' Joanna wanted to scream at them to stop, to escape from Margaret's bright curiosity, to take her shame and her humiliation somewhere far, far away and to be left to suffer in peace.

'Perhaps he's gone to find a champion,' said Margaret. 'He can certainly afford the best. I wonder who he will choose?'

'If Sir Tristram wins,' replied her husband, 'Gryffard might have to look elsewhere for his bride. After today, if Burgeys plays his cards right and can find the dowry, he might catch that knight for his daughter.'

'Not if she's already made her betrothal vows,' declared Margaret. Joanna could stand no more of it.

'I must get out, I must get away,' she mumbled, jumping to her feet.

'You cannot go now, Joanna,' exclaimed Margaret. 'This is likely to be the best of the whole tournament. Don't you want to see how your knight acquits himself? Don't you want to see him win?'

And if he won, thought Joanna in an agony of despair, how could she bear it when he claimed Mariota? Too intensely miserable to be capable of any action save flight, she fought her way out of the crowded loge, stumbling over people's feet and pushing past their unyielding knees, scarcely knowing what she did, deaf to the indignant protests and blind to the curious stares which followed her.

Once outside in the anonymity of the milling crowds, she wandered aimlessly, her mind in chaos, prey to a thousand thoughts, each one more depressing than the last. She saw nothing of the winkle-sellers, did not hear the cooks crying their wares; she walked past pedlars with their trays of coloured ribbons and tantalising trinkets, impervious to temptation; she did not even notice the lewd comments of the young journeymen and apprentices.

The whinnying of a horse suddenly startled her. Looking up she saw a knight in black armour and on his shield a row of small green sea-horses. Beyond him there were other knights mingling and she realised that she must have wandered, as if drawn irresistibly by the power of her love, to the place at the back of the lists where the knights were assembled. It brought her to her senses and she looked round in dismay, terrified that she might see Tristram, but to her relief there was no sign of him. Instead she saw a man talking to the black knight and to her surprise she recognised William Gryffard. The thought of an encounter with Gryffard at this moment was unbearable and she immediately began to retreat. But it was too late, he had seen her. He was shaking hands with the black knight and before she could get well away had caught up with her.

'Mistress Joanna,' he said, 'what a pleasure to find you here. Can I escort you back to the loge? You're sitting with the Philpots, are you not?'

'I wasn't feeling well, I thought I'd go home,' she stammered.

'You surely have not grown tired of the jousting already? The most exciting part is about to begin.'

'I don't much care for single combat, I thought the mêlée yesterday was by far the best of it.' Even to her own ears it sounded lame and she shot a quick, guilty glance at him to see if he believed her.

159

His watchful eyes were appraising her thoughtfully and she looked away quickly again. He did not look at all defeated or miserable, she thought with a tiny shock of surprise, not like a man who was about to lose the woman he loved. If anything, he looked triumphant.

'You know, you don't want to give in so easily,' he said suddenly. 'You must learn to fight for what you want.'

'I don't know what you mean,' she said, shaken.

'Oh yes you do, Mistress Joanna. And don't think I cannot share your dismay, for it is much like my own. You and I are in danger of becoming losers, are we not? But I do not want to lose your sister Mariota and you do not want to lose the foolish young man who thinks he can solve everything by force majeure.'

'He's not a foolish young man,' she retorted, stung into betraying herself. 'He's a brave and chivalrous warrior.'

'Then fight for him,' he replied with a smile. 'Don't run away.'

'How can I, any more than you? You cannot fight Sir Tristram, you're not a knight.'

'It's true I am not entitled to bear arms in a tourney such as this but that does not prevent me hiring a champion to fight my battles for me,' he said. Joanna looked over her shoulder at the knight in the black armour, waiting like an avenging demon on his powerful destrier. She recognised those arms. He was the knight who had triumphed over Tristram yesterday.

'De Chevigny?' she asked, and shivered.

'De Chevigny,' he confirmed. 'He's already proved himself the better fighter. I don't think Sir Tristram's challenge will succeed, do you?' Fear shot through her, making her knees weak and her hands clammy, fear for Tristram and his defiant challenge, fear that he would be defeated by this knight who had triumphed against him yesterday, fear that he would not, and in winning would marry Mariota and be lost to her for ever. But was he not lost to her already?

'Come, Joanna,' said the wool merchant, taking her arm, 'we will go back to the loge now, and we will watch de Chevigny knock this brave knight out of the saddle and make a mockery of his challenge. Then once Mariota and I are betrothed perhaps your father can arrange a marriage for you with de Maudesbury. It is what you want, after all, is it not?'

Joanna said nothing. This man with his all-knowing eyes and his subtle smile was dangerously persuasive. She could not repress a small flicker of hope, although she knew that there was a flaw in the merchant's confident reasoning: for he took no account of love. That Tristram, loving Mariota as she now knew he did, would ever look at her instead was impossible. But what of Mariota? Did she love Sir Tristram? How could she not?

Confused and helpless, she allowed Gryffard to escort her back to the city's loge and took her seat again beside Margaret Philpot. In an agony of conflicting emotion, she heard the heralds call upon Sir Tristram de Maudesbury and the Sieur de Chevigny to come forth and do battle for the hand of the Demoiselle Mariota Burgeys, and when Margaret asked her if she felt better, she could only numbly nod her head.

Sir Tristram pulled down his visor and stared through the narrow slits at the knight in black armour at the other end of the lists. He had not expected the Sieur de Chevigny. It would take all his skill and a great deal of luck to defeat so formidable an adversary, but he was not afraid. He was elated. This was his chance to avenge himself for yesterday's defeat.

He settled the end of the heavy, nine-foot lance into the hook on the right side of his breastplate. He could feel Orion's great strength beneath him. The horse was no longer fidgeting; like his rider, he waited, muscles tensed, for the moment when the final trumpet would ring out and together they would perform an act of violence and precision practised many, many times before. Tristram's mind was entirely concentrated on outwitting the man waiting at the other end of the lists. No good trying to unhorse so experienced a fighter as de Chevigny. In the first encounter he would not even go for the helm but try to stay out of trouble and perhaps go for a hit on the black knight's shield if he could. The trumpets sounded. Orion trembled, ears pricked, waiting for the charge.

'In the name of God and St George, come forth and do battle,' shouted the marshal, waving his white baton.

Tristram lowered the lance, took a firm grip of Orion with his legs, Robin let go of the bridle and the stallion surged forward. Through the slits of his visor Tristram saw the knight thundering towards him. He steadied Orion with his left hand, the one that held his shield, keeping him on a straight course, his right gripping his lance. He watched his opponent's lance, ready to duck out of its reach, keeping his shield close to his body where it would be difficult for the other man to hit.

The knight was upon him now, his lance streaking for his helmet. Tristram jerked his body sideways at the last minute and let de Chevigny's lance pass harmlessly over his shoulder while driving his own lance straight at the black shield with the green seahorses. But de Chevigny saw the move just in time and jerked his shield away. Tristram yanked his arm up and over the knight's head as he thundered past, neither knight having scored a hit.

Orion hurtled on towards the wooden stockade at the end of the lists and Tristram reined him sharply back. The horse slithered to a halt and turned quickly, but hardly quick enough, for de Chevigny was already thundering down upon them again. This time, Tristram was slightly off balance, with Orion charging down on his prey and his lance barely in position. The black knight was upon him, his lance aiming straight at his head. Instinctively he put up his shield to protect himself. With a crack of splintering wood de Chevigny's lance shattered against Tristram's shield and although he managed a glancing blow on the black knight's helmet he failed to knock it off.

Galloping to the end of the lists, Tristram waited while the black knight fetched a new lance and considered his strategy. De Chevigny was fast and he was accurate; it was going to be difficult to beat him. He had no more time to think before the knight was at him again. This time Tristram managed a hit on his shield but failed to prevent de Chevigny doing the same.

They rode course after course. Tristram wheeled Orion faster and charged down upon the black knight with such fury that he twice broke his lance against his shield, but all the time de Chevigny was scoring more hits and once Tristram felt the tip of de Chevigny's lance beneath his chin and knew he was within an inch of losing his helmet. Had Orion not jinked sideways at that moment, all might have been lost. The sweat was streaming down his face inside his helmet and it was becoming harder and harder to see through the narrow slits of his visor. His right arm was aching now and the reins were slippery with Orion's sweat. He had to acknowledge that de Chevigny was by far the more subtle jouster; his only hope now was to unhorse him.

He charged again. Watch, watch, keep watch until the last minute, that was when the black knight would make his hit. The two knights met, Tristram's lance outstretched, aiming for de Chevigny's shield; then at the last moment Tristram reined back, Orion checked, Tristram dodged that fiercely probing lance and then kneed Orion forward. The great stallion slashed at the black knight's destrier with his forefeet. De Chevigny's horse reared and Tristram seized his advantage; his lance lunged towards the knight's helm. Quick as a flash, de Chevigny brought up his shield to counter the blow. Tristram stood up in his stirrups and hefted his shield against the other's with all his weight behind it. Orion, acting in complete concord, pushed with his shoulder against the black knight's destrier. The horse staggered back and Tristram slammed his shield hard against the black knight's body and felt him suddenly yield. His lance fell from his hand and slowly he toppled from the saddle and pitched head first upon the ground.

For a moment Tristram sat panting in his saddle, oblivious of everything, even the prize for which he had fought, overcome with joy. The unbelievable had happened, he'd unhorsed de Chevigny, the Black Prince's champion. Then the cheers echoing round the arena pierced his tired mind and raising his visor he saw the Duke of Lancaster himself riding out to greet him. Leaving the defeated champion lying on the ground, he rode with his liege lord round the lists, Mariota's ribbon streaming from his helmet and the crowd roaring itself hoarse.

CHAPTER 16

'Joanna, I thought you had more courage. Are you going to sit here and mope or are you going to try and be of some use to me again?'

'I'm sorry, I can't help it.'

'Of course you can help it.' Petronilla looked down at Joanna sitting crouched over the ledgers in the counting house. What was she to do with the child?

The coronation was over. Richard II was crowned King and John of Gaunt had accepted his nephew, acting as the King's seneschal throughout the coronation festivities. A fortnight into the new reign there was no sign of civil war and the city had settled down to enjoy a peaceful succession. But it had been a worrying and difficult time for her husband, Petronilla knew. Northampton no longer counted in the city and Petronilla supposed that at the next elections he would lose his office of Sheriff. She sighed. John was taking his political ostracism hard, as hard as Joanna was taking the collapse of her romantic idyll.

They were not unalike, her husband and this rebellious child, thought Petronilla with a start. Both idealists, both determined to push the frail craft of their own will against the mighty tide of custom and the established order. It seemed that God had seen fit to burden her with the task of making their paths smooth for them. But she did not seem to be having much success with Joanna. The child would not eat, she would not work. At first Petronilla had tried kindness, taking her with them to all the coronation celebrations, hoping that the spectacular pageants and processions would prove a sufficient diversion. But though the fountains had run with wine and the streets had been full of dancing and music, every window and balcony along the King's route from the Tower to Westminster hung with ribbons and flowers, though the whole city had rejoiced, Joanna had remained unmoved, so wrapped up in her own misery she seemed to see nothing.

Joanna did not hide her heart well, thought Petronilla ruefully. When she was happy the whole household benefited from her exu-

163

berance, but when she was sad she cast a great cloud of gloom over everyone around her, and Petronilla was getting tired of it. Somehow she had to reach her. Somehow she had to shake her out of her black mood of despair.

'Joanna, you must stop feeling so sorry for yourself,' she said. 'Do you think life is supposed to be easy? Do you think God gives us everything we wish just because we wish it?'

'God has deserted me,' said Joanna bleakly.

'Sweet Jesus, do not say such a thing, it's blasphemous,' exclaimed the shocked Petronilla. 'God never deserts us, you know that. He may send us trials to test us. He may ask us to do things we dislike. He may even make us suffer, but if He does, it is not because He has deserted us, it is for our own good, for our spiritual development. Through suffering we reach a closer understanding of God and a better love for each other.'

'I don't want to be perfect, I want to be happy.'

'How do you know what will make you happy? Does having our own way in everything make us happy? Do we give little Katherine everything she wants just because she wants it? If she had all the sweetmeats she wanted, they would make her sick, would they not? Do you think God does not know what is best for us?'

'I thought God wanted me to have Tristram.'

'Joanna, it's time you came to terms with life and stopped all this silly daydreaming,' said Petronilla in exasperation. 'You are a mercer's daughter and he is a knight. There was never any possibility of your marrying Sir Tristram. It was all madness and I blame that silly, vain woman Margaret Philpot for encouraging you.'

'Mariota's going to marry him and she's only a mercer's daughter,' said Joanna stubbornly.

'Your sister Mariota is promised to William Gryffard and she will marry him as your father has arranged. She is a good, obedient girl who accepts that her father knows what is best for her and she will obey him even as you must when the time comes.'

'Obey! Obey! Obey!' shouted Joanna wildly. 'Why must I obey? Where does obedience get you except misery and unhappiness for the rest of your life? If I'd obeyed Father in the first place I would not be here now,' she added, breaking into uncontrollable sobs. 'I'd be in St Helen's Priory.'

Petronilla waited calmly, even a little pleased at this glimpse of temper. It was better than the dumb despair Joanna had shown ever since the tournament. Perhaps this was what she needed. Perhaps when she had finished crying she would be prepared to listen to reason at last. When the worst of Joanna's weeping had subsided, Petronilla tried anew to comfort her.

'Do not take it so hard, Joanna. This pain will pass. Nothing lasts for ever and one day you will look back on all this and laugh at your-self for a romantic fool.'

'We're losers, all of us,' said Joanna staring at her blankly. 'William Gryffard, me, and Master Northampton too. We're all losers. God has turned his face from us and we're lost.'

Petronilla stared back in horror. It was a dangerous thought, a contagious thought, the counsel of despair. If she were to believe it, then she too would be lost. Her patience snapped.

'What am I to do with you? See, your tears have fallen all over the ledgers. That page will have to be copied out all over again. What possible use to me are you, behaving like this? You are upsetting the whole household. If you can't do better than this, I shall have to send you home.'

'And they will send me to the nunnery. You will condemn me to that? You could not be so cruel!'

Petronilla swallowed hard and turned away from Joanna's huge, expressive eyes staring up at her out of her stricken face.

'Enough of this nonsense, Joanna,' she said brusquely, more brusquely than she meant. 'If you cannot keep the ledgers for me without spoiling them with your tears, then you'd better go out to the garden and see about replenishing the stillroom. And this evening you must come with me to All Hallows the Great and ask Father Paul to give you a penance for your loss of faith.'

Without a word Joanna got up from her seat. Petronilla watched her go, feeling tired and depressed. Life was hard enough as it was, without Joanna upsetting everything all the time. The trouble was she did not really see any way out for the child.

With a heavy heart, Petronilla set about copying out the spoilt page in the ledger. Perhaps the nunnery was the best place for her after all.

Outside in the garden it was hot. Joanna sank down on her knees in the herb garden beside a clump of lady's mantle and started picking off the flowers and storing them carefully in her apron. The scene with Petronilla had shaken her. Ever since the tournament she had been in a daze, like a sleepwalker, performing the tasks Petronilla set but unaware of her surroundings, scarcely knowing she was alive. Now she was awake and conscious that at any moment she might hear the nunnery gates closing behind her, shutting her out from the world for ever. She shivered in the hot sunshine. That she could not bear!

She looked at the herb lying in her palm. The lobes of the leaves resembled a mantle, which was why the plant was dedicated to the Virgin Mary. But the Virgin had forsaken her. Joanna crushed the delicate little plant in her clenched fist, and looking up saw Tristram coming into the garden. He was dressed in a short blue surcoat with a long sword hanging from his hip. She shut her eyes quickly. Now his beautiful form had come to haunt her waking hours as well as her sleep!

'They told me I might find you here,' he said. At the sound of his voice her eyes flew open in amazement. He was not a dream, but living flesh and blood. She gazed at him in wonder. He had come here, seeking her out. Hope, the irrepressible flame which could never quite be extinguished, flared briefly as she scrambled to her feet.

'Joanna,' he said, 'I need your help. I must see Mariota, speak to her.' Hope quenched, Joanna stared down at the fresh brown soil, disappointment rendering her speechless.

'Joanna,' he pleaded, 'you can help me. I must see her. You can take a message to her. Make some excuse to go home.'

'What if she doesn't want to see you?' said Joanna to her shoes.

'You can persuade her, can't you? Tell her she cannot marry the wool merchant, cannot throw herself away on such a worthless fellow. She loves me, I know she does. I don't know what your father's reasons are, but he is forcing your sister into this marriage against her will. You must help us. You can do it. Only you can help us!'

As she listened to his voice, begging her to help him she was choked with pain. She had dreamed so often of how he would plead and beg – for a favour, for a kiss, for her hand. But he was pleading not for her but for Mariota. She could not bear to look at him. Could not bear to see his face. Was there no end to it? It will pass, Petronilla had said, but it would never pass. Not if he were married to Mariota. Suppose she were to refuse? He was making her suffer. Let him suffer too. Yet it was not his fault. He had done nothing to make her love him, shown her no favour, asked nothing of her till now. She loved him for no good reason except that she could not help herself. So what else could she do but help him to be happy?

'What do you want me to do?' she asked.

'Tell her I shall be in the chantry of St Mary le Bow every evening after vespers, every evening until she comes.'

'I'll do my best,' she said, 'but Mariota is very good. If Father has set his heart on this marriage with William Gryffard, I can't see Mariota refusing to do it.'

'If I can just talk to her once more. Hear from her own lips that she doesn't love me, then I might be able to accept it,' he said.

It was strange to hear him talk about acceptance. Tristram de Maudesbury was a man of glorious deeds, accustomed to getting his own way by force. Yet he was as helpless as she was, as crossed in love as he was fortunate in war. Did it amuse God to arouse such longing in the human heart only to deny it satisfaction? she wondered, quickly looking at him and as quickly away. Oh, she understood why he wanted to see Mariota once more. He thought it would help, while he was with her. Just to be with her would be a solace. But afterwards, nothing helped.

'I'll do it,' she said, 'but I may not be able to get permission to go home immediately.'

'Thank you Joanna, but please try to make it soon. The Duke is talking of retiring to Kenilworth. He and Percy have been left out of the council which is to advise the King, in spite of Percy's having been made Earl of Northumberland. The real power now lies with his enemies the Earl of March and the Bishop of London, and with the Queen Mother. The Duke intends to let them stew in their own juice.'

It was not difficult to get permission from Petronilla to go home. In fact she seemed almost relieved. 'You can leave after prime,' Petronilla said. 'Take as long as you like but be sure to ask your father for some of his fine silk. It's time you had a new gown to wear. You're a pretty girl, Joanna, far too pretty to waste your life sighing after the unobtainable. When you come back we'll make a fresh start, find you a good honest man to chase those silly dreams away.' Joanna had shuddered. Nobody could replace Tristram in her dreams. But she was glad to escape. Glad to have something to do. It was better to be able to help him be happy, even if she could never be happy herself.

When she arrived in the Mercery, she found the family breaking their fast in the hall. Mariota ran to her with a little cry of pleasure, throwing an affectionate arm about her waist and leading her to the table. Owen and Dickon grinned, Joan clucked contentedly like a mother hen as she cut a large slice of fine crusty white bread and filled Joanna's cup with ale. Even Matilda seemed pleased for once.

'You can help Mariota in the bakery this morning, Joanna,' she said. 'We're so behind after all the coronation celebrations, I'm at my wits end to know how to manage the household.'

Her father said nothing, sitting at the head of the table morosely toying with his bread, ignoring her presence. Joanna felt uneasy. Was something wrong? Had the Northamptons complained to him already?

'Are you not going to give me your blessing, Father?' she said, walking round the table to stand at his side. He looked up startled and seemed to see her for the first time.

'Why Joanna, you here? Not sent home in disgrace, I hope?' It was not exactly the welcome she had expected from him, but she tried to laugh it off. He asked her briefly how she was and enquired after the Northamptons, but he did not seem to be listening to her answers. Shortly afterwards he drained his ale and left the table without another word to any of them. Joanna's feeling of unease increased.

After breakfast, Matilda accompanied the two girls to the buttery and Joanna was afraid that she would have no chance to talk to Mariota alone. But after inspecting the dough which Mariota had made at break of day and satisfying herself that it had risen enough to be ready for knocking back, Matilda left them with a parting warning not to waste time in idle talk for there was much spinning and weaving to be done and the rushes to be changed on the chamber floor – all before noon.

Left alone in the buttery with her sister, Joanna waited for a rush of confidence. But Mariota said nothing. She picked up a lump of dough and gave it a good punch with her fist, then began to slap it about in the bowl. Joanna stood and watched her, wondering how to begin.

'Well, don't just stand there, Joanna. You heard what Mother said, there's work to be done.' She was right, thought Joanna, there was no time to waste.

'Mariota, is it true,' she asked, 'that you're to marry William Gryffard?'

A sigh 'It's what Father wants.'

'And do you want it, Mariota?'

Another sigh. 'I must do as Father wishes, of course.' Mariota sprinkled her piece of dough with flour, pushing it out and folding it over on itself, kneading busily.

'Sir Tristram is your secret lover, is he not? What of him?'

'Oh, Joanna, was he not wonderful at the tournament? The way he unhorsed the Sieur de Chevigny. I felt so proud and so happy, even though he should never have done it. Father was furious.'

'Then he has not changed his mind?'

'No, he's more determined than ever.'

'And what about you, Mariota?' Joanna made herself ask the question. 'Do you still love Tristram?' In spite of herself, her voice broke on his name and she was sure that Mariota would suspect something, but her sister's fair head was bent over her work, her hands busy slapping the dough on the board, turning and folding, turning and folding.

'It doesn't matter who I love, I must do as Father says,' she murmured.

'But Mariota, if you love him, surely something can be done? After all, what can Father have against Sir Tristram? He's a wonderful match for you.'

But Mariota was not to be drawn. She laid the dough aside, now round and neat and ready for baking, and began on another piece. 'Aren't you going to help me, Joanna?' she said. 'It'll be much quicker with two of us doing it.' Joanna seized a piece of risen dough.

'Master Gryffard, how did he take Sir Tristram's triumph?' she asked, as she smacked her fist into the puffed and spongy mass.

'Oh, poor William was dreadfully cross. He thought he'd been made a fool of, but he still comes here every day, and nearly always brings me presents. Only yesterday he brought me a beautiful cloak of green samite lined with marten's fur.'

'You don't want to marry Gryffard, do you?' asked Joanna, wondering whether in fact Mariota had any heart to break.

Mariota said nothing, just kept turning the dough over and over on the board, folding and kneading with practised movements, but two tears slid slowly down her cheeks and splashed onto the bread in her hands. Instantly, Joanna regretted her unworthy thought.

'Can't Mother Matilda do something? She hasn't turned against Sir Tristram too has she? Can't she persuade Father to change his mind? She nearly always gets her own way in the end.'

'Oh, she's tried, they have rows every day about it. I cannot stand it, Joanna, everything is so terrible now. I've begged Mother to stop. It makes me so unhappy when they fight and it's all because of me. All my fault.' The tears were coursing down Mariota's cheeks now.

'Mariota, you must fight for what you want. Your whole happiness is at stake. A little unpleasantness now is better than a lifetime married to the wrong man.' Silence. 'Sir Tristram loves you, Mariota. Sacrifice yourself if you must, but what about him? Do you want to break his heart as well?' Oh, how it hurt her to say it! But once begun, she felt determined to see the task through to the end. It was the only thing she could ever do for Tristram and she would have died for him.

Mariota said nothing. She went on kneading bread while more tears slid slowly down her cheeks.

'I've brought you a message from him.'

Mariota put her hands up over her ears. 'I don't want to hear it. Father forbids me to speak to him. I don't want to know. I mustn't listen. Stop torturing me, Joanna. I must marry Gryffard and there's an end to it.' Joanna stared at her in exasperation. Mariota did not deserve Sir Tristram. She would not even try to help herself. Joanna was almost sure now that she would not agree to meet him in church, but the message must be delivered all the same. But before she could decide what to do, her father suddenly appeared in the buttery. Joanna gave a guilty start.

'Joanna, will you come to the counting house? I must speak to you,' he said and she trembled, wondering how much he had heard.

He led the way down to the warehouse and she followed full of foreboding. She had achieved nothing with Mariota, she had even failed to deliver Tristram's message, and now she was in trouble with her father as well.

When they reached the counting house he sat down on the corner of the desk and looked at her gravely. Joanna clasped her hands in front of her and bowed her head, prepared for the storm. But instead

169

of accusing, her father seemed to be asking her to do something for him. Joanna was so surprised at first she was unable to take in properly what he was saying. Something about a fleet of war galleys attacking the Isle of Wight and landing on the Sussex coast. It was so unexpected that she did not know what to make of it all. She stood and stared at her father. He looked very worried and for the first time it struck her that her handsome, confident father looked old.

'It is rumoured that Rye, Portsmouth and Plymouth have been sacked,' he was saying. 'I do not know what damage has been done.' It was then that the full import of his words began to sink in. The French had invaded, important seaports has been sacked. Her thoughts flew to Tristram. He would be leaving. He would be going into battle. 'You are friendly with the Philpots, are you not, my child?' he went on.

'Yes,' she stammered, still thinking of the knight. If there were a battle, he might be wounded! He might be killed!

'Joanna, are you listening? I said I want you to try and find out if anything has happened to Black Nick. If anybody knows, it would be John Philpot.'

'Black Nick?' She gazed at him blankly, trying to concentrate on what he was saying.

'The sea captain Black Nick has a consignment of wool, a large consignment, which he was to take to Calais for me. He left London a few days ago and may have been caught by the Spanish and French squadron anywhere along the coast. I must know what has happened to my wool.' So it wasn't imminent danger of invasion. It was only Black Nick and some wool on its way to France. Cargoes were often lost, she knew that, and if that black-hearted rascal had gone down with it, so much the better.

'Joanna, you must go at once to Philpot's Inn, see what you can discover. Be discreet. Do not mention my name.'

'But Father, I haven't seen Mistress Philpot since the tournament. She may not wish to see me. I have never been there uninvited.'

'Make up some excuse – you're a resourceful girl. Too resourceful at times. It is something I have failed to cure you of; now perhaps I may be grateful to God for that. I must know if my cargo is safe.'

'But what about William Gryffard, does he not come here every day to visit Mariota? Surely he can tell you what's happening? He seems to know everything.'

'Not Gryffard,' said her father with a shudder, 'he must know nothing of this. Now go quickly and come back as soon as you can.'

Joanna left the house with her mind in a whirl. As she hurried through the hot, dusty streets towards East Chepe she tried to make some sense of it all. But try as she might, the pieces did not fit. Mariota believed she was doomed to marry Gryffard, yet her father could not trust the merchant of the staple enough to ask him for news of the invasion. It was all very mysterious. Suddenly she stood stock still in the middle of Chepeside. Suppose her father was afraid that, if Gryffard knew he had lost his wool, he might withdraw from the marriage? Suppose he wanted to find out so urgently in case it was necessary to hurry up the betrothal?

Slowly she walked down Chepe, thinking deeply. If William Gryffard withdrew, Sir Tristram would be once more welcomed in the Mercery. Did Tristram love Mariota enough to take her without a dowry? Of course he did. He was a knight, wasn't he, and knights did not worry about such mundane things as dowries. A host of conflicting emotions swirled through her but chief among them was the realisation that if the wool had been lost then there was still hope for Mariota and Tristram. Suddenly the errand, which she has been so reluctant to perform, became of vital importance and she hurried on towards Philpot's Lane, consumed with anxiety to find out what had happened to Black Nick and his valuable cargo. But when at length she stood outside Philpot's Inn she hesitated, wracking her brains for a convincing excuse for her visit. None came.

The beggars gathering outside the gate for the noonday crumbs were staring at her. Some of them began holding out their hands, calling to her, beseeching her in the name of God to take pity on their plight. She could not stand there all day. Throwing caution to the wind she raised her fist and hammered on the door, praying to the Virgin for inspiration. The door swung open and a servant she did not know peered at her suspiciously across the threshold.

'Is Mistress Philpot at home?' Joanna asked with her brightest smile.

'Mistress Philpot is lying down. She's not well.'

'Oh!' This was something Joanna had not thought of. She twisted her hands together in her gown and the servant began to close the door again in her face.

'Well, Master Philpot then?' said Joanna, slipping her foot neatly into the closing crack of the door.

'He's in council, I'll see if he'll be disturbed. Who shall I say wants to see him?'

'Joanna Burgeys,' she said faintly. This was worse than anything. Whatever had made her ask for Philpot himself? What was she to say to him if he did see her? She could not ask him what had happened to her father's wool.

The servant came back and opened the door wide. 'The master will see you,' he said. Fearfully she followed him into the house. He led her through the hall and into a small parlour leading off the far end of it.

The chamber was full of men. They turned to stare at her in sur-

171

prise as she entered but Joanna was too confused and too deeply embarrassed to be capable of recognising any save one. Black Nick was standing by the window, dressed in the shabby sea-stained garments he had worn the first time she'd met him, his hair and beard as wild as a baited bear's. He seemed as disenchanted to see her as she him, and turned his back with a scowl. Disconcerted, she gazed about her helplessly and met William Gryffard's watchful eyes. Sweet Mary, let me get away from here, she prayed, wishing fervently that she could just turn tail and leave them all, but she couldn't. Philpot was approaching her.

'Well, Joanna, you wished to see me,' he said kindly.

'I heard that your wife was not well,' stammered Joanna, 'and I wondered whether she would like me to sing to her. She's so fond of music and it sometimes helps when you're not well.' There was a long pause; Joanna was sure they could hear her heart beating. She fixed her eyes on Black Nick's uncompromising back and noticed a long jagged slash across the padded leather of his gambeson.

'Why yes, I think she might like that,' said Philpot at last. 'What a very kind thought, my dear. Ivan,' he bawled, so loud that she nearly jumped out of her skin. The door opened to reveal the little black slave. 'A visitor for your mistress,' Philpot told him. 'Take her to the bedchamber.'

Thankfully Joanna followed the boy out of the room. She felt like Daniel escaping from the lion's den.

On the way up to Margaret's chamber, Joanna wondered what ailed her and hoped it was nothing catching. With a sudden gut-wracking fear she thought of the plague. There had been no outbreaks so far this year, but the Philpots were in contact with all manner of seamen and who knew what might have been brought in on the ships from the East. In this heat, plague would spread quickly. Still, she was committed now and could not draw back. Sweet Cecilia, she prayed crossing herself, let it not be plague.

Margaret Philpot was lying fully dressed on the sumptuous bed, her eyes closed and a servant sitting on the bed board, applying a cold compress to her head.

'Who is it?' she asked weakly, not opening her eyes.

'It's me, Joanna.' She approached the bed. 'I heard you were sick and I thought you might like me to sing to you.'

Margaret opened her eyes and groaned. 'You can try, but I don't know if it will do any good. They've purged me and bled me, and even had that idiot chantry priest here, but so far nobody's tried singing.' She had closed her eyes again but her hands were clenched tightly on the covers.

Joanna stared at her, dismayed that Margaret, always so bright and lively, really was ill. The servant holding the damp linen to her mistress's head watched Joanna jealously. The little black slave was curled up like a dog at the foot of the bed. What to sing? She began with the Ave Maria but Margaret waved at her with her eyes shut. 'No more prayers, I beg,' she muttered. So Joanna chose a lullaby. It was one she often sang to little Katherine to send her off to sleep. Softly she began to sing, her eyes on Margaret's tense, white face. Gradually her fingers uncurled from their hold on the bedcovers. Joanna finished the lullaby and began another. The tension left the sick woman and Joanna could see that she slept.

The servant got up from her place by the bed. 'Sleep will do her more good than anything now.' She snapped her fingers at the slave and held open the door. Joanna knew there was no point in trying to outstay her welcome. She would get no information out of Margaret at present and so she followed the slave out into the gallery.

The door of the chamber was firmly shut behind her and she stood looking down into the hall below, wondering what she should do next. Two servants were busy setting up the trestle tables for dinner. In the parlour below Margaret's chamber they would all be discussing the present crisis. That was where she would get her information. But she did not dare intrude on them again. Besides, William Gryffard was there, and Black Nick. If he was safe and sound, her father's wool might be all right, but she had to make sure. Black Nick had seemed angry and there was that long slash across his shoulders. He looked as if he had been in a fight. He was the person to question, but how was she to get him away from the others?

The little black slave stood at her side rolling his eyes enquiringly. She could not stand there all morning. The two servants working in the hall below – they might know something! Certainly the servants at the Hood knew all the Northamptons' secrets.

She was halfway down the stairs when suddenly the parlour door opened and the sea captain strode out, alone. Holy Mother be praised, it was her chance. She flew down the rest of the stairs and almost collided with him at the bottom.

'If you were coming up to see how Margaret does, I've left her sleeping,' she said rather breathlessly.

'I wasn't,' he said with a bitter smile, 'but I'm glad to know that your visit has been of some use. Did she enjoy your singing?'

'She seemed soothed, at least,' replied Joanna. He stared down at her with his black brows drawn together so that they almost met above his piercing blue eyes.

'Now tell me, what was the real reason for your visit?' he asked. She backed away from him, leaning against the wall for support, and clenched her hands together in front of her.

'I wanted to know what had happened to my father's cargo.'

'By God, the vultures don't take long to gather. What is wrong with

173

your father? Is he too afraid to come asking after his precious wool himself, but not too ashamed to send his daughter to do his dirty work for him?'

'I don't know why you should always think the worst of everyone,' she retorted quickly. 'Just because you never have an honest thought in your head does not mean that others cannot.'

Nick's face was dark and expressionless, but his eyes were bleak. 'I lost your father's cargo,' he said. 'Along with my ship and most of my crew. The French and Spanish sailed up the Thames and attacked us at anchor in Gravesend Harbour.'

She stared down at the floor. So it had gone. Her father's wool, Mariota's dowry. Tristram had a chance again. She did not know until now how very much it mattered to her. Would hope never die?

'Are you afraid you've lost your dowry,' he taunted, ruthlessly, picking over the pieces of her broken heart like a hungry bird of prey. 'Did you think your father could buy you that knight you want so much?'

'What do you know about it?' she blazed at him. 'What do you know of what it is like to be a woman, to be bought and sold like any slave or bond serf, to depend on the success or failure of a business deal for a husband? Or to be sent to a nunnery to pray for souls, black, bad souls, for the rest of one's life because a father thinks it good to have a nun in the family.'

'Well, at least he won't be able to send you to a nunnery now. No convent will have you without the price of a dowry. Your father may be ruined and I've only lost my ship and crew, but you'll be all right.'

She stared up into the dark face above her and did not know when she had hated anyone more.

'I don't know what you've got to be so sorry for,' she cried. 'You're young and strong and a man and free to go out and start again. John Philpot's your friend and will give you a new ship to fight the French with. Isn't that what he promised?'

'I know you wish I'd gone to the bottom of the sea with the rest of them,' he said more gently. 'But I daresay God has a worse fate in store for me. I don't die easily, I'm afraid.'

'You enjoy it!' she accused him. 'You enjoy gambling with death.'

'Your father's a gambler too,' he said suddenly. 'Other merchants spread their risk, divide their cargoes over several ships. But he was in a hurry, he wanted to get ahead of the others. He was greedy and he risked everything in one throw.'

'I thought you were supposed to be the best, I thought you bore a charmed life.' Somehow she could not resist needling him. He was so harsh, so utterly unrepentant for what he had done.

'I'm not one of your heroes, Joanna,' he answered bitterly, 'and you can't forgive me for that, can you? One day you'll find out that there's no such thing as a hero, only a man trying to prove something to himself. Well, I trust I know myself better than that. I don't enjoy it when the dice are stacked against me. I don't enjoy having my ship and my livelihood and all I possess taken from me when I'm lying in harbour unable to fight properly, and all because of the incompetence of a government run by a lot of praying priests who know nothing of what should be done to protect this country.'

She did not know what more to say. She had the information her father needed and now all she wanted to do was escape from him and from this house. She remained rigidly silent.

'Go and tell your father that his wool is gone,' he went on, 'and take your dreams of love and knights in their shinning armour and try and live on them.' He turned his back on her and walked up the stairs without a backward glance. Blinded by tears of rage and mortification, she half ran, half stumbled across the hall, past the startled servants, and out into the lane beyond.

CHAPTER 17

Richard Burgeys took the news of his loss badly.

'All gone? All of it?' he asked in a voice that shook.

'Black Nick said he'd lost his ship and most of his crew, so it must have all gone,' said Joanna, feeling guilty, as if somehow it was her fault.

'Sweet Jesus, all gone and none of it paid for yet,' he whispered. Joanna stared at him, not understanding but frightened by the change in him. His face had a sick, grey tinge to it and was crumpled like an old man's. He was panting, as if he'd been moving sacks around the warehouse all morning, and the knuckles of his hands as they gripped the edge of his desk were quite white.

Black Nick has said that her father was ruined, but she had not taken it in, had not believed him. How could Father be ruined? she thought, gazing round the warehouse at the bolts of bright-coloured silks and taffetas, the bales of fine linen, the damasks and velvets, all brought in, she supposed, by Black Nick on his last voyage. But looking at her father now, slumped in front of his ledgers, she felt a cold chill run over her. What was to become of them all if he were ruined?

'You saw Black Nick himself?' he asked. 'He was there, at Philpots Inn?'

'Yes, Father, he was there.'

'Then the whole city will know by tomorrow.' He buried his head in his hands.

'Why should they? Why should they care?' she said, trying to reach him, trying to bring him comfort. 'Black Nick may not tell them. He only told me because I asked him, when we were alone.' But she did not believe it. Black Nick did not have one grain of chivalry in him, but Father might be comforted for a while.

'Who else was there, at Philpot's Inn?' he asked, his head still buried in his hands. When she told him he looked up and stared at her wildly.

'Gryffard there?' he cried. 'Merciful Christ, then he'll know!'

Joanna did not know what to do. The earth had suddenly tilted on its axis and she felt lost, as if she had strayed into a new and terrifying land. Her father whom she loved and feared and whose word was law in all things had suddenly become a stranger, was staring at her helplessly, unable to find his way in this hostile world they had stumbled into together. It was frightening and Joanna felt a rush of longing for those times when she had stood before him trembling on her own account, when she had endured his wrath and been beaten for her transgressions. He had been mighty then, the fount of all her certainties, appointed by God to be honoured and obeyed. That had been so much better.

He was still staring at her and she thought of something which might offer him a glimmer of hope. 'Father, will it mean Master Gryffard will not want to marry Mariota now, do you think?'

'I don't know what it means,' he snapped.

'Mariota's so beautiful, does it matter if you lose Gryffard? Sir Tristram de Maudesbury would have her. He wanted her so much he fought for her at the tournament.'

He did not say anything, just stared down blankly at the rows of neat figures in his ledgers.

'Father,' she pleaded, creeping closer and laying a hand on his sleeve, 'Sir Tristram would take Mariota with nothing, I'm sure he would. They say that the fight at the tournament was just a pretty game, to entertain the spectators, that it meant nothing. But I know he loves her. Father, wouldn't a knight be even better than a merchant of the staple?'

'Don't mention that young man's name to me!' he exclaimed, thrusting her hand away.

'But why, Father?' she persisted, standing her ground. 'What have you got against him? Why will he not do instead of Gryffard? Mariota loves him, I'm sure she does.'

'You don't understand, Joanna,' he said with a sigh. 'Gryffard lent me the money to buy the wool. If Gryffard backs off now I'm done for. Our only hope is Mariota. She's all I've got left and I just pray that Gryffard wants her enough to take her in her shift. He should do, he's hot enough for her. If he stands by me, gives me time, I can still trade myself out of this somehow. He may even lend me the money to pay the woolmen when the time comes, and if he wants her enough, he will. But it won't be easy.'

Joanna was stunned. There was no hope for Tristram, she could see that now; Mariota was to be sacrificed to save them all. Poor Mariota! Should she tell her the truth? It might help. There seemed nothing else she could do, no sacrifice she could make to ease her father's plight. She would go into the nunnery willingly now, if it would save

177

her family. But it wouldn't. It was Mariota's beauty and goodness which was to rescue them from disgrace and ruin. All Joanna could do was to reconcile Mariota to her fate.

But when Joanna broke the news to her sister, she did not seem in the least distressed.

'I must look my very best for him,' she said, jumping up from the loom where she had been weaving and peering at herself in the polished steel hanging on the chamber wall. 'He may call at any moment. Joanna, you must help me.'

'What if he doesn't come?' Joanna could not resist saying it. 'He may not want you now.' Mariota stood stock still in the centre of the chamber, staring at the sister in dismay.

'Joanna, you don't really think that, do you?'

'Of course I don't,' said Joanna, instantly contrite. 'I'm sure William Gryffard loves you every bit as much as Sir Tristram, in his way.'

'What do you think I should wear, my pink silk or the blue damask?' Mariota was busy rummaging in the chest at the foot of the bed. Joanna said nothing. She was thinking of Sir Tristram waiting night after night in Bow Church. Even now, when his case was hopeless, she had to give Mariota his message. She could at least do that for him.

'Mariota, Sir Tristram wants to see you. He asked me to tell you that he will wait every evening after vespers in St Mary le Bow until you come.'

'Of course I must wear the silver girdle he gave me,' said Mariota. 'I think the pink sets it off the best, don't you?' She had taken off her apron and her wimple and was swiftly discarding surcoat and kirtle. She held the pink silk gown she had worn at the tournament up against her shift. 'What do you think, Joanna?'

'Mariota, what of Sir Tristram? Is he to wait in the church until doomsday?'

'I cannot go to meet him, not now. You must see that.' She was struggling into the pink gown, smoothing it down over her slender hips.

'Not even to say goodbye,' said Joanna, 'after all he's meant to you?'

'I dare not, Father would be furious,' replied Mariota, busy with a row of little buttons down the front of her gown.

'But Mariota, don't you think you owe it to Tristram to see him just once more, after he fought for you at the tournament and everything? He said if he heard it from your own lips that you did not love him, he would accept it.'

'No, Joanna, I cannot. It would be wrong. Father has forbidden me to speak to him again and I shan't,' said Mariota. She picked up a brush from the table and held it out to Joanna. 'Will you brush it for me? Nobody does my hair like you used to do. You cannot believe how much I have missed you every evening at bedtime.'

'Could you not write a letter to him?' persisted Joanna, gently teasing out the long silken tresses.

'What would be the use, when Tristram cannot read? You go, Joanna, explain for me. I must wait here in case William Gryffard calls. Think how terrible it would be if he came and perhaps found out where I had gone, and why?'

'Don't you love Tristram any more?' said Joanna, brushing vigorously.

'How can I, when it is William Gryffard I must marry? Now, what sort of headdress would he like? I know.' She whirled round and ran to look in the chest again. 'I've a new net caul he hasn't seen yet. I'm sure he'll like it.' She piled her silken hair into the caul and fixed it in place with a jewelled filet round her brow.

'Did he give you the filet as well?' asked Joanna incredulously.

'He nearly always brings me something,' said Mariota, peering at herself in the polished steel. 'Do you think I ought to wear the new cloak he gave me? It's not as hot as it was earlier on.'

Silently Joanna picked up the green samite cloak and draped it round her sister's shoulders. Impossible to believe that Mariota could forget Tristram already. But it certainly seemed like it. She appeared far more concerned now at the thought of losing Gryffard than with any regrets for her lost knight. Was conquest, then, all that Mariota cared about? She was studying her reflection with the utmost concentration.

'You look wonderful, Mariota,' said Joanna, an empty feeling somewhere around her heart. 'Gryffard cannot help but want you.'

'Enough to take me in my shift?' asked Mariota with a laugh.

'I don't see why not. If he's as rich as all that, he's not going to worry about your dowry, is he?'

'I think perhaps he will, and I shall do my best to please him. Don't look so worried, Joanna, I'm sure he will be able to advise father how best to recover from his losses.'

'I don't set too much store on Gryffard's advice,' said Joanna scathingly. 'If it hadn't been for him, Father wouldn't have bought more wool than he could afford and be faced with the problem now of finding the money to pay for it.'

'William wasn't to know that Father would send all the wool to Calais in the same ship.' Mariota walked over to the window and positioned herself so she had a good view of the street below. 'Poor Father, I wonder why he took such a terrible risk?'

Greed! That's what Black Nick had said, thought Joanna with a shiver.

'Poor Joanna,' said Mariota from the window, 'you're cold. The

179

heat has quite gone out of the day. I think perhaps it's going to rain. You'd better take my blue cloak, I don't need it now that William has given me this beautiful new one.'

Through the open window Joanna could hear the bells ringing for vespers. It was time for her to go. She kissed Mariota goodbye and for a moment her sister clung to her. Joanna wondered whether, in spite of all outward appearances, Mariota really loved Tristram as much as ever. If so, she was a saint, thought Joanna as she kissed her tenderly. Such courage in the face of adversity was magnificent. Was Mariota as brave as that? Joanna thought ruefully of her own behaviour since the tournament and felt ashamed. With a sigh she picked up Mariota's cloak and wrapped it round her. She could never be as beautiful as Mariota, and it didn't look as if she'd ever be as good either.

Outside, the first few drops of a summer shower were beginning to fall, and Joanna pulled her hood up over her head as she set out for the church, glad of Mariota's cloak. Her mind was so full of all that had happened she barely knew what she was doing, but when she saw the distinctive stone arches atop the steeple of Bow Church the full realisation hit her. Tristram was waiting there and she was bringing him nothing but sorrow and disappointment. Slowly she walked along Chepeside, wondering how she was going to break the news to Tristram and how much it would be right to tell him. She was conscious of an overwhelming sense of failure. Nothing she did seemed to help anybody it seemed.

She entered Bow Church fearfully. The fading day, already darkened by rain clouds, was unable to penetrate the heavy stained glass in the windows. Pinpricks of light from the many candles pierced the shadows, here and there falling upon a face in one of the wall paintings, or throwing a pool of light on the stone-flagged floor, but she could not make out Sir Tristram among the worshippers taking part in the service. Not wanting to be recognised by any friends of her family, Joanna hovered in the shadows while Father James intoned the office for the night. When people began to leave, she slipped into one of the side chapels and knelt, head bent as if in prayer, waiting until the chattering voices drifted away. At last, silence.

Cautiously Joanna raised her head. Father James was extinguishing the candles on the altar. Quickly she bowed her head again, praying that he would not notice her. What could she say to him? What possible excuse could she give for wanting to remain? He would probably insist on walking home with her in the hope that he might be offered supper. Peeping though her spread fingers she saw him give a perfunctory glance round the church and then disappear quickly through the chantry towards the door of the vestry. Perhaps he already had a destination for his supper. Better to wait a little longer just to make sure.

She said two more paternosters, her heart beating uncomfortably fast, then cautiously she got to her feet and crept down the nave to the chantry. It was empty. A great feeling of desolation swept over her. He wasn't there. But then reason returned. The chantry was not a good place to hide. Perhaps he was somewhere else. Down each side of the thirty-foot nave, arched bays opened into a series of small side chapels. Carefully, stopping all the time to look and listen, Joanna searched each one until she came to a chapel on the south side of the nave, more elaborate than the rest. In the centre of the chapel stood an elevated tomb and standing by it a hooded figure in a long black cloak. Joanna gave a gasp and shrank back against the wall of the chapel. The man threw back his hood and from the light of the single candle burning on the little altar Joanna could see that it was Tristram.

'Mariota,' he cried, throwing himself on his knees before her, 'you have come. I'd almost given up hope.'

'No, no,' she whispered as he seized her hands and covered them with kisses. 'You don't understand.'

'But I do! I know it's been difficult for you to get away, but I knew you would come whatever the risk.' As he knelt before her Joanna succumbed. It was so easy, just for one moment to pretend to be her sister, for just one minute more feel his lips on her hands. He might even kiss her goodbye. One kiss, that's all she asked.

'Why did you not come before?' he asked. 'I've almost worn out my knees in prayer waiting for you.'

'I couldn't,' she said haltingly, drawing further back into the shadows. 'You don't know how difficult it is for me to get away.'

'Mariota,' he said taking hold of her hands and holding them against his heart. 'You know I love you, that I want to marry you. I can give you a better life than he can.' He began to talk about his manor and the serfs who would wait on her, of the forest where they would go hunting together, of the merlin he would buy for her and how he would teach her to fly it, of all the wonderful things they would do together.

Dear God, he was making it all so much more difficult! She snatched her hands away in anguish. 'Stop! Stop!' she whispered, head bent. 'I cannot bear it. Don't make it harder for me.'

'Then marry me, Mariota! What has your father got against me? What has happened since I went away?'

Would it help him to know the truth? She thought, panic-stricken. But she could not betray her father. 'It's nothing to do with you, I promise,' she said, in as strong a voice as she could muster. 'Father has nothing against you. It's just that he needs William Gryffard to help him.'

181

'You don't want to marry me, is that it?' He bent forward trying to see her face, but she backed away.

'It's not that,' she managed to stutter, 'I love you more than life itself, but I cannot, cannot marry you.'

'Mariota, let me come home with you now and speak to him. Make him see how much he has to gain by agreeing to our marriage. I can do so much more for you and your whole family than this miserly wool merchant.'

She tried to marshal her thoughts. Now to tell him. But would it help him to know that Mariota had not come? Would it not help him more to have one last kiss to remember, thinking it was Mariota?

'I came to say farewell,' she whispered, 'that's all. It's no use. Once I thought that God had destined us for each other, but I was wrong. Goodbye, my love, I'll always be true to you in my heart.' She reached up swiftly and pressed her lips against his cheek and turned resolutely to go. But to her astonishment he pulled her back, sweeping her to him and smothering her face with kisses. She tried to push him away, but the more she struggled, the more inflamed he became. His lips were on her throat, his hands fumbling at the neck of her gown. It was too much ecstasy to bear.

With a small moan she fell against his chest, all thoughts of where she was, who she was, what she was doing driven from her mind by the sensation of his lips on hers. Suddenly before she knew it, she was lifted off her feet by strong arms, carried quickly through the church and out into the small arched court beyond. Dazed, bemused and weak with desire, she let him throw her up onto his horse and make off. Swiftly they rode down Chepeside, scattering people in their wake, Joanna too terrified of falling off to do anything but cling desperately to him. With her arms about his waist and her face pressed against his chest, she closed her eyes and tried not to think.

Soon there was the ring of shoes on cobbled stones and the cry of a gatekeeper wishing Godspeed, and she guessed they must be passing out of the city. She opened her eyes and recognised the Lud Gate; she realised that he was taking her to the Savoy. She ought to stop him, make him turn back before it was too late, before the city gates closed for the night. But he quickened pace as soon as they were in open country, and the horse was galloping so fast she had neither breath nor wits to do anything but cling on and pray he would not kill her when he discovered how she had deceived him.

All too soon they were clattering under the gatehouse of the Duke of Lancaster's Savoy Palace. In the lower court Tristram dismounted. Joanna waited, head bent, trying to summon up the courage to throw back her hood and reveal all. Then she was whisked off the horse as if she'd been no more than a pound of meal and carried through a small crowd of curious knights, while Tristram shouted for a priest.

'What is it? Who's been hurt?'

'What have you done this time, Tristram?' All around her voices and questions, while she cowered beneath the false colours of Mariota's cloak.

'I've brought me a bride, straight out of London, that's what I've done!' she heard him shout. 'Fetch the priest. We'll be married at once.'

'You dog, Tristram, you haven't carried her off, have you?'

'Sweet Jesus, that'll show the Londoners who's master!'

The voices rang in her ears, laughing, shouting ribald comments, congratulations and lewd advice as she was carried from the lower court. She blushed with shame. What would he do to her when he found out who she was? What would this jostling mob of men say then. Would he cast her out among them? She remembered the day when she'd been caught by the fishmongers' apprentices and fear ran through her. But it was Tristram who had rescued her, she reminded herself. He would not let anything happen to her now. Besides, they were knights, not unruly apprentices. Knights did not deflower helpless maidens. They were different.

He was carrying her up some stairs, along a passageway. He crossed a grass courtyard, and she was aware of some snatches of song floating from an open window. He kicked open a door and carried her up another flight of stairs. He was panting now. More passageways, down another flight of stairs and then all of a sudden cold, quiet stillness. He put her down.

He had brought her to the chapel. There were wax tapers burning, lighting up the brilliant colours of the stained-glass window behind the altar, a red, gold and blue banner hanging above her head, and Tristram casting aside his long black cloak, so handsome and flushed with triumph she did not know how she would live through the next few minutes.

A tall friar emerged from the sanctuary; she knew him for a Franciscan by the grey of his habit and the long knotted scourge that dangled from his waist beside his crucifix.

'What is this then, Sir Tristram?' he said.

'This, Brother William, is my bride, whom I won in fair combat in the tournament and I want you to marry us here and now.'

'Marry you! What madness is this? My child, if you've been carried off against your will, you need have no fear. You are under the Duke's protection here and none will do you harm.'

'You mistake, Brother William,' put in Tristram. 'She loves me as much as I love her. Isn't that so, Mariota?'

'Then why this unseemly haste?' asked the friar severely. 'You should be married in her parish church with her family and friends about her.'

'Her father's against the match, doesn't like the Duke or Lancaster – a crazy notion he's taken into his head.'

'And so you would force her to disobey her father?' put in the friar more sternly than ever. 'My child, whatever this knight may have told you –'

'I didn't force her, she was willing!' interrupted Tristram.

'Stop! Stop!' cried Joanna. She couldn't allow this farce to go on any longer. She threw off her hood. 'It's all a mistake, a terrible mistake.'

'Of course it's a mistake,' said the friar, 'and even though you may have encouraged Sir Tristram a little, the mistake is mainly his.'

'No, no, you don't understand,' she whispered, fighting back the tears. 'I'm not Mariota. He carried off the wrong one.'

'Merciful Christ!' exclaimed Tristram, seizing a torch from the wall and holding it up so the light fell upon her face.

She stared down at the floor in an agony of shame.

'Joanna! What magic is this?' She glanced up and saw genuine fear on his face as he made the sign of the cross.

'No magic, but a case of mistaken identity, it would appear,' said the friar calmly.'Perhaps this will be a lesson to you, Sir Tristram, not to think you can always take matters into your own hand, nor solve every problem with deeds of arms. Meanwhile, we must think what is best to be done. It will do the Duke's reputation in the city no good, I fear, and I'd better inform His Grace straightaway.' So saying the friar hurried away, leaving them alone.

'Bewitched!' he said staring at her in horror. 'You bewitched me, the pair of you. What do you want from me, you she-devil? What does she want?

'No, no, I didn't mean to, please believe me. I came because Mariota couldn't.'

'But in her cloak?' he said, still too bemused to be angry.

'I only borrowed it because of the rain.'

'And speaking in her voice.'

'Well, we are sisters, sisters' voices quite often sound alike.'

'You tricked me,' he declared, anger banishing fear and astonishment alike. He shook his head like a confused, baited bear. 'Why? Was it a joke between you, a joke to make me look a fool?'

'No, no,' Joanna pleaded earnestly. 'It was no joke, believe me. I was only trying to make it easier for you. Mariota knows nothing. She sent me to tell you that she could not come herself. I came to bid you farewell from her. I only meant... I thought...' She broke off, blushing furiously. Impossible to try to explain to him what it had meant to her. 'I never thought you would try to carry her off,' she stammered lamely.

'Didn't you! Yet you didn't cry out. You didn't tell me then.'

'It was all so quick, so unexpected. And you are so strong.'

184

The memory of his arms round her sent a shiver of desire through her body and she watched him hungrily for a sign that he too was remembering how he had kissed her with such passion. But he was staring down at the floor morosely.

'What's to be done now?' he said, beginning to pace up and down the chapel. 'You can't go back tonight, the city gates are closed. You'll have to spend the night here at the palace. I suppose there'll be a hue and cry for you at home. It's the devil of a fix.'

The Northamptons! Joanna began to think about them for the first time. Petronilla would never take her back, not after this. This was the final straw. She knew that. There was nothing for her now but the nunnery – not even that, for her father could not now pay to send her there. She was nothing but a burden to everyone. The last thing her father needed in the midst of all his trouble was for his daughter to be sent home in disgrace.

These melancholy thoughts were interrupted by a deep, powerful voice outside the chapel. 'Where's that lovesick knave? He's keeping me from my supper. I hope the maiden is worth it.'

A tall, broad-shouldered man came striding into the chapel, dressed in a tight-fitting surcoat embroidered with lions in gold, and a cloak lined with scarlet taffeta so full and long that it swept the floor behind him as he descended the stairs. Following in his wake, his long, pale face even more worried than usual, came John of Northampton. Joanna gasped and Northampton stopped at the top of the steps into the chapel, staring at her in astonishment.

'So you've carried off a bride, my impetuous young fool,' said the Duke. 'Let's have a look at her.' He seized Joanna by the chin and tilted her face to the light. She gazed back at him a little defiantly. 'Not bad, not bad at all,' he said, releasing her with a chuckle. 'My congratulations, young Tristram, I didn't know you had so much imagination. She may not be a beauty yet, but she will be one day, I'd hazard my best falcon on it. I think perhaps you'd better marry her. You should have been married long times past. I doesn't look as if the King's Council has much use for my service, so you get married and go down to your manor and breed an heir. There'll never be a better time.'

'But Sire, I can't, there's been a mistake.'

'Nothing that can't be put right, I'm sure,' replied the Duke. 'Now it so happens that by God's good grace Sheriff Northampton came to see me today. Perhaps he can advise us. Now let me see if I have this aright. These two young lovebirds want to marry, but her father will not permit it because Tristram here is a retainer of mine. What do you say, Northampton? Should we let the marriage proceed, or will the citizens of London mount an attack upon my palace? You say you speak for the disaffected guilds in London. Do you undertake to persuade the girl's father of his great good fortune in having secured one of my knights for his daughter? Or is he not one of your party? Is he one of these victuallers you've been telling me about?'

'No, he's a mercer,' replied Northampton gravely, 'and the mercers are a law unto themselves.'

'Which usually means they prefer to follow where their best interests lie – isn't that it?'

'Sire, it is true that the victuallers are in power now,' replied Northampton. 'They will use their power to keep out foreign workers, to force many crafts out of the city for lack of cheap labour, to keep food prices so high that the poor will starve. When that happens Brembre will lose his support. There are numerous crafts who hate the powerful victuallers. Individually, they are small and weak, but if I can unite them to fight the bigger one, not with riot and affray but through the constitutional means at our disposal, through Common Council and the Court of Aldermen, and with the poor people of London behind us, then we will be a match for Brembre and his friends.'

'A deadly picture indeed,' drawled the Duke. 'But I've always had the greatest contempt for the constitutional process. I doubt if I can help you to win over the Common Council.'

'We need a champion,' said Northampton, urgently. 'Brembre is strong because he has the ear of the King, he lends him money. He is able to negotiate through strength. Nobody can win in the city without some influence outside it. But like us, you too need friends now. If you become our champion, help us to throw off the oppression which is threatening us, then the people of London will not fear you as they do now. They will support you and welcome you into their city.'

For a moment the Duke stood staring up at the banner above his head, at the three lions passant in gold on a red field, and the fleur-de-lis on blue. Then he swung round to face Tristram, his cloak sweeping the stones of the chapel floor in a graceful curve.

'You see, Tristram,' he said lightly, 'you have to marry her, the fate of England depends upon it.'

'But I don't want to marry Joanna,' protested Tristram. 'It's Mariota I want.'

'You must make up your mind, Tristram, you can't keep chopping and changing from one sister to the other. You should have made up your mind which one you wanted before your daring abduction.'

'But it was all a mistake, she bewitched me!' he exclaimed.

'Ah, women! Are we not all bewitched by them at one time or another,' replied the Duke laughing.

Joanna could not bear it. 'I must go home,' she whispered, 'why can you not just let me go home?'

'Quiet, Joanna,' said Northampton coming to stand beside her. 'You cannot go home now. It is too late.'

'But Mistress Petronilla, and Father and everybody! Oh, what will they think?' The recriminations, the accusations – they would never forgive her.

'Be quiet, I say, and leave it to me,' Northampton insisted with such intensity that she was frightened into silence. His eyes were shining with excitement, his pale face had a tinge of colour, his hands were clenched together so tight the knuckles shone white in the candlelight. She looked at Tristram scowling down at the floor and her heart sank. They were pawns, Tristram and she, in a game being played between the great Duke of Lancaster and John of Northampton. It was a game which did not interest her. All she cared about was Tristram. They wanted her to marry him. That she understood. But she did not want him forced to marry her. He looked up and she tried to smile, her eyes full of pleading.

'I don't want her,' Tristram said, turning away, and Joanna felt sick.

'Well, it looks as if you're going to have to have her,' said the Duke. 'You've made enough of a business over her. Fighting at the tournament, carrying her off in the middle of the night. You can't just take her back tomorrow morning and say you don't want her.'

'I cannot do it,' said Joanna, plucking at Northampton's sleeve. 'Please do not make me do it.'

'What! Not you as well,' exclaimed the Duke, clearly beginning to lose patience. 'Is this the way you reward your lover? You've no choice now. We can't have my retainers pillaging women and sending them back to their families the next morning like used goods, not if I am to become the champion of the poor of London against the Mayor Brembre and his victuallers. Isn't that the role you wish me to play, Sheriff?'

'But he doesn't want me,' she wailed. Why, oh why did the Duke keep ignoring the fact that she was not Mariota. He was either very dim-witted or else determined to ignore the truth because it was inconvenient.

'Tell her not to be so faint-hearted, Sheriff. Reassure the girl.'

Northampton laid his hand on her shoulder and his fingers pressed into her flesh fiercely. 'Joanna, I do not know how it has come about that you have been carried here but you have put yourself in a position fraught with peril, not only for yourself but for the whole city. You cannot now do anything else but marry him. If you do not, there will be a scandal. Your good name will be besmirched, it will bring shame to your father and to your family. But more than that, it will bring dishonour to the House of Lancaster. A retainer of the Duke carries an innocent girl away from her family. Do you not see what a prize you have given to the Duke's enemies, all those wicked men who snatch at any chance to stir up the city against His Grace? You are afraid that your father does not want you to marry this knight because he is a retainer of the Duke but I tell you that you must, for that very reason. Otherwise there may be more rioting. Your friends and family may be hurt, even killed. Do you want to be the cause of all that?'

'No,' she murmured, overawed.

'Good,' said the Duke, 'then we can get on with the marriage before I faint from hunger. Brother William, are you ready?' The friar had been standing patiently, taking no part in the argument; now he stepped forward and took Joanna's hand in his.

'My child,' he said gently, 'you are still troubled. Do you truly want to marry him? No one can force you to say your vows before God.'

She raised trusting eyes to his, praying that he might see into her soul and understand. 'I only want it if he does,' she whispered. 'I love him, you see.'

The Friar nodded. 'May God grant you the wisdom and strength you will need,' he said. Then, turning to the Duke, 'I shall need a few minutes to prepare for the Nuptial Mass, Sire,' he said. He did not ask Tristram anything.

'The saints be praised, that's done,' said the Duke, clearly delighted. 'Have the girl taken to my lady Swynford, tell her to make her look a little more bridal. We'll have the wedding feast immediately the deed is done.'

CHAPTER 18

The Duke of Lancaster's London home was like a small city in itself. Some four hundred people were housed and fed in it, people who were necessary to the great state maintained by the Duke and for the running of his considerable empire. There were smithies, barracks, armourers, shops, the falcon mews, kennels, cellars and dungeons, as well as the chapel, the Offices of Chancery and the Great Treasure Chamber. As a page escorted Joanna up spiral staircases, along passageways, in and out of various chambers and courtyards, she felt dazed with the immensity of it all. Occasionally she caught the sound of music, and once, looking out of a window as they walked through a chamber, a glimpse of the river not far away beyond a green sward where a group of knights strolled in the twilight.

Coming at last to a tower in the south-west corner of the palace, the page led her up one final stairway to a large round chamber at the top. It was a room full of colour, lit by many flaring tapers. Rich tapestries hung upon the walls and the floor was tiled in blue and red and gold. A woman was sitting sewing by the huge hearth, two young girls seated demurely at her side, and Joanna recognised her as the lady the Duke had escorted into his loge on the day of the tournament. She was very beautiful, dressed in a gown of green damask beneath a clinging sleeveless surcoat of cloth-of-gold. A thin jewel-studded filet encircled her high arched forehead, and her dark auburn hair shone in the light from the candles. She looked up. What sad eyes, Joanna thought, as the page delivered his message and withdrew.

'A wedding! And in the chapel at dusk, how very romantic,' said Lady Swynford, getting up and coming towards her with both hands held out in welcome. 'Trust Tristram to do something like this. How lucky you are to be marrying your heart's desire – it doesn't often happen, except in minstrels' tales.' Joanna smiled nervously as the lady looked her up and down. 'That dress is a little too severe for a wedding,' she went on. 'I think we might do better for Sir Tristram, but we must hurry. The Duke does not like to be kept waiting!'

She disappeared into an adjoining closet leaving Joanna to the silent scrutiny of the two young girls. Quite unconscious of their wide-eyed interest, Joanna stayed where she was in the middle of the chamber, trying to think, but her mind refused to function properly. So much had happened to her that day she seemed to have lost all hold upon reality.

Soon Lady Swynford returned. Trance-like, Joanna shed her own surcoat and linen kirtle and submitted patiently while she was eased into a low-cut, clinging gown of tawny silk taffeta. 'Why it fits you so well it could have been made for you,' said Lady Swynford, beginning to unravel Joanna's thick braids. Joanna glanced down at herself bemused and was shocked to see the mounds of her near-naked breasts straining against the fine silk.

'Oughtn't I to wear a veil or something?' she ventured timidly.

'No, no, brides don't wear anything on their heads,' replied Lady Swynford, laughing. 'Tonight is your wedding night. You want to inflame him, don't you? Though from what I hear he's probably inflamed enough already.' But he doesn't want me, Joanna longed to cry out, to tell this well-meaning lady with the sad eyes the truth, to share the burden of guilt and shame and uncertainty.

'What beautiful hair, it's the colour of beechwoods in autumn,' Lady Swynford was saying as she brushed out the thick mass of Joanna's unruly tresses, letting them fall in a cascade of rippling chestnut curls to her waist. For Joanna it was too much. Nobody had ever told her she had beautiful hair, and before she knew it she was pouring out the whole story, unburdening herself to this sympathetic lady just as if she was in the confessional. Katherine Swynford listened quietly as she brushed the lustrous hair.

'You say that your sister must marry this wool merchant to save your father from ruin?' she asked, when the tale was done. Joanna nodded miserably. 'Then I do not see how you can have stolen him from her, when she has already lost him.'

'But that I should seize my happiness and leave her to sacrifice herself for the family,' pleaded Joanna.

'We women must learn to live with whatever we can get in this life,' said Lady Swynford with a sigh. 'God has answered your prayers, my child, what more do you want from Him?'

'But Tristram doesn't want me. I tricked him. I didn't mean to but I did.'

'Keep still,' said Lady Swynford, rubbing cochineal paste onto Joanna's lips to redden them. 'There are many ways a woman can make a man want her and you will soon learn how to please him, I feel sure. There, I think you'll do. Courage, my dear. Remember, love conquers all. Have you not already succeeded against all possible odds? Why draw back now? There are not many girls as lucky as you, so do not throw away your good fortune. It won't come again.' She turned Joanna round to look at herself in the polished steel on the wall and Joanna was almost shocked at what she saw. With her hair hanging loose and her breasts bursting from the tight gown, she looked positively wanton.

'Smile, Joanna, it's your wedding you're going to, not an execution,' said Lady Swynford. 'That's better, you look truly beautiful when you smile. I don't think it will be long before Tristram realises that he ran away with the right sister after all. Now we must hurry, before the Duke loses patience altogether.'

A little encouraged, Joanna followed Lady Swynford and the two small girls out of the chamber. Lady Swynford was right, God had wrought a miracle and it would be a sin not to seize her opportunity and be grateful. If God could do so much, surely He could make Tristram love her in time.

Tristram was waiting at the door to the chapel. She glanced up at him shyly. He looked at her startled, and his eyes dropped to her breasts. She blushed from her head to her toes, as a warm rush of desire coursed through her body. Everything would be all right, after all. He may not have wanted her, but she could make him love her. She had enough love for two. She would give him everything she had and surely he could not help but love her in the end.

She made her vows, stumbling over the words in her anxiety, and then in loud ringing tones Tristram made his. It was done. The unbelievable had happened and he was hers. In a daze she walked beside him to the altar for the Nuptial Mass. With a full heart she poured out her thanks to God who had not deserted her, and heaped praises upon the Virgin who had not forgotten her. But as they approached the altar, Joanna tripped on the hem of the unfamiliar gown and stumbled awkwardly, entangling herself in Tristram's sword as she did so. It fell with a clatter to the ground and lay between them on the cold stone, its hilt towards her and its point directed straight at Tristram.

Joanna shivered and crossed herself fearfully, as Tristram with a muttered oath picked it up. After that she heard nothing of the Mass, the familiar Latin phrases brought no reassurance, haunted as she was by the significance of the fallen sword. What did it mean? In spite of everything that Lady Swynford had said, in spite of all reason, she knew in her heart of hearts that she had stolen this man. Stolen him from her sister, even though Mariota could never have him, did not even, perhaps, want him. She ought to make some promise to atone for – what? For her disobedience, the still small voice of her conscience whispered. A vow, something to buy God's forgiveness for having snatched at happiness instead of being prepared to wait patiently for it as she should. The Mass was nearly over. Before she could think of a suitable penance, the friar spread his hands and said, '*Benedicite*, go in peace, my children.' It was too late. The time for penitence and forgiveness was past.

The Duke of Lancaster kissed her first, then stood back and waited for Tristram to embrace his bride. When he did not, the Duke merely shrugged and quickly led the way out of the chapel. Joanna stifled her humiliation and disappointment as her husband grasped her firmly by the hand, pulled her sharply round and marched her unceremoniously down the aisle in the Duke's wake.

The great hall, blazing with colour and crowded with people, rang from rafter to rafter as the trumpets proclaimed the Duke's progress towards the high table. Joanna hesitated, hardly daring to enter so magnificent a place, but Tristram's grasp on her wrist was relentless and he pulled her along after the Duke, between long lines of men waiting on either side of many trestle tables. By the dais at the far end a squire was standing with a large dish of scented water and the Duke washed his face and hands before taking his place at the high table. Joanna watched as Lady Swynford dipped her fingers elegantly in the water, and copied her carefully. The trumpets ceased and there was a silence while the friar said grace, then with a great rustle of silk and a loud scraping of wood against stone the company sat down to supper.

Gingerly Joanna sat down on the hard bench beside Tristram and gazed around her in fascination. The room seemed full of strange beasts; heraldic griffins, leopards, seahorses, phoenix, dragons and unicorns leapt across the rippling arras on the walls and on the banners hanging above her head, or pranced on the breasts of the knights seated in serried ranks down each side of the hall. Even the women had heraldic symbols on their surcoats. Music played. The sound of fiddle, pipe and drum filled the air as pageboys ran hither and thither with flagons of rich, ruby-red wine from Bordeaux. Here was the enchanted world which she had hungered for that day of the tournament and thought so far beyond her grasp. Now, by some miracle, she had entered it, was now a part of it all.

Joanna sipped her wine and gazed about her, still not convinced that in a moment she would not wake up and find herself in the women's dorter in the Hood. John of Northampton was talking earnestly across Lady Swynford to the Duke, and for the first time that evening it occurred to Joanna to wonder exactly what he was doing here in the Duke's palace. The Duke sat at the head of the table with an empty chair beside him.

'Whose chair is that?' she asked Tristram.

'Why, the Duchess's, of course,' he replied.

'Is she not here tonight?'

He laughed. 'The Duchess is hardly ever here. She's at Hereford Castle most of the time, praying and scourging herself and fasting. Constanza is heir to the Spanish throne, she's the Duke's entry into Spain. All that's needed now is money to mount a big enough army for the Duke to lead into Spain to restore Constanza's father to his rightful inheritance. That's what the Duke really needs, Parliament's support for a Spanish campaign, not all this pother about London and its factions.'

A long line of pages were staggering into the hall bearing the dishes of the first course and Joanna watched in amazement as fish-liver turnovers, a meat stew, ox-marrow fritters, an eel stew and a large loach in broth with a green sage sauce were all laid out on the table in front of them. She was surprised to find that she was hungry but did not dare begin to eat in case she should let Tristram down in some way. She watched the others, looking for guidance.

'Will the Duke be leading an army to repel the French invaders?' she asked timidly, averting her eyes from the tantalising stew in front of her.

'What French invaders?' he asked, staring at her.

'The ones who sailed up the river and burnt the shipping in Gravesend and other seaports,' she answered, wondering if perhaps they had not heard the news at the Savoy. But Northampton would have told the Duke by now.

'Oh that,' said Tristram, stretching across her and whipping a slice out of a large piece of meat with a deft flick of his knife. 'There's no point in going after a small raiding party like that. They'd be back at sea before we left London. The people to deal with them are the knights who live locally. A couple of men who have manors on the Sussex coast left after noon today.'

'Will you – will we – be going to your manor then?' she asked. It seemed so stupid, but she did not even know where his manor really was.

'I don't know,' he said morosely.

She waited, hoping that he would tell her something about her new home, but he seemed far more interested in the food in front of him. All around her people were attacking the dishes with gusto and so she dipped her fingers into the dish in front of her and popped a piece of meat into her mouth. It had a sharp cinnamon sauce and she licked her fingers appreciatively. Beside her, Tristram ate steadily without looking up, only pausing to drink deep draughts of wine from his goblet. The vast hall reverberated with talk and laughter. She gazed at her husband, her heart so full of love she thought it must burst, yet she could not think of anything to say to him.

'What are you staring at?' he asked, looking up suddenly and catching her gaze.

'Nothing,' she stammered, blushing. 'Who is Lady Swynford?'

'The Lady Katherine is governess to the Duke's daughters, that's her official position, but in reality she's his mistress,' he replied, draining his goblet. Joanna looked down the table to where the Duke sat beside the Lady Katherine with the empty chair on his right. Even someone as grand and important as the Duke of Lancaster could not marry the woman he loved, she thought. No wonder the Lady Katherine had such sad eyes.

Tristram was shouting to a knight at the table below the dais, ignoring her as a bevy of pages came to clear away the dishes of the first course. An arm bearing a flagon of wine appeared at her elbow and turning round she saw Robin Swynbrook in attendance behind Tristram's chair. She smiled at him warmly and he blushed and looked away.

'When do you eat, Robin?' she asked him.

'After the knights and before the poor,' he replied as he filled her goblet.

'Don't you get very hungry?'

'You become used to it, my lady,' he replied. My lady! It was true, she really had married a knight. She hugged herself, feeling the joy bubbling up inside her. Robin was looking at her with such open admiration in his eyes that she felt a little less forlorn. Here at least was someone who might prove to be a friend, someone who might initiate her into the mysteries of this new enchanted world, show her how to be like all these others.

'You must help me, Robin,' she said impulsively, 'teach me what to do so that I am not an embarrassment to you all. It's all so new and strange to me, you see.'

'There's not much to it,' he replied, 'although I'll gladly serve you in any way I can.'

Easy for him, she thought, watching him take up his position again behind Sir Tristram. He had been living in such surroundings since he was a page and the ritual was second nature to him. She sighed. It was all frighteningly new and different but she would learn to fit in, for Tristram's sake. She would pluck her hair from the front of her forehead and get used to men's eyes resting on her half-naked breasts. She would even learn how to play these games of love, if it would help to make her husband notice her. She would learn everything she needed to know to be a perfect knight's lady.

The trumpets sounded again and the pages returned with even more dishes for the second course – a roast swan, a piece of mutton larded and boiled, a spiced chopped meat dish garnished with crayfish tails, capon pasties and crisp pancakes, bream pasties, eels and blancmange. Joanna had never seen so much food in her life. Her head began to ache and her stomach to revolt against the highly spiced and ornamental dishes set before her. The music which had at first entranced her now seemed incessantly loud.

It had been a long, long day and she was quite exhausted. She longed to find some quiet place where she could be alone and think about everything that had happened since she had left Northampton's Inn that morning. All around her there was shouting and laughter. Tristram was ignoring her completely. They all ignored her. Even Robin, the squire. He waited on her and on Tristram as he was trained to do, but she could not engage him in conversation. She was an outcast, but for now she was too tired and too bewildered to care.

As the interminable meal dragged on, she concentrated all her thoughts on the moment when she and Tristram would be alone together, savouring the rapture in Bow Church when he had showered kisses on her. She had aroused him then, she thought, even though he had mistaken her for Mariota, and tonight she would arouse him again, make him love her. Then she would be an outcast no longer. He would look at her as tenderly as the Duke was looking at Lady Swynford and everything would be perfect.

But when at last she lay between silken sheets waiting for her husband, she began to be assailed by doubt once more. The Duke had leant them the Duchess's own solar for their bridal night. The room was large, almost as large as the hall at home, but it was very gloomy. The walls were painted with horrifying pictures of Christ's suffering on the Cross, and a plain gold crucifix dominated the centre of the room above the fireplace. By the prie-dieu in the corner, instead of a picture of the Virgin there was a miniature chapel with aisles, statuettes, transepts and altar. For all its spacious luxury, it was more fit for a nun than a bride and Joanna felt depressed.

Cautiously she stretched out in the big bed, and the silken sheets caressed her naked flesh. Would he never come! She wished she knew more about what would happen, wished she had questioned her sister Alice more about her wedding night. There were many ways, Lady Swynford had said, in which to make a man love you, but what were they? Joanna wished she knew but one. The ladies who had brought her to bed, giggling as they undressed her, had told her nothing. They had been in too much of a hurry to get back to the revels. Here in this vast palace with more than four hundred souls, Joanna felt more truly alone and abandoned than ever before in the whole of her life.

The bed was so big. It was the first time she had ever been in a bed by herself and she felt lost in it. She propped herself up on one elbow and looked out of the open window. The light from an almost full moon was flooding the river, turning it ghostly pale against the silvery grass of the lawn running down to its banks. A group of knights were walking in the moonlight and she could hear their laughter echoing in the summer night. Was Sir Tristram there? Would he never come!

She shivered and threw herself down in the bed again. How did one seduce one's husband on the wedding night? What would Mariota do? Mariota would know what to do, Mariota always knew how to behave. But at the thought of Mariota, Joanna began to shake. Suppose William Gryffard no longer wanted Mariota. She had not thought of that, not until now. They would never forgive her. She had run away from her family in their deepest need, left them to bear the burden of her father's ruin without her. It did not occur to her that in looking after herself she had removed one burden from her father's shoulders, that there was little, if anything, she could do to help them now. Guilt, fear and an overpowering sense of her own inadequacy began to assail her. Still he did not come. At long last, worn out by the day's adventures, she drifted into an uneasy sleep.

The crash of the door being thrown open woke her. She heard laughter and shouting, and at first could not think where she was. Then she remembered. Trembling, she lay holding the sheet up to her chin, listening to Tristram shouting at them to go away. She prayed they would not insist on seeing him bedded, dreading their drunken pranks, the ribald comments, her greatest joy being reduced to a spectacle for all to see. The door slammed. The laughter and the shouting died away.

She could hear his heavy breathing and the thunderous beating of her own heart. She ventured to look. He was alone, standing with his back to the door, a silver goblet in his hand, staring at her. She gazed back, devouring him with her eyes over the top of the sheet. Suddenly he plunged towards the bed, grabbed hold of the sheet and with one violent thrust stripped it off. She lay with only her hair to cover her while he stared down, frowning at her naked body. He swayed a little, still staring at her over the rim of his goblet. She gazed up at him like a rabbit transfixed by a stoat, unable to move or speak.

He tossed off the rest of his wine, threw the cup over his shoulder and grasped her arms so roughly that she had to bite her lip not to cry out. With one movement he pulled her up off the bed and hard against him. Lips, cold and hard, covered hers, crushing them brutally. The hilt of his sword pressed against her thigh, bruising it. An overpowering stench of wine filled her nostrils. She wriggled to try and avoid the steel which was cutting into her, and the sword hit the steps round the bed with a resounding clang.

'Keep still, by God's blood,' he swore hoarsely.

'How can I, with your sword digging into me?' she retorted before she could stop herself.

'Take it off,' he muttered, releasing her. She began fumbling with shaking hands at the buckles on his belt, but she made poor work of it.

'Here,' he said impatiently, undoing the sword and throwing it on the floor. 'You'd better get Robin to give you some lessons.'

'I will,' she whispered boldly, starting to undo the buttons on his surcoat, 'I'll be your squire.' He caught her to him again, one hand clamped behind her back, the other holding her chin in a vice-like grip as he covered her mouth with his. She gasped and instantly his tongue was in her mouth, probing and searching like a great hungry snake so she could hardly breathe. She waited for the ecstasy to swamp her but all she could feel was the buttons down the front of his surcoat bruising her naked flesh. She cried out.

'What is it now?' he said, flinging her from him.

'I'm sorry, I'm truly sorry,' she said, 'but your buttons – they're hurting. Can we not take it off?'

'Very well,' he said, standing glaring at her. 'Do it.'

Blushing furiously, very conscious of her nakedness, she unbuttoned the row of silver buttons while he stood swaying on his feet. She helped him out of his surcoat and began to untie his laces which attached his hose to his short overshirt. 'Hurry!' he said. Her hand brushed against proud proof of his manhood and its size frightened her. Keeping her eyes averted she knelt down and tore at the red and blue hose. Before she could finish he grabbed her by the hair and yanked her to her feet again. She would have wound her arms round his neck, offered herself to him, but he pushed her violently and she fell onto her back on the bed. Then he was upon her. She yielded him her mouth, opening it, trying to welcome the brutal, thrusting tongue.

'That's right,' he muttered, 'show me how you love me.' His hands, hard and calloused from work with sword and lance, were everywhere, digging into her delicate flesh, his tongue in her mouth so deep she almost choked. Would it never end? Suddenly he raised his head. He was panting. She watched him warily. Her bruised lips were bleeding, but she did not dare turn her head away. This was not how she thought it would be, not what she had imagined.

'Show me how you love me,' he repeated, leaning over her, seizing great handfuls of her hair and twisting it round her throat. She could not move. Did not know what to do. How could she please him? Suddenly he let go of her hair and rearing up leant back on his heels. Then placing a hand on each of her thighs he parted her legs and plunged into her. The pain, Blessed Virgin, the pain! She bit her lips, determined not to cry out again, while he thrust relentlessly. He was groaning now, groaning and panting and the sweat was dripping off him onto her bruised and aching body. He gripped her breasts, one in each hand and pummelled and pumped as he thrust. She closed her eyes and willed herself to bear it. She was disgusted, frightened, appalled. She could not reconcile this panting, slavering beast with the golden god of her dreams. Once, just once, a low moan of pure terror escaped her.

'That's it,' he cried, covering her mouth with his so she could scarcely breath and thrusting ever more urgently. Then at last, when she thought she must surely suffocate or die from the pain of it, he suddenly gave a great cry of triumph and slumped down on top of her, crushing the breath out of her bruised and battered body. She lay in shock beneath him, until the regular sound of his breathing told her that he was asleep. Then carefully she wriggled out from underneath him and lay staring wide-eyed up into the purple canopy above her head.

This then was love, this pain and humiliation. But if this was love, why did the minstrels make so much of it? Suddenly she remembered something that Black Nick had said on the day of the tournament. 'Forget about all that knight errantry – that's minstrels' tales. They are men, like any other, with all the faults and sins of men.' She remembered the day when she had been at the mercy of the fish-mongers' apprentices, when the one they'd called Kurt had tried to take her. Were they all the same? It's not true, she thought, it can't be true. She slid out of bed and tiptoed across the chamber to kneel at the prie-dieu in front of the Duchess of Lancaster's elaborate miniature chapel. Was this to be her reward for having defied them all and seizing what she wanted? Was this to be her penance for not waiting upon the will of God?

'Help me still to love him,' she prayed. 'Oh, Blessed Mary, don't let me lose that.'

PART II

'Ah freedom is a noble thing
Freedom all solace to man gives
He lives at ease that freely lives!
A noble heart may have none ease
Nor elles naught that may him please
If freedom fail!'

John Barbour – Archdeacon of Aberdeen 1360/70

CHAPTER 19

London 1381

William Gryffard left Calais and went to live in the City of London when he married. The house he built for his bride was on a plot of land just south of the Priory of St Helen's in the north-east part of the city looking down onto Cornhill. Here the fine houses of merchants, knights and noblemen, set apart by their fine gardens and orchards, vied with each other in splendour. Gryffard's Inn was amongst their number, as large as any in the neighbourhood, with no fewer than fourteen rooms, more than twice the norm, set in an orchard and flower garden, with a dovecot in its midst. The walls of the house were of stone, plastered and painted inside, the roof thatched, the ceilings vaulted, the brick floors polished and waxed, the windows fitted with heavy wooden shutters opening inwards on hinges, the main door made of oak and framed by hewn stone. It had taken a long time to build, but by the spring of 1381 it was finished.

On the first Tuesday after Easter, Mariota looked out of the small solar window overlooking Lime Street and shivered as she lowered the oiled cotton covering. The wind, moaning down the narrow street like a demented dervish, was sweeping stray pieces of refuse from its path and tossing them playfully in the air, where they hung for a few fleeting moments, as free as the mischievous breeze, before plunging earthwards into the churned mud and pools of water in the street below.

'Why could it not have been fine today of all days?' Mariota said, turning back into the chamber, where a servant girl was busy stoking the fire. 'It's more like Christmas than Eastertide. How can anyone rejoice on a day such as this?'

'It doesn't matter much, mistress,' said the servant girl. 'There be room for everyone in this grand new house.'

It was true, thought Mariota. The house, William's monument to his success, was large enough for the great feast they were to give today. It had been designed for just such an occasion and the feast was to celebrate its successful completion. For weeks Mariota had been working towards this day, checking carefully every detail, leaving nothing to chance. Now, everything that could be done had been done, and all she had to think of was her own appearance.

'Have you seen the master this morning, Bridget?' she asked, seating herself in front of a small table covered with trinkets, pots and potions.

'Happen he went to the counting house after Mass,' replied the girl.

The counting house, thought Mariota, exasperated. 'Well, I hope he comes to dress soon,' was all she said. 'Perhaps you ought to go and remind him.'

'There be time,' said the girl. 'It be not long past prime.'

True, thought Mariota, there was plenty of time – too much time. Time to think about all the things that could go wrong. William did not like anything to go wrong.

The girl began to brush her hair. William had so many fears and uncertainties, Mariota reflected, his daily dread of war, pestilence, famine and insurrection, his constant expectation of bad news, his obsession with work and dogged attention to detail. This magnificent house was the result of all sorts of worry and care, yet the people coming to their feast – the King, the Bishop of London, the knights, the Mayor – they would see her jewels, her successful husband, her grand new house, her beauty. They would not know what hard work it all was.

'Will you wear a veil, mistress?' asked the girl, her deft fingers busy plaiting the silky tresses into two long braids and arranging them into a square round her head in the latest fashion. Mariota peered at herself critically in the polished steel hanging on the wall behind the table.

'No, I don't think so,' she said. 'Just a jewelled filet.' The broad band of gold studded with precious stones which the girl fixed round her brow was heavy. Mariota anxiously examined her reflection. Would he approve? She now had more jewels and beautiful dresses than she knew what to do with, and William was so very particular that she should show off his wealth properly.

'You looks beautiful, mistress,' said the girl and Mariota frowned. Was there a hint of reassurance in Bridget's voice? She got up and surveyed herself full length. The red silk gown clung to her body down to the hips, from where it swirled in billowing folds to the ground. The neck was cut low, with a row of tiny buttons down the front to her waist. The sleeves were long and tight with another row of buttons to the wrist, and from the elbows long streamers of white silk swept to the ground. At her throat a large ruby sparkled against her white skin. Her body was as slim as ever, her small breasts swelling gently beneath the rich red silk, her stomach flat, her waist tiny. She needed no reassurance, she knew she was beautiful.

Then she caught the girl's eye peering over her shoulder into the polished steel. Just for a moment she saw a flash of pity in the girl's glance. Was William laying her? She looked at the girl as if seeing her for the first time. She was not a bad-looking girl, ruddy-cheeked and buxom with a mouthful of healthy teeth. William was probably laying her. Mariota stared at her reflection, pondering her husband's inexplicable behaviour. Her beauty was undiminished. In fact, with her jewels and fine clothes it was, if anything, even more dazzling than before, yet the man who had once trembled at one smile from her now bedded any passable female in the household, even her own maid. She simply could not understand why he did it. She obeyed him in all things, did everything he asked without complaint, carried out his every command to the letter. What more did he want? A son, that's what he really wanted. Mariota sighed. Nearly twenty years old and still no children. Sometimes she felt God was very unjust.

There was a scratching at the door and Bridget went to open it. A small bundle of fur came rushing into the room.

'Catch him,' screamed Mariota, 'before he ruins my gown.' The servant girl threw herself at the dog and pinned him to the ground. Girl and dog rolled in the rushes, the one laughing, the other yapping furiously. At that moment William walked into the chamber.

'The minstrels have arrived, and the tumblers,' he said, ignoring the fracas on the floor. 'I think you should go down. Are you ready?'

'Yes,' she said standing in the middle of the chamber while Bridget, keeping a tight hold on the little dog, scrambled hastily to her feet. Gryffard looked at his wife as she turned slowly round for his approval.

'Where's that girdle I gave you last New Year's Eve?' he demanded. Quickly Mariota went to the painted chest and rummaged about until she found a chain of gold and silver set with precious stones. She clasped it round her slender waist where it lay like a jewelled serpent, flashing fire.

'That's better,' said William, satisfied. 'I want you to outshine everyone today, especially the two Stodeye sisters, Margaret Philpot and Idonia Brembre.'

'I'm worried about the Northamptons,' she said. 'Suppose he walks out in disgust? He's grown very touchy.'

'Then he'll miss a very good dinner,' said William calmly.

'Why did you have to ask them? Northampton always makes me uneasy and Petronilla is so clever I never know what to say to her,' she persisted, panic gripping her.

'Because, my dear, John of Northampton is building up a large following in the city. It's even rumoured he has Gaunt's support as well.'

'Oh, politics,' she said with a small shrug. 'I can't think why you want to meddle in politics.'

'I don't, that's why I must ask everybody to my feast.'

'Well, if inviting the leaders of the victuallers and the mercantile guilds at one and the same time isn't meddling in politics, I don't know what is,' she said faintly.

'That's not politics, that's prudence. I must have all the leading London merchants to my feast, but that doesn't mean I have to take sides with one or the other. Your father can look after the Northamptons. Now, if you just keep your head and say as little as you can, we should be able to make a success of it. But I think you should go down and keep an eye on the entertainers. I'll join you as soon as I'm dressed.' She looked at Bridget standing with her mouth agape, the little dog wriggling in her arms.

'Come, Bridget,' she said, snapping her fingers, 'and bring the dog. I must have him with me, no court lady ever goes anywhere without her dog.'

'Wait,' said William, and she trembled, wondering whether he might defy her in front of the girl. 'If you're going to have that ridiculous dog with you, you must do it properly. He'll have to have a jewel too.'

Without a word Mariota held the wriggling bundle of fur while Bridget fixed a large pearl onto a red ribbon to match her mistress's gown and tied it round the dog's neck. Mariota handed the animal back to the girl and left the bedchamber.

Making her way down the carved stone staircase into the hall, she thought that it was all very well for him to invite everybody to show his impartiality, but it would be she who would have to soothe ruffled feelings and smooth over any difficulties. The more she thought about it, the more nervous she became at the thought of the ordeal in front of her. All these people who were coming to their house today were coming because her husband needed them for some purpose of his own. They were not friends, some of them were total strangers – like the King. What was she to say to him, how amuse him? He was only a boy, too young to appreciate the only thing she really knew how to do well – you could not flirt with a boy of fourteen. Or could you?

In the hall, glittering from the light of thousands of beeswax candles and laid from end to end with long trestle tables all covered with sparkling white damask cloths, she found her brother Tom being helped to his feet by one of the tumblers.

'Hello, Mariota,' he said slightly breathlessly, 'this splendid fellow here has just been trying to teach me how to do that terrific hand spring of his. It's more difficult than it looks.'

'For goodness sake, Tommy, you should have more sense. You'll break your neck.'

'That would really be a pity,' he retorted with a grin. 'For you'd have to find yourself another cup bearer today.'

'Thomas, you will be sure to serve the Mayor after the King,' she said, straightening his smart new *cote-hardie* which had become somewhat rumpled after his fall. 'He takes precedence over all the others.'

'What about the Bishop of London, doesn't he take precedence over the Mayor?'

'Sweet Jesus, I hadn't thought of that. You must ask William.'

'And then there's Robert de Vere, the King's playfellow. Don't you think he might be insulted to have to wait until the Mayor has quenched his thirst before he gets a drink?'

'Dear God, Robert de Vere! He's not an earl, is he?' she cried, staring at him horrified.

'Yes, but relax, you can trust me not to get it wrong. You're getting as bad as Mother. Who's to do the carving? Not John Constantyn, I hope.'

'No, no, one of the knights with the King will do that, William's arranged it. Tommy, do you think Alice and John may be hurt at having to sit with the servants?'

'I don't know. Alice isn't one to stand on ceremony.'

'You will be kind to Alice and John, won't you? Make them feel welcome. I may not have much time to talk to them.'

'Of course I will. I'm not ashamed of my family. Honestly, Mariota, why did you have to go and ask them in the first place if it was going to cause all this trouble?'

'William didn't want me to and I suppose I was wrong to insist. William's usually right. It's just I wanted all the family here today. I didn't want them to feel left out.'

Thomas shook his head. 'Why do you always want to please everyone all the time? You never can, you know.'

'Your sister can't bear unpleasantness, isn't that it?' said William, appearing so suddenly Mariota jumped nervously. It was a habit of William's to appear at her side noiselessly and with no warning. Even after almost four years of marriage she still had not got used to it. 'Well, Thomas,' William went on, 'and how is the law?' You must be very nearly at the end of your time.'

'The law's no better than it's ever been and that's the truth of it,' retorted Thomas. 'I'd far rather be a knight any day. Did you know, Mariota, I asked Joanna if Tristram would take me as a squire when Robin was knighted, but she wouldn't hear of it. Don't you think that was mean of her? What's the use of having a knight in the family if he can't make me his squire?'

'Still singing that old song, Thomas,' said William. 'You'll not make your fortune following the Duke of Lancaster, you mark my words. Look at what happened when he led that expedition to St Malo in the second year of King Richard's reign. Months spent marching about France trying to entice the French into battle and all for nothing. Du Guesclin is a wily commander who knows better than to do battle with our English archers. The French have learnt their lesson and you'll do better to learn yours. Use your brain and forget about all these fine deeds.'

Mariota tried not to listen. Any mention of Sir Tristram always made her feel unhappy and she did not want to be unhappy today. She took the small dog from Bridget and went to stand by the great carved entrance into the hall, trying to look calm, telling herself she was rich and beautiful and much to be envied but still she felt sick with fright. The dog, sensing her tension, wriggled and barked vociferously.

'For sweet Christ's sake, put the animal down,' commanded William coming to stand beside her. 'If he gets any more frenzied he'll foul your gown and then where will we be?' She put the dog down and he rushed away yapping excitedly and then immediately proved William right by relieving himself on the highly polished floor.

Richard Burgeys and Matilda were the first to arrive. As Mariota greeted them warmly, she thought how well they looked. Matilda had a new headdress and her best gown had been freshly trimmed with marten's fur. She looked around her happily, pouring effusive praise on everything she saw, and Mariota basked in the warmth of her approval.

'How beautiful you look, Mariota,' said her father, beaming at her proudly. He was still handsome, she thought, in his brocade, fur-trimmed gown. Handsome and prospering again, thanks to William.

'Can you be kind to John of Northampton tonight, Father?' she said, beginning to feel better.

'Does William want me to?' he asked.

'Yes, William wants it,' she replied.

'Then of course I'll speak to him,' said her father. They moved away and Mariota went to stand by her husband as he welcomed his guests.

William Walworth, the fishmonger who had been elected Mayor in October, arrived with his wife and Nicholas and Idonia Brembre. Mariota smiled and looked beautiful while William said all that was necessary. For a while it was easy with William at her side. But when the Philpots arrived William had moved away and she was left to greet them on her own. They brought a stranger with them, a tall man whose massive frame seemed too robust for the delicate silk of his tightly fitting tunic. He looked familiar but Mariota could not place him.

'I apologise for bringing this rogue to your feast, Mariota,' said John Philpot, 'but he's just arrived from Italy and I did not want to let him loose upon the city before I had time to hear what he's been up to.'

She smiled and held out her hand, all the time cudgelling her brains to remember where she had seen him before.

'They call me Black Nick, mistress,' he said, his blue eyes twinkling at her as he kissed her hand. Black Nick? Wasn't that the name of the sea captain who had sometimes worked for her father? Dear God, what was she to do with him? William would be furious.

'What a wonderful room,' cooed Margaret Philpot, 'such brilliant wall paintings. Wherever did you find a painter to produce such colours?'

'William found him in Genoa,' muttered Mariota. She glanced over her shoulder nervously. Her husband was hurrying forward to greet the Philpots.

'Nick,' said Margaret turning to the intruder, 'you must bring me back an Italian painter the next time you go to Venice. I shall have the bedchamber entirely redone, the bedhangings can be painted to match the walls. It will make my sister Idonia wild with envy.'

'For goodness sake, Nick, you must do no such thing,' said John taking his wife's arm. Idonia is quite upstaged enough already, without her having to better her bedhangings.'

To Mariota's surprise William did not seem in the least put out as he welcomed Black Nick with every show of cordiality before leading the Philpots away, leaving Mariota frantically wondering what to do with the uninvited guest. A sea captain ought to sit with the household servants and below the Constantyns, yet he was not dressed like a sea captain and the sword he wore had an elaborately embossed hilt of chased silver.

'I should be happiest if I could sit beside you,' he said as if reading her thoughts. 'It is the best chance either of us have of enlivening what looks like being a tedious afternoon.'

'Tedious!' she gasped not knowing whether to be pleased by the compliment to herself or indignant at the insult to her hospitality.

'Yes, tedious,' he insisted. 'All these merchants, these men of money, they look a sadly troubled lot.'

She did not know what to say. Here, gathered together under her roof, was the cream of the city, the most successful men of her aquaintance. 'I don't know what you mean,' she said. 'They're all very successful.'

'But at what cost? Constant worry, nightly poring over letters, incessant attention to the details of business. It makes for a weary life, is that not so?' She was shaken that anybody should be able to describe her life so accurately. 'Such a shame,' he murmured, 'when a man takes so much trouble bedecking his beautiful wife with so many fine jewels and then does not have time for her as well.' She looked up quickly. He was studying her boldly and she recognised the look in his eyes. It made her feel better – better than she had felt all day.

207

'You mustn't think that because my husband is so successful he has no time for his wife,' she said, pouting prettily.

'I wouldn't say that, I'd say William Gryffard knew how to take care of his possessions,' he said. She rewarded him with a quick upward glance and a smile, but before she could say anything more the sound of a trumpet rang through the hall.

'The King!' she said. 'Sweet Jesu, it's the King already.'

'The King!' he exclaimed. 'By the Rood, then you must not waste any more time here with me.' William was hurrying to the door and she flew to her husband's side, her thoughts in a whirl.

'Where did you seat Black Nick?' asked William watching the door anxiously.

Where indeed!

'I thought with the Constantyns,' she stammered.

William stared at her aghast.

'He's only a sea captain, isn't he?'

'He's a hero,' snapped William, just as the King accompanied by Robert de Vere, the Bishop of London, the Earl of March and some half-dozen knights entered the hall. 'Put him next to the Mayor,' he hissed, bowing low before a small, pretty boy dressed in a short silk doublet embroidered with the lions couchant of England and the fleur-de-lis of France. On his head he wore a small golden circlet which crowned his fair curls like a halo. Mariota sank into a graceful curtsy which she had been practising for weeks; out of the corner of her eye she saw Black Nick calmly join John Philpot at the high table.

'Sire,' said William bowing low over the hand the boy was holding out to him. 'You do me much honour in gracing my humble house today.'

'I hope you've got plenty of entertainers,' said the King. 'I can't stand a long, boring feast with no entertainers.'

'Rest assured, Sire, there are musicians, a minstrel, tumblers.'

'Good, I like tumblers,' replied the King, washing his hands in the chased silver rosewater dish which William had brought specially from Florence. He dried his fingers on the fine linen cloth that John Constantyn offered him on bended knee. Then the trumpets sounded once more as William led his royal guest to the dais at the far end of the hall.

The trumpets ceased and the Bishop of London offered a prayer in Latin, then embarked on an appropriate expounding of the tale of Dives, the rich man with the beggar at his gate. To Mariota, anxiously watching while the King fidgeted and frowned, it seemed as if the Bishop would never finish. Thomas grimaced at her; he was standing behind the King's chair with a flagon of wine ready to pour into the royal goblet.

At last the extempore sermon was over and with another

triumphant trumpet call the company sat down.

As the elaborate pageant of the feast unfurled, Mariota found that their royal guest was even more difficult to amuse than she had feared. He made no response to her tentative sallies, took no interest in her pretty speeches, and failed utterly to respond to her attempts to flirt with him. Instead, he lay back almost lost in the vast, throne-like chair William had commissioned specially for this occasion, frowning and chewing his bottom lip in a right royal sulk. Mariota was at her wit's end to know what to do next. She glanced at William and caught him scowling at her. He thinks it's my fault, she thought terrified. Dear God, William would never forgive her if the King was bored.

A peacock was being presented to the King. Perched upright on a platter, it had been cooked and then sewn back into its skin, complete with feathers. Its beak and feet were gilded. The knight acting as carver sliced off the head and neck and laid them ceremoniously on the King's trencher, but Richard just glanced at them moodily. Mariota, looking round her wildly for something, anything, that might please him, caught the eye of Robert de Vere. He was a good-looking boy of about the King's age, tall and slender with a merry grin and a quick bright eye. He pulled a face at her and then suddenly plunged beneath the table to reappear seconds later with her little dog struggling and kicking in his hands.

'What's this?' he cried, standing the dog on its hind legs upon the table. 'The King of Misrule!' He cocked his head at Richard. The King's sulky expression did not change, but Mariota thought his eyes brightened a little.

'The King must be crowned,' Robert de Vere went on, grabbing a piece of bread and moulding it into a makeshift crown for the dog's head. The little dog shook himself vigorously and the bread crown slipped over one ear. He looked so comical that Mariota could not help laughing. De Vere then plucked a feather from the partially dismembered peacock before him and began tickling the dog with it. Instinctively the dog made a dive for the feather, worrying and snapping at it. Suddenly the King laughed. Robert de Vere bent down so his eyes were on a level with the dog's and barked in clever imitation. The dog cocked his head and listened fascinated.

'By the saints, Robert, he think you're a dog,' cried the King showing interest at last. 'What's his name?'

'His name is Tristram, Sire,' replied Mariota.

'Tristram the troublemaker,' said Richard jabbing at the dog with his dagger. The animal, thinking it was another feather dived at it ferociously and gave a yelp of terror as he felt the sharp point. Richard gave a shout of laughter and lunged at the dog as it turned to run. A bright speck of blood appeared on his little white rump. The King was enjoying himself at last. Eyes shining excitedly, he made another lunge at the dog with his dagger while the animal raced away in terror down the centre of the table. Other daggers appeared in imitation of the King and poked and prodded the poor little dog as he barked and raced about the table in a frenzy, upsetting goblets of wine and scattering trencher bread in his wake, while Richard leant back in his chair laughing and uttering bloodcurdling whoops of glee.

Mariota, much relieved, glanced at William happily, but he was staring at the dishevelled table in obvious disapproval. She lowered her eyes quickly, and noticed a spreading stain of wine in her lap from the overturned goblet in front of her.

When at last the dog, his immaculate white coat dotted with splashes of blood, managed to escape by throwing himself off the end of the table, it was time for the tumblers, who kept the King sufficiently amused with their antics. But as soon as their act was over, he announced that it was time to leave.

Mariota watched the royal guest depart with relief tinged with disappointment. The King had not wanted to stay for the dancing, and she trembled in case the rest of the guests drifted away in his wake. But as the musicians struck up a merry jig, William Walworth, the Mayor, led his wife out onto the floor and others soon followed his lead. Mariota let out a long sigh of relief. The worst part of the day was over. Now perhaps she could begin to enjoy herself. But with whom?

William was listening carefully to the Bishop of London's warning on the dangers of travelling about the country. 'From reports we've heard it's much more than the usual petty crime,' the Bishop said. 'There are more runaway serfs and freemen wandering loose than is healthy. We've been having a lot of trouble lately keeping the villeins on the land. Now that the cost of labour is so high they want to leave their unprofitable farms and hire their labour out to the highest bidder. Of course we can't have that.'

'I don't see why not,' said William. 'As long as it is carefully done, so much for the harrowing, the reaping, or the tribute in eggs. You build up a staff of skilled men by commuting all other work from ploughmen and shepherds. By commuting services which involve food at the lord's expense, like the harvest days, when beer, bacon, herrings and barley bread has to be provided, it can save money. Wage rates can be kept down by statute and enforced by the justices of labourers and every labourer put on oath to obey the statutes.

'I didn't know you were a landowner,' put in Brembre sharply.

'I'm not yet, but when I am I like to think that I shall know how best to run my manor,' said William smoothly.

'It isn't really a question of wages,' said the Bishop, 'it's more a question of freedom, and that is a very dangerous plant once it takes root in a man's mind. I blame that priest from the north, John Ball. He's been preaching freedom to the lower orders for the past twenty years. He should have been sent to the Tower for treason years ago – the Archbishop's too soft.'

'Freedom is not so easily stifled, my friend,' said Philpot. 'It's not the voice of one man, but hundreds. If you silence Ball, you just make a martyr of him. I blame the friars, setting class against class, and worst of all Wycliffe with all his reforming nonsense.'

'Wycliffe makes it clear that even a wicked master must be obeyed and that resistance and revolution are justified by God only under certain strictly limited conditions,' said Northampton quietly.

'Try preaching that sort of doctrine to the simple men and women in the villages,' retorted the Bishop scornfully. 'Try that in the mouths of the poor parish priests. Do you think an uneducated man who cannot read or write can express the metaphysical juggling of a brilliant mind like Wycliffe, or if they could that their congregations could understand it? "When Adam delved and Eve span, who was then a gentleman?" How many times do you think I have heard that doggerel recently? How many times have you? It is the sort of easy doctrine that these people understand. It's the stuff that rebellions are made of.'

'If anything could set off a rebellion, this incompetent poll tax could,' said Brembre angrily.

'What would you?' replied the Bishop. 'The wars have to be paid for. You merchants will not give the young King's government enough credit.'

'It's not a question of giving credit to the government,' retorted Brembre. 'There's not enough money in the whole of the city to pay for the sort of sums needed today.'

'Better to get the money from the people than from a small band of elite men who get rich on privileges in exchange for their loans,' argued Northampton. Brembre glared at him, but he was not to be put off. 'A shilling a head is not excessive. The rich are to pay as much as a pound, the poorest only four pennies. Surely that is fair?'

'It is not the tax itself, perhaps,' put in Philpot, 'but the method of its collection. During this winter the commission sets about gathering the tax, then it discovers that the returns are inadequate, so what do they do? They send another set of commissioners out into the country to scrutinise the lists of inhabitants and forcibly compel payment from those who evaded it before. But what will people think? Why, that a lot of strangers from London have come down to levy an entirely new poll tax not yet voted by Parliament. The heavy burden incurred for an unsuccessful war has made the people suspicious and quarrelsome.'

'Then they must send men-at-arms with the commissioners,' replied the Bishop. 'They are poor, ignorant, harmless fools, nothing that a knight and a company of archers could not put down in an instant.'

Mariota gazed longingly at the dancers twirling merrily around the hall. Tommy was dancing with Mistress Philpot and they both appeared to be thoroughly enjoying themselves. Then she caught sight of Black Nick. He was standing a little apart from the group of merchants arguing so intensely among themselves, and he was watching her. He bowed encouragingly and so she went to join him.

'A remarkable feast,' he said, looking at her with a very satisfying degree of warmth in his blue eyes.

'Was it? I'm not sure that the King enjoyed it very much,' she said, longing for a little sympathy, a word of reassurance.

'But he did — enormously. The King does not like long ceremonial feasts, it's well known. He gets bored very easily. Your performing dog was a masterpiece. The King went away in high good humour.'

'Do you really think so?' For all his ugliness he was really a very charming man to be with. Should she allow him to dance with her? she wondered. William had said he was a hero, perhaps he would not mind. But Nick showed little sign of wanting to dance. She tapped her foot impatiently to the time of the music and stood looking at him, her grey eyes full of an open invitation. He smiled down at her appreciatively.

'Poor Mistress Gryffard, is it very hard for you?' he asked.

'I don't know what you mean,' she said baffled.

'Being married to William Gryffard.'

'But I have everything a woman can possibly want. I have riches, a beautiful new house, my husband is always bringing me presents, he never beats me.'

'But he never seems satisfied, does he?'

'I'm afraid I fall very far below what he expects of a wife, his standards are so exacting,' she explained, surprised at herself.

'Perhaps he expects the wrong things. Don't feel judged by William. Just because he can judge a bale of wool to a nicety, doesn't mean he knows how to appreciate a woman. It's like a man who can't hear music when he listens to the perfect counterpoint. He doesn't hear the harmony but that doesn't mean to say it isn't there.' He was really very sympathetic, and understanding. She gave him a long grateful look from under her lashes, but he was not looking at her. He was gazing over her shoulder at where her husband was talking to Nicholas Brembre. 'He's an interesting man, your husband, you know, he has the enterprise and audacity of the travelling pedlar.'

'That doesn't sound at all like William,' she said with a little frown.

'The city is run by men who take big risks, people with audacity and nerve, who know how to seize an opportunity and profit from another man's misfortunes.'

'William never takes risks,' she said.

'The only difference between William and other less successful risk-takers is that William leaves nothing to chance. He distributes his fortune in as many places as possible, never sinking too much in any single company, never trusting too much to any one partner, always prepared to cut his losses and begin again, to recover in one field what he has lost in another. Does your husband want to be Mayor, I wonder?'

'I don't think he can, he's not a member of any guild.'

'No, of course not, but your father,' he suddenly fixed her with a penetrating stare, 'is now the Master of the Mercers. Perhaps he hopes to be Mayor?'

'I don't know but I'm sure, if he did, William would do all he could to help him. William has been more than kindness itself to Father,' she replied, disappointed in Nick. A promising little flirtation had suddenly died, like a feeble flame round a damp log, and the conversation was beginning to bore her.

'He would, of course,' mused Nick. 'A man like your husband wouldn't want to rule from in front, there's too much danger in being Mayor of a city like London. He prefers being in a position to influence events from behind the arras, that way he can scuttle back into the wainscot when things go wrong.'

Mariota shrugged. She had thought this ugly man with the bold eyes was interested in her. Now it seemed that it was William who concerned him. She turned her head to look back at William and show her perfect profile. 'My husband is a very jealous man,' she said, 'he guards me closely.'

'I never thought he was a fool,' he replied. She peeped at him, a swift provocative glance, then dropped her eyes demurely and waited for the magic to work. Surely now he would ask her to dance? But he seemed content to stand and watch, enjoying the music but making no attempt to share his pleasure with her. She felt piqued.

'Don't you dance, master seaman?' she asked before she could stop herself.

'What! Dance with a man's wife under his nose at his very own feast, when I have it from her own lips that he guards her most jealously! I'm not such a risk-taker as that,' he said, grinning wickedly. 'I'm going to dance with Margaret Philpot, having first obtained her husband's permission.' He wandered away and she was left feeling foolish and not a little mortified. For the first time in her life a man had turned her down for another woman. It was not a pleasant experience. She watched him take Margaret Philpot away from Tommy and went to sympathise with him.

'Isn't she wonderful?' said Tommy, eyes glued to Margaret's lively countenance as she whirled away in Nick's arms. 'I never knew dancing could be such fun! Don't you think she's beautiful?'

'She's old enough to be your mother.'

'I like older women,' he said with a grin.

'Well, you lost her easily enough,' she retorted.

'Oh, I can't compete with Black Nick,' he said ruefully.

'Thomas, who is he?' she asked. 'I thought he was an ordinary sea captain who sometimes used to take cargoes for Father to Calais, but William says he's some sort of hero.'

'Mariota, you goose,' said Tommy shocked, 'don't you take any interest in what's going on? He's only the man who captured the Scottish pirate, John Mercer.'

'Oh, a pirate,' she said with a shrug. 'It takes one to catch one, I daresay. What's one pirate the less?'

'Mercer wasn't just an ordinary pirate,' explained Tommy. 'He's the man who led the French attack on our coast back in the first year of King Richard's reign. He sailed right up the river as far as Gravesend and sank all the ships at anchor there, including Black Nick's. That's why he was so intent on capturing him.'

'I thought it was John Philpot who was responsible for capturing the Scottish pirate,' said Mariota. 'I thought that's why they call him the Sailor King.'

'John Philpot doubtless provided the ships, but it was Black Nick who did the dirty work. I'd love to sail across the Channel with him. I should think he'd be a hell of a fellow in a fight.'

'Well, Margaret Philpot certainly seems to like him,' she said. 'Poor Tommy, you've lost her, I'm afraid. You'll have to dance with your poor sister instead.'

'Oh, he'll soon be off to sea again, and then I shall be able to console her,' he responded unabashed. 'She's invited me to visit her at Philpot's Inn.'

'Be careful, Tommy, the Philpots are powerful people. You could find yourself in deeper water than you know and even William wouldn't be able to protect you.'

'Don't worry, Mariota, I shall be as sly as a fox. William should be grateful to me for the trouble I'm taking. I shouldn't be surprised if Mistress Philpot doesn't have a good deal of influence over her husband. Tell you what,' he said grinning wickedly as he led her onto the floor, 'if you like I'll ask her to put in a good word for William with her husband.' It was useless, she thought, to try to restrain someone like Tommy. He was as bad as Joanna, the more you warned him to be cautious the more reckless he became.

For Mariota, the dancing was not a success. Tommy soon left her in search of food, for his cup-bearing duties had prevented him from

214

partaking of the feast with the others and, though she had many other partners, none of them made up for Nick's rejection. She told herself that he was little better than a pirate and ugly into the bargain but it was a serious blow to her pride that any man should be able to resist the pull of her beauty. It quite spoilt the rest of the day for her.

When at last Nick came to take his leave, she was standing by William.

'Will you be in London for long this time?' William asked.

'I don't know, not for very long,' Black Nick replied. 'I have business to attend to in Bristol.'

'You're going to Bristol! I'm going to the Cotswolds to buy cloth and I'd be glad of your company on the way. The roads are becoming perilous as the sea, if we are to believe some of the travellers' tales we hear.'

'I'd be pleased to bear you company,' said Nick with a slight bow. 'Why don't you bring your wife with you? She has a sister living near Cirencester, has she not? Would you not like to visit her, Mistress Gryffard?' Mariota, taken unawares, was startled, but she was also pleased. So he was a little interested after all! She looked at her husband quickly, expecting him to refuse, but to her surprise he seemed to think the idea a good one.

'Why not, Mariota? I can leave you at Maudesbury while I do my business, then we can travel back together when we're ready.' She bowed her head in dutiful acquiescence and did not even look at Black Nick as he kissed her hand.

As she got ready for bed that night, Mariota wondered at William's agreement to the projected visit to the Cotswolds. Always before when she suggested going to see Joanna, he had found some excuse to forbid it, and she had given up. They had not seen each other since Joanna's marriage over four years ago. Tristram's name was never mentioned, and Mariota suspected that William either knew or had guessed her secret. She had not thought of Tristram for a long, long time, but now she did. Would he still remember her? Would he still want her? That he could marry Joanna in her place had been such a bitter blow to her self-esteem that for a long time she had never wanted to see him again. But now the thought of him made her spirits rise, that and the thought of Black Nick. He was something of a mystery and a challenge. It would be fun flirting with him on the journey. Of William she thought not at all.

She was still at her prayers in front of the prie-dieu when William came into their bedchamber. She heard him moving about the room behind her while she repeated the paternoster, knowing she made a pretty picture of piety in her white shift and her hair hanging loose down to her waist. She finished her prayers and got up slowly, waiting for some comment from him about the day, some indication of relief that the great feast had been accomplished without mishap. But he said nothing, no word of approval or condemnation.

'I want you ready to leave in two days,' he said as he removed his rich, fur-trimmed gown, folding it meticulously and laying it on the painted chest at the foot of the bed. He then began to list what she should take with her on the journey, and she, listening in dismay as he embarked upon the minutest detail of her clothes, her jewels and all the household amenities he considered necessary for them to take, became once more borne down by the burden of preparation, work and worry which he laid upon her.

'I can't possibly be ready in only two days,' she said at last, driven by sheer weariness to demur for once.

'You must,' he said. 'Black Nick waits for no man and it's too dangerous to make the journey alone.'

With a sigh she slipped out of her smock and into bed. He joined her quickly. His hands moved over her naked skin, exploring her body with the meticulous care with which he did everything. She wanted only to be left alone as she was on other nights, to curl herself up into a corner of the big four-poster bed and sleep.

'Oh William, must you?' she said, pushing his hands away, for once too tired to comply with her usual instant obedience.

'Yes, Mariota, I'm afraid I must,' he said, catching her hand and making her feel him. 'Perhaps tonight we will beget a son.' She sighed. She had given birth to a stillborn girl a year ago, but since then – nothing. Alice had four children now. What was she doing wrong? Obedient, good and compliant, she lay and let him take her. A son, she thought, as he grunted and struggled for the release he wanted. Blessed Mother, let him get me with child and then perhaps I won't have to endure this endless striving.

CHAPTER 20

Spring came at last on the day they set out for the Cotswolds. The sun was just rising behind the distant wall of the city, bathing the spire of St Andrew Undershaft in a pale rosy light. William strode about impatiently trying to marshal the two menservants, the woolpacker, Mariota's maid and the two packhorses into some sort of cavalcade. Mariota stood beside the new palfrey William had bought specially for this journey, cradling her small dog in her arms and eyeing the horse nervously. She was dressed in a simple loose gown of fine blue wool, pulled in at the waist with a girdle of linked silver. Her only other jewellery was a cameo of pearls to fasten the neck of her gown. Her hair was hidden by a linen veil which tightly framed her face and hung down her back in two tails. She had been pleased with her appearance when she had left her chamber at daybreak.

'You can't go like that!' exclaimed William impatiently, seeming to notice her for the first time. 'You'll be covered in dust and mud within the hour. Where's your travelling cloak?' Meekly she waited while Bridget unpacked the cloak from one of the saddlebags and enfolded her in it. One of the menservants then lifted her onto the palfrey, as William, casting a last critical eye over the party, mounted his own strong gelding.

Mariota twined her fingers in the palfrey's flowing mane and followed her husband into Lime Street, trying not to feel afraid. It should have been a relief to be at last upon the way after all the hard work, worry and attention to detail of the last few days, but all she could think of was the danger and difficulty of the long journey that lay ahead of them. They were such a small band, just two heavily armed servants, two helpless women, a woolpacker – and William. Round William's waist, she knew, were two heavy moneybags, coin for the cloth and the wool he travelled to the Cotswolds to buy, and she trembled at the thought of all the robbers lying in wait for them ahead.

'Can you not make that animal move faster?' shouted William, turning round in his saddle in exasperation. 'Black Nick will not wait all morning for us.'

The thought of Black Nick brought comfort. The man who had captured the Scottish pirate and braved the French and Spanish so very many times would surely be able to get the better of any bandits. They would be safe with Black Nick. She began to look forward to seeing him again. It was, in truth, for his sake that she had dressed so carefully this morning, had scorned the ugly travelling cloak. But perhaps William was right. How terrible if the effect should be spoilt by mud and dust! Better to reveal herself little by little, when they stopped upon the way.

She prodded the palfrey's rounded side gently with her heel, but the horse continued to amble contentedly along Lime Street until William reined in alongside and gave him a great buffet with his sword. Mariota gave a little squeal of fright, the dog jumped from her arms, but the palfrey bore no grudge, merely breaking into a sort of shuffling run which seemed to satisfy William. They continued more swiftly across Cornhill Street and the busy corn market, down towards the river, with Tristram yapping at the palfrey's heels and Mariota bouncing about in the saddle clinging to the high pommel in front of her and trying to find a comfortable way to sit.

At London Bridge Black Nick was waiting. He was dressed in a fine doublet of green – no armour or chain mail, not even a leather padded gambeson. His hood was thrown back from his head and lay in festoons of gaily coloured cloth round his neck, and across his back hung a lute. Apart from the sword dangling from his hip, he looked more ready to go Maying than on a long and dangerous journey. Beside him waited a scarred ruffian, who looked menacing enough, armed with a sword and a longbow over his shoulder.

'I thought you would be bringing more men with you.' said William, and Mariota could see that he was disappointed.

'Sam's worth ten of any others,' was the laconic reply. Without waiting to see if they followed, Black Nick wheeled his horse and set off across the bridge. Mariota, too, was disappointed. Why, he had not even bade her good morning! He was nothing but an ill-mannered seaman, for all he dressed to look like a man of nobler birth.

Although it was still early, London Bridge was teeming with life. Houses lined the bridge on both sides, and hawkers, loaded carts, horses and people on foot all jostled in the narrow thoroughfare. Halfway across the bridge there was an open space without houses and here the noise from the river roaring and breaking against the bridge's great pontoons almost drowned the considerable din caused by the traffic struggling across it. Mariota clung to the palfrey's mane, terrified that he might shy and send her hurtling over the high wall of the bridge into the fast-flowing flood below, but he was too well-trained to do more than amble forward, squeezing past all obstacles with a dogged perseverance all his own. Towards the end of the bridge a row of pike staves above the Drawbridge Gate bore the decaying remains of the heads of recent criminals. Mariota shuddered at the sight and closed her eyes. At the far end was the Stone Gate which was closed each night at curfew. Here an armed guard was stationed in the gatehouse and a watchman was on duty at all times. To the east just outside the wall lay the Tower of London, its stonework gleaming in the first rays of the sun.

At the foot of the bridge, Mariota looked back across the wide stretch of the Thames at the city she was leaving behind. It looked so beautiful, hundreds of church spires rising from it like a forest of spears, with the great spire of St Paul's Cathedral stretching up into the heavens so high above the rest. Just then the bells began to ring for prime, and Mariota drew a deep breath of longing – to be going to Mass at St Peter's Upon Cornhill, then home to break her fast, inside the city, listening to the reassuring sound of the bells behind its impregnable walls, instead of here on the wrong side of the only bridge across the river. The bells seemed to be calling to her, telling her not to go. A shiver ran down her spine, and fearfully she crossed herself, praying to St Christopher, patron saint of travellers, to bring her back in safety before too long.

They swung west past the Priory of St Mary Overy and on past fine churches and noble houses in spacious surroundings, but gradually the scattered houses became meaner till they were little better than shabby hovels giving on to lanes deep with mud and filth. Mariota wrinkled her nose in disgust. She was accustomed to smells in London but this stench was beyond anything that would have been permitted in the city. Had they no scavengers in Southwark? It was as they were leaving the unsavoury huddle of houses behind and turning south to pick up the Richmond road that Mariota first missed her little dog.

'Merciful Mother,' she wailed, tugging at the reins of the palfrey, 'Tristram's disappeared.' Her horse, obedient to the rein and all too eager to seize an excuse for a rest, stopped dead in the road. William turned round in his saddle with a savage oath.

'What's the matter now, Mariota?' he cried. 'Can you not make that animal keep up. By St Vitus, the rascal who sold him to me shall pay for this. He swore he was a perfect conveyance for any lady.' When Mariota explained it was not the palfrey's fault and begged to be allowed to go back for the dog, he lost all patience.

'Of course you cannot go back for him,' he said, seizing hold of the palfrey's bridle and jerking him forward. 'I can't think why you

219

wanted to take a dog with you on a long journey like this. Now keep that horse of yours moving. We'll not reach Maudesbury before the month is out at this rate.'

'But the dog, what will happen to him?' she said, her eyes full of tears.

'How should I know what will happen? You were not too concerned about the wretched animal performing for the King's pleasure at our feast, as I remember. Stop pretending, Mariota and save your tears for when we are attacked by brigands,' snapped William, venting his anger with a resounding blow to the palfrey's ample rump. The horse broke into a smart trot and Mariota gasped, clutching his mane again. Through a haze of tears she followed William, thinking not of her poor little dog running about the mean streets of Southwark searching for them in vain, but of William and his insensitivity. She did not notice that Black Nick had disappeared. The palfrey was now trotting beside William's gelding quite briskly and it took all her concentration just to stay in the saddle. When at last she did notice that Black Nick had gone, she felt even worse. He must have grown impatient, even more impatient than William, and now they were at the mercy of every robber and bandit upon the way. It was all her fault for being so slow.

The tears blinded her as she struggled to keep up with William, bouncing about in her high-sided saddle, her fingers entwined in the palfrey's mane. After a time she thought she heard the sound of hooves thudding on the road behind. Terrified, she turned round expecting to find a party of bandits falling upon them. To her surprise she saw that it was Black Nick, cantering after them with the little dog held tightly under one arm.

'Oh, you found him, thank you, thank you,' she called, smiling brightly at him through her tears. 'Was he quite forlorn, poor little fellow?'

'On the contrary,' replied Nick with a grin, 'he was busy pursuing some amorous adventure of his own and not at all interested in being rescued. In fact I had the devil's own job catching hold of him.'

'Naughty, naughty Tristram, how could you give me such a fright?' she chided holding out her arms. 'Let me take him.'

'You will do no such thing,' William's voice broke in sternly. 'Let the wretched creature go, he's wasted too much time already. My wife had no business bringing him on a journey such as this.'

Mariota trembled and cast an appealing look at Black Nick. What would he do? Would he stand up to William for her sake? William would not like it, she knew. It was no use defying William when he was angry. There would only be trouble.

'And what do you think we shall do if the first tavern we stop in happens to be rat-infested?' said Black Nick pleasantly. 'Why do you think

I went back to find him? This little fellow here might well turn out to be just what we need to keep the vermin at bay. Here, do you think you can keep a tight hold of him, my girl?' he said handing the dog to Bridget. 'If you don't, I'll see you walk all the way to Cirencester.' The maid, riding pillion behind one of the menservants, took the dog and wrapped him in the kerchief she wore round her shoulders, binding him tightly against her breast, while Black Nick watched appreciatively.

'Lucky dog, I wouldn't mind being in his place,' he said. Bridget giggled and blushed, the battle-scarred seaman winked crudely at his master and William, his face expressionless, urged his gelding on again.

'Summer is acoming in' sang Nick, taking the lute from his back and accompanying himself with skill:

'Loud sing cuckoo!
Grow seed, and blow wind
Spring makes the world new
Sing cuckoo!'

It was a cheerful song, with an easy rollicking rhythm to it. As Nick sang, his long body moved with the rhythm of his horse in a way Mariota envied. Verse followed verse and Sam, Nick's ruffianly seaman, joined in the chorus with raucous shouts of 'Sing cuckoo!' Mariota forgot her fears as she watched Black Nick, wondering whether he had gone back to rescue the dog to please her, and if the story of the rats was just a clever way to outwit William. Apart from that incident, he had ignored her completely this morning. But was he ignoring her, or was he courting her subtly and cleverly right under her suspicious husband's nose? She wished she knew.

The April sun shone warm on their backs, blackbirds sang in the trees and here and there a lark was pouring out its song of welcome to spring. They rode past heavily laden packhorses with their drivers, carts of all descriptions and numerous travellers on foot. Once they passed a party of pilgrims riding towards London. They were singing and laughing merrily, as if the pilgrimage had done them much good. For a while there was enough to interest Mariota on the busy thoroughfare, but as the sun climbed high overhead, she grew tired and thirsty. She longed to discard the heavy travelling cloak, but looking down she could see that it was well covered in dirt and knew that William had been right to make her wear it.

'How much further before we can stop?' she asked, urging her palfrey faster so she could catch up with William.

It was Black Nick who answered. 'We'll stop in Richmond,' he said, reining his horse back to ride alongside her. 'The Green Falcon's a passable tavern and if you're as hungry as I, mistress, you'll be ready for some dinner. You'll feel better with some food inside you and there's no point in trying to do too much on your first day.'

'How far to Richmond?' she asked.

'A few more miles.'

'A few more miles,' she wailed. 'I don't think I could ride another yard.'

'Oh yes you can, you'll be surprised how far you'll be able to ride once you get used to it,' he said. 'The trick is to think of something else.'

'I've not ridden much before. William bought the palfrey for the journey and I know I ought to be grateful, but I wish all the same he'd allowed me to travel by litter.'

'William bought well,' replied Black Nick. 'What will you call him?'

'Juniper,' she said, giving him her most bewitching smile. He was looking at her in a very encouraging way, but William turned round in his saddle, shouting at them to make haste, and she was so weary she could barely summon up the energy to flirt any more.

'Courage, fair lady,' he said gently, 'the walls of Richmond are in sight.' Ahead of them she saw a small, pretty castle floating like a swan on its broad moat beside the river, with behind a small town built on the slopes of a hill. With a heartfelt sigh of relief she prodded Juniper with her heel and the obedient palfrey, sensing respite, broke into a decorous canter.

Mariota sat and studied the cobbled yard of the Green Falcon while Juniper drank thirstily from the water trough. William had disappeared inside the tavern.

'Aren't you going to help me down?' she said to Black Nick when he too had dismounted.

'Wouldn't you like me to bring you something to eat out here?' he said, coming to stand beside her. 'It's not much of a place inside, though the water looks clean enough for the horses.'

'I'd like to get off,' she said, holding out her hands to him. He held her round the waist, lifting her out of the saddle and holding her suspended above the ground so that her eyes were on a level with his own. She pursed her little rosebud of a mouth and lowered her lashes demurely.

'Surely you're not going to take advantage of another man's wife when she's tired and faint from hunger,' she whispered.

'I never take advantage of unwilling females,' he replied, setting her on her feet so abruptly she almost fell. He turned away and Mariota, feeling unfairly rebuffed, walked alone into the tavern. Inside, it was dark and stuffy, and rank with odours of sour ale, sweat and stale food. She looked down at her feet and saw that the rushes were filthy and covered with old bones and discarded scraps. She was sure it was rat-infested.

'William,' she said as her husband came into the room followed by the tavernkeeper bearing a covered dish. 'I'd rather we didn't sleep here tonight. Isn't there some abbey in Richmond where we could find lodgings for the night?'

'Sleep here!' he exclaimed incredulously. 'Of course we don't sleep here. We've only stopped for dinner and then we'll be on our way.'

She gaped at him. So the agony was not over. She had more of it to endure.

William was wolfing down his food, eating with single-minded concentration as if every minute spent was precious time wasted. She picked at the mess of meat in a warm sticky sauce. It was tough and stringy and stuck in her throat as she tried to swallow it down. She looked round for Black Nick. He was nowhere to be seen. All too soon she was out in the yard again eyeing the patient palfrey with loathing in her heart.

'How much further must we go today?' she asked plaintively.

'Until nightfall,' said William, grasping hold of her firmly and hoisting her up into the saddle.

'Please, William, must we?' she said, gazing down at him imploringly. 'I don't think I can ride any more today.' But he had already turned away and was mounting his horse.

'We must make the best of the weather,' he said over his shoulder. 'It may not stay fair for long. Today the road is good and the mud's dried well, but you cannot rely on it at this time of the year. A day or two's rain can make the way impassable. We must make the best possible speed until we join the Roman road at Speen, just north of Newbury. It's a good road which runs straight to Cirencester. You can ride it in a thunderstorm and not get stuck in the mud.'

'How far to Speen?' she asked faintly.

'Four days' ride, at this pace maybe more, though I've done it in much less.' So saying he swung out of the yard and she had no choice but to follow.

Black Nick joined them as they left the town and she cast him a look full of sorrowful reproach. He grinned at her as he brought his horse alongside hers.

'Poor lady, is it very bad?' he asked and the sympathy in his eyes unlocked all the misery of her suffering.

'How could you be so cruel?'

'Why, what have I done?' he exclaimed, genuinely surprised.

'Making me think my ordeal was over for today, letting me believe that when we arrived in Richmond we need go no further.'

'Far be it from me to give a beautiful lady the lie, but I said no such thing,' he protested.

'You said there was no need to do too much on the first day,' she accused.

'Well, perhaps I did, but too much is a relative term and sometimes when in a hurry we ride all day without stopping for more than a drink of ale and a slice of pie as we ride. I thought maybe that would be too much for you on your first day.'

Almost she disliked him – why he was no better than William. She rode on slowly, nursing her grievances, making no attempt to keep up. Already William was far ahead; the servants passed her leading the two packhorses, closely followed by the woolpacker and the seaman. Black Nick stayed behind, restraining his impatient stallion to the palfrey's amble. She could not resist shooting a glance at him and found his eyes too full of laughter for her liking.

'You cannot know how much I suffer,' she said.

'Ah, the mortification of the flesh. Suffering is supposed to bring you closer to God. Doubtless by the time we reach Cirencester you will be well advanced into a state of grace.'

'I think you're making fun of me and I don't think it's very kind,' she said staring out over the ears of her palfrey.

'And if I am kind to you, what will you do for me, fair mistress? Will you give me your sweet lips to kiss?'

She looked at him then, a long cool glance from beneath her lashes. 'How could I?' she replied. 'For then my husband would surely beat me. You wouldn't want that, would you?'

'He might never find out.'

'William always finds things out. He seems to know everything.'

'It's a useful gift for a merchant to have,' he replied with a shrug.

For a while they rode on in silence. Mariota, very conscious of the man at her side, forgot her grievances and was happy knowing she was admired. He took up his lute and began to sing.

'Nothing is to man so dear
As woman's love in good manner
A good woman is man's bliss
There her love right and steadfast is
There is no solace under heaven
Of all that a man may name
That should a man so much gladden
As a good woman that loves true.'

He broke off suddenly. 'It's not true, is it, Mariota?' he said. 'A bad woman is more fun than a good one any day.'

She gave a little gasp and stared at him. 'I don't know,' she said. 'I've never met a bad woman.'

He threw back his head and laughed long and loud. 'And I've yet to meet a good one,' he said. 'Oh, don't look so offended, Mistress Gryffard. You think you're good, but that's because you've never been

224

tempted. You like to rouse a man's passions, to watch the poor creatures burn themselves at the flame of your beauty like the helpless
moths which singe their wings on a candle flame. But then you've
never been in love.'

'Of course I have, often,' she said indignantly.

'There! Condemned, and by your own admission. Anyone who
loves "often" cannot love true. You're no better than I am, sweet mistress. Shall I swear to love you till this journey's end?'

'I cannot help it if you do,' she said, stroking the palfrey's neck gently.

'And if I do, will you love me in return?' he asked. She looked up
swiftly and saw that he was grinning at her, while the devil's own merriment danced in his eyes.

'You are forgetting that I am married to William,' she rebuked him.

'No, I hadn't forgotten,' he said. His eyes were on her still, appraising her knowingly.

She smiled back at him a gentle resigned little smile, then urged her
palfrey forward to catch up with William.

She felt pleased with the progress she was making. His eyes told her
that he admired her. He said he wanted her kisses. Already he was
halfway under her spell. No man could resist the lure of her beauty
for long.

But as the days passed and they progressed uneventfully west-
wards, Black Nick proved a disappointment to her. Certainly he
courted her, with words and with song, as they rode through the
green countryside, making her forget her aches and pains and the long
hours in the saddle. When they passed through dense forests he rode
close beside her, soothing her fears. He helped her from her horse,
and at times paid her such audacious compliments that she trembled
lest he arouse William's jealousy, but William was too absorbed in
making the best of progress, in keeping anxious watch for any trouble ahead, to pay attention to their chatter. But attentive though he
was, Nick showed little sign of being in love with her; he accepted all
too easily her plea of William's jealousy and never attempted to take
advantage of her when William was not near.

At last they approached the crossroads where the Ridgeway across
the Downs joined the Roman road. A crowd was gathered where a
hermit's small shelter stood at the crossroads. Black Nick rode forward to investigate with so casual an air that Mariota had not been
at first alarmed, but then Sam unstrung his longbow and hurried after
his master so purposefully that she immediately feared the worst. At
William's command the two menservants followed reluctantly after
them while William waited behind with the woolpacker and the
women. Soon Nick returned, saying it was nothing to worry about,
just some local farmers and shepherds who had gathered to listen to

225

a group of glee singers. As they rode past they could not help hearing the gleemen's song:

> 'John the Miller hath ground small, small, small
> The King's son of heaven shall pay for all
> Beware or ye be woe
> Know your friend from your foe
> Have enough and say "ho"!
> And do well and better and flee sin
> And seek peace and hold therein
> And so bid John Trueman and all his fellows.'

'The last time I heard that song was in London,' remarked William.

'I've heard it in Gravesend and I've heard it in the Kentish seaports,' Nick told him. 'Now it's here as well.'

'It's an odd song, I can't think what makes it so popular,' said Mariota. 'It doesn't even have a very good tune.'

'I agree, Mistress Gryffard, it has a very poor tune.'

'What do you think it means?' asked William.

'I don't know, but it sounds more like a message than a song.'

'A message?' queried William. 'What sort of message? Who from and who to?'

'I wish I knew,' Nick replied and it was the first time Mariota had ever seen him looking really serious. 'A warning perhaps, or a signal passed from one end of the country to another for those who cannot read. But by whom?'

William looked very worried and Mariota's fears, which had been to a large extent forgotten, now swept back. For the rest of the day she peered around her fearfully, glancing over her shoulder and constantly urging the good-natured Juniper to keep up with Black Nick at all times. But they encountered no more gleemen. The travellers they passed on the road all seemed harmless enough.

Soon they were riding along the fine Roman road into the rolling Cotswolds, dotted with churches and sheep, and Mariota began to look forward more and more to their journey's end. She was weary of strange beds and indifferent food. The weather had broken as they crossed the Berkshire Downs and Bridget had caught a cold. Her doleful sneezes and raucous snores at night had driven Mariota wild. Even the dog had been more of a nuisance than a consolation, always arousing William's anger and proving only partially successful as a rat catcher. But at last William pointed out the town of Cirencester in the distance, and Mariota felt her spirits rise. Maudesbury was only a short ride from Cirencester, so William had said. They were nearly there.

Bright visions of comfort beguiled her. Soon, instead of a snivelling

226

Bridget, she would have Joanna to spoil and coddle her, an army of serfs to unpack and lay out her beautiful clothes, a soft feather bed to lie in, delectable food to tempt back her lost appetite and a stillroom full of remedies for her aching limbs. And when she was cleansed of the dirt of the journey, with her hair properly brushed and her jewels and silks adorning her once more, then there would be Tristram. The nearer she got to Maudesbury the more the thought of Tristram occupied her mind and, when William announced that they would stop that night at the abbey in Cirencester, she was terribly disappointed.

'Can we not ride on to Maudesbury?' she asked. 'It cannot be much further.'

'Why Mariota, I thought you would be glad! All the way from London you have done nothing but beg me to stop, yet now you want to go on. Does nothing I do please you?'

'Yes, of course, William,' she said hastily. 'If you want to stop now, then by all means let us stop. I'm sorry, I just thought that as we were so near you would want to press on until we reach Maudesbury.'

'The sun is already sinking, it will be gone by the time we reach the town. We cannot ride to Maudesbury in the dark.'

'No, of course not, I'm sorry.'

William proved right as usual. By the time they rode through the Norman arch of the abbey, it was almost dark. There were already quite a number of travellers making themselves comfortable in the abbey guest house. Mariota took off her heavy cloak and tried to make herself look respectable in her travel-stained dress.

'Do you think we could unpack some of our things?' she asked William. 'I don't want to look like a peasant woman in front of the Abbot.'

'I doubt whether we will eat at the Abbot's table,' said William, 'since it's usually only knights and the nobility who are invited inside the monastery. You look well enough to eat here with the others in the guest house.'

Joanna would be allowed inside the monastery, thought Mariota with a pang which she instantly stifled as being unworthy. But the Sacristan had taken a knowing look at their well-fed horses, at the woolpacker, the armed servants, the two packhorses and the thick and voluminous travelling cloaks. Soon the sub-Prior came seeking William and invited him and his wife to his table.

Supper was an excellent meal of well-cooked meats, oats and wholemeal bread with plentiful supplies of locally produced wine and cheese. The sub-Prior was interested to know how they had fared upon the roads and seemed surprised when they had nothing more eventful to report than the incident of the miller's song. He regaled them with lurid travellers' tales of pilgrims set upon, stripped of their clothes, jewels and money, and left naked as they came into the world. Mariota did not want to listen to such horror stories and looked around her for Black Nick to set her fears at rest. But she could not see him in the refectory and supposed that he was having his supper with the ordinary travellers in the guest house. From the opposite side of the table a young monk was gazing at her admiringly and, warmed by his attention, she immediately set about capturing his heart.

'What's your name?' she asked, smiling at him.

'Gervase de Haen,' he replied with a blush. She asked him about the abbey and he told her that the Canons Regular of St Augustine were the first religious order to consist entirely of priests who lived a collegiate life. Unlike monks, they were not ascetic and did no manual work. There were no illiterate lay brothers. They fed well, had warm clothes and proper shoes to wear. They were allowed to own private property and moved at will in and out of the abbey precincts.

'It must be much more fun being an Augustinian than a Benedictine or a Carmelite,' she said.

'Perhaps.' He told her that he came from a long line of fighters but that both his parents had died of plague and he had been brought to the abbey as an orphan at a very early age. 'So I wouldn't know what it was like in any other order – though nothing could be as much fun as being a knight.'

She told him that she was on her way to stay with her sister who was married to Sir Tristram de Maudesbury and he seemed impressed. She would have liked to have heard more about Tristram but all he could tell her was that he sold his wool to the abbey.

CHAPTER 21

Next morning William for once was in no hurry to leave. Mariota found him talking to the sub-Prior.

'Short staple Cotswold wool,' the sub-Prior was saying, 'carded with teazles and treated with fuller's earth from Stroud or Dursley. It's only uncoloured broadcloth, but there's a market for it in Flanders where they do the finishing.'

'Don't you do any dyeing here?' asked William.

'Sometimes we do. There's a good supply of woad for dyeing in Wootton and Painswick, so we tend to specialise in blue cloth.'

'What about the fulling?'

'Abbot Blake built two fulling mills,' replied the sub-Prior.

Mariota delicately stifled a yawn and watched the sleepy monks scurrying into the chapel for prime, wondering whether William would want to go to Mass before leaving.

'I'd like to see some of your cloth, if I may,' said William.

'Are you a cloth merchant?' asked the sub-Prior in surprise. 'I thought you were here to buy wool.'

'I buy anything if the price is right.' They walked away towards the abbey warehouses and Mariota turned towards the chapel uncertainly. Should she attend Mass without him? She was still trying to make up her mind when she saw Black Nick come striding round the side of the chapel towards her.

'Good day, fair lady,' he called. 'I trust you slept well.'

'Not very, I'm afraid, for our lodgings were next to the chapel and I could not help hearing the monks coming and going for the night office. Are you going to Mass?'

'Not this morning. I must be on my way.'

'But you're coming with us to Maudesbury, are you not?' she said, panic seizing her.

'Alas, fair lady, I cannot, I have already delayed too long on the way and I mean to reach Bristol by tomorrow night if I can.'

'But you cannot leave us now! The countryside is crawling with vagabonds and escaped villains.'

'There's been no trouble here, the Abbot says. Besides, you have barely fifteen miles left to travel and William, two stout menservants, the woolpacker, not to mention that ferocious little dog of yours to protect you. You don't need me.'

'But I do,' she wailed, looking up at him piteously, the tears gathering on her lower lashes. 'You would not leve me now?'

'Indeed I must. I would have been gone already had I not wanted to bid you farewell.' He took her arm, guided her quickly past the chapel door and pulled her into a gap between two buttresses where they were hidden from sight. She gave a little gasp of fright and looked round fearfully.

'My husband, he will kill me if he sees us,' she whispered.

'Your husband is in the warehouse with William of Tresham and has thoughts only of cloth. Everyone else is at Mass. Are you not going to give me a farewell kiss?'

'I don't think I should,' she said, looking up at him invitingly.

'Do you not want to?' he asked. She dropped her eyes, then peeped up at him coyly from beneath her long lashes.

'Do you?' she countered.

'I always want to kiss beautiful ladies,' he replied. 'But I never force a chaste maiden against her will.' She peeped at him again, searching for some sign of the worshipful reverence she was wont to inspire in her suitors and finding nothing but amusement in his eyes. Her back was against the stone wall of the abbey church. She could hear the chanting of the monks at Mass. Black Nick towered over her, blocking out the light. Jesu, but he was ugly! Perhaps if she let him kiss her, he might be persuaded to see them safely to their journey's end. She closed her eyes and held up her face. He kissed her long and hard on her pretty little mouth, while she waited passively for him to finish.

'Now, you will surely come with us to Maudesbury,' she whispered, when at last he raised his head.

'By the Virgin, sweet mistress,' he said with a shout of laughter, 'if that's your game you'll have to do better than that.'

'I don't know what you mean.' She was genuinely puzzled.

'Don't you?' He stared down at her, an odd expression in his intense blue eyes. 'Almost, fairest of ladies, I believe you.'

She was confused and a little frightened that he might kiss her again. She put two hands against his chest and pushed him gently away. 'William,' she murmured. 'I cannot betray my husband.'

'No, of course not,' he said with a wry smile. 'William is a fortunate fellow indeed to have found such a beautiful and obedient wife. I hope he knows how to appreciate it.' He stepped aside and she slipped past him to the open courtyard. There was no sign of William or the sub-Prior, only Black Nick's ruffianly seaman waiting with the horses.

'How long will you be in Bristol?' she asked as Nick caught up with her.

'Not long, I hope.'

'Will you come back this way? Can I tell William you might ride back with us?'

'Who knows?' he said as he mounted his stallion. 'Can you say how long it will take your husband to do his business here? I cannot tell how long it will take me to do mine. Who knows what plans God has in store for any of us.'

She watched him go, feeling confused and somehow deprived. She would miss him and not only for his fighting ability. He had made a long and difficult journey bearable for her and she was more than sorry to see him go. Yet he would be a dangerous lover, she thought, with a shiver of fear. She expected her admirers to swear undying devotion not to bargain for reciprocal passion as Nick did. Of course she could not possibly love him, he was too ugly for that, and yet love was clearly what he had wanted. That was why he had refused to go with them any further. What a fool she had been! Surely she could have pretended to love him a little, just enough to persuade him to not leave them unprotected.

'Black Nick has left without us,' she informed William when he reappeared. 'Do you think we could get some of the Abbot's men to accompany us to Maudesbury?'

'No need,' said William. 'The country round here is peaceable enough and it's not far. If we hurry we should be there by noon.' She was not entirely convinced, but since she never argued with her husband she dutifully mounted Juniper and followed him.

It began to rain as they left the town and the fifteen miles dragged until they seemed like thirty. Soon the highway was nothing but a muddy lane with here and there patches of sticky clay which sucked at the horses' feet. Juniper stumbled and struggled through the mire, and at every step Mariota expected him to fall. She huddled inside her thick cloak, her hood pulled so far over her head she could barely see where she was going. For a time they rode through a large beech wood, and she clung tightly to the palfrey's mane, urging him along, her little heel drumming against his side, expecting at every moment a party of outlawed vagabonds to pounce out from behind a tree.

When at last they came out of the wood she saw rich pastureland, with pools of water lying in the fields and sodden sheep grazing on every spare patch of untilled land. The land was flat pasture, huge enclosed fields divided into strips by long, raised, roundbacked ridges, alternating with woods and wasteland. Suddenly the going became steeper and they had to climb sharply up a thickly wooded slope. The road narrowed until it was barely a path and the tree branches met above their heads. Peering anxiously through the trees, Mariota caught the gleam of water and saw far below a small, oval-shaped lake. At the top of the hill stood a church, a few wattle and log huts full of holes, and two turrets showing above the top of a high stone wall encircled by a moat.

William reined up in front of the drawbridge. 'The man in the gate-house is as deaf as a post and so old he can hardly stand,' he told Mariota. 'There's no point waiting for him to admit us.'

'You've been here before then?' she said in surprise.

'Two years ago, when I was wool buying, I spent the night here.'

He'd never mentioned it! She was used to William's secrecy, but he might at least have brought back news of Joanna.

William led the way over the drawbridge and through the open gate into the courtyard beyond. There was nobody about, only a few scrawny hens busy scratching for food in the mud. Mariota looked about her curiously. Round the outer courtyard were stables, a byre, a falcon mews. William was already disappearing through an arch in the centre of the stables and she followed him into the inner court beyond. She gazed with a strange mixture of emotion at a two-storeyed building with a turret at either end and creeper climbing up its stonework like an invading army. So this was Maudesbury, this was the manor over which she might, had things been different, been mistress. It looked empty and forlorn. She did not know what she had expected but somehow she was disappointed. Where were the hard-working serfs, the pageboys, the steward – all the people who might be expected to be part of a knight's household?

'Come, Mariota, let me help you down.'

'Shouldn't we wait until someone comes?' she said uncertainly. 'We can't just walk in surely?'

'Well. I'm certainly not waiting outside in this rain.' He lifted her out of the saddle.

Mariota looked at their party standing about in the courtyard: the muddied packhorses, heads hanging dejectedly, the woolpacker still sitting on his amiable rouncy, unperturbed as always, the two manser-vants looking at William and waiting for their instructions, and Bridget, sneezing and trying to keep hold of the little dog who was yapping and wriggling determinedly. Suddenly Mariota remembered why she had brought the troublesome creature all this way. She might not be wearing her best gown, her cloak might be soaked and covered with mud, but she could at least make her entrance carrying her lit-tle dog, symbol of her fashionable London life. She took the dog from Bridget and followed William into the house.

The hall was cold, dark and empty save for two large shaggy-haired hounds, who bounded baying at her across the stone floor. Mariota gave a gasp of dismay and shrank back against the wall.

'They'll leave you alone if you put that ridiculous dog down,' said William fiercely.

'I can't, they'll kill him!' she cried. 'Do something, William.'

But William just pursed his lips and looked away. At the dais end of the hall, a flight of stone steps wound out of sight, round the corner of which a woman suddenly appeared with a lighted taper in her hand. She was tall and thin, dressed in a style which Mariota guessed must once have been fashionable about the middle of the last King's reign. The woman began lighting the tapers on the walls, paying no attention to the dogs who were standing in front of Mariota, still baying loudly.

'My lady, could you call your dogs off?' shouted William above the din.

'You can put your dog down, they won't hurt him,' she said with no more than a cursory glance at Mariota. Terrified, Mariota obeyed.

Slowly and meticulously the lady continued with her taper lighting, while the two wolfhounds chased Mariota's little dog around the hall until he found a temporary hiding place behind a trestle table leaning against the wall. Mariota stared around her in dismay. Upon the whitewashed stone walls hung a number of rusty weapons and the heads of a great variety of wild animals all grinning at her with bared teeth. The windows, merest slits no wider than a crossbow's bolt, let in the cold air but little light. The elegant lady, having at last finished lighting all the candles, was looking at William enquiringly and it was clear she did not recognise him.

'It's William Gryffard,' he explained, 'and this is my wife, Mariota, sister of Lady de Maudesbury.'

'I don't know where Joanna is, out in the village, I expect, trying to get the serfs to come and do their boon work, although I've told her to leave it to the bailiff. Joanna's too soft with them. It's hard enough getting the work out of them as it is. Spoiling them just makes them lazier.' She looked at the half-burnt logs lying cold in the hearth and sighed. 'I'll see if I can find someone to do something to that fire,' she said and disappeared through an arch at the far end of the hall. No word of welcome, no curiosity about where they had come from or how long they meant to stay.

'Who is she?' Mariota asked in a whisper.

'She's the Lady Isabel, Sir Tristram's mother,' he replied.

'She's not very friendly, is she?'

'She's nobly born,' said William as if that excused everything.

'She hasn't got a very good memory, she didn't seem to remember having ever seen you before.'

'Lady Isabel knows how to behave,' William retorted. 'You would do well, while you are here, Mariota, to study her in all things.'

Mariota stared round at the vast, forbidding hall, at the two large wolfhounds snuffling curiously at her terrified little dog still quivering behind the trestle, at the pools of water dripping off her sodden travelling cloak and soaking the rushes at her feet, at William standing patiently waiting.

'Yes, William,' she said meekly.

Soon Lady Isabel returned, driving before her a thin boy who threw himself on his knees by the hearth and proceeded to try and rekindle the dead logs. His mistress watched him, clearly more interested in the making of the fire than in her visitors. Mariota was beginning to wonder if they were to be left to wait in this chilly fortress of a hall for ever, when suddenly the clatter of hooves sounded in the courtyard outside. The two huge dogs raised their heads and immediately ran whining to the door. Lady Isabel looked up quickly, her pale, expressionless face suddenly transformed by an eager joy which was almost frightening in its intensity. Mariota heard spurs clashing against stone and her heart began to beat faster. There was a loud oath followed immediately by an agonised yelp as one of the dogs came flying back into the hall with his tail between his legs.

Sir Tristram de Maudesbury, clad in chain mail and carrying a falcon on his fist, came striding into the room. He paused on the threshold and stared at Mariota in amazement, while she held her breath, wishing she had removed her cloak, wondering if there was mud on her face, longing for a piece of polished steel to seek assurance from her reflection.

'This is William Gryffard and Joanna's sister, his wife,' the cool, quiet voice of Lady Isabel explained. Mariota looked at her feet shyly.

'Yes indeed,' Tristram said. 'I remember Joanna's sister very well.' He crossed the hall, spurs jingling, and came to stand at her side. She peeped at him then, a quick upward glance, and was relieved to see that he was gazing intently down into her face with every appearance of delight.

'I'm sorry if we've arrived at an inconvenient moment,' William's flat, quiet voice broke the spell.

'Inconvenient! How could any visit of yours be inconvenient?' replied Tristram and Mariota, stealing another shy glance at him, knew herself to be welcome at last. 'Are you hungry? Here, let me take off your wet cloak.' Thrusting the falcon at a squire who had followed him into the hall, Tristram unfastened her cloak and threw it on the floor. She smiled at him gratefully, and his eyes sweeping over her slender form told her all she needed to know.

'My wife is tired, travelling wearies her. I expect she would like to lie down.' Now, when it no longer mattered, when she was basking in the warmth of admiration from the one man she had ever really wanted, now William showed concern for her wellbeing!

'Of course she shall have everything she wants,' said Tristram. 'Mother, where's Joanna?'

'I don't know. I expect she's in the village,' replied Lady Isabel.

'Well, send for her! And you,' he said cuffing the housecarl over the head impatiently, 'if you can't make a better fire than that, go and fetch some wine and some bread.'

The boy disappeared at a run and Tristram strode after him to where three arches guarded the entrance to the hall. He shouted and cursed into each one alternately, to no avail. The squire was despatched to see to the woolpacker and the servants outside. Lady Isabel drifted away, presumably in search of Joanna, and William, bending over the fire, succeeded in coaxing it into life. Mariota sat down on a stool by the fire and held out one small foot to the flame. The wolfhounds resumed their persecution of her little dog.

'Oh, my poor dog,' Mariota cried, holding out her arms. 'Will you not save him for me?'

Tristram strode over to where his hounds had cornered the intruder and aimed a savage kick in their general direction. They dodged him with the skill of much practice and watched resentfully while he scooped up their victim from his hiding place.

'There, he's none the worse,' he said depositing a frantically wriggling bundle in Mariota's lap.

'Poor, poor Tristram,' she crooned, as she held the dog against her breast and stroked him gently.

'Tristram?' he queried, staring at her rather hard.

'Yes, Tristram,' she said, dropping a light kiss on the dog's head. 'I named him after you.' She looked up at him coyly and it was then that she caught sight of Joanna standing staring at her from the doorway. Joanna, in a tight russet sheath like Lady Isabel's, and a belt worn low on her slender hips, with her brow plucked and her thick bright hair braided and coiled round her head like a crown, looking so slender and poised, so different from the old scapegoat Joanna she'd always taken for granted. Why, she was almost a beauty! Mariota stared at her half-sister, consternation and surprise rendering her speechless. It was not at all as she had expected. Joanna did not rush across the hall to throw herself into her arms as once she would have done. She just stood staring, as cool and lifeless as an alabaster saint, and about as welcoming.

'Joanna, where have you been?' demanded Tristram. 'Your sister is here, come to visit you at last, and there is no welcome for her. Where are all the housecarls? Why is there no fire? What sort of welcome is this?'

'Of course... I didn't expect... You've taken us so much by surprise,' Joanna stammered, coming forward slowly. Mariota jumped up but still Joanna did not embrace her. She lent forward, kissed the air in the general direction of her sister's cheek and then shot a quick, frightened glance at her husband.

'Well, don't just stand there,' Tristram snapped. 'Mariota's tired from the journey and wants to lie down. Get a chamber prepared for her, find some serfs to unload the packhorses. Make her comfortable, Joanna.'

'Yes, of course, I'm sorry. It's just that...' Joanna shot another agonised glance at her husband and, receiving no encouragement, hurried away. He doesn't love her, thought Mariota with relief, and once more sank down upon her stool.

The housecarl returned bearing wine and Tristram's squire offered it to Mariota on bended knee. She sipped it gingerly, aware that it was vinegary and thin but happy in the knowledge that she was the centre of attention at last. William had gone to supervise the unloading of the packhorses and Lady Isabel had not returned. The squire filled Tristram's goblet and withdrew to the shadows while Tristram just stood staring down at Mariota as if in a trance. She would have been content to sit there indefinitely, enjoying his bewildered silence, knowing that the mere sight of her had reduced him to helplessness, but all too soon Joanna returned to say that the chamber was ready. Gracefully Mariota rose from her stool, favoured Tristram with one of her secret little smiles and followed Joanna demurely out of the hall.

The chamber was at the top of the east tower. It was roomy enough but bare. A bed with faded bedhangings, a stool and an oak coffer were its only furnishings. Mariota sat upon the bed caressing her little dog and watched as one by one all the possessions William had deemed necessary for this visit were carried in: the arras cloths, the polished steel mirror, the pillows of old scarlet taffeta with pillowcases worked in drawn-thread work and cross-stitch, the leather box in which she kept her rings, and the little coffer, containing her clothes, carved all round in ivory, which came from Avignon. Seeing the bare chamber gradually transformed into something resembling the luxury she was accustomed to at home gave Mariota a feeling of virtue well-rewarded. She had obeyed Father and married William and all these things were her just rewards.

'It looks better, Joanna, don't you think?' she said when at last everything was in place. 'William likes it all to be right. He says that comfort has to be worked at like everything else.'

'Tristram isn't interested in comfort. He's interested in war and war is never comfortable,' said Joanna.

'All the more reason for making him comfortable at home,' said Mariota.

'Oh, Tristram's almost never at home,' Joanna replied. 'He's only at Maudesbury now to fit out a lance for the Scottish wars. The Duke of Lancaster leaves for Scotland at the beginning of May and expects his retainers in London by Pentecost.'

'Pentecost!' exclaimed Mariota. 'Why, that's in no time at all.'

'No time,' agreed Joanna. 'Soon Tristram will be gone and then it will be very quiet here on the manor. I'm glad you came, Mariota, to keep me company.'

Mariota got up off the bed and began to pace restlessly round the chamber. It was not at all what she had in mind, to be alone on this spartan manor without male attention. Bridget was unpacking her coffer, shaking out gowns and kirtles and surcoats and laying them carefully on the bed. Mariota looked at the fine velvets, the brilliant silks, the lavish fur trimmings. She had not brought them all this way just to impress the Lady Isabel and Joanna. She began to feel dispirited, but then she remembered the look of wonder in Tristram's eyes and her vanity told her not to despair. Tristram was here, was he not, even now eagerly awaiting her return to the hall? She had a few days before he was due to leave. Could she keep him from his duty to the Duke, could she so entrance him that he would be unable to leave? It would be fun to try.

Swiftly Mariota struggled out of her warm surcoat, her eyes raking the cornucopia on the bed. What should she wear to begin her siege? The royal blue velvet with miniver trimming, that would show off her beauty without leaving her delicate skin blotched and goosepimpled from the cold. What headdress? Or should she follow Joanna's lead and leave her pale gold hair to proclaim its own glory? Would it bear comparison? She looked at Joanna waiting impassively by the bed, apparently unimpressed, and felt the old peculiar combination of pity mingled with exasperation which had always been part of her feelings towards her half-sister. What was Joanna doing married to a man like Tristram? How had she managed it? She had certainly changed, turned herself into a perfect copy of the Lady Isabel, but what had she got? A knight who was never at home. Joanna always made a mess of everything she did. She, Mariota, would show her what a mistake she had made in running off with someone else's lover.

CHAPTER 22

Joanna stood on the village green, holding the stirrup cup and shivering in the chill April dawn. Never did she think that she would be glad to see Tristram ride away from Maudesbury, but now she gave thanks to God from the bottom of her heart.

The last week had been torture ever since she had walked into the hall and seen her husband's expression as he stared down into Mariota's lovely face. It was the moment Joanna had been dreading from the day of her marriage, the moment when Tristram and Mariota should meet again. It had haunted her dreams so often she should have been more prepared for it, but the reality had far outstripped her worst imagining. It was then that she realised the futility of her struggle to win his love. Everything she had endured during the four years of her marriage, the self-abasement, the indignities suffered, the hurt borne silently, the terrible loneliness, the suppression of her will and her true nature in a superhuman effort to please — all had been wasted. Tristram did not love her, could not love her; he was for ever bound in love to Mariota.

Helplessly she had watched Mariota flirting with Tristram, deploying all her familiar tricks — the fluttering eyelashes, the downcast looks, the little sighs, the averted head to show the perfect profile, the grey eyes brimming with unspilt tears. She had seen Tristram lose interest in his preparations for war and become utterly fascinated. Terrified and at the same time deeply envious of Mariota's ability to make Tristram her slave, Joanna became haunted by the fear that, when the moment came, he would find it impossible to leave. That was when she had gone to William.

'Tristram is finding it very hard to get everything he needs to go to war,' she'd said.

'I thought Tristram's sword was a match for anyone's,' William replied.

'Well yes, of course, but other knights bring archers and foot sol-

238

diers with them and never ride their war horses except in battle. It's so difficult for Tristram with just the one manor; everything that can be squeezed out of it he takes, but I know that it is a constant source of shame to him that he's not able to bring with him the numbers of men and horses other knights, with more than one manor, can provide.'

'I see.'

He wasn't making it very easy for her. How much did William suspect? Sometimes she thought that with every glance, every word, every deed Tristram and Mariota betrayed themselves, but William had seemed to notice nothing. Perhaps it was only because she herself was so sensitive to the lovers that their every act seemed to proclaim their secret. Perhaps it was because William did not care.

'What Tristram really wants,' she said, determined, having started, to see it through, ' is a "lance" — the basic tactical unit of an army.'

'Then we must give Tristram what he wants,' William had replied with the curl of the lips which was his apology for a smile.

How it had been done Joanna did not know, but for the last few days the manor had been seething with bustle and activity — the blacksmith's anvil had rung day and night as weapons were sharpened, horses shod and arrow heads made. The walls of the hall were denuded of their decoration as armour was taken down to have every trace of rust removed, to be polished and repaired. Tristram had made several journeys to Cirencester and elsewhere, scouring the countryside for horses, and William instead of leaving immediately on his own business had stayed behind at the manor to help with all the preparations.

This morning, long before the sun had risen, the church bell had rung to call the villagers to bid Godspeed to their manor lord. Joanna gripped the stirrup cup tightly and stared at the men and horses trampling the grass that the peasants, goats and geese were wont to graze, wondering whether she had been right to appeal to William. Right or wrong Tristram was leaving today, and with the sort of retinue that any knight could be proud of. In the end that had proved a stronger temptation to Tristram than all Mariota's armoury of enticement.

The serfs standing round the edges of the green raised a ragged cheer and Joanna saw Tristram come striding through the gatehouse. She let out her breath in a long, slow sigh; not until now had she dared believe that she had won. He was dressed in gleaming armour, on his head the padded leather arming cap, and over his chain-mail hauberk a tight-fitting shirt embroidered with his arms. It was Mariota who had lovingly mended the linen jupon, with many sighs and pretty poutings which Joanna had pretended not to notice. Watching him, Joanna felt relief tinged with shame. Last night, long after she had retired to bed, Tristram had come to their chamber stinking of wine.

239

He had thrown himself upon her, pulling her roughly to him, wrestling with her breasts, bruising her mouth with brutal kisses. She would not have minded the physical pain if she had thought for one moment that he wanted to make love to her. But she guessed that he was only using her to assuage his longing for Mariota, that when he crushed her lips so fiercely, it was Mariota's little rosebud mouth he sought to ravish, that when he seized her breasts, it was the memory of Mariota's small twin mounds of perfection he was trying to destroy and that when he cruelly parted her legs and thrust into her relentlessly, it was his raging desire for Mariota he was trying to kill. Even so, she had tried to please him; she ignored the pain and arched her back to take him deeper inside her, had tried to show her love for him by answering his desperate demands with passion of her own. He came to her bed little enough and only when he was drunk. It was one of her deepest humiliations, that her husband, whose touch she craved so desperately, only laid hand on her to hurt her and could not bring himself to lie with her except when drugged with wine.

She watched him as he walked across the drawbridge. How glorious he looked in his armour, so strong and invincible. He turned when he reached the foot of the drawbridge to look up at the east tower where the guest chamber was. Joanna, too, looked up at the tower and caught the flutter of a white hand from the window below the battlements. He stood staring back at the tower until joined by William dressed in a long travelling cloak and soft velvet cap pulled well down over his ears. William was leaving today also. He and the woolpacker and one of the menservants were to ride with Tristram as far as Cirencester. With his hunched shoulders and his fleshy, pallid face, he cut a poor figure beside Tristram and for a moment Joanna's heart went out to Mariota probably even now weeping in her chamber. She did not blame her for wanting Tristram. But Mariota was lucky, she told herself, at least she had the knowledge that Tristram loved her. If I had that, she thought sadly, as William came to take his leave, I could bear almost anything.

'Godspeed, William,' she said, proferring the cup. 'May God keep you and bring you safe back to us soon.'

'Aren't you going to ask for His blessing on my endeavours?' he said.

'You always prosper, William.'

'Not without God's grace,' he said as he drank. 'I know I leave Mariota in safe hands and that you will deal much better together when we are gone.' She glanced at him startled and he smiled his knowing smile. So he had noticed something.

For a moment Joanna felt a chill hand on her heart. She remembered how her father had nearly been ruined when he had overstretched himself, thanks to William, and now here was Tristram with the lance he had always coveted. How much money had he finally borrowed from William, she wondered, and how would he pay it back if he did not manage to capture some rich Scottish prisoners?

William was watching her. She returned his gaze coolly enough, though there was something about his darting eyes which always made her feel uncomfortable. She reminded herself that her father had brought his troubles upon himself and that it was William who had come to his rescue when the cargo had been lost.

'Here's Father Luke,' William said, 'coming to bless us, no doubt. I should be careful of that man if I were you, Joanna. I wouldn't be surprised if he hasn't been listening too much to Wycliffe's seditious talk.'

'He's a good man,' she said. 'The villagers love him and he's the only one that can do anything with the serfs when Tristram is away.'

'That's just what I mean, he has too much influence over the people on the manor,' replied William. 'The bailiff is the one that they should answer to, not the priest.'

'Well, of course they do what the bailiff tells them, most of the time,' Joanna put in hurriedly.

'That painting in the church, the one of Christ of the Trades, when did that appear? That wasn't here the last time I came.'

Jesu! but he missed nothing, she thought. 'I don't know, sometime since Christmas, I think. Father Luke organised the people in the village to paint it. They each put in their particular craft. They're rather proud of it.'

'Don't you see the significance?'

'I see that he cares enough to want to beautify Christ's church. There's no harm in that, and in its simplicity I think it's rather fine.'

'Christ as a craftsman? A labourer? It's dangerous, Joanna, all part of the stirrings for freedom that are causing trouble up and down the country.'

'Father Luke knows nothing of Wycliffe,' she said, watching the priest walking slowly towards them from the church, pausing to talk to the villagers making way for him. 'What would a man, poor and ill-educated such as he, know of Wycliffe? Why, he's little better than a peasant himself, which is why he understands them so well.' William's watchful eyes never left her face, and she had the uncomfortable feeling that he was sifting everything she said, storing it up in his capacious memory in case it should be useful one day. What was it about him that always made her talk too much, tell him things that it was unnecessary for him to know? He would be a merciless adversary, she thought with a sudden pang of fear, and then hastily pushed the thought away. He was family, wasn't he? He had saved them once from ruin and under his protection Father was doing very well, so Mariota had said.

With a heart full of pride and love, Joanna watched Tristram as he knelt on the ground to receive the priest's blessing and added her own fervant invocations to St George and the Blessed Mother for his safe return from the wars. William and the rest of the company followed suit. Then Tristram climbed the mounting block and swung easily into the palfrey's saddle. Joanna went to stand by him and held out the cup. He took it from her and drank. 'God keep you, Joanna,' he said, looking over her head at the window in the east tower.

'And you, my lord and husband,' she returned, smiling up at him, though her heart beat painfully. He was going into battle and this time through her own conniving. Would God punish her? 'Guard him well, Godfrey,' she said, her dazzling smile moving to his squire. She must not show her fears in front of Tristram. He hated long faces around him.

Godfrey bowed expressionlessly as Joanna handed him the cup, and she went on smiling at him, trying to smother her feeling of dislike for this pretty boy who had replaced Robin. Robin had been such a comfort when she had first come to Maudesbury. If it had not been for Robin she did not think she would have survived. But Robin had been knighted after the Duke's disastrous French campaign in the second year of King Richard's reign, and was serving with Sir Robert Knollys she knew not where.

The brief ceremony over, Tristram urged the palfrey forward. His eyes were shining and she wondered if he was halfway to forgetting Mariota already. How she envied him, riding away to excitement and danger. Soon he would be with the Duke once more, among fighting men, surrounded by knights and all the glittering panoply of a great army on the move. How many times had she watched him ride away, hopes high, expecting to bring back booty and ransom money from a successful compaign only to return empty-handed.

It was not his fault, of course, she knew that. Nor even the fault of the great Duke of Lancaster. It was the fault of his enemies. They were too afraid of the English to fight. Pray God this time it would be different. If it wasn't, then the manor would just have to make more from the woolclip, that was all. Somehow they would manage, she and Lady Isabel, if they were careful and if the sheep were well enough cared for, and if the serfs could be made to work harder. She would ask Father Luke to help her. The bailiff was useless. As soon as Tristram rode away he would be at the ale butt and they would get little sense out of him for weeks. But Father Luke was a shepherd's son. He understood sheep and he understood the serfs.

Tristram led his lance out of the village. Behind him a young lad was struggling with Orion. The old stallion, highly excited to be once again dressed in the colourful caparison, the high-fronted saddle and all the trappings of war, was prancing and sidling, snorting at the angry geese that had been driven to seek sanctuary by the edge of the moat, and lunging at the palfrey's rump with laid-back ears and bared teeth, showing his superiority. Behind him came Godfrey whose job it was to carry Tristram's lance and act as his valet while learning the art of soldiering. He also carried an iron half-lance, which he had once told Joanna was used to slit the throat of any prisoner refusing ramsom. Godfrey had a lust for blood which Joanna hated.

Behind the squire rode the six mounted archers, each wearing a leather baldric across his chest to carry the long quiver full of arrows, and each clasping a deadly longbow. They were followed by three foot soldiers with a variety of pack animals bringing up the rear, including a spirited little mare for Tristram's personal provisions. It was a proud day for the manor, to be sending such a numerous company to war, and a proud day for Tristram too. Dear God keep him safe from harm and bring him back to me triumphant, prayed Joanna watching the costly lance follow Tristram slowly out of sight behind the church.

The space in front of the drawbridge now was desolate and empty. The villagers had departed to work either in home or field. The geese were wandering over the trampled grass reclaiming their territory. The sun was rising, bringing promise of a fine spring morning. Joanna felt exhausted and bereft. She longed to turn and run into the house, to let loose her grief in the privacy of her own chamber, but the priest was coming towards her. She braced herself and gave him her brightest smile.

'Sir Tristram leaves the manor the poorer for his going,' said Father Luke.

'Indeed, we shall all miss him sorely,' she replied calmly.

'Those who are left will have to work doubly hard to make up for all those who have gone with him.'

'Yes indeed,' she smiled at him encouragingly. 'I hope you'll help me to see that everyone does his boon work. I want a record woolclip this year.'

'Young Bill the shepherd can't do his boon work, he's dead,' said the priest flatly. She stared at him blankly. A shepherd dead, that was a pity. 'He left a widow and four young children under seven and only one of them a boy to work their land.' He was mopping his perspiring face with a corner of his worn, claret-coloured gown and looking at her hopefully.

'That's no reason why I should be expected to feed them,' she said sternly, more sternly than she meant for he made her feel guilty. Tristram had barely been gone a paternoster time and already the priest was trying to take advantage.

Father Luke said nothing, just stared at her, disappointment replacing the simple trust on his face like a cloud blotting out the sun.

'If we made exceptions, everyone would soon produce a hard-luck story, and then what would we live on?' Joanna felt forced to justify herself.

'But when your best beast is also your only cow and it's gone to pay the heriot . . .' He sighed. 'It's hard to know how they will manage.'

'You surely don't think they shouldn't pay heriot!'

He coughed apologetically. 'No, my lady, of course I know that when a tenant dies, if the family are to be allowed to stay, they must forfeit their best beast to the lord of the manor as is his right.'

'There's nothing more to be said then.' She turned away quickly, but he caught at her cloak.

'My lady, you have a kind heart, I know it. I can remember once when you first came here, you gave me some money to say Masses for a poor old man's soul, who had no kin to mourn him.'

'If I did then I've forgotten,' she said, staring disdainfully down at his restraining hand. The fingers were swollen and engrained with dirt from years of manual labour.

'I have not forgotten,' he said, releasing her. 'A poor man's soul may rest with God thanks to your loving pity.'

She did not want to be reminded and sought refuge in the dignity of her position. 'It is time for Mass — I will attend it.'

'Just a little bread and some milk — they miss their cow, you see.' It was not much to ask, but Tristram was always telling her not to spoil them.

'Why don't you speak to the bailiff?' she said. It was quite easy really, with practice she had grown used to repressing all feeling of sympathy for the serfs. Tristram would have been proud of her.

The priest was staring at her coldly now. Disgust, disappointment, even contempt flickered in his eyes. She looked away quickly and saw Lady Isabel still standing at the foot of the drawbridge. She was clinging to the bridge rail with one hand, shading her eyes with the other, staring out across the empty green. Her face was expressionless, and her body sagged as if drained of all life. Tristram was the centre of Lady Isabel's universe, the meaning of her very existence. When he went away, it was as if he took her with him, leaving nothing but an empty shell. We both of us suffer so for loving him, thought Joanna sadly, it's such a pity we cannot help each other more.

She walked over and took Lady Isabel gently by the hand. 'It's almost prime. Father Luke is going to say Mass,' she said. 'Come, we'll light a candle to the Virgin for Tristram's safe return.'

Lady Isabel stared at Joanna blankly, looking through her as if she wasn't there. But Joanna was used to being ignored by Tristram's mother. She drew the cold hand through her arm and led her unprotesting towards the little church, wishing she could get closer to the older woman. But Lady Isabel had never forgiven Joanna for mar-

244

rying her son without a dowry, and no matter how hard Joanna tried to atone, how hard she worked to get more out of the manor, how much she tried to please her, the Lady Isabel remained cool and aloof.

They walked into the church side by side and Joanna was overwhelmed with a sense of utter hopelessness. The serfs she was not allowed to help, and this woman who shared her hopes and fears for the manor, for Tristram, and for whom she could have done so much, wanted nothing from her. Gazing around the little church, she tried to find consolation and inspiration from the pictures on its walls. All she saw was Dives, the rich man with the beggar at his gate, and it only reminded her of the starving family of the dead shepherd. She turned to look at the crude painting on the wall of Christ naked, lacerated and bleeding, with a carpenter's tools haloed round his head. Absently she studied the mallet, hammer, knife, axe, pincers, horn and wheel. Now that William had pointed it out, perhaps it was an odd form of embellishment to find on a church wall. Was Father Luke trying to stir up trouble among the serfs? She could not believe it. Father Luke might be poor, his speech that of the rough country peasants, and his learning closer to nature than to the Church's liturgy, yet he was in his own way a man of God with a stronger faith than many an educated churchman and certainly than any of the monks at the abbey. William surely was wrong. She prayed that he was wrong. Tristram would be away a long time and if she was to get the demesne lands planted, let alone harvested and its sheep sheared and the wool sold with the few able-bodied men left at her disposal, she would need the priest's full support. Perhaps it would do no harm to give Bill's family a little milk after all.

With Tristram gone Joanna felt terribly depressed. She missed the way he strode through the hall with his hounds or his hawk, the sound of steel ringing on steel as he and his squire fought their daily practise duels or battled at the quintain in the tilting-yard together, his shouting and cursing, even his demanding criticisms and cruel practical jokes. And their dinner table missed the game he killed in the woods and neighbouring forests. Without his presence, the manor was a desolate, silent tomb. For in truth, as Joanna had very soon discovered when she first arrived, the manor had nothing save Tristram to recommend it.

It was a small manor, with a few freehold tenants in various tenures and two score customary tenants, the serfs, who gave their services as labourers on the demesne by way of rent. Tristram had inherited the manor from his father but its resources hardly supported them and he supplemented his income by his retaining fees from the Duke of Lancaster. The manor house was old and crumbling but Tristram did not care. He was seldom at home and when he was, his main concern was to squeeze as much out of the manor as he could to finance his campaigning. Under Lady Isabel's careful and frugal management, the manor was able just about to fulfil his needs, but there was nothing left over for luxuries.

With Tristram's departure Lady Isabel withdrew to her chamber and Joanna let her be, understanding only too well her wish to be alone with her grief. It was what she longed to do herself. But she dare not. There was too much to be done. The spring sowing was still not finished, many of the sheep were lambing and needed constant care, which they were unlikely to receive with two shepherds gone to the wars with the manor lord, and one dead. The drunken bailiff would not notice if Tristram's sheep were the ones that were neglected. The house serfs too had to be supervised, food found for all, herbs planted for the stillroom, and all the while, Joanna was conscious of Mariota, beautifully dressed in costly silk, with her jewels and her elaborate headdresses, loitering in the hall or haunting Joanna's own chamber, her pouting little mouth turned down, wanting to talk, needing attention, craving company, miserable without Tristram.

Mariota's unhappiness was the price Joanna had known she would have to pay for getting Tristram away. Every time she looked at Mariota she felt silently accused. She would like to have been noble and self-sacrificing, have sat back and let Mariota and Tristram love each other as they were clearly meant to do, but she could not. She was a slave to her unrequited passion for Tristram, as unable to break free from his power over her as any of the serfs on his manor. Her guilt made her want to make up to Mariota for the misery she had caused, but she did not know how.

About a week after Tristram's departure, Joanna entered the hall after a morning's work which had started at dawn to find Mariota sitting hunched in front of the fire cradling her little dog in her lap. 'Poor little Tristram's shivering,' she said. The hall was dark and cheerless. A heavy spring shower was drumming on the roof, seeping through in various places and splashing onto the rushes on the floor. How Joanna had come to hate that sound of dripping water! Soon the rushes would be sodden and begin to smell. They would have to be cleared away once the rain was over and she would have to tell someone to do it, because no one would think of doing it for themselves.

'Blessed Mother, his coat's soaking wet!' Mariota jumped up and held the wriggling creature out in front of her accusingly. 'He hates the wet, as do I. You ought to get something done about that roof, you know.'

'I do, frequently. But as soon as the tyler mends one hole, another one appears,' Joanna replied wearily.

'Well, if you can't mend the roof, why don't you brighten the hall up? It's so dark and dismal. Why don't you have some wall paintings done? William brought a very clever artist back from Genoa for our new house — our wall paintings are the talk of London. Margaret Philpot was green with envy.'

Margaret Philpot! With a sharp pang of longing Joanna thought of the comfort and gaiety of Philpot's Inn, of the songs she and Margaret used to sing together. There was no music at Maudesbury and at times her soul craved it.

'I don't think Lady Isabel would want wall paintings. She likes to keep the house exactly as it was in her husband's time. I think she's afraid to change.'

'And I think she's lonely,' Mariota persisted. 'It's company she lacks. You're always so busy, Joanna.'

'To tell you the truth, I'm worried about Lady Isabel,' said Joanna, ignoring the plaintive plea.

'Why, what ails her? It's not the sweating sickness is it?' asked Mariota alarmed.

'No, no, nothing like that. In fact she doesn't appear ill at all. She came back from Mass the morning Tristram left and took to her bed. That in itself is not unusual when Tristram leaves, but she's lain there ever since. I've never know her mourn his departure like this before. It's as if she's given up.'

'Would you like me to go and sit with her for a while?'

'She has Martha with her,' said Joanna, with a shake of the head. Martha was a small shrivelled stick of skin and bone who had looked after Lady Isabel since the day she was born and answered to no one else. Joanna did not think a visit from Mariota would go down well with Martha. 'She should be purged or bled, I daresay. I ought to go to Cirencester. Get one of the monks from the abbey to come and look at her.'

'I'd like that,' said Mariota, brightening immediately.

'Are you sure you can face the journey, Mariota?' Joanna asked in surprise. 'I'm afraid we can't take any men from the fields, they're far too busy with the spring sowing.'

'We can take the manservant William left behind to look after me,' said Mariota. 'And the bailiff — surely he's not too busy?'

'If he's not drunk,' replied Joanna, suppressing a smile. Mariota seemed far less frightened of being set upon by brigands when no susceptible males were present, but at least here was an opportunity of doing something which might please her.

'If you like we could go tomorrow,' Joanna offered. 'It's market day.'

Mariota was soon happily planning what she wanted to buy in the market and Joanna went off to see what there was for dinner, relieved.

CHAPTER 23

Joanna enjoyed the ride to Cirencester. It was three months since she had left the manor and she could not help feeling a sense of freedom as for a while all care was left behind. The sun shone warm on her face, the trees were beginning to put on fresh new green and Mariota showed more interest than alarm in the countryside around her.

'Who lives there?' she asked, pointing to a small castle in the far distance, rising out of the morning mist and dominating the flat lands around it.

'Sir Edmund de Cher,' replied Joanna. 'He's an invalid, so they say. He's been to all the holiest places, even the Holy Sepulchre in Jerusalem, but nothing does any good.'

'Don't you ever visit him? He must be lonely.'

'Tristram will not permit it,' replied Joanna. 'It's something to do with Sir Edmund's younger brother. They both went to fight with the Black Prince, years ago, against Don Pedro the Cruel of Castile. Sir Edmund sustained the wounds from which he's never recovered and the younger brother was never heard of again. There were rumours that he was captured and broke his parole, escaped without paying ransom. Tristram won't talk of it. All I know is that he won't allow the name de Cher to be spoken at Maudesbury.'

'Well, if the family's dishonoured, of course you cannot go there.'

Joanna said nothing, unwilling to admit to Mariota that it was one of the many disappointments of her life at Maudesbury that she was not allowed to know their nearest neighbours. Their tragic story intrigued her and she longed to know more. And when Tristram's cruelty made her deams of him a mockery, it was to her mysterious neighbours that she escaped in her mind. She had whiled away many a lonely hour weaving her own embellishments to their story, in which both brothers, but particularly the younger one, became endowed with heroic qualities far beyond mortal man. The de Chers, even if it was only in Joanna's imagination, provided an escape from the harsh reality of her life at Maudesbury.

248

Cirencester was a partly walled market town held in villeinage on a great ecclesiastical estate, ever since the day when King Richard I for the sake of his soul and that of the Queen had made it over to the Austin Abbot of St Mary's. Built on the site of an old Roman fortress where four roads met – the Fosse, the Icknield Way, Ermin Street and Ackman Street – it attracted woolmen, cloth merchants, clerics, men of God and men of money, in pursuit of Cotswold wool. Necessities such as salt and luxuries such as silk, imported into the port of Bristol, passed through the town. The abbey dominated the town and a higgledy piggledy mass of little wooden houses huddled beneath its protective walls like chickens sheltering under their mother's wing.

It was still quite early when the party from Maudesbury arrived in the town. Leaving their horses with the manservant, Joanna and Mariota went straight to the marketplace, an open rectangle about the size of a jousting arena which on market days was completely filled by a jumble of stalls and pens. Farmers from the surrounding countryside were selling their animals, their butter, bacon, honey and milk, fishermen had salmon, eels and lampreys fresh from the River Severn, purveyors of every kind had set up their stalls in front of the tightly packed houses overlooking the square. The noise was deafening as stallholders tried to shout each other down and at the same time make themselves heard above the lowing, bleating, squawking or snorting of the various animals waiting in their pens to be sold or slaughtered. The air was laden with conflicting aromas, the smell of hot pies and roasting meats from the cookshops mingling with incense and spices and animal dung.

Mariota was immediately absorbed, stopping at each stall to study its wares, frowning with delighted concentration, like a child faced with a basket of sweetmeats. The choice was infinite. There were clogs in neat rows, iron nails heaped in piles, linen lying as smooth and unmarked as fresh fallen snow, rich silks hanging in a rainbow of colour, piles of hemp coiled like sleeping snakes and blocks of wood of such shapes and sizes as to satisfy any carpenter.

Joanna followed in Mariota's wake. Freed from any compulsion to buy from her lack of the wherewithal to do so, she was content just to browse and feast her senses. Gazing about her idly, her attention was caught by a huge, golden carriage parked beside the stone cross at the head of the marketplace. It had solid beams resting on heavy iron axles, and above this framework an archway rounded like a tunnel. The wheels were carved and their spokes widened near the gilt hoop beams. Square windows pierced the sides, hung with silk curtains. Four horses, harnessed one in front of the other, rested patiently, while a postilion mounted on the second horse and armed with a short-handled whip of many thongs waited with them. She gazed at it fascinated, trying to catch a glimpse of its occupants through the silk-screened windows and wondering who it belonged to.

Mariota was studying the silks at a nearby stall and the silk seller, sensing a serious buyer, unravelled a bolt and flung the length of it over her where it hung in a shimmering cascade of brilliant green. Joanna caught her breath. I could wear that, she thought, surprised by an unaccustomed stab of acquisitiveness. It was the colour of emeralds, jewel-bright with a myriad lights dancing in the sunshine as it lay draped across Mariota's shoulders.

'No, no, no, I cannot permit you,' said a deep voice, 'it's too strong a colour for your delicate beauty, Mistress Gryffard.'

Joanna knew that voice! Slowly she turned and saw Black Nick raising Mariota's hand to his lips. He was handsomely dressed in a short tunic of blue embroidered with silver. His legs were encased in colourful hose and she couldn't help noticing that they swelled with muscle and tapered to his long pointed shoes almost as well as Tristram's. His hair was shorn and hung in a neat bob below his jauntily feathered cap and he had shaved off his bushy black beard. It made him look years younger and almost handsome. No, not handsome; passable. He raised a quizzical eyebrow at Joanna.

'Good day, Lady Maudesbury,' he said.

Inclining her head in a manner borrowed from Lady Isabel at her most detached, she acknowledged his presence. Mariota on the other hand welcomed him joyously as she disentangled herself from the silk.

'Have you done everything you wanted in Bristol?' she asked as she gave him one of her arch sideways glances.

'Everything,' he replied, 'and more quickly than I expected. So I came back to wait for you.'

'You're going to ride back to London with us then?' Mariota clapped her hands joyfully.

'That depends.'

'On when William comes back?'

'That and other things.'

Joanna was bemused. What was he doing here, in Cirencester of all places, and laughing and flirting with Mariota like an old friend?

'Has Lady Maudesbury taken you to meet my mother and my brother?' he asked and receiving a confused stare from Mariota swung round to confront Joanna. 'What, deny poor Edmund a chance to feast his eyes on the fairest face this side of paradise! Where is your Christian charity, Lady Maudesbury?' A dreadful premonition seized Joanna. It couldn't be true. It was unthinkable. She shrank back against the silk stall and to hide her confusion seized the emerald silk, her mind in turmoil. The stallholder revived his patter, reducing his price, urging her to make the most of her good fortune, praising her good taste.

'Come, my lady,' Nick said, taking Joanna by the arm. 'You can return later, the silk seller won't run away.' Well she knew the strength of those fingers. With a disdainful glance at his restraining hand she acquiesced coldly.

As he shepherded them through the crowded marketplace, Joanna desperately tried to collect her scattered wits. This man, this ruffian of a sea captain could not be the missing son. This man who had not an ounce of chivalry in him; who hated the very idea of knighthood and all it stood for, it could not be. One by one Joanna felt her dreams turn into dust and ashes beneath her feet as she was born relentlessly towards the splendid equipage waiting at the head of the marketplace. Nicholas was not a misunderstood hero, but a scoundrel who had betrayed his knighthood and brought disgrace upon his family; Tristram was right not to want to have anything to do with them.

They reached the coach. Black Nick stood aside to allow them to enter, and Mariota, her face bright with eager curiosity and her gown held just high enough to show her little velvet slippered feet, climbed quickly up the steep narrow steps. Joanna hesitated.

'Well, my lady, is the ascent too much for you? Has my improved station in life robbed you of your triumph?' If he hoped to goad her into losing her temper he failed, for she was barely listening, trying instead to decide what to do. She could not make an unladylike scene here in the marketplace, and yet to enter that coach and meet the de Chers would mean defying her husband's express command. What would Lady Isabel do?

'The steps are not the easiest, I know,' he went on pleasantly. 'Would you like me to carry you?'

Without a word, Joanna picked up her skirts and swiftly negotiated the three steps into the coach.

The inside was hung with tapestries, and on a seat covered with embroidered cushions a knight was stretched out, half sitting, half lying, propped up on pillows reading a book. Beside him sat a slim lady tightly clad in pale lilac silk. Her surcoat was embroidered with a device of griffins on one side and on the other a gold chevron on a sable field, which Joanna took to be the de Cher coat of arms. On her lap she held a small dog.

Nick made the introductions and Mariota greeted the Lady Elizabeth demurely with eyes cast down as befitted her station as a mere merchant's wife. But when presented to Edmund she gave one brief flick of her eyelashes and sent him a speaking glance full of gentle sympathy. Joanna would have been amused had she not felt so ill at ease. To the Lady Elizabeth's words of welcome she mumbled an inadequate reply and did not look at the knight at all.

Once the initial civilities were completed, an awkward silence fell. Outside, the din of the market continued unabated, but here inside the coach it was as if a spell had been cast. Joanna looked at Nick and

251

he smiled at her ruefully. So he was not as confident as usual, she thought with surprise. She returned his smile with a challenging stare. It was Sir Edmund who broke the silence at last.

'I suppose you knew Nick in London?' he said.

'We met when he came to our Eastertide feast,' Mariota replied. 'The Philpots brought him. John Philpot is known as the Sailor King, on account of his having arranged the capture of the Scottish pirate. Only it was Nick who led the fleet and captured the pirate. He's a hero in London now, you know.' Mariota smiled archly up at Nick.

Joanna noticed a shadow of something resembling distaste cross Edmund's face. She wondered how much he knew of Nick's seafaring exploits and felt sorry for this knight, so wasted and thin, his face marked by deep lines of suffering. Only his eyes, bright with curiosity, were full of life.

'What, heroics! That'll take some living down, Nicholas,' Edmund said.

'Didn't he tell you?' Mariota gazed proudly at Nick. 'My husband is a merchant of the staple and travels constantly to Calais. Nicholas often used to take him and what with the pirates and the French and the Spanish it was very, very dangerous. Now, thanks to Nick, at least the pirates are not such a threat and the French who used to get help from Joe Mercer no longer raid our seaports.'

'Nicco didn't tell us,' said Lady Elizabeth, smiling at her son. 'But then he has only just returned to us and there is so much of his life we have yet to hear about. For now, we are just thankful to have him safely home at last.'

'Indeed, it must be the most wonderful comfort to you,' Mariota chattered on. 'It gave me such courage having him by my side all the way from London, for he came with us, with me and my husband, when we came from London. I don't think I could have survived the journey without him.'

'A hero and a knight errant,' said Nick's brother. 'I can see there's much of Nicholas we have to come to terms with.'

Nick moved restlessly and Joanna felt intrigued. There were strange undercurrents here, and no wonder. Nick's sudden return must have upset them all! They obviously knew very little of what he had been doing during his long absence and she was not surprised. There was not much that Black Nick had done in his life that people such as the de Chers would be proud of, she felt sure.

'I'm so afraid of travelling without a proper escort,' Mariota was now confessing to Edmund. 'I hope that when my husband has bought all the wool and cloth he came for, Nick will ride back to London with us. I don't think I could bear to face the journey otherwise, you hear such spine-chilling tales of innocent people being attacked on the road.'

'I hope Nick won't think of leaving us yet awhile,' said his mother gently. 'Of course it's not very exciting here after what he's been used to but we shall have to see what we can do to make it attractive enough for him to want to stay.'

'Nicholas wants danger, Mother. You'll have to find him a dragon or two that needs slaying,' Edmund mocked.

'I think perhaps he's had enough of danger,' replied Lady Elizabeth with a quick warning glance at Edmund.

'Perhaps you and your sister will come and visit us at Cher Castle, now that he's home, Lady Maudesbury,' said Edmund. 'I'm afraid I've never been much company for a lively young bride but now that Nick's back we should be able to entertain you better.'

Joanna opened her mouth to refuse before Mariota could say anything, but was forestalled by Nick.

'My mother is holding a May Day feast, to celebrate my return. You will come, won't you, and bring your sister? The whole county is to be there.'

Joanna, wracking her brains for a convincing excuse, detected a shadow flit across the calm, smiling face of Nick's mother – just the merest flicker, gone almost before it had come. She doesn't want us, thought Joanna, we're not good enough.

'I'm afraid it would be impossible,' she said quickly. 'Sir Tristram is away and Lady Isabel is sick. We've only come into Cirencester to consult the infirmarer at the abbey. We couldn't possibly come.' She did not dare look at Mariota.

'I'm sorry to hear that Lady Isabel is ill,' said Nick's mother. 'I hope it is nothing to worry about.'

'I don't think so, but I'd like to consult the monks about her all the same,' said Joanna. 'I think we ought to be going. I don't like being away from the manor too long, leaving her on her own.' She glanced at Nick to see if he meant to oppose her. He was standing, his huge frame slightly stooped to fit into the low-roofed carriage, and looked out of place and not entirely at his ease.

'I'll escort you,' he said.

'There's no need,' she said quickly.

'I have business with the Abbot,' he said. 'Mistress Mariota, allow me to offer you my protection as far as the abbey, lest the wild animals burst from their pens and savage you on the way.'

Joanna could not help but smile as Mariota started in alarm, and over the top of her head Nick smiled back. It made Joanna feel guilty to have enjoyed a joke with him at her sister's expense and she left the coach feeling confused and ill-prepared to do battle over the matter of the May Day feast. Nick never accepted no for an answer – not in her experience, anyway – and in Mariota he would find a good ally. It was clever of him to have whisked them out of the carriage so quickly, away from his own opposing forces and onto neutral territory where he could use her sister against her.

But once outside the coach, Joanna heard shouts coming from beyond the stone cross and saw that another battle was taking place. A man was being dragged struggling and cursing towards the abbey by two burly lay brothers. 'What's he done, do you think?' she said, thanking God for the diversion.

'Probably been grinding his own corn instead of using the abbey's mill,' replied Nick. 'As overlord, the abbey of course has a monopoly on the grinding of all household corn, but I understand from the Abbot that there's been a lot of trouble from the burghers who object to paying the high cost of the grinding.'

'You sound as if you feel sorry for them,' said Joanna. 'Don't your tenants have to bring their corn to the castle to be ground? Or perhaps you don't know.'

'I imagine they do,' he replied. 'But I would think that my brother's bailiff knows how to pitch what he charges them someway between extortion and providing a free service.'

'Poor man. What will they do with him?' asked Mariota with a shudder.

Nick shrugged. 'Throw him in the quiet churn until he mends his ways, I expect.'

'Stupid fellow,' said Joanna. 'It's not worth losing a day or two's work, when you think of the lost trade – on a busy market day too. He'd have been better to pay the abbey its due.'

'There are always fools ready to sacrifice their best interests for a principle,' Nick responded.

Joanna knew by the challenging look he gave her that he was expecting an argument but she turned away, intending to proceed to the abbey.

'It's better if we don't go to the abbey just yet,' Nick advised, 'not while there's liable to be a brawl. Wait there. I'll tell you when the way is clear.' He disappeared into the market and as soon as he had gone Mariota rounded on Joanna.

'How could you refuse such a splendid invitation? Everyone will be there – you heard what they said.'

'Lady Elizabeth didn't really want us,' said Joanna. 'You didn't see her face.'

'Her sons did. Edmund has taken a fancy to you, I could see that, and Nick is madly in love with me, poor man.'

'Nick? In love with you?' Joanna stared at Mariota.

'You need not look so surprised. He courted me all the way from London. Of course I did not dare to encourage him; how could I with William there watching me all the time.'

254

'You never told me,' said Joanna, 'that Black Nick came with you all the way.'

'Nicholas, Joanna. We must not call him Black Nick any more. Isn't it exciting that he should be a knight in disguise? I always knew there must be some mystery, that he was more than he seemed. He had such perfect manners – and he loves me quite desperately, I know it.'

'He doesn't know the meaning of the word,' said Joanna without thinking. 'Love is just a game to him. Black Nick or Sir Nicholas de Cher, he's still a blackguard. He only wants to bed you, Mariota, and when he's done it, he'll lose interest immediately.'

'Don't you think I don't know that! It's what all men want, after all. It's their base nature. But it's for us to teach them what love is, to make them worship us from afar.'

'And what about William? Doesn't he mind that you flirt with other men? Do you think he doesn't notice?' At last she could say it without the spectre of Tristram coming between them.

'William is far, far worse. He sleeps with every woman in my household and doesn't care that I know it.'

'Merciful Mother! Mariota, I had no idea. William!' Joanna could not imagine it. The careworn, watchful, pallid William sleeping with everyone in sight when he had beautiful Mariota to bed? It was unthinkable. 'My poor Mariota, how dreadful for you.'

'Dreadful? It's not at all dreadful,' replied Mariota with a toss of her head. 'You don't think I want him in my bed at night, do you? The trouble with you, Joanna, is you live in a dream world. You won't face up to life as it really is. Don't tell me that you like what goes on between a husband and wife together in bed any more than I do. It's necessary to get babies but that's not love, is it? Love is what a man feels for a woman when he can't have her. Perhaps it is a game. It's certainly a lot of fun. And Nicholas de Cher knows how to play it better than anybody.'

Joanna stared at her, so shaken she did not know what to say. But there was little time to say anything in any case. Black Nick was coming back. She could see him shouldering his way towards them carrying a bundle of something under his arm.

'Peace is restored,' he announced when he reached them. 'We can approach the abbey in safety.' Joanna was too confused thinking about what Mariota had said about love to pay much attention to him. Of course it was true that on the rare occasions when Tristram came to her bed it was torture, and now that she knew Mariota did not enjoy it either, Joanna felt a small sense of relief. Perhaps Mariota was right after all and love was just a game, an elaborate passage of arms between men and women with rules and formalities just like a tournament.

255

But the love she felt for Tristram was not like that. The agony of her craving was for the physical feel of him, the smell of his skin, the touch of his hand on her bare flesh, the longing for him to caress her gently. Love was shame and torture, a bondage of the spirit. Its power was more potent than anything in heaven or on earth. Because of her love for Tristram, she had learnt to do things she despised herself for. She did not understand the compulsion that made her his slave, she did not understand this terrifying thing called love, but it was not a game.

On the way to the abbey, Nick renewed his invitation to the May Day feast.

'We may go, may we not, Joanna?' Mariota asked and Joanna, looking into those beseeching grey eyes, suddenly realised that in Black Nick she had found what she sought. Someone to make it up to Mariota for having lost Tristram. To go would be to defy Tristram for the first time, but he need never know, since Lady Isabel was shut up in her chamber, taking no interest in life at all. Mariota deserved a little pleasure and if Black Nick did succeed in seducing her, would it matter? Mariota knew what she was about. She was not likely to get too seriously hurt, her feelings did not run deep enough. Why, already she seemed to have put all thought of Tristram out of her head entirely.

Turning upon Nick her most glowing smile, Joanna accepted his invitation graciously.

He escorted them to the abbey gates. Then, as he was about to take his leave, he suddenly thrust the parcel he was carrying into Joanna's arms. 'For you,' he said, 'to go Maying in.' He kissed Mariota's hand and departed before Joanna had time either to refuse the gift or to thank him.

Tearing off the wrappings she saw the green silk she had coveted in the marketplace. Wretch! He must have been very sure of getting his own way. Almost she thought of finding an excuse not to go to the feast. But she knew it was unthinkable. Mariota's disappointment would be too much to bear. But of course she wouldn't wear it.

'Joanna! How stupid of him,' said Mariota frowning at Nick's departing back. 'Did he not say himself the colour was far too strong. It'll look terrible with that bright hair of yours. But you'll have to wear it, since he's given it to you. Perhaps if you wear a linen cap and a plain surcoat it won't make you look too bad.'

It will look wonderful, thought Joanna, her anger against Nick dissolved by Mariota's scorn. She would wear it just to show him – to show them all. What it was she wanted to show them she did not think to ask herself.

Chapter 24

Cher Castle perched on its hilltop on May Day morn like a vision of chivalry seemed to Joanna far too beautiful and mysterious a home for so earthbound a creature as Black Nick. From a haphazard circuit of towers a fanfare of trumpets rang, proclaiming the arrival of each guest, and Joanna could not help but thrill to the sound as she and Mariota rode across the lowered drawbridge.

In the outer bailey a Maypole had been set up. The great golden coach with the four horses harnessed one in front of the other sat waiting, while round it buzzed a gaily dressed crowd, like bees beseiging a hive: a mêlée of knights informally clad in tunics and short cloaks, armed only with swords and daggers, ladies in fine silk, their surcoats embroidered with colourful quarterings and escutcheons, squires carrying not lances but hooded hawks, dogs and pages darting about. Nick was moving among them, greeting his guests, and Joanna watched him nervously as she waited to be noticed. Apart from Nick, she could not see a single face she knew.

Beside her, Mariota was sitting serenely upon her palfrey, unperturbed by the admiring stares cast in their direction, like a goddess aloof upon her pedestal, but Joanna, unaccustomed to causing men's heads to turn, felt ruffled. The green silk which she had hurriedly had made up by the manor's most skilled needlewoman had a scooped neck and long tight sleeves. The gown was just a simple loose-fitting sheath; there had been no time to do anything elaborate. She had tied a thin cord of plaited twine round her waist and the silk fell in glorious folds of shimmering colour to the ground, so soft and pliant it clung to her body and caressed it as she moved. Her hair, brushed and shining, flowed down her back in a mass of bright chestnut curls. She had no costly jewelled filet like Mariota's to wear round her brow; instead she had made herself a garland of primroses and bluebells. The effect was sensational, she knew. Her image when she had looked in the polished steel in her chamber told her that. Then she had felt pleased, but now as she sat on her palfrey growing hot under the admiring stares of the men around her, she began to wish she had worn something more demure.

A page brought them wine and Joanna sipped it gratefully, for the ride that morning had made her thirsty.

Suddenly Mariota pointed. 'That's Gervase de Haen. I met him when we stayed at the abbey on our way here.' He had exchanged his monk's habit for green doublet and hose and looked quite different.

He saw her too and immediately came hurrying across the crowded court to greet her. He had come with his Abbot, he explained, and when Joanna asked him if he knew who some of these people were he launched into an exact description of their pedigrees. 'The short squat little man over there is Sir Philip Mansell, and the pale girl in green and gold talking to my lord Abbot is his wife. She's not long left her fourth lying-in – she gives birth to nothing but stillborn babes, poor child. Sir Philip owns the large manor of Bisley and is building himself a beautiful new house in Lypiatt Park. His sister Joan is married to William Whittington of Gloucester – I think his younger son went to London to be a merchant, a mercer, I believe. Perhaps you know him, Mistress Gryffard?'

Mariota smiled at him and admitted that she had met Master Whittington on several occasions. De Haen blushed and became tongue-tied, smitten by Mariota's smile.

'Who's the knight on the white horse, talking to the Lady Elizabeth?' prompted Joanna.

'Why, that's the Lord Berkeley, overlord to the de Chers. Surely your know him?' replied the monk in surprise. It was Joanna's turn to blush. She wished for the tenth time that morning that Tristram was with her. She had thought that just getting away from the manor where she was reminded of him constantly might help her to forget, but here it was worse. This was where he belonged. He would have known who all these people were. He would have shone among them. 'And the lady with the Lady Elizabeth,' Gervase continued, 'that's Agnes Proudfoot, the betrothed of Nicholas de Cher.'

'Betrothed!' exclaimed Mariota.

'Yes, is it not a triumph for hope and constancy? They've been betrothed since he was eleven and she seven. Why they did not marry before he went to the wars I know not. I'm told she had the pox or some such and was not expected to live. Her father, Sir Owen Proudfoot, owned some score different manors in the counties of Wiltshire, Gloucestershire and Somerset. When Nick was lost, there was talk of her marrying Edmund but that came to naught, and Sir Owen died before he could find someone else for her. I think the girl herself would like to go into a convent, but when her father died she became a ward of Lord Berkeley and I don't think he's too anxious

258

to give the Proudfoot manors to the Church. Now it seems the girl will have a husband after all; Lady Elizabeth is anxious to have the marriage ceremony as soon as possible.'

No wonder there were undercurrents, thought Joanna , delighted. Agnes Proudfoot was dressed demurely in a drab linen sheath and sur-coat embroidered with her father's arms, a veil covered her hair and swathed her throat, and her eyes were cast modestly down as she stood beside Nick's mother, taking no interest in the merry scene. She looked well fitted for a convent. Far from being a triumph for con-stancy, it was a huge jest on the part of fate! Joanna watched Black Nick approaching, so amused at the thought of the bold, pirate-slay-ing womaniser having to marry that she was for once able to feel quite well disposed towards him.

When he reached them she thanked him for the silk but he stared at her almost angrily. For a moment she wondered whether perhaps he had meant the silk for Mariota after all. She held his gaze defiantly.

'It suits you,' he said smiling suddenly, 'as I knew it would. We shall be ready to set out soon. We shan't go far, a small hawking expedi-tion, a little Maying in the wood, and later dinner back at the castle. Will you come hawking?'

'I don't know how to,' she said without thinking.

'What! Sir Tristram's lady these four years and doesn't fly a hawk?' There was genuine surprise in his voice.

'Sir Tristram isn't at home very often and when he is, he's too busy,' she answered rather lamely.

'We shall have to do something about this. Sam,' he called over his shoulder, 'tell the falconer to bring a merlin from the mews for my lady Maudesbury. We'll take advantage of Sir Tristram's absence to teach his lady how to handle a hawk.' Sam nodded and went to do his master's bidding. Joanna caught sight of Mariota looking just a lit-tle less serene than usual and felt annoyed with him again. It was Mariota he was supposed to flirt with.

'Teach Mariota,' she said. 'She'd be a much better pupil than I.'

'I could teach you both at the same time.' He grinned at her. This was not what she had intended. Now the rogue was trying to play them off one against the other. Casting around for some way to extri-cate herself, she caught sight of Lady Elizabeth, still with Nick's betrothed in tow, not far away. She dug her heel sharply into her horse's flank and rode forward to pay her respects to her hostess.

Elizabeth de Cher acknowledged Joanna's greeting with just the slightest hint of condescension in her manner and enquired politely after Lady Isabel.

'Your son is to teach Mariota how to fly a hawk,' said Joanna gaily. 'Perhaps I could keep you company in the coach with Sir Edmund.'

'Why of course you must go in the coach with Edmund since you

259

have not brought any hawks with you,' Elizabeth said. 'Agnes, my dear, now you may come hawking with us. Lady de Maudesbury will be company enough for Edmund in your place.'

Agnes looked at the ground and mumbled that she could not bear to see the poor rabbits killed by the cruel hawks, but Elizabeth de Cher brushed her protestations aside. Joanna dismounted swiftly and offered Agnes her palfrey, delighted at having been able to turn the tables on Nick so completely. Now he would have his mother and his betrothed to play off against Mariota. That should keep him busy enough for the rest of the morning!

She entered the coach feeling well prepared to make herself agreeable to Edmund.

'So you came,' he said. 'Nick said you would. He's a persuasive fellow, isn't he?'

'He certainly likes to get his own way.' Joanna sat down on a large cushion on the floor beside him. 'Was he always such a bully, when he was young?'

'Not to me,' said Edmund. 'Nick is four years younger than I am and I could beat him in all things.' He closed his eyes as the coach lurched forward and lay back against the cushions which supported him. Joanna watched him sympathetically, bracing herself against one of the solid beams of the superstructure as the coach lurched from side to side, thinking that he must find it very uncomfortable.

'Don't you want to confide in me?' he asked, opening his eyes suddenly and fixing her with a baleful stare. 'People generally do. They think that because I'm like I am, I'm a sort of substitute for the confessional.'

'How fascinating! You must learn all sorts of secrets! Just think of the trouble you could cause if you had a mind to.'

'It's not fascinating being treated as a receptacle,' he said bitterly. 'Just because I can't fight, and hunt and dance, people forget that I'm a man.'

Joanna thought of Tristram, of the vigorous, violent life he loved, and felt acute pity for this knight who would never ride into battle again. 'You fought with the Black Prince, didn't you?' she said, thinking that if he could not fight, maybe he would enjoy talking about it. Tristram always loved to talk of war. 'What was he like?'

'He was a wonderful soldier. He had the ability to seize the opportunity of the moment, to make up his strategy according to the way things happened. Campaigns never work out the way they're meant to, you know. Najera was a great victory, won against terrific odds, like all his victories. But he was let down by his allies.'

'Najera?'

'It's in Spain. I fought at Najera, it was a great battle.' He lapsed into silence.

'Why Spain?' she prompted trying to keep him from brooding.

'When Don Pedro the Cruel of Castile was deposed by his bastard brother Henry of Trastamare, he appealed in the name of chivalry and kinship to the Black Prince for help to regain his throne. So we went to Spain, defeated the Spaniards and the French at Najera and won back Don Pedro's throne for him. But what thanks did we get? All that summer we waited on the burning Castilian plain for the gold that was to have been paid for our services. There was no water, just a few stagnant pools which gave us all the bloody flux. The countryside was bare and soon we'd no food, only our dead horses left to eat. Not one man in five saw England again.'

Joanna felt embarrassed, awkward, at a loss for words. This tale of misery and defeat was so different from Tristram's glowing visions of the glory of war.

'Eventually we returned to Bordeaux.' Edmund continued. 'All we had to show for our trouble was a handful of jewels in place of the million crowns Don Pedro had promised. The troops were unpaid and the Black Prince was already worn out with illness. We had to try and recoup our losses from the French in Aquitaine, but the local inhabitants didn't take kindly to heavy taxation and most of our army – those that were well enough – were left behind to garrison our castles. Nick was one of them. The rest of us made our way back to England, harried and plagued by the French army who were too cowardly to fight us in the open but managed to do quite well by picking off the stragglers. I was one of the unlucky ones.'

'And you never saw your brother again – from that day to this?' Joanna, consumed with curiosity, could not help questioning him.

'We knew he wasn't dead,' Edmund replied. 'From time to time he sent word to my mother that he was alive and well.'

'But he never came to see you – until now?'

'I used to think it was because he was too ashamed, but now that he is back I know that whatever it was kept Nick from us for so long it wasn't shame.'

Joanna did not know what to say. Edmund was lying back against his cushions scowling at her, wincing with every lurch of the lumbering coach and she wondered pityingly when it was that he sustained the injuries which had turned him from a brave young knight into a weak and bitter invalid.

'Did the French treat you very badly?' she asked, her amber eyes glowing with sympathy.

'Knights don't get treated badly by other knights,' he said, 'provided their families can pay the ransom. It's only the foot soldiers who have to suffer in war. It nearly ruined the manor, my ransom.' He said it almost proudly. 'Don't look so troubled, the manor recovered eventually, thanks to the sheep and our hard-working tenants. Better than I did, alas.'

Joanna felt a chill hand on her heart. Ransom was a word often on

Tristram's lips. It was his justification for the sacrifices the manor made every time he went to war. Ransom for the Scottish knights captured in the current campaign would repay all that he had borrowed from William, it would put a new roof on the manor house, enable them to entertain their neighbours as the de Chers were doing, fulfil all Tristram's extravagant demands. But suppose it happened the other way? Suppose instead of capturing, Tristram himself were to be taken prisoner? It was something that had never occurred to Joanna. Death, yes, always she was terrified that he might be killed in battle, but never the disgrace of capture. Now for the first time she considered the possibility and it was as if a great pit had opened up beneath her feet. If the manor of de Cher had nearly been brought to ruin in paying for Edmund, what would such a demand do to Maudesbury? Stretched as it was to the limit merely to provision Tristram's lance, it would be quite impossible for them ever to find the money to ransom him if he should be captured. Edmund had said that knights treated each other well, provided the ransom was forthcoming. She did not dare ask what happened if it were not. She had seen the half-lance carried by Tristram's squire and knew what its cruel, hooked blade was for.

They stopped in a clearing in the woods. Edmund was helped from his coach. Food and drink was laid out by the pages. The ladies who had not gone hawking dismounted, clustering round Edmund as he was laid upon the grass, vying with suggestions to improve his comfort, bringing cushions, offering help, adding to his irritation. Someone produced a lute. Relieved to be able to escape from her self-appointed task of entertaining Edmund, Joanna wandered to the far edge of the clearing and sat down with her back against a large beech tree, content to be on her own. Sipping her wine and listening to the music of the lute mingling with the birdsong all about her, she began truly to enjoy herself for the first time that day.

When the hawking party joined them at last, Joanna was not surprised to see Nick and Mariota together and Agnes attended by Gervase de Haen. As Nick helped Mariota down from her palfrey, Joanna glanced curiously at Elizabeth de Cher hovering over Edmund. She was looking strained, as well she might, thought Joanna. Nick's arrival in their midst must have been about as peaceful as a storm at sea. The feast today put Joanna in mind of the story of the prodigal's return and she wondered whether Edmund, like that other brother, was jealous of all the attention Nick was getting. But Nick was no prodigal, she realised with a start. Far from coming home when he was poor and in need, he had waited until now when he seemed once more to be prospering. It was Edmund who had cost the manor dear with his ransom. It was all very confusing and Joanna did not know what to make of it. She noticed Edmund's eyes fixed on Mariota. He was watching her with so much anguish on his pale face that Joanna felt renewed sympathy for him. He could not dance, nor fight, nor hunt but he could still love without any hope of fulfilment.

But Mariota had clearly enjoyed her morning. 'You should have come hawking, Joanna,' she said, as Nick brought her over. 'It was such fun. My merlin caught a lark and Nick said the hawk flew so well for me, he made me a present of her. He's going to bring her over to Maudesbury very soon and take me out hunting again.'

'I hope you managed to keep my brother amused, Lady Maudesbury,' Nick said.

'I tried,' Joanna replied. 'But I'm afraid it's Mariota he would rather have had with him in the coach. Be kind to him, Mariota. Like all the others, he's dying of love for you, I fear.'

'Ah, the poor invalid!' exclaimed Mariota, all instant sympathy, and hurried across the grass to bestow her favour upon Edmund.

'Why do you persist in playing second fiddle to that spoilt beauty of a sister of yours?' asked Nick, scowling at her.

'She's not spoilt,' Joanna retorted, startled. 'She's as good and obedient as she's beautiful. Everybody loves Mariota.'

'Yet it was you Tristram made off with, and I can't say I blame him. I'd like to have run off with you myself!'

She was not in the least flattered. 'I suppose kidnapping is the sort of thing pirates do all the time.'

'Tell me, how did you persuade him to do it?'

'Do what?' she asked, her eyes as wide as Mariota's at her most beguiling.

'To marry you, of course.'

'Oh that!' She laughed. 'That was the Duke of Lancaster's idea. No, come to think of it, it was really John of Northampton's. There was some very important political reason for it at the time!' Whether it was the warmth of the sun, or the seduction of the music, or the new May wine, she could not be angry with him.

'No, Joanna, you'll have to do better than that,' he said. 'Far be it for me to deride your father's aspirations, but I'll not believe the marriage of his daughter to a retainer of Lancaster's could make the least difference one way or the other.'

'It wouldn't have done if he hadn't abducted me,' she admitted.

'Against your will, of course?'

'No,' she said throwing back her head and meeting his eyes steadily, 'not against my will.'

'I'm sorry, I forgot,' he said almost harshly. 'You never do anything against your will, do you, Joanna? But I'm still at a loss to know how you persuaded him to do anything so foolish.'

'Come, come, sir, don't be so unchivalrous,' she parried lightly.

'You said yourself you'd like to run off with me.'

'I'd like to think I've more discrimination than Sir Tristram,' he said with a shrug. 'I never would have credited him with so much good sense. So, having got your way, are you happy, Joanna?'

'Of course I'm happy,' she said turning away.

'You're not a very good liar, Joanna.'

'I miss Tristram, that's all.' Mariota was chattering away to Edmund quite unselfconsciously, she noticed. No arch looks, or lowered lashes. It made Joanna suddenly feel terribly sad. 'Why does everyone treat your poor brother as if he's a eunuch?' she burst out, unthinkingly. 'Mariota's not even bothering to flirt with him. It's a shame. No wonder he feels so bitter at times. It's not enough that he's dying slowly and painfully, unable to do all the things he wants to, but people make him feel so useless. I wish she'd flirt just a little with him.'

'What, and drive the poor fellow right out of his mind?'

'There,' she said triumphantly, 'you do find her attractive.'

'I find her irresistible, but she can't hold a candle to you in one of your rages.'

'I don't have rages any more,' she said coldly. He was grinning at her with the devilry dancing in his eyes. 'Your betrothed looks as if she will make a good and dutiful wife,' she simply could not resist saying it, 'she should give you no trouble at all.'

'But trouble is what I like,' he retorted, 'which is why I like you, Joanna.'

'Then it looks as if you are about to be indulged because here's your mother come to upbraid you for neglecting your betrothed.' With that parting shot she left him, knowing that he could not pursue her in front of Lady Elizabeth.

When the sun was high the whole party returned to the castle for dinner. The men dined in the hall and the women in a separate chamber. Sweet-smelling herbs covered the stone floor and great boughs of may, apple, sycamore and flowering cherry decorated the walls. They dined on a wonderful array of meats and fish and intricately fashioned pastries, drank wine perfumed with wild thyme and violets, and were beguiled by a minstrel for an hour or more. When at last they were sufficiently refreshed and beginning to tire of each other's company, Lady Elizabeth led them down to the great hall, where the trestles had been cleared away for dancing.

To Joanna's surprise she found herself much in demand. Men whom she had never met came to commiserate over the absence of Sir Tristram and beg to dance with her. It was a completely new experience and she found it intoxicating. She had a good sense of rhythm and loved to dance, so she cast care aside and abandoned herself to the music, flying on winged feet about the hall, treading the different measures with a variety of knights young and old, enjoying it all the more after the long isolation of her life at Maudesbury. Mariota, too, seemed to be enjoying herself, dancing with Nick. He moved well, Joanna noted, surprised. He was twirling Mariota around the hall with a skill born, Joanna supposed, of much practice. Mariota's head was tilted back so that she could look up into his face and her eyes were shining. He was staring down at her but it was impossible to tell what he was thinking.

Later, when Joanna was sipping wine with a young squire from Sir Philip Mansell's household and trying to get her breath back after a particularly lively jig, Lady Elizabeth came up to her.

'Come and talk to Edmund,' she said. 'Dear Agnes has been keeping him company and missing all the dancing. He likes you, he told me so.'

Edmund was lounging on a pile of cushions on the dais at the far end of the hall, with Agnes Proudfoot sitting silent at his side. Lord Berkeley, the Abbot of Cirencester, and Sir Philip Mansell were grouped round him, talking among themselves. Joanna thought Edmund looked exhausted, his face pinched and white, his eyes sunk far back in his head.

'I suppose Mother's chosen you to entertain me now,' Edmund said, glancing at her wearily. 'The disadvantage of being an invalid is that I am a captive audience for all Mother's visitors. On the pretext of keeping me amused, she dumps the most dreadful dowagers on me for sometimes days at a time, while she slips off hawking.'

'If you're tired, why don't you retire to your chamber?' Joanna replied. 'Blame me. You can say the tedium of my company drove you away. One of the advantages of being an invalid, I would have thought, must be to do exactly what you feel like and use your illness as an excuse.'

'The tedium of your company, my dear lady, is as nothing to the tedium of my own should I leave this merry scene. I have enough of that as it is.' It was on the tip of her tongue to say she wasn't surprised he found his own company tedious but she was rescued by Lord Berkeley who enquired very kindly after her husband.

'Tristram's gone to fight in Scotland,' she said, 'with the Duke of Lancaster.'

'It's a pity John of Gaunt has taken it into his head to make war on the Scots just now. This new poll tax isn't at all popular, and what with that and the trouble Wycliffe and his priests have been stirring up, the countryside's very unsettled.' Lady Elizabeth had managed to prise Nick away from Mariota, Joanna noticed, but he had slipped away from his mother to talk to some knight, and Lady Elizabeth had no choice but to return without him to where Agnes Proudfoot was still waiting, her hands folded in front of her and her eyes fixed firmly on the floor. Joanna turned her attention back to Edmund.

'Lord Berkeley wants us to go and stay at Berkeley Castle,' he explained to her. 'He says it's not safe enough for us here. I've never heard such nonsense.'

'It's not nonsense, Edmund, it's serious,' said Berkeley. 'There have been mob rescues of fugitive bondsmen as they were being hauled back to their villages; the woods are full of them, swelling the usual numbers of robbers and outlaws, and they assemble at night to poach the woods and slay game up and down the country. The peasants are becoming restive, refusing to do their boon work. Look what happened in Harmsworth. The villeins stayed away from the haymaking and the villagers deliberately opened the river sluices to flood the hay.'

'Harmsworth's near London, isn't it?' said Edmund. 'And the property of a Norman abbey. Those serfs were protesting against a foreign overlord and I can't say that I blame them.'

'Have you not been having trouble with the serfs on the manor?' asked Joanna, thinking of the constant struggle to get her own serfs to do their boon work.

'Some,' replied Edmund. 'Doesn't everyone have a few serfs who have run away? We're lucky we have a good bailiff. The tenants like him and the serfs work well for him. If the peasants do rise, they'll attack the monasteries and the abbeys rather than a castle such as ours.'

'I don't think you should count on that,' said the Abbott. 'If the peasants were to rise, we'd all be in danger.'

'Well, then we draw up the bridge. We've nothing to fear from our own serfs, of that I'm sure.'

'The castle's hardly in a fit state to stand a siege, Nick says,' put in Lady Elizabeth. 'I'm afraid it's deteriorated a lot since Sir Simon de Cher fortified it in Edward I's reign. It didn't seem to matter, being so far away from the coast and with Edmund so out of things. I'm afraid I spent the money that should have gone on repairing the walls and refitting the cannons on comforts for Edmund and myself.'

'And so you should,' Lord Berkeley assured her. 'You must come to us, you'll be quite safe at Berkeley Castle. Just until this poll tax is safely gathered in. The country should settle down again after that. I know Edmund doesn't like long journeys, but he can travel in easy stages. Stay one or two nights on the way. You know how much we'd like to have you.'

'Nick says, does he?' Edmund grumbled as he moved restlessly on his cushions. 'Why do you have to listen to everything he says all of sudden? I suspect this is just a plan of his to be rid of me from Cher so he can have everything his own way.'

'I put it down to the rise in the cost of labour,' said Sir Philip Mansell quickly with a worried glance over his shoulder. 'The serfs want to leave their unprofitable farms and hire their labour out to the highest bidder. Of course we can't have that.'

'Why not?' asked Nick, materialising suddenly at Joanna's side. 'Why not set them free and pay them for their services?'

'Nicholas, you sound almost as if you sympathise with them,' protested Lord Berkeley. 'You've not come back here to stir up trouble in the neighbourhood, I trust?'

'No, but I always believe that the way to beat my enemy is to put myself in his place and see things from his point of view.'

'My dear chap, we can't free the serfs, what would we live on?' expostulated Sir Philip.

'Their rents,' said Nick. 'Charge them a proper rent for their land and pay them a wage for the labour they do, then they might be more willing to work for us.'

'You couldn't charge our serfs rent,' said Joanna, 'they could not possibly pay. They barely scratch a living as it is.'

'The peasants aren't a serious threat,' insisted Edmund. 'They'd never turn on their manor lord, they need him for their own protection.'

'"When Adam delved and Eve span, who was then the gentleman?"' quoted Nick. 'Once ideas of freedom get into men's minds, there's no knowing where it might end.'

'A little unrest, some troublesome priests, a few serfs who prefer preying on helpless travellers to doing a hard day's work in the fields, you're not frightened of them, are you?' demanded Edmund.

'I just wish the young King's uncles weren't all so far away,' replied Berkeley. 'John of Gaunt is in Scotland, Thomas Woodstock is in the Welsh Marches and Edmund of Cambridge is about to sail to Portugal. The seeds of rebellion are here, there've been too many isolated incidents for my comfort of late. All it needs is for them to find a leader – John Ball has prepared the ground. If the peasants do rise, there will be others ready to take advantage of our weakness to further their own interests.'

Joanna stifled a little trickle of alarm. It could not happen, surely? She found it impossible to imagine the serfs at Maudesbury taking part in anything so dramatic as rebellion. They were awkward at times, slow to do her bidding and adept at disappearing when there was a lot of work to be done, but that was because they were so poor, because the struggle to keep their own few acres tilled and their families fed was so dire. She could not imagine them ever turning against their manor lord. She looked anxiously at the men standing around her and caught Nick's gaze. He smiled reassuringly.

'Well, Joanna, shall we dance?' he said. She would not have gone with him if it had not been for Lady Elizabeth's disapproving stare, but opposition was something that never failed to stimulate a reaction in Joanna's soul, and so she gave him her glorious smile and allowed him to lead her into the dance.

It was a lively jig and he whirled her round and round with an expert if energetic ease until she was completely out of breath. Then before she knew what he was about, he had whisked her out through the carved screen at the end of the hall into a small grass-covered court beyond.

'Where are you taking me?' she asked breathlessly.

'To cool off in the fresh air,' he replied, and suddenly he bent and kissed her swiftly on the mouth. It was so quickly done she was completely taken by surprise. 'Well, aren't you going to slap my face?' he asked, grinning at her.

'I wouldn't dream of giving you that pleasure,' she said, still breathless, but no longer now from dancing. He was standing very close, looking down into her eyes, but she was determined not to let him see how shaken she was.

'There's no one can see you,' he teased. She looked quickly round the little court. He was right. They were quite alone. Blessed Mother, let me stay calm, she thought, trying to forget the feel of his lips on hers. They had been warm, enticing.

'The Lady Isabel has trained you well, my poor tamed creature,' he said. 'But you don't fool me. Underneath that cold manner there's still a warm heart and flesh and blood.'

Stay cold and distant, Joanna told herself firmly – and try to bring him to a sense of the duty of his hospitality.

'You wouldn't be so dishonourable as to take advantage of me here in your own castle, when I am at your mercy?'

'Of course I would! You know I'm not a hero. I believe in making the most of my opportunities.' He went on to prove it by sweeping her into his arms and kissing her properly. It was quite different to anything Joanna had ever experienced before. She didn't know a kiss could be like this. She thought all kisses were like Tristram's, a suffocating business of thrusting tongue and clashing teeth. This was different, this was warm and gentle and so insistent she yielded without knowing what she was doing.

A melting sweetness engulfed her as her lips opened under his and fire shot through her whole body. Somewhere in the far reaches of her mind she was conscious of a need to stop, to put an end to this madness, but desire such as she had never known was urging her onwards until she thought she might drown in the tide of passion which was sweeping over her and making her cling to him helplessly. He tightened his hold and she felt the firmness of his body beneath the velvet doublet. It warned her. With a superhuman effort she tore her mouth away from his, picked up her skirts and fled, as if pursued by all the devils in hell, back into the hall.

CHAPTER 25

Back at Maudesbury, Joanna tried to forget all about Black Nick, but it wasn't easy. The memory of that scene with him lived in her mind and kept coming back to torture her at odd moments of the day. She felt ashamed. The feelings he had aroused were quite new to her. It wasn't what she felt for Tristram at all. It was lust, she supposed, and went to Mass and lit a candle to the Virgin, promising to purge the sin. Mariota helped. Mariota had thoroughly enjoyed the May feast and was fulsome in her praise of everything at Cher Castle, in particular Black Nick.

'Did he kiss you?' Joanna asked, to punish herself.

'No, he did not,' Mariota had replied. 'Of course he tried, he's still madly in love with me, but I wasn't going to let him kiss me.'

Joanna felt even more ashamed. She encouraged her sister to talk about Nick as much as possible, listening to every detail of his devotion, to remind herself what a terrible flirt he was. She knew him for an inconstant rogue, a black-hearted seducer who preyed on all women, good and bad alike, and yet she could not forget the magic of that moment in his arms. She lived in dread of his coming to Maudesbury.

When they had taken their leave, Nick had promised to come soon and bring the hawk. The promise had been made to Mariota but his wicked, dancing eyes had held hers and she had felt herself blushing until her face must have almost matched the colour of her hair. It was the only thing she could remember about the rest of that day. She was so concerned with regaining her composure, making sure no one suspected anything, avoiding Nick, that she had been unable to concentrate. Lady Isabel's schooling stood her in good stead. Somehow she had managed to hide her turmoil behind a distant manner, until at last it had been time for them to leave.

To the daily dread of his coming was added a tiny rebellious longing, one which all her prayers and promises to the Virgin did nothing to suppress and she made up her mind that when he came she would hide in her chamber until he had gone. Let Mariota play with fire if she dared; Joanna knew that she herself would be very likely to get burned.

Nick did not come. Mariota pined as Joanna threw herself into all the demanding work of the manor, relieved to have so much to do and resolutely thanking God each night for deliverance from temptation. When at last, towards the end of May, they did have a visitor, it was not Nick but William. He brought bad tidings of trouble in Essex and Kent. John Bampton, a commissioner of the peace, had been driven out of the village of Brentwood by a crowd of hostile peasants while attempting to collect the poll tax and when Sir Robert Bealknap, the King's Chief Justice, was sent to restore order, he too was ignominiously driven back to London.

'It's not safe in the country any longer,' William declared. 'I'm going back to London and taking Mariota with me.'

When Mariota heard, she was distraught. Afraid of the journey, afraid of remaining at Maudesbury, she threw herself into Joanna's arms, weeping hysterically.

'Calm yourself, Mariota,' William reproved her sternly. 'The Abbot of Cirencester is going to London with a strong force and we are to travel with him. In five days you'll be safe behind the walls of London.'

'Five days!' yelped Mariota. 'I can't do the journey in five days.'

'My dear, I don't want to frighten you but we must lose no time. At the moment the trouble is confined to local pockets of unrest, but we don't know that it might not escalate into a full-scale rebellion. We must get to London as quickly as possible. You will manage it, I'm sure.'

'Not without Joanna,' Mariota sobbed, clinging to her sister. 'You'll come with us, won't you, Joanna? You won't make me do that journey alone.'

'Mariota, you won't be alone, you'll have William and all the Abbot's men-at-arms, as well as Bridget to attend you.' Gently Joanna prised her sister's arms from round her neck. 'You don't need me, and I can't leave Lady Isabel here all alone. It's just a little bit of nonsense from some unruly peasants far away from here. There's nothing to worry about.'

'Joanna, I don't think you appreciate the danger you face,' interrupted William. 'These rebels have chased out the Chief Justice of England and a considerable force. It is not just a little nonsense, it is a sign that the unrest which has been plaguing the country these last few months is in danger of getting out of hand. You would be most unwise to stay here, you or the Lady Isabel. You must persuade her to come with us, but we must leave without delay.'

Mariota was looking so frightened Joanna thought she might faint at any moment and she inwardly cursed William for his insensitivity. Better not to argue with him if she didn't want to upset Mariota any more, and maybe he was right. He was saying what Lord Berkeley had been saying at the May Day feast. If ever they were to leave the manor, this was her and Lady Isabel's opportunity. She must get Tristram's mother out of her bed. Maybe the danger was what she needed to make her snap out of her lethargy. Maybe if she had a change of scene it would cure her.

Joanna entered the chamber at the top of the west turret prepared to stand no nonsense. William's fear had been palpable and Joanna did not welcome the thought of being left alone on the manor with a bedridden woman and the surly serfs to face whatever danger was brewing. She went over to the large bed standing in the centre of the room and drew back the faded bed curtains embroidered with Tristram's arms. It was several days since she had visited her mother-in-law and she was shocked now at the change in her. Her face was the colour of parchment and her breathing was so shallow Joanna wondered if she were still alive.

'Why didn't you tell me she was so much worse?' she said rounding accusingly on the serving woman.

'What would be the use? There's nothing you could have done,' replied Martha stubbornly. 'She's in God's hands and it won't be long before she's with Him in paradise, by the look of her.'

Joanna stared down in dismay at the sick woman. Her hands lying loosely on the covers were moving, the bony fingers plucking aimlessly at the sheet. Suddenly Lady Isabel opened her eyes and caught hold of Joanna by the hand.

'The woolclip,' she said hoarsely. 'Is it done?' Joanna was startled. Not since she had taken to her bed had Lady Isabel shown any interest in the manor.

'The woolclip's all done,' Joanna lied reassuringly. 'William is here. He's come to buy it.'

'Good. We must get the money for Tristram. The next time he comes home he will want horses. He wants a lance, you know.' The hand holding Joanna's was hot and dry. 'The haymaking,' Lady Isabel went on. 'They must get on with the haymaking.' Joanna promised that she would find the hayward and tell him to start on the haymaking that very day. Lady Isabel seemed to relax a little and Joanna went on talking about the manor, saying nothing about her struggles with the serfs, or the bailiff's drunkenness, pretending everything was as well as could be, until Lady Isabel drifted off to sleep.

'She just lies there, won't eat nor sleep, just lies there aworrying about the manor,' said Martha. 'She seems happier now that you say it be well. She's sleeping.'

Joanna stared down at the shrunken features of Tristram's mother and knew that there was no question of Lady Isabel leaving her bed. Even in a litter. It would be the utmost cruelty to try to move her. Let her die peacefully at home in the manor where she belonged.

Joanna went back to the hall where she found William pacing restlessly and told him that Lady Isabel was too ill to move, that she must stay behind and look after her. He did not try to persuade her otherwise. He was too concerned with getting Mariota on the road that day to spare much time arguing with her sister. All Mariota's beautiful possessions were to be left behind and William promised that as soon as this trouble was over and the roads fit to travel again, he would come back to Maudesbury to collect them. Joanna could see that Gryffard was a frightened man, in a frenzy to be gone, and it did not make her decision to stay any easier. Her sister, too, increased her fear; Mariota clung to her, weeping, begging her to come with them, saying she was mad to stay unprotected at Maudesbury, that she would never see her again.

Finally Joanna lost her temper. 'Don't be such a wet goose, Mariota,' she cried. 'If I could come with you I would. You're just making it harder for me. Underneath that pose of goodness and obedience you're nothing but a spoiled, selfish little coward. Now go, before William leaves without you, and give thanks to God that he cares enough about you to take you with him.' Immediately her words were out Joanna regretted them, but they had the desired effect. Mariota's face crumpled as she relinquished her hold round Joanna's neck. Still weeping, she allowed the manservant to lift her onto her palfrey. She turned hurt, reproachful eyes upon Joanna.

'You don't understand,' she gulped between her tears. 'It's you I'm afraid for. I shall blame myself for the rest of my life if anything happens to you once we're gone.'

'Nothing will happen to me,' said Joanna with a confidence she was far from feeling. 'I know the people here. They're like children, awkward, lazy, difficult perhaps, but they'll not harm me.'

'Go to the abbey if there's trouble.' said William. 'They'll shelter you.' Joanna couldn't help feeling that if the Abbot had thought fit to run away to London taking all his men-at-arms with him, the abbey was the last place to seek refuge!

With a sinking heart she watched the little cavalcade ride out over the drawbridge – William, the woolpacker, the two menservants and Bridget cradling Mariota's little dog in her arms. Mariota in their midst was hunched into her travelling cloak, a piteously dejected little figure. Joanna hoped she would turn round just once to show that she was forgiven. But although she watched until they were all well out of sight, Mariota never looked back. It was very quiet when they had gone. Joanna wondered about the manor aimlessly, telling herself that she had been a fool to stay. Tristram's mother did not care for her. She had never shown her the slightest warmth in all the time she had been married to Tristram. What difference would it make to Lady Isabel if she were here? Martha looked after her and resented any interference. She had sacrificed the only hope of escape from an unknown peril and for what? For Tristram's sake, she supposed. But what did he care? What did anybody care – except Mariota and she had sent her sister away with angry words.

For two days the Lady Isabel hung between life and death. Joanna made a half-hearted attempt to persuade the serfs to begin haymaking but the weather was wrong, the hayward said, and Joanna pretended to believe him, unable to do battle while the Lady Isabel lay dying. Joanna spent most of her time in the sick woman's chamber and Martha, to her surprise, accepted her. Lady Isabel was very restless, tossing and turning and muttering all the time. Her mind wandered. The only time she seemed to rest was when Joanna sat beside the bed and talked about the manor. Hour after hour she wove fairy tales of how the manor was prospering, how the woolclip was the best they'd ever had and the hay already nearly made, of the improvements they would make when Tristram came back triumphant from the wars. The Lady Isabel listened with her eyes closed and her hands still, almost smiling. But by the morning of the third day even this failed. The sick woman was struggling for every breath she drew, her fingers plucking convulsively at the sheet and when her eyes opened they were blank and unknowing.

'You'd better get the priest,' said Martha. 'It can't be long now.'

Glad to escape from the terrible rattle of Lady Isabel's laboured breathing, Joanna hurried out into brilliant sunshine. The priest was not in the church or in the village. Maybe he was working in the fields. She ran into the large open field with its long raised ridges divided by the furrows which drained the land, where each tenant had his allotted strips. There was nobody working, neither on the strips belonging to Tristram nor on any of the serfs' plots. She ran into the meadows beyond, where the hay stood tall and green, waiting to be cut. Nobody. She ran back to the village and tried the priest's cottage. It too was empty. Where was everybody? Alarmed now, she ran back to the manor house. There was nobody in the stables, nobody in the falcon mews. Swiftly she searched the kitchens, the buttery, the bakehouse and found them all deserted.

Back in the hall she stood panting and listening, but all she heard was her own rasping breath. The silence was eerie. It made her afraid. One of the wolfhounds got up and padded slowly across the rushes to greet her and she seized hold of his strong hairy coat gratefully. With her fingers tightly entwined in his fur she climbed the winding stairs back to the Lady Isabel's chamber.

One look at Martha's face told Joanna that it was too late anyway.

273

'I'm sorry, I couldn't find him,' she said, feeling terrible that she had failed Lady Isabel in her last hour.

'It doesn't matter,' Martha sniffed, much to Joanna's surprise. 'The priest heard her confession on Holy Rood Day. She was a saint, my lady, she'll go straight to paradise.'

Joanna went to the bed and gazed down at Tristram's mother, overcome by a sense of helplessness. The restless hands were still, folded by Martha across her chest, her eyes staring calmly up at the tester above her head, vacant and untroubled. Joanna knelt down and began to say the prayers for the dead, while Martha rocked backwards and forwards in an agony of grief.

Suddenly the wolfhound stiffened. With hackles raised he stood facing the door and growled. Joanna stopped praying and crept to the window. Beneath lay the village huddled up against the manor house wall with, beyond, the open field, meadows and common land, bathed in sunshine. Nothing moved. Joanna stood still, listening intently, but she could hear nothing above Martha's noisy lamentations.

'Stop that racket, can't you, Martha,' she snapped. The dog growled again and from the hall below Joanna heard the deep baying of the other wolfhound. Joanna thought of an ancient battleaxe still hanging in the hall, which Tristram had left behind. Grabbing hold of the wolfhound she set off down the stairs. Halfway down, the dog bounded away from her, baying furiously, and Joanna rushed after him, hoping that while the dogs were busy she would be able to seize the weapon in time to use it on any intruder. Rounding the corner into the hall with the light of battle in her eye, she was completely taken aback to find both wolfhounds cowering in a corner and Black Nick blocking the foot of the stairs. The relief was so great she wanted to throw herself into his arms but she restrained herself and leant weakly against the cold stone of the stairwall.

'I'm afraid Mariota's not here,' she said, struggling for calm. 'William arrived unexpectedly and swept her off to London.'

He frowned. 'You should have gone with them.'

'I know, but I couldn't leave Lady Isabel, not when she was dying, and now she's dead and I was unable to find the priest in time.' Almost she lost control of herself.

'Where are all your serfs?' he demanded roughly.

'I don't know. I can't find anyone. The place is deserted.'

'You can't stay here, Joanna, you'll have to come with me.'

'To Cher Castle?'

'No. My brother and mother and various local families have gone to Berkeley Castle where they will be safe. I'm on my way to London. We'll have to leave right away.'

'William said I should go to the abbey if anything happened.'

'The abbey is the last place I would have thought of sending you. How long will it take you to get ready?'

'But Lady Isabel – we can't leave her corpse unburied.'

'We'll bury her,' he said. 'Now go and get ready, there's no time to lose. And don't bring too many things with you, we shall be travelling fast.'

She stared at him. Just for one moment she was tempted to surrender to him, to be swept along wherever he cared to take her. Just for one moment she had a glimpse of freedom, from the manor and all its cares, from the struggle to be what Tristram wanted, from Tristram and his cruelty. Then she remembered. Nick was just a flirt, a skilled player in the game of love. She could never trust herself to him. She began to retreat slowly up the stone stairs towards Lady Isabel's chamber, shaking her head.

'I cannot leave Maudesbury,' she said. He leapt up the stairs after her and took firm hold of her arm.

'You have no choice, Joanna,' he said. 'Leave now with me, or stay here and face death. You're a survivor, aren't you? Now go and get ready. But be quick. We leave as soon as we've buried the Lady Isabel.' He dragged her down the stairs and across the hall and with a start she noticed a rough-looking man standing guard over the two wolfhounds. Then she recognised him from the May Day feast. It was Sam, the seaman who at the feast had been as close to Nick as any squire. He was dressed in leather and armed to the teeth; Nick too, she realised, as his long sword caught her a crack across the shins, was dressed in chain mail over the old padded gambesons he used always to wear.

'You can let me go,' she said, with all the dignity she could muster. 'I'll come with you.' He left her then and strode towards Lady Isabel's tower with Sam following. 'Be gentle with Martha,' she called after him as she ran towards her chamber.

She was ready and waiting by the time they had finished digging the grave. She watched dry-eyed while they laid Lady Isabel to rest, too shocked by all that had happened to be able to feel anything at all.

Apart from Sam, Nick had two other men-at-arms with him, one of whom saddled her palfrey. Nick lifted her onto her horse and Sam dumped the still wailing Martha behind her.

'Does she have to ride with me?' Joanna asked Nick. 'Can't she ride behind one of your men-at-arms?'

'A man can't fight with a woman clinging round his waist,' Nick said, climbing onto his powerful gelding. 'Since you insist on her coming, you'll have to put up with her.'

But even then Joanna did not feel really frightened. It was all so unreal. The open field bathed in sunshine, the sheep grazing calmly on the common land, the manor house with its crumbling, ivy-coloured walls, silent as the grave. It was all so strange without the toiling oxen and sweating, grumbling serfs. Where were they? She could not believe that the serfs would take up arms. Would leave their homes and their farms for some stupid ideal of freedom. Or that they could possibly constitute a threat to anybody. It was a silly mistake, that was all.

They rode in silence at a fast pace and at first Joanna was too busy trying to keep up to worry about anything else. As she became accustomed to the horses' steady trot, she began to think more clearly about her predicament. God, instead of delivering her from temptation, had placed her straight into Nick's hands. She did not doubt that Nick would try at some time to make love to her and her pulses raced and her senses leapt at the very thought of it. Perhaps God was trying to test her. Perhaps if she resisted this terrible temptation, Tristram would one day come to love her as she loved him. She must not on any account let an inconstant seducer like Nick spoil her dream of love. After all, her love for Tristram was all she had – that and the hope that one day he would come to look at her as he looked at Mariota.

In Cirencester the townspeople were attacking the abbey. A team of strong burghers carrying a huge wooden stake were using it as a battering ram against the closed door, while a mob stood cheering encouragement. Nick drew rein and sat studying their endeavours with professional interest.

'It will be some time before that door yields, if it ever does,' he said, as she came up beside him.

'Do you think they'll let us pass?' she asked nervously.

'Certainly they will. I doubt if this has anything to do with what is happening in the rest of the country. This looks more like the good burghers of Cirencester taking advantage of the general malaise to try to address their grievances. They hate having to take their corn to the abbey. I don't think they'll give us any trouble – they're much too busy with that door.'

He was right. Nobody tried to stop them as they rode through Cirencester and out onto the Fosse Way and for the rest of the day they travelled without incident. Nick kept up a steady pace, and the sun was sinking behind them when he finally called a halt at a wayside tavern.

'I'm sorry, it's not much of a place,' he apologised, dismounting and coming to stand beside Joanna's palfrey. 'But in another hour it will be dark and I think perhaps you've done enough for one day. Let me help you down.' Cirencester was about as far as Joanna ever rode, and she was so stiff she could barely move.

'I can manage, thank you.'

'I daresay you think you can,' he said putting two hands round her waist. 'but you don't fool me. The way you've been lolling about in your saddle this hour or two past you can't have a muscle left in your body that's any good.' So saying he lifted her out of the saddle and set her on her feet. She looked round quickly for Martha but Sam must have whisked her quickly away. Of the other two men-at-arms there was no sign.

'What are you afraid of, Joanna?' said Nick, taking hold of her hands and pulling them up and round his neck. 'Is it me, or is it perhaps yourself?'

This then was the first trial. She could feel his breath, sweet and warm on her cheek. His eyes, intensely blue, looked down into hers and her fatigue vanished. She tried to pull her hands away but he held them clasped round his neck as slowly, gently, he kissed her on the lips. She thought of Tristram, of his golden hair and his perfect chiselled features, of how he had looked in full armour the last time he had ridden away from Maudesbury. She willed herself not to think of the panting beast who leapt on her when he was drunk.

'You think I want to, don't you?'

'I know you want to. Don't fight me, Joanna. I know you wanted me when I took you unawares the other day, as much as I want you.'

She bit her lip and glared back at him. 'But I don't want you,' she said, her candid eyes looking up at him. 'Oh yes, my body does, for you know too well how to make a woman's body crave your kisses and caresses, but my soul does not want you. My heart and mind and soul belong to Tristram. I love him, you see. That is something you cannot understand – love. When you hold me in your arms and look at me as you are doing now, it is my weak body that welcomes you, not my mind and soul. Is that what you want?' She stared at him, believing every word she said. He gazed down at her angrily and she saw that he too believed it. Without a word he turned on his heel and strode away into the tavern.

It was an awkward night. Nick, scowling and distant, bought a mess of stew and some black bread for them. The meat was tough and stringy and tasted vile, but Joanna had eaten nothing all day and was hungry enough to eat whatever was put before her. Nick avoided her as if she were a leper and Joanna told herself that she was relieved.

As soon as she had finished eating, she wrapped herself in her travelling cloak and with Martha beside her lay down on the earth floor to sleep. The tavern began to fill up as night fell and Joanna noticed that some of the latest arrivals looked rough and troublesome. Peering through the smoke-filled gloom, she saw that Nick had flung himself down in the corner of the room furthest from her, with his back to everyone. It would have been comforting to have had the benefit of his protection, she thought wistfully. But God was a hard taskmaster and if such was the price she had to pay for staying true to Tristram, then so be it. God would protect her. She was so exhausted she sank almost instantly into deep sleep.

As she slept she dreamt a man was crawling across the room

towards her. Wake up! she told her sleeping mind. Wake up! She fought up from the depths of sleep, trying to wake, aware of danger – and woke to feel fingers tugging at her cloak. She gave a cry which was instantly smothered by a heavy hand clamped across her mouth. She struggled and squirmed and kicked out vigorously, but she was hampered by her heavy cloak. At first she thought he was only trying to rob her until to her horror she saw the glint of steel in his other hand. She raised both hands, still wrapped inside her cloak, and desperately pushed aside the knife as it plunged towards her. To her surprise he gave a grunt and pitched suddenly forward on top of her, knocking all the breath out of her body. He didn't move and as soon as she could breathe again, she wriggled free – to see Black Nick, with his back to her, blood dripping from his dagger.

'You killed him,' she said, awestruck.

'Yes. Are you all right?' he called over his shoulder. With drawn sword in one hand and his dagger in the other, he was cutting and thrusting two more men who were almost on top of them.

'I'm all right,' she said, scrambling to her feet. The whole room was in an uproar, ringing with the sound of stamping feet, panting, cursing, grunting and the occasional scream.

'Good,' said Nick, extricating his sword from a second victim with a neat flick of the wrist. 'Do you think you can get to the horses? We've got some more work to do here, but we'll join you as soon as we can.'

She seized hold of Martha and with her back pressed to the wall worked her way carefully round the edge of the room towards the door. She could see nothing but a mass of struggling bodies indistinguishable in the gloom, but they were all far too hard-pressed to attempt to waylay her. Outside, it was cool and clear; a full moon lit the yard and Joanna was relieved to see that their horses were all still where they had left them to graze behind the tavern. She untied their hobbles and those of two more horses she found. They were restless and uneasy, disturbed by the din from the tavern and it took all her concentration to hold them.

Soon Nick came out of the tavern with Sam and the other two. 'Good girl,' he said, only slightly out of breath.

'Did you kill them all in there?' she asked, fascinated and horrified at the same time.

'No, but enough to discourage the others,' he said with a grin. 'I'm sorry it's been such a short night's rest. Can you bear to get back in the saddle again?'

'I didn't like it much here anyway,' she said, infected by his calm. 'I found an extra horse for Martha. It'll be better not to leave any behind.' He was standing looking down at her with a mixture of concern and pride. It warmed her and at the same time weakened her.

She longed to lean on him, to feel his arms holding her tightly, comforting her. Angry with herself, she turned away and tried to mount. But she found she was trembling so much she could not raise one leg off the ground.

'I'm afraid we'll have to keep going all night,' Nick said, lifting her into the saddle. 'I don't know how many more there might be in the neighbourhood. By God's mercy there's a full moon.'

'Who were they?' she asked as they set off at a quick trot.

'Outlaws, runaway serfs, thieves and robbers. There were some branded men in there. It's most unusual for them to come out of the forests like that. They've grown very bold all of a sudden. But you needn't be afraid. None of them are mounted. They'll not give us any more trouble as long as we avoid the taverns.'

'I'm not frightened,' she said, and began to shake. Now that the danger had passed she was overcome with fear, revulsion and a trembling worse than the palsy. She seized hold of the palfrey's mane to still her shaking hands and willed herself not to vomit.

'It's all right, Joanna,' Nick said gently. 'We all of us feel fear after a battle, and before one, too! Some – the cowards – feel it during the fighting. You're the bravest lady I've ever had the good fortune to meet and I'd be proud to share a tight corner with you any day. Weep if you want to, it will do you good.'

She didn't weep and she didn't vomit, but she continued to shake, convulsively and uncontrollably, as they rode through the rest of that night while Nick kept pace beside her, talking. She heard his voice and she knew he was trying to take her mind off what had happened. She was glad of his presence so close beside her but she did not hear a word he said. Her mind was too full of the gruesome scene in the tavern, of the sights and sounds and smell of death.

As dawn broke they left the Fosse and rode up towards the high Downs. It was then that Nick began to sing. The deep melodic baritone stole through her shocked mind like balm, easing her pain, and at last her shaking stopped.

The fight in the tavern healed the breach between them. Nick was his old self again, only now he no longer tried to rile her. Instead he was charming, considerate, amusing and kind. He made no more attempts to seduce her and Joanna began to relax and enjoy his company. She forgot the danger they were in, laughed with him, sang with him and felt free for the first time in her life.

They crossed the broad rolling uplands on the top of the Ridgeway, safe in the knowledge that they could see for miles on either side. They slept the next night out under the stars. The third day found them riding through a forest of beech trees, the tall trunks arching high overhead like the walls of St Paul's Cathedral. Sam and one of the men-at-arms rode ahead scouting; Nick stayed close to the women, and the other man-at-arms guarded the rear. Towards nightfall they found a suitable place to camp beside a stream. 'It seems safe enough,' said Nick, inspecting the small clearing carefully, 'but I think I'll take a look around to make sure.'

One of the men-at-arms started to build a fire. Sam was unslinging his bow ready to hunt for their supper and the two wolfhounds were fawning at his side. Martha slid off her horse and onto the ground where she collapsed into a little ball with a moan. Joanna looked at her anxiously. Far from being a fierce chaperon, Martha was proving a poor traveller, so exhausted by the pace they set that at the end of each day she was barely conscious. Joanna did not know what to do with her. They could not leave her behind, but she suspected that much more of this unaccustomed exertion might well kill the poor old soul. Nick, when she sought his advice, had said if she died it was God's will and that she had anyway outlived her usefulness the day Lady Isabel died. It was practical advice but it still shocked Joanna. There was about Nick a hardness which shook her romantic soul and which she found difficult to equate with his acts of gentleness and consideration.

She left Martha lying on the ground to recover and wandered a little way along the bank in search of a place where she could wash and make herself look better after the long day's ride. It was a beautiful summer evening. She sat on the bank of the stream and dipped her feet in the water, listening in delight to the birdsong, feeling at peace with the world. Presently Sam would come back with a rabbit and a pheasant perhaps, or even a deer. They would skin them and roast them on the fire and Nick would talk to her about the books he'd read, or maybe they would sing together.

She bent forward to scoop up a handful of water and as she did so caught sight of a torn piece of pink silk clinging to a thorn bush. It was an odd thing to find in a forest. Curious, she got up to examine it and saw another scrap of pink further away. She frowned as she noticed that on the far bank the bushes were broken, beaten. Someone had come along in a hurry, someone in a pink silk gown that had caught on the thorns in the way.

Joanna crossed the stream and began to search the ground anxiously. A little further the undergrowth became thicker. She saw a slipper peeping out from a patch of bracken. She picked it up. She knew that slipper.

She ran on frantically, searching. Then she saw it. A pale form, lying half in, half out of the bushes. White skin gleaming in the twilight, marred by a multitude of big purplish bruises, long silken tresses of corn-ripe hair spread over the ground and caught like a spider's web on the twigs and branches, eyes wide and filled with horror, staring at her blankly. Naked, abused, dead. It was Mariota.

CHAPTER 26

It was Nick who found her retching into the bushes. Nick who cleaned her up, held her tightly against his chest, who soothed and comforted her until the wracking sobs came, who let her weep and who finally, when the first storm of grief began to subside, picked her up and carried her in his arms back to the camp. There he set her down beside the fire and, crouching in front of her with her hands held tightly in his, told her what he knew.

He had found a small convent with its gates torn off their hinges, its door hanging open and its church violated. After a careful search he had discovered the terrified nuns, huddled inside the refectory. They told him that the day before, a band of men had broken into their convent, defiled their church, stolen their food and then departed.

'Who were they?' she asked, groping through a mist of grief and shock to make some sense of what he was telling her.

'Peasants mostly, armed only with knives, pitchforks, wooden clubs. The nuns recognised some of their own serfs amongst them. Mariota ran out into the forest in panic at the first hint of trouble and the nuns were too afraid to go looking for her.'

'Mariota?' she asked, staring at him blankly.

'It appears that William and the Abbot's party passed through four days ago and stopped to spend the night at the Convent of the Sacred Heart. Mariota was so exhausted by the journey she had vowed she could go no further without a day's rest. But the Abbot was anxious to reach London as quickly as possible. So at William's suggestion they left Mariota in the care of the nuns and went on without her. Her maid stayed with her, and is at the convent now, unharmed.'

'Poor Mariota, she was so afraid,' said Joanna. 'She begged me not to leave her to make the journey alone. Pleaded with me to come with her. And I didn't listen, I let her go alone.'

'She wasn't alone,' Nick said, 'she had William and the Abbot and countless men-at-arms. They should never have left her here – that's all.'

281

Joanna barely heard him. She was thinking of her sister, lying out there in the forest, naked for all men to see. 'We must bury her,' she said, trying to get up, but Nick still held her hands firmly.

'Don't worry, Joanna,' he said. 'I've taken care of everything. Sam is taking her body to the convent now. He has your cloak. He will give her into the care of the nuns.'

'I must go there,' she insisted. 'Where is it?'

'Not more than a good bowshot from the forest edge,' he said. 'But it would be much better if you were to stay here. There is nothing you can do for her now.'

'I can pray for her,' she said simply. 'Will you show me the way?'

'If I must.' He was clearly reluctant to take her to the convent and she wondered whether there were worse horrors in store.

'The nuns – were any of them...?' She could not bring herself to put it into words.

'No, the nuns are very frightened, but none of them is harmed.'

She walked beside him along the narrow track through the forest and every step of the way she thought of Mariota, flying along this very path on her little slippered feet, with her pink silk kirtle hampering her every step and behind her the hue and cry, gaining at every step. Mariota so beautiful and so chaste, who had every man at her feet and yet still managed to keep them all at arm's length – until now.

'Why?' she burst out. 'Why did she run? It's so unlike her. Mariota was much more likely to have remained frozen to the spot.'

'You never know how people will behave in extreme danger. Don't torture yourself, Joanna. She took the wrong course and lost, that's all. There's no profit in the whys and wherefores.'

Poor obedient, beautiful, gentle Mariota. In all her life she had never tried to break free. Joanna could see her now getting ready for William Gryffard the day of her father's ruin. She had been too good to take her chance of happiness and meet Tristram in the church after vespers. She, who had sacrificed herself without thought, should have been at Maudesbury married to Tristram, not dying unshriven and alone at the hands of brutal, lust-crazed peasants!

'It's my fault she's dead!' she cried, in an agony of guilt.

'Stop it, Joanna!' he said. 'It's no good going over and over it like this. There'll be many more dead before this thing is through and if you're not to be one of them you must stop all this nonsense.' But Joanna could not stop, could not stem the tide of guilt and shame which swept over her.

'I should have gone with her,' she insisted. 'It would never have happened if I'd been there. I shall never forgive myself for what I've done to her.'

'Rubbish!' he retorted. 'She's dead because she was a silly little fool and lost her head. There was no danger if she'd stayed with the nuns. Stop blaming yourself, Joanna. It's fruitless.'

It was as if he'd whipped her and she recoiled, hurt. Just for a moment she almost gave way. She wanted to weep, to scream and cry and rage against an unjust God who could let such a thing happen to Mariota of all people. But Nick pulled her along unceremoniously, and his expression was not encouraging. He looked so dreadful when he scowled, really terrifying. He did not understand why she felt so guilty and she could not bear for him ever to find out. He was clearly furious with her for being such a nuisance. Well she would show him, she told herself savagely, putting one foot firmly down in front of the other, grimly concentrating on each step, determined to show no more weakness. He need not fear that she would be a burden.

They had laid Mariota's body in the ruined church, decently wrapped in a shroud. Her hair had been combed and braided and lay in two silken cords across her folded hands. The broken remains of a candle burned at head and foot, and at each corner of the bier a nun knelt in prayer. Mariota's horrified eyes were closed and in the dim light of the candles her face looked calm and peaceful, the livid bruises no longer visible. The rest of the church was a shambles, silver chalices bent and dented lying where they had been hurled to the floor, windows smashed and stained glass scattered into a million pieces, the painting on the walls scarred and criss-crossed by a myriad of knife thrusts.

Throwing herself on her knees before a pile of crushed beeswax, Joanna scrabbled among the debris looking for a piece of candle for Mariota but found nothing left worth lighting. It was then that the full enormity of what was happening hit her. She had been so absorbed by Nick, by the challenge of matching her wits against his, by the knowledge that he wanted her and would not give up trying, by the enticement of his subtle courtship, that she had forgotten the danger. Nick had made it all seem like an adventure. But now Mariota was dead. Killed by peasants who had broken the bonds of service and dependence which for centuries had bound them to the manor. She saw here in the ruined church the evidence of their violent rejection of all law and order, and now she knew it was not an adventure but a disaster which was steadily growing worse.

As she knelt there beside the nuns and tried to pray for her sister's soul, fear slowly began to seep through her sorrow and guilt. The relentless chanting of the nuns beat in her head, driving the message of doom, disaster, death deeper and deeper until she wanted to run from this terrible place to find somewhere to hide where she could no longer hear that dismal dirge. But she must not run, she told herself, biting her lip and clenching her hands firmly in front of her, she must stay and pray for the swift passage of Mariota's soul to paradise. She had robbed Mariota of her chance of love, had taken Tristram when he loved Mariota, had left Mariota to save the family from ruin and had let Mariota ride away to her death.

The hours passed and the nuns relinquished their place to others, but Joanna remained, determined to keep vigil throughout the night. When her knees gave out, she lay full length in front of the bier and with her head pressed against the cold stone of the floor wrestled with the twin demons of grief and guilt.

Some time after the night office, exhaustion must have taken its toll because the next thing she knew she was being carried out of the church. Too drugged with sleep to protest, she knew in whose arms she lay and instinctively snuggled closer. Nick tightened his grip and in her confusion she thought they were alone in the forest. For a moment she let the warm comfort of his strength bring peace and security. Then as her body began to stir in response to the feel of him, she drifted nearer consciousness. She heard in the distance the sound of the nuns' dismal chanting, opened her eyes and saw four bare white walls, unadorned save for a plain carved crucifix hanging above a straw pallet.

'No!' she cried, her overwrought mind a prey to every kind of fear. 'Don't leave me here!'

'Don't be afraid, my love,' Nick replied. 'I'll not leave you. Not now, not ever. But there's barely two more hours till dawn and you need sleep. I'll be here with you – only outside the door. I don't think the good sisters would take kindly to my sharing your cell.' Still dazed, confused, she let him lay her down on the hard pallet, unable to think. He kissed her lightly on the brow and retreated as far as the door while she watched him anxiously.

'Trust me, Joanna,' he said and smiled at her as he lay down across the threshold. Reassured, she closed her eyes and drifted almost immediately back into deep, dreamless sleep.

She woke to the tolling of the convent bell and full realisation. Mariota was dead and danger lurked everywhere. The forest was full of lawless rebels, the convent no sanctuary and many miles of difficult travel lay between it and the safety of London.

Nick was picking himself up off the floor outside her cell. 'They are going to bury Mariota,' he said. 'Will you come?'

She scrambled to her feet and followed him to the churchyard. He had lain outside her door, like a knight errant, all night! Black Nick, the despiser of all forms of knightly chivalry! He was such a difficult man to understand, so tender and understanding one moment, so hard and distant the next. She could not recall much about the previous night, but she distinctly remembered his calling her 'my love' and promising to say with her always. It helped her to get through the next hour.

As soon as the burial was over, the nuns gathered round Nick, wondering helplessly what was to become of them. At the sight of all their anxious faces, Joanna's heart sank. There were so many of them;

284

some were old, others infirm. They could not walk far and there were not nearly enough horses for them to ride. What would he do?

'My men have worked much of the night in your forge repairing the gates and the door only needs to be rehung, it's not damaged at all,' Nick told them briskly.

'Yes, that struck me as strange,' said the Prioress. 'I cannot understand how they broke in so easily.'

'I expect your own serfs helped from within,' said Nick. 'Are any of them left?'

'Only the old and the very young,' replied the Prioress. 'But we are not afraid of work. We shall do all we can to help you.'

She expects us to stay, thought Joanna, and a cold chill ran down her spine.

'I'm afraid we haven't got much for you to eat as most of our provisions were taken by the intruders,' the Prioress went on, 'but your men, I'm sure, are skilled archers and the forest is full of game. Our overlord cannot object to our taking some of his game at a time like this.' The Prioress seemed confident that he would not leave them and Joanna looked at Nick, unaware that her eyes were full of appeal. Let him not abandon them to their fate, she prayed, longing for just one noble act from him.

'I'm afraid we cannot stay,' said Nick, smiling at her encouragingly. 'We have to get to London as soon as we can.'

He doesn't understand, Joanna thought, appalled! He may be able to leave them here, unprotected amid the ruins of their convent, but I cannot.

'Ah yes, you should be safe enough in London,' the Prioress retorted bitterly. 'London's walls are much higher than ours and a good deal thicker. London isn't hard to defend.' Nick frowned and she changed her ground quickly. 'London doesn't need you as we need you. There are knights and men-at-arms aplenty to defend it. Would you leave us unprotected to go to London's aid?'

'I cannot agree that London does not need me,' Nick answered. 'London may need every sword that can be drawn, for I believe that it is in London that this crisis will be solved and a greater crisis averted.'

'God in His infinite mercy has sent you to us in our hour of need,' the Prioress insisted stubbornly. 'The poor child we have just committed to His care was the instrument of His will. She led you to us. Her death will have been in vain if you deny His purpose.' It seemed to Joanna then that she must stay here and help them. Persuade Nick to help them too. He had said last night he would never leave her. If she stayed, he would stay too. She'd allowed Mariota to ride off to a terrible death. She couldn't leave these other women to the same fate.

'God's purpose has always been too deep for a simple fighting man

285

like myself.' Nick was saying. 'I'm a survivor, by God's grace, but I've found that there's a difference between blind trust in God and in helping Him along a bit. I don't believe in praying for deliverance and leaving the rest to Him. I prefer to use the wits God gave me, to get close to my enemy, to seize the opportunity – any opportunity – and then to trust to God to help me see it through.'

'You are my opportunity. Do you blame me for trying to seize it?' retorted the Prioress. He grinned then, acknowledging the hit.

'And what of the King? The King needs me too, he is a mere boy of fourteen summers. He has no army, his uncles are all away campaigning on the country's furthermost borders, he is advised by clerics with no experience of war. Do you ask me to put your convent before my duty to the King?'

'What can you do in London?'

'I don't know, but I believe I may do something, with God's help.'

'You cannot leave us here to starve,' exclaimed Joanna. 'They have no food, no servants, how are we to manage?'

'Us?' he queried sharply.

'Fasting is no hardship to a nun,' said the Prioress, ignoring him. 'If Nicholas de Cher thinks he can help the King put down this rebellion, then of course he must not let our small needs deter him.'

'I do not believe you are in too much danger here, Reverend Mother,' Nick tried to reassure her. 'We have made your house secure again. Sam has killed a deer for you and there is still flour and yeast in your storehouse. You should be able to manage. Come, Joanna, let me help you onto your horse.'

'I'm staying here,' Joanna said, not looking at him.

'What nonsense is this?' he retorted. 'They do not want another mouth to feed.'

'Reverend Mother,' Joanna appealed to the Prioress, 'can I not be of assistance to you here?'

'I can understand your concern.' The Prioress turned her stern gaze on Joanna. 'It is not right for you to be travelling alone with Nicholas de Cher and his men. I believe that in the circumstances you had no choice but to accept his protection when you had to flee from your manor. But God has brought you here to us and it would be more fitting for you to wait here until your husband returns. Perhaps Nicholas de Cher can send a messenger to the Duke of Lancaster in Scotland to tell your husband where to find you.'

Nick was scowling at her and she could see that he was not likely to change his mind. So much for all his honeyed words! It would be better if he went without her, Joanna told herself fiercely. Nick was temptation. Why, he had almost made her forget Tristram, her one love. Nick made her no better than Mariota, transferring her affection to whatever suitor happened to be courting her the hardest.

Immediately she stifled the unworthy thought, guilt overwhelming her at the thought of her sister. But certainly, it would be best if Nick left without her. She would wait for Tristram here and by praying night and day for Mariota's soul atone for her sin. She bowed her head submissively to the Prioress but before she could speak, Nick intervened.

'What of your family?' he demanded. 'What of your father and mother? Who will break the news of Mariota's death to them? You cannot hide away here wasting your time in prayer when your father and mother need you. Dame Mariota was a favourite child,' he explained to the Prioress, 'and her mother is not strong. I am afraid I must insist that Lady Maudesbury comes with us, if only to help avert another tragedy.'

The Prioress gave him a long hard look. Joanna thought of the tiny cell she had slept in, with its cold bare walls enclosing her on every side. Could she bear it? Was staying really the right thing to do? Or was Nick right? Was it her duty to comfort Matilda?

'If I were to come with you, perhaps the Reverend Mother would be content?'

Startled, Joanna looked at the speaker. She was a handsome woman in spite of her nun's habit, tall and straight, with finely chiselled features, who met Nick's gaze unflinchingly.

'I am the sub-Prioress of the Priory of St Helen's by Bishopsgate,' she explained. 'I was on my way back to London from a pilgrimage to Glastonbury and sought sanctuary here at the Convent of the Sacred Heart. I am as anxious to return to London as you, and it is true they do not need any extra mouths to feed. Will you take me with you?'

'The journey may not be easy,' Nick warned. 'We must travel fast and I do not know what we may find on the way. Lady Maudesbury has proved herself a brave and hardy traveller, able to endure long hours in the saddle without food or water. Can you do as well?'

'You need not worry about me,' the nun said. 'I come from a long line of knights. My father fought at Crécy and Poitiers and my mother's father helped Edward III defeat Roger Mortimer at Nottingham. I'm no coward, I promise, and can face, with God's help, whatever danger the journey may bring. I'll not hinder you.'

'We'll take the Mistress Gryffard's maid,' said Nick. 'She is young and strong and can attend Lady Maudesbury and the sub-Prioress in Martha's place. I'm afraid I must leave Martha in your care, Reverend Mother. I regret adding to your burdens but I fear it would kill her to take her further. Joanna, are you ready?'

Joanna went to kneel before the Prioress with her mind in turmoil. Nick was riding roughshod over all her best intentions and she did not know how to gainsay him.

'Tell me what I should do, Reverend Mother,' she pleaded.

'It seems as if God wants to test you a little more before you are ready to join us,' replied the Prioress. 'And, with God's help, we shall be safe here. Go to your family in London and do your best for them. I know that one day you will come back to us. I feel it in my heart. Meanwhile, pray for us, as we shall pray for you.'

'Of course I shall come back,' Joanna promised, knowing it was not what the Prioress meant. 'As soon as this is over, I will bring William Gryffard to you here. He will want to do something for the salvation of Mariota's soul, found a chantry perhaps, restore your ruined chapel. I am sure you will not find Master Gryffard ungenerous. Will you have your nuns continue to pray for her?'

'We shall pray for her anyway, you did not need to ask it,' the Prioress rebuked her gently. 'God go with you and preserve you in safety until you reach London.'

'And with you, Reverend Mother,' Joanna replied.

Riding through the forest with Sister Teresa at her side, Joanna could not help feeling relieved. The thought of staying behind in the convent filled her with an abhorrence far greater than the fear of what dangers lay before them on the road to London, and for the first time since she had known him she was grateful for the obstinacy which made Nick always determined to get his way.

Once they were out of the forest and riding along the open road towards Reading, he ordered them to ride spread out one behind the other, with one of the men-at-arms scouting ahead, the other guarding Bridget, Mariota's maid, and Sam protecting the nun.

'I thought you hated convents,' Nick said conversationally as he brought his horse alongside Joanna's palfrey.

'I thought I did too,' she replied quickly. 'But I found I was wrong.'

'As I've said before, you're not a very good liar, Joanna' he chided her gently.

'I wanted to stay and pray for Mariota.'

'Let the nuns do that, it's what they're there for. You've got to rid yourself of this ridiculous idea that you're to blame for your sister's death. It won't do you any good.'

'You don't understand and I can't explain.'

'I understand more than you think. You're a survivor, Joanna, you, and, I suspect, the next Prioress of St Helen's there. Occasionally survival has to be won at the expense of someone else – it's the price you have to pay. But don't destroy yourself with guilt. You'd do it again, it's in your nature.'

'I can change my nature, with prayer and God's help,' she said.

'Don't, you're perfect the way you are.' If the Prioress could see the way he was looking at her now, thought Joanna, she would never have given her assent to the departure.

'You should have left me there,' she said, hastily looking away.

'I'm no William Gryffard.'

'Then it's not true what you told them? They're still in danger?' Immediately she felt guilty.

'Anything could happen, there are unknown forces loose in the land. I don't know where they are or what they want, what their strength is or who, if anybody, leads them. That's why I'm anxious to get to London as quickly as possible, to find out.'

'And so you left them to their fate!'

'I couldn't take them all to London. In war you have to save the strong and let the weak go to the wall. It's the only way to win.'

She'd been betrayed by him once more. And by allowing herself to be persuaded to leave the nuns, she'd betrayed them too! 'Tristram would not have abandoned them thus,' she accused him. 'A knight always comes to the aid of the weak.'

'Tristram!' he exclaimed angrily. 'Do you really know your husband at all, Joanna? You're in love with a creature of your own imagination, a white knight you've dreamed up out of that ridiculously romantic nature of your. One day you'll discover that the man you love doesn't really exist at all!'

'How dare you!' she cried, stung. 'Just because you thought so little of your knighthood that you threw it away rather than abide by the rules of capture, you think all knights are false.'

'Is that what you thought, that I allowed them to think they'd get a ransom from me, then slipped away without paying it? I know I'm not a hero but I'm not a complete scoundrel.' It was what Tristram had told her but she dared not say so.

'Then are you a knight or aren't you?' she asked, her anger deflated by her confusion.

'I'm still entitled to bear arms, but I don't choose to,' he said with a grin. 'It's an expensive business being a knight and one of them in the family is quite enough, I'd say.' She didn't know whether he was mocking her or not but she was curious.

'How did you manage to excape then?'

'When the French captured me, I made it clear there'd be no ransom. I was so weak from plague they didn't bother to guard me too well. Just threw me in the dungeons with Sam to care for me. Misplaced chivalry you see. They couldn't bring themselves to kill me in cold blood; they thought I'd die anyway. And I would have done had it not been for Sam. He managed to break out of the dungeons and took me with him. We lived off the Gascon countryside until I got my strength back, then made our way to Bordeaux where we caught a ship for home. I might still have been a knight, if God hadn't willed it otherwise. The ship was captured by the French and we were sold to the Turks. By the time I'd served three years at the oar of a Turkish galley, the glory of knighthood had begun to fade a little.'

'But you escaped?'

'One day the galley was captured by pirates, a sailing cog which needed men-at-arms more than oarsmen. So Sam and I changed our oar for a longbow, until I succeeded in taking over the ship from the pirates and Black Nick the sea captain was born!'

'You could have gone home then,' she said.

'I could and I did, but I found my name blackened, my brother happy at Cher, my mother fully occupied in looking after him. There did not seem much point in upsetting them all. So I set about carving a fortune of my own, as Black Nick, and had a good deal of fun.'

He made light of it, but she realised how very hard it must have been. She was beginning to understand how he was able to appear so callous and uncaring at times. To survive the sort of life he had led, he must have done many things he was not proud of.

'But then you came back. Why now?'

'I thought perhaps I had been away long enough?'

She knew it was not the real reason. 'So you are not a knight, yet you are riding to London to serve the King?'

'In whatever way I can.'

'And afterwards – will you go back to sea?'

'Not if I can help it.' He grinned. 'A sea captain's life is hard and uncomfortable. I've prospered since the capture of the Scottish pirate, made enough to buy my own ships and hire a crew to sail them. I'm a ship-owner now, respectable enough to marry and settle down.'

'With Agnes Proudfoot?'

'You see why it was too complicated for me to come back before,' he said. 'I could not expect Agnes to keep her betrothal vow to a disreputable sea captain.'

From his expression it was hard to tell whether he was joking or not. He did not pursue the subject any further, and she let it drop, feeling suddenly depressed. He too became silent, riding along lost in thought.

Once they left Reading the going became harder and there was little time for idle talk. Sister Teresa proved as good as her word. Straight of back and calm of mien she rode through river, forest, field and stream, up hill and down dale with a cool disregard for any discomfort that was a challenge to Joanna to match. At night the women slept huddled together on the ground, while the men took turns on guard. But no matter how exhausted she was, the nun never failed to scramble to her knees and say the night offices. Nick treated her with respectful deference and Joanna with a kind of comradely familiarity which she found more difficult to contend with than obvious attempts to flirt with her. They encountered no more trouble, whether thanks to Nick and Sam's careful scouting and the avoidance of all public pathways, or whether because the danger had gone, Joanna was not sure.

Early in the afternoon of Tuesday, 11 June, they came to Windsor, hungry, weary and not a little anxious, for during the last hour's ride the road had been so thronged they could scarcely move at all. People from all the surrounding shires seemed to be flocking to seek sanctuary and those who could not be accommodated in the castle were encamped on the plain below the walls. Sam's voice grew hoarse from shouting 'Make way, make way!' while they wormed their way through the streets of Windsor towards the castle, jostled by prosperous merchants, beggars, palmers, whores in hoods of scarlet ray, respectable goodwives with their children, crowded waggons, merchants, all clamorous with fear.

'Wouldn't we be better to go straight on to London?' Joanna asked Sam. 'There's still a good few hours of light and there can't be so much as a cranny left vacant in the castle.'

'If we cannot find lodgings for the night in the castle, there is always the church,' said Sister Teresa imperturbably. 'We can keep vigil there for one night to give thanks for our safe journey so far and pray for a speedy entry into London.'

'The master wants to find out if the King's still at Windsor. I doubt if he means to spend the night here,' replied Sam with a judiciously aimed blow of his longbow at a heavily laden mule. The mule broke into a smart trot, trampling on the foot passengers in his path while the merchant on its back cursed and clung on precariously.

They rode through the portcullis to the lower ward where Nick dismounted, threw his reins to a stable urchin and disappeared, leaving them to wait for him in a corner by the curfew tower. The great paved courtyard was as full of confusion as the streets. One or two mounted knights with their squires came and went, servants ran panting from building to building, a noble lady arrived in a gilt and blazoned chariot, was received by a bowing chamberlain and vanished through one of the myriad doors. Rumours and counter-rumours were running wild: a large army of peasants was marching upon London from the south-east; Maidstone was in a state of anarchy; Rochester Castle had fallen and the governor, Sir John Newton, taken hostage.

The confusion and fear which gripped all those about her unsettled Joanna. They were in no condition to defend themselves, she thought; even an army of peasants armed only with sticks and staves could wreak havoc amidst such overcrowded chaos. She began to understand for the first time what Nick had been trying to tell them. Why he had thought it more important to leave the Convent of the Sacred Heart to their fate and press on. There was much that a man like Nick could do here, she thought, resigning herself to a long wait. But he returned soon, with the news that the King was not at Windsor. He had left for London that morning and the court was even now preparing to follow.

'I've arranged for you to travel to London with the rest of the royal household,' he said to Joanna. 'You'll be safe enough with them.'

'What about you? Are you not coming with us?'

'Alas, I cannot – not yet. This is one of Sir Aubrey de Vere's pages, he will take you to the Chamberlain of the Household.'

'You're staying behind to arrange the defence of the castle?'

'No, no, nothing so chivalrous as that, I promise you,' he replied, his eyes dancing.

'Then why can you not come with us to London?' For the life of her she could not keep the disappointment out of her voice.

'Because you don't need me any longer and I don't choose to,' he said, staring out over her head at the milling crowds. Once she would have taken offence at such provoking lack of gallantry, but now she knew him better and guessed that he was deliberately trying to anger her to disguise his real purpose.

'What are you planning?' Why won't you tell me? Is it some silly heroic quest you don't want me to know about?' She knew by the quick, unguarded flicker of recognition in his eyes that she had guessed right, and she felt afraid. 'You love danger, don't you?' she accused him.

'Not as much as I love you,' he said, and for once there was no mocking laughter in his eyes, only an intentness which drove the anger out and left her shaking. For a moment the world stood still, she was unaware of the bustle around them, of Sister Teresa, of the stones beneath her feet, of anything save his eyes looking down into hers. 'Don't be afraid, my heart,' he said. 'I was a hard man to kill before I knew you and I'm not going courting death now – not when I've so much to live for.' Swiftly he bent down and kissed her lightly on the lips. Then without waiting for a word from her, he turned and leapt onto his horse. Blushing, confused, her heart soaring in spite of herself, Joanna watched him ride out of the castle.

'You need not be afraid for him,' Sister Teresa consoled her drily. 'He'll be back to reap his reward, I don't doubt, for the devil knows how to look after his own.'

'How ungrateful, Sister Teresa,' replied Joanna, crossing herself with a guilty glance at the nun. 'How can you say such a terrible thing about a man who has brought us so far, through so much peril into safety?'

'I can say it,' Sister Teresa replied severely, 'because I know that the devil does not always come distinguished with horns and a tail, but in many very appealing disguises. Look into your own soul, my child, and you will know if I speak the truth or not.'

Joanna looked at her feet. It was true. Nick was a consummate charmer, a champion in the tournament of love, and she was in danger of succumbing as easily as all the other ladies who fell at his feet. She had thought that her all-enduring love for Tristram would be armour enough against his charm. But now she knew differently. How fortunate that she had the nun with her to save her from herself.

CHAPTER 27

It was not until the Eve of Corpus Christi that William Gryffard learnt of the death of his wife. Safely arrived in London with the Abbot of Cirencester, William had witnessed the King's entry into the city. The Mayor and the aldermen had ridden out to welcome their young sovereign and escort him through the city on his way to seek a safe lodging in the security of the Tower of London. On the morning after the King's arrival, the first of the Kentish rebels bearing banners and pennons had begun to arrive at Blackheath, and those who had welcomed the King so eagerly the day before realised that his arrival in their midst had only made things worse as it drew the rebels after him, marching upon London on both sides of the Thames estuary.

William, desperate to know what the city leaders proposed to do to keep the rebels out of London, hurried to the Mayor's house, where much to his surprise he encountered Black Nick.

William Walworth welcomed Gryffard. 'You already know Nicholas de Cher, I believe,' the Mayor said, 'but perhaps not in his new colours. We merchants have much to be grateful to him for when he sailed the seas as Black Nick, and he has come here today to help us in our hour of need.'

William Gryffard was astonished. This man in whose company he had travelled all the way to the Cotswolds was the missing son of the de Chers and he had never guessed! William who prided himself on discovering the best-kept secrets was so completely thrown off balance that he was at first unable to concentrate on anything else. Then he realised that Nick brought bad news, that he was telling him that Mariota was dead. William received the news with detached calm. It was not that he did not mind, would not grieve when he could, but just then he was already so tormented by thoughts of what he stood to lose that he had not enough anguish left to spare for the loss of his pretty wife.

In addition to Nicholas de Cher, the men who gathered in the

Mayor's house on that Wednesday, 12 June were the Mayor William Walworth, Nicholas Brembre, Robert Launde, Nicholas Twyford, John Philpot and the three aldermen – John Horn, Adam Karlyll and John Fressh – whom the Mayor had sent to meet the rebels at Blackheath. Gryffard, watching and listening as they argued what was best to be done, deduced that, with the exception perhaps of John Philpot, none of them had known Black Nick's secret. To them he was still Black Nick, the brave sea captain who had prospered sufficiently after his capture of the Scottish pirate to turn ship-owner. Of the de Cher family they knew nothing. It was a relief to William to know that he was not the only one kept in the dark, and in the back of his mind he was busily trying to work out what – if any – advantage could be wrung from this sudden change in Nick's circumstances. But for the moment it was his instinct for survival which was uppermost in his mind.

John Horn was all for allowing the rebellious peasants into the city, and vowed he would go surety for their good behaviour. To William Gryffard's surprise most of the others welcomed the idea of appeasement. Perhaps there was a chance after all of a peaceful settlement, a way out of their difficulties without resort to violence and bloodshed?

But Nick rudely shattered William's growing confidence. 'It's madness,' he pronounced. 'What are a city's defences for if not to keep the enemy out? The city is impregnable. The best-equipped army in Europe could not take it in a year and you want to open the gates to a rabble without arms or the remotest idea of siege warfare.'

'They've promised to pay for everything they take and do no damage to the city.' John Fressh supported John Horn. 'They're starving out there on the heath.'

'Let them starve!' Nick replied. 'Nothing demoralises an army more than starvation.'

'But they swore to set fire to Southwark if we don't open the gates,' Fressh explained.

'Much good may it do them.' Nick was unimpressed. 'They'll starve all the quicker when they lay waste the south bank. In two or three days their empty bellies will start them thinking of the homes they left behind them. Once they do that, the fight will soon go out of them.'

'But there's valuable property in Southwark,' objected William Walworth.

'Much of it yours,' Nick retorted and the Mayor looked at his feet uncomfortably. In the ensuing silence William thought of his beautiful new house behind the city's walls and decided that Nick was talking much sense.

'All very well to talk of sitting out a siege,' Nicholas Brembre said, breaking the silence. 'To do that you have to have the support of the besieged and the trouble is that half London sympathises with the rebels. I doubt if we could keep our own citizens under control with the peasant army beseiging our gates. Besides, we want to look a little further ahead than this immediate crisis. We want to look at what is happening in this city of ours. John of Northampton has been gaining a lot of support recently and now has most of the mercantile guilds behind him. There is a real danger he may become elected next Michaelmas.'

'St Michael protect us,' declared Nick, glaring at him fiercely. 'You'll never win if you cannot learn to fight one battle at a time! The peasant army is the enemy you have to defeat today. John of Northampton can be defeated later. Can't you pack the Guildhall with your supporters for the election, like you've done before?'

'That won't work this time, I'm afraid,' Nicholas Twyford the goldsmith put in. 'John of Northampton has done his preparatory work too well. He has succeeded in winning the support of many of the mercers and even a few goldsmiths, as well as the lesser guilds. He'll pack the Guildhall with his supporters too and probably outnumber us.'

'He must be stopped,' Brembre declared vehemently. 'And now it looks as if God has given us a chance to do it. Remember that time back in the last year of the old King's reign when I ousted that fool Adam Staple? You helped me to do it, Nick, and found us not ungrateful, I think. These ignorant peasants can be used in the same way to destroy Northampton for ever. If we allow them into the city on our terms we can do a deal with them, and deliver them to the King once the time is ripe.'

Nick glowered at Brembre. 'Have you seen these ignorant peasants?' he demanded. 'Have you been to Blackfriars, listened to them, talked to them, as I have? They're men who've left sheep that need shearing, hay standing in the fields, wives big with child; they've abandoned the land they've been bound to for generations and the protection of their overlords to demand their freedom. You can't use men such as that to serve your own ends, they'll rend you to pieces.

'Serfs!' Brembre scoffed. 'Men who until now have never left the manors on which they've been born, who all their lives have done nothing but take orders from the bailiff, or the reeve, who depend on their overlord for all they have. All they need is to be led.'

'They have a leader,' Nick insisted. 'Wat Tyler, a veteran of the French wars who knows how to fight a campaign. They also have a preacher – John Ball. They destroyed Maidstone gaol where the Archbisop of Canterbury had Ball imprisoned and he marches with them. John Ball will rouse their will to fight and Tyler will show them how and where to strike. Do you think you can lead such a combination as that by the nose?'

'I haven't seen the peasants but I have been to the Tower to see the King,' Brembre announced and they were all impressed.

'Who's there with him?' Philpot asked.

'The King's half-brothers – Thomas Holland, and Sir John Holland. Henry Bolingbroke, Gaunt's son, the Earls of Salisbury, Warwick, Arundel and Suffolk, and Robert de Vere of course. Some knights in the King's household. Sir Robert Knollys, Sir Thomas Percy, the Archbishop of Canterbury and the Treasurer.'

'Old men, young boys and too many clerics,' retorted Nick scornfully. 'How does the King's Council propose to save us from the peril at our gates?'

'The King proposes to sail down to Greenwich tomorrow morning to meet the rebels,' answered Brembre.

'Perhaps the King's grace will be able to pacify them and persuade them to return to their homes,' Walworth said but William knew from the look on all their faces that they did not have a great deal of faith in the persuasive powers of a fourteen-year-old boy. It made William feel frightened and he wanted to feel secure. He wanted to feel, like the Mayor, that everything could safely be left to the King.

Brembre had no comfort to offer. 'The King is frightened,' he said, 'although trying his best not to show it, and the Council is divided. If we can but do a deal with these rebels, I believe that the King would be eternally grateful. It is our opportunity to capture the King's favour and that of the city as well.'

'Isn't it rather risky, letting them into the city?' Timidly William voiced his growing fear and saw from the anxious glances cast at Brembre that he was not alone.

'Of course it's risky,' Brembre retorted, 'you don't win without taking chances, as we did before when we defeated Northampton and his friends. The young King was grateful then, was he not? How much more grateful will he be now?'

The men in the Mayor's parlour were clearly more inclined to follow Brembre. They wanted to have their say but, in the end, leave it to someone else to take the decisions and shoulder the responsibility. Brembre had saved the city before, back in the last king's reign. His devious tactics had achieved everything the Victuallers had wanted. He had been right before, why should he not be right again? To them Nicholas de Cher was an outsider. He knew nothing about the complicated tangle of interests dividing the city's loyalties; he was no more than an accomplished mercenary when all was said and done. De Cher had no easy solutions and was too much in love with danger to trust completely. Whereas to the worried men gathered in the Mayor's parlour it seemed that Brembre offered an easier and safer way if the rebels could be bought off with promises. They sided with Brembre because they knew and trusted him and because they wanted his solution to work. They were terrified of the damage the rebels might do to their property in Southwark. They wanted easy solutions, the King's approbation and above all to maintain their hold over the city. They did not understand war. They were merchants and politicians not soldiers.

So it was that early the next morning William, despite many misgivings, rode with the others to the Tower to present to the young King their plan for the salvation of the city. He hated leaving his precious house at such a time, but he had allowed his instinct for caution and self-preservation to be overruled by an even stronger desire for gain. For Brembre had convinced him that if the scheme worked, as it could not fail to, then it would be those who had gone to the King on Corpus Christi morn who would reap the reward, of which a knighthood would be the very least each of them might expect.

They arrived at the Tower just as the King returned from his meeting the rebels. The boy was looking dejected and it was clear that the meeting had not been a success. With him in his barge he had taken the Chancellor and the Treasurer, and four further barges had carried the remaining members of his household. With some state they had rowed down to Greenwich but when the King's councillors saw the unruly multitude massed on the south bank below Blackheath, they had dissuaded him from landing. The commons of Kent had drawn up a petition asking for the heads of those close to the King whom they considered to be traitors. John of Gaunt, Sudbury the Archbishop of Canterbury, Robert Hales the Treasurer, John Fordham the Keeper of the Privy Seal, and many others. Since the King could not agree to execute all his principal advisers, he prevaricated by suggesting a further meeting at Windsor on the following Monday, and told the rebels to disperse. As the royal barges had moved off upstream to return to the Tower, there were cries of 'Treason!'.

The young King was delighted when told that the Mayor had succeeded in opening negotiations with the rebels. For a time the city's leaders basked in the warmth of royal approval and William congratulated himself on having had the sense to stick with Brembre. The ex-Mayor knew how to get on in the world. He knew how to seize opportunities, how to claw back profit out of disaster. But later in the day, while they were still gathered in the Tower, Nicholas de Cher arrived with the news that the peasants had entered London and were running amok. The Mayor's plan had failed and London was at the rebels' mercy. The angry King accused the Mayor of failing to defend the city and withdrew with his Council, leaving the city representatives to contemplate the failure alone.

297

Amongst their number was William Gryffard, his anxiety and alarm now turning to the most profound anguish. He was consumed with fear – for himself, for his precious possessions, and most of all for his new house, the heart of his far-flung commercial empire. As evening came, he watched from a turret window in the Tower the sky glowing vividly from some twenty or thirty fires burning in different parts of the town. How much everything had changed since the optimism of early this morning. How much better things would have been if they'd only listened to Nicholas de Cher.

He turned away from the window, unable to bear the message of doom written in fire across the sky, and saw the same tale proclaimed large on the worried faces of the other men in the room. Restlessly, William walked the chamber, consumed by a burning desire to know what was really happeing out there in the city. Without information he was powerless to help himself. Warily he glanced at Nick, who as the bearer of bad tidings had been banished from the King's presence and left to share their disgrace. He would have news. Nick grinned at him with a most unnerving cheerfulness. William crossed himself surreptitiously. There was something positively unnatural in the way that man loved danger. But William was prepared to talk with the devil himself if he could learn anything thereby. Nervously he approached Nick, glancing cautiously over his shoulder. No one else was within earshot.

The rebels had first made for the Marshalsea prisons in Southwark, Nick told him, released the prisoners, destroyed the buildings and razed to the ground the fine houses belonging to the keeper of the Marshalsea, Richard Imworth. After this, some of them had moved west along the river to Lambeth where they broke into the Archbishop's palace, destroyed his goods and burnt all the books and records they could find. Others destroyed a brothel run by a Flemish woman who rented the tenement from William Walworth, the Mayor. After this Walter Sibil the Alderman of Bridge had lowered the drawbridge and the rebels entered London unopposed. At the same time, Alderman Tonge of Aldgate ward had given up and opened the city gate to the Essex rebels. Once the rebels gained access to the city itself, they split up into separate bands to carry out individual acts of plunder, to settle private quarrels or merely to carouse in the city taverns at no cost to themselves.

'My house?' William asked, trembling. 'Did they break into it, do you know?'

'I have been to your house,' Nick reassured him. 'The Burgeys family have taken refuge there and with them is their daughter, Lady Maudesbury. They very sensibly did not open their doors, unlike some Londoners, and all is well.'

'Then the house is safe? It has not been sacked?'

'Not as yet,' replied Nick. 'At the moment the rebels seem intent on more important targets and when I left the city were in the process of sacking the Duke of Lancaster's Savoy Palace.'

'I ought to be at home, to make sure nobody breaks in. I should never have come here. It was Master Brembre who persuaded me. Do you think if I were to ride out now I could get back into the city unharmed?'

'Don't worry, your house is in good hands.'

'But suppose they should be frightened into letting the rebels in?' William found it difficult to accept Nick's assurances; he could think of many who might bear a grudge against him.

'Lady Maudesbury is not afraid of anything,' Nick said with a laugh. 'She will guard your house well for you.' William's sharp ears, so atune to seeking out a man's vulnerable point, detected something in the other man's laugh. Was it joy? A ring of pride? He looked at Nick sharply.

'Lady Maudesbury,' he said. 'She's in London? How did she get here?'

'I brought her,' said Nick. 'She was alone, the Lady Isabel had just died, the serfs ran off. I could not abandon her there.'

'No, no, of course not.' Through his fear, William's brain began groping towards an interesting idea. 'Lady Maudesbury was with you when you found my poor dear wife at the convent. Did she not want to remain with the nuns, to pray for her sister's soul?'

'I did not consider it safe for her, after what happened to Mariota.' Nick turned away brusquely. Too brusquely! A tiny bolt of triumph, quicker than an arrow's flight, shot through William's soul. He had stumbled on a secret. He did not know how he would be able to use it yet, but a secret was better than gold if put to proper use.

Nick was staring out of the window and something about the intentness of his gaze alarmed William.

'What is it?' he asked.

'The first of the rebels, come in search of the King,' Nick replied. 'You can forget about trying to ride back to the city, you wouldn't get past St Catherine's Hill.'

William joined Nick at the window. A small party of rebels was settling down beyond the Tower walls beneath a banner of St George, and from further afield he could see more running towards the Tower.

'Blessed Virgin save us, we're trapped.' William felt his knees turn to water. 'What do they want?'

'What they've always wanted, to talk to the King,' said Nick calmly. 'At least while they're here they're not plaguing London. The city lies at the mercy of the peasants any time they care to return. We must keep them here or draw them away – from the Tower and from the city. London must be regained. If they defeat us now, here in the cap-

299

ital, they will defeat us throughout England.'

William trembled as he thought of the wool he had bought making its way by packhorse to London, and he suddenly remembered with a shiver another investment he had made which now looked as if it might have been a serious mistake.

'And if we succeed in driving them out of the city, do you think they'll ever go back to the land?' he asked.

'Where else can they go? They're peasants, remember.'

'But the land, what will become of it if they don't?' William cast a frightened glance out of the window again. The numbers on the hill were swelling alarmingly.

'There must be many a landowner asking himself that very question today,' Nick replied, turning his back on the window and raising a quizzical eyebrow. 'You believe in taking a chance, Master Gryffard, in profiting from the misfortune of others. How big a chance are you prepared to take? Would you buy land now it's cheap?'

'Would you?' William countered. It was as if the man had read his thoughts.

'I'm a ship-owner not a knight. What would I do with land?' Nick replied carelessly.

William's brain began to race. His continued success he owed not so much to his willingness to take risks but to his ability to recognise failure and cut his losses. It was the failure of one of his most recent ventures which was worrying him now.

'I bought Sir Tristram de Maudesbury's wool from him – not only for this year but for many years to come.' At the time it had seemed like a brilliant bargain. A guaranteed supply of wool for the future with a chance of becoming lord of the manor should the wool fail. But now, if the battle with the peasants was lost, he would have no wool and be lord of nothing but trouble. 'You'll be manor lord of Cher one day,' he went on. 'Your manor lies not far from de Maudesbury.' Nick was gazing round the room as if totally uninterested, but William felt compelled to persevere. 'I'd be willing to sell you Sir Tristram's pledge. I only did it to help Lady de Maudesbury, for my poor dear wife's sake, you know. But what do I want with land? It was the wool I was after and I thought Mariota would be pleased to visit her sister each year when the woolclip was ready. But now Mariota is dead, and to be frank with you, I'd rather have money in my hand at a time like this.' Would the rascal want it? he wondered. Nobody else would. It all depended on whether he had guessed Nick's secret correctly. If Nick was in love with Joanna, it just might provide him with an unlooked for opportunity. But Black Nick said nothing.

From outside, the sound of shouting, singing and occasional chanting floated through the narrow window. William could see the rebels massing on the hill beyond the Tower, and he fought down rising

300

panic. Here inside the Tower they were safe – weren't they? A chill ran down his spine as he thought of the city with its impregnable walls and how easily the rebels had entered.

'If Sir Tristram defaults on the wool, his land is no use to me,' he continued, more to take his mind off the immediate danger than in any hope of succeeding. 'What do I know about running a manor? I'm a merchant. I may be ruined by the time this is finished. But you'll be set fair. Your ships are safe at sea away from all this. You can afford to wait. It's an opportunity that might never come your way again.'

Still Nick said nothing. He had turned away and seemed engrossed in the view from the window. William wondered if he'd been wrong. It was not often his intuition let him down. 'I did it for Lady Maudesbury, she begged me to help Sir Tristram mount his lance.' A muscle in Nick's cheek twitched. 'But of course I cannot go to her now and ask for it back and I don't think there's much chance of my seeing the wool. All the sheep will have strayed and it may be years before the manor is able to produce what Sir Tristram promised me.'

Nick swung round. 'How much for your bond?'

At the look in his eyes William quailed. Fighting a desire to remove himself to the furthest corner of the chamber, he said, 'What is it worth to you?'

Nick turned back to the window. 'There must be nigh on a thousand of them,' he said and William trembled, afraid that he had lost interest or was merely teasing him, afraid that he had misread the man and in so doing made him a present of a most valuable piece of information.

'I have a round ship, the *Margaret*. She left Bayonne at Rogationtide with a cargo of fine Gascon wine and twenty bales of leather – the best Spanish cordwain,' Nick said quietly, so quietly William had to strain his ears. 'Her cargo in return for your bond.'

'Of course I'd rather have gold,' said William, looking down quickly to hide his exultation.

'But you'll take my cargo,' Nick said without even bothering to turn round. 'Have you the wool options with Sir Tristram's mark on them?'

'At my house. Where is the *Margaret* now?'

'At anchor in the Pool of London.' So close at hand and yet out of harm's way – William could scarcely believe his ears. Only a man seriously in love could make such a generous offer at a time like this. 'And the bills of lading?' he asked eagerly.

'Gently, gently, my friend. If the King doesn't do something soon to placate that rabble out there, your bond may not be worth very much. I hate to think what they'll do to London if they get no satisfaction here.'

His words plunged William instantly back into a paroxysm of fear.

Terrified, he peered out at the hill beyond the moat and stout walls of the Tower. It was dark with the massed ranks of rebellious peasants. They were drawn up beneath a variety of banners and pennons and had all the appearance of a large determined army settling down for a long siege. To William, who had never faced any kind of army, let alone been besieged by a screaming horde clamouring for the heads of their enemies, it was a sight to freeze the blood and drive from his heart all pleasure in the deal he had just struck with Nick. He began to doubt whether he would ever leave the Tower alive, and with this painful thought came the even more agonised one that he had been so busy trying to preserve his worldly goods that he had made no provision for his soul in the life to come. His hands grew clammy and he began to tremble violently at the thought of the chantries he should have endowed, of the gifts he ought to have made to the poor, of bequests and benevolences he might have devised to buy his way to paradise.

He was aroused from these painful reflections by the sudden arrival of the King. Instantly the sombre chamber was transformed by a bustle of noise and colour, the clangor of armed men in chain mail covered with surcoats emblazoned with their arms, the weighty authority of the clerics in their swirling scarlet trimmed with precious fur. The King, a slight figure, with the Lilies of France in white and blue and the Lion of England in red and gold embroidered across his chest, looked apprehensive. Most of the men with him were known to William: the old Earl of Salisbury owed him twenty crowns; Suffolk and Arundel had also frequently allowed him to lend them money.

The city representatives bowed low and an expectant hush fell upon the chamber. The boy King looked helplessly at his mother, the Princess Joan, who laid a hand on his shoulder with an encouraging smile.

'How would you suggest we take the city again?' The Queen Mother looked at them all quite pleasantly as if she at least did not hold them responsible for having lost it.

'There are six hundred armed men in the Tower. If we lead them out against the rebels encamped on St Catherine's Hill, can you arrange for a simultaneous attack on the insurgents in the city?' demanded the Earl of Salisbury.

'Willingly,' promised the Mayor, eager to restore his claim to authority. 'If we strike at once we might take them by surprise, while they are still sleeping off the effects of their debauch.'

'Just listen to the mob out there howling for poor Sudbury's blood,' Brembre exclaimed with brutal practicality. 'Do you think there'll be many sleeping on St Catherine's Hill this night? How can you hope to reach London to rouse them, let alone take anybody by surprise?'

'It's a pity you did not think to employ such vigorous action while the rebels were still outside the city gates,' the old Earl accused them. The merchants looked at each other uncomfortably and William shrank further into the shadows, hoping he'd not been recognised.

'There are archers in the Tower,' the Earl of Suffolk said. 'Let them fire a volley into that crowd down there. Let them feel the sharp point of an arrow. That'll soon put them to flight.'

'And drive them back into the city,' Nick broke in savagely. Then he went down on one knee before the Queen Mother. 'If the King were to offer to ride out to meet the leaders of the rebels and to hear their wrongs—'

'I've tried talking to them already,' interrupted the King, ' but they wouldn't listen to me.'

'If the King had been allowed to disembark and talk to them, they might have been less angry.' Nick, still kneeling, turned his head in the direction of the Archbishop of Canterbury. 'I was in the rebel camp that day and listened to what they said. They are simple people weighed down by a great grievance which they wish to relate to their King. They are loyal to you, Sire. It is your uncle John of Gaunt they blame. It seems to them that he stands between them and their ruler, and they swear they will have no king called John.'

'What should I say to them?' asked the boy.

'Promise them what they ask,' said Suffolk. 'Say that if they will but disperse to their homes again you will grant them all their demands.'

'Give in to them, you mean,' sneered Brembre.

'He need not keep his promises,' Suffolk retorted. 'They can always afterwards be repudiated as obtained under duress.'

'You surely do not mean that my son should risk his life by going out to talk to that ravening horde,' exclaimed the Princess Joan. 'You would throw a mere child to the wolves because you yourselves have not the courage to fight!'

'The mere child's father commanded a wing of the army at Crécy when only a year older and led them to victory,' replied the old Earl of Salisbury. 'Would you deny him a chance to win his spurs?'

'The boy Daniel, you will recall, with God's protection came unscathed out of the lion's den. God will protect the King's grace.' The voice of the Archbishop was calm, although his face was white and strained; the repeated calls for his head were taking their toll.

'His youth and innocence is an advantage, don't you see, Ma'am?' Walworth tried to persuade her. 'If we take a good escort of knights and men-at-arms, he'll come to no harm.'

'Not too many armed men.' Nick spoke directly to the King. 'They trust you, Your Grace. If you were to show you trusted them in return, they might be prepared to listen to what you say.'

'If you say they trust me, then I will go,' said the King. 'Who will come with me? The whole Council?'

'Not the Archbishop, it's him and the Treasurer they're after.' Brutally Brembre spelled out what all knew and none up to now had dared say.

Robert Hales, the Treasurer, stiffened. 'The rebels enter London, Rochester Castle falls without a blow. How safe is the Tower?' One or two of the merchants again looked at each other uncomfortably.

'The safety of the Tower is not in question,' Nick put in impatiently. 'It is the safety of the city we have to worry about. If the peasants get no satisfaction here at the Tower they will return to the city and wreak vengence on it and on all its inhabitants. Somehow we must draw them away from here without driving them back to London. If the King will arrange to meet them in Mile End fields, that might draw enough of them away for us to slip back into the city and organise its defence.'

'And then the Archbishop and Treasurer could make good their escape,' added Brembre. The Treasurer gave a nervous nod of agreement but the Archbishop, William noted, seemed not to take much interest. He was staring pensively at the luxurious trimming on his scarlet gown. He looked resigned and William had a premonition that Hales was right and that the Tower, should he and the Archbishop not succeed in making good their escape, would prove as susceptible to the rebels as had Rochester Castle and the city.

'We shall accompany the King,' said Salisbury. 'As soon as we leave for Mile End fields, the Archbishop and the Treasurer must slip away by river. You too, Ma'am.' he added, turning to the Queen Mother. 'You should leave with your ladies and take Henry Bolingbroke with you. I wouldn't give Gaunt's heir much of a chance if the rebels should find him here.'

'You're mad, all of you,' Sir John Holland, the King's half-brother broke out. 'What could be safer than the Tower? Why don't we all stay here and wait for succour?'

'What succour?' demanded Arundel. 'John of Gaunt's in the north, which considering how that mob hate him is doubtless just as well. The Earl of Cambridge has already set sail for Portugal with his army. The knights in the shires are themselves under siege. There is nobody to come to our rescue but ourselves.'

There was silence in the chamber, broken by the sound of shouting once more from St Catherine's Hill. Involuntarily the boy King glanced towards the window. Then he squared his shoulders and looked at his mother.

'I will rescue you,' he said.

304

CHAPTER 28

Early next morning – Friday, 14 June – the heralds proclaimed the King's intention of meeting the rebels in Mile End fields. Soon afterwards the cobbled court just inside the entrance of the Tower began to fill with mounted men. They were unarmed save for their daggers but one or two had taken the precaution of wearing chain mail beneath their fur-trimmed gowns.

William Gryffard had no chain mail and, as he waited for the King to appear, he wished devoutly that he did not have to follow the King upon this hazardous mission. In an agony of apprehension he gazed up at the Tower's fine battlement and the reassuring sight of the archers posted on it. He longed to stay behind in this greatest of fortresses. He looked nervously around him. They were all here, Walworth, Brembre and the others, waiting to ride out with the King; he had to go if he wanted to be counted among the leaders of the city; he wanted the power that leadership brought and all the advantages that came with it, but he longed to hide away in the Tower and let others do the fighting for him.

A fanfare of trumpets announced the arrival of the King, surrounded by his nobles. William fixed his eyes on the bright circlet of gold ringing the boy's fair curls, seeking courage from its symbolic power, but he could not rid himself of the thought that the wearer was an untried boy desperate to live up to the heroic deeds of his father and grandfather. The portcullis rose with a tremendous rattle of its well-oiled chains, and William gagged on the bile that rose in his throat as he looked through the open gateway and saw the lowered drawbridge leading out into unknown peril. Now that the moment had come he could not move, could not bring himself to leave this blessed, well-defended shelter, could not endure the thought of what waited for him outside the Tower's immense security.

'Courage my friend,' Nicholas Brembre smiled all too knowingly as he caught his eye. 'When we settle this affair we'll be knights all of us.'

Knighthood! There was a thought worth clinging to! Gryffard gathered up his reins in hands that shook, and urged his horse forward, sustained by bright visions of knightly glory, the summit of all his ambition.

A cry arose as they crossed the drawbridge, a howl of glee which shook William to the core and pierced his threadbare courage. He was so frightened his heart was pounding in his chest and he could feel the sweat trickling down his back inside his velvet gown. The rising ground opposite the Tower seemed to him to be completely covered with a heaving, threatening, noisy mass – like a piece of putrid meat alive with vermin. He looked back longingly over his shoulder at the haven of security he had so foolishly left. The portcullis was being quickly lowered again and he was cut off, retreat impossible.

Silently he cursed Nicholas de Cher who it seemed to him had persuaded the King upon this foolhardy enterprise, but who now had stayed behing with the Queen Mother and her ladies, the Archbishop and the Treasurer, safe and protected in the Tower, leaving them to face the mob.

They rode up the hill accompanied but unmolested, and a little of William's panic subsided. No one had dragged him off his horse as yet and as they breasted the hill and left the Tower behind, only the most fleet of foot were able to keep up with their swiftly trotting horses. William looked back and saw a great crowd following in their wake and was reminded of a story he had once heard in Bruges, about a piper who had been able to rid a city of a plague of rats. The King was their piper and he was drawing the rats away from the stricken city. Perhaps the plan might work after all! Then one of the rebels suddenly leapt up and seized hold of the King's bridle and William felt his gut go liquid with fear. The King's horse threw up its head nervously but the boy kept his seat, as Walworth and Brembre pressed forward to be at the King's side.

'It's Thomas Farringdon, leader of the Essex rebels,' muttered someone in William's ear. 'What's he saying?'

William could not hear and he did not care. He could stand it no longer. Any minute now a large calloused hand would be laid on his own bridle and he would be dragged from his horse and clubbed to death. The price of knighthood came too dear. He looked round wildly and saw the King's two half-brothers easing away. Nobody tried to stop them. A second rebel now had hold of Brembre's bridle and was arguing hotly. It was his moment! His skin crawling with fear, every second expecting a shout or an angry face to appear at his knee, William slipped away. Once he looked round but no one followed. He bent over his horse's neck, dug frantic heels into the animal's sides and galloped after the fast-disappearing Hollands.

He had ridden a mile or two before the fear which had so overwhelmed his reason subsided sufficiently for him to be able to think coherently. It was then that he realised that the King's half-brothers were riding not towards the city but north and he began to consider the unpleasant alternatives now facing him. He could continue this frenzied pursuit of the Hollands and perhaps find himself in greater danger than that he had just escaped, or he could return to London. All his instincts were to return to London, to his home and his possessions. But was it safe? Nowhere was safe any more.

He drew rein. Out here he was alone and at any moment could be set upon, with none to come to his rescue. In London there was his house, as secure a refuge as any he could think of, if he could but reach it safely. Nick had assured him his inn was unharmed, staunchly defended by the Burgeys family. But was that still the case? The peasants had sacked the Duke's Palace of Savoy and burnt half the Mayor's property in Southwark; suppose his house and all his valuable records had been burnt to the ground?

He could not bear the thought a moment longer. Forgetting his fear in his anxiety for his possessions, he turned his horse round and galloped back towards London.

He entered the city through the Aldgate and was greatly relieved to see that the Priory of Holy Trinity on his right appeared unharmed. The Priory gates were firmly closed and in the street nothing stirred. William trotted swiftly past the closed doors and shuttered shops, watched by many an anxious eye from the windows above. His horse's hooves rang in the silence, adding to his nervousness. He kept peering to right and to left, missing the raucous cries of the shopkeepers calling their wares, the ringing clangor coming from the open workshops along the way, the persistent apprentices touting for trade, the normal noisy hullabaloo of every working day in the city. It was not the peaceable quiet of a holy day; it was a brooding, ominous quiet like the heavy threatening stillness that comes before a storm.

Once he heard shouting and a high-pitched cry for help which seemed to come from the direction of Chepeside. Crossing himself fearfully and praying for deliverance he hurried onward. Once his horse shied and hesitated, blowing alarm though distended nostrils. Something, which might have been a bundle of rags or could have been a body, was lying in the gutter, but William didn't stop to investigate. He kicked, frantic in his haste, until the horse bounded forward, ears back, head swinging from side to side, snorting his suspicion.

Not far now. By St Andrew Undershaft at the top of Cornhill he drew rein and anxiously scanned the jumble of towers, roofs and spires to his right, trying to pick out his own three-storey mansion. He saw the arched stone cloisters of St Helen's Priory set in its acres of green and nearby he could just make out the lofty roof of his own house with the sun shining on its bright new thatch. 'Merciful Saviour be praised,' he whispered in relief. Then he began to shake as his muscles, tensed and strung tight as a bowstring all morning, suddenly relaxed.

Feeling much better, he urged the horse forward once more, relieved of his worst fears and longing to be home, looking forward to hours of quiet in his counting house, alone with his ledgers, when he could plan in peace and solitude how to survive the worst effects of the crisis. He turned into Lime Street and approached St Peter Upon Cornhill. Once past the church he would be within sight of his gates. He was nearly home.

Suddenly two men leapt out from behind the church.

'Where are you going?' they demanded as they seized his bridle.

'Home!' replied William with a small squeak of terror. 'It's just round the corner.'

'That your house? The fine new one, all built of stone? Big as a nobleman's inn.'

'Yes, yes.' William was fumbling for the moneybag he always kept tied to his waist. He knew to the last groat how much there was in it – more than these two might earn in a year, but he was so desperate to reach the safety of his house he was willing to part with it all if they would only let him pass in peace.

They took the money and without even bothering to count it let him go. With a hasty prayer of thanks to the Almighty for this lucky escape, William rode round the side of St Peter's Church. There, at last within sight of his home, he stopped dead in his tracks and trembled at what he saw.

His house stood firm, its great door barred and all the shutters on the ground floor firmly in place, but encamped before it, some lying, some standing, with all the appearance of those who waited for a purpose and who would not be easily put to rout, were some of the meanest-looking men William had ever seen. How could God be so cruel as to give him a house so stout and strong and then leave him on the wrong side of it?

'Be this here the man you want?' The voice of one of William's recent captors sounded like the Death Crier in his ear. 'Says he lives here. Wants to go home, he says. Pay anything, that's what him says.' Harsh laughter echoed all around him as a man detached himself from the crowd and came to examine William. He was barefoot and dressed in rags, although he carried a long, sharp knife. His hair and beard were matted and his face tinged with prison pallor. He grasped the mane of William's horse in one bony hand and peered up at him. Quickly William looked away but not before he'd seen bitter recognition in the other's eyes.

'That's him, the devil take him!' The man hawked and spat at William's knee. 'I've dreamt of this day, many's the day and night I've

308

dreamt on it but never until now did I dream that God in his mercy would be so good.'

'I don't know what you mean,' stuttered William, desperately trying to gather his scattered wits. 'I've never seen you before in my life.'

'You don't remember my face maybe, but you'll remember my name perhaps, Ben Smale. And you'll remember my debt to you – that's summat your kind never do forget, what's owing.'

'If it's money you want, I can let you have some. Alas I've given all that I had in my purse to your friends back there, but there's more in my house for you if you let me go.' Bitterly William regretted having thrown away so impetuously the entire contents of his moneybag.

'Ah, what would you give to be allowed into that fine new house that's all shut and barred against us now?' the hoarse voice taunted at William's side. 'What'll you pay?' Quickly William calculated the sum he had already parted with and wondered whether the two men would tell their friend how much they had got. He doubted it. He offered half as much to his tormentor, expecting him to haggle and prepared to raise the sum a little if he did.

'Do you hear him now,' squealed Ben Smale. 'He'll pay me now, all right, to save hisself. Though he'll trick me again if he can. He'd lend his soul to the devil and still try to buy his way into paradise – that's what a dirty-dealing trickster he is. Lends me fifty golden guineas to get me own place as a master bladesmith but he doesn't say, when he gives me the money, that it'll cost me more than that when I comes to pay it back. And when I keep him waiting for his dues, what does he do? He seizes my house, that's what he does, and my goods, and has me thrown into the Fleet for debt. Usurer! That's a sin against Holy Church, but what do the fat churchmen care? Nothing, that's what.'

William clutched the mane of his horse and trembled as with the ague, darting frightened glances at the sea of grinning faces crowding round him.

'Usurer!' they shouted. 'What shall we do with him, Ben?'

'Throw him in the Fleet, let him see what it's like to be a prisoner,' shouted Ben Smale, hopping up and down in his excitement.

'The prison's gone, we burnt it down, remember?'

'Then we'll throw him in the river instead. Let him have a taste of Fleet water – I've had to endure the stench of it these three years past.' Eager hands reached up and grasped William's fur-trimmed gown. Desperately he clung to his horse's mane, but they prised his fingers loose, dragged him from his saddle and hurled him to the ground.

It cannot be happening, he kept thinking. This cannot be happening to me. They drove him into the middle of the road and thrust him down on his knees in the gutter. He knelt there with the liquid waste oozing through the rich velvet of his gown, an abject, trembling, broken vessel of fear, unable to think, unable to fight, convinced his last hour on earth had come.

'Blessed Mother save me!' he screamed to himself, and in his agony he did not even realise that he had shouted it out loud.

Joanna heard the shriek. She was in the solar overlooking the street, sitting with her mother and her sister Alice, the maid Bridget and Alice's two youngest children. She was reading to them tales of suffering and heroic endurance from the Book of the Saints, trying to ignore the man Ben Smale clamouring for his rights as he had been doing all morning. They had let him rant and rave unanswered, knowing that they were safe behind the shuttered windows and firmly barred oak door. They had hoped that Smale would grow tired of his vigil and seek reparation elsewhere, but he did not leave, and Joanna had for the last three hours lived in dread of what would happen to anyone who tried to come to them. At the sound of William's scream she ran to the window.

'The brutes,' she said. 'They've got William!'

'Sweet Jesus have mercy,' moaned Matilda from where she lay prostrate upon the large bed. 'What will become of him?'

'We must do something.'

'No, Joanna!' shrieked Matilda sitting bolt upright on the bed. 'I beseech you, don't! Don't cause trouble, you'll get us all killed.'

Joanna hardly heard her. She was counting them as they pelted William with refuse. Too many for the servants in the house to deal with. She thought of the men who served William, last seen cowering together in the kitchen as Smale and his friends hammered on the door outside, and she knew any idea of armed rescue was out of the question. Black Nick and Sam would make short work of them. If only he would come! Yesterday he had called to see that she was safe and promised to return soon, and she had been secretly relying on his timely return to rout the besiegers at the gate.

It wasn't the first time she'd thought of Black Nick. She had fought so hard to do as Sister Teresa had commanded, had stifled the leaping sense of joy which thinking about him brought, had almost succeeded while the nun was still with her, but when Sister Teresa had returned to St Helen's Priory, Nick kept popping into her thoughts unbidden at all times of the day and night. Resolutely she thrust all thought of him out of her head.

'If John were here,' said Alice, 'he would know what to do.'

John Constantyn had brought Alice and the children to take shelter in William's house two nights ago, when the peasants had first appeared outside the city walls. Then he'd taken their two eldest boys and some of William's menservants, armed with what he could find in the house, to defend London Bridge. Alice had not tried to stop him and that was another worry to add to everything else. Where was John? What had happened to him and the two boys? Alice was bearing it calmly, looking after her two youngest children, soothing Matilda's fear and helping to keep the house running smoothly, while all the time she must have been torn apart with worry for her husband and two eldest children.

Such courage, thought Joanna, admiring her sister's calm serenity. There she sat on the wooden ledge running round the bed, quietly feeding her youngest babe, as placid and unruffled as the still waters of the moat at Maudesbury. Joanna was glad that Alice was here. She never panicked, never lost her temper, never did anything in a hurry. But sometimes one had to act quickly, without pausing for thought.

'I'm going to find Father,' said Joanna jumping up. 'Maybe he will know what to do.'

'Don't do anything rash, Joanna,' said Alice, head bent over her suckling babe. 'We don't want to let any of them in.'

Richard Burgeys was in the bakehouse checking the bread. 'There's food enough and ale for a day or so – a week if we're careful. Let them rant and rave, we can sit it out. William need not fear, his house is in good hands,' he said quite cheerfully.

'Father, William Gryffard has come home and they've got him captive outside.'

'William here? God in His mercy!' He stared at her horrified, the confidence draining from him like wine running out of a cracked vessel.

'We must do something quickly. They'll kill him if we don't act soon.'

'The fool! Why did he not stay where he was in the Tower? He'd have been safe enough there.'

'Father!' He was gaping at her, his mouth slack with shock, his eyes blank. Her heart sank as she realised that he was going to be no help at all. 'We must rescue him,' she insisted.

'Of course we must,' her father mumbled. 'I'll go out to them, plead with them. Offer to take his place. They can have me instead—'

'No, Father!'

'It's the least I can do for him after all that he's done for me.'

'It won't do any good, it's not what they want. That man Ben Smale, he thinks he's been cheated, robbed; that's what he's been shouting all the time. Perhaps if we were to offer him the bond – that's what he's come for, isn't it? Let him have his house and his goods in exchange for William.'

'William won't like it. He lent that rogue Smale a considerable sum which he'll never see. William never lends money unless it's secured. He's got plans for Smale's property which he won't like losing.'

'Father, if we don't do something quickly, William isn't going to

311

live long enough to regret it!' she exclaimed. 'We must find that bond.'

'It'll be in the counting house, but I daren't go through his papers without his permission. It's more than my life's worth,' he said, wringing his hands and gazing at her helplessly.

'Then I'll go. You go back to the solar. Talk to them from the window. Ask for the man Smale. Tell him he can have his bond if he'll let William go.'

'How will you know where to look?' He was still doubtful. 'It might take hours.'

'I know my way round a counting house from my time with the Northamptons,' she said. 'And you know how to drive a bargain. Drive one with Smale. It won't be easy but you can do it – keep him talking until I come.' She threw her arms round his neck and kissed him on the cheek. He hugged her back, then squaring his shoulders strode off towards the solar.

In the counting house Joanna paused for a moment, overawed by the number of ledgers, the tally sticks, the letters of credit, the deeds of partnership, bills of lading, letters of advice and bills of exchange which represented William's daily toil. How could any one man do so much? On the table in front of her a ledger lay open and she stared down at it, vaguely marvelling at the sheer scale of William's enterprise. A name leapt out of the page at her. Sir Tristram de Maudesbury. In all the trouble and anxiety and excitement of the last few days she had not thought of him once. He who used to occupy her every waking hour. She gave a little shiver, and peered closer at the ledger. What was her husband's name doing in William Gryffard's book?

There in William's small spidery writing was the transaction by which he had bought the wool of Maudesbury manor for seven years to come. Joanna stood looking down at her discovery and saw in her mind's eye Tristram riding away in all his glory. It was a large sum, the money William had given Tristram, but it would all be gone, she knew that. Tristram did not think of money the way William and her father and his friends thought of money. Money was not a tool to be used to forge one's fortune with, money was for spending, for show or for equipping armies.

Holy Mother! The empty sheds at Maudesbury! The sheep with their wool still on their backs would all be stolen or strayed by now. The serfs – where were they? Suppose Tristram came back from Scotland empty-handed, which he would if the Scots refused to fight. He would come back to Maudesbury expecting to replenish the cost of war, and there would be nothing. He would be like the man out there pelting William with horse dung. Would he have to forfeit his manor? She did not know. She only knew she had delivered Tristram into William's power. It was she who had asked William for help, to

312

get Tristram away from Mariota.

She stood in the middle of the counting house and thought of how her father deferred to William in everything. She thought of Tristram, of his high-handed, autocratic ways, and then she thought of the manor being run the way William thought fit. But William was kneeling in the gutter at the mercy of his enemies. She could leave him there. She could let vengeance take its course. Perhaps it was the will of God.

She stared down at the ledger while the small spidery figures danced before her eyes. What had William done? He had come to their rescue when her father was ruined. He had sent Tristram to Scotland as proud and as happy as could be. He was family; he was poor Mariota's husband. She could not leave him out there and do nothing to try to save him. Forgive me, Blessed Mary, Mother of God, she whispered, appalled at herself; help me to find the deed. She slammed shut the ledger as if to shut out temptation and set about searching for Ben Smale's quit claim.

When she got back to the solar with the bond they all turned to her expectantly.

'They won't let him go unless we bring the paper out to them,' said her father. 'They don't trust us.'

'Well, we certainly can't trust them,' said Alice, cradling the now sleeping baby gently. 'You won't go, will you, Father? Joanna, tell him he must not go.'

With a sinking heart Joanna realised that without meaning to she had taken command, that it was she who had to decide what was to be done next, she who had to bear the pain of choosing, and she who would suffer the consequences if she chose wrong. It made her feel frightened and alone. She was not equal to the task, did not want it. She realised, then, what it must have been like for Nick in the convent in the forest and how unfair she had been to him. The thought of Nick gave her strength.

She went to the window and looked out. William was still kneeling in the gutter, his once fine gown covered in mud and filth, his fine hat knocked from his head and his hood hanging in folds round his neck like a noose – bareheaded, dishevelled, helpless.

'We've got to risk it,' she said, turning to face them. 'We can't leave William out there any longer. What is he, after all, this Ben Smale? A failed craftsman, one who was unlucky and has been made to pay for it. He's not a bandit, none of them are. They'd have killed William by this time if they were murderers. I think once he has his rights restored to him he'll be satisfied.'

Richard Burgeys stretched out his hand. 'Give me the bond, Joanna. I'll take it out to the villain.'

'You'll do no such thing.' Matilda launched herself off the bed and, throwing her arms round her husband's neck, clung to him. 'You cannot go out there among that rabble. Do you want to end up in the gutter like William? Do you want to embrace death before your time? What about us? You cannot leave us here alone and unprotected!'

'Then I'll go,' said Joanna.

'Oh Joanna, don't!' Alice got up and laid a restraining hand on her arm. 'You don't know what they might do to you.'

'Of course she must not go,' Burgeys objected. 'Send Bridget.' Immediately the maid cast herself at Joanna's feet, wildly weeping and beseeching her not to be so cruel.

'Be quiet, Bridget.' Alice spoke sharply. 'Bridget would be useless, Father. They will make a performing bear out of her. Joanna, if you're determined to go, I'll come with you.'

'No, Alice, you've the children to take care of. I'll go alone. It's better.' Now that she had decided, Joanna was anxious to be gone, before her courage failed her. She glanced briefly at her father; with Matilda hanging from his neck like a ball and chain, he looked defeated and absurd. Quickly she looked away.

'Richard, go and open the door for her,' Matilda said, 'and see that you close it quickly behind her in case they rush the house.'

Joanna stood in the street and heard the door shut behind her with a resounding thud. The finality of the sound sent a small tremor down her spine. Blessed St George, give me courage, she prayed, as she looked at the sea of grinning faces all turned towards her. They were just peasants, she said to herself, treat them like the serfs at Maudesbury and they will obey.

Resolutely she marched towards Smale, trying not to show that she was afraid.

'Here is your bond,' she said. 'This will give you back your house and goods in it. Now take it and be thankful.'

'How do I know what's awritten there?' he said, staring at the parchment in her hand suspiciously.

'I will read it to you,' she said unrolling the deed.

'How do I know you be reading it aright?' he asked, unimpressed. 'He tricked me before – I'll not be tricked again.'

She ignored him and began to read, pleased to see that her hand holding the parchment hardly trembled at all.

'I swear by the Holy Rood that I have read what is written on the paper,' she said when she had finished.

His hand shot out and he tried to take the paper from her, but she twitched it up above her head.

'Not so fast,' she said. 'First you must let him go, then I will give you your bond.' He glared at her and she waited, the precious document held above her head, not daring to look at the sea of bearded, unwashed faces gathered around her, knowing that it would not be difficult for any of them to snatch the paper out of her hand. 'Don't

314

think you can get your property back with this paper alone,' she said, fixing him with a steely glare. 'You'll have to go to court to prove it and take him,' she inclined her head to the kneeling figure in the gutter, 'with you. If you destroy him or the paper you'll never see your house again. That's not what you want, is it?'

He stared at her suspiciously, scratching his matted head of hair, puzzling it over. She felt a thrill of pure joy shoot through her tensed body. He believed her, she could see it in his eyes.

Suddenly he turned away as the sound of shouting came from the direction of Cornhill. Joanna tensed. What now? Several of the men ran towards St Peter's to see what was happening.

'It's the predator,' they cried, disappearing round the side of the church, leaping and punching the air with their fists. 'They've done it – they've done for the Archbishop at last.' The others followed them, scampering down the street towards Cornhill, shrieking with joy.

'Quick, William,' said Joanna, darting across the road to where he still knelt bemused and cowed. 'Get into the house, while their attention's elsewhere. Hurry.' But he could not hurry. He knelt where he was, frozen with fear while she tugged and pulled. 'For the love of Jesus our saviour, William, try, will you?' she urged as the shouting swelled to a roar. The mob was rounding the corner of St Peter's, bearing before it a long pole, on top of which was a severed head decorated with the magnificently jewelled and embroidered mitre of the Archbishop of Canterbury. 'Death to the predator!' they shouted. 'To London Bridge, that's where he belongs!'

One look, that was all Joanna took. One look, and instead of fainting away with horror at the grisly sight, she rounded on William and kicked him hard. 'Get up, William,' she hissed at him angrily. 'Save yourself while you can. Do you want to end up like the Archbishop?'

Somehow he stumbled to his feet. Somehow she dragged him to the side as the rebels swept down upon them with their horrible trophy.

'London Bridge! Stick the traitor up where he belongs. On London Bridge.'

She watched them pass, chanting and singing, thankful that they were so intent on their purpose that they had no time for lesser victims.

'Now, William,' she said, 'run!' He shuffled after her as she dragged him towards the house, and they reached the door with Joanna praying to God and all His saints that someone would not be too afraid to open it for them.

'Where do you think you're going?' A rough hand caught hold of her skirt and she was spun round to find Ben Smale glaring at her. 'Trying to cheat me, mistress?' he said. 'I told you, I'll not be cheated twice.'

315

'Here's what you came for,' she held the bond like a talisman clutched to her chest. 'Take it and let me go.'

'I'm not sure,' he said, licking his lips and staring at her boldly. 'I'm not sure I wouldn't be a fool to let go such a pretty one as you be, eh lads?' From behind him came lewd shouts and ribald encouragement.

Still too angry to be afraid, she waved the bond in his face. 'Stop this nonsense. It's not what you came for. This will give you back your house – do you want it or not?'

'I want you, my lovely lady, you with your fine eyes and red juicy mouth – that's what I want now and the devil take the deed and a hundred houses with it.' He lunged for her and she strained backwards. With supreme effort of will she fought her instinct to hit out at him and tried to stay calm. Beside her, William was on his knees scrabbling at the door, weeping and cursing alternately.

She looked down her nose at the man whose face was but an inch from her own, coldly, calmly, as Lady Isabel had taught her, but she knew from the lewd leer he gave that whatever authority she had once held over him had now been swept away by the excitement of the Archbishop's murder. Infected by the behaviour of the mob, he was beyond reason and beyond restraint. He leant forward and with his body pinned her against the unyielding timber of the door. How strong he was, for all his emaciated frame; his hands roved her body, tugged at her skirts. She abandoned her dignity and her calm and fought him desperately, but knowing it was useless, that he was stronger than she, and knowing too, as the jeering of the others rang in her ears, that when Smale had finished with her it would not be the end.

'Stop! In the name of Jesus Christ our saviour!' A small tree trunk crashed down on Smale's head. He fell back cursing, and Joanna found herself looking up into the face of Father Luke. He was out of breath and sweat dripped from his round countryman's face but the sight of his bulky figure standing between her and her tormentors was as good as the Archangel Gabriel himself. She drew a deep breath and smoothed down her dishevelled skirts.

'You're far from home, Father,' she said.

'And you, my lady,' he replied levelly – no guilt, no embarrassment at being found so far from his parish, only compassion for her plight. It didn't seem odd to see him here, it didn't even seem wicked that he should have abandoned his parish at Maudesbury and come to London. The whole world had gone mad and nothing made sense any more. Ben Smale, rubbing his head ruefully, began to mutter and curse and the others who still remained growled their support. The priest rounded on them like an angry bear.

'Shame on you,' he shouted, seizing Smale by the back of his jerkin and shaking him like a dog. 'We came here to seek a remedy for our

ills. What justice can you expect from the King if you prey on innocent women? Behave like dogs and you'll be treated like dogs.' They
backed away, cowed by his fury and heavy ashplant staff.

From behind them came another voice. 'The Archbishop – you
killed the Archbishop,' accused William, slowly getting to his feet.

Now he chose to interfere! thought Joanna furiously, wondering
how to silence him. Father Luke was all that stood between them and
these animals, it was not the time to antagonise him.

But the priest seemed more abashed than antagonised. 'We never
meant to kill the Archbishop, my lady,' he said looking at her with
such sad eyes that she believed him. 'I tried to stop them, many of us
tried, but it was useless. Once the mob got into the Tower they went
mad. There were too many of them you see. Blood-crazed, they
were.'

Ben Smale began whining about his wrongs but Joanna could see
that his tale of distrained goods and quit claims was way beyond the
priest's comprehension.

'Father Luke,' she said as inspiration struck. 'This man Ben Smale
thinks I'm trying to cheat him. Will you take this and tell him it isn't
so.' She thrust the rolled parchment into his hand. 'Read it. Tell him
what it says. Then perhaps they'll let us go. You can read, Father
Luke, can't you?' she added as he gazed at her in obvious perplexity.

He took the precious document in his large, roughened hands,
carefully unrolled it and laboriously spelt out the words, while Joanna
held her breath and watched William, terrified that he might refuse
to part with his bond. But William had slumped back against the door,
muttering and moaning to himself, and appeared to have lost all
interest in the means of his salvation.

It seemed to Joanna that the priest would never finish. When at last
it was done, none of them looked as if they had understood a word.
The priest turned to Joanna and she gazed back earnestly, her candid eyes fixed on his. 'Tell him he can trust me,' she said. 'As God is
my witness, I do not try to cheat him. Give him the paper, it will
restore to him his house and his goods. He may have it if he will leave
us alone and go.'

The priest looked at Smale. 'You've heard my lady Maudesbury.
You may believe me when I say that she is speaking true.'

Ben Smale took the parchment from the priest's hand and stuffed
it down the front of his jerkin. Father Luke raised his staff and, like
a shepherd with a flock of recalcitrant sheep, herded them down the
street. Joanna turned and hammered on the door. It opened instantly
and she pushed William across the threshold. She felt no joy at her
triumph, no relief at her escape, only deep and utter exhaustion as she
followed William into the house on legs that trembled so much she
could barely stand.

317

CHAPTER 29

William sat in his huge carved oak chair rocking backwards and forwards, muttering to himself. 'God have mercy on him, God have mercy on us all,' he kept saying as if obsessed by the fate of the Archbishop of Canterbury.

'Get some wine,' said Richard Burgeys, ineffectually trying to wipe some of the filth from William's face. When Matilda held the cup to William's lips, his teeth clattered against the rim of the goblet.

'The Tower! It must have fallen!' William gazed about him wildly. 'De Cher was right. Sweet Jesus, I did well to leave.'

'You've seen Nicholas de Cher?' Joanna exclaimed before she could stop herself.

'All put to the sword! Perished, every one of them.' He was shaking uncontrollably, and Joanna clenched her hands together tightly to stop herself from screaming.

'Nicholas,' she repeated and her voice sounded strange in her ears. 'Where is he?' He stared at her, wine dribbling from the corners of his mouth.

'He stayed behind in the Tower with the Archbishop and the Treasurer when we rode out this morning. The fool! He'll be dead by now, I don't doubt. God have mercy on him, God have mercy on us all,' he moaned again as he crossed himself. Joanna felt the room tilt.

'Have some wine, Joanna. You look done in.' Alice was at her elbow holding a brimming cup and Joanna swallowed the drink gratefully. It was strong, laced with honey and spices to kill the vinegary taste. The room steadied again.

Nick couldn't be dead. She wouldn't believe it. Nick wasn't like the Archbishop of Canterbury. He was a hard man to kill – hadn't he said it himself? It was a straw to cling to.

They were helping William out of his chair and taking him to his chamber, the servants running to the kitchens to fetch hot water and

318

Matilda and Richard fussing round him like two anxious sparrows with a fledgling cuckoo.

'Poor Joanna, it must have been terrible out there,' said Alice anxiously, 'but you did it, you saved William, and we're all so proud of you.'

Joanna did not hear. She stared at Alice blankly, full of bitter regret. Nick dead! Only yesterday she'd been so proud of herself for keeping him at arm's length, for treating him as a friend who had done her great service, nothing more. She had known by the light that danced in his eye that he was undaunted, that he would go on trying to make love to her until she succumbed. She had believed then that she would be strong enough to resist him, to remain true to Tristram. Now she would probably never have the chance. He was more than likely dead. Not until now did she realise how much a part of her life he had become. Not until now did she appreciate how much he towered above other men. Always different, always challenging, and always temptation. How could she ever have thought him ugly? Dear God in heaven, how could she endure life without Black Nick to tease and plague her. Sweet Jesus, let him not be dead, she prayed silently; anything else I could bear, but not that.

It was a long afternoon, the longest of Joanna's life. She took her seat once again by the window in the solar, while Alice sewed and Matilda slept and Richard went with William to the counting house. She tried to read but she could not concentrate. Foreboding, as dark and insidious as the dense fogs of winter, crept over her as the shadows lengthened in the street below and the sun moved round to the west. She could not bear the silent deserted street, with its air of waiting for the next catastrophe, but she could not tear herself away from the window either. From time to time a band of rebels would run by and from other parts of the city came intermittent sounds of shouting and the occasional scream. Then she would shiver and turn away, unable to endure the thought of what might be taking place. She tried then to distract her mind with thoughts of Tristram. But she found she had no happy memories of her husband to cling to. All her good times had been with Nick. With Tristram there had been only pain and humiliation and an endless, vain struggle to please.

Someone was coming down the street on a horse. She looked out quickly once more, hope soaring crazily. It was only another group of rebels with a stolen packhorse, heavily laden with their looted gains. She leant out of the window and watched them disappear, drawn against her will to keep looking up and down the deserted thoroughfare, as if by the very force of her longing she could conjure him up out of the cobblestones. She knew it was hopeless but she could not help herself. Would it never end, this waiting? Almost it would be better to know the worst.

The bells in the city began to ring for vespers and Matilda woke demanding to know what was to be done about supper. Food! The very thought of it made Joanna queasy, but she left the solar and went to find William's cook, glad to have a task to perform, something to distract her from the false promise of the window. She was halfway across the great hall when a knock came at the door. She stood stock still, listening, holding her breath, heart hammering. 'Holy Mother, let it be him,' she whispered. 'Blessed Mary, Mother of God, bring him back safe and well.' She was almost at the door when Alice came flying down the stairs from the solar.

'Open quickly, Joanna,' she said, relief transforming her normally rather plain face. 'It's John and the two boys, come back safe, most blessed Mother be praised.'

Joanna threw herself on the great wooden levers which secured the door, fighting her disappointment, thrusting it down deep inside her, trying to be glad for Alice that her husband and children were safe.

They crowded round John, eager for news, the servants creeping out from the buttery and the pantry, Matilda hurrying down from the solar with her cap askew. But John had little comfort to bring. 'It's feared that the King may be dead and the Mayor and all the city's leaders likewise. They've got the Archbishop's head, and Treasurer Hales's too, up on the Drawbridge Gate. The city's swarming with rebels. John of Northampton is preparing to step into the Mayor's shoes forthwith. I've only come back to see that all's well here with you and then I shall be gone again.'

Alice did not scold or complain. She took his sword and helped him off with his leather basinet as she proudly greeted her two elder children. They had been fighting and had had a splendid time. A brewer from Wood Street with a band of ruffians had broken into the Sheriff's compters at the Guildhall looking for the Jubilee Book. They had taken part in its defence.

'It just shows what can be done if the masters will but lead their men out and fight,' said John. 'It's no good cowering behind shuttered doors. We've got to stand up to them. We saved the Guildhall today; tomorrow we'll drive them out of the city. It's a pity we weren't in time to prevent them opening the bridge yesterday. That was a bad day's work and no mistake. Heads will roll for that when this is all over.'

'Will it be over?' asked Alice, throwing an arm round each of her sons, clutching them close to her. 'If we ever recover from these terrible times, will we find anything left, I wonder?'

'The shop's safe,' John reassured her. 'Nobody's broken into it yet. We came back by Cordwainer Street to make sure.'

'You must be hungry,' said Joanna. 'Supper will be ready soon.'

'You'd have been proud of our boys today,' John said to Alice. 'Harry's got as good an aim with a stone as any archer, and Roger can wield that club of his better than Thomas at his age.'

'Thomas! Is it news of Thomas?' Richard Burgeys, coming into the hall at that moment, looked eagerly at his son-in-law.

'The Temple was attacked yesterday,' Harry informed them jauntily. 'So Uncle Thomas must have been in the thick of it. He'd have liked that, Uncle Thomas loves a good brawl.'

Joanna caught her breath and looked at her father uneasily as Alice quickly cuffed her firstborn. Richard Burgeys' face had crumpled and he looked old. Not Thomas, thought Joanna, full of a deep, dark dread. With a heavy heart she went in search of something to feed them all.

In the larder she found pieces of sucking pig and chicken and meat pasties all piled on wooden plates. It was the remains of yesterday's dinner which in normal times would have been put out on the alms dish, but now even the poor had fled from the gates. The chicken and pork could be put into the cauldron for a hotchpotch and the Constantyn children would doubtless be pleased to eat up the pastry.

Having instructed the cook, Joanna went out into the garden to look for some sorrel for a puree to disguise the tired meats. The birds were singing cheerfully as they prepared for bed, the sky a pale washed blue above her head, the air fragrant with the scent from the herbs and humming with bees. But the peace and tranquillity of nature did nothing to soothe Joanna's troubled spirit; it seemed merely to make disaster the harder to bear. Suddenly John Constantyn came bounding into the garden.

'Two men,' he said. 'Dangerous-looking customers. Demanding to be let in. Dark as Beelzebub the one and a giant to boot.'

Could it be? Joanna stared at John, not daring to hope, unable to speak for the pounding of her heart in her breast.

'Says you'll vouch for him,' John went on. 'Nick the something said he's known by.'

She wanted to throw her arms round his neck and kiss him. Instead she hitched up her skirts and ran out of the kitchen and through the garden into the hall. John lifted the wooden levers which secured the door, the door swung open at last, and there stood Nick all dirty and dishevelled, grinning down at her, with Sam by his side. She just stood gazing at him speechlessly, her magnificent eyes shining with joy.

'By my faith, Joanna, I believe you are pleased to see me for once,' he said.

'Well, and so I am,' she replied somewhat breathlessly. 'For I thought you were dead.'

'And willingly I'd have died,' he said taking her hands and raising

321

them to his lips, 'just to see you look at me like that.'

'I'd much rather that you live,' she told him and blushed furiously under his intent gaze. She stood as if turned to stone, her eyes locked with his, her hands clasped against his chest, helpless to resist him any longer. It was as if all her life she had been wandering in the wilderness and now at last she had come home.

'Where have you come from?' It was her father's voice behind her and the spell was broken.

'From the King,' Nick replied as Joanna pulled her hands away guiltily.

'Then he's not dead?' John asked.

'No, he's not dead.'

'What of the Queen Mother, William said she was in the Tower when he left. Did the rebels not harm her?' asked Joanna.

'The Queen Mother got safe away by barge, with Gaunt's heir, Henry of Derby, disguised as one of her ladies,' replied Nick. 'She took refuge in her Tower in the Royal. The Queen's Wardrobe is strong and defensible and the King has joined her with such of his councillors as survived the day. His clerks are even now writing out charters, patents and letters of protection granted to the commons.' Although he answered their questions, Nick was still looking at Joanna and the expression in his eyes made her blink and turn quickly away.

'Then he has agreed to all their demands, given in to them?' John sounded disappointed.

'For the time being,' Nick replied.

'Why don't they go home then?' asked Burgeys. 'They've got what they came for, haven't they, why don't they go home?'

'It is not enough,' Nick replied. 'Wat Tyler, like many a soldier before him, has tasted power and it's made him hungry. He wants more. The men of Kent are still angry and they are loose in the city. They are simply unmoved by the King's promises.'

'Who can be found to change their minds?' asked Burgeys.

'The King, I believe, could do it. He has tried once and only half succeeded. Pray God there are those even now persuading him to try again. Then if the city rallies behind his lead—'

'That's what I say,' John interrupted eagerly. 'We've got to fight. We beat the buggers at the Guildhall today, we can do it if there's enough of us.'

Nick wanted to know all about the attack on the Guildhall and they walked back into the hall, discussing tactics, Nick cheerful and matter-of-fact, John eager and full of fight. Joanna drifted after them, content just to feast her eyes upon Nick's broad, reassuring back. It was strange, she thought as she watched the faces of her family crowding round him, how Nick inspired confidence. Now that he was here, defeat no longer seemed inevitable. His zest for danger was infectious, imbuing them all with courage and the will to resist. Even her father brightened up.

'Where's William?' Nick asked suddenly, looking round the hall.

'In the counting house.' replied Richard.

'I must speak to him.'

'He doesn't want to see anybody,' Richard protested. 'He is still very shaken by his narrow escape.' He went on to tell Nick what had happened to William and when he heard Joanna's part in the story he was furious.

'Christ God, will you never learn not to meddle!' he shouted at her. 'Sweet Jesus, you could have been killed – or worse.' She bowed her head meekly and tried to look crestfallen but in truth she found his fury easy to bear, because he cared. It was an experience entirely new to her and quite exceptionally pleasing. Her submission seemed to inflame his wrath and he continued to rant and rave, accusing her of reckless lack of sense and a genius for headlong flight into trouble at the least opportunity, until Alice came to her rescue.

'Stop it,' she said severely as if reprimanding one of her naughty children. 'You don't understand Joanna at all. What she did was brave and timely and I won't have a word more spoken against her.'

He whirled round to stare at Alice, then suddenly smiled warmly at her. 'That's where you're wrong, mistress,' he said. 'I understand Joanna very well and know her worth to be beyond price.'

Joanna did not dare look at him. She knew that he would be watching her, waiting for a quick riposte. She would not give him that satisfaction, not in front of the others. But she felt alive, aware of herself, confident and ready to show it.

When Nick departed to the counting house in search of William, she hurried to the solar to make herself look better for him at supper. In Mariota's chest she found an embroidered surcoat with low-cut sides which she slipped on over her old gown. She brushed her hair and rebraided it neatly, arranging a fine linen veil becomingly over her head and throat. There was not a great deal more she could do but when she peered at herself in the polished steel on the wall, she was pleased with the effect.

Returning to the great hall with a spring in her step and her heart singing, she found supper already laid out upon the tables and William sitting in his carved oak chair with her father pouring wine into his goblet.

'Joanna, how fine you look tonight,' said William. 'Won't you come and sit here by me?' Joanna glanced quickly round the room. Sam was seated with the rest of the household servants but of Nick there was no sign.

'Where's Nick?' she said, unable to believe he could have left already, so soon and without a word of farewell.

'Nick had to leave,' said Alice, shepherding her children to the table.

'Without any supper?' Dazed with disappointment Joanna stared at Alice baffled.

'There wasn't time,' replied Alice. 'He and John went off together. There's much to be done if we're to win through – much waiting for us and fighting, no doubt, for them.' Alice busily ladled hotchpotch onto the trenchers, clearly hiding her own anxiety beneath a calm practicality. Joanna felt ashamed. How could she be so self-absorbed at a time like this, when Alice was being so brave and sensible? William was watching her with that close attentive scrutiny which she used to find so unnerving. But she would never fear William again, not now, not since she had seen him disintegrate in front of her very eyes. Instead, she felt sorry for him. So she took the stool he proffered beside him at the table and asked solicitously how he felt.

'I have recovered, I thank you,' he said gravely, rewarding her with a long, serious stare full of quite unusual appreciation. 'And you? I'm glad to see that you look none the worse for your ordeal.'

'We were lucky,' she said. 'God sent Father Luke to us in the nick of time.'

'I warned you about that priest,' William muttered as he handed her the wine cup. 'I could see at Maudesbury that he was up to no good. It's he who enticed your serfs away from their land, and he who will be to blame for the unshorn sheep left straying in the hayfields. He set out to ruin you and has succeeded, I daresay.'

'If the manor is ruined then we shall recover,' she said looking at him defiantly over the rim of the goblet. 'The serfs want to eat too, remember; when they return they will work all the harder to put things right.'

'And if the King grants them their freedom, how will you work the demesne lands?' he challenged her.

She gave him a long, cool glance and held his eyes unblinking. 'You need not be afraid,' she said, 'we'll manage somehow. You shall have your wool.' It was William who looked away.

'You've been in my counting house,' he accused.

'Yes,' she said sweetly. 'I have been in your counting house, and I saw what you did for Tristram. It was a great deal of money you lent him, much more than he needed for his lance.'

'You had no business there,' he said sharply. 'Nobody goes to my counting house.'

'I had to,' she said. 'To find the bond which saved you.'

For a long moment he examined her, frowning, while she stared back disdainfully, looking down her nose at him in the way Lady Isabel would have done. What had she to be afraid of? she told herself. He was a coward and she had no time for cowards. She gave him a sweet smile and addressed herself to her trencher, scooping the pieces of chicken and pork up with careful fingers and delicately popping them into her mouth so that she spilt no sauce on Mariota's embroidered surcoat.

To her relief, William said no more. He sat beside her picking at the dishes in front of him and occasionally darting small speculative glances in her direction as he ate. Soon she did not notice him any more. Her thoughts were with Nick, engaged on some enterprise out there in the rebellious city. That it would be dangerous she did not doubt, but that he would come back to see her whenever he could she was equally sure. He had lived with danger as his most constant companion and there was nothing he did not know about the art of survival.

Her eyes lighted on Sam sitting among the timorous household servants shovelling food into his mouth with obvious relish. Nick might have gone, but he had left Sam behind to guard them and it gave her a warm, secure feeling just having him here.

She slept well that night, exhausted by all that she had endured, and woke next morning refreshed and ready to face whatever the day might bring.

Nick returned not long after terce. 'I want to talk to you, Joanna,' he said and without explanation or excuse marched her out into the garden away from the curious eyes of her family. She went with him quietly, a deep foreboding driving out all pleasure at the thought of being alone with him at last. For his face told her that the news was bad.

'What is it?' she asked, alarmed. 'What has happened during the night?'

'Thirty-five Flemings were dragged from the Church of St Martin in the Vintry in open defiance of the laws of sanctuary; many more from the Austin Friars church were beheaded without judgement or cause.'

'How could they?' she exclaimed, horrified. 'Why slaughter the poor aliens in the name of freedom?'

'It's not the peasants, it's the London craftsmen seizing the chance to settle their grievances against the Flemish weavers. It's what happens when law and order breaks down.' He was staring out into William's perfectly laid-out garden, frowning at the beauty all around him and she knew that there was more, that he had not brought her out just to tell her about the Flemings.

'That's not all, is it?' she asked, bracing herself.

'No,' he said, taking both her hands in his, 'it's not all.' She waited, holding her breath for the blow to fall. 'The Temple was attacked on the first day of the revolt...'

'Thomas?' she whispered, and knew by the pity in his eyes and the way his grip tightened that her fears were correct.

'Dead?'

'I thought it better to tell you first, so you could break it to your father, but I'll tell him for you if you'd like me to,' he said.

'Why Thomas?' she cried in anguish. 'He did them no harm.'

'They hate lawyers. In their simple minds they are connected with the making of the laws which keep them enslaved, and they chose the Temple because it is in the hands of the Order of St John and Treasurer Hales was Prior of the Order.'

'But Thomas hated the law, all he ever wanted was to be a knight. He asked Tristram to take him as his squire but I persuaded him not to, for Father's sake. He could have been with Tristram now, in Scotland, out of harm's way.' Wild-eyed, she stared at him, racked with guilt.

'Joanna, when are you going to learn to stop blaming yourself for other people's tragedies?' He held her by the shoulders and shook her gently.

'I don't blame myself for everybody. Not for the Flemings or the Archbishop of Canterbury or all the others. But Thomas was so young, so innocent. He never did anyone any harm. Why did it have to be Tommy?'

'I don't know, Joanna,' he said, drawing her to him. 'But we all of us have to die one day and only God can choose when.'

She laid her head on his shoulder and felt the rough, padded leather of his gambeson hard beneath her cheek. It was a comfort to feel his arms about her and she leant against him in silent anguish, too grieved for tears, empty of all emotion save a deep, enduring sadness. He held her close and after a while she felt a tension creep through his body and the steady rhythmic pounding of his heart beneath her breast begin to quicken. She stiffened, afraid of her response. He pulled her closer, no longer comforting and she looked up. Swiftly he bent to kiss her parted lips. It was a long kiss, deep and sweet and infinitely satisfying, yet when at last he raised his head her body was on fire, clamouring for more.

'You see,' he said. 'Love can conquer all. Would you have believed, my sweet, beautiful Joanna, that you could break out of that ridiculous dream world of yours and find that love is much better than anything you've ever imagined it to be?'

She was dumb, shaken to the very depths of her being by the strength of her desire for him. But he pushed her away, almost savagely. 'No, not here, not now,' he said hoarsely, 'but one day soon, I'll make you mine.'

Suddenly he whipped out his dagger and with a swift deft stroke sliced a piece of green silk from her hanging sleeve. 'Until then I'll keep true,' he promised, 'and with this favour next my heart dream only of thee.' She stretched out her hands to him in supplication, desperate that he should not go. He knelt before her and pressed her hands to his lips while she stood gazing at his bent head, unable to believe that Nick, the proud, bold, cynical Nick should kneel to her. Then he sprang to his feet and without another word walked swiftly out of the garden.

Joanna watched him go in a turmoil of conflicting emotions. She loved him. Until now she had not known what love was. What she had felt for Tristram had been stupid, girlish nonsense. She had been bewitched by his knightly glory and his golden beauty. It had not been love, it had been bondage, and Nick had freed her. She could not help feeling a surge of triumphant pride that a hardbitten unromantic philanderer such as Nick should throw himself at her feet and swear to be true.

Tingling, her whole body alive and glowing with happiness, she floated through the garden until she saw her father coming to look for her and remembered with a sharp stab of grief that Thomas was dead and her father yet to be told.

CHAPTER 30

The great hall at Philpot's Inn was full of armed men, some in leather basinets, some in steel helmets, some with sword and breastplate, others in padded leather with pikes, staves, or longbows. They were merchants mainly, with their servants and apprentices; a determined, angry crowd of well-to-do citizens who had suffered enough and had come to John Philpot, the man they called the Sailor King and who they hoped now would help them fight for their city. Margaret Philpot looked down at them from the musicians' gallery and wondered whether she was expected to give them all dinner. Suddenly she saw a tall, broad-shouldered figure, standing a head above the rest, and with a quick intake of breath left her vantage point and hurried down into the crowded hall.

He was talking to her husband when she finally reached him, or rather listening while John Philpot outlined his plan of attack.

'Sir Robert Knollys has a force of nigh on a hundred men in his house and garden, which he has been mobilising to send to Portugal,' John was saying.

'Nick,' said Margaret, sliding between them and holding out both her hands to him. 'You've been in London these three days past and never come to see me. What have I done to deserve such neglect?'

'Don't be a goose, my dear,' said her husband with only a touch of impatience. 'Nick's been too busy.'

'I was afraid that if I came to see you it might deter me from my duty,' Nick replied as he raised her hands lightly to his lips.

'If Sir Robert leads his men out,' Philpot continued, 'the rest will follow. These men here are ready and we'll get the aldermen to raise the men in their wards.'

Nick shook his head vehemently. 'You can't wage war in the narrow streets of London, when the peasants outnumber us so. You need to be able to round them up and drive them out. Somehow we must get them out into the open, that is when your men-at-arms will have the advantage, and the only person who can do that is the King.'

'It wasn't very successful at Mile End fields,' objected Philpot.

'That's because the London citizens did nothing to repel the rebels when they marched back into London. The Mayor should get the aldermen together, tell them to have the men in their wards armed ready and waiting – Knollys too.'

'The Mayor's gone to the Queen's Wardrobe with Nicholas Brembre, to be with the King.'

'Then you must go too. Persuade the King to meet the peasants again, somewhere outside the city walls. That's the time for Sir Robert to lead his men out.'

'What of the King, suppose the peasants take him hostage?'

'The risk of war, my friend,' said Nick with a grin. 'That's what you and the Mayor and Brembre and the knights of the King's escort will be there to prevent.'

'Aren't you coming with us?'

'No indeed, I'm staying here to look after Margaret. It's not fitting she be left alone in the house with all these impatient warriors.'

John Philpot looked round the room, startled. 'You think not? I hadn't thought of that. By the Rood, you're a good friend, Nick, the best a man could have. I'm grateful to you.'

'She'll be safe with me,' replied Nick solemnly, and Margaret, smiling happily at her husband, knew that she would forgive Nick anything for his sheer audacity. Never mind that the city was in a state of anarchy, never mind that people had been slaughtered mercilessly, that nobody knew what fresh horrors were about to be perpetrated; in the midst of peril, Nick was still full of his own devilment and it made her feel excited – and safe. Just before he had left for the Cotswolds Margaret had learnt Nick's true identity. John Philpot had told her. At first she had been angry with her husband for keeping such a momentous secret to himself for so long. But her anger had soon been banished by curiosity and she had wormed out of her husband all he knew of Nick de Cher's past. The story was a strange one, better than any minstrel's tale, and it made Nick more exciting and irresistible than ever.

'Have you had any dinner, Nick?' she asked him as soon as her husband had gone. It would have to be quick, she thought, her whole body tingling with expectation, but she did not mind. Sometimes the quicker the better! The knowledge that at any time they might be interrupted, caught, punished, made the act of love doubly exciting. Today would be especially so, with all of London in the grip of terror and the hall packed with armed men! Nick was someone who paid no heed to danger or emergency. Danger only made him the more outrageous. He would be at his best today.

She looked at him expectantly. He had not answered her question.

'You look hungry,' she said, wondering if there would be time while the servants were bringing the dinner. 'Come to my solar. I don't want to have to feed everyone, our pantry is bare enough as it is.'

'I'll just have a cup of wine in the hall then,' he said. 'I'd like to keep a watch on some of these fellows out here.'

'We'll be safe enough in my solar,' she assured him with a quick provocative glance, but he did not seem to notice.

'Your husband has some odd men at his counsels,' he said, frowning as he studied the crowded room. 'I wouldn't trust some of them not to follow their own interests, should the opportunity present itself.'

Disappointed, Margaret went to the board at the side of the room, picked up a silver goblet and a flagon of wine and brought them to him. He took the goblet from her absently, still watching the men who thronged the hall.

'I thought you stayed to look after me,' she said, avid eyes trying to catch his, before she bent to pour the wine. He glanced at her low-cut gown thoughtfully and she waited for him to challenge, tease or take advantage but he did none of these things. If anything he looked bored. Disappointment turned to dissatisfaction as she realised that today he was not to be tempted.

'Why Nick, whatever is the matter with you?' she said, head on one side, red lips pursed invitingly. 'Don't tell me that you're afraid to, just because the city is in such mortal danger. I thought nothing put you off your stroke.' He did not rise, just smiled, an amused tolerant smile, which only made her more hungry. She took the cup from him, placed her lips where his had been and drank deep, her eyes on his face.

'Don't you want to?' she said, emboldened by the wine and unable to bear the knowledge that he did not.

'Want to what?' he replied, looking not at her but out into the hall. She could have hurled the goblet at his head but she was an old campaigner in the game of love and never lost control of herself.

'I've never known you like this before. Something's happened to you,' she teased. 'Can it be that you are in love?'

'I do believe I am,' he replied.

'I thought you didn't believe in love,' she exclaimed, needled.

'I thought so too,' he said, 'but we can all of us be wrong sometimes.' He seemed bent on making her angry today. Maybe that was it. They had never had a row, always she had preserved a lighthearted approach to their affair; she thought that was what he wanted. But perhaps today he wanted her angry, in tune with the violence all around them.

'Are you trying to tell me that you've lost your heart?' she accused, allowing her anger some rein. 'You've no heart to lose.'

He shrugged.

'You don't believe in love, you've said so a hundred times,' she insisted.

'Perhaps that was because I'd never found someone worth loving, someone who doesn't play games, who when she loves does it with her whole heart and would be true unto death and beyond. You wouldn't understand that, would you, my dear?'

'And she loves you?' Margaret said, shaken as she realised that he meant it. 'Poor, stupid little innocent! I suppose she thinks you'll be true.'

'On the contrary, she thinks I'm a worthless rogue bent on dragging her down with me to hell. She remains true to her husband – unlike you, my lovely Margaret.' So he hasn't bedded her yet, thought Margaret with a glimmer of hope. Some virtuous female had managed to hold out for longer than all the others, that was all.

'I never would have thought, Nick, that you would lose your heart to a paragon of virtue,' she said, throwing back her shoulders to present a little more of her bared white breast to his view. 'You always told me that you found virtue boring in a woman.'

'She's not at all good,' he replied with a grin, 'that's what's so refreshing about her. In fact, she's no better than I am, but she has the capacity to love, wholly, completely and destructively, and that, my dear Margaret, I've discovered is the most wonderful of all God's mysteries.'

'And you think you'll play the unrequited lover, foresworn to all others, worshipping your lady from afar, true until death,' she taunted. 'You're not cut out for such a part, Black Nick. I thought you knew yourself better than that.'

'Maybe. Who knows what God has in store? Death may come to save me before I pine away altogether.'

'Whose death, hers or yours?' she snapped.

'Maybe the husband's,' he said with a grin.

Who was it? she wondered, staring at him in dismay, as frustration, anger and jealousy raged within her. Nick was watching the door and suddenly his eyes narrowed.

'Well, if it isn't William Gryffard,' he said softly, 'with sword and breastplate too. I wonder what that wily merchant hopes to discover here at Philpot's Inn?'

Margaret was speechless with annoyance. She wanted to be alone with Nick to prise his secret out of him, not forced to dissemble before William Gryffard with his prying eyes and his ingratiating manner.

She watched William working his way towards them. It was a slow progress, as he paused to greet various merchants on the way, listening with grave attention to each one, like a busy bee, extracting pollen from every flower in the garden. He collected information like other men collected silver and gold, thought Margaret irritably, and then it suddenly occurred to her that if William knew so much, he might know who it was that Nick had lost his heart to.

'Welcome, Master Gryffard,' she said, giving him her hand and her warmest smile when at last he reached her side. 'Are you looking for John? He's gone to the Queen's Wardrobe to be with the King.'

'I came to offer my services,' William replied, holding her hand just a little longer than was necessary. 'But if your husband has already left, perhaps I may be able to be of service to you, dear lady.'

'Well, Nicholas de Cher promised my husband to look after me,' she said with an indignant glance at Nick, 'but he tells me he feels unequal to the task, so perhaps you will be able to help him.'

'Surely you are in no danger here?' William said, casting an anxious glance around the room.

'Alas, I fear not,' she replied and was pleased to see that he looked thoroughly confused.

'There'll be plenty of fighting before the day's out,' Nick said. 'How many men did you bring? We want everyone we can get.'

'I tried to bring that archer of yours you left at my house,' retorted William, 'but he refused. Said he'd instructions from you not to leave my inn until you yourself came to fetch him. So I brought three of my servants with me instead, but they're timid fellows, I'm afraid. They won't be much use if there's to be fighting.'

'Have you seen Alderman Sibil or John Horn today?' asked Nick.

'I have seen no one,' William replied. 'Aren't the aldermen all with the Mayor?'

'That is what I am wondering,' said Nick.

'Come to my solar,' said Margaret, laying a hand on William's padded sleeve, 'there are far too many armed men here, getting noisier and more restless every minute. Nick cannot leave the hall, he says, but that's no reason why you and I should endure their hurly burly any longer.' She glanced at Nick, but he said nothing, as impervious to her taunts as he was to her temptings. It was as if she had ceased to exist for him.

Margaret Philpot was not used to being ignored. Who is it? she thought as she led the way to the solar. Halfway up the stairs she suddenly paused as an idea struck her. Gryffard was married to that beautiful Burgeys girl! Of course the creature was incapable of the sort of love Nick imagined he wanted. She was beautiful but cold, just the sort of combination to drive Nick into his present state. Men were such fools.

She resumed her progress towards the solar, turning over in her mind how best to help Nick achieve the seduction of Mariota. Once the girl had given in to him, Nick would lose interest and then he would come back to her. Gryffard's watchful eyes were upon her. Did he know? How very diverting if Nick should cuckold Gryffard and Gryffard never find out. Or should he? Which would be the most amusing?

Feeling much better, Margaret entered the solar and arranged herself carefully on the stool beside her harp. 'Are you fond of music, Master Gryffard?' she asked as she leant forward and ran her long white fingers over the strings. 'I find it a great solace, especially now.'

'I can't find solace in anything,' William replied. 'The streets are piled with bodies, countless fine houses have been destroyed, the King and his advisers are helpless. What is to become of us all?'

'You must not give up hope,' she told him, determined not to let his despair strip her of her own courage. 'My husband has a plan to save us all. Soon it will all be over and then you must bring your beautiful wife here to dinner and we shall laugh and sing and forget all the terrors we have been through.'

'My wife is dead, Mistress Philpot,' he said, wandering over to the window and peering nervously down into the narrow street below.

'Dead!' exclaimed Margaret, completely taken aback. 'When? How?'

He proceeded at length to tell her and she listened with sympathy, although it was only one of many tragic tales Margaret had heard in the last two days. Mariota she had known only slightly and she had found her too cool and beautiful to want to make her a friend. But if she was dead then it couldn't be her Nick was in love with. Who then? There was some connection between William and Black Nick, she could feel it in her bones. Else why was Sam, Nick's devoted shadow, on guard at William's house? It was William who provided the clue, when he mentioned Lady Maudesbury.

'Lady Maudesbury?' she said, instant attention.

'My wife's sister, Joanna, she married Sir Tristram de Maudesbury in the first year of King Richard's reign.'

Of course she knew who Lady Maudesbury was. She had been consumed with curiosity to know how that madcap girl had succeeded in catching her knight. But what was Joanna doing here in London?

'Nicholas de Cher brought her with him,' William told her.

'How extraordinary,' she said, thinking busily. Maudesbury was in the Cotswolds almost next door to de Cher. Before Nick left for the Cotswolds he had not been in love with anybody, of that Margaret felt quite sure. Joanna and Nick? It was impossible. That unruly child with her silly fantasies, who lurched from one scrape into another like a disorderly puppy, could not capture the heart of a man like Nick. She had no style, no looks, no self-control. It could not be Joanna.

'Sometimes I wonder,' said William, turning at last from the window, 'whether Nicholas de Cher is not a little more interested in Lady Maudesbury than he should be in another man's wife.' So William had noticed something. But Joanna had hated Black Nick, and she had loved her knight to distraction. Did she love him still? That would play havoc with Nick's pride, especially as the knight was none other than Sir Tristram de Maudesbury.

Margaret looked at William and found him watching her closely. What was he up to? He was a dangerous playmate, she thought, but his passion for information might be put to good use.

'It's not Lady Maudesbury who interests Nicholas de Cher,' she said, 'so much as Sir Tristram. But Sir Tristram is under the protection of the Duke of Lancaster and not easy to harm. Perhaps Nick sees a way to be even with him through the wife.'

'Even?' William prompted, eyes bright with curiosity. From outside came the sound of shouting but William did not go immediately to the window. He was too intent upon extracting from her the reason why Nicholas de Cher needed to be avenged. So she told him what she had recently learnt from her husband, while the noise of shouting grew ever nearer until the words came quite distinctly through the solar window.

'They're killing the King, they're killing the King.'

White-faced, William rushed to the window.

'Who is it?' asked Margaret, feeling frightened.

'It's Alderman Horn. He says the rebels have killed the King and are advancing on London again. We're to man the walls. Close the gates. Keep them out whatever happens.'

'Christ have mercy on us! What of the others?' She ran to the door, pulled it open and heard from the hall below a great bellow above the hubbub of armed men preparing to depart.

'Who says so?' It was Nick, standing by the great door, arms spread wide, holding them back by the sheer force of his personality. 'Let no man leave until we know who brings this tale.'

They didn't like it, Margaret could see. They were angry, eager to rush to the city's gates, to shut them in the face of the returning rebels as they should have been shut before. But with drawn sword and blazing eye Nick kept them at bay, and Margaret, who had never seen him except as an amusing, albeit accomplished lover, marvelled at the ferocity of the man even as she trembled with excitement and fear.

'What's the matter, what's he waiting for? Why won't he let them go?' William, white with fear, burbled at her side.

'I don't know. He doesn't trust Alderman Horn.'

'Why not? We'll be lost if we let the rebels back into the city again.' But now a new sound could be heard outside and Margaret ran through the open door of the solar to her window to see her husband come galloping down the street with his horse in a lather.

'It's John,' she said, 'open the door.' Nick heard her and stood back while a half score flung themselves at the door to throw it wide.

John Philpot came striding into the hall, calling them to arms.

'Horn's a traitor,' he cried. 'Don't listen to him. The King's still alive but we must rescue him.'

Nick had been right, thought Margaret, hurrying down the stairs to welcome her husband. If it had not been for him the men now rallying to her husband would all have been gone to do Horn's bidding. Nick had suspected something like this which was why he had stayed behind when John left that morning. He had not stayed to look after her as he had pretended. It made her feel more unwanted than ever.

Joanna stood in the hall in William's inn and watched her father call for his sword, while John Constantyn waited breathless and impatient, urging him to hurry.

'Must you go, Father?' she said. 'If anything happens to you, Mother will never recover.'

'I must go,' he replied, struggling with the stiff leather buckles of his sword belt, 'if only for Thomas's sake, don't you see?'

'Wouldn't it be better to wait?' said Alice, drawing her elder children to her with a quick appealing glance at her husband. 'They said the King was dead before and he was safe all the time in the Queen's Wardrobe. Shouldn't you wait until we know more?'

'And let the vermin back into the city?' exclaimed John. 'I had it from Alderman Sibil himself – come at the gallop from Smithfield. We're to close all the city's gates, he says, man the walls, let no one back into London. It's what we should have done at the very beginning.'

'Goodoh!' shouted Harry, dodging out from Alice's protective embrace. 'I'll throw stones at them from atop the walls.'

'Not this time, Harry,' said John. 'You must stay and look after your mother and the rest of the women in the house.' Harry's face fell but he did not argue. John turned to his father-in-law. 'Are you ready?'

Richard Burgeys snatched up his leather headpiece and Joanna could see that it was pointless to try and prevent his going. Since Thomas's death he had thrown off his lethargy and regained some of his old recklessness. If she had not been so afraid for him she would have been pleased he was showing spirit at last. But with Mariota and Tommy dead, she dared not think what would become of them if her father were to be killed too.

'Sam, you'll go with them, see they come to no harm,' she said as she tied her father's basinet firmly in place.

'My master told me to stay here and not set foot outside the house, no matter what, and that's what I'll be doing,' said the archer, shaking his head.

'But Sam,' she protested, 'the city needs you. If your master were here he'd want you to go out and fight with the rest of them, I know he would.'

'I never asks meself what he wants,' replied Sam stubbornly. 'I just does as he says. When he gives an order he expects it to be obeyed. He'd half kill me else. He's a hard one to please at times,' he added with obvious pride, 'and I don't cross him, not for the Archangel Gabriel himself, that I dursn't.'

'We're wasting time,' John said, flinging open the door, 'let the man stay here if that's what he wants. We've got to get going if we're to keep the rebels out.'

Down the street a horse was flying, slithering to a halt outside the house. It was William, hot and out of breath. They crowded round him, begging for news.

'Wat Tyler's dead,' he informed them.

'And the King?' demanded John. 'Is he not dead also?'

'No, no, the King's alive and at the head of the rebel army.'

'The King leading the peasants, by the Rood I'll not believe it,' swore Burgeys.

'If the King hadn't taken command in Wat Tyler's place, they'd all be dead by now,' said William.

'Who killed Wat Tyler then?' demanded John.

'It was the Mayor who did it,' replied William. 'When Tyler tried to make a stab at the King, Walworth whips out his dagger and Tyler stabs him instead. But the Mayor's wearing armour beneath his gown and he sticks his own dagger up to the hilt into Tyler's breast; Tyler falls from his horse and when the rebels see their leader fall, each man bends his bow to shoot and that's when the little King shows the stuff he's made of. "Be still," he commands, "I am your King, your leader and your chief, and those of you who are loyal to me should go immediately into the field." So saying he claps spurs to his horse and sets off northwards towards Clerkenwell, and the miracle of it is they follow him like lambs to the slaughter.'

'Were you there, William?' asked Joanna impressed. But he could not meet her candid gaze.

'I was at Philpot's Inn,' he said dismounting. 'First we hear that the King is dead and some of Alderman Horn's men want to rush out and close the gates, but Black Nick stopped them, God be praised. Back comes John Philpot. The King must be rescued. Sir Robert Knollys is to lead his men out and with him the Gascon knight Sir Perducat d'Albret. The aldermen are even now collecting bands of armed men from the wards.'

'How do we know it's not a trick to let the rebels back in?' asked John suspiciously. 'The Mayor let them in before, didn't he? What's he up to this time, that's what I'd like to know. I have it from Alderman Horn—'

'Horn's a traitor,' said William. 'He it was who let the peasants into the city in the first place. His schemes have gone awry and now he seeks to save his neck by delivering the city to the peasants.'

'We'll deliver the city to the peasants right enough if we all march out and leave it undefended,' retorted John.

'Then stay here and let others do the work for you,' said William with a shrug. 'It should all be over, with God's help, by nightfall.'

'Then by Jesus, John, we'll go,' said Burgeys, seizing his pike. 'If we're not quick we'll be too late to kill some of those bastards! I'll not let Thomas go unavenged.' He leapt into the street without a glance at William, and Joanna could not help feeling proud of him.

'Are you not going too, William?' she challenged sweetly.

'I shall stay here and look after you,' he replied, quite unperturbed.

'We've got Sam to do that,' she retorted.

'Of course, Sam,' he said, smiling at her. He looked pleased with himself, smug almost, and she did not know why but it made her feel uneasy.

She followed him back into the hall, telling herself that William was nothing but a coward without a conscience and not worth worrying about. Sam closed the door behind them and she watched him swing the levers back into place, thinking with a lifting of the heart of Nick. William seemed to think it would all be over soon and then Nick would come back. She dared not think of what would happen then, but a little shiver of delight ran through her, making her body tingle.

The hall was full of shadows, with splashes of light from the long narrow windows falling in patches on the colourful tiled floor. The room was a tribute to William's wealth and industry, with its painted walls and glittering array of silver vessels arranged upon the board table at the side, and the rich tapestries hanging down from the gallery above. A servant brought wine and Joanna watched William drink, hoping that soon he would take himself off to his counting house. She longed to be alone with Sam, to question him about Nick, to feed her newborn love with all the stories that a devoted servant might be able to tell.

William was looking at her, waiting expectantly, and she realised with a guilty start that he had asked her a question and she'd not been listening. 'The summer air will make you feel better,' he added when she did not respond.

What had he said? Whatever it was she was not eager for his company, and so she made a quick excuse about having to attend to Matilda.

'Let Alice do that,' he said, tossing off the last of his wine. 'I want to show you my dovecot.' She had no choice but to go with him – out into the garden, into the soft warm stillness of the June evening. There was much to admire in the garden, the carp pond full of succulent fat fish, the kitchen garden with its row of fragrant herbs, the orchard with its tender young fruit trees. As William described how it had all been done, she caught a glimpse of the effort which had gone into it, of the will and determination and attention to detail which drove him. At the dovecot, he paused to gaze proudly at his creation and to watch with

337

obvious pleasure the pigeons fluttering in and out, bringing food to their fledglings. Then before Joanna knew what he was about, and as if it was the most natural thing in the world, he drew her to him and kissed her on the mouth. She leapt back as if branded.

'What's the matter, Joanna?' he asked, quite at ease. 'Did I surprise you? You're a beautiful woman, my dear, as well as a brave one and I find it a challenging combination.'

Blessed Mary, Mother of Jesus, what to say? She muttered something about not being able to think of anything save the danger her father and John were in.

'You're overwrought, Joanna – of course you are, and so am I,' he responded calmly. 'We've been through much together, but our troubles are nearly over. I need release, as you do if you'll but admit it. Let me help you.' He had hold of her arm and was stroking it beneath her hanging sleeve, running a soft, smooth finger caressingly from her wrist to her elbow. 'And what of my duty to Tristram?' she said, pulling away. 'Would you have me be untrue to my husband?'

He laughed. 'Tristram loved my Mariota,' he said and she winced at the careless certainty in his voice. 'You know that and I know that. I've always admired you for the way you managed to trick him into marriage. One day you must tell me how it was done. Alas that you were not able to cure him of his passion for your sister. I saw that at Maudesbury. A girl like you needs a man to make love to her for her own sake. You're wasted keeping yourself for that unappreciative fool.' He slipped an arm round her waist and started trying to draw her to him again. 'I can show you how you should be loved, Joanna. Forget Tristram, for you may be sure that he has forgotten you.'

She pushed him away, shaking her head vehemently.

'What are you saving yourself for?' he demanded. 'Is it Nicholas de Cher?'

She could feel his shrewd eyes upon her, noting her confusion, the telltale blush which swept up her neck and over her cheeks to the edge of her wimple.

'Don't throw yourself away on that rascal,' he said. 'He's only trying to make love to you to be avenged upon Sir Tristram.'

'Avenged?' she whispered, shocked into betraying herself. 'I don't know what you mean.'

'Of course you don't, my poor little Joanna. You don't know, do you, that your husband was once squire to Sir Nicholas de Cher, that he ran away from the castle in Aquitaine when his master lay dying of the plague, that he took most of the garrison with him so that when the French came, the castle fell without a blow and Nick was captured.'

'It's not true,' she said, staring at him horrified. 'Tristram's a retainer of John of Gaunt. He's been in his service ever since . . . ever since . . .'

'Since when?' William prompted.

Joanna realised she knew nothing of Tristram's past life. She had always assumed that he had been brought up in the Duke's household, but she did not know for certain.

'It's not true,' she repeated. 'Tristram's not a coward! Why, he's the best fighter in the Duke's retinue.'

'He thought himself safe at first,' William went on, and Joanna in spite of herself hung upon his every word. 'Tristram the runaway squire. He was sure that de Cher had perished in the castle and his secret with him. He found the Duke of Lancaster in Bordeaux and spun some convincing tale. He was a good fighter, taught by one of the best knights in the Black Prince's train. The Duke took him into his household, knighted him, but then the rumours began that the commander of the castle had escaped. What was your knight to do then? Why, he blackened his name, spread the tale that de Cher had broke his parole, betrayed his knighthood—'

'Stop!' she cried, hands over her ears. 'I will not listen to any more. It's a lie, all of it. I don't know where you got this stupid tale but I'll not believe a word of it.'

'Believe or not as you will,' he said with a shrug. 'You'll find out one day the true nature of the man you married. I'm surprised you have not fathomed him yet. But sooner or later you will have to come to me for help. I can wait, my pretty, until you're ready.'

She ran from him then, fleeing through the garden as if all the demons of hell were in hot pursuit. She did not stop until she was back in the hall and there she saw Sam, still on guard by the door, patiently waiting for his master to come back. Sam would know. Sam had been there. He would tell her the truth. She waited in the shadows until her breathing had returned to normal and then approached him.

'You're fond of your master, aren't you, Sam,' she said with a friendly smile.

'Follow him into hell if I had to, your ladyship,' Sam replied.

'Why is that?'

'Been through a lot together, the master and I. Got me out of some ticklish spots once or twice.'

'You were with him in Aquitaine were you not?'

'That were a long time ago.' Suddenly Sam looked wary.

'But you were there, I know because he told me so. He said that you nursed him through the plague, saved his life.'

'I don't know as I saved his life. The plague either gets you or it don't. The master's a tough man to kill, he'd have lived anyway.'

'Yes, he was born under a lucky star, was your master. And he had his squire to look after him too, or did he die of the plague?'

'Better if he had, the whoreson chicken-livered varmint.' Sam spat contemptuously on the ground. 'Him and the priest, they were the first to run and the rest of the garrison not long behind them. I'd have stopped them if I'd known what was happening but I was tending to the master there and when I got out it was too late, they'd gone.'

'Did you ever see the squire again?' she asked as casually as she could. Sam looked at her, a quick guilty glance that slid away and would not meet her gaze.

'No, never,' he muttered.

She knew, then, by his very evasiveness. Yet she wanted it spelt out, to be doubly sure.

'Do you remember the squire's name?' She watched him carefully and his embarrassment was all too plain to see.

'It were a long time ago, mistress,' he said, not looking at her.

'It was Sir Tristram, wasn't it, Sam?' He tried to deny it but he was not a good liar.

'Will you swear by the Holy Cross that it was not Sir Tristram?' she insisted, desperate to believe him.

'I can't remember, your ladyship. It were so long ago,' he said shuffling his feet and looking utterly miserable.

'I'm sorry, Sam, of course it was a painful time for both you and Sir Nicholas, and I'm not surprised you should want to forget all about it. It was just a silly fancy I got into my head, that's all. The last few days have been so hard, I think it's made us all a little mad.' Sam grinned, looking so relieved she knew William had been telling the truth, and cursed him for his passion for nosing out secrets. Sam seemed anxious to talk then, about Nick and when he would return, but she could not bear it. She left him with a plausible excuse and went to the solar, where Alice was vainly trying to feed her babe, control her energetic elder children and look after Matilda.

'Joanna! Sweet Mary be praised you're here,' she said. 'Could you read to us again? It might help to pass the time until supper and Mother always feels better for your reading.'

Joanna sat down on the ledge running round the bed and took up the Book of the Saints, but she read in a daze, not aware of a single word. She was thinking about Tristram, remembering not the glorious knight in his shining armour but as he was at home, petulant, cruel, stupid. Nick had tried to warn her, several times. What was it he had said that day at the tournament, the day she discovered that it was Mariota Tristram loved? 'The creatures inside all that shining armour can be small and mean, soft and slimy as a snail without its shell,' that was what Nick had said to her and she had thought it was because he was jealous of the knights. What a fool she'd been, a silly, romantic, impressionable fool to be taken in by Tristram. He was but the shadow and Nick the substance.

Nick! Had she been taken in by him as well? William said he was only courting her for revenge, to punish Tristram. Was he? What did she know about Nick? That he was a master in the art of seduction, that he preyed on women for his own amusement. What had Nick been doing at Philpot's Inn when all the rest were at Smithfield with the King? All too clearly Joanna remembered Nick and Margaret Philpot teasing each other in Margaret's solar. Nick did not believe in being true, love was a game, he'd told her that many times. He was only pretending to love her because he knew that was the way to make her yield to him, to get what he wanted.

'What a fool I've been!' she exclaimed out loud, dropping the book.

'Why Joanna, whatever's the matter?' asked Alice, staring at her in surprise. Joanna mumbled some excuse and hastily began again at the top of the page.

'You've just read that,' complained Matilda. 'We'd got to where she was about to be swallowed by Satan disguised as a dragon.'

Joanna found the place and continued with the reading but she could not concentrate on the trials and tribulations which Margaret the virgin martyr had suffered for her Christianity. Her own trial would come when Nick returned expecting her to fall into his arms, and she knew she was not strong enough to resist.

It was almost dark when at last John and Richard Burgeys came home. They brought wonderful news. The revolt was over. At Clerkenwell the rebels had been encircled, just like sheep in a pen, and shown Wat Tyler's head stuck on top of a long pole. When they realised that the King was now backed by an effective armed force, they had fallen down among the corn and begged for mercy. And the King had shown mercy. Much to John's disgust, the young Richard had refused to allow his subjects to be slaughtered but had instructed two of the knights to escort the rebels back through London across the bridge and so home to Kent. The streets of the city were being patrolled by armed men from the wards and the rowdy opportunists who had wreaked such havoc were now nowhere to be seen. Law and order had returned.

Supper that night became a celebration. When they had finished the somewhat sparse fare the servants managed the lay before them, William told his cellarer to broach a keg of his finest Rhenish wine. It was the last night when they would all be together. In the morning the Constantyns would be able to return to Cordwainer Street and Joanna would go home with her father and his wife to the Mercery.

Joanna tried not to think too much about what lay ahead. Nick had not come and, in spite of everything, her greatest feeling was one of disappointment. Was he with Margaret Philpot? she wondered and looked up to find William's eyes on her.

'There will be great rejoicings at Philpot's Inn,' he said as if he'd read her thoughts, 'and in the Guildhall too. The King has knighted many who were with him today, and William Walworth, Brembre and John Philpot are bound to have been among their number.'

'Don't you wish you had been there then?' she retorted and was pleased to see the thrust went home. She hoped that he would be repelled but he surprised her by his quick recovery.

'I always thought that obedience and gentleness were what I admired most in a woman,' he said, turning round on his carved oak chair so that he was able to look her fully in the face, 'but I've come to see that a woman of spirit is much more exciting.'

'Mariota was too good,' she said, and wanted to add 'for you' but checked herself in time. 'I've tried hard to be like her, but it's not easy.'

'Mariota would not have done what you did for me,' he said, laying his hand on her and squeezing it gently, 'and believe me when I say that you will not find me ungrateful.'

She did not know what to make of him. Was he her enemy, or her only friend? Her instinct told her to beware, and her reason that she could not afford to offend him, not while he owned all the wool Maudesbury manor could produce for years to come.

William turned to her father, seated on his other side, and Joanna was left alone to consider her position. Sooner or later she would have to return to the manor and start putting it to rights. Sooner or later Tristram would return and there would be nothing left of the money William had given him, of that she was sure. What would they do then? William was right, sooner or later she was going to need his help.

Her mind slid away from these problems and she thought with longing of Nick. He would return for Sam, and then what? But Nick was lost to her for ever. Had never, in fact, been hers. Because of Tristram. For better and for worse, Tristram was her husband, and she could not let Nick use her to gain his revenge. She was married to Tristram through her own fault, her own headstrong, wilful fault, and if she could not love him any more, it was her duty to be at least loyal and faithful. Tristram needed Maudesbury, and who was left to care for Maudesbury now that Lady Isabel was dead except herself? If she could get William to give up the wool, to cancel their debt to him, if she could free the manor from William's clutches, that would be something worth achieving. There might be a way, she thought, staring out into the hall, a way to save the manor and at the same time finish with Nicholas de Cher for good. Could she give herself to a man she did not love? Mariota had done it. Joanna could see Mariota now, dressing for William that last day in the solar of her father's house, making herself look her very best to entice the man who would save their father from ruin. But Mariota was dead. And so was Tommy. Miserably Joanna stared around the hall. The trestles had been cleared away. The candles were guttering on their prickets. It was growing dark. Why had they died and she been spared? To atone? For her disobedience, her selfishness in pursuing love so relentlessly. The men she had loved – Tristram, Nick – did not want her. But William wanted her. Could she do less than Mariota? It was her duty to save the manor if she could. Alice and her family were leaving the hall. Her father, worn out with his exertions and full of William's wine, was nodding off where he sat. Matilda had already disappeared, would be waiting in the solar – brokenhearted, demanding, troublesome Matilda. Joanna was too tired to face Matilda just now. All she wanted was to curl up in a corner and cry herself to sleep.

'Have some more wine, Joanna.' William held a brimming goblet and she took it from him, drank deep, to give her courage. 'You look quite exhausted. You've been so strong in the face of our adversities; now that it's over the strain is taking its toll.'

'You said you would not be ungrateful,' she said, quick to grasp her chance. 'What will you give me – for saving you from Ben Smale and his friends?'

'What's your price?' he replied amused. 'A jewelled filet, a new dress?'

'The wool you bought from my husband before he went to Scotland – the years of Maudesbury wool, not yet grown on the sheep's back nor likely to be for many a year to come,' she said, head high, daring him to deny it.

'A high price indeed!'

'Too high for a life?' she shot back.

'Come, come, my dear, I've already lost the deed to Ben Smale's fine house and shop. You can't expect me to pay for my life twice in one day.'

'What then, for the wool?'

'It's worth a great deal of money,' he said, eyeing her thoughtfully, 'and there's many who would be glad to have it.'

'Not today or even tomorrow,' she said quickly. 'You know as well as I that the manor will be in a dreadful state. You might have to wait a long time.'

'Whereas you think you could give me something worth having now?'

'You helped us out once before,' she said, still hoping to prevaricate, hoping that perhaps she might be able to prevail on his good nature, if he had one.

'And received Mariota for my help,' he nodded, smiling. 'But you, Joanna, as you pointed out earlier to me today, are already married to Sir Tristram.'

How he was enjoying himself, she thought, turning away from the triumph in his eyes to look out into the hall. The servants were lying down to sleep. Only Sam still waited, watching her and William.

He's like a dog left guarding his master's slippers, she thought. She took another great draught of wine, looked William full in the eye, lowered her lashes as she had seen Mariota do so many times.

'There is nothing I would not do in my husband's interests,' she said into the empty goblet.

'What a true and loving wife,' he said softly, laying a finger against her cheek. Then he got up and stretched out his hand. 'Shall we retire to my chamber? It's been a long day.'

Only for a moment did she hesitate. 'The deeds?'

'In the morning,' he promised. She was surprised that he gave in so easily. She had expected more haggling, a harder bargain. In her heart of hearts she had not really expected him to agree. Now she was committed she felt panic rising within her, dreading the brutal assault, the pain, the humiliation. She told herself that it was her penance, that it would not last for ever.

Meekly, she followed him to his chamber off the hall, feeling Sam's eyes boring into her back and not daring to turn round. Let him tell his master, she thought fiercely. He has to know!

It was a large chamber, magnificently painted. In the flickering light of the candles, Joanna could dimly discern an array of gambolling gods and goddesses chasing each other around the walls. The bed was curtained with rich vermilon velvet and seemed to fill the room. She was surprised. She did not expect a man like William to have such a chamber. There were many things about William which were a surprise.

He was standing by the painted chest at the foot of the bed, and she watched him warily, waiting for him to pounce. But William did not pounce. He helped her out of her clothes as gently and skilfully as any maid, unbound her hair and shook out the thick lustrous tresses which covered her nakedness to her waist. Then he held up the candle and examined her, almost as if she were a rare article for sale in the marketplace. I am for sale, she thought, and shuddered.

'You're cold, my dear,' he said, carefully setting down the candle on top of the chest. 'I'm an inconsiderate lover, putting my own pleasure in looking at your loveliness before your comfort.' He took her by the hand and led her to the bed. Quickly she slipped between the cold, smooth sheets, hoping that he would not expect her to undress him. A sense of unreality possessed her as she waited, cocooned in darkness dense as the womb, all sound stifled by the thick velvet of the bed curtains.

Too soon he was there beside her, and she tensed, bracing herself for the onslaught, for the brutal attack upon her fragile flesh, the bruising and the pain. But William did not throw himself upon her as Tristram would have done, instead he stroked her gently, softly and knowingly until, in spite of herself she began to move in response to

344

those exploring, expert fingers. Then he kissed her. His lips were cold and hard. As his mouth closed on hers she thought of Nick and instinctively turned her head away.

'Don't be like your sister,' he said, 'so good and dutiful and so cold. You can do better than that.'

Dear God. Think of Tristram, think of Maudesbury, of the manor, of the Lady Isabel – but do not think of Nick. He was kissing her again, his tongue flicking in and out between her teeth like a hungry snake. What would the Lady Isabel say if she knew what I was doing for her beloved manor? thought Joanna and wanted to laugh hysterically. William moved on top of her, hands busy once more and to Joanna's amazement and shame she began to enjoy it. He was inside her now and instead of the pain there was an insistent pleasure building steadily until she could scarcely bear it. She gave a little cry of pure delight.

'There, you see!' he muttered into her ear. 'You were made for love. Has that fool of a husband not found out how to pleasure you?' She opened her eyes and although it was dark she imagined him watching her, measuring her enjoyment with his coldly calculating eyes. Her pleasure went, swiftly gone. He took his own, rhythmically, while she lay beneath him feeling used and dirty and sinful. Part of her had enjoyed what she'd done and that had made her sacrifice worthless.

Nick waylaid her after Mass the following morning. The Church of St Peter Upon Cornhill, like every other church in the city that morning, was crowded with all those who had come to give thanks to God for the safe deliverance of the city. As Joanna came out of the church she saw him making his way towards her through the churchyard and her knees began to knock.

'Why Joanna, have you no welcome for me this morning?' he asked, grinning down at her confidently. 'You can look more pleased to see me sometimes, or do I have to ride out of the jaws of death every time to win one soft look from my lady's glorious eyes?' So Sam hadn't told him yet.

'You were not then at Smithfield yesterday, with the King?' she said.

'No, I stayed behind in the city and glad I was that I did!'

'Was Margaret Philpot glad too?' she flashed before she could stop herself.

'You need not worry about Margaret Philpot,' he said, and how she wished she could believe him. But she did not dare.

'What will happen now?' she asked, turning away from his intent blue gaze. William was walking on ahead with her father and if he had seen her talking to Black Nick he showed no sign.

'The King has called for a support force of loyal knights to come armed and mounted to his aid,' he said. 'The Mayor and his fellows will be at work tomorrow hearing indictments against suspected rebel sympathisers. The accusations and counter-accusations will go on for months, I expect.' She wanted to feel angry with him, but all she felt was love and a natural affinity, a sense of partnership with him which overwhelmed her, and for one dangerous moment made her think of throwing herself on his mercy, telling him everything and trusting herself to him.

'And you?' she asked. 'What will you do? Will you answer the King's call and take up arms again?'

People were standing about in groups, lingering in the churchyard as they swapped tales of the terrible ordeal they had come through. Nobody seemed interested in the large man dressed in short surcoat and hose and the girl in the sheath of green by his side.

'I thought I'd escort you back to Maudesbury when the time is right,' Nick said, and there was no mistaking his meaning.

'My husband will take me back to Maudesbury,' she said, avoiding his eyes. 'When the Duke hears what has happened here, he is bound to hasten to the aid of his nephew and Tristram will come with him to London. Until then I shall try to be a help to my father and Matilda in their sorrow.'

Nick scowled at her, 'What's the matter, Joanna? Do you want me to start courting you all over again? It's a game some ladies like to play, blowing hot and cold all the time. But I thought you were different.'

Now it had come, the moment to cut herself off from him once and for all. It was best done here in this public place, with people around her.

'I'm no different,' she said to the grass at her feet. 'But the game's over now, that's all.'

'What nonsense is this!' he exclaimed, seizing her roughly by the arm. 'Look at me, Joanna, and tell me that you've only been using me to amuse yourself all this time, for by the Rood I'll not believe it.'

'Haven't you been using me?' she retorted. 'To avenge yourself on my husband?' She looked at him then, hoping that he would deny it, that it wasn't true, that there was still hope for them. But he was frowning at her, obviously taken aback, and her heart sank. 'Tristram was the squire who ran away from you, who ruined your life, dishonoured your name. Wasn't he?' she demanded.

'He set me back a bit but he certainly didn't ruin my life and though he tried to dishonour me he didn't succeed,' he said slowly.

'I don't blame you for hating him, for trying to get even. I don't blame you for all that you have done to try and,' she glared at him defiantly, 'cuckold him! Just don't talk to me of love, you don't know what it means.'

'I admit that I started out with the idea of amusing myself with you, to spite Tristram, but I believe even then that I was fooling myself. In truth I've been under your spell, Joanna, since the first day I met you in your father's counting house when you tried to cover me with ink. I was furious when I met you in Philpot's Inn that day I lost my ship, furious because I wanted to help you and I couldn't. I was even more furious when I heard how you'd married Tristram to save yourself.'

'I married Tristram because I loved him!' she said. 'And I still love him in spite of everything.'

'No you don't Joanna,' he said grasping both her arms and staring down at her fiercely. 'You love me, as I love you.'

Summoning all her courage she glared back at him. 'I belong to him,' she said. 'And I belong to Maudesbury. Last night I sold myself to William Gryffard for the sake of Maudesbury.'

'You what?' he shouted and she thought for one moment he would kill her.

'William Gryffard bought the wool from the manor for years to come,' she gasped, eyes watering with the pain of his fingers gripping her arms, 'so that Tristram could have his lance to take to the Duke. If the wool fails, which it surely must, Maudesbury will belong to William. I could not let that happen. I went to his bedchamber last night, let him take me, in exchange for the wool.'

'Jesus Christ, you harlot!' he swore, almost throwing her from him. She staggered backwards, clutching her bruised flesh and angry at last.

'Did you think I was a saint?' she flung at him. 'You taught me there are no heroes. You taught me that survival is all. What I've done I've learnt from you. Are you not pleased with me?' Blessed St Mary, how terrible he looked in his fury.

'Pleased!' he hissed at her, teeth bared, eyes staring wildly like a wounded boar in pain. 'Yes, I'm pleased, for now my revenge will be doubly sweet. You made a mistake. With your usual genius for impulsive action you sold yourself to the wrong man. I bought those deeds from William, did he not tell you? When the wool fails, it is to me you will have to crawl for Maudesbury, for Tristram. But I don't want you, not now, not ever – not after William! And I shall have the manor.'

'Blessed Mary, what have I done,' she whispered, backing away from him in horror.

'Idiot! Blind, stupid fool,' he hurled abuse at her. 'Do you think Tristram cares whether I take you or not! Do you think he wants your constancy? A poor revenge that would be, to take something from a man he doesn't value, never wanted. But the manor, he'll care when I take his manor from him, as I will one day, and there's nothing you or he can do to stop me!'

He left her then, striding past the little groups in the churchyard with such fury in his face they stared after him curiously and some even crossed themselves as he passed. But Joanna stayed where she was, stricken, her world in ruins about her. She had found love and through her own folly destroyed it for ever. There was nothing she could hope for now, no peace, no solace, no future.

CHAPTER 31

London after the rebellion was a city ill at ease with itself as the search for those who had betrayed it during what came to be known as the 'Hurling Time' began. Recrimination, suspicion, fear and guilt walked hand in hand with grief as the rival factions sought to blame each other for the disaster. Five aldermen went to prison, including Sibil the Alderman of Bridge who had opened the gates to the Kentish rebels, Tonge the Alderman of Aldgate who had let the Essex men in, and Horn the fishmonger who had been Walworth's chief negotiator with the rebels. In addition there were seventeen others – three butchers, three brewers, two wine-drawers, three drapers, one saddler and one goldsmith – arrested for their activities.

Mayor Walworth himself was above reproach since it had been his hand that had despatched the rebel leader Wat Tyler. But there were rumours of double-dealing, whispers of complicity, dishonourable compromise, and innocent sacrifices which clung like wisps of a November fog about the reputations of the city's leaders and friends of the Mayor. Men like Brembre and Philpot, who had once been idolised by the Londoners for their strong-arm tactics, were now suspected of having put their own self-interest before the safety of the city.

While the hunt for scapegoats was at it height, William skulked in the shadows, scurrying after every scrap of scandal, like a terrier after a rat. He was made welcome by Richard Burgeys who waited eagerly for each new titbit of news, seeking in his inconsolable grief to find someone to blame for the loss of his son.

To Joanna, William's constant presence in the Mercery was like a knife turning in an open wound, an incessant reminder to her of her gross and unforgivable folly. She tried to avoid him but he sought her out, following her about the house with the latest gossip, like a persistent dog bringing his most treasured and smelliest bones to her for approval. She did not know whether William did it out of a perverse

348

desire to plague her or whether he was genuinely trying to please. Perhaps he felt guilty for the wong he'd done her and was trying to make amends. Whatever it was, she did not care. She was not interested in his news. She had nothing to hope for from any investigation. She knew whom to blame for her trouble and found the knowledge insupportable. What she did not have was a purpose. Tristram had once been her obsession and love her justification. But Tristram was flawed, and love? She had betrayed love.

All her certainties were gone and she was like a ship without a rudder, tossed hither and thither by every puff of wind, a survivor no more but a helpless victim unable to care whether she sank or swam. She wished William would leave her alone but since he would not, she bore his attentions with a resigned and distant politeness, hiding her misery behind a mask of indifference which only seemed to make him more determined to arouse her interest. He continued to beseech her to take better care of herself, to eat more, to get out and see her friends.

'I have no friends,' said Joanna, and meant it.

'You have the Northamptons,' he retorted swiftly. 'Have you been to see them since you came to London?' So that was it. His daily visits to her father's house were caused not by feelings of guilt or admiration, but by fear. William Gryffard was a frightened man, hiding away in the Mercery with those who were not important enough to attract too much notice. His friends were now in disgrace and he wanted to change sides, to make up to the Northamptons whose star was in the ascendant. She saw no reason why she should help him.

'I haven't seen Petronilla since my marriage,' she replied. 'I doubt whether she'll want to see me, it was all so long ago.'

'All the more reason for going to see her now, to show that you haven't forgotten her, that the change in your fortunes has not made you too proud to remember old friends.'

She glanced at him swiftly. Was he mocking her? His watchful eyes held hers and she wondered how much he knew of the circumstances of her hasty marriage to Tristram. Let him think what he liked, it made no difference now.

'If you do not care for yourself, you should care for your father's sake,' William went on. 'John of Northampton used to see a great deal of your father.' Before you encouraged him to drop him, thought Joanna, with a tiny pinprick of indignation. She did not want to help him, but what was the use? He would have his way in the end and it was easier to give in now.

So she went to the Northamptons, expecting rejection, and was surprised when Petronilla welcomed her with joy. 'I can't tell you how pleased I was when I heard my Joanna had married her knight,' she said when they were alone together, sitting on the big bed in the solar. 'When John came back from the palace that day and told me what he had done, I threw my arms round his neck and kissed him. I was so proud and happy for you.'

Joanna swallowed hard and clenched her hands tightly in her lap. Petronilla bore her no ill will, was not jealous, or piqued, or angry, just glad for her supposed good fortune. In the face of such transparent goodness, it was difficult not to break down and weep.

'I've missed you, Joanna,' Petronilla went on. 'We all missed you. It wasn't the same after you left; so quiet and dull. Little Katherine was inconsolable.'

'I thought you might be angry with me for running away. I didn't really mean to, it was all a mistake somehow,' muttered Joanna, confused and embarrassed by Petronilla's enthusiasm.

'It was God's will,' said Petronilla, nodding vigorously. 'I know that it's a little frightening sometimes when our prayers are answered, especially when He gives us more than we deserve. You mustn't feel ashamed of asking for too much. There was a time when I gave up all hope, when I thought the powerful families who have the city in their grip could never be beaten. It wasn't easy being ostracised and ignored because of what John was trying to do. He made enemies, so many enemies, and wherever we went we could feel their hatred. But John has such courage. He knew what he wanted to do and he never gave up. You have it too, Joanna, that courage. You're not afraid to reach for the impossible.'

'Well, the tide seems to be turning in his favour at last,' Joanna responded, getting up and going to look out of the window. But Petronilla was not to be so easily distracted.

'I remember when you first came to us, so rebellious and troubled. My goodness, you were difficult at first, Joanna,' she said with a laugh. 'But you got what you wanted by being difficult, just as I hope John will get what he wants and the city needs. There is so much he wants to do, so many improvements to make. The world needs people like you and John, to fight against the established order of things.'

Joanna stared out of the window at the river below, braced tight against Petronilla's praise, trying not to listen as all her sins and wickednesses were transformed into virtues. She must not give way before Petronilla. Must not disillusion her.

'You once said to me that you didn't want to be good, you wanted to be happy. Do you remember?' Petronilla asked. 'You're happy now, are you not, Joanna?'

'Of course I'm happy, I married the man of my dreams. What girl could want for more?' The sails on the river barges hung idly in the breathless air and she watched the flashing blades of the oarsmen as they toiled to bring the heavily laden graft to the warehouses along the bank.

350

'Children perhaps. Have you little ones to keep you company when Sir Tristram is away?'

'Two babies, buried in the churchyard,' Joanna replied. 'God does not give without also taking away.'

'I'm so sorry.' Petronilla got off the bed and came to lay a sympathetic hand on Joanna's shoulder. 'Well, I know what it's like to lose a little one – what woman doesn't. It's the worst part of the suffering of childbirth. But there will be others and when at last you hold your healthy babe in your arms, it will mean all the more because of the ones you lost. Believe me, I know.'

She must not give way. Must not weep. Must not spoil Petronilla's happy trust. Carefully she counted the barges out on the river's unruffled surface. There were sixteen of them.

To her relief Petronilla reverted to the subject of Northampton's chances of ousting Mayor Walworth at Michaelmas.

'My father thinks, indeed hopes, Master Northampton will be elected Mayor,' said Joanna, seizing her chance to put in a good word for him and at the same time bracing herself for Petronilla's scorn.

'Does he? That's good,' she said without a trace of rancour. 'John needs all the support he can get, but I believe his time has come at last. The victuallers are discredited beyond hope of recovery. The ways of God are passing strange at times, and God forgive me but I doubted Him, but now I feel that He really does want John to be Mayor.'

'Mariota and Tommy were both killed by the peasants,' said Joanna, still staring at the unruffled river. 'You'd have thought God would have managed to bring Master Northampton to power without quite so much pain and suffering for the rest of us.'

'My poor Joanna,' exclaimed Petronilla as she gathered her into her arms and held her close, 'so that's why you look so sad. I knew there was something wrong the moment you walked in. It's your eyes, they've always given you away, and they still do, no matter how poised and grand you've grown. Don't try to lock your sorrow away, my dear, it won't do you any harm to let it out. Not here with me. I can imagine that at home, with your father and Matilda, you've had to bear it bravely for their sakes, but you can let go now. That's what friends are for.'

How Joanna longed to abandon herself to the miracle of Petronilla's friendship, to let loose her despair and grief and weep the bitter tears she did not dare indulge in. Petronilla would think it was for Tommy and Mariota. There would be no need for explanations. But she didn't. Once she let go she would never be able to control herself again. She stood stiff and straight within Petronilla's encircling arms, holding her breath and counting slowly. When she got to thirty, Petronilla released her.

'You must not think God caused the terrible things which hap-

351

pened in the city during the Hurling Time,' Petronilla said with a sigh. 'Of course He did not, but even out of the greatest evil God can always bring good.'

'Can he?' asked Joanna, turing her back upon the river at last and looking directly at Petronilla for the first time. 'Do you think, if we were to do a great wrong, He could find a way to make it right again?'

'I think there is nothing that God cannot do, but if we err, we have to bear the consequences as punishment for our sins.'

'If God were not a vengeful God, He would be able to bring good even out of our sins.'

'How do we know that He does not?' Petronilla chided her. 'It is not for us mortals to question the ways of God.'

Joanna walked home through the hot, dusty city to the Mercery, thinking about God. God had answered her prayers, it was true. But God had also taken Mariota and Tommy and spared her. Why? What did He want? The question would not go away. She went to church at St Mary le Bow. She lit her candles to the Virgin and to St Peter and St Paul, to St Swithin, St Thomas and St Benedict, each one on their appointed day. She listened to the plainsong and the familiar Latin phrases of the Mass. She said her paternosters and her Ave Marias and the Angelus, while all around her she heard the chatter of the mercers and their families praising God and discussing trade. She learnt that black silk was highly prized and worth twice what it had been before the Hurling Time, that the King had reached Reading, where he met up with John of Gaunt who had hurried down from Scotland to put himself and his retainers at the King's disposal. She heard that there would be shortages of wheat and wool and even ale in the coming winter, that the weavers were demanding double wages and it looked as if they would have to be paid since so many of the Flemings had been murdered. There was talk that the country-side around London was peaceable and safe to visit again but that there were still pockets of rebellion in the north and in the east, that the Mayor's closest friends and advisers had left the city as soon as it was safe to do so and were hiding on their country manors. But she never heard the voice of God.

William noticed her sudden excess of religious fervour, as he noticed everything.

'I've brought you an indulgence,' he said to her one day, when he met her in the Mercery on the way back from Mass. 'I bought it for you from a friar in Chepe. Take it, and may it bring you rest.'

She turned sorrowful eyes upon him in wordless reproach. How could he be so insensitive to the harm that he had done her? He examined her carefully and she looked away, unable to bear his scrutiny.

'You do not fool me, Joanna,' he said. 'I know that beneath that disdainful manner there's a passionate woman. You cannot fight it for ever. It's so silly of you to deny your true nature. Think what you're missing. Why don't you let me help you? I can show you all manner of pleasures you've never dreamt of.'

'And will you buy me a fresh indulgence for each one?' she demanded indignantly.

'I'll buy you whatever you like if you'll but humour me a little,' he said, and tried to take her arm, but she twitched away from him and walked on, head bent, holding her skirts up out of the dust, determined not to let him touch her.

'What you need, what we all need, is a change of air,' he said, scurrying along beside her on his spindly little legs. 'I think we should visit the convent where Mariota is laid to rest. It is time I did something for my poor wife's soul. I might found a chantry for her. You shall come with me, of course, and Matilda too. Perhaps a pilgrimage to her daughter's last resting place might help her come to terms with her grief.'

Joanna stopped so suddenly he almost fell against her. She stared at him as if spellbound. She knew now what God wanted. Of course she knew, had always known, but would not admit it. She was meant to be a nun. 'One day you will come back to us,' that was what the Prioress had said to her and Joanna had known in her heart what she had meant. Could she do it? Was her life so desperate that the convent was her only escape? She had fought against it once, was there any point in fighting any longer?

She agreed to go, although she felt ill at the very thought of the journey, so queasy and sickly that in the mornings she could not face her bread and ale. William was impatient to leave. Joanna knew that he was going to the convent because he wanted to get away from London, to escape any awkward questions; to do what Brembre and Philpot and the rest of them had done and remove himself from harm's way. But it did not bother her. God moved in mysterious ways. William was God's instrument and the convent her destiny.

At first Matilda had been anxious to come with them, and her father, too. But William had persuaded her father that he would be more useful to him in London, renewing his friendship with Northampton and keeping an eye on the business. Matilda, when the moment came to leave, could not face up to the journey and so it was that Joanna and William left alone with only Bridget and two of William's servants to accompany them. William assured Joanna that the road had never been safer. With so many knights and their men-at-arms scouring the countryside for escaped serfs, all the robbers and bandits were hiding in their lairs and would not dare venture forth again until many a moon. Joanna did not care about her safety.

Whether she lived or whether she died was a matter of supreme indifference to her now.

The Convent of the Sacred Heart, Joanna was relieved to see, was still standing. The Prioress welcomed them warmly. 'We have survived, as you see, through God's good grace,' she said, holding out her hand to Joanna. Joanna took it awkwardly, not knowing whether she ought to kneel and kiss the badge of office. She compromised by bobbing vaguely in the direction of the Prioress's silver signet ring.

'We have been fortunate,' the Prioress continued. 'Apart from that first dreadful attack we have been left alone, and fared better, I fear, than you in London. I have heard nothing but the most appalling rumours, which I hope like all travellers' tales have been much exaggerated in the telling.'

William launched into his version of London's tribulation, while Joanna looked around her in growing dismay. It was much poorer than she remembered, the buildings small and mean, the tower of the little church so squat and ugly, the dark cloisters full of nuns hovering like a bunch of expectant crows. Joanna shivered and tried to reason with herself. It was just that she had never really seen it properly. She had been too stunned by Mariota's death to notice her surroundings and of course there had been Nick. A stab of anguish pierced her, so sharp it made her catch her breath.

'The chapel is sadly spoilt, I'm afraid,' the Prioress was saying, 'and I fear it will take many months before we are able to find the resources to restore it to its former glory.'

Even the Prioress looked drab – defeated somehow. But she cheered up as soon as William spoke of a chantry for Mariota, seizing on the idea with joy, sending for two of the nuns to escort their benefactor immediately to the church so that he could choose where his wife's memorial should be built without delay.

Left alone with the Prioress, Joanna was overwhelmed by the sense of panic which had been growing ever since they had ridden through the convent gate and she had heard it bang behind her.

'So, Joanna, you have come back to us,' said the Prioress.

Joanna felt clammy with fear and her breath caught, as if a hand had her by the throat. She could not speak.

'Last night I had a vision,' the Prioress continued, smiling benignly, 'a vision of you, Joanna, standing in the church once more restored to its full glory. You were wearing our nun's habit and you were singing. It was very beautiful.'

No, no, no, she couldn't do it. God did not really want her to be a nun. There was a reason, a good practical reason why she could not. The Prioress would understand. She must.

'I didn't come here to stay,' Joanna began, but hesitated at the look in the Prioress's eyes. 'I meant to when I left London, I thought God wanted...' She looked away, unable to meet that serene and piercing gaze. 'But I don't think I can, not now.' Blessed Mother, let her understand. 'You see, I think I may be with child,' she finished all in a rush.

'You will not be the first,' replied the Prioress quite calmly. 'We have had nuns here before who have sinned in such a way, even once or twice among our own flock, alas. Even here we are not entirely free from the temptings of the flesh and the devil. I would not turn you away for such a reason as that. What did Christ die for, if it was not to save sinners?'

'But I'm not a nun, I'm a married woman,' cried Joanna without thinking.

'And Sir Tristram far from home these past four months,' replied the Prioress sternly. Joanna was dumbfounded. What did a nun know of childbearing? What did a woman who had never been married or felt the quickening of her womb know of the signs and portents of pregnancy? How did she know when this child might have been conceived? But she could not look the Prioress in the face and swear that it was Tristram's.

She bit her lip and stared at the ground uncomfortably while the silence lengthened between them. The bell began to toll for tierce and from all directions black-robed figures appeared and began scuttling towards the church. Joanna watched them in dismay as she listened to the inexorable bell that ruled their lives, tolling every three hours throughout the day until compline at eight o'clock. Even in bed there was no rest, for soon after midnight they were called forth again for matins and then again for lauds. How could she endure it, day after endless day?

'I have no dowry,' she said, remembering suddenly.

'You have a manor,' the Prioress replied steadily.

'I don't know that it will be able to provide anything,' said Joanna. 'With all our serfs gone, the land will be untended, the sheep stolen or strayed. I doubt if there will be enough to feed us through the winter, let alone anything left over.'

'Do not despair. It may not be as bad as you fear,' the Prioress replied. 'Our serfs are back now, much chastened by all they have endured. They have fled the King's progress, and the hangings of Judge Tresilian. They have thrown away their charters of freedom and are only too glad to be allowed to return with their lives.'

Joanna said nothing. She looked at the ground and wondered if Nick would be able to seize the manor or whether he would simply hound them, year in, year out, waiting for his wool.

'Does he love you, your husband?' asked the Prioress suddenly and Joanna jumped.

355

'No, he's never loved me,' she said, shocked into admitting the truth.

'Then if things are bad,' the Prioress advised gently, 'perhaps he will be better off without a wife. He will be comfortable in the Duke of Lancaster's household or content as a soldier of fortune. You can only be a nuisance to him.'

'And you would take me undowered?' Joanna said, wincing under such a cruel understanding of her situation.

'Alas, I cannot. I would not be too greedy. You did after all bring us Master Gryffard. Our nuns are growing old and their dowries have long since been used up. It is not easy finding well-dowered novices. Parents do not like to confide their daughters to impoverished provincial houses, and there are many convents besides ours, all of them anxious for benefices. Perhaps Nicholas de Cher could be persuaded to dower you, he seems a wealthy man.'

Joanna was aghast. The Prioress thought the child was Nick's. But she could not tell her about William, that would be testing her Christianity too far.

'Sir Tristram would never forgive me if I allowed Nicholas de Cher to pay for his child to be born in a convent,' she said.

The Prioress looked at her long and hard. 'Not if the child were his,' she said.

'There is great enmity between them,' Joanna rushed on, ignoring the unspoken question, 'a family feud, caused by something which happened long ago but which I have only just discovered. I cannot ask Nicholas de Cher for favours, for Sir Tristram's sake,' she said.

'Then the child is not Nicholas de Cher's?' It was a relief to be able to meet the Prioress's steady gaze.

'No,' said Joanna. 'The child is not fathered by Nicholas de Cher.' Somehow the Prioress seemed disappointed.

'What will you do then, if your manor is in ruins and your husband does not want you?' The Prioress was nothing if not frank.

'I will save the manor for him.' Joanna stared at the Prioress defiantly, hardly knowing what she said and certainly not knowing whether she could do it but determined not to be defeated by this woman.

'I do believe you will,' said the Prioress, smiling. 'And then perhaps you will hear God's call at last and save this convent for Him.'

Part III

'Two goshawks pursue me;
one of them will die of love.

Two goshawks of mine
move round me in this dance;
one of them will die of love.'

From the Portuguese of Gil Vicente

CHAPTER 32

Maudesbury, 1383

Joanna gazed down at the unbleached broadcloth laid out upon the trestle in the hall at Maudesbury and felt a surge of possessive pride. In its unfinished state it was scarcely a thing of beauty and yet to her it was as precious as a newborn babe, for it had been borne of much struggle, hard work, and anguish. She turned to William.

'Well, what do you think?' He picked it up, felt it, smelt it, held it up against a shaft of sunlight stabbing through the arrow-slit window.

'Is this all there is?' he asked.

'For now, but there will be more.'

'Do you want me to sell it for you?'

'I just want to know what you think of it.'

'You'd do better to sell it to me than to the abbey – they're bound to rob you.

'And you wouldn't?'

'Joanna, still so cruel! When will you learn to trust me? Did I not find you the weaver to work the broadloom?'

'And I am grateful.'

'Yet you spurn me still.'

She turned her back on him and began to roll up the cloth. Yes, she could spurn him now, she thought with a feeling of elation. She did not need him now, not now she had her cloth. But it had been hard, so much harder than she had imagined. If she had known how difficult it would be, would she ever have left the convent?

She stared lovingly at the thick felt beneath her fingers, stroked it proudly. 'It's good,' she said confidently. 'And the next ones will be better.'

'I'll give you two pounds a bale for it,' he said. 'The abbey would not pay as much.'

'I do not need your help to sell my cloth,' she said.

He moved closer, so close that his sour breath fanned her cheek. 'The time will never come, Joanna, when you do not need my help.

Why will you not learn to accept the truth? Allow me to be your friend. You know there is nothing I would not do for you, if you would only give me what I want.'

He was gazing at her so intently that in spite of herself she could not help a small shiver of fear. What did he know?

'John of Northampton has lost the election,' he said, suddenly changing tack. She looked at him blankly. John of Northampton had been elected Mayor of London at Michaelmas after the Hurling Time and his popularity since had known no bounds. He had been re-elected again the following year, curbing the power of the fishmongers, enjoying the support of the King and the minor craftsmen of London alike.

'I supposed Northampton could not remain Mayor for ever,' she said carefully.

'It is not so much his going but the manner of it that bodes ill for his friends in the city,' replied William. 'He was defeated by Brembre, who packed the Guildhall with armed men and forced the guildsmen to vote for him. The fishmongers and the victualling crafts are out to avenge themselves and I fear that the time is coming when it will not be a good thing to have been a strong supporter of Northampton – like your father.' He was watching her closely and she would not give him the satisfaction of seeing that she was disturbed by his news.

She picked up the heavy bale of cloth, thrust it between them. 'We must put this away before Tristram sees it,' she said. 'He hates me making cloth.'

'Sir Tristram, of course, is above such things,' said William as he helped her stow the bale of cloth out of sight beneath the trestle table.

'Of course,' she agreed pleasantly.

'Will he be back today?'

'I never know when Tristram will be back. He may be hunting game, or scouring the forest in search of adventure. He may even have set up his standard at some crossroads ready to challenge any unfortunate knight who happens to pass by. He finds time tedious while waiting for another war.'

For the last two years Gaunt had been trying to obtain Parliament's backing for his Spanish ambitions. At first the Lords had been in favour and in November of '82 Gaunt had called up his retinue and begun his preparations for the invasion of Spain. Tristram had left the manor with high hopes, but the Commons had been against the Duke. In January 1383 they had voted taxes to fit out an expedition for the succour and comfort of Ghent instead. The command of these forces had been given not to Gaunt but to Bishop Spencer of Norwich. Gaunt had retired to his estates in the north and Tristram had come home again in disgust.

So for six months Tristram had been hanging about the manor with nothing to do. Meanwhile Bishop Spencer had arrived in Flanders and marched against the coast towns, displaying the papal banner of St Peter's keys. He had taken Gravelines, Dunkirk, Nieuport, Furnes without too much difficulty and then he had met the French army at Sluys. The Bishop, although a fighting man who had campaigned most effectively against the peasants in East Anglia at the time of the Rising, had no experience of full-scale war. He was beaten back to the coast, losing town after town almost without a struggle. He had now returned home, leaving part of his army under a few officers to defend in vain England's last foothold in Flanders, the town of Bourbourg. It was a source of severe irritation to Tristram that such an opportunity for military glory should have been entrusted to an incompetent priest while the Duke of Lancaster and his well-trained knights were left to kick their heels in idleness at home.

'And do you not also find time tedious, Joanna?' William asked, sidling up to her once more, 'while your husband terrorises the countryside with his pranks?'

'You'd love to be a knight, wouldn't you, William?' she retorted. 'You'd love to ride about the countryside terrorising people, only you haven't the courage and you haven't the skill so you try and frighten me into submission. Well, I don't frighten and I'm not unhappy, so spare me your sympathy, I beg you.'

'You are angry with me because I speak the truth,' he said. 'You have a hard husband who has little inclination towards women, and yet you will not let me make you happy for an hour.'

He did not understand. For all his intense watchfulness, he did not see beneath the surface of Tristram's bravado. For that, at least, she could be thankful.

'Why can you not accept that I love my husband,' she said, 'that what I did once I did for his sake? And I have not forgotten the villainous way in which you tricked me.'

'What man does not try to take advantage sometimes of a beautiful woman?' he replied with a shrug. 'I have not forgotten that night either. I brought you pleasure once, the memory of it lingers ever with me, which is why I live in hope that I can persuade you to repeat it.'

From outside the hall came the sounds of shouting and the clash of iron on stone. 'It's Tristram,' she said coldly. 'He's back from the forest. There'll be fresh game for supper tonight.'

Her husband came striding into the hall with his squire and two hounds padding purposefully beside him.

'There, my lady,' he said, as he hurled a brace of rabbits at Joanna's feet. 'You can have your cony pie for supper.'

'Is that all?' she said, bending swiftly to retrieve the rabbits and holding them high above her head but only just out of reach of the wolfhounds' snapping jaws. Tristram shouted at them and the dogs backed away warily.

'No, it's not all,' he said. 'There's a fine young buck in the court outside, it'll need skinning. You're lucky William, there'll be venison for dinner tomorrow – if she doesn't give it all away to the serfs before we have a chance to eat it.'

'Starving men can't work properly,' said Joanna. 'Have they started ploughing on the demesne lands? Did you notice as you rode by?'

'No, I didn't notice,' he said, throwing himself down upon the chair at the head of the table. 'I was too busy trying to get my horse past those cloths hanging up all over the place like a lot of shrouds. Took me the devil's own time, the poor beast was half demented with fright. It's your fault, William. I thought I'd knocked all that merchant nonsense out of her, then you have to come here encouraging her to make cloth.'

Joanna glanced at William and he gave her a small, understanding smile. She looked quickly away. Tristram was alway worse when William was here, bullying her and ordering her about as if to demonstrate his mastery.

Supper that evening was almost worthy of a knight's table, since Joanna felt that with Tristram's successful hunting she could for once let plenty triumph over necessity. There were capons, in addition to the rabbit pie, pease pudding, and a respectable number of apple and quince tartlets. All the same, she knew William would not be impressed. She was all too conscious of the lack of music, the bitterness of the ale, the smoking fire, the huge shadowy hall with its leaking roof, its unpainted walls hung with weapons and grisly trophies of the chase, and of the pitifully limited company. The cowed household servants huddled at table with the bailiff, casting occasional furtive glances at the three of them sitting in isolated splendour on the dais, while Tristram showed off and William treated her with the exaggerated courtesy he always used in front of Tristram. The squire poured wine, carved the meat and waited on bended knee with such perfect grace, it only served to emphasise that he was used to better things. Then William and Tristram began arguing about the Duke of Lancaster's desire to invade Spain. Joanna was not interested in the lastest news from Flanders. She had little time now for the glories of war. But she was not prepared to side with William against her husband, and so she left them arguing and went to bed.

Alone in her chamber, she pondered Northampton's fall from power. Could it really mean trouble again, for her father, for her family, or was William merely trying to frighten her? He could not bear that she had survived in spite of everything and without his help. She had hoped that by now he would have grown tired of her. She had given him no hope or encouragement, treated him with the utmost disdain, and yet the worse she treated him, the more he tried to please her. Why could William not find himself a fine rich widow

362

to marry and leave them all alone? she thought as she curled up in the middle of the big bed. Still, with Tristram at home to tease and plague him, William would not stay for long, and with that comforting thought she fell asleep.

She awoke in darkness to the sound of Tristram stumbling about her chamber, cursing. The bed curtain was twitched aside and she blinked in the bright light of a full moon flooding the chamber.

'You're drunk!' she accused him.

'Not as drunk as the merchant,' he replied with a grin. 'He had to be carried to bed.' He seemed in a good humour and it made her suspicious.

'You haven't borrowed from William again, have you, Tristram?'

'Why not? It's what merchants are for.'

'How many times do I have to tell you there will be a day of reckoning.'

'Never! Merchants like William love lending money. It makes him feel important. He hasn't ruined us yet, has he? He wouldn't come here so often if he didn't want to lend us money.'

'William wants the manor, don't you know that?'

'Is it the manor William wants, or is it you, the manor's lady?'

'And if it is, do you think I enjoy being nice to him so that you can plunge us further and further into debt?'

'Nice to him! You're not nice to him – you're not nice to anybody.'

'Tristram, that's not true, you know it's not. Everything I do, I do for you.'

'Is it? I wish I could believe you,' he said.

She lay and watched him, feeling a great weariness sweep over her. He was as handsome as ever, tall and straight and muscular, his hair pale as flax in the moonlight, his chiselled features perfectly formed. Why, oh why could she not love him still? She tried to think of something to say that was loving and kind, but her mind defied her. He sat down on the edge of the bed.

'You need not worry about William Gryffard any more,' he said suddenly brightening. 'He wants my help.'

'Your help?' she repeated, bewildered.

'Yes, mine. That surprises you, doesn't it? But I'll not sell it cheap, I promise you. This is what I've been wating for.'

'Be careful,' she said. 'William will trick you if he can.'

'Just because I can't read and write you think I can't outwit a man like William,' he accused her. 'I'm a match for him any day. William's been very useful to us, but I'm getting tired of him hanging round you like a lovesick squire. This is my chance to get even with him at last, to free the manor from any claim he may think he has on it.'

She stared at him in horror. It was going on for three years now since Tristram had pledged the manor's wool to William and in all that time he had said nothing about it. Joanna was not surprised. It was typical of Tristram conveniently to forget such a debt. Of Nicholas de Cher there had been no sign, and as long as he stayed away it did not matter that Tristram was kept in ignorance of the true state of things. And William had kept quiet – while it suited him.

'What does William want you to do for him?' she asked, deeply suspicious.

'He wants me to intercede with Gaunt, get him to declare the recent election for the Mayor of London null and void – have a new one.'

'But what can you do? If Brembre has been elected, the damage is done, it's too late.'

'Not if we can have the election declared unlawful. It appears that Brembre took a lot of armed men into the Guildhall, terrified the electors into voting for him. So I get my lord Duke to pursuade the King to grant a royal writ to hold new elections. Then we pack the Guildhall, same as Bumble, and we get your Northampton in. Should be a good scrap if Bumble's as big a villain as the merchant says he is.'

'Then you'll be no better than Brembre,' she objected.

'But they want Northampton – that's what Gryffard says. They'd have voted for him if they'd been allowed to.'

Merciful Jesus, what was William up to? He had been one of Brembre's followers before, hadn't he? He had changed sides so often, he could change sides again. But maybe this time he'd gone too far, identified himself too closely with Northampton's reforming zeal, benefited too much in the last two years from Northampton's persecution of the victuallers. Besides, William liked manipulating people. If he succeeded in restoring John of Northampton to the Mayoralty, he would be in a position to demand many favours.

'The Duke will never agree to help,' she said, still doubtful. 'He's lost interest in London.'

'William says if we help Northampton, he'll get the city's vote for the Duke's Spanish campaign.'

Oh, he was wily, was William, and of course Tristram was eager to go, anything to escape from the drab austerity of his own manor to the splendid opulence of the Duke's household.

'We'll have your John of Northampton back as Mayor before Christmas,' Tristram went on, happy now in his enthusiasm.

'Don't go, Tristram,' she said, seized with a dreadful premonition. 'Stay here with me.' She looked at him then, trying to summon up the courage to warn him about Nicholas de Cher. But he had hold of the sheet and was pulling it away from her, staring at her naked breasts.

'That's right, you want me, don't you, Joanna?' he whispered hoarsely. 'You'll do anything for it, won't you, my hungry little wife.' Her heart sank. He was drunk but not nearly drunk enough to be incapable.

She got out of bed and helped him undress. He caught hold of her flowing hair, jerked her head back so violently her eyes watered. 'Show me how you love me,' he moaned as he pulled her towards him. She wound her arms round his neck, offered him her lips, forced herself not to turn away as he bruised her mouth with hard, hateful kisses. He could get very nasty if he thought she didn't want him.

She moulded her body against his and he bent over her so fiercely she stumbled and fell backwards onto the bed. He leapt upon her and she made herself lie still, arched her body to receive him, moaned a little. She must not let him think that she was not in ecstasy. The rampant desire could so quickly drain from his loins if he lost confidence, and then he would torture himself and her for half the night trying to achieve some sort of satisfaction. There would be indignities, bruising, sometimes beatings if he could not get arousal.

'Let it be quick,' she prayed as he straddled her, one hand on each shoulder, pressing her down into the feather bed so she could hardly breathe. She closed her eyes so as not to see the hard, joyless determination on his face as he rode her, like a charger in the tilt-yard, humping her again and again and again, grunting and muttering to himself until she thought he would never be done. Then at last he gave three savage thrusts and she clenched her teeth so as not to cry out. He gave one more satisfied grunt and collapsed on top of her. Within minutes he was asleep, his face buried in her luxurious hair. She lay pinned beside him, wide awake and worrying.

Part of her wanted Tristram to go with William. Never before had Tristram been at home for so long and she didn't know how much longer the manor would withstand his extravagant demands, practical jokes and restless, unchannelled energy. A deeper part of her wanted him to succeed, to oust Brembre and restore Northampton or perhaps even her father in his place. If only Tristram could prove his worth, overcome her enemies, then perhaps she could love him again. If she could love him as she once had done, there might be hope for them after all. But another part of her, the practical side that the hardships of the last three years had done much to hone and polish, told her to keep Tristram away from William. Even as she formed the thought, she knew it was useless. Tristram would do as he pleased and if he wanted to go, she could do nothing to stop him. She consoled herself then with the thought that Tristram, once he was back with the Duke of Lancaster, would soon forget about William's schemes – assuming the Duke made him welcome and asked him to stay. And it would be a relief to be free of him for a while.

CHAPTER 33

Tristram and William left together on 13 October. Joanna bade them farewell and Godspeed without regret. There was much to be done preparing for the winter and at first she did not feel lonely. There were cattle to be husbanded; the best chosen for breeding, the rest to be slaughtered and the meat salted or smoked above the huge open fires in the kitchens. There was fruit in the orchard to be picked and stored, preserves to be made, the stillroom to be filled. There was the autumn woolclip to be made into cloth. First the matted wool had to be washed and beaten clean. Then it had to be carded, then spun. The women on the manor would be hard at work with their children while the men and boys laboured all the daylight hours in the fields. When the yarn was ready it was woven on the huge broadloom, so wide a man had to have an assistant just to pass the warp.

As Joanna went about the village and the outlying farms, watching over each part of the process, listening to complaints, urging and encouraging and driving them on to get the work done, she was conscious of a feeling of harmony, of the interdependence among serfs and free tenants alike. This was now a thriving community not only battling together against the wild and predatory forces of nature but also striving to get the better of their neighbours, and showing a new pride in its self-sufficiency. She was content that autumn of 1383, knowing that there would be no starvation for any of them this winter, that whatever befell, she had her cloth to sell. Yes she had done it. Against all the odds, she had finally found a way.

As she went about her many tasks, the serfs smiled at her and did her bidding willingly, the parish priest blessed her when she passed, the free tenants stopped to share with her their small triumphs and sorrows; even the bailiff treated her with respect. She was alone in the great manor house, but she was not lonely. She had poured everything she had into the manor and it was beginning to bear fruit.

It had not always been so. Often Joanna had thought with longing of the Convent of the Sacred Heart during those first despairing months back at Maudesbury. She had come home under armed guard with Tristram and a score of men-at-arms. Tristram had immediately called a special meeting of the manor court and had the serfs dragged before him one by one. They had come, each one clutching his charter of freedom from the King like a talisman. But Tristram had seized their charters and torn them up in front of their eyes.

'Serfs you are and serfs you will remain,' he had shouted at them while they cowered before him. Joanna had watched horrified, cringing as she thought of her own humiliation when she must entice him into her bed. Not because she wanted him, but because he needed to believe that the child she bore was his.

Once, her love for him had bound her to him, helplessly, hopelessly; now, that was dead but she was still bound to him because of the child – William's child. She must lie with her husband still, even though he did not want her. Tristram would not notice dates or count months, would probably be far from home when the child was born. He would accept the child gladly – he wanted a son – provided he thought that it was his. So she had had to pretend that nothing had changed, that she loved him as much as ever, had to wait until he was drunk enough and then beg him to come to her. She was still a slave, because of her duty to the unborn child.

Tristram had enacted swift and terrible punishment on his serfs, instructing the bailiff to raise the rents of the free tenants. Then he had departed with his men-at-arms to carry on the fight against the rebellious serfs elsewhere, leaving the manor destitute, the sheep dying from a murrain, the serfs defeated and hopeless, their harvest in ruins, their livestock stolen or strayed, and the parish priest weeping in despair. How vain her proud boast to the Prioress had seemed then. How impossible her task.

That first winter after the Hurling Time, after Tristram had left, there had been nothing but despair and discord. In the face of severe shortages, the normal co-operation between villagers, so vital in regulating the use of common fields, pastures, waters, had broken down. There had been too many helpless women and children, too many mouths to feed, and everyone fighting everyone else for the little that there was. Christmas had come and Joanna had spent it alone and hungry in the empty manor house, with rain dripping through the roof of the hall, and only the rats scuttling in the wainscot to keep her company.

A few weeks later she received a letter from Petronilla Northampton describing the King's wedding to Ann of Bohemia – the processions, the pageants, the conduits running with wine, the banquets, the tournaments and Tristram's glorious conquests in battle. It was the time of Joanna's deepest despair. Huddled in her cold solar with no music but the howling of the wolves outside and reading by the light of one poor tallow candle, she realised how appalled Petronilla would be if she knew how all her golden dreams had ended. At the end of her letter, Petronilla gently upbraided Joanna for being such a poor correspondent, hoped nothing was amiss, and expressed surprise that Tristram had not brought her with him to watch his triumph in the lists. Joanna, as much to comfort herself as to reassure Petronilla, had written back a glowing account of all the pleasures of Maudesbury, inventing the sort of life for herself she once thought marriage to Tristram would bring, letting her fantasy carry her away for just a little while, away from the loneliness, the fruitless struggle and the hopelessness of it all.

All through that winter, she had struggled on, barely able to keep starvation at bay. Every time she went to church she dreaded her meeting with the priest. Always he had some tale of disaster for her and there was nothing she could do to help any more. All the time she thought about Nick, wondering when he would come to take his revenge, believing in her desperation that it would be the best thing for all of them when he did, clinging to the idea of seeing him again, of throwing herself on his mercy, dreaming occasionally of obtaining his forgiveness.

But Nick never came and spring brought William Gryffard just in time for the birth of her baby. That he knew about the child did not surprise her. William always knew. What he intended to do with the information she never discovered because after a long and agonising labour the child was born dead, strangled by the cord caught round his neck at the moment of birth. Joanna ought to have been relieved, but she was not. Looking at the frail, lifeless body of her son whom she had struggled so hard to bring into the world, she felt an overwhelming sense of loss, and fear. It was a sign that God had not forgiven her, that nothing would ever go right again until she gave up all hope and became a nun.

William had taken his leave soon after and Joanna, worn out by the rigours of winter and long hours of agonising labour, had abandoned all hope of saving the manor and sunk into the lethargy of despair.

It was Edmund de Cher who gave her the courage to go on. One fine morning at the beginning of May, when the wind was warm and gentle as a benediction and the birds poured out their song in clamorous welcome to spring, the golden coach had lumbered over the drawbridge at Maudesbury and come to rest in the outer court. Joanna had looked out of the solar window in surprise and seen Edmund being helped from the coach by the postilions. All she could think of was that perhaps he had come with a message from Nick. She flew down to greet him without so much as stopping to change her cap.

He had come, he said, because he was bored. His mother and her guests had taken advantage of the fine weather to go hawking and he was sick of being left with Agnes Proudfoot, his brother's betrothed. Her goodness got on his nerves. Joanna settled him into Tristram's chair, and plied him with ale, while trying to hide her disappointment. All too conscious of the gloomy hall, the cold hearth, her old gown and that her cap was not quite clean, she felt unable to amuse anyone, let alone Edmund. But to her surprise, Edmund entertained her. He launched into a wicked and vivid description of his mother's guests, for his sufferings had made him an acute observer of human nature, and he disposed of each one in turn with such a sharp but neat thrust of wit that she could not help laughing. Indeed, she discovered that when he wanted to be, he was the most stimulating of companions. He put her on her mettle and for a time, while they talked, she was able to forget her troubles.

'Admit you feel the better for my visit,' he said when they had talked and argued most of the morning away, 'as do I. You're much more fun than those women my mother surrounds herself with. I can never enjoy a good argument with them, they always agree with me all the time – they're frightened of upsetting the invalid. Will you come and visit me at Cher sometimes?'

'I can't,' she said, panic making her more abrupt than she intended. 'Tristram would not like it.'

'And you are content to live shut up in his manor like an anchoress in a cell?'

She stared at him, realising the truth of his accusation. Even a nun was better off than she was here. There was music, company and the benefit of God's grace in a convent.

'Oh, you make shift to show a happy face to your servants and tenants,' he continued, misinterpreting her dismay, 'but what delights or pleasures have you to enjoy? No wine, no books, no music, no gentlewomen even to keep you company. How do you endure it, day after day? I could improve your life a little, if you would but let me. If you would but come to Cher Castle. I could pamper you.'

'I don't want to be pampered,' she said quickly.

'What do you want then?'

'To make things better here,' she said. 'To see the manor prosper, the serfs working happily, for there to be enough to eat.'

'It will come if you're patient,' he told her. 'There've been bad harvests before, sheep are always falling prey to disease, but nature is a bounteous provider, there's always one or two left to breed and multiply. You'll have wool this year and wheat and hay. The serfs have learnt their lesson, hunger makes a good bailiff. They'll work harder than before the rebellion, you'll see.'

'The trouble is our wool never seems to make enough to supply all the manor's needs, even in good times and now I'm afraid we're too far behind ever to catch up.' He was being so understanding she could not help confessing just a little.

'Then why don't you make cloth. You'll get twice the price for it.'

'Cloth!'

'The wool tax is killing the trade in wool,' he explained. 'But cloth, that's different. There's hardly any tax on cloth. By making up your wool into cloth here and then sending it to Calais, you can undercut the Flemish who still have to buy English wool and pay the tax on it.'

Joanna listened, a glimmer of hope lightening her despair. The wool had been sold in advance to Nick but he had not claimed it yet. Before he did she could use it, couldn't she, to make money – to buy him off by paying him its value.

'But I don't know how,' she said, daunted by the enormity of the risk she was contemplating.

'You can learn, can't you? The monks at Cirencester know all about cloth-making. Gervase de Haen – he's a friend of mine. He'll tell you how it's done. We'll go there now and afterwards you can come back with me to Cher.'

She told him then the reason why she could not come to Cher. Not the whole story, just enough to convince him that her visits to his castle were impossible.

'So Tristram ran away,' Edmund said when she'd finished. 'That's bad, but he was only a boy and plague is a terrifying thing. As for the rest, I wouldn't blame Tristram for Nick's disgrace. Nick's quite capable of bringing it upon himself. He told us very little about what he'd been up to in all the time he'd been away. I don't doubt there's much in Nick's life he's not very proud of. My brother's not really cut out to be a knight; he has the soul of a brigand. Not an ounce of chivalry in him.'

'That's not true,' she countered. 'He only pretends to be a villain to hide his true nature. Beneath that rough exterior of his, he's the only really chivalrous man I've ever met.'

'Joanna, I'm disappointed in you,' Edmund exclaimed. 'I thought you were the one lady whose good sense was proof against all my brother's magic.'

She bit her lip and turned away from his amused gaze, annoyed with herself.

'You need not be afraid, Nick's never at Cher. We haven't heard of him since the Rising. Apart from that one brief visit he paid, he's still lost to his family. It would make my days less long if you were to come and see me sometimes.' he pleaded.

'I'll come with you to Cirencester, to see Gervase de Haen,' she said. 'But I cannot come to Cher – for Tristram's sake.' He looked at her sceptically and she wasn't sure whether he believed her or not. But he did not press further.

Edmund showed her the way to recovery but it was not easy persuading the free tenants to pay their rents in wool, for they were selling it to the abbey again. And the women and children had little time to spare to card and spin; they were needed to tend their livestock or help in the fields. The bailiff, the parish priest and the reeve all told her it couldn't be done, that they needed all the hands they had for the crops, the swine, the cattle and the sheep, that wool was their business not cloth – cloth was for the Flemings. Joanna cajoled and pleaded and lost her temper, and when that failed she learnt how to use diplomacy and rank. She visited the tenant farmers one by one, and slowly her will prevailed. At every obstacle she refused to consider defeat, though there were times when she was sorely tempted to give up. Tristram came home and scolded her for interfering with the old ways, for squandering the rent money on her merchant's obsession. Then they couldn't find anyone on the manor to work the huge broadloom. But a year ago William had paid them another visit and it was he, much to Joanna's surprise, who had found her a skilled weaver. Edmund de Cher also took an interest in her venture, making the journey to Maudesbury in his golden coach as often as the weather and his health would permit. When they couldn't get the shrinkage of the cloth right, it was Edmund who suggested they take the cloth to the experts at the fulling mill at Painswick, a manor not more than ten miles away on the other side of the valley.

Now at last she had her cloth, rolled up in bales in the wool shed, waiting for a buyer. She would have to sell it to William, dearly though she would have loved to ship it to Calais and sell it there. But she had no agents in France and was deterred by the transport problems. If only Tristram would take an interest. But Tristram was a knight. He was above such things. He could not be expected to burden himself with carting bundles of cloth about the countryside.

Tristram did not like the cloth-making, but when her child was born dead Joanna ceased to care what Tristram wanted. In those far off days when Tristram had been the centre of her universe, it had seemed as if he was all the manor had to offer; now, after all the effort and struggle she had put into it, she had come to love the manor for its own sake. To her amazement, she found that the colder she was to Tristram, the more impressed with her he became. Sometimes she caught him looking at her with puzzled fascination. It was not the way he had looked at Mariota, but she sometimes wondered whether, if she could only learn how to feel for him again, he might not perhaps come at last to love her in return. But she no longer wanted his love; it was a relief to be alone on the manor again, unhampered and free to deal with the practical problems of the cloth-making as she saw fit.

At the end of October Joanna, accompanied by the bailiff as protector, rode through the splendour of the dying year to Cirencester. She was worried about Edmend de Cher and thought they might be able to give her news of him at the abbey. When Tristram was at home, she was unable to see anything of Edmund. She had tried, at Edmund's prompting, to persuade Tristram to visit Cher, but he had reacted so violently she had never dared mention the subject again. For the last six months she had seen nothing of her friend and adviser and she had missed him, and not only for his encouragement with the cloth-making. His sharp tongue had been a whetstone for her own wits. He had lent her books and introduced her to a fascinating world of ideas and literature which was far more satisfying than the silly fantasies she had once woven for herself. She longed to show him her cloth. He would rejoice for her, might even know how she could best sell it. Gervase de Haen at the abbey would let him know that Tristram had gone, and Joanna prayed that Edmund would be fit enough still to make the journey to see her; he had been failing for some time. If he could no longer leave his bed, Joanna wondered whether she dared go to Cher Castle to visit her friend.

Her dilemma was rudely resolved by Gervase de Haen, who told her that Edmund de Cher was dead. Joanna was shocked and distressed although she knew she should be glad for poor Edmund. He had often, quite calmly and sincerely, longed for a merciful release from his suffering, but she would miss him sorely. Her sorrow over Edmund was, however, driven from her mind by Gervase de Haen's next piece of news.

'Maybe the prodigal son will return now to step into his brother's shoes,' Gervase went on. 'A poor son and a poor brother he's been to them all these years, leaving the Lady Elizabeth with all the trouble of ministering to Edmund unaided, that on top of the manor and all its cares. You'd have thought he'd have been to see them once in a while, wouldn't you? Jealous, I don't doubt, couldn't bear to see the elder brother getting all the attention.'

'I don't think Nicholas is at all interested in Cher,' said Joanna, stifling the quick leap of her senses at the thought of his return. It was typical of him, she thought with a quick spurt of anger, to have acquired such a black reputation among his family and the local people.

'The Lady Elizabeth expects him,' Gervase informed her. 'She has invited Agnes Proudfoot into her household permanently to keep her company in Edmund's place. She clearly means to have the marriage bond tied as soon as Sir Nicholas reappears, and not before time either. That poor girl has been kept waiting for too long. You'd have thought the Lord Berkeley would have found another husband for her by this time, but I daresay he's enjoyed the fruit of his wardship from her lands too much to want to give them up.'

Joanna rode home thinking about Nick's return. She had given up all hope of his forgiveness long ago, that out of love he might relent.

But at least she had her cloth; he could not harm the manor now. Still she could not help feeling depressed. The thought of his coming to Cher, marrying that insipid girl, living on the next-door manor was unbearable. All her newfound peace of mind, her acceptance, her affection for the people – her people – was threatened by Nicholas de Cher's return.

In November Joanna received a letter from Petronilla. Nicholas Brembre had been sworn in as Mayor. Petronilla was afraid that her husband was taking his defeat badly and was stirring up trouble among the craftsmen and mercantile guilds. Joanna's father was hopeful of bringing the mercers to his support and her brother-in-law John Constantyn swore the cordwainers could be relied upon. Petronilla was fearful of where it might all lead, although William Gryffard had assured her John would win in the end.

Joanna laid down the letter and stared out of the window at the rain drumming on the surface of the moat. If Brembre had been sworn in it meant that the royal writ to overrule his election had not been granted. Tristram must have failed to persuade John of Gaunt to intervene. What was William Gryffard up to? Was he trying to implicate her family in a bid to overthrow the elected Mayor, or was he genuinely helping Northampton back to power? William hated violence, that she knew. She could not believe that he would not now accept Brembre as Mayor and simply change sides once again. And where was Tristram? Petronilla made no mention of him. If he had got no further than the Duke of Lancaster's castle, he would not be likely to leave until after Christmas. Feeling depressed at the thought of another Christmas alone and uncelebrated, she sat down and wrote back begging Petronilla to be careful of William and not to trust him in any way.

In the third week of Advent it began to snow. Joanna watched the big fat flakes falling past the window of her solar as she sat on the board round the edge of the big bed, spinning. Every spare moment of her life she spent spinning for the broadloom; she could spin in her sleep, she could spin and think of nothing at all. The fire was smoking and making her cough. She got up, eyes watering, and hung her head out of the window, drawing great breaths of cold air deep into her lungs.

Two horsemen were approaching the drawbridge. She peered at them through the falling snow, surprise and a tiny tingle of disquiet driving out her calm. They were muffled up in their heavy travelling cloaks, but she had no doubt that it was Tristram come home for Christmas after all. What did it mean?

She turned from the window to peer through the smoke at her reflection in the polished steel. If her husband had come home to spend Christmas with her, she should make him welcome. Tristram liked her to look her best. Swiftly she changed her old serge gown for a sheath of green wool and added a close-fitting surcoat lined with fur and a cloak of scarlet samite; she brushed and rebraided her hair and wound the glowing chestnut ropes round her head. There was no time to find a fresh veil so she left her head uncovered and swiftly descended the winding staircase to the hall below. A housecarl was hard at work coaxing the glowing embers of the fire into leaping life. 'You can leave it, Huw,' she said, pleased. 'Now go to the door, you know how he hates to be kept waiting.' The man gave her a frightened look, and scurried from the hall.

She stood in front of the fire, the flames leaping up behind her lighting the crowning glory of her hair, confident that she looked good, glad in a way that her husband had come home to her in time for Christmas. She would make it a good one for him. Be kinder, try to love him. She had loved him once, perhaps now that the manor's future was more secure, it would be easier.

Someone was coming down the passage outside. She turned towards the screen at the far end of the hall, ready with her smile of welcome. But it was not Tristram who came into the hall shaking snow from his heavy cloak. It was Nick. Her smile froze.

He took off his heavy travelling cloak, threw it to the servant. 'I've a man outside with the horses – show him to the stables,' he ordered and the servant scuttled quickly away.

Joanna opened her mouth but found she had no breath. It was trapped somewhere between her stomach and her heart. He was staring at her in a very alarming manner. She seized a taper and busied herself with lighting the candles on their wall sconces.

'Aren't you going to give me good day?' he asked and she mumbled some sort of greeting over her shoulder. He took the taper from her hand.

'Let me do that for you,' he said. She relinquished the taper and backed quickly away from him as if he had the pox. Calmly he lit the rest of the candles while she struggled to gain control over her breath, her shaking limbs, her beating heart.

He was well dressed in a velvet surcoat trimmed with fur and belted with a sword belt of leather chased with silver. His hair was shorn neatly and he was clean-shaven but his face was weatherbeaten to a dark red-brown colour which made the brilliant blue of his eyes all the more startling. He finished lighting the candles and came to stand in front of her.

'You've grown more beautiful,' he said almost belligerently. She dared not look at him. Stay calm, she told herself fiercely. Don't give in to his magic. Remember he says that to every woman. She took a deep breath, raised her eyes to his face. He was frowning down at her with his big bushy brows drawn together fiercely.

'I'm afraid Tristram isn't at home,' she said, letting out her breath slowly.

'I know.'

'What do you want?' She meant to sound defiant but only achieved a terrified whisper.

'I've come to buy your cloth,' he said.

'Buy it or take it?' This time defiance won.

'Buy it, if you will sell it to me. Gervase de Haen says it is good, the best quality. I'll give you a better price than the monks in the abbey.'

'William has offered me two pounds a bale for it,' she said deliberately.

'With or without you thrown in?' he demanded, glaring at her angrily.

She turned her back on him with what she hoped was regal disdain, walked to Tristram's chair and sat down unable to trust her trembling legs much longer. He followed her and stood staring down at her in silence, while she nervously waited for him to attack her. But he said nothing.

'You've been away a long time,' she said when she could bear the silence no longer.

'I went to fight for Philip van Artevelde the Flemish leader in his revolt against the French.'

'I thought you didn't believe in that sort of thing.'

'I developed a taste for lost causes. It seemed a good idea at the time.' He was not looking quite so angry, and his eyes searching her face made her pulses begin to race.

'Was it a lost cause?' she asked quickly, looking away.

'It might not have been if the English had sent help sooner,' he said. 'Van Artevelde was a great leader and a clever fighter. I was with him when he captured Bruges. He did it by sheer force of will against all odds and then the other towns opened their gates, the nobles emigrated and the country districts submitted. He was master of all Flanders, and if we'd sent an army then, when he asked us to, under a proper command instead of that lunatic Bishop, we could have kept the French out of Flanders for good. Instead of which, by the time the English army got to Calais it was already too late.'

'Were you one of the garrison left defending Bourbourg?' she asked.

'No, I came back with the Bishop. I knew it was only a matter of time before Bourbourg fell too and I didn't want to risk surrender and ransom a second time.'

'The Bishop returned more than two months ago. Your brother was still alive then. He was lonely at Cher with only your mother and her friends,' she accused.

'You think it hard of me to stay away from them. In truth I did it for their sakes.' He began wandering around the hall, examining the trophies on the walls and the weaponry, as if he'd never seen armour before. 'Edmund could not have borne to have me at Cher, hunting the forests and playing the knight. I realised that when I came home before. He was happy being the centre of my mother's life and she was content to be ruled by him. Weakness is a powerful weapon if used skilfully and Edmund used it well.'

'You sound as if you did not love your brother.'

'I never really knew him. He was four years older, and when we were young he always beat me in everything. Edmund hated to be bested in anything; it made him a powerful fighter and it was hard for him when he was brought down. But he fought on in his own way with the only weapons at his disposal. I can match strength with strength, but I cannot fight weakness, so I stayed away.'

'We used to meet,' she told him, 'in Cirencester – at the abbey or here when he was well enough to make the journey. He was very good company when he wanted to be. I know many people found him moody and bitter, but I didn't and I shall miss him sorely, for he was my friend.'

'As I am, Joanna,' Nick said. He was standing now in front of her, looking at her solemnly, and she knew then that he had not come to ruin her. Had he forgiven her? Once before he had offered her friendship and she had spurned it because she hated him. She didn't hate him now. She loved him. She got up from her chair and walked to the fire, telling herself not to be a fool, that he was nothing but a proven breaker of hearts. His own brother had confirmed it.

'I hear that Agnes Proudfoot is living now at Cher. Will you honour your betrothal vow at last?'

'It's what my mother wants, but not Agnes, and it's not what I want either,' he said.

'And you always do exactly what you want, don't you?'

'It's certainly what the people here expect of me,' he said with a bitter laugh. 'But I thought you might be different, might know me better, Joanna.'

'Why do you always let everyone think the worst of you? You don't even try to clear your name,' she burst out, suddenly angry.

'I've never cared much what people thought of me,' he retorted. 'I try to live with myself and obey God's law, that's all any man can hope for, in my belief.' He was glaring at her furiously again.

To Joanna's relief Huw returned bearing a pitcher of ale and a loaf of new-baked bread which he laid on the trestle table. Joanna sat down in Tristram's chair, broke the bread and offered it to Nick. The servant filled his goblet with ale. He tossed it back, walking about the hall impatiently, while the servant made up the fire again, refilled the goblets and at last withdrew.

Joanna sipped her ale and stared miserably down at the table. Why was it she always had to fight with him? How could they ever even be friends when all they did was quarrel? He came to stand beside her chair and she glanced up. He was glowering down like a huge black thundercloud and she trembled, waiting for the storm to burst, feeling the great gulf of misunderstanding stretching between them, wanting to bridge it, not knowing what to say.

'It's no use, Joanna,' he suddenly burst out. 'For three years I've fought it. Done everything I could think of to cut you out of my heart. But I cannot. Jesu, I had no idea love could be like this and I'm the worst kind of a fool for having become its victim, but I cannot help it.'

She gripped her goblet tightly with both hands, looked down into the muddy brown liquid. 'You mean you've forgiven me?' she whispered into its depths.

'Forgiven you? For lying with that serpent?' he shouted. 'By all the saints, I'll never forgive you. Never!'

She could not go on sitting there with him leaning over her, bullying and shouting. She got up swiftly, clung to the back of the chair for support. 'I only did it that once, I swear it.'

'I don't care! I don't care what you did. Don't you see, I love you no matter what you do. You're an unscrupulous, tenderhearted, meddling, impulsive, beautiful vixen who just will not ever accept defeat. That's why I love you, because of all your faults not in spite of them.' His eyes were blazing with so much passion she instinctively tried to put the table between them, but he was too quick. He seized her by the wrist, spun her round, held both her hands in a grip of steel. 'Joanna, it's no good pretending any longer. We were made for each other, you and I. Can't you see that?'

'And what of Tristram?' she whispered. The hiss of his indrawn breath was like arrow's flight. She thought he would strike her, but he didn't. He kissed her hard, crushing the breath out of her body until she squirmed in protest. Instantly he released her, slipped his hands round her waist, gently drew her close and kissed her again, but this time with infinite tenderness. In the magic of that moment she felt all her doubts subside, all her difficulties disperse. She wound her arms round his neck, closed her eyes and returned his kiss with all the pent-up passion she had tried for three long years to stifle.

At last he raised his head. 'Now tell me that you still love Tristram,' he said.

It was too late for that. She couldn't deny him the truth. She couldn't deny him anything.

'I love you,' she said.

'Heart and mind, body and soul?' he demanded.

'Heart and mind, body and soul, God have mercy,' she whispered.

'As do I thee,' he swore. Then lifting her gently into his arms, he carried her slowly up the long winding stone staircase to her solar.

CHAPTER 34

Tristram spent Christmastide with John of Gaunt at Leicester Castle. But on the morning after Epiphany, the Duke was on the move, bound for France. Tristram travelled in his retinue as far as London, expecting to accompany his liege lord on his mission. But when they reached Westminster the Duke bade him farewell. 'I go to pay my respects to the King,' he said, a wry smile twisting his handsome mouth, 'and think it better not to antagonise my nephew by a show of strength. Nor have I work for you in France, since I'm going there in pursuit of peace. But keep your sword sharp, by the end of the month our truce with the Scots comes to an end and I don't doubt we shall be needed with an army on the border again.'

Tristram was not too downcast. He knew he could not be kept by the Duke for ever. He was a knight of little standing, unlike Richard Scrope and Michael de la Pole. All he had to offer his powerful and royal overlord was his sword. He consoled himself that it would not, after all, be much fun in France while the Duke haggled endlessly with the Dukes of Berri and Brittany. The talks were to take place in the benighted town of Lelinghen, a halfway house between Calais and Boulogne. Tristram had been there in November in search of the Duke and the place did not even have a decent tournament ground. So he rode on towards London, accompanied only by his squire, looking forward to the Duke's promise of another campaign against the Scots. The last expedition to that land had been all too tame and had ended in a bloodless truce. But the Scots were a warlike race and might yet be provoked into a profitable battle.

Finding himself approaching the city at dinner time, Tristram thought of William Gryffard. The merchant had a comfortable house, or such was his boast, and there was always the chance he might be able to borrow some more money from him. But when Tristram arrived at William's house in Cornhill, he found the merchant was just setting out for Northampton's Inn.

'You'd better come with me,' William said. 'John of Northampton will be very pleased to see you. Your influence with the Duke of Lancaster could be very important to us at this time.'

Tristram swore softly as he watched William climb onto a well-fed palfrey. He had forgotten all about that business of the Mayor's election. He didn't feel guilty, Tristram never felt guilty, but he did feel defensive.

'That writ you wanted from the King,' he said. 'I did my best for you but the Duke couldn't do anything, he's been in France these past two months. I had to chase all over the place after him.'

William merely smiled knowingly, which infuriated Tristram. He felt himself silently accused.

'You merchants are never satisfied, are you?' he said petulantly. 'You talk all day long about it not being safe to ship your goods across the Channel and when the Duke goes over there to try and bring about a peaceful settlement, you want him back in London settling your quarrels for you. Well, a man can't be in two places at once.'

Instantly William was anxious to placate him. 'You must pardon us,' he said, 'if sometimes we are too preoccupied with the travail of our trade and plague you with all our little difficulties. If we seem ungrateful we don't mean to be. We need you and your fellow knights to fight for us, don't think we don't, and that is why you'll be so welcome at Northampton's Inn today. It will put heart into the waverers to see a knight of such prowess among the ex-Mayor's supporters.' So saying, he urged his horse forward and Tristram felt obliged to follow, somewhat mollified by the man's obvious good sense. He wasn't a bad fellow, Gryffard, just so long as he was kept in his place.

John of Northampton welcomed them warmly. 'You are timely,' he said, 'for we are just about to sit down to dinner.'

The hall was bright and warm, with a myriad beeswax candles alight upon the walls and a huge fire blazing in the hearth, but Tristram's heart sank as he studied the men gathered about the long trestle tables filling the room. They were cowled and hooded, with soft hats pulled well down over their brows, wrapped up well against the cold in gowns of velvet, or fine wool much trimmed with fur, and he searched in vain for the gleam of chain mail or steel. In all the company he could not see one tabard decorated with a recognisable coat of arms.

A servant proffered a silver dish and as Tristram washed his hands in the lukewarm water, he cursed William for having made him come. He could think of many better ways of spending his day than in dining with these solemn-faced traders, grumbling about their taxes or their cargoes lost at sea, or even, St Michael spare him, the need for peace. John of Northampton, his pale face as long and dismal as any

379

sheep, enquired most anxiously after the Duke of Lancaster.

'The Duke's busy trying to get a peace treaty with the French,' said Tristram, shaking scented water from his fingertips, 'so we can go to Spain and knock the bastard usurper Don Juan off his throne.' That ought to give Northampton something to look sad about, he thought, pleased with himself.

Northampton received this information with a wintry smile and led the way to the high table. Tristram followed, thinking longingly of the lavish entertainment no doubt taking place at Westminster Palace where the Duke would be dining with the King. Not that Northampton's table was wanting, there were dishes aplenty being carried in from the kitchens by an impressive procession of servants, but if the only entertainment was to be city politics it would make for a long afternoon. Tristram's squire seemed to share these misgivings. His face was long as he leant over his master's shoulder and handed Tristram a fine silver goblet filled with good new Rhenish wine.

'What's the matter, Godfrey?' he said, drinking deep. 'I can assure you the wine's as good as in the Duke's household, although the company's hardly what we're used to. Are you afraid to go and take your meats with those rough-looking apprentices down there? Or are you worried that by the time you've finished serving me they'll have cleaned up all that's remaining and you'll have to go scramble for the scraps with the poor at the gates?' Enjoying the squire's obvious discomfiture, Tristram drew his dagger and began to attack the dish in front of him.

'How fares my daughter?' asked a man seated opposite, leaning forward and helping himself to the same dish.

'She was well when I last saw her,' Tristram replied, his mouth full of venison pie.

'You didn't bring her to London with you then?'

'I haven't come from Maudesbury, I've come from the Duke's castle in Leicester,' Tristram replied, glancing at Richard Burgeys carelessly. He had done his best to forget Joanna's low-born parentage, but now face to face with Burgeys, he saw not Joanna's father, but the man who had once stood between him and Mariota. Mariota! It was ages since he had thought about her. He found it difficult now to remember the madness that had engulfed him, to believe that once he had been so desperate to have her that he had offered to take the girl in her shift. He could not remember what had possessed him, but he could remember this man, cowering behind his ledgers in his mean little counting house and having the temerity to turn down a knight for his daughter. He could remember humiliation and unjust treatment.

'When are you going to bring Joanna to London to visit us?' Burgeys said, watching him anxiously from the other side of the table.

'Or has she grown too grand for the likes of us?'

'Mariota was too grand for the likes of me as I remember!' retorted Tristram. 'You should have let me marry her. I'd have known how to take good care of her and she'd still be alive today.' Tristram was pleased to see from the pain in Burgeys' eyes that his taunt had gone home. It made him feel better.

'You have our Joanna and I have to be thankful for that,' replied Burgeys, with a quick warning glance at William seated at Tristram's side. Tristram turned to stare arrogantly at the merchant but he was deep in conversation with his neighbour on the other side.

The dishes for the second course were being brought in and laid out upon the table and Tristram applied himself with renewed vigour, bored with baiting Burgeys. But Burgeys was not so easily snubbed.

'I'm glad you're here,' he said. 'We need strong men like you to help us in the battle to overthrow Brembre.'

'Well, if you want any fighting done, I'm your man.' Tristram speared a piece of sturgeon on the point of his dagger and popped it swiftly into his mouth. A fight – now that might be a bit of fun. He wondered whether they would pay him for his services. They looked prosperous enough.

'That's it,' said Burgeys with a grin. 'That's the sort of talk we need. It wouldn't be difficult to start a rebellion. The city's ripe for it. They all hate Brembre.'

'Pay no heed to him, he's too hotheaded,' said Northampton on Tristram's other side. 'Now that Brembre has been sworn in, what we have to do is convince the King he's unfit to govern.'

'A riot or two ought to convince him of that,' said Burgeys.

'What we do, we must do by peaceful means,' replied Northampton. 'I will not be a party to Brembre's tactics of rioting and disorder.'

'What do you propose to do then? Pray?' Tristram scoffed.

'Something like that,' Northampton responded calmly. 'On Sunday we shall meet at Bow Church in Chepe and march to Mass at the Carmelite church by Fleet Bridge. Will you come with us? I've summoned five hundred guildmen on pain of a fine if they don't appear. I want to show the King that the city has not accepted this unlawful election of its Mayor. We will go on marching and demonstrating, peacefully, until the King or your Duke takes notice.'

Tristram was disappointed. He had expected at the very least a large-scale riot and all they were planning was a procession to church. He gazed around the hall and wondered how much longer he would have to sit here. Gryffard, he noticed, took little part in the discussion. Perhaps he too was disgusted with Northampton's timid approach.

381

When dinner was over, to Tristram's dismay the hall was invaded by some of the wives who had been dining in a separate room. He was preparing to make good his escape when he found himself accosted by Petronilla Northampton.

'Sir Tristram, this is an unlooked for pleasure. What brings you here?'

'William Gryffard brought me.'

'William Gryffard? Do you lodge with him while you are in the city?'

'I might,' he replied.

'I hope you will. It would be a relief to me, and to Joanna, to know that you were there at a time like this.' She was richly and fashionably dressed but for all her worldly appearance there was something about the innocent enquiry of her gaze that reminded him uncomfortably of a nun. He muttered some excuse and backed away, but she was not be so easily shaken off.

'Tell me about my Joanna,' she said, laying a hand on his arm and drawing him with her to a far corner of the hall. 'She's happy, I know, and it's all because of you. You and Joanna are my Troilus and Criseyde, you know.'

Tristram was bemused. As Petronilla went on to eulogise the delights and pleasures of living at Maudesbury, he could not believe she was talking about his manor. He had never regarded it as anything other than a source of replenishment for his needs, somewhere to return to only when he had nowhere more congenial to go. Yet this extraordinary woman seemed to think of it as some sort of love bower, that he and Joanna might actually be happy just being there. It was absurd. He felt uncomfortable, as if he'd strayed by chance into the middle of some minstrel's tale.

'I had a letter from Maudesbury not so long ago,' Petronilla continued. 'Joanna seems well. She says the harvest is all in and it is a good one, thanks be to God. All she waits for now is your safe return. I will write to her this night and tell her I have spoken to you. Can I tell her when she might see you again?' She was looking at him with a sort of eager expectancy and he did not know what to say. He muttered something about trouble in Scotland when the truce ended, of having to be ready when the Duke came back from France. To his relief she forgot Joanna and returned to the subject which seemed to occupy all their thoughts so entirely.

'You will try and ask the Duke to help us, Sir Tristram?' she pleaded.

'I did, but he believes your husband's cause was lost with the election,' Tristram replied, heartily sick of the whole business.

'John doesn't think so, and he has remarkable powers of recovery.

382

But I'm so afraid for him. All these meetings and marchings could well result in more bloodshed.'

He grimaced. 'I can't see much harm in going to church to say Mass,' he retorted.

When Tristram stood in Bow churchyard that Sunday, 7 February, and saw the massed ranks of guildsmen all dressed in their various liveries, he wasn't so sure. None of them were properly armed, but the sheer weight of numbers was impressive. It reminded Tristram of that fateful day back in the last year of the old King's reign when they'd escorted Wycliffe to St Paul's and nearly been trampled to death in the cathedral.

'All we need is some interference from the Mayor and this orderly crowd could turn very nasty,' he said to William as he flexed the fingers of his sword hand and felt the customary thrill of approaching combat.

'I hope the Mayor will have more sense than that,' replied William with a shudder.

Tristram glanced at him contemptuously. 'Well, I'm glad I didn't wear full armour. We'll be crushed to death in the city's streets if we meet a like force along the way.' William's pale face grew paler, Tristram noticed with amusement. He had not wanted to come but Tristram had been determined to see to it that he did. The man was plainly terrified of any form of violence and Tristram was looking forward to making the wily old rogue fairly crawl with fear. If there should be a scrap, he intended to make sure that the merchant was in the thick of it.

As soon as they were all assembled, John of Northampton led them out through West Chepe and up the hill towards St Paul's. In the churchyard they were met by a nervous messenger who had been sent to order them to halt in Paul's yard and wait for the Mayor. But they did not stop. They marched on and out through the Lud Gate, while the messenger vainly tried to prevent them. Three times he repeated the Mayor's orders and on the third, Northampton suddenly obeyed. They had reached Fleet Bridge. There on the banks of the stinking tributary which carried so much of the city's unsavoury waste into the sweet waters of the Thames, Northampton deployed his forces. Beyond them lay the grand, turreted manor belonging to the Bishop of Salisbury, and behind that, barely discernible in the distance, the cloistered walls of the Convent of the White Friars, their destination.

The ranks of liverymen lined up on either side of the bridge. Each guild had its own distinctive colour and the massed purples, reds, greens, blues, yellows and black told an impressive story to anyone versed in the liveries of the guilds. Tristram frowned as he gazed at Northampton's gesture of defiance. He knew nothing of the significance of all those coloured gowns, but he did know an easy target when he saw one.

'If the Mayor brings archers, they'll be done for,' he said to his squire. 'Someone ought to tell that fool Northampton.' He looked round for William, but there was no sign of him. 'Where's Master Gryffard?'

'Must have hopped it in Paul's yard, when that messenger of the Mayor's first tried to stop us,' replied Godfrey. Tristram swore fiercely, annoyed with himself for letting the merchant off so easily.

'You should have kept a better watch, Godfrey,' he accused his squire. 'I'd like to have seen him piss himself when the fun starts.' Then he went to remonstrate with Northampton over his tactics.

'There will be no fighting,' Northampton replied with what Tristram thought was the confidence of blind folly. 'We are on our way to Mass at the Carmelite church. There is nothing unlawful in that.' Tristram was about to argue, but at that moment five horsemen came cantering down the hill from Lud Gate and he realised from the way in which Northampton stiffened expectantly that it must be the Mayor. Tristram watched the riders approach in utter disbelief. Where were the archers, the men-at-arms?

The Mayor drew rein in front of Northampton and, without more ado, arrested him for breach of the King's peace. In vain Northampton protested that there was nothing wrong in going to church, that outside the city wall the Mayor had no right to arrest him but Brembre had him off his feet and across his saddle before he had finished his protest. Roger Comberton, Northampton's brother, sprang forward as if to remonstrate and he too was summarily arrested. Then the small party galloped back the way they had come, leaving the protestors leaderless and dumbfounded.

Tristram could not help being impressed. It was the boldest, bravest, simplest piece of effrontery and had he not witnessed it with his own eyes he would not have believed it possible. Richard Burgeys appeared at his side, looking decidedly crestfallen.

'Aren't you going to do something?' Tristram demanded.

'What can we do?' Burgeys replied.

'Rescue him! You are five hundred and the Mayor and his companions number five. You're not going to let him get away with it, are you?'

'By the time we catch up with him, he'll be back in his own inn, or the Guildhall. We dare not storm his house. The King would not tolerate it. The Mayor is a law unto himself in the city. We cannot give the King an excuse for taking away our privileges.'

Almost Tristram gave up and went home then. He was beginning to think that he was on the wrong side. Suddenly a thickset, bearded man dressed in a green gown thrust himself forward.

'You're right, sir knight,' he said. 'We should do something. The time for peaceful demonstration has passed.'

'Northampton would not like it,' Burgeys put in quickly. 'Has he not always said he doesn't want bloodshed?'

'What's he been stirring us up for all this time then?' demanded the other fellow fiercely. 'You can't take on someone like Brembre if you're afraid of a little blood.'

'Well spoken,' encouraged Tristram. 'You're a man after my own heart.'

'John Constantyn, married to Joanna's sister, Alice,' Richard Burgeys introduced him. 'He's a cordwainer.'

'What we need to do is to take a leaf out of Brembre's book,' said John. 'Remember that time when the Earl Marshal had that prisoner held in Northumberland's Inn? He encouraged us to attack it and we got the prisoner out. And then the Mayor was sacked by the King for failing to maintain order in the city.'

'That was poor Adam Staple, a mercer,' said Burgeys.

'It worked then, why shouldn't it work now?' John continued. 'We'll go and get Northampton out of the Mayor's house and the King'll blame the Mayor for failing to maintain law and order.'

'You'll come with us, Sir Tristram?' asked Burgeys but Tristram barely heard him. He was remembering how he and Hugh d'Aycliffe had come upon the mob outside Percy's Inn. It had been a blood-chilling sight, the whole street a mass of screaming men packed from wall to wall and advancing like a huge angry wave. He remembered lowering his lance and charging into their midst and how their leader, a huge man with black bushy hair and beard had urged them aside, how they had parted like the waters of the Red Sea must have parted before Moses. Orion had charged through them and it had taken all Tristram's great strength to force him to turn – that was all he could remember, the strain on his muscles as he yanked the charger round, and the laughter on the face of the huge black-haired man as he charged, then nothing more until he had woken on the floor of the Burgeys' warehouse.

'Sir Tristram, you'll help us, won't you?' Burgeys prompted.

'What do you want me to do?' Tristram began to feel uneasy.

'Nothing today,' John said. 'We must be sure that the whole city comes out in force. It may take several days to get enough support. Where are you staying?'

'He's with Master Gryffard,' put in Burgeys before Tristram could prevaricate.

'Good,' said John. 'I don't trust that one not to try and change sides. You can keep him from straying, make sure he comes out with us when we're ready.'

'And when will that be?' Tristram demanded.

'Soon, I promise you,' replied John. 'I'll give the signal for revolt by closing my shop in Bread Street.'

Tristram left them then, still anxiously conferring among themselves. As he walked back to Lime Street, he began to wonder whether it was entirely dignified for a knight to become embroiled in what they were planning. It was after all a matter of supreme indifference to him which side won and he had only gone along today for the fun of it, in the hope of finding a bit of action.

By the time he got back to William's house he determined to have nothing more to do with them.

He found the merchant busy getting ready to leave. 'For Calais,' William informed him, 'on urgent business.' It didn't suit Tristram to have him leave for Calais. He intended to wait here, comfortably ensconced in Gryffard's house, until the Duke's return from France, and meanwhile think of a way of getting back his promise of the Maudesbury wool.

'You're running away too soon, Master Gryffard,' he said. 'Northampton's not finished yet. If you go now you'll be on the wrong side in the end.' The merchant paused in the act of mounting his palfrey, and from under the brow of his soft, head-hugging hat, his watchful eyes were curious.

'Why?' he asked.

'Just because Northampton's in prison doesn't mean it's over,' said Tristram, delighted to be able to tell the merchant something he didn't know for once. 'It's only just beginning.'

William listened carefully to the plan for Northampton's rescue and by the time Tristram had finished, his business in Calais appeared suddenly less pressing. As the packhorses were led back to the stables, the armed servants disbanded and William turned back into the house, Tristram congratulated himself. The merchant was a coward and a rat. Out of sheer perversity Tristram decided that William should be one of the mob to storm Brembre's house when the message came.

It came four days later, on 11 February. Immediately, Tristram went in search of William and found him, as was to be expected, in his counting house.

'The shops are shut in Bread Street, West Chepe and Budge Row. Come on, it's time,' said Tristram.

William made no sign of having heard. He just went on writing carefully in his ledger.

'Are you with them, Master Gryffard?' Tristram demanded scornfully. 'Or are you throwing in your lot with Brembre and his friends?'

'You know I don't hold with violence.'

'You cannot always sit here and wait for others to do your fighting for you.' Tristram took him by the arm and pulled him to his feet. 'It's time for you to use force.' William was paler now and Tristram noted with pleasure that the quill pen he still clutched in his fingers was quivering a little.

'Let me go. You don't know your own strength,' protested the merchant with an attempt at a placatory smile.

'You're in this up to your neck and I'm going to see you're there – this time,' replied Tristram, tightening his grip and watching the beads of perspiration break out on the fellow's brow. 'You'll bless me for it when we win.'

'No, no, I can't.' It was a squeal. 'I beg you not to make me.'

Suddenly Tristram had an idea. 'Very well,' he said. 'I'll go and do your fighting for you.' The relief in the man's eyes made him want to laugh. 'If first of all you'll do something for me.' The eyes grew wary once again and it occurred to Tristram that William was not nearly as frightened as he made out. He released his arm and put two hands on the fur round the neck of the merchant's gown. 'Give me back the options on Maudesbury wool and I'll do your fighting for you.'

'I can't,' William squeaked. Tristram twisted the fur round his neck and lifted him bodily from his stool.

'Yes you can, or you can come with me now to fight for Northampton. Which is it to be?'

'I can't, I can't. I'm no good at fighting. You can bully me as much as you like but you'll never make me fight.' There was defiance in his eyes.

'If I can't make you fight, I can make sure you're there in the street storming Brembre's Inn,' Tristram retorted. 'Don't you want friend Northampton to know how much you helped him when he gets back into power? Or are you more afraid of the Mayor?'

'I can't give you back your wool options,' whispered Gryffard, half-strangled by the grip on his gown. 'I haven't got them any more. I sold them at the Hurling Time to Nicholas de Cher.'

'Liar!' shouted Tristram. 'De Cher's dead.' But his grip slackened.

'You'd like to think he was dead,' countered the merchant. 'But you knew he escaped from that castle in Gascony. What you didn't know was that he made a new life for himself as Black Nick, was befriended by John Philpot, captured the Scottish pirate and did so well out of it that he's a prosperous ship-owner now.'

'Liar!' Tristram shouted. This was the moment he had dreaded for a long time – the return of Nicholas de Cher. But with the passing of the years and no news of Nick, he had grown more confident, until he had almost forgotten de Cher.

'De Cher bought your wool off me during the Peasants' Revolt,' continued the merchant. 'It didn't seem much of an investment to me, but he paid me well for it. He seemed to have an interest in Maudesbury.'

Tristram grabbed the merchant by the throat and shook him like a dog until his teeth rattled. 'Lying cur, I'll not believe it.' William's fear was genuine enough now, Tristram could smell it and see it in his terrified eyes. With an oath of disgust he released him.

William staggered back against his stool, overturning it. 'It's no good you half killing me just because I'm the bearer of bad tidings,' he said as he picked himself up. 'It won't alter the truth and the truth is that Nicholas de Cher is alive and well and at home at Cher, making love to your wife.'

But Tristram wasn't really listening. His mind was in turmoil, bewildered by the revelation that de Cher was alive and well known to all these city merchants as Black Nick, the sea captain. It seemed impossible that the chivalrous young knight he had served as squire could have become little better than a pirate. He was vaguely conscious of William back at work on his ledgers.

'Here,' said William holding open a ledger and stabbing at an entry with an ink-stained finger. 'Read for yourself if you don't believe me. The transaction is there, inscribed these three years past at the Hurling Time.'

Tristram stared down uncomprehending at the bleached parchment covered with black loops and lines like a snail's trail. Like many others who couldn't read, he distrusted anything on paper. There was only one thing to do and that was to get down to Maudesbury immediately and find out the truth.

The streets around William's house were silent and deserted. Tristram swept through them with his squire unimpeded until he came to the wide thoroughfare of Chepe. There by the Standard a small crowd had gathered, so engrossed in something that no one paid him any heed. Forced to draw rein or mow them down, he pulled Orion to a halt, cursing loudly, and saw the block beside the Standard bright with fresh blood, and the headless body of a man lying spread-eagled on the cobblestones, still twitching involuntarily.

'Who is it?' he asked.

'It's John Constantyn, the cordwainer,' they told him. 'Beheaded by the Mayor, without right, justice or legal process.' The bold bid to rescue Northampton suddenly came back to Tristram through the turmoil of his thoughts.

'What happened to the others?' he asked. 'Did they not come out, did the city not support him?'

'The Mayor took us by surprise,' they said. 'He was waiting for us, with a great number of armed men. Richard Burgeys the mercer and John Bere the haberdasher are in prison. We're finished.'

Tristram stared at the bloody scene of the execution and frowned. Richard Burgeys was Joanna's father. What was it Gryffard had said about Joanna? Something about Nicholas de Cher making love to her. Of course it was lies. Joanna wouldn't look at another man. She was devoted to him. She loved him to distraction, he knew it. Petronilla had confirmed it. William Gryffard lied, and if he had lied about Joanna perhaps he had also lied about de Cher. But Joanna's father was in prison.

A woman came running down the street with two boys behind her. A murmur like the whisper of ripe corn in a strong breeze ran through the crowd as it made way for her. She stood looking at the thing that lay at the foot of the block and a tremor shook her from head to foot. Then she turned swiftly to intercept the two young boys who came running after her and pressed their faces against her, while someone at last had the sense to throw a cloak over all that remained of a brave husband and father.

Tristram watched Joanna's sister being led away feeling that he ought to help. But what could he do? The revolt was over before it had begun. He must get himself with all possible haste to Maudesbury to break the news to Joanna, and then confront Nicholas de Cher before he took his manor, and possibly his wife too, away from him.

CHAPTER 35

It snowed on the way to Maudesbury, so much so that Tristram was forced to spend two nights at Reading Castle waiting for the weather to ease. The Constable made Tristram welcome and passed on the news that the Scots had lost no time in celebrating the end of the truce with England. He told Tristram that Archibald Douglas, Lord of Galloway, had surprised Lochmaben Castle on 5 February and a few days later the Earl of March captured the Baron of Greystoke and carried him off to Dunbar where he had set before him a feast served from his own plate in a hall hung with his own tapestries. 'You'll be on the march again, sir knight, as soon as your Duke returns from France,' the Constable had stated with more than a little envy. 'We cannot let the loss of Annandale go unavenged.'

The news cheered Tristram. As soon as he had put things to right at Maudesbury he could be gone to Scotland, fighting the Scots with the rest of the Duke's retainers. He would be among his own kind again doing something he understood and all his confusion and uncertainties could be forgotten. The Constable, pleased to have one of John of Gaunt's retainers to keep him company, would have kept Tristram at the castle drinking and talking about knightly pursuits or riding practise bouts in the tilt-yard for as long as Tristram cared to accept his hospitality, but for once he was impatient to be gone. As soon as the snow stopped, he left, ignoring the Constable's dire prediction of more snow to come.

The riding was treacherous and slow across a white, unmarked wasteland, yet Tristram pressed on regardless of the cold and the danger. The biting east wind whipped the snow off the ground and hurled it in his face; the hungry wolves howled and tracked him and his squire at a distance. The rigours of the journey numbed Tristram's brain. He ought to have been thinking about Nicholas de Cher and what he was going to do about him; but instead he found that it was Joanna he couldn't get out of his mind.

390

How she irritated him! He had not wanted her at first, with her lovesick, slavish devotion, her meddling, merchant's ways. Then just when he had grown used to her adoration, come to expect it, become accustomed to her huge amber eyes following him in wonder, she had changed. Once she had wanted only to please him, but now she had grown cold and aloof, treating him with thinly veiled contempt and scant regard for his wishes. It mattered not that she seemed to treat all men the same – certainly poor William Gryffard fared no better. Petronilla had said Joanna was proud of him, loved him as much as ever, but William Gryffard said she was being unfaithful with Nicholas de Cher! Who was right? Which did he want to believe? He did not want Joanna, she was nothing but trouble to him. But he wished he knew how to handle her, how to master her. Somehow, no matter whether he used her for his pleasure or beat her until her white flesh was bruised and angry, he never really felt he had won. Her soft compliant body was his for the taking but he never seemed to possess her; always it seemed she eluded him. And now, if Gryffard was telling the truth, she had committed the additional sin of having allowed Nicholas de Cher to use her for his revenge. She should be punished. But how? As he drove his poor horses and his long-suffering squire on through the snow-covered plain and brooding forest, over windswept hill and through fast-flowing river that was the one question that filled Tristram's troubled mind.

He came to Maudesbury on a bright frosty morning. The snow was lying thick upon the ground, unmarked save for the patterns made by many paws crisscrossing his path. The sun, shining through the trees, dappled the virgin whiteness with blue-grey shadows and sparkled on the ghostly fingers of frosted twigs hanging from the bare branches. As the horses trotted steadily through the wood towards the village, only the creaking of steel on leather broke the muffled silence all around. The village lay quiet beneath its cold white blanket, with the open fields frozen into immobility and no sign of the villeins; all huddled inside their cottages with their livestock and their families, no doubt. A few ducks were forlornly exploring the frozen surface of the moat, but the gate to the manor house yawned wide in welcome.

The gatekeeper thrust a startled head out of the window of the gatehouse as Tristram and his squire rode over the lowered drawbridge. Dismounting in the inner court, Tristram flung his reins to Godfrey and strode swiftly into the house. The hall was empty save for the wolfhounds who pounced upon him in raucous welcome. Tristram quietened them with a buffet from his sword hilt and in the ensuing silence became aware of music. He stood in the hall and stared round him, frowning at the rusty armour decorating the old walls. Drifting down from the solar above came a soaring, joyful melody. It was an alien sound to hear at Maudesbury and for a moment Tristram could not believe the evidence of his own ears. Then with an oath he bounded up the wide stone circular stairs and burst into the solar like a charging boar.

A man was standing with one foot on the runner round the bed, holding a lute, and at his feet sat Joanna. Tristram stared at the man in reluctant recognition. He was older, thicker in build, but the blue eyes were the same. It was Nicholas de Cher all right, the man whom, Tristram had thought never to see again. The man he had once worshipped, and then betrayed, and who now had come back to steal his wife and his manor from him.

'Welcome home, Sir Tristram,' said Nick, plucking a sweet note from the lute. 'Is the Duke of Lancaster able to spare you at last?'

'Joanna, I thought I'd told you that the de Chers were not welcome here at Maudesbury.' Tristram did not look at her, he was transfixed by the unyielding steel in de Cher's eyes.

'Not to you, perhaps,' she said, 'but to me Sir Nicholas will always be welcome.' Nick's eyes blazed in triumph and Tristram turned to hurl abuse at his wife. But his anger drained away as he looked at her. She was dressed in some silky green stuff which became her well. Round her brow she wore a jewelled filet which Tristram did not remember having seen before and her hair, loose and unbraided, hung to her waist in rippling luxuriant waves of glorious colour. He stared at her in astonishment, feeling exactly as he had felt the first time he'd been unhorsed by the Duke of Lancaster – breathless, surprised, lost in admiration. He fought an uncontrollable urge to throw himself at her feet and proclaim his homage, and forced himself to confront the man who stood beside her.

'Master Gryffard tells me you bought my wool from him. Why?' he demanded.

'Poor William, so he's finally had to show his empty hand at last,' said Nick. 'I hope you didn't threaten to fight him for it.'

'I can't fight a merchant,' retorted Tristram, seizing on something he understood. 'But I can fight you.'

'I thought you said Nicholas de Cher was disgraced and, even if he lived, which you seemed to doubt, couldn't bear arms any longer,' Joanna interrupted.

'Keep out of this, Joanna, you know nothing of the matter.' Tristram turned to Nick. 'You'll fight me, won't you?'

'No,' he said, and it seemed to Tristram that he was amused. 'I don't believe in settling business arrangements at the point of a lance.'

'There's no need for any fighting,' said Joanna, rising swiftly and standing between them. 'The cloth-making can pay for the wool. You owe him nothing.'

Tristram looked down into her face, met her steady gaze, felt his breath come faster, his heart race. Jesu, but she was desirable! The white skin of her naked throat was delicate as the snowflakes falling past the window and the green silk of her gown moulded itself to her body so that he could see the inviting curve of her breast and her swelling hips encircled by a snake of plaited gold. De Cher had had her, Tristram knew from the lazy contentment in her lustrous eyes, the warm smile hovering over those inviting lips.

'I shall have to fight him if you've made me a cuckold,' he said with the bitter taste of humiliation sour in his mouth.

'And in that case I shall certainly have to defend your lady's honour,' Nick said. That shook her. Tristram could see fear drive out the contentment and it made him angry.

Joanna swung round to challenge Nick. 'I thought you didn't believe in trial by combat.'

'I don't approve of play-acting,' Nick replied, 'but I don't mind fighting for what I want.' He wasn't laughing now, he was in deadly earnest and Tristram felt the joy of battle tingling in his veins.

'And do you think that I could with honour come to you if you should kill my husband?' Joanna asked Nick softly. The joy vanished and Tristram felt humiliated anew. Where was their shame? he thought, bewildered, injured, excluded.

He thrust himself between them. 'He won't kill me. When did Nicholas de Cher last hold a lance?'

'Then you'll be a murderer,' she flashed at him. 'Do you want to drive me to a nunnery with your fine words of fighting? Whatever the outcome, no one will be the winner.'

There was silence then in the chamber. A log crashed in the fireplace, sending a shower of sparks up the chimney, and Nick casually walked over to the open hearth to attend to it. Tristram watched, baffled. He did not know what to do or say next. He could not draw his sword and set about an unarmed man in his wife's solar. He could call up his serfs and try to have de Cher thrown out, but Nick was strong as an ox and it would take some doing. He could not begin to punish Joanna until Nick was safely out of the way. So he stood, feet planted wide apart, in the middle of the room and glowered belligerently.

It was Joanna who broke the silence. She walked up to Nick, who was now standing with his back to the fire looking fierce and immovable, laid her hand on his arm and smiled up into his face.

'Enough of this talk of fighting,' she said. 'You would do well to depart and let Tristram rest. He has doubtless ridden far and is fatigued from the journey.' The words were innocent enough, but the smile was not. Tristram could not bear to see the dazzling splendour of that smile, nor its bewitching effect upon Nicholas de Cher.

'To please you, fair lady,' Nick said with obvious reluctance, 'I'll take my leave. But I shall return soon, and be assured, Sir Tristram, if you hurt one hair of her head, I'll kill you or be for ever damned.'

'You seem to have forgotten she's my wife and I'm entitled to do what I will with her.' Merciful Saviour, but he had forgotten the murderous intensity of those eyes when Nicholas de Cher was moved to anger. For a moment Tristram thought he meant to attack him there and then and his hand flew to his sword, but suddenly Nick laughed, a wild, dangerous sound which reminded Tristram of something he couldn't quite place.

'She's your wife, it's true I had quite forgot,' Nick said. Then he raised Joanna's hand to his lips, murmured something as he kissed it tenderly and without so much as a backward glance at Tristram left the chamber.

Tristram gazed at his wife, completely bewildered. What was a man to do when he found his wife had been unfaithful, except fight? They were so open about it, so unrepentant. If he had caught them in bed together it could not have been more obvious. He ought to beat her but he didn't want to. He wanted to make love to her. Joanna was standing by the window with her back to him, watching her lover ride away and Tristram felt a surge of intense desire such as he'd never known, not even for Mariota in his madness. He strode across the room and siezed great handfuls of her magnificent hair, buried his face in its perfumed sweetness.

'You must be hungry after so long a ride, would you like me to send for wine?' she said coldly, calmly, still with her back to him. He could feel the heat of her body through the cloud of hair, smell the warm spicy fragrance of her skin. He took her by the shoulders, turned her round to face him, bent to kiss her wide, tender mouth. She stood still as a graven image beneath his hands. Her lips were closed against him. He could have forced them open, could have picked her up and thrown her across the big bed in the centre of the room. But now he wanted to please her, wanted her lips to part of their own accord, to see the slavish adoration back in her magnificent amber eyes. Her body was his for the taking, her submission he could command, but what he craved was her willing participation. He looked into her face. She stared back at him unflinchingly. I am ready for anything you care to do to me, that look seemed to say. Slowly he released her. She walked away from him and sat down by her spindle. He stared at her as she began to spin, ignoring him. He felt quite helpless.

'Your father's in prison and your sister's husband is dead, killed by the Mayor,' he said abruptly, determined to pierce the armour of her disdain. He had her attention now. She stopped spinning and her head came up like a spirited horse reined in by too heavy a hand. He told her of Northampton's arrest and the abortive attempt to rescue him.

'Couldn't you have stopped them?' she exclaimed when he'd finished.

'It was a good plan and would have worked, but someone must have betrayed them.'

'Betrayed them?'

'Yes, the Mayor was waiting for them with a great number of armed men. He took them by surprise. Nipped the revolt in the bud before it had time to get going.'

'And William knew what they were going to do?' She jumped up. 'I warned Petronilla not to trust him, they should never have let him into the secret.'

He went to stand beside her, tried to take her in his arms again. 'I'll get your father out of prison for you. We'll go to London. Get the Duke to intercede for him on his return. Arraign Brembre for unlawful arrest and get Northampton released.'

'I thought you'd already tried to get the Duke's help and he wasn't interested,' she said, pushing him away.

'He'll do it for you, if you speak to him. The Duke's always willing to listen to a pretty woman, especially now Lady Swynford isn't with him any more. There is nothing a man wouldn't do for you.' He caught hold of her wrists, pulled her close. 'Joanna, be kind to me,' he whispered. He bent to kiss her lips and saw in her eyes such pity that it made his blood run cold. No one had ever pitied Tristram de Maudesbury before. It was as if she'd stripped him of his manhood. All desire quenched, he flung her from him and stormed out of the chamber.

Joanna watched him leave without remorse. She dwelt in a realm of enchantment so far beyond the real world that she was unable to feel guilt, or pain. Nick had brought her there. Into her lonely, hard existence he had brought colour, music and love. Every day had seen new joy as they explored each other's minds and bodies, laughing together, singing together, making love together. To Joanna it seemed as if she had been born again into a new world. When it rained, she exalted in the fresh clean smell of the earth; when it blew, she lay and listened to the wind howling outside, secure in her lover's arms; when it snowed, she delighted in the soft feathery flakes falling past her window; and when the sun shone upon the crisp white world as it had this morning, she felt it was a special blessing devised by nature to celebrate the miracle of their happiness together. How could she feel remorse, or guilt, or regret now that she had discovered love and found it to be all that she had ever dreamed and much more? Nothing could touch her, now that she had love.

Nick called early next day and found her waiting for him in the solar.

'Are you all right?' he asked, holding her at arm's length and searching her face carefully. 'He did you no harm?'

'No, he got blind drunk and went to sleep in the hall. Before dawn he went out with his squire and his hawk and his hounds.'

Nick looked haggard, his face harsh in the morning light, and she laid the back of her hand against his cheek, stroked it lightly.

'You need not fear for me. He'll be hunting in the forest and may not be back for days perhaps.' He captured the hand, turned it over and planted a kiss in her palm.

'I've been on the rack every minute of every hour since I left you yesterday,' he said.

'I thought you were used to affairs with other men's wives,' she said with a mischievous smile. But there was no answering laughter in his eyes.

'This isn't an affair,' he said, 'it's love, and love, as I've discovered, can be torture.'

'What do you want me to do?' she asked.

He moved away from her to the window and stood looking down into the court below. 'Merciful Jesus, if you knew how many times I asked myself that last night.'

'You mustn't fight him,' she said.

'Do you think I don't know that!'

'He might try and force a fight. Promise me you will not give him the chance to kill you.'

He came back to her, took her hands in his, held them against his chest. 'Such lack of faith, my own true heart,' he said, smiling down into her anxious eyes. 'Do you think so little of my skill? I haven't stayed alive this long without learning how to defend myself.'

'He unhorsed the King's champion, I saw him! And every day he practises at the quintain.'

'Don't worry, I'm not going to fight him. It's ironic, is it not? I thought once that if I could steal you from him I'd be avenged, but love makes fools of us all, it seems. Instead it's he who is the victor. For he has what I most prize in all the world and there is nothing I can do about it. My hands are tied because of you, and he is safe.' He was back again at the window, frowning down at the court below.

'We must be patient and bear it as best we may,' she said, knowing it was little comfort, but unable to offer anything better. 'It is our penance.' He swung round, still frowning, and she walked over to him. 'Pray God that Lancaster is back soon from France. Then Tristram will be off to Scotland again.'

'If God hearkens to all my prayers, a wild Scot may despatch him for us,' he said, the laughter back in his eyes.

'Do not say that, even in jest.' Hastily she made the sign of the cross.

'It wasn't a jest. It is our best chance. Don't you think God might grant us that one small mercy? I cannot see what useful purpose Tristram can serve by remaining upon this earth and indeed his death upon the battlefield would be just the sort of end he would like best for himself.'

'I prayed to God once, how I prayed, when I thought Tristram was my heart's desire. And God granted my request, he gave me Tristram. My knight married me! How He must laugh as He grants our requests! Do not ask God's help, I beg you, lest He mock us by giving us more than we deserve.'

'He has given me more than I deserve or ever thought existed this side of paradise.' Nick took her in his arms and kissed her. For a moment she let herself surrender, rejoicing in the wild expectancy that seized her body as she kissed him back. Then she pushed him from her.

'Tristram wants to take me to London with him, and I think I should go.'

He held her still, studying her upturned face intently. 'And you know that I will follow,' he said. 'Where does he hope to hide you in London?'

She told him then about Northampton's fall and her family's plight.

'I don't think you should go,' he said when she had finished. 'The city's a dangerous place, especially for someone like you. I don't trust you not to mount some crazy rescue attempt.'

'But I must do something.'

'Why, Joanna? Why must you do something? Northampton has brought this trouble upon himself and his unfortunate supporters. Anything you try to do to help will only make matters worse.'

'You only say that because you're a friend of Brembre. You helped him before and you'll help him again. Even though he murdered poor Alice's husband!'

'Nicholas Brembre doesn't need my help. He has been elected Mayor, he has the King's support. Northampton's a clever man, a man of great courage and one with a zealous desire to change things for the better. But like all reformers he doesn't know when to stop. The city's tired of Northampton and his reforms. Oh, he did well enough to begin with when he broke the power of the Fishmongers and brought down the price of food. That pleased the people, but then he went too far, started meddling with their morals, tried to change everything, and people don't like that. Now he won't listen to reason, won't accept defeat.'

'One cannot abandon one's friends just because they're in trouble,' she retorted. She wanted sympathy and understanding, not a lecture.

'Northampton's dangerous, Joanna. Brembre had to restore order the swiftest, cleanest way. If he had not acted as he did, far more blood would have been shed in the end.' He tried to take her in his arms again but she backed away, shaking her head.

'I must go to London, my family needs me.'

'Then I will bring them to you here,' he said. His patience made her all the more obstinate.

'And leave my father to languish in prison! Tristram is going to ask the Duke to intervene.'

'The Duke's influence isn't worth much these days,' said Nick. 'The King doesn't trust him, he's afraid of his powerful uncle and is determined to keep him out of his Council. Whatever the Duke says, the King will do the opposite. Don't meddle in things you don't understand, Joanna, you'll get hurt. Let Tristram go to Scotland with the Duke, they'll both be better employed defending our borders.'

Joanna shook her head sadly. 'Poor Tristram. He so wants to be a hero.'

'Poor Tristram indeed,' he declared, stung at last. 'Are you sure you're not still trying to make of him a hero? If he could do one good shining deed, you'd love him still, wouldn't you? You're still trying to turn him into Sir Galahad. You won't recognise the truth, can't see that beneath that handsome knightly exterior Sir Tristram de Maudesbury has a mean and cowardly soul. God damn you, Joanna, why do you have to have such a faithful heart?'

'And may God have mercy on you,' she retorted. 'Do you think I don't know what he is after all this time? Love! I thought it was bondage – shame, humiliation, God's curse upon us for our human-ity – until I knew you. Do you think I don't recognise the counterfeit coin now I've found gold? Do you think I like being bound to Tristram, even if it is through my own folly? Do you think I have not learnt to dread his return more than I dread the loneliness and the hard daily struggle and the cursed sheep bleating at each other every weary endless day?'

He crossed the chamber in two strides and gathered her into his arms. 'Forgive me, my beloved,' he said, 'I never knew what jealousy was till now. But without the serpent it would not be true paradise, I suppose. How much I find I have to learn about love.'

Her anger and pain dissolved in the warmth of his embrace as he swept her up and laid her tenderly in the middle of the large bed.

'Tristram?' she said as he began to unbuckle his sword. 'Suppose he should return?'

'Don't worry, I've left Sam on guard,' he said, planting warm ten-der kisses on her brow, her cheek, her throat. 'He's been watching the manor all night. How else do you think I knew I'd find you alone this morning?'

'Poor Sam, out all night in this weather,' she murmured as the first tremors of excitement coursed through her body.

'Sam has slept out in worse weather than this. He's an old campaigner, as am I, my queen.' He had removed her wimple and was exploring the exposed white flesh with his lips, working expertly over her throat and neck down towards the edge of her low-cut gown. 'Sam was honoured to keep vigil for me – he lost his heart to you many moons ago.' His fingers were busy among the row of tiny buttons down the front of her gown. 'Your heart is beating like a snared bird,' he added, laying his hand on her quivering breast.

'Do you blame it?' she retorted, smiling up at him in joyful anticipation. He kissed her then on the mouth and she forgot everything – her family, her husband, everything save the magic of his kisses. Eagerly she matched him but then he raised his head and began to kiss her eyes, her nose, her ears, her throat with infinite care until he reached her breast and took one erect quivering nipple between his lips. When she thought she could not bear the longing a moment longer and began to squirm with desire he suddenly claimed her mouth again and she soared with him anew, passion building upon passion until her clamouring flesh could hardly bear the wanting. Then at last he moved inside her, filled her, and she relaxed, knowing it would be soon now, that she was near fulfilment. But still he kept her with him, soaring upwards and ever upwards, until at last with a great explosion of joy they burst through together into the light, their spirits joined as one. Then she knew he was as completely hers as it was possible for one human being to be to another and nothing could ever come between them.

Later, much later, she opened her eyes and found him looking at her tenderly.

'Let me go to London for you,' he said, holding her tight. 'See what I can do to get your father out of prison.'

'Can I not come with you?' She traced the line of his strong obstinate mouth with her finger.

'No, my heart,' he said, picking up the long tendrils of her hair and winding them round his wrist. 'It would be best for you to remain here. We don't want to force Tristram into a corner. Do you think you can manage to keep him at arm's length until he goes to Scotland?'

'I ought to be able to do that at least,' she said. 'He's never wanted me much anyway.'

'He always was too much in love with himself to notice women, for which I thank God now,' said Nick, smiling at her. 'I'll return as soon as I can and I'll bring your family with me. They'd be safer here out of harm's way.'

'Oh, Nick, would you?' she said. 'Father and Matilda and Alice and the children. Then I can help Alice to come to terms with losing John and the children can have the run of the manor. It will be good for the house to have some children in it at last.'

CHAPTER 36

It was the middle of April when William Gryffard returned from Calais, whither he had prudently removed himself immediately after the execution of John Constantyn. From his network of informers, he knew that John of Northampton had been incarcerated in the isolated stronghold of Corfe Castle in Dorset, pending the King's pleasure. William also knew that the Duke of Lancaster had returned from France and had immediately been despatched by the government to invade Scotland. He hoped that Tristram would be in Scotland with his liege lord, having first killed Nicholas de Cher, leaving Joanna alone at Maudesbury in need of comfort and consolation.

Informing Tristram that his wife was being unfaithful with de Cher had been a master stroke, William believed, since it provided the knight with the perfect excuse for trial by combat, a chance to rid himself of an unfortunate skeleton in his closet and at the same time redeem his honour. Coward that he was, William had an exaggerated regard for brute force and although he had a poor opinion of Tristram's mind, he had no doubts about his physical ability – he had seen it exercised to deadly effect against the King's champion in the lists. To William, Tristram was nothing more or less than a tool, a dangerous weapon to be used against men like Nicholas de Cher, whom William found too astute for his lasting comfort.

As he rode across London Bridge, William looked up at the heads impaled above him on the Drawbridge Gate. The skulls were picked clean, bare and anonymous as all old bones. It was impossible any longer to know which, if any, had once been John Constantyn's. Time, and the scavenging birds, had erased all distinguishing features of flesh and blood, and time, William trusted, would also have blurred his own part in the recent turmoil.

Slowly he rode across the crowded bridge, pushing through the welter of stalls and carts and stout matrons pursuing the necessities of life, reassured by the normal noise and bustle of it all. Once clear of the bridge, he made his way towards Cornhill, pleased to be assailed on all sides by persistent apprentices crying their masters' wares, to be cursed on occasion by water carriers for obstructing their way, to make room for busy citizens all battling each other towards one common end – trade. There was nothing, to his watchful eye, that betokened anything other than a prosperous capital city; and it certainly seemed as if London had settled down again to business as normal.

Reaching his splendid mansion, with the sound of the bells all over the city ringing the Angelus and bringing another day to its close, William bowed his head and gave thanks in his heart to God for a dangerous journey accomplished in safety. He spent the evening and much of the night with his clerk and his letters, and found nothing to give any cause for alarm, no news to disquiet him unduly. When all was done he sat back in his counting house and considered his position.

In betraying John Constantyn's plan to Mayor Brembre, William had made, for him, an unpleasant choice. He had probably lost the chance of ever siding with the merchant guilds again. His days of sitting on the fence were over. He was henceforth irreconcilably committed to the victuallers. And yet, if he could save Richard Burgeys from the unpleasant consequences of his own action, he might still be able one day to make the mercer Mayor – when Brembre's unpopularity brought him down, and Northampton was no more. It would take patience and much skill, but William was used to waiting. It was a pleasant thought, one worth considering further, but first of all he would have to engineer Burgeys' release. It was now time to test whether his prudent absence from the city had lasted long enough and whether the singular service he had been able to render before his departure was sufficient to secure the Mayor's favour. The season of the woolclip was approaching and he could not afford to delay setting out for the Cotswolds. If he were successful, he could go to Maudesbury with Joanna's father. Here at last was something he could do for Joanna, something which would ensure his welcome when he reached her. With such a thought to sweeten his dreams, William retired to bed, well pleased with himself.

He rose with the dawn and went first of all to Mass at St Peter Upon Cornhill, there to light a candle to St Christopher for safely bringing him home across the treacherous English Channel and afterwards to mingle with corn merchants, some mercers, a few drapers, one or two knights, many acquaintances, his debtors and his creditors, greeting all alike with a smile and a deprecatory bow. It took time, but William always had time to listen to others; patience and a ready ear brought him many useful titbits of information.

From a knight who lived in a large house called the Wey on the north side of Cornhill he learnt that the Duke of Lancaster had done little in Scotland, apart from burning a few villages, and had suffered more from the adverse spring than on the battlefield. After repairing the truce, the Duke was probably back in Salisbury where Parliament was called for the end of April. From John More, a mercer and erstwhile friend of Northampton, he learnt that Sir John Philpot lay dying. In the church that morning it was the most important topic of conversation. They were all afraid that, with the passing of the Sailor King, the voice of moderation would be silenced in the Mayor's chamber and the city fall a prey to untold trouble at the hands of the extremists.

Returning home to break his fast, William pondered his next move. He was a man who always preferred the more devious approach and so, instead of visiting the Mayor, he decided to call at Philpot's Inn and proffer sympathy to Dame Margaret. He had purchased in the market in Paris a fan of peacock feathers set in a clasp of fine French enamel, as well as a silken veil from Venice, and he thought that they were just the sort of gifts that might cheer a woman such as Lady Philpot, as he must now remember to call her, when her husband lay dying.

The great hall of Philpot's Inn was as crowded as on an election day, the blues, greens, vermilions, blacks, yellows and purples of their coloured gowns mingling with, here and there, the bright splash of aldermanic scarlet. There were fishmongers, grocers, vintners, not a few aldermen; William knew most of them and those he didn't know he could identify by the colour of their gowns. They were Victuallers to a man and his mouth went dry, even as he congratulated himself on having come to the right place to try out his popularity. Cautiously he greeted the men he knew, ever ready with his ingratiating smile and his sympathetic ear, and was relieved to find them pleased to see him, anxious to learn the latest news from across the Channel, some even prepared to voice their fear for the future of the city with poor Philpot gone.

He was beginning to feel almost at home in their company when a ripple ran through the crowded hall and he saw the door to the sick man's chamber open. Margaret Philpot came out, dressed in dark velvet which swept in elegant folds to the ground; a wimple of fine lawn swathed her head and throat, her only jewel a gem-encrusted crucifix hanging on her breast. She seemed perfectly composed, and William drew back into the shadows to watch as she moved from group to group with a nod and a smile, accepting their sympathy with graceful calm. She saw him and approached.

'I expected you before,' she said, 'if only to visit our prisoner. Wasn't Richard Burgeys your friend and partner for a time?'

So direct an approach took him aback but he explained his absence in Calais, produced his gifts, sought refuge in flattery. She seemed pleased with the gifts. She was still an attractive woman, a little past her best perhaps, in need of a little more praise, some extra cajoling.

William well knew how to tell a woman what she wanted to hear. She accepted his compliments as she had accepted his gifts, with alacrity, then returned to the attack with unexpected suddenness.

'Do you mean you did not know Burgeys was a prisoner?' she asked him. 'I thought you knew everything, Master Gryffard.'

'I came as soon as I could, to put in a good word for Burgeys and ask your husband to release him into my care, but I would not wish to plague a sick man.' He did not like being forced onto the defensive, to have to improvise.

'You're too late,' she said. 'Richard Burgeys is no longer a prisoner. He's been released on the understanding that he would leave the city forthwith. He's been gone a se'enight, to stay with his daughter – the one who married that knight.'

The news took William by surprise.

'Dear me, did you hope to buy the daughter's favour by helping the father? I wonder, is it Lady Maudesbury or the manor that you want, Master Gryffard?' Margaret's bright eyes were fixed on him inquisitively. He stared at her, hardly noticing the taunt. Who had secured Burgeys' release and why had he not been told?

'It was Nicholas de Cher who got him out,' she informed him, reading his mind. 'My brother-in-law and my husband seem to think they have to grant Black Nick any favour he cares to ask.'

William was dismayed. De Cher ought to have been dead by now. He kept his shock hidden beneath a mask of polite solicitude as he enquired after the health of her husband.

'He's dying,' she said. 'The priest is with him now. You think I should be more sad? Well, I am sad. He has been a good husband to me, but he wasn't my first and he won't be my last. A woman cannot let her heart rule her head when it comes to thinking of her future.'

'No indeed,' muttered William.

'That's what that little fool Joanna would do. Isn't it?' she demanded suddenly. 'The silly chit dotes on that husband of hers. And you men love her for it, isn't that so? All except Sir Tristram of course. He doesn't love her, or he would not leave her alone so much.'

'He has his knight service to perform for the Duke of Lancaster,' William replied absently, wondering what she wanted. Did she not know that Joanna and Nick were lovers? Was she seeking his confirmation or his denial? It was certainly an odd conversation to be having with a woman when her husband was on his death bed.

'You'd like to be a knight, wouldn't you, Master Gryffard?' she continued. 'Only you weren't lucky enough to be with the King at Clerkenwell on that great day of glory when Wat Tyler was stabbed and the peasants conquered. You should have been there, you might have been knighted with all the others. Now you'll just have to find some service you can render. Lend the King money perhaps – he's always short of it, so they say.'

'I'm afraid I must leave that to your brother-in-law, the Mayor,' William said. 'But perhaps I can be of service to you.'

'To me? You don't think Sir John means to die and leave me penniless, surely?'

'No, but you said yourself you'll have to think of marriage again.'

'Are you proposing to me before my husband is in his grave, Master Gryffard? A pox on you.' But she wasn't angry.

'Alas, I know you would never look at a mere merchant of the staple like myself when Sir Nicholas de Cher is looking for a wife.'

'Sir Nicholas is betrothed to Agnes Proudfoot,' she said a little too quickly.

'And has been for very many summers,' William agreed, and waited to see whether she would confide in him. She looked away and he thought that perhaps he had pushed her too far, been too direct. She was gazing round the room restlessly as if looking for someone else to talk to.

'Have you ever imagined yourself in love, Master Gryffard?' she asked him suddenly.

'Every time I look at you,' he replied with his deprecatory bow. But for once she ignored the compliment.

'Nick believes he's in love with Lady Maudesbury. The fool! It's only because she's so faithful to that knight of hers.'

'How do you know she's faithful?'

'She is, isn't she? Joanna would never betray that handsome husband of hers.' She looked at him almost angrily, while he wondered how she could be of use to him.

'Every woman has her price,' he said, making up his mind.

'Not Joanna, surely?'

'Even Joanna,' he replied with a conspiratorial wink. 'I know.'

Suddenly she laughed gaily. 'You're a man of many surprises, Master Gryffard! Wait till I tell Nick.'

'He knows,' William said. He watched with secret amusement the good humour of a moment replaced by anger again, and thought with detached interest how some women looked so much better when they were angry than others. Joanna always looked more desirable, whereas Margaret Philpot looked like a shrew.

'An adulteress!' exclaimed Margaret savagely. 'We have laws for adultery in London now, thanks to that meddling old fool Northampton. What a pity she never leaves that manor of hers. I'd like to have seen Joanna being paraded about the city in sight of all with her head shaven and the trumpets and pipes sounding her shame. That would teach Northampton to go poking his nose into what doesn't concern him – catching one of his own dear friends with his new adultery law.'

'And have Sir Nicholas galloping to her rescue? That would not serve our purpose in the least.'

'What then?'

'We must be patient. Wait for him to tire, as tire of her he must. Then we shall see.'

'He doesn't show much sign of tiring of her.'

'There are many ways to tarnish the bright image of love, especially between two such impetuous beings as Nicholas de Cher and Lady Maudesbury,' William told her. 'An opportunity will present itself if we are watchful. I have to go into the Cotswolds for the woolclip and I shall visit Maudesbury and see what I can discover. You do what you can and keep me informed. Write to my house, here in the city. My clerk will know where to find me.'

'What do you want to know?' she asked him, puzzled.

'Anything and everything,' he replied. 'It should not be too difficult to drive them apart.'

William left Philpot's Inn pleased that he had acquired a useful ally, but anxious too, having learnt that morning more to confound than comfort him. He did not like to be taken unawares and he wondered why he had not heard from Maudesbury. The weaver who worked the broadloom had always been a reliable informant in the past. Prior knowledge of events, that was how William worked. By using his superior knowledge to twist whatever fate flung in his path, he had contrived to turn many a potential disaster to his own advantage. It meant constant vigilance and a great deal of fast travelling. He ought to be setting out for the Cotswolds to get ahead of the Italians, or for Salisbury to find out what Parliament was up to; most of all he longed to be at Maudesbury to see Joanna again and to find out the true state of affairs. But he could not leave London until after Sir John Philpot's funeral. It would be one of the most important occasions in the city that year and he could not afford to miss it.

Joanna found that bringing her family to live with her at Maudesbury was not as satisfactory as she had imagined. She tried so hard to make them all feel at home, but none of them were really happy. Her father had begun well by getting rid of the drunken bailiff for her, but it soon transpired that he had little idea of how to run a manor. He did not understand the manorial courts, had no patience with the reeve, treated the serfs as if they were apprentices, instructing them in quite unnecessary skills, and was always inspecting the broadloom, wasting hours of the weaver's precious time with searching questions. And his absence from the Mercery made him fretful. Matilda complained and interfered and criticised all day long, while Alice, dear hard-working, practical Alice roamed about the manor house like a lost soul. She was used to having to do everything herself and did not know how to order the serfs to do her bidding. Once Joanna even found her sister in the kitchens looking longingly at the scullions as they toiled over the huge open fire.

It made Joanna sad. She had thought that Alice, once she got away from London, would begin to forget the horror of her husband's execution and be able to enjoy the new and better life for her children running free at Maudesbury. But she pined for London. The space and the silence all around terrified her. Instead of rejoicing in the children's freedom she became over-protective towards them. She lived in constant fear that they might be trampled to death in the stables, or drowned in the moat's mysterious depths, or break their necks tumbling down the long, winding stone staircases, or be savaged by the boisterous wolfhounds haunting the hall. Joanna had no idea that a manor could contain so many hidden perils and she felt personally responsible for every one. Once she had been proud of all that she had achieved and wanted to share it with her family. But they were clearly ill at ease in their new surroundings and it made Joanna feel inadequate. And she missed Nick. At first he had visited them at Maudesbury frequently but it was impossible for them to be alone for more than the briefest moment – enough for a snatched kiss but not long enough to satisfy the craving it aroused. The need for concealment began to prey on her nerves and on his too, she knew. She was not surprised when he announced that he had to go to Bristol where a ship of his was expected soon. That was two weeks ago, longer than it took to ride to Bristol and back.

Nick had still not returned when William arrived at the beginning of May. To Joanna's surprise and dismay, her father welcomed him with undisguised delight. As soon as she could get her father on his own, she tried to persuade him to turn William out, but he would not hear of it.

'I'm disappointed in you, Joanna,' he said. 'I thought that you knew the rules of hospitality better than to turn away a traveller from your door, especially one who has been such a friend to your family as William.'

'But Father, he betrayed you all,' she protested, unable to believe that he could be so blind. 'He's responsible for your arrest, for poor John's death. I don't know what he wants now but you must have nothing more to do with him.'

'What nonsense is this? If anybody betrayed us it was Northampton with all his talk of new elections. We made a mistake, William and I, in staying loyal to him for so long, and it has cost me dear. But William has been clever. The truth is, he has always been just that bit cleverer than I and now he's back in favour with Brembre and his friends. But I've not yet given up hope of being Mayor one day. If I am to do it, it will only be through William Gryffard's help. We can't afford to offend him now, you must see that. Maybe he does show you a little too much attention, and with Tristram away it makes it awkward, but I'll not leave you alone, you can trust your old father to look after his daughter when her husband's away. Just treat him kindly – for my sake.'

'Father, listen to me. William Gryffard saved his own skin by betraying you all to Brembre. It was obvious from what Tristram told me.'

'What does Tristram know about it? He never showed the slightest interest in the city's problems.' She was about to interrupt him to explain but he held up his hand angrily. 'Now say no more. I don't want to talk about it. You stick to looking after your manor and don't go trying to interfere in what is man's work. You know nothing about it. Just because you're a knight's lady doesn't mean you can forget the respect you owe your father.'

At dinner, William entertained them with the details of Sir John Philpot's funeral, quite one of the best and most well attended the city had seen for some time; not since Sir John Stodeye was laid to rest back in King Edward's reign had there been such a funeral. 'And the widow,' he added, his eyes fixed intently on Joanna's face, 'looked magnificent in her black, as you would expect a Stodeye daughter to look.'

'Poor Margaret, what will she do without Sir John?' said Joanna, selecting a piece of stewed carp from the dish in front of her and popping it into her mouth.

'Why, marry again, with all possible speed,' he replied. 'Sir Nicholas de Cher seemed very attentive throughout the funeral feast.'

Nick was in London, with Margaret Philpot? The carp felt like sheep's wool in Joanna's mouth and she seemed unable to swallow it. She took a sip of wine, gulped the fish down in one eye-watering lump, and almost gagged. William fussed over her, blaming the fish, but she knew from the gleam in those shrewd eyes that he was well aware what had made her choke. How long did he mean to stay this time? she wondered, angry with her father for his short-sighted dependence on this evil man, with Nick for deserting her, and with William most of all for his unpleasant tenacity. Would she ever be free of him?

William left the next morning, taking Richard Burgeys with him. Joanna was so relieved, she did nothing to prevent her father going. He wouldn't have listened anyway; he was very anxious to get back to the Mercery, and William had convinced him he would be quite safe now in London.

'You'll take care, won't you, Father?' she said as she stood on the village green to wish them Godspeed.

'I'll be fine with William, never fear,' he replied, looking happier than he had in weeks. 'There's a party of woolmen bound for Northleach. William thinks we ought to catch up with them in Cirencester, if we hurry. Look after your mother and get on with that cloth-making of yours. You ought to take it to Winchcomb for St Kenelm's Fair in July. I'll come back in good time to sell it for you.' She thanked him and knelt for his blessing.

William was waiting at her side. She turned and stretched out her hand to him as far as possible to keep him at arm's length, but he bent forward and kissed her familiarly on the cheek. It was done quickly, before she could protest, but it made her feel all the more anxious. He had taken the liberty as if to show her that her father was in his power and there was nothing she could do about it.

Nick came a few days later. Joanna was in the tilt-yard with her nephews Harry and Roger, who were taking it in turns to ride her palfrey at the quintain. They had provided themselves with a stout ash-plant to act as a lance but it was not very straight and they were not having much success in hitting the post.

'You should have a proper lance for that sort of work,' Nick said as he rode into the yard.

Joanna watched him take the stick from Roger while relief and resentment battled for supremacy. He rides in here as if it were only yesterday that he went away, she thought, but told herself she would not quarrel with him. She had no right to question his comings and goings. If he were growing tired of her, nothing would make him more disenchanted than a clinging mistress.

'Don't hold it out in front of you like a spear,' Nick tucked the makeshift lance firmly into his side, 'you couch it like this.' Then he kicked his tired gelding into a trot and attacked the quintain. The stake hit the post with a dull thud, the sandbag swivelled round with alarming speed and caught him a buffet on the back of his head. He swayed alarmingly, but was saved from falling by the high-fronted saddle. The boys whooped with unsympathetic laughter and clamoured at him to try again, but Nick waved them away, rubbing his head ruefully. 'Later,' he promised them. 'My horse has done enough for one day and besides I want to talk to your aunt. Take my horse round to the stables and see he's well rubbed down.'

'I'm not sure that's wise,' said Joanna. 'Alice hates them going to the stables. She's afraid they might get trampled.'

'Sam can go with them,' he replied, dismounting. 'He'll see they come to no harm. Those boys should be learning to fight with proper weapons. When I was their age I knew how to couch a lance and use a two-edged sword.'

'It's plain you've forgotten in the meantime,' she retorted.

'I'm out of practice,' he said, grinning at her. 'Do you want me to find some knight who's in need of a squire?'

'I don't think Alice wants them to learn how to fight,' she said.

'Apprentice them to a good master craftsman then. They're too old to be dancing attendance on a household of women.' He was right, Joanna knew, but the future was too fraught with difficult choices. Only by living day by day could she manage to keep all the anxiety at bay. She longed to throw herself into his arms, feel the reassurance of his caresses, but although they were alone in the empty tilt-yard, they were not safe from prying eyes. He was studying her thoughtfully and she wished he had not caught her in her oldest kirtle with her head and neck swathed in a formidable linen wimple.

'You look down, my heart,' he said. 'What's the matter?'

'William was here,' she said. 'He came for the night and when he left he took father with him.'

Nick swore softly. 'You should never have let him leave, especially with William. I thought you knew better than that.'

'What could I do? I can't keep my father tied down at Maudesbury for the rest of his life. He's a mercer, not a knight. He's not happy unless he's buying and selling things. He hated having to leave his shop in the Mercery and William says he had the Mayor's promise not to punish Northampton's old friends as long as they behave themselves. Father thinks William will protect him. He wants to get back to what he knows best.'

'Sweet Jesu, Joanna, until Northampton is brought to trial, none of his friends are safe.'

'What harm can Northampton do shut up in Corfe Castle?'

'Unfortunately things have become more complicated thanks to that fool Northampton trying to involve the Duke of Lancaster in his cause. The Duke's become implicated in a plot on the King's life.'

'Sweet Mary have mercy,' she whispered. 'When?'

'It was at Salisbury, during a session of Parliament. Suddenly a Carmelite friar came forward with some story of a conspiracy against the King's life organised and controlled by the Duke of Lancaster. Of course the Duke denies it and offers to prove his innocence by wager of battle. Wiser counsels prevailed, but before the friar could be properly interrogated he was tortured and put to death by the King's half-brothers without revealing anything.'

'Then the Duke is innocent?' she asked, puzzled.

'Innocent or guilty, it doesn't much matter. What matters is that the King fears his uncle and his fear makes him suspicious. He dare not move against the Duke himself, he's too powerful, but he's looking for a scapegoat, and who better than John of Northampton? All this time Northampton has claimed the Duke's protection. It looks bad for him.'

'But not for my father, surely? He has done nothing wrong.'

'Your father has many enemies in London. He wants to be Mayor one day and who knows, if Northampton is executed, the dissatisfied crafts might rally behind your father. He's a mercer, not a victualler. Nicholas Brembre is ruthless when it comes to holding on to power and the trouble with your father is he has no sense of self-preservation. I don't trust him not to do something silly and land himself back in prison again. If that happens, there'll be nothing I can do to save him this time.'

'What did you have to do last time?' she asked before she could stop herself. 'Pleasure Mistress Philpot?'

'St Michael bring me patience,' he swore. 'Joanna, why do you persist in thinking I'm interested in any woman but you? We've gone beyond that. Surely we can trust each other?'

'You were at Philpot's funeral, weren't you?'

'He was my friend, I owed him a great deal. Of course I went to his funeral.'

'And his widow – she was your friend, was she not? How does she bear her loss?' Once started, Joanna couldn't stop herself.

'With fortitude,' he said with a grin. 'Joanna, you look magnificent when you are angry.' He took a step towards her.

She caught her breath, unable to stay angry with him when he looked at her in such a way. Then Alice thrust her head out of the window in the turret above. 'Joanna,' she called. 'Where are the boys? I thought they were with you.'

Joanna looked at Nick helplessly. 'I'll have to go to the stables and bring them back. Alice will not rest if she knows they're there.' He took hold of her wrist, stayed her.

'I saw Tristram in Salibury,' he said. 'He'll be on his way home as soon as Parliament is over.' He paused. 'It's better that I go to London,' he said.

Her heart sank. He was going back to Margaret Philpot. She knew it.

'Don't go,' she said.

'Don't you want me to look out for your father? Persuade him to come back to you here?'

'Father promised to come back for the St Kenelm's Fair – he's going to help me sell my cloth.'

'That's not until July, I doubt if it's safe for him to stay until then.'

'You want an excuse to leave me, to go back and court Lady Philpot. That's it isn't it?'

Nick's expression darkened once more. 'And you're determined to think the worst of me. What do you want me to do, lie in wait for your husband and challenge him on his return?'

'No,' she said. 'Not that – never that. You must not kill Tristram for my sake.'

'For mine then, he's my enemy too, remember.' She stood and looked at him helplessly, caught in a web of her own sinfulness so fast she seemed to be beyond mercy. He was scowling at her fiercely and she longed to say something to make him take her in his arms, kiss away her fear. But she could think of nothing to say.

'If William's been here I'd better go and have a word with that weaver of yours,' Nick said abruptly. 'Find out if he's been passing on any more secrets.'

'Don't frighten him too much,' was all she said. 'He's the only man can work the broadloom and we're behind with the weaving as it is.'

Tristram came home at Pentecost. Sitting by his side that first night at supper, sharing his cup and eating what he chose to put upon her trencher bread, Joanna felt completely trapped. Her whole being cried out with the need to remain faithful to Nick as with every glance and possessive gesture Tristram made it plain that in all the long weeks away he had lost none of his newfound hunger for her. When she left the hall, his eyes followed her and she knew it would not be long before he came to her chamber, and when he did it would be her duty to let him make love to her. She knew that she deserved nothing less, that loving Nick the way she did meant that every day she was in a state of mortal sin. She could not go to Father Luke to confess and receive forgiveness, since she did not repent, would die if she had to give Nick up. And could not pray for deliverance from Tristram; she did not expect God to forgive her. When Tristram arrived in her chamber, she steeled herself to submit obediently to his lovemaking. It was her penance, her punishment for all the hours of pleasure with Nick. She was prepared, but it was not easy. She had forgotten just how rough Tristram could be. After it was over, he did not go to sleep as he usually did.

'Happy, Joanna?' he asked, clutching her in the darkness. She mumbled something which she hoped sounded like appreciation as she lay rigid in his arms and fought the desire to curl up in a ball as far away from him as possible. She could accept his use of her to satisfy his lust, she could close her mind and detach it from her bruised and aching body, but she could not pretend to love him. Sweet Jesus, she prayed in the darkness, do not ask that of me.

But to Joanna's increasing dismay it seemed as if Tristram would be content with nothing less. As slowly spring turned into summer, Tristram seemed to spend every hour of every day in a vain attempt to win her love. Instead of cursing Joanna for having installed her family in his manor, he surprised her by winning them to his side. Harry

411

and Roger soon began to follow him around like shadows and he took them hawking and hunting, brushing aside Alice's protestations with an arrogant surprise, which to Joanna's chagrin appeared to reassure the anxious mother far better than all her painstaking care. Soon the two boys were like extra squires, waiting on Tristram on bended knees, polishing his armour, spending hours with him in the tilt-yard learning how to hit the quintain without being knocked off the long-suffering palfrey. Matilda too deferred to him in everything and Alice was so overawed by his presence that she came to believe that while her boys were with Tristram no harm could befall them.

Joanna felt she was no longer mistress in her own household, but that was not as bad as having her husband courting her like a lovesick swain. Day by day he embarrassed her with his clumsy attempts to please. The nights were torture for them both. Tristram had no idea how to pleasure a woman. He only knew how to take by storm. There was nothing she could do any longer to disguise his failure to arouse her passion and it drove him to lengthy drinking sessions with his squire in the hall and fiercer and fiercer lovemaking. All the time Joanna missed Nick desperately, knowing that he could not come to her with Tristram at home. It made Tristram's pathetic gestures of good will all the more frustrating. She waited, with what patience she could, for him to get bored and take himself off on a long hunting expedition but he never went far from home.

About a week after Tristram's return Alice took her aside and upbraided her.

'I can't understand you, Joanna. I used to think you had the best head of all the family. Here you are, married to the finest, the hand-somest knight anyone could wish for, and yet you seem determined to throw away a good man's love for the sake of a rake like that jumped-up sea captain.'

'He's not "jumped up" – Nicholas de Cher is better born than Tristram,' Joanna replied hotly.

'And head over heels in love with you, I suppose you believe.'

'No, I don't,' Joanna lied. 'Sir Nicholas loves all women. He can't resist making them feel good. It's his way. But you don't understand, Alice. It's fashionable. Every lady at court has her own true knight – he doesn't have to be her husband.'

'Black Nick's a practised seducer, Joanna. I can see that,' Alice declared. 'He's been paying court to ladies all his life, I shouldn't won-der. Whereas, poor Tristram has never been in love before. He doesn't know how to treat women. All his life he's spent in the company of men.'

'Tristram was in love with Mariota, once,' Joanna replied, stung into defending herself with the unpalatable truth. 'I loved him then, Alice, so much that I stole him from Mariota.'

'I doubt if you could steal anything from Mariota if she'd truly wanted it,' said Alice to Joanna's great surprise. 'She was as ruthless as Matilda in getting her own way. She could have done what you're doing now and there would have been no harm in it. But you're not cut out for these court games, Joanna, no matter how much you act the lady. You're looking for true love, I know that even if you don't, and Black Nick isn't the kind of man to love for ever someone he can never have. He takes love where he finds it.'

'I sometimes think that love is God's way to make fools of us,' said Joanna. 'I loved Tristram so much, I lay down and crawled beneath his feet and he walked all over me. Tristram only loves me now because I'm cold. Being treated like a dog seems to stimulate him. I don't know what it is that Tristram wants, but it isn't love.'

Much though she would have liked to ignore it, Joanna could not get Alice's unwelcome advice out of her head, perhaps because it embodied her own fears; nor could she ignore the fact that this time Tristram's homecoming had brought zest to the manor. The men Tristram brought back with him were a much needed addition to the labour force and the game he killed out hunting restocked the larder. The adverse spring gave way to a hot dry spell so that by mid-summer the haymaking was all but done, the corn ripening in the fields, and tentering cloth stretched out in every spare corner of the village. With so much going well, Joanna felt all the more isolated in her misery. Once it was all she would have ever asked – a prosperous manor and Tristram her slave. But love had spoilt it, and capricious fate mocked her with its cornucopia come too late.

Then one day she received a letter from William Gryffard and knew that she should have been thankful for what she had. William informed her that on 15 June, Roger Comberton, John of Northampton's brother, and her father had been arrested by the King's decree and sent to Corfe Castle to join Northampton. William blamed himself for having left London when he did and promised to make all possible speed there to see what could be done. 'Sir Nicholas Brembre has much influence with the King. He might be able to do something to help your father,' William wrote in his neat spidery handwriting. 'Believe me, I shall do everything in my power to save him.'

The letter had been sent from Calais where William had heard the news. As Joanna read it, a still, small voice suggested to her that if William in Calais knew of her father's trouble, so must Nick, wherever he might be, but he had found no way of telling her. At first Joanna felt too distressed by the catastrophe to be able to think of what to do. Tristram had gone hunting at break of day and in the meantime the news so devastated Matilda it took most of the afternoon just to calm her down enough to make her drink a soothing posset and get her to bed. By the time she finally dropped into an uneasy sleep, Tristram was back.

'We must rescue them,' he declared as soon as he heard the news.

'Rescue them from Corfe Castle? It's impossible,' said Joanna.

'I could probably bribe the garrison, or the Mayor of Corfe, or else lie in wait for them on the way. The trial won't be at Corfe, they'll have to be moved. It'd probably be better to ambush them on the move.'

'If you did succeed in rescuing them, what then?' Alice asked. 'You can't bring them back here – or London. Where would you hide them?'

'I'd take them to France, seek the Duke's protection. They'd be safe in France until the Duke is able to help.'

'Exile?' said Alice. 'Poor father.'

'Better than execution,' he replied. 'They're dead men if we don't try something before they come to trial. The King was very frightened by the plot on his life. He needs to execute someone before he can feel safe again.'

Joanna sat and listened to them arguing. It was madness, she knew that. She ought to stop him from going on such a crazy adventure.

Tristram was standing in the middle of the hall, still encased in chain mail, his handsome face eager with the prospect of action, his eyes fixed on her beseechingly, the very picture of a true knight waiting for her to send him on his quest. Joanna burst into tears.

'Don't weep, Joanna. I'll rescue your father, never fear. Does William say when the trial is to be?'

She wiped her eyes, read the letter again. 'William doesn't know. He's on his way to London to find out what he can.'

'We can't trust that cowardly rascal,' Tristram declared. 'I'd best go to London, see what he's up to. You'd better come too, Joanna. We've got to find out when the trial is to be.'

Joanna stared at him in dismay. She did not want to go to London. She wanted to stay at the manor and wait for Nick. Nick would know what to do. But Nick wasn't here and Tristram was, longing to fight, to perform some great heroic deed to prove his love. And someone had to help her father.

'Joanna can't go to London, it wouldn't be safe.' Alice objected. 'Where would you stay?'

'With Petronilla Northampton,' said Joanna. 'She'll know when the trial is to be.'

'Don't go, Joanna. You're playing into their hands,' Alice begged. 'What will become of us here if you go?'

'She'll be quite safe with me,' said Tristram. 'As for the manor, it can take care of itself – it always has. Joanna wants to come, don't you, Joanna? I'll look after you.'

414

I ought to love him, thought Joanna, overwhelmed with guilt. Alice was right. He was her husband, after all, and he was trying hard to win her. Perhaps if he could perform one shining deed of chivalry she could love him still. At least he ought to have the chance.

'I'll come,' she said.

But next day as she stood beside her palfrey in the pale morning dawn, her heart was full of foreboding and she had a fearful premonition that she would never return. Alice stood in the outer court surrounded by her children, a forlorn little group, standing apart from the stamping horses and busy men-at-arms. Tristram, dressed in full armour was already mounted, impatient to be gone.

Joanna looked up at the turreted walls of the manor. Home or prison? She had poured such effort into it, suffered so many humiliations, yet spent some of the happiest days of her life here, that now she did not really know whether she was glad to be escaping or sorry to have to leave its sanctuary. All she knew was that she must give Tristram his chance. It was as if she was in the grip of destiny, swept along helplessly, like the serfs who had abandoned their homes and plots of land to march to London in search of their freedom. Her love for Nick had made her weak and she could no longer fight for what she wanted, because she didn't know what she wanted any longer. She clutched Alice to her tightly.

'If Nick should come, tell him where I've gone,' she whispered. 'Promise me, Alice,' It was all she could do.

With tears in her eyes, Alice promised.

Chapter 37

They arrived in London at the end of July and went straight to Northampton's Inn. There they found everyone as busy as usual, as if the estate was not about to be forfeited and all Northampton's goods confiscated. Petronilla welcomed them warmly. 'My dear, I am so sorry for all that your family has suffered in supporting us. I wish such trust and loyalty could have been better rewarded.'

'You've suffered, too,' said Joanna.

'One's own sufferings one can bear, with God's help,' Petronilla replied. 'It is the knowledge that we have brought down with us those whom we most love and wish to be happy which I find so very hard to bear. But what brings you to the city? Oh, do not tell me that the Duke of Lancaster is back from France! Might he yet do something to save them all?'

Swiftly Tristram disillusioned her and explained his plan for Northampton's rescue. At first Petronilla was afraid.

'No more bloodshed, I beseech you,' she cried wringing her hands. 'I cannot have another death upon my conscience.'

'There may be three more if we let them stand trial,' Tristram pointed out with brutal frankness. She grew pale, but refused to despair.

'John will fight well – at his trial,' she said. 'He will not let them convict him easily. He has done nothing deserving of death. A period of imprisonment perhaps, but not execution. No, I do not believe it.'

'I too am a fighter,' retorted Tristram, 'and I mean to put it to good use.' Full of enthusiasm, he set about persuading her, and Joanna listened impressed. Confident, strong, untroubled by doubt, he was a different man from the one who tortured her with his clumsy attempts to please. Fighting was what Tristram understood – it was the only thing he truly did understand. How wonderful to be a man, she thought, to ride out into the forest, lance couched, and slay one's enemies, to know that might was right and the solution to every obsta-

416

cle in one's way a swift cut of the sword. Perhaps for once Tristram's approach was the right one. She prayed it was – for all their sakes.

'Do you know when the trial is to be?' she asked Petronilla.

'I had a letter from John – they allow him to write to me, but I think his letters are written by a scrivener, for it is not his hand and he says very little. Just that they have been summoned before the King's Council at Reading on the Wednesday after the Feast of the Assumption to answer for themselves. He wrote not long after your father's arrest.'

'Poor Father, if only I had been able to keep him with me at Maudesbury. But he would not stay, Petronilla, he only wanted to get back to London. He wasn't happy in the country. He was never one to hide away out of danger and now look what's happened to him.'

'Your father bears his fate with fortitude, John says,' replied Petronilla. 'He says that he's a great source of strength to them both.'

'The Feast of the Assumption – that's in a se'ennight,' said Tristram. 'I'd best be off right away. There's no time to lose if I'm to intercept them before they reach Reading.' Petronilla did not argue any more. Tristram's belief in his own invincibility had conquered all her doubts.

'When will we see you again?' Petronilla asked.

'Not for some time I fear,' he replied but it was Joanna he was looking at. 'As soon as I have them, I'll make straight for France. Then I'll seek out the Duke of Lancaster, throw myself on his mercy.'

'Oh dear, I should not permit you to do it,' Petronilla was concerned again, 'sacrificing your own future – suppose the Duke refuses to help us?'

Joanna felt ashamed. She should have been the one worrying about Tristram. But he had no such fears.

'Don't worry about the Duke, he stands by his retainers. It won't be the first time he's helped me out of a scrape. I shouldn't wonder if he doesn't relish a chance to show his muscle. I should think he's had just about enough of being cold-shouldered by the babes and sucklings the King's got round him nowadays. Lancaster knows he's far too powerful for the King to touch and it won't do the King's Council any harm to realise it.'

Petronilla hurried away to find food and drink for Tristram and his men before they left. Alone with her husband in the large lofty hall, Joanna knew she ought to feel grateful. He was going away on a dangerous quest, risking his life and his career, and she did not know when she would see him again. She should feel proud. But all she felt was relief.

'You'll be all right here, Petronilla will look after you,' he said. 'You're not frightened of her, are you, Joanna? She's a bit formidable, but I believe she's fond of you in her way.'

'No,' she said, 'I'm not frightened of Petronilla.'

'Take care of yourself until I get back. And don't worry about your father, I'll see he comes to no harm.'

'I know you will,' she murmured.

'And Joanna . . .' He paused and swallowed hard, stood glaring at her, struggling with something that was hard for him to say. She could not bear it. He was going to make her promise not to see Nick, not to be unfaithful to him while he was away, and sinner that she was it was all she could think of – that soon her husband would be gone, maybe for many months, and Nick would be free to come to her again. She stood looking down at her feet, feeling shame and fear that he would somehow extract a promise from her which she could not keep.

He cleared his throat and looked at her wistfully. 'I love you, Joanna,' he said. 'What I do, I do for you. You know that, don't you?' Blessed words. What she once would have given to hear him say them! They came too late now. The fire that once had blazed so fiercely it had almost consumed her had burnt itself out for want of fuel and in the cold ashes of disillusionment not one spark remained to rekindle it anew.

She looked up at him and there were tears in her eyes, tears for the lost chances and the might-have-beens.

'I will pray for you,' she said.

'Don't look so sad, Joanna,' he said, pulling her roughly into his arms. 'The Duke will make all come right, you'll see. I'll be back with your father and John of Northampton before the year's out and we'll all spend Christmas together at Maudesbury.'

The Wednesday after the Feast of the Assumption in the year 1384 fell on 17 August. William Gryffard was in bed wracked by sickness, headaches and a bad attack of the gravel he was so prone to, prey to the knowledge that his bodily discomfort was a direct result of the magnificent banquet given by the Mayor to celebrate the recent holy day. To have been invited to such a feast was for William a considerable triumph and there was self-congratulation as well as mortification in his musings, for although his flesh suffered from the aftermath of Sir Nicholas Brembre's lavish hospitality, his mind was filled with all the possibilities of what might be achieved now that he was the trusted servant of Brembre.

It had not been done without some painful choices, for Brembre was a tough customer. Burgeys had been the price of his present favour and in sacrificing Richard Burgeys, William had had to abandon his plan of having a tame Mayor in his pocket. Burgeys would never be Mayor now, even if he escaped with his life. And William realised it was anyway a mistake to concentrate on trying to control the government of London. Politics in the city were too much at the mercy of the free citizens, too many independent spirits were united within the individual guilds, and the guilds were powerful bodies with votes and a corporate wealth that could not easily be confiscated. No, Brembre had the right of it, and it had taken a taunt of Margaret Philpot's to make William see it. The key to his future ambitions lay with the King himself.

The King was now in his eighteenth year and beginning to assert himself. His favour was monopolised by a small coterie of friends and courtiers, the most conspicuous being the two young Earls, Nottingham and Oxford. Thomas Mowbray and Robert de Vere were like the King himself, young, arrogant and eager to show off their power with extravagant display. Of course it would cost money and, although William was not a poor man, he had nothing like the resources of Nicholas Brembre. But still he thought he could contrive a loan or two, just enough to secure a useful favour from the King – something like collector of the wool subsidy which Richard Lyons had received a decade ago. He had used it to line his pockets very successfully, until he met his unfortunate end at the hands of the peasants during the Hurling Time. And he could marry a rich widow. It was time he married again. Margaret Philpot, for instance, was well dowered with two husbands in the churchyard and her father one of the wealthiest merchants in London in his time.

Restlessly William turned over onto his back and stared at the embroidered canopy above his head. The widow was bearing her bereavement uncommonly well. At the Mayor's feast she had looked radiant in her black velvet. She had been gay, she had been outrageously flirtatious, but when he had tried to ask her for news, she had fobbed him off with taunts and teasing. If only he knew what had become of that rascal de Cher. No news from Maudesbury since his last visit, which could only mean that his informer, the weaver, had been silenced. William hated being in the dark; it was like buying cloth without a yardstick. He had been taken completely by surprise when he'd discovered Joanna was at Northampton's Inn.

He flung himself from side to side in his splendid feather bed and groaned in anguish. His flesh, his all too frail and disobedient flesh! Joanna upset all his careful calculations. He knew that she was trouble, told himself that she was no longer much use to him; yet he could not stop himself from wanting her. It was not just her body, although the thought of that one night he had enjoyed her still made him groan out loud; it was her courage, her honesty and her spontaneity that attracted him against all his better judgement. But he had lost Joanna the day he decided to sacrifice her father. He sat up in bed and cursed himself for the fool that he was.

His angry shout brought a manservant hurrying into the chamber, closely followed by the young physician whom William had himself sent to Florence to be trained in medicine at the city's prestigious medical school.

'That's good,' said the young man, thrusting half a bowlful of theriaca – an antidote compounded of many mysterious ingredients stirred together in a great cauldron, which he believed to be a panacea for all ills – into William's hand. 'To get angry and shout at times will keep up your natural heat; what displeases me is your being grieved and taking everything so much to heart. For it is this, as the whole of physic teaches, which destroys the body more than any other cause.'

'I can't help worrying, laid here helpless as I am,' muttered William, staring into the unappetising contents of the bowl. 'If I drink this mysterious compound of yours, will I be able to get back to work?'

'Not if you insist on work as an end in itself,' replied the doctor. 'You should strive to be fit to give thanks to God, for I've found that in sickness men can scarce remember God nor find the energy to say as much as a paternoster.'

'Then send the priest in to me,' replied William, handing back the empty bowl in disgust. 'Maybe he, through God's grace, can inspire my mind, since your potions do so little to heal my body.'

But it was not the priest who cured him of his torments. It was a message he received three days later, which had him out of bed, dressed, and into a barber's shop to be shaved before scurrying round to the Mayor's house in the Royall. He was shown directly into Brembre's parlour where he found the Mayor, dictating to a clerk in holy orders.

'Well, my assiduous watchdog, I don't doubt you bring me news that's as fresh as new-baked bread,' Brembre said, not at all perturbed by the interruption.

'Indeed,' said William, still slightly out of breath from the exertions of his journey after so long a period of fasting. 'I have it from a young squire in the Earl of Oxford's train. The prisoners have escaped.' From the scowl on the face of the Mayor, William surmised with a sinking of the heart that his news was not so fresh after all.

'You disappoint me,' Brembre said. 'I thought you'd be able to tell me something I didn't know. I have already received instructions from the King to arrest Northampton's friends and keep them in prison until the King should order otherwise.'

'Who are you going to arrest?' William asked.

Brembre took the scroll from the clerk's hand and read impassively: 'John More, mercer, Richard Norbury mercer, William Essex draper, Robert Franceys goldsmith, John Lincolle goldsmith, Robert Riseby draper, John Willardby and John Maudeleyn, tailors. Is there anyone else you would like added to the list? I owe you a favour for delivering Burgeys to me.'

'John of Northampton might give himself up for the sake of Petronilla, his wife,' suggested William.

'I don't make war against women,' replied Brembre.

'Richard Burgeys' daughter, Lady Maudesbury, has come to London and is staying with Northampton's wife at the Hood. I know her to be both resourceful and headstrong. I cannot but feel that this escape is somehow her doing.'

'Least of all a knight's lady.'

'Her husband, Sir Tristram, is a retainer of Gaunt.'

Brembre's scowl deepened as he gazed thoughtfully at his informer. 'You think Gaunt may be behind this? The King will want more than a few hostages if Gaunt has robbed him of his prey.'

'I don't know for sure,' William replied, ignoring the scowl. He had learnt not to give way before Brembre's aggression; the Mayor did not want flattery or crawling subservience. If he were to ingratiate himself with Brembre, he knew he had to do so by offering positive advice. 'Joanna, Lady Maudesbury, was once a good friend of your wife's sister, the Lady Philpot. Could you not send her to Philpot's Inn under house arrest? You know you can count on one of your own family to guard her carefully but still treat her according to her rank.'

'By the Mass, friend Gryffard, you're cunning as the fox,' exclaimed Brembre, his face relaxing into a broad grin. 'It's the perfect solution – and Mistress Northampton can come here. Best keep the ladies apart in case they get to plotting their escape. Have some wine, you look pale. I heard you'd been ill. You must look after yourself, you're going to be very useful to me for a long time yet, I trust.' Brembre's smile was even more daunting than his scowl.

William drank the wine eagerly. It was not easy serving such a one as Brembre. Still, it had been a good morning's work, William reflected, listening with a feeling of pleasant anticipation while Brembre instructed the clerk to add the names of Petronilla Northampton and Lady Maudesbury to the scroll.

When Joanna arrived at Philpot's Inn she did not know whether to be glad or sorry. Expecting the Fleet Prison, it was a relief to find herself being ushered into Margaret's comfortable solar and welcomed like an honoured guest.

'I can't tell you how pleased I am to have you with me,' Margaret cried with a disdainful nod of dismissal to the two men of the Watch. Then she held out both hands to Joanna and swept her into the chamber, saying joyfully: 'It will be like old times again. You must tell me everything that has happened to you since we last met.'

She noticed Joanna looking round the chamber eagerly, and sighed. 'I'm afraid there is no one here but me, so we must make do with each other's company. But we shan't mind that, shall we, Joanna? See, I have a fine new guitar. It was a gift from –' She broke off and laughed artlessly, her eyes quizzing Joanna from beneath her plucked eyebrows. 'But I need not tell you who it was from, you will have guessed already.'

Joanna knew then that the Fleet would have been by far the easier. 'Am I your prisoner?' she asked.

'Prisoner is such a horrible word,' Margaret said. She picked up the guitar and plucked once or twice at the strings, listening critically. 'That doesn't sound quite right, does it? You must forgive me, he only gave it to me last week and I have not mastered it properly yet. But you shall learn to play it. You have such a quick ear, and then you can accompany me on the harp. We shall make some splendid music together. You'd like that, wouldn't you, Joanna?'

'How long do you mean to keep me here?'

'My dear, don't look so angry,' chided Margaret, laying down the instrument and taking Joanna's cold hand in hers. 'I do not think of you as my prisoner, but as my friend. Let the men play their stupid games. I don't understand what it is all about. All I know is that we women have no quarrel between us.'

'And what of Petronilla Northampton? What have they done with her?' asked Joanna.

'She has gone to my sister where she will be well cared for and out of harm's way. You have William Gryffard to thank that you were sent here to me. You're to be congratulated, Joanna, in your choice of lover – so rich, and the Mayor does nothing without consulting him; a powerful friend. You never cease to surprise me. You were such a romantic dreamer, were you not? But I never thought that all your dreams would come true. Now you have it all, a knight to husband and a lover who's rich and powerful. Tell me,' Margaret leaned forward and drew Joanna down beside her onto the bed, 'is Gryffard as generous to his mistresses as they say he is?'

'Is that what they say?'

'Gryffard told me every woman has her price,' Margaret persevered. 'What was yours?'

'William Gryffard could not pay my price,' said Joanna, getting off the bed and walking to the window.

For a while there was silence in the chamber. Joanna stood looking out of the window, her back straight, her face pale and still. Margaret paced restlessly about, from time to time glancing at her uncommunicative guest. 'Have you not brought any better clothes with you?' she asked after a while.

'I didn't think I'd be needing anything very good, in the Fleet.'

'What a shame. You could have had some of mine, I haven't worn any of them since I put on my black, but now that I'm getting married again I shall need them. Do you think that's very wicked of me,

422

Joanna, to put off my black so soon? Don't look so shocked. I can see you still believe that love ought to last one's whole life long. But I'm not like you, Joanna, I cannot love for ever. Although this time,' she sighed soulfully, 'this time perhaps I might, for I have loved him secretly this many a year.' Her hard, bright eyes watching Joanna belied her lovelorn words.'Now I know I have shocked you. I can see it in your face. Don't hold it against me that I snatch at happiness before it's too late. We none of us know, do we, how long we have here on earth and it behoves us not to waste too much time.'

The next few days were torture for Joanna. Margaret kept her with her at all times. They slept together in the commodious bed, ate together either in the solar or with the rest of the household in the hall, made music, sewed, read together. In all that time Margaret Philpot never mentioned Nick by name but his spectre hung between them like a tangible presence. Pride and a paralysing, dark despair kept Joanna silent and she spent each long day in an agony of fear lest at any moment Nick might appear in the flesh to shame her for ever with his betrayal. It was a most blessed relief therefore when suddenly Margaret whisked Joanna out of her solar and down to the vaulted cellars beneath the hall.

'I'm so sorry to have to do this to you, Joanna,' Margaret apologised, 'but my betrothed has returned and of course he will want to have me to himself. You do understand, don't you? I'm afraid I have to keep you under lock and key when you're not with me.'

A bed, candles, books, a lute – and solitude. Joanna sat in the cool dark and tortured herself with imagining Nick and Margaret together. Were they, at this very moment, making love in the solar above, laughing at the silly little romantic fool whom Nick had seduced so easily? But then Joanna thought of all the happy times she had spent with Nick and a tiny piece of her optimistic nature clung to the belief that it was not true, that Nick could not have fooled her so completely. Many and many were the times when he had sworn that Margaret Philpot meant nothing to him. But if that were so, why had he not come to her? Where was he? Why had he deserted her? Was Margaret teasing or was she really going to marry Nicholas de Cher? Who was she to believe – Margaret, her rival and now her gaoler, or Nick her own true love? Sometimes she upbraided herself for her lack of faith, but then she would remember him as she first had known him, she heard the voices of all those who warned her against him and was plunged once more into darkest despair.

She lost count of the days. Her spacious prison was so far below ground she could not hear the bells ringing out the daily offices, nor see the sun rise. Only a gradual transformation from Stygian gloom to grey twilight marked day from night, and the meals brought to her regularly indicated the passing of the hours. The food was good and plentiful; the wine better than anything they'd had at Maudesbury, and Joanna consumed it all.

She was confident that her present isolation was a temporary lull, that eventually her capricious hostess, tired of her present occupation and in search of further entertainment, would seek amusement with her prisoner. Then Joanna would need all her wits and her strength. Peril hung waiting, like a falcon high in the sky, threatening her father, Tristram, John of Northampton, Petronilla and all their friends. Their lives were all at risk. One false move and the hawk would swoop upon its prey. Now was not the time to give way to emotion. Death owed no homage to love, and anyway love was delusion. If she was to survive whatever new horrors fate had in store, Joanna told herself firmly, she needed to use this period of solitary confinement to help her gather her dignity, her self-confidence and her presence of mind.

One morning when she was beginning to think Margaret must have forgotten her entirely, the servant, instead of bringing bread and ale, invited her to accompany him to Lady Philpot's chamber. When she entered the solar, Margaret was alone.

'My dear, forgive me for keeping you down in the dungeons all this time. I had meant it to be so much more fun for you but I have had so many things to do for the wedding, and my betrothed – he's so demanding, so impatient. Never mind. It's all over now, you are free to go.'

'Free!' Joanna was not reassured. 'Why am I free?'

'John of Northampton and his brother and your father have all appeared in Reading. They were three days late for the trial but now the King has sent word that his friends need not be held hostage any longer.' If the prisoners had appeared in Reading, then Tristram must have failed. She noticed that far from being triumphant, Margaret was looking at her with genuine sympathy in her eyes.

'What has happened?' she whispered.

'My dear, sit down. I'm afraid I have some bad news for you. Sir Tristram has been killed.'

'He can't have been.' Of all the things that Joanna had prepared herself to hear, she had never thought of this.

'You must not blame yourself, although what he did he did for you. Your knight loved you after all, Joanna, you can take comfort in that,' said Margaret and maybe she meant it to be kind.

'Who?' The question forced itself from Joanna's shocked mind yet already in her heart she knew the answer.

'Why, by Nicholas de Cher, of course,' replied Margaret.

The room spun and Joanna would have fallen had not Margaret caught her. From far away she heard Margaret's voice, urging her to sit down, to drink some wine; kind, gentle, understanding Margaret, sympathising with her in her loss. With hands that shook, Joanna held the cup to her lips and drank slowly, letting the wine do its work.

'Tell me,' she said at last.

'Tristram was trying to take them to France. Nick waylaid them, somewhere between Corfe Castle and Southampton. Challenged Sir Tristram. They fought. He killed your husband and escorted the prisoners back to Reading to face trial.'

'Nick killed Tristram?' Joanna could not accept the terrible truth. If Nick had killed Tristram, he was lost to her for ever.

'Why would he not?'

'But Tristram was invincible. Nobody could kill him in single combat.'

'Except Nick, who taught him everything he knew, when Tristram was his squire, before Tristram ran away and left him. Didn't you know Joanna? What your knight was?'

Joanna stood up. Looked at Margaret blankly. 'You say that I'm free to go.'

'William Gryffard's waiting in the hall below,' Margaret nodded. 'I've promised to release you into his care.'

'No, oh no.' Instinctively Joanna backed away.

'My dear child, where else have you to go? Your husband is dead. Your father on trial. You are alone and unprotected unless you marry again. Who better than William Gryffard? He's not a knight, I know, but he's rich and well thought of by my brother-in-law, and hot for you. Of course it'll take some doing. Gryffard's set his sights high, he'll be looking for a rich wife and you haven't much to offer him now, my poor Joanna. But you're a clever girl and if you're skilful, you might get him to church. But not if you go down to him looking like that. Let me lend you something of mine. I'd like to help you if I can.'

Joanna studied her reflection in the polished steel for a long time. 'You're right,' she said finally over her shoulder. 'Your dungeon hasn't done much for my old gown. I'll take your black velvet, since you won't be needing it any longer.'

Margaret was taken aback but she helped Joanna out of her old gown and into the luscious black velvet. 'Black suits you,' she said, standing back to admire the result. 'Gryffard won't be able to keep his hands off you.'

'I need a headdress,' said Joanna.

'Much better leave your hair uncovered,' Margaret urged. 'That colour's so good with black. It's almost as if God meant you for a widow.'

Joanna ignored her. Rummaging in Margaret's chest, she found a wimple. She stood in front of the polished steel and proceeded to swathe her neck and head in the fine linen. Then she turned and stared defiantly at Margaret. 'I'm ready,' she said.

425

William Gryffard was waiting in the hall. He came forward over-flowing with sympathy and took the hand Joanna gave him, holding it clasped in both of his like a precious piece of porcelain, while he poured out condolences on her loss.

'Sir Tristram was a brave knight,' Joanna cut him short. 'It was right that he should die in battle.'

'No braver than his lady,' said William, his watchful eyes fixed on hers. She glanced down disdainfully at her hand still imprisoned in his.

'I'm ready to leave,' she said.

He led her out into the hot August morning and the courtyard full of horses and men. In spite of her velvets and the bright sun already beating down out of a cloudless sky, Joanna felt cold.

'Ar armed guard?' she said.

'I brought a litter for you,' William explained. 'I thought it would be easier for you, not having to walk on such a hot day.'

'I'm not an invalid.'

'I would spare you the curious glances of our friends and neighbours. I felt sure you would want to be alone with your grief.'

'Yes, I am quite alone, so Lady Philpot reminds me,' said Joanna. 'But free now, she says.'

'William will take care of you.' Margaret, who had followed them out, exchanged a swift conspiratorial smile with William. 'I know you will be in good hands.'

'Well I know how much Master Gryffard can be relied upon,' replied Joanna. 'He has always been near our family at times of our deepest need.'

'Do not think I will abandon you now,' he said, leading her towards the litter. 'You are my responsibility and I mean to take good care of you.'

Joanna let him help her in. She sat down, arranged her skirts carefully round her, while he mounted his gelding. Until that moment her chief concern had been to get out of Margaret's house without breaking down, to show no weakness, no emotion. But Margaret, who professed to be her friend, had delivered her into William's power and all her senses were now alive to the danger that once inside his house, she would be at his mercy.

The litter swayed and dipped as the bearers shouldered their burden and the armed servants closed in on either side. Joanna pictured the short journey ahead to William's house. In Lime Street and Cornhill there was room to ride abreast and to keep up a good pace – too good for her to be able to leap from the litter. She leant back against her cushions as they moved out of the spacious courtyard into Philpot's Lane, visualising the narrow pathway which connected East Chepe to Fenchurch Street, listened to the servants shouting to make way and the sound of their stout clubs being used to good effect.

The pace was brisk at first, but soon the bouncing of the litter slowed and Joanna, peering out, saw that the street was partially blocked by a man pushing a cart filled with heavy stones. Already William had ridden past the obstacle and his mounted servants had dropped back to leave room for the litter to squeeze through. She might never have a better chance. She seized her black velvet skirts in one hand, with the other threw back the curtain and, quick as a cat, dropped out of the litter. She landed in the cart, much to its handler's surprise, but even as he drew breath to cry out she had scrambled to the ground and was off and running, past the mounted servants, back towards Philpot's Inn before they could wheel their horses in the confined space.

With her skirts hitched up above her ankles she raced along the busy lane, dodging the outstretched hands which tried to detain her and pushing past people who got in her way. Somewhere she knew there was a turning which led into the maze of little passageways north of Thames Street, where mounted men would find it difficult to follow. Behind her the hue and cry grew louder, but she forced herself not to look round, to resist the urge to run faster, terrified that in her haste she would miss the turning and find herself back at Philpot's Inn.

A water carrier with his wide yoke stretching on either side of his shoulders and two heavy buckets suspended in mid-air stood in front of her, mouth agape, blocking her path, but she had reached the turning. She ducked beneath his shoulder, spinning him round like a quintain, and plunged down the narrow street, running fast now, her breath coming in short painful gasps as the shouting swelled behind her and fear lent wings to her feet.

The maze of little lanes became darker, narrower, smellier as she followed each twist and turn, not knowing where she was going, hearing the pursuit grow fainter, until she was running through mere passageways between a higgledy piggledy jumble of mean little houses built so close together they seemed to lean against one another for support.

She paused then to catch her breath. She had lost her pursuers, but in the process was herself lost. She thought about what she should do, where she should go when she found her way out. She could smell, above the noxious odours all around her, the all-pervading tang of tar. She must be near the Ropery – and Northampton's Inn. Should she go there? But that was the first place that William would look for her. She could not burden Petronilla with her problems. Could not expect protection from the wife of a man on trial. If Northampton were to be found guilty, Petronilla and her children would be left penniless. Petronilla had enough problems of her own. Where then?

She could go to Maudesbury – if she could get there. But at

Maudesbury she would never be safe from William. Besides, Margaret would be married to Nick and living nearby at Cher. She could not bear to go back to Maudesbury. She had been so intent on escaping from Margaret, from William, she had not been able to think about Tristram's death, her father's fate, Nick's betrayal. Now she began to feel overwhelmed by the full enormity of the disaster.

Two seamen came lurching down the alleyway and called out to her. A woman stuck her head out of a window above and spat angrily at her. It brought Joanna up sharp. One thing was certain, she could not loiter here. She began to walk hurriedly away, glancing over her shoulder. The seamen followed and she quickened her step, as anxious now to find her way out of the maze of dark alleys as before she had been to lose herself in them. But where could she go?

She walked on, peering round corners, earnestly praying that she would not come round in a complete circle and find herself face to face with William, until at last she came into a slightly better street. The seamen must have lost interest in her; they were nowhere to be seen. Cautiously she looked up and down the street but there was no sign of William or any of his entourage. Instead she saw a building with a long pole sticking out halfway across the street and a creaking sign attached to it on which was painted a black swan. It was a tavern and Joanna, suddenly realising how very tired and thirsty she was, approached it with care. The yard in front of the tavern was filled with a motley collection of men and women and horses. From their dress and their talk, Joanna deduced that they were pilgrims and she asked one motherly-looking matron where they were going.

'To Glastonbury, to the west country,' she was told. 'Are you wanting to join us, sister?' Joanna stared at the round, kindly face, as if at a divine vision. The road to Glastonbury would take them past the Convent of the Sacred Heart! Indeed, these pilgrims might well be happy to take shelter there for one night. She could go with them to the convent. She would be safe there, and the Prioress would welcome her back like a lost sheep into the fold.

Joanna stood there in the yard of the black swan, surrounded by the merry bustle of the pilgrims' preparation for departure, and felt the weight of God's will. It seemed to her then that everything that had happened – her marriage to Tristram, Mariota's death, her father's arrest, Tristram's death at the hand of Nicholas de Cher – was her fault, a direct result of her determination to escape the convent. God wanted her to be a nun. She would find no mercy and no justice outside the convent. What she had always regarded as a prison was now her only refuge. Relentlessly, God was bending her to His will. Her only chance of achieving atonement in this world and salvation in the next was to become a nun.

Chapter 38

'Joanna, the Reverend Mother wants to see you.' Joanna's heart sank. What had she done wrong this time? She looked in dismay at the crowned M of the Blessed Virgin she was attempting to embroider in blue and gold thread and knew that no matter how hard she tried, she could not make neat, even stitches. She never had been able to.

'Hurry, Joanna,' urged Sister Agnes. She was the Prioress's chaplain, who acted as her companion and assisted her in the choir and as witness to her good behaviour. Every year, to prevent favouritism, the Prioress's chaplain was changed but Joanna did not think it would make much difference. They none of them liked her.

As she walked demurely along the quiet cloisters to the Prioress's private room, Joanna reviewed the hours and minutes of each tedious day since the last time she had been summoned before the Prioress, examining her conscience carefully. It was a depressing exercise. There seemed to be so many lapses from the path of righteousness. She told herself it was all part of God's plan for her redemption. She had expected discipline and self-denial, had embraced it eagerly. She had prepared herself for the eight hours in church each day, welcomed the prayer and meditation, to her surprise had found joy in the singing, amusement even when she realised that Sister Agnes pitched the chant three notes higher to show off her own voice at the expense of some of the nuns who were less favoured by God. It was the little everyday pettinesses Joanna found so hard to overcome. Perhaps the Prioress had heard how she told Catherine de Sifart she was slower than a lame-footed ox in the bakery yesterday. Catherine de Sifart was a proper little tale-bearer.

Joanna sighed. How hard it was to subdue her natural impulses, her unruly tongue and her quick temper. She knew she was a disappointment to the Prioress. The Reverend Mother had such high hopes for her. She had said as much when Joanna had arrived at the convent over a month ago.

'I always knew you would come back to us one day,' she had said. 'God sent you to us for a purpose and I will be frank with you Joanna, as you have been frank with me. We are having trouble attracting well-dowered nuns. There are times when I have been afraid that we might have to close. I have prayed and God has answered my prayer. He has sent you to help us.'

'I'm afraid I cannot bring very much. Maudesbury is prospering again thanks to the cloth-making and with a good bailiff should continue to do so – enough to pay my widow's portion, all of which you will have. But it is not great riches.'

'It will be a start,' replied the Prioress. 'After what you have achieved on your own manor, alone and unaided, I feel sure that here you will be able one day to do great things.'

Joanna's heart sank. Was there no sanctuary from the pressing need to find money? She had come to the convent to escape from the world, but even here she seemed condemned to have to fight to make ends meet. 'I will not treat you any differently from the others, Joanna,' the Prioress continued. 'In fact, if anything I shall have to be harsher, for there is much for you to unlearn having spent so much time in the world. But I have great hopes for you, my child, and every day I shall pray that you will find your way to God, for I know that you have had many troubles to bear and that only He can help you to find peace.'

The Prioress had certainly been strict, but somehow the others had sensed that Joanna was in some way special, that she was being singled out for extra attention, even though it always took the form of extra penance. In the long hours of meditation, there was too much time to brood, every small slip was watched for and pounced upon by the frustrated women all living together in such close-knit isolation. There were those who were jealous of Joanna, who guessed that once her time as a novice was over she would quickly rise through their ranks to be assistant Prioress and they resented her. Joanna bore it as best she could, accepting the glee of the other novices and the severity of the nuns every time she fell from grace, embracing all punishment as a necessary mortification of the spirit, an essential debasement of her nature to bring her closer to God.

She knocked at the Prioress's door and waited patiently until bidden to enter.

'You sent for me, Reverend Mother,' she said, walking into the room, hands folded meekly in front of her, eyes cast down, spirit braced for the wrath to come.

'Yes, my child, I sent for you because you have a visitor,' said the Prioress. 'You may look up.' Joanna's eyes flew to the Prioress's face in startled surprise and then followed her gaze. There, with his back to the window, his face in shadow, stood Nicholas de Cher.

'No, I don't want to see him,' Joanna stammered, turning to run from the room.

'Joanna, be calm, please.' The stern authority of the Prioress's voice brought Joanna up short. She took a deep breath, clasped her hands more tightly in front of her and stared down at the points of her shoes.

'Sir Nicholas de Cher has told me a sad tale,' the Prioress continued more gently. 'He has been very honest with me. I think you should listen to what he has to say. He has asked my permission to speak to you in private and I have granted it. It will do you no harm at least to hear what he has to say.' With that she smiled serenely, pressed Joanna's shoulder and swiftly left the room.

'I don't blame you,' said Nick, as the door closed softly behind the Prioress. 'I don't blame you at all, but perhaps when you hear what I have to say, you will not judge me so harshly.'

'I don't want to hear anything,' she burst out, putting both hands over her ears. 'I won't listen. You can talk your way out of anything. I've heard too many explanations, too many wonderful tales. You can charm anyone, even the Reverend Mother herself, but I don't want to hear any more.'

'Not even when commanded by the Reverend Mother? I can see you haven't made much progress in learning to obey.'

She glanced at him, angry that he dare to tease her at such a time. With his back to the light she could not see his face clearly, but the mere sight of his broad shoulders and strong powerful frame, so out of place in the Prioress's little solar, brought her close to panic.

'Go away and leave me alone,' she beseeched him. 'Are you so vain, so proud of your effect on women that you have to conquer every one of us?'

'Oh Joanna, my beloved, why do you persist in thinking that I am nothing but a relentless seducer? I love you, truly I do. I love you, only you. How many times do I have to prove it to you before you will believe me?' He knelt in front of her and bent to kiss her hands. She jumped at the touch of his lips as if she'd been scalded.

'What about Margaret Philpot?' she said.

'Margaret Philpot!' he exclaimed. 'What in the name of the Blessed Virgin has Margaret Philpot got to do with it?'

'But aren't you going to marry her?'

'Marry her! Sweet Jesu, Joanna, you don't think . . . Margaret Philpot means nothing to me. I swear it, on the bones of St Nicholas himself.'

'She may mean nothing to you, but you certainly mean a great deal to her,' retorted Joanna with some of her old fire.

431

'Margaret Philpot's only interested in Margaret Philpot. She didn't tell you she was going to marry me, did she?' he demanded, suddenly looking grim.

'She told me she was getting married again. I always thought that you and she . . . She let me think . . .'

'Margaret Philpot's married Adam Bamme the goldsmith, you silly goose. Didn't you ask who it was she was to marry? Joanna, how could you let yourself be taken in by that woman?'

'It doesn't matter, makes no difference now.' Wearily Joanna moved away from him. 'Can you not leave me to find my own peace?'

'Peace!' He laughed a bitter, mocking laugh. 'What peace can a hot-tempered, passionate woman like you find in a place like this?' Two long strides brought him to her side. He glowered down at her and she glared back defiantly, telling herself that he was an emissary of the devil sent to tempt her, but all she could think of was how gaunt and haggard he looked. He suddenly seized her by the shoulders and shook her angrily.

'Little fool. You'll never make a nun.' His fingers bit deep but her flesh gloried in the feel of him.

'Let me go,' she said breathlessly. 'You're hurting.'

He released her instantly. 'I'm sorry, Joanna,' he said. 'I didn't mean to hurt you, but you're enough to drive a man mad at times.' Watching him warily, she backed away and sat down trembling on a stool by the fire. 'Joanna, don't look at me so. Jesus, I'm making such a mess of this but how can I think straight with you sitting there in that pathetic white robe and your wounded eyes upon me, like a dying hind waiting to be put out of its misery?'

She could not bear the look of suffering on his face and so she fixed her gaze on the bright embers in the hearth.

'Will you listen to me now?' he asked.

She bent her head in acquiescence, clenched her hands tightly in her lap, tried to stay calm.

'I was in London at the time your father was arrested,' he said at last. 'I knew that it was useless to appeal to Nicholas Brembre so I went to see the King. I hoped he might remember me from the time of the Peasants' Revolt. I hung about the court, ingratiating myself with that fop de Vere. I'm afraid the King is a different person from the young boy who showed his courage at Smithfield. He's older now but not wiser. He listens to all the wrong people. When the prisoners failed to appear on the Wednesday after the Feast of the Assumption, I learnt that the King had ordered the arrest of all Northampton's supporters. I hurried to London and discovered you were under arrest. I went to Philpot's Inn but I wasn't allowed to see you. I dared not use force, already the King was very angry. To attack Philpot's Inn would have been playing into the Mayor's hand. I knew that the only hope of securing your release was to persuade John of Northampton to give himself up.'

'You did not think that perhaps we were prepared to make the sacrifice for him and for my father?'

'I thought there was a good chance of your father's being acquitted. The evidence against him was very slight, a trumped-up charge concocted by Gryffard and Brembre. But if he did not appear for trial, he convicted himself by default.'

'How did you know where to find him?'

'It wasn't difficult to guess that Tristram was behind Northampton's escape – it was the sort of stupid thing he would do. It also wasn't difficult to guess where he would take his captors. All I had to do was wait for him in a quiet glade somewhere along the way, dressed in full armour. I knew Tristram wouldn't be able to resist the challenge.'

'And you killed him,' she accused.

'I intended to knock him off his horse. Make him yield his prisoners. But I underestimated his ability as a jouster. I haven't done a great deal of tournament work and it wasn't easy unhorsing him. In the end we both of us came down together. He was up and on his feet with his sword out quicker than I and I thought he'd got me. I've fought in every kind of battle with some fairly desperate adversaries, but Tristram was one of the very best. And he really wanted to kill me. I had to break his leg in the end before he would yield.'

'And you left him in the forest to die?'

'He had his squire and men-at arms. They were confident of their ability to get him back home. It was but two days' travelling from Maudesbury. They could send to the abbey at Cirencester for medical attention. I had to get to Reading with my prisoners. I didn't know then that they had the pox at Maudesbury and none of the monks would go near the place.'

'Merciful Jesus,' Joanna whispered.

'When they reached Maudesbury, Tristram had a fever. His squire and his attendants did not dare go further. The manor was deserted, all those well enough to do so had run away.'

'Mother Matilda, Alice and the children?' Joanna asked, horrified.

'Safe in the abbey. At the first outbreak of the infection they fled to Cirencester and escaped unharmed. Tristram's squire stayed by him, nursed him devotedly but then he caught the pox and died. No doubt he'll get his due reward in heaven.'

'And Tristram?'

'He died of the pox, Joanna, because he could not run away. God has a terrible sense of justice, after all.'

'Poor Tristram, he so wanted to be a hero.' Her eyes filled with tears as she thought of the man who all his life had been chasing vainly after an image of chivalry which had always eluded him.

'There aren't any heroes, Joanna. Just brave men and cowards. Tristram fought bravely. In battle he'd have been a worthy warrior. It was his misfortune that he never got the chance he wanted. If he'd lived in the Black Prince's day he'd have probably ended up as revered as Sir Robert Knollys.'

For a while she sat staring into the fire, thinking of Tristram, who hadn't died as he would have wanted, in battle, but slowly in painful agony, of smallpox. She felt confused. Somehow it didn't seem to matter whether Nick had killed Tristram or not. The hand of God which had seemed so clear had suddenly become indecipherable again.

'What about my father?' she asked, remembering.

'Your father was acquitted, eventually. John of Northampton bought time by demanding what right the Council had to try any man for his life in the absence of its chairman the Duke of Lancaster. The prisoners were sent back to Corfe Castle, Northampton and his brother outlawed, their lands and goods forfeited to the Crown. In September they were tried again, this time in the Tower of London, and condemned to death.'

'Oh, God have mercy,' whispered Joanna.

'By that time the Duke of Lancaster had returned home from France and was persuaded to act on their behalf. The sentences were commuted to banishment and exile from the city. Northampton is detained in Tintagel Castle in Cornwall. Your father was released, and has since been allowed back into London.'

'A ruined man,' she said.

'No, not ruined, but sufficiently encumbered to keep him busy building up his business and out of city politics for a while. Mistress Burgeys and your sister Alice and the children are all back safely in London, helping him re-establish himself.'

Joanna looked down at her hands. From far away came the sound of the Angelus. Work was over for another day, soon it would be time for compline.

'And Petronilla?' she asked. 'Poor Petronilla, she and the children, they'll be penniless.'

'The Drapers Guild are supporting her now and some of Northampton's friends in the city are trying to save something from Petronilla's dowry. Perhaps an annual grant from the steelyard that formed part of her inheritance. If it hadn't been for Petronilla, I'd have found you sooner. As soon as I reached London I went to see Dame Petronilla, who I don't think approves of me. She sent me to Margaret Philpot who told me you were going to marry Gryffard and he'd left for Calais. I wasted a great deal of time chasing halfway across Europe after William Gryffard.'

'Did you find him?' she asked, despite herself intrigued at the thought of William when finally confronted by Nick in vengeful mood.

'I eventually caught up with him in Bruges, laying siege to a rich widow, the head of a fine company with useful Venetian backing. From him I discovered your trail had gone cold at Northampton's Inn. So I did what I should have done in the first place and went to Maudesbury. There I found all in order under a new bailiff, who I discovered had been installed by Gervase de Haen. So I hurried to Cirencester Abbey and was informed by that worthy monk that you were safe from blackguards like me, and had gone to fulfil your destiny. That was when I knew where to look for you.'

She got up, walked to the window, and stood looking out at the round squat tower of the little church. 'It is my destiny,' she said and wondered that her voice hardly trembled at all. 'I cannot fight it any longer. God wants me for a nun.'

This time he did not shout or shake her. Gently he took her by the shoulders, turned her round to face him and when she would not meet his gaze, placed a hand beneath her chin and forced her to look at him. 'Do you think God gave us love such as ours for nothing?' he asked. 'Don't throw away the only chance we have of being happy together.' Before she could speak, the door opened and the Prioress came in. Joanna started back guiltily, but the Prioress only smiled.

'That's the bell for compline, Sir Nicholas,' she said. 'It's time for you to leave now.'

'But I haven't said anything like all I want to say yet,' he protested.

'Never mind, you can come back tomorrow and talk to Joanna again. The poor child will be confused enough with what you've told her today, I'm sure, and she needs time to think about it, to examine her conscience and to pray.' He frowned and his jaw stuck out obstinately. He was not used to being thwarted. The Prioress saw the familiar signs of rebellion and was quick to forestall them.

'No arguments, Sir Nicholas, please,' she said sternly. 'I have already bent the rules of this house considerably for you. Novices are not normally allowed visitors at all. If you do not comply with my request I shall have to forbid you to visit us again.' If Joanna had not felt so utterly depressed, she would have been amused as she watched Nick realise he could not fly in the face of Holy Church.

He raised her hands to his lips. 'Until tomorrow, Joanna. Promise me you will think kindly of me?'

She could scarcely speak for the great weight in her heart, dared not look at him. 'Goodbye,' she whispered. She heard his indrawn breath, felt his hands tighten on hers.

'Sir Nicholas.' The Prioress was stern. He had to leave.

As soon as he had gone, Joanna broke down. The Prioress gathered the weeping girl into her arms and let her cry, as all the months of pent-up misery, the shock of seeing Nick again, and with it the over-whelming love so vainly stifled, came pouring forth in a torrent of tears. The Prioress waited until the storm had almost subsided. Then she fished in the pouch hanging from her girdle and produced a fine linen handkerchief.

'Here, child, blow your nose. I don't know what you have to weep for.'

Joanna looked up at the Prioress, eyes streaming with tears. 'God wants me to be a nun, I know it, but He makes it so hard, so dread-fully hard. Will you tell Sir Nicholas tomorrow – that I cannot see him ever again? Then pray for me, Reverend Mother, pray that I may have the strength to bear it.'

The Prioress led her to the stool by the fire, made her sit down. 'Joanna,' she said, 'listen to me. God asks us to make many sacrifices, to test us, just as iron is put through fire to make it stronger. But some-times He does not require us to make the sacrifice, just to show that we are willing.'

'I know He wants me to be a nun,' Joanna cried, shaking her head vigorously. 'Every time I have run away it has ended in disaster.'

'Sometimes faith is enough,' said the Prioress gently.

'No, no, not faith – a sacrifice. God wants a sacrifice!'

'Abraham once was asked to make a sacrifice, do you remember, Joanna? Abraham did what God asked of him. He took Isaac, his most beloved and only son, into the land of Moriah and there he built an altar and piled wood around it for the fire. He bound his son and laid him on the altar and took a knife and stretched forth his hand to slay the son whom he loved beyond price. And the Angel of the Lord called unto him out of heaven and said, "Lay not thine hand upon the lad neither do thou any thing unto him for now I know that thou fear-est God seeing thou hast not withheld thy son, thine only son from me." Abraham lifted up his eyes and saw a ram caught in a thicket by his horns. He went and took the ram and offered him up for an offer-ing instead of his son.

'It is not for us, child, to question the will of God,' the Prioress said firmly, 'but to show that we are willing to trust and obey Him in all things. Now dry your tears. It is time we were in church. I shall pray for you, that you may find your way to God.'

It was surprising how quickly the whole priory knew that a knight had come awooing. After compline that evening, the sole topic of all the gossipings and whisperings was Joanna's lover. When Nick called next morning, an unusual number of nuns found it necessary to be working between the gate and the Prioress's private chamber. Inquisitive eyes watched his huge, richly clad figure pass purposefully along the quiet cloisters, and the nun in charge of the novices was so intrigued that she quite forgot to chide her charges when they too lifted their eyes from the ground and stared in open admiration at this splendidly masculine intruder.

When Sister Agnes came to inform Joanna that the Prioress wanted to see her again, she was ready. For the first time since she had come to the Priory, her heart did not sink. She flew along the cloisters, her novice's habit billowing out behind her, and the nuns, instead of being shocked at such unseemly behaviour, smiled. Never before had such romance come to the Convent of the Sacred Heart.

Reaching the Prioress's sanctum, Joanna paused to catch her breath. Then she lowered her eyes dutifully and when the Prioress bid her enter walked into the room as meekly and obediently as the most devout postulant. But her heart was singing.

'What's this?' Nick teased, as soon as the Prioress left them alone together. 'Don't tell me you've learnt meekness at last? Have I been cheated? Just when the Reverend Mother assures me that your temper is quite untamed.'

'That's not fair,' flashed Joanna and he gave a shout of laughter as he swept her into his arms.

'No vocation, no vocation at all, poor child,' he declared as he kissed her. 'How could they ever have put up with you all these months?'

'I'm not as bad as you think,' she retorted somewhat breathlessly between kisses. 'Why, I can sing better than anybody in the whole Priory, and read and write and speak French with the best of them.'

'I believe they are all even now in the church on their knees praising God and thanking him for a merciful deliverance.' She tried to protest but he was kissing her and she had no breath left to protest with.

'What I can't understand,' Joanna said when at last he released her, 'is how you were allowed in.'

'I told the Prioress that I had come here to marry you and that if she did not let me see you I would bring a dozen knights and ravish the entire Priory.'

'Oh Nick, you didn't,' she said, shocked. 'I'm surprised she didn't threaten you with excommunication.'

'Not in so many words, perhaps, but the Prioress is nothing if not a realist and when I told her that I could bring an eager novice of impeccable vocation and lands of great worth, which would make her priory the best in the diocese, she saw the wisdom of bowing to force majeure.'

'Who?' she asked, impressed by his resourcefulness.

'Agnes Proudfoot, my betrothed. She's never wanted anything but to enter a convent. It seems I don't succeed in winning every heart, my beloved.'

'The ram in the thicket,' murmured Joanna, not knowing whether to admire the Prioress most for her wisdom or her sense of the practical.

'So you see, in helping the Prioress I have freed myself from my betrothed, and can ask,' Nick threw himself on is knees before her, 'for your hand in marriage, Lady Maudesbury.'

Marriage! In her confusion, excitement and struggle to understand God's will, Joanna had thought no further ahead than being free to accept Nick's love. Now she had a moment of doubt.

'Your mother,' she said. 'She was so set on Agnes and her lands, and I have nothing much to bring. If you're to be a knight again, can Cher support you without a substantial dower?'

He got up and took both her hands in his. 'You will have to be patient with my mother,' he said. 'She has had a difficult time, but you'll manage her as you manage everything in the end, and she's not nearly as hard as the Lady Isabel. Once she gets to know you, my angel, she will love you as much as I do. Besides, I do not intend to leave you behind at the manor all the time. My mother will be happy running it as she has always done. We'll live in London too. You and I are going to build the biggest fleet of ships the city has ever seen.'

Still she hesitated. 'Oh Nick, you'll not be like all the rest of them, bartering for power and trying to win the little people's confidence for the sake of your own pride?'

'No, I do not want to be Mayor, but there is much we can do for your friends who have suffered in the city – when we're married. You are going to marry me, my sweet love, are you not? For I have vowed not to leave the Sacred Heart without you as my wife.'

'In that case,' she said, smiling up at him with shining eyes, 'I shall have to say yes without more ado, for I fear the Priory would never survive a prolonged wooing. The nuns would die of curiosity.'